ESSENTIAL TALES AND POEMS

ESSENTIAL TALES AND POEMS

EDGAR ALLAN POE

Edited by
Stefan Dziemianowicz

Introduction and Notes by
Jeffrey Goddin

BARNES & NOBLE

NEW YORK

SIGNATURE B&N EDITIONS

Barnes & Noble

NEW YORK

387 Park Avenue South
New York, NY 10016

Introduction, Annotations, and Further Reading
© 2012 by Sterling Publishing Co., Inc.

This 2012 edition published by Sterling Publishing Co., Inc.

ISBN 978-1-4351-3767-7 (print format)
ISBN 978-1-4351-4109-4 (ebook)

For information about custom editions, special sales,
and premium and corporate purchases,
please contact Sterling Special Sales at 800-805-5489 or
specialsales@sterlingpublishing.com

Manufactured in the United States of America

4 6 8 10 9 7 5

www.sterlingpublishing.com

CONTENTS

THE LIFE AND TIMES OF EDGAR ALLAN POE

1809 Edgar Poe is born to David Poe, Jr., and Elizabeth Arnold Hopkins Poe in a boardinghouse in Boston on January 19; his actor parents are on tour at the time.

1810 David and Elizabeth Poe separate; Edgar and his older brother, William Henry Leonard, remain with their mother.

 The third US census records a population of 7,239,881 people.

1811 Poe's mother, Elizabeth, dies. He is taken in by John and Frances Allan, a childless couple; Edgar's baby sister, Rosalie, and older brother, William Henry Leonard, are taken in by other families.

 The first steamboat to travel down the Mississippi River makes its journey.

1812 The War of 1812 commences, and the term "Uncle Sam" is first used as a name for the federal government.

1813 Oliver Hazard Perry defeats a British fleet at the Battle of Lake Erie and sends the message, "We have met the enemy and they are ours."

1814 "The Star Spangled Banner" is written by Francis Scott Key.

1815 Poe goes to Scotland with the Allans, then to school in London.

 Napoleon's forces are defeated at Waterloo.

1818 Mary Shelley's *Frankenstein* is published.

1819 "The Vampyre" by John Polidori, a gothic vampire tale that achieves great popularity, is published.

 Herman Melville is born on August 1.

 Washington Irving's *Sketch Book* is published in several parts during this year and the subsequent one; it becomes a best seller, whetting the American public's appetite for colorful tales.

1820 Poe's family comes back to the United States, settling in Richmond. Poe attends Joseph H. Clarke's Academy and William Burke's School; he excels at athletics and Latin.

1825 Poe's guardians, the Allans, become rich through inheritance. The Erie Canal is opened.

1826 At age seventeen, Poe enrolls at the University of Virginia, where he is said to have set a running broad jump record of 21 feet, 6 inches. He excels at Latin and French, but develops a reputation for drinking and gambling.

1827 Ballet is introduced into the United States.
 When John Allan won't help him pay his gambling debts, Poe quits school.
 With no job and no support from his parents, Poe goes to Boston, where he pays a printer to publish a small edition of his first book, *Tamerlane and Other Poems*, a now extremely rare small book of forty pages with a buff cover. Poe joins the US Army and is stationed at Fort Moultrie on Sullivan's Island, South Carolina, which will become the setting of his story "The Gold Bug."

1828 Andrew Jackson is elected president.

1829 Poe does well in the Army, reaching the rank of sergeant major, but when Frances Allan dies, he moves back home, and tries unsuccessfully to reconcile with John. Poe applies to West Point.
 Al Aaraaf, Tamerlane, and Minor Poems is published.

1830 John Allan remarries.

1831 Poe tires of West Point and gets himself court-martialed and expelled on purpose. He moves in with his aunt Maria Clemm and her eight-year-old daughter, Virginia, in Baltimore.
 Poe's brother, Henry (William Henry Poe), for whom Edgar felt strong affection, dies.
 Poe's *Poems* is published.

1832 Andrew Jackson is re-elected president, continuing a populist trend in American government.
 The *Saturday Courier* publishes Poe's "Metzengerstein," as well as some of his other stories.

1833 "MS. Found in a Bottle" wins a literary prize of fifty dollars given by the *Baltimore Saturday Visiter.*

1834 Poe's former guardian John Allan dies, but out of continuing dislike for Edgar, the wealthy Allan doesn't leave him anything in his will. Edgar is struggling financially, as he will for most of his life.

1835 Poe and the Clemms move to Richmond, where Poe takes a job with the *Southern Literary Messenger* at $520 a year.

His stories "Berenice," "Morella," "Shadow," and "King Pest" are published.

Poe begins to achieve some recognition for his fiction.

Samuel Clemens, who will write under the pen name Mark Twain, is born on November 30.

1836 In May, Edgar Poe marries his thirteen-year-old cousin Virginia. His aunt fully approves of the marriage, and the three continue to live together.

1837 Poe leaves the *Southern Literary Messenger* and moves to New York City.

Nathaniel Hawthorne's *Twice-Told Tales* is published; it will later (1842) receive a favorable review by Poe.

1838 Poe moves to Philadelphia.

His short story "Ligeia" is published, as is his only novel, *The Narrative of Arthur Gordon Pym of Nantucket.*

Tennessee passes the first prohibition law in the United States.

1839 *The Conchologist's First Book* is published. Poe edited and partly rewrote this guide to a type of large marine snail for a popular audience. It was the only book bearing his name that went into a second edition during his lifetime.

Poe joins *Burton's Gentleman's Magazine.*

In December, Poe's first collection of short stories, *Tales of the Grotesque and Arabesque*, is published (with "1840" printed on the title page); this two-volume set includes "William Wilson," "The Fall of the House of Usher," and "MS. Found in a Bottle." Poe doesn't make any money from the book, but his stories do receive some public notice.

1840 Poe leaves *Burton's* and tries to found his own magazine, the *Penn Magazine.*

1841 Poe joins the staff of *Graham's Magazine.* He publishes "The Murders in the Rue Morgue," "A Descent into the Maelström," and "The Island of the Fay."

The Deerslayer by James Fenimore Cooper is published.

Ralph Waldo Emerson publishes *Essays.*

Henry Wadsworth Longfellow publishes his very popular *Ballads and Other Poems.*

1842 While playing piano, Poe's wife, Virginia, ruptures a blood vessel.

Poe meets Charles Dickens while Dickens is touring the United States.

Poe leaves *Graham's* in May. His attempts to make his new magazine, the *Penn Magazine*, successful are plagued by illness, and no issues are ever published.

Poe's stories "The Masque of the Red Death," "The Pit and the Pendulum," and the first two installments of "The Mystery of Marie Rogêt" are published.

The New York Philharmonic is founded.

1843 Poe's story "The Gold Bug" wins a one-hundred-dollar prize.

"The Tell-Tale Heart," "The Black Cat," and the final installment of "The Mystery of Marie Rogêt" are published.

1844 Poe returns to New York City.

His story "The Balloon Hoax," published in the *New York Sun*, fools many readers, who believe that the fictional tale (about a hot air balloon crossing the Atlantic in seventy-five hours) is an actual news account.

The first telegraph message is sent by Samuel Morse.

Poe's stories "The Premature Burial" and "The Purloined Letter" are published.

1845 Poe's poem "The Raven," is published for the first time in the *Evening Mirror*.

He joins the *Broadway Journal* and has literary duels with Henry Wadsworth Longfellow.

Tales and *The Raven and Other Poems* are published by Wiley and Putnam; *The Raven and Other Poems* contains thirty-one poems and sells for thirty-one cents.

The first baseball club, the New York Knickerbockers, is organized.

1846 Poe's essay "The Philosophy of Composition" and his short story "The Cask of Amontillado" are published.

Poe moves to a cottage in Fordham, New York.

He receives letters of praise from Elizabeth Barrett Browning and Nathaniel Hawthorne.

Poe successfully files a libel suit against Hiram Fuller and Augustus W. Clason of the *Evening Mirror* for statements made about Poe by a contributor to the publication. He receives $225 and court fees in 1847.

Henry David Thoreau is jailed overnight for refusing to pay his poll tax, inspiring his famous essay "Civil Disobedience."

Herman Melville's first novel, *Typee*, somewhat based on his own experiences in the South Seas, is published; it is quite successful.

1847 On January 30, Virginia Clemm Poe dies from tuberculosis. Poe collapses and is nursed back to health by Virginia's mother (his aunt/mother-in-law), Maria.

Poe's poem "Ulalume—A Ballad" is published.

The first official US postage stamps are issued.

1848 Poe returns to Richmond.

The cult of spiritualism in the United States begins with the Fox sisters of New York.

Karl Marx and Friedrich Engels' *The Communist Manifesto* is published.

1849 Poe joins the Sons of Temperance in an attempt to give up drinking (or possibly to give the appearance of giving up drinking).

He delivers his famous lecture "The Poetic Principle" in August.

At the end of September, Poe disappears for five days; after being found in a coma in Baltimore, he dies on October 7. He is buried in that city on October 9 in the Presbyterian cemetery at Fayette and Greene Streets, in the lot of his grandfather David Poe.

Rufus Griswold writes a nasty obituary of Poe for the *New York Daily Tribune*. The obituary is widely reprinted.

Poe's poem "Annabel Lee" is published two days after his death.

1850– Griswold publishes the multivolume *The Works of the Late Edgar*
1856 *Allan Poe*, which is the first comprehensive edition of Poe's works, but which also contains an essay called "Memoir" depicting Poe from a highly negative personal perspective. This becomes the most widely accepted commentary on Poe's life until scholars begin to seriously research Poe in the early twentieth century.

1875 Poe's grave is moved to the southwest corner of the cemetery, where the current monument now stands. In 1921 the French Literary Society and the Alliance Francaise sent an elegant bronze memorial wreath for Poe's grave. This wreath was later stolen, but in 1986 it was replaced by a replica plexiglass plaque, and the memorial was rededicated with a personal visit by the French Consul.

INTRODUCTION

How many major league sports teams have been named for a 150-year-old poem? Such is the enduring fame of Edgar Allan Poe's "The Raven" that it provided the name for Baltimore's professional football team. Poe's writing has claimed a unique place in American literature. Almost every American student has at some point read "The Fall of the House of Usher," "The Black Cat," "William Wilson," or "The Pit and the Pendulum," and has at least a vague idea of what Poe looked like, with his high pale forehead and the black clothes he habitually wore. Poe's stories and poems are not only read for their richly descriptive style and the eerie enjoyment they bring, but are, along with his essays, closely analyzed by critics to uncover the many allusions and levels of symbolism that Poe wove into them. As well as crafting gripping stories of lost love, obsession, and madness that set the standard for future writers in the horror genre, Poe is credited with inventing the modern detective story, with "The Murders in the Rue Morgue," "The Mystery of Marie Rogêt," and "The Purloined Letter." Reading Poe is an experience that is both engaging and disturbing, because no other American writer so illuminated the dark side of the human soul.

Poe is probably best known today for his horror and detective stories, written mostly from the 1830s to the mid 1840s. His works have been praised by such writers as Arthur Conan Doyle, Ray Bradbury, H. P. Lovecraft, Stephen King, and Thomas M. Disch. Many of his tales are quite scary and disturbing, and in showing us the emotions and thoughts of his heroes and heroines, Poe was one of the first writers to give us a character's "interior monologue." His horror, rather than revolving around vampires, werewolves, and the like, is usually *psychological horror*, bred from

a character's obsession and paranoia; in this respect, his brand of horror is very modern. The contemporary reader who is exposed to Poe's tales, the twists and turns of his essays, the evocative magic of his poetry, and the weird mystery of his one novel is in for a strange journey into the world of one of the most creative minds in literature.

Edgar Poe was born in Boston on January 19, 1809, while his actor parents, David Poe, Jr., and Elizabeth Arnold Hopkins Poe, were on tour. His parents soon separated, and his mother died of tuberculosis in 1811. His father died in 1810 or 1811 (exact date unknown). This left the three Poe children—Edgar; his older brother, William Henry Leonard; and his younger sister, Rosalie—to be raised by different families. Edgar was taken in, though not actually adopted, by John and Frances Allan, a well-to-do couple from Richmond, Virginia. In school, Poe was sometimes called "Edgar Allan," and in later years often wrote his name as Edgar A. Poe. Poe showed an interest in literature at an early age, and by the time he was five, he was reciting passages from the English poetry of the era.

The Allans moved to Scotland, then England, and Poe attended a manor house school in Stoke Newington, now a part of north London, from 1817 to 1820. The Allans then moved back to the United States, settling in Richmond. At Joseph H. Clarke's Academy and William Burke's School, Poe excelled at Latin and athletics, but his mind was not entirely on his studies. With his dark hair, high forehead, pale eyes, and slender build, Poe was popular with members of the opposite sex. In 1825, at age sixteen, he was secretly engaged to his childhood sweetheart, the lovely Sarah Elmira Royster, but her parents disapproved of the engagement so intensely that they intercepted his letters; thinking Poe had abandoned her, Sarah married someone else.

At age seventeen, Poe enrolled at the University of Virginia, excelling at Latin and French. At the university, Poe proved fond of drinking and gambling, incurring serious debts from the latter vice. John Allan wouldn't help pay those debts, and with no money and no immediate prospects of getting any, Poe dropped out of the university (or was expelled). He self-published his first book of poems, *Tamerlane and Other Poems*, in 1827, but the book made no money and drew little attention. As a matter of survival, Poe enlisted in the US Army under the assumed name of Edgar A. Perry. Within nineteen months, Poe was promoted to the highest rank an enlisted man could achieve, sergeant major, and he later used Sullivan's Island, South Carolina, where he was stationed, as the setting for his tales "The Gold Bug" (1843) and "The Balloon Hoax" (1844).

Poe tired of the Army, and resigned his office. He suffered one of the first of his nervous breakdowns when John Allan subsequently refused to see him. Poe then enrolled at West Point, where for a brief period, he did well. While at West Point, he was actively writing poetry. One poem from this period is "Israfel" (1831), which provides an example of how similar images often appear in Poe's poems and stories. Inspired by an angel mentioned in the Koran (though not one with that name), "Israfel" is a lyrical description of the beauty of the angel's song, which literally charms the stars of heaven. A line describing the angel, "Whose heart-strings are a lute," is echoed by a quotation from a poem by De Beranger placed, years later, at the beginning of "The Fall of the House of Usher" (1839):

> Son Coeur est un luth suspendu;
> Sitôt qu'on le touche il résonne.

This translates to: "His heart is a lute that's been suspended (hung up). As soon as you touch it, it makes sound."

Poe soon tired of West Point, as he had the Army, and he deliberately got himself court-martialed for drinking and other offenses. He was, however, so popular with his fellow students at West Point that they took up a collection to help him publish his third book of poems, entitled simply *Poems*, which appeared in 1831, after he left the Academy.

Poe moved to Baltimore to live with a paternal aunt, Maria Poe Clemm, and his young cousin Virginia. Virginia adored him, and she once made a valentine for him crafted so that the first letter of each line, read from top to bottom, spelled out his name. In 1831, Poe's beloved brother died—yet another in the series of personal losses that would punctuate the author's life (Frances Allan had died in 1829). During the Baltimore years, Poe wrote many stories and poems and received some encouragement when, in 1833, his story "MS. Found in a Bottle" won a literary prize of fifty dollars. In 1835, he and the Clemms moved to Richmond, and Poe began working for the *Southern Literary Messenger,* his first major association with one of the periodicals of the era. He left the *Messenger* after about a year, possibly having been forced out because of his drinking.

Poe's weaknesses are somewhat legendary, and perhaps exaggerated, in that much of the image of Poe as a strange alcoholic character comes from obituaries written by Rufus Griswold, a fellow who didn't like Poe, but became literary executor of Poe's estate. It does seem, however, that

Poe did drink frequently. He was chided for his drinking in a letter (September 29, 1835) from his boss, Thomas White, at the *Southern Literary Messenger.* "No man is safe who drinks before breakfast! No man can do so, and attend to business properly."[1]

In 1836, Poe married his then thirteen-year-old cousin Virginia. The couple continued to live happily together with Poe's aunt (and mother-in-law), Maria, who is probably the unsung heroine of the whole saga of Poe's career. She loved Poe deeply, provided stability in his life, and would later nurse him through a variety of illnesses and breakdowns, as well as look after his soon-to-be invalid young wife.

In the following years, Poe worked as an editor for a number of periodicals, including *Burton's Gentleman's Magazine, Graham's Magazine,* and *Godey's Lady's Book.* He frequently published stories, poems, sketches, and essays, but was chronically short of money. While he wanted to be a popular writer, during much of his life, he was probably better known for his critical work in various magazines than for his fiction or poetry. Totaling all the reviews, fillers, and hack work that Poe did for a few dollars, he probably published over 350 pieces of writing (rather impressive for an alleged alcoholic), but during his lifetime, his writing brought in very little income. Well into the 1840s, his letters are sprinkled with references to his poverty—and requests for money.

Poe's only novel, *The Narrative of Arthur Gordon Pym of Nantucket,* was published in 1838. It is a strange story of a young man's dramatic adventures (involving storms, bloody mutiny, and cannibalism) after stowing away in a sailing ship. The novel shows Poe's ability to craft scenes of both heightened tension and surprising grotesqueness, as when the beleaguered protagonist encounters a ship from which he hopes to find rescue, only to discover that it's a ship of dead men; the apparent animation of one sailor in the bow is caused by a seagull that has tunneled into the back of the dead sailor's head. The scenes that take place in a fantastical South Pole region are among the most surreal in American literature. It's possible that *The Narrative of Arthur Gordon Pym of Nantucket* (as well as Herman Melville's *Moby Dick)* was influenced by a popular book, Owen Chase's *Narrative of the Most Extraordinary and Disturbing Shipwreck of the Whaleship Essex* (1821), which recounts the true story of the ill-fated voyage of a whaling ship whose crew endured harrowing adventures ranging from shipwreck to cannibalism. Poe's novel is also notable for the extended symbolism of the color white (also found in *Moby Dick)* as being of particular ill omen.

Regarding Poe's short fiction, H. P. Lovecraft commented: "Surely, it may be said that Poe invented the short story in its present form."[2] By the time *The Narrative of Arthur Gordon Pym of Nantucket* was published, Poe's short fiction had also begun to appear regularly in various periodicals. Some of the influences on Poe's poetry and fiction are easily traced. Poe was very fond of the English Romantic poets Lord Byron, Samuel Taylor Coleridge, and Elizabeth Barrett Browning. Byron particularly captured Poe's imagination, with his dramatic poems and equally dramatic lifestyle. Like Byron, who once held a ghost story competition that gave rise to Mary Shelley's *Frankenstein* (1818) and John Polidori's "The Vampyre" (1819), Poe was fond of the trappings of gothic tales—or at least recognized their commercial potential. A good gothic story would have a gloomy castle, ghosts, perhaps a fallen nun or two, darkness, death, torture, madness, and a family curse. The true gothic story goes back to Horace Walpole and *The Castle of Otranto* (1764), and Poe brought many of the gothic trappings into his own era with such stories as "The Pit and the Pendulum" (1842) and "The Fall of the House of Usher."

When in 1839 (title page dated 1840) Lea and Blanchard published a two-volume set of twenty-five of Poe's short stories, *Tales of the Grotesque and Arabesque*, which included "The Fall of the House of Usher," Poe's literary reputation received a solid boost. "The Fall of the House of Usher" employs a motif that would later become common in horror fiction (and was often used by H. P. Lovecraft): someone visits an old friend whose residence is the site of terrible happenings and/or possesses a sinister past. This tale features another theme used by Poe in several stories—that of premature burial. In this case, the narrator visits his old friend Roderick Usher, who is convinced that his sister Madeline has been buried alive. As the story of dark obsession evolves, it turns out that Usher may not be entirely wrong.

"The Fall of the House of Usher" also provides a good example of how Poe works his magic of wordcraft at the very beginning of the story, creating an instant mood with three adjectives in the first sentence.

During the whole of a dull, dark, and soundless day in the autumn of the year, when the clouds hung oppressively low in the heavens, I had been passing alone, on horseback, through a singularly dreary tract of country; and at length found myself, as the shades of the evening drew on, within view of the melancholy House of Usher.

Also included in *Tales of the Grotesque and Arabesque* was "William Wilson," a story which may have been inspired by a Washington Irving story with a similar theme—that of the doppelgänger, or double, which frequently appears in Poe's work. This somewhat autobiographical tale begins with the young William Wilson attending a private academy in England, as Poe did. At the school he meets a boy also named William Wilson, who becomes his only competitor in athletics and scholarship. This boy gradually assumes the main character's mannerisms until the two boys are nearly indistinguishable. The protagonist leaves the school to attend the university (and escape his double), and falls into a decadent lifestyle that leads him to theft, dissipation, and the attempted seduction of a married woman; at a pivotal point in each of his adventures, his old adversary, the other William Wilson, appears and reveals the protagonist's intentions. Finally, at a ball in Rome, the main character meets his double once again and determines to murder him on the spot, with truly weird results.

In 1841, Poe joined the staff of *Graham's Magazine*. He worked there for about a year before leaving to attempt, unsuccessfully, to found his own magazine. Although Poe's wife, Virginia, ruptured a blood vessel while playing piano in 1842 and never recovered her health, some of Poe's most interesting fiction was published in the early 1840s, including "The Masque of the Red Death" (1842), "The Pit and the Pendulum" (1842), "The Mystery of Marie Rogêt" (1842–43), "The Gold Bug" (1843), and "The Tell-Tale Heart" (1843).

It was in 1841 that Poe published a story that was to change the future of fiction. The appearance of "The Murders in the Rue Morgue" is said to mark the birth of the modern detective story. For his three detective stories, Poe created the character of C. Auguste Dupin, a mildly eccentric private investigator, and precursor of Sherlock Holmes, who uses the deductive method to solve crimes and catch criminals. The other two Dupin stories are "The Mystery of Marie Rogêt" and "The Purloined Letter" (1844).

In "The Murders in the Rue Morgue," Dupin must solve a double murder. Madame L'Espanaye is found with her head nearly cut off, and her daughter's body is found stuffed in a chimney. Fortunately, Dupin discovers an important clue at the scene—a hair that didn't come from a human being. Dupin is depicted as something of a mind reader, to the point of completing the thoughts of those he converses with. He uses what Poe calls "ratiocination"—a combination of scientific logic and imagination—to put himself in the mind of the criminal, thus gaining insight on the crime. Dupin's outwitting of the more slow-minded police presages the style of

many modern fictional detectives. Both Arthur Conan Doyle and Agatha Christie paid direct tribute to Poe's Dupin. Sherlock Holmes' friend Watson compares Holmes to Dupin in *A Study in Scarlet* (1887), and Agatha Christie's famous detective Hercule Poirot writes a book on Poe in the novel *The Third Girl* (1966).

The year 1843 saw the publication of a number of Poe's most famous works, among them the poem "The Conqueror Worm" and the story "The Black Cat." The former is an allegorical poem in which angels watch a play produced by "mimes" and chase a phantom they can't catch. The appearance of a sinister shape on the scene is described in the following lines:

> But see, amid the mimic rout,
> A crawling shape intrude!
> A blood-red thing that writhes from out
> The scenic solitude!

The crawling shape eats the mimes, and it turns out that the play is called "Man," and its hero is the Conqueror Worm. This poem was also worked into a short story that Poe considered to be his best, "Ligeia" (1838), titled after the heroine's name, which is Greek for "clear-voiced."

"The Black Cat," one of Poe's best-known and most often dramatized stories, is an eerie tale of guilt, psychological horror, and revenge. "The Black Cat" was also instrumental in spreading Poe's reputation abroad. Not long after its publication, the French poet Baudelaire discovered the story and began to translate Poe into French. The French Symbolist writers Arthur Rimbaud, Paul Verlaine, and Stéphane Mallarmé came to know Poe's works through Baudelaire's translations; fascinated by Poe's charting of the darker areas of the human consciousness through the use of striking images and subtle symbolism, they began to work similar themes into their own poetry. The French became so fond of Poe that after his death they sent a plaque for his grave.

In 1844, Poe moved back to New York City, where he worked at the *Evening Mirror* and bought and briefly owned *The Broadway Journal,* which soon failed. It was during this period that Poe wrote "The Balloon Hoax."

"The Balloon Hoax," which is quite different from his horror stories, created a stir when it was published on April 13, 1844, in the *New York Sun.* The response somewhat presaged the public reaction to Orson Welles' narration of "The War of the Worlds"—a 1938 Mercury Theatre

radio production dramatizing H. G. Wells' novel of the same name that was taken by some listeners to be a true account of an attack on the earth by Martians. Poe's story, which relates the more peaceful event of an imaginary transatlantic crossing by hot air balloon in seventy-five hours, was believed by thousands and generated a lot of publicity for the *Sun*, which wound up retracting the story.

In 1845, the publication of *The Raven and Other Poems* and *Tales* established Poe's literary reputation (the two volumes were combined in 1846). In "The Raven," a lover is brooding over his lost love when a mysterious talking raven appears and perches on a bust of Pallas, Greek goddess of wisdom. Although the man soon discovers the raven speaks only one word, he nonetheless asks the creature a number of personal and philosophical questions, only to have his grief punctuated each time with the refrain, "Nevermore!"

With *The Raven and Other Poems* and *Tales*, Poe began to make a modest sum of money from his writing. Although his biographers sometimes depict him as a man who took himself too seriously, Poe's comments (from May 4, 1845) on a copy of "The Raven" that he sent to his friend Frederick Thomas reveal someone with a sense of wit and practicality: "'The Raven' has had a great 'run,' Thomas—but I wrote it for the express purpose of running—just as I did 'The Gold Bug,' you know. The bird beat the bug, all hollow."[3]

In addition to his fiction and poetry, Poe's essays contributed to his growing reputation. In "The Philosophy of Composition," published in *Graham's Magazine* in 1846, Poe discusses the process by which he wrote "The Raven" as a way of developing a set of theories of what creates good writing. In this essay, he talks about how to craft all the elements of a work to unify the themes, characters, setting, and several other aspects for the strongest effect. Among his conclusions is that the death of a beautiful woman is the most poetic theme—and that the writer best suited for developing this theme is her grieving lover. A particularly interesting passage is one in which Poe contrasts Truth (as the satisfaction of the intellect) and Passion with his idea of Beauty: "Truth, in fact, demands a precision, and Passion, a *homeliness* (the truly passionate will comprehend me) which are absolutely antagonistic to that Beauty which, I maintain, is the excitement, or pleasurable elevation, of the soul." Critics have debated whether Poe actually followed the process so beautifully described in "The Philosophy of Composition" or simply made the whole thing up after the fact.

In 1847, Poe's wife died of tuberculosis. Poe suffered a complete collapse, but was again nursed back to health by the ever-loyal Maria. At this point in his life, after losing his parents, his second mother, his brother, and his beloved wife/cousin, the exact state of Poe's psyche is hard to gauge. In 1848, he moved back to Richmond, but he seemed to be somewhat adrift, having at one point a liaison with the poet Sarah Helen Whitman. He then began to pursue an engagement with his childhood sweetheart, Sarah Elmira Royster, now Elmira Shelton, who was both widowed and wealthy. In August 1849, Poe gave a famous lecture on "The Poetic Principle," which was well attended, widely praised, and generally considered to be the last great accomplishment of his career. After joining the Sons of Temperance in an effort to give up drinking (or to create the appearance of doing so), possibly to impress his fiancée and her family, Poe mysteriously disappeared for five days while en route from Richmond to New York. On October 3, he was found and recognized in a delirious state in a tavern in Baltimore and taken to the hospital. Poe died on October 7, and was buried in Baltimore in the Presbyterian burying ground on Greene Street. The cause of Poe's death remains a mystery, as does how he came to be in Baltimore at the time of his death. Poe might have fallen victim to cholera, which was epidemic at the time, or meningitis. A popular theory of his death is that he was used as a phantom voter and made drunk until he became ill as he was taken from one polling place to another. Another theory has the brothers of his fiancée, who hated Poe, following him and getting him drunk to break his temperance vow, but overdoing the job. In all there are more than forty theories of how Poe died and, most likely, we'll never know what really happened.

One of Poe's best-known poems, the melancholy "Annabel Lee," was published two days after his death. "Annabel Lee" is about a childhood love so sweet that it is envied by the angels in heaven, who indirectly kill the beloved. The bereaved lover's devotion is so strong that each night he lies down in the tomb of his lost love. The poem is a suitable coda to Poe's life.

Although Poe's popularity declined somewhat in the first half of the twentieth century, the last few decades have seen a revival of interest in his works. The dark themes of death, melancholy, loss, horror, and madness—and his marvelous writing—are connecting once again with modern readers.

Since the 1950s, Poe's original grave marker has been the site of a peculiar phenomenon called the "Poe Toaster." Every year on Poe's

birthday, January 19, a small group of people gathers at Poe's grave, and a tall figure in a black cape and top hat appears, places three roses on the grave, and makes a toast of cognac to Poe's memory.

Doubtless Poe would have approved.

Jeffrey Goddin is the author of two horror novels and some sixty short stories and articles, as well as essays on writers such as Lafcadio Hearn, Algernon Blackwood and David Case. He holds a Master's Degree in English Literature from Indiana University.

Tales of the Macabre

METZENGERSTEIN

Pestis eram vivus—moriens tua mors ero.[1]

—MARTIN LUTHER

HORROR AND FATALITY HAVE BEEN STALKING ABROAD IN ALL AGES. WHY then give a date to this story I have to tell? Let it suffice to say, that at the period of which I speak, there existed, in the interior of Hungary, a settled although hidden belief in the doctrines of the Metempsychosis.[2] Of the doctrines themselves—that is, of their falsity, or of their probability—I say nothing. I assert, however, that much of our incredulity (as La Bruyere says of all our unhappiness) *"vient de ne pouvoir etre seuls."*[*]

But there were some points in the Hungarian superstition which were fast verging to absurdity. They—the Hungarians—differed very essentially from their Eastern authorities. For example, *"The soul,"* said the former—I give the words of an acute and intelligent Parisian— *"ne demeure qu'un seul fois dans un corps sensible: au reste—un cheval, un chien, un homme meme, n'est que la ressemblance peu tangible de ces animaux."*

The families of Berlifitzing and Metzengerstein had been at variance for centuries. Never before were two houses so illustrious, mutually embittered by hostility so deadly. The origin of this enmity seems to be found in the words of an ancient prophecy—"A lofty name shall have a fearful

[*] Mercier, in *L'an deux mille quatre cents quarante*, seriously maintains the doctrines of the Metempsychosis, and I. D'Israeli says that "no system is so simple and so little repugnant to the understanding." Colonel Ethan Allen, the "Green Mountain Boy," is also to have been a serious metempsychosist.

fall when, as the rider over his horse, the mortality of Metzengerstein shall triumph over the immortality of Berlifitzing."

To be sure the words themselves had little or no meaning. But more trivial causes have given rise—and that no long while ago—to consequences equally eventful. Besides, the estates, which were contiguous, had long exercised a rival influence in the affairs of a busy government. Moreover, near neighbors are seldom friends; and the inhabitants of the Castle Berlifitzing might look, from their lofty buttresses, into the very windows of the palace Metzengerstein. Least of all had the more than feudal magnificence thus discovered, a tendency to allay the irritable feelings of the less ancient and less wealthy Berlifitzings. What wonder, then, that the words, however silly, of that prediction, should have succeeded in setting and keeping at variance two families already predisposed to quarrel by every instigation of hereditary jealousy? The prophecy seemed to imply—if it implied anything—a final triumph on the part of the already more powerful house; and was of course remembered with the more bitter animosity by the weaker and less influential.

Wilhelm, Count Berlifitzing, although loftily descended, was, at the epoch of this narrative, an infirm and doting old man, remarkable for nothing but an inordinate and inveterate personal antipathy to the family of his rival, and so passionate a love of horses, and of hunting, that neither bodily infirmity, great age, nor mental incapacity, prevented his daily participation in the dangers of the chase.

Frederick, Baron Metzengerstein, was, on the other hand, not yet of age. His father, the Minister G——, died young. His mother, the Lady Mary, followed him quickly. Frederick was, at that time, in his eighteenth year. In a city, eighteen years are no long period: but in a wilderness—in so magnificent a wilderness as that old principality, the pendulum vibrates with a deeper meaning.

From some peculiar circumstances attending the administration of his father, the young Baron, at the decease of the former, entered immediately upon his vast possessions. Such estates were seldom held before by a nobleman of Hungary. His castles were without number. The chief in point of splendor and extent was the "Palace Metzengerstein." The boundary line of his dominions was never clearly defined; but his principal park embraced a circuit of fifty miles.

Upon the succession of a proprietor so young, with a character so well known, to a fortune so unparalleled, little speculation was afloat in regard to his probable course of conduct. And, indeed, for the space of

three days, the behavior of the heir out-heroded Herod, and fairly surpassed the expectations of his most enthusiastic admirers. Shameful debaucheries—flagrant treacheries—unheard-of atrocities—gave his trembling vassals quickly to understand that no servile submission on their part—no punctilios of conscience on his own—were thenceforward to prove any security against the remorseless fangs of a petty Caligula. On the night of the fourth day, the stables of the Castle Berlifitzing were discovered to be on fire; and the unanimous opinion of the neighborhood added the crime of the incendiary to the already hideous list of the Baron's misdemeanors and enormities.

But during the tumult occasioned by this occurrence, the young nobleman himself, sat apparently buried in meditation, in a vast and desolate upper apartment of the family palace of Metzengerstein. The rich although faded tapestry hangings which swung gloomily upon the walls, represented the shadowy and majestic forms of a thousand illustrious ancestors. *Here,* rich-ermined priests, and pontifical dignitaries, familiarly seated with the autocrat and the sovereign, put a veto on the wishes of a temporal king, or restrained with the fiat of papal supremacy the rebellious sceptre of the Archenemy. *There,* the dark, tall statures of the Princes Metzengerstein—their muscular war-coursers plunging over the carcasses of fallen foes—startled the steadiest nerves with their vigorous expression: and *here,* again, the voluptuous and swan-like figures of the dames of days gone by, floated away in the mazes of an unreal dance to the strains of imaginary melody.

But as the Baron listened, or affected to listen, to the gradually increasing uproar in the stables of Berlifitzing—or perhaps pondered upon some more novel, some more decided act of audacity—his eyes were turned unwittingly to the figure of an enormous, and unnaturally colored horse, represented in the tapestry as belonging to a Saracen ancestor of the family of his rival. The horse itself, in the foreground of the design, stood motionless and statue-like—while, farther back, its discomfited rider perished by the dagger of a Metzengerstein.

On Frederick's lip arose a fiendish expression, as he became aware of the direction which his glance had, without his consciousness, assumed. Yet he did not remove it. On the contrary, he could by no means account for the overwhelming anxiety which appeared falling like a pall upon his senses. It was with difficulty that he reconciled his dreamy and incoherent feelings with the certainty of being awake. The longer he gazed, the more absorbing became the spell—the more impossible did it appear that he could ever withdraw his glance from the fascination of that tapestry. But

the tumult without becoming suddenly more violent, with a compulsory exertion he diverted his attention to the glare of ruddy light thrown full by the flaming stables upon the windows of the apartment.

The action, however, was but momentary; his gaze returned mechanically to the wall. To his extreme horror and astonishment, the head of the gigantic steed had, in the meantime, altered its position. The neck of the animal, before arched, as if in compassion, over the prostrate body of its lord, was now extended, at full length, in the direction of the Baron. The eyes, before invisible, now wore an energetic and human expression, while they gleamed with a fiery and unusual red; and the distended lips of the apparently enraged horse left in full view his sepulchral and disgusting teeth.

Stupified with terror, the young nobleman tottered to the door. As he threw it open, a flash of red light, streaming far into the chamber, flung his shadow with a clear outline against the quivering tapestry; and he shuddered to perceive that shadow—as he staggered awhile upon the threshold—assuming the exact position, and precisely filling up the contour, of the relentless and triumphant murderer of the Saracen Berlifitzing.

To lighten the depression of his spirits, the Baron hurried into the open air. At the principal gate of the palace he encountered three equerries. With much difficulty, and at the imminent peril of their lives, they were restraining the convulsive plunges of a gigantic and fiery-colored horse.

"Whose horse? Where did you get him?" demanded the youth, in a querulous and husky tone, as he became instantly aware that the mysterious steed in the tapestried chamber was the very counterpart of the furious animal before his eyes.

"He is your own property, sire," replied one of the equerries, "at least he is claimed by no other owner. We caught him flying, all smoking and foaming with rage, from the burning stables of the Castle Berlifitzing. Supposing him to have belonged to the old Count's stud of foreign horses, we led him back as an estray. But the grooms there disclaim any title to the creature; which is strange, since he bears evident marks of having made a narrow escape from the flames."

"The letters W. V. B. are also branded very distinctly on his forehead," interrupted a second equerry; "I supposed them, of course, to be the initials of Wilhelm Von Berlifitzing—but all at the castle are positive in denying any knowledge of the horse."

"Extremely singular!" said the young Baron, with a musing air, and apparently unconscious of the meaning of his words. "He is, as you say, a remarkable horse—a prodigious horse! although, as you very justly

observe, of a suspicious and untractable character; let him be mine, however," he added, after a pause, "perhaps a rider like Frederick of Metzengerstein, may tame even the devil from the stables of Berlifitzing."

"You are mistaken, my lord; the horse, as I think we mentioned, is *not* from the stables of the Count. If such had been the case, we know our duty better than to bring him into the presence of a noble of your family."

"True!" observed the Baron, dryly; and at that instant a page of the bedchamber came from the palace with a heightened color, and a precipitate step. He whispered into his master's ear an account of the sudden disappearance of a small portion of the tapestry, in an apartment which he designated; entering, at the same time, into particulars of a minute and circumstantial character; but from the low tone of voice in which these latter were communicated, nothing escaped to gratify the excited curiosity of the equerries.

The young Frederick, during the conference, seemed agitated by a variety of emotions. He soon, however, recovered his composure, and an expression of determined malignancy settled upon his countenance, as he gave peremptory orders that the apartment in question should be immediately locked up, and the key placed in his own possession.

"Have you heard of the unhappy death of the old hunter Berlifitzing?" said one of his vassals to the Baron, as, after the departure of the page, the huge steed which that nobleman had adopted as his own, plunged and curveted, with redoubled fury, down the long avenue which extended from the palace to the stables of Metzengerstein.

"No!" said the Baron, turning abruptly towards the speaker; "dead! say you?"

"It is indeed true, my lord; and, to a noble of your name, will be, I imagine, no unwelcome intelligence."

A rapid smile shot over the countenance of the listener. "How died he?"

"In his rash exertions to rescue a favorite portion of his hunting stud, he has himself perished miserably in the flames."

"I—n—d—e—e—d—!" ejaculated the Baron, as if slowly and deliberately impressed with the truth of some exciting idea.

"Indeed," repeated the vassal.

"Shocking!" said the youth, calmly, and turned quietly into the palace.

From this date a marked alteration took place in the outward demeanor of the dissolute young Baron Frederick Von Metzengerstein. Indeed, his behavior disappointed every expectation, and proved little in accordance with the views of many a maneuvering mamma; while his

habits and manners, still less than formerly, offered anything congenial with those of the neighboring aristocracy. He was never to be seen beyond the limits of his own domain, and, in this wide and social world, was utterly companionless—unless, indeed, that unnatural, impetuous, and fiery-colored horse, which he henceforward continually bestrode, had any mysterious right to the title of his friend.

Numerous invitations on the part of the neighborhood for a long time, however, periodically came in. "Will the Baron honor our festivals with his presence?" "Will the Baron join us in a hunting of the boar?" "Metzengerstein does not hunt"; "Metzengerstein will not attend," were the haughty and laconic answers.

These repeated insults were not to be endured by an imperious nobility. Such invitations became less cordial—less frequent—in time they ceased altogether. The widow of the unfortunate Count Berlifitzing was even heard to express a hope "that the Baron might be at home when he did not wish to be at home, since he disdained the company of his equals; and ride when he did not wish to ride, since he preferred the society of a horse." This to be sure was a very silly explosion of hereditary pique; and merely proved how singularly unmeaning our sayings are apt to become, when we desire to be unusually energetic.

The charitable, nevertheless, attributed the alteration in the conduct of the young nobleman to the natural sorrow of a son for the untimely loss of his parents; forgetting, however, his atrocious and reckless behavior during the short period immediately succeeding that bereavement. Some there were, indeed, who suggested a too haughty idea of self-consequence and dignity. Others again (among whom may be mentioned the family physician) did not hesitate in speaking of morbid melancholy, and hereditary ill-health; while dark hints, of a more equivocal nature, were current among the multitude.

Indeed, the Baron's perverse attachment to his lately acquired charger— an attachment which seemed to attain new strength from every fresh example of the animal's ferocious and demon-like propensities—at length became, in the eyes of all reasonable men, a hideous and unnatural fervor. In the glare of noon—at the dead hour of night—in sickness or in health—in calm or in tempest—the young Metzengerstein seemed riveted to the saddle of that colossal horse, whose intractable audacities so well accorded with his own spirit.

There were circumstances, moreover, which, coupled with late events, gave an unearthly and portentous character to the mania of the

rider, and to the capabilities of the steed. The space passed over in a single leap had been accurately measured, and was found to exceed, by an astounding difference, the wildest expectations of the most imaginative. The Baron, besides, had no particular *name* for the animal, although all the rest in his collection were distinguished by characteristic appellations. His stable, too, was appointed at a distance from the rest; and with regard to grooming and other necessary offices, none but the owner in person had ventured to officiate, or even to enter the enclosure of that horse's particular stall. It was also to be observed, that although the three grooms, who had caught the steed as he fled from the conflagration at Berlifitzing, had succeeded in arresting his course, by means of a chain-bridle and noose—yet no one of the three could with any certainty affirm that he had, during that dangerous struggle, or at any period thereafter, actually placed his hand upon the body of the beast. Instances of peculiar intelligence in the demeanor of a noble and high-spirited horse are not to be supposed capable of exciting unreasonable attention, but there were certain circumstances which intruded themselves per force upon the most skeptical and phlegmatic; and it is said there were times when the animal caused the gaping crowd who stood around to recoil in horror from the deep and impressive meaning of his terrible stamp—times when the young Metzengerstein turned pale and shrunk away from the rapid and searching expression of his earnest and human-looking eye.

Among all the retinue of the Baron, however, none were found to doubt the ardor of that extraordinary affection which existed on the part of the young nobleman for the fiery qualities of his horse; at least, none but an insignificant and misshapen little page, whose deformities were in everybody's way, and whose opinions were of the least possible importance. He (if his ideas are worth mentioning at all) had the effrontery to assert that his master never vaulted into the saddle, without an unaccountable and almost imperceptible shudder; and that, upon his return from every long-continued and habitual ride, an expression of triumphant malignity distorted every muscle in his countenance.

One tempestuous night, Metzengerstein, awaking from heavy slumber, descended like a maniac from his chamber, and, mounting in hot haste, bounded away into the mazes of the forest. An occurrence so common attracted no particular attention, but his return was looked for with intense anxiety on the part of his domestics, when, after some hours' absence, the stupendous and magnificent battlements of the Palace Metzengerstein,

were discovered crackling and rocking to their very foundation, under the influence of a dense and livid mass of ungovernable fire.

As the flames, when first seen, had already made so terrible a progress that all efforts to save any portion of the building were evidently futile, the astonished neighborhood stood idly around in silent, if not apathetic wonder. But a new and fearful object soon riveted the attention of the multitude, and proved how much more intense is the excitement wrought in the feelings of a crowd by the contemplation of human agony, than that brought about by the most appalling spectacles of inanimate matter.

Up the long avenue of aged oaks which led from the forest to the main entrance of the Palace Metzengerstein, a steed, bearing an unbonneted and disordered rider, was seen leaping with an impetuosity which outstripped the very Demon of the Tempest.

The career of the horseman was indisputably, on his own part, uncontrollable. The agony of his countenance, the convulsive struggle of his frame, gave evidence of superhuman exertion: but no sound, save a solitary shriek, escaped from his lacerated lips, which were bitten through and through in the intensity of terror. One instant, and the clattering of hoofs resounded sharply and shrilly above the roaring of the flames and the shrieking of the winds—another, and, clearing at a single plunge the gateway and the moat, the steed bounded far up the tottering staircases of the palace, and, with its rider, disappeared amid the whirlwind of chaotic fire.

The fury of the tempest immediately died away, and a dead calm sullenly succeeded. A white flame still enveloped the building like a shroud, and, streaming far away into the quiet atmosphere, shot forth a glare of preternatural light; while a cloud of smoke settled heavily over the battlements in the distinct colossal figure of—*a horse.*

MS. FOUND IN A BOTTLE

Qui n'a plus qu'un moment à vivre
N'a plus rien à dissimuler.[1]

—QUINAULT, *ATYS*

OF MY COUNTRY AND OF MY FAMILY I HAVE LITTLE TO SAY. ILL USAGE
and length of years have driven me from the one, and estranged me from
the other. Hereditary wealth afforded me an education of no common
order, and a contemplative turn of mind enabled me to methodize the
stores which early study very diligently garnered up. Beyond all things,
the works of the German moralists gave me great delight; not from any
ill advised admiration of their eloquent madness, but from the ease with
which my habits of rigid thought enabled me to detect their falsities. I
have often been reproached with the aridity of my genius; a deficiency
of imagination has been imputed to me as a crime; and the Pyrrhonism[2] of
my opinions has at all times rendered me notorious. Indeed, a strong rel-
ish for physical philosophy has, I fear, tinctured my mind with a very
common error of this age—I mean the habit of referring occurrences,
even the least susceptible of such reference, to the principles of that sci-
ence. Upon the whole, no person could be less liable than myself to be led
away from the severe precincts of truth by the *ignes fatui* of superstition. I
have thought proper to premise thus much, lest the incredible tale I have
to tell should be considered rather the raving of a crude imagination, than
the positive experience of a mind to which the reveries of fancy have been
a dead letter and a nullity.

After many years spent in foreign travel, I sailed in the year 18—, from
the port of Batavia, in the rich and populous island of Java, on a voyage to

the Archipelago of the Sunda islands. I went as passenger—having no other inducement than a kind of nervous restlessness which haunted me as a fiend.

Our vessel was a beautiful ship of about four hundred tons, copper-fastened, and built at Bombay of Malabar teak. She was freighted with cotton-wool and oil, from the Lachadive islands. We had also on board coir, jaggeree, ghee, cocoa-nuts, and a few cases of opium. The stowage was clumsily done, and the vessel consequently crank.

We got under way with a mere breath of wind, and for many days stood along the eastern coast of Java, without any other incident to beguile the monotony of our course than the occasional meeting with some of the small grabs of the Archipelago to which we were bound.

One evening, leaning over the taffrail, I observed a very singular, isolated cloud, to the N. W. It was remarkable, as well for its color, as from its being the first we had seen since our departure from Batavia. I watched it attentively until sunset, when it spread all at once to the eastward and westward, girting in the horizon with a narrow strip of vapor, and looking like a long line of low beach. My notice was soon afterwards attracted by the dusky-red appearance of the moon, and the peculiar character of the sea. The latter was undergoing a rapid change, and the water seemed more than usually transparent. Although I could distinctly see the bottom, yet, heaving the lead, I found the ship in fifteen fathoms. The air now became intolerably hot, and was loaded with spiral exhalations similar to those arising from heated iron. As night came on, every breath of wind died away, and more entire calm it is impossible to conceive. The flame of a candle burned upon the poop without the least perceptible motion, and a long hair, held between the finger and thumb, hung without the possibility of detecting a vibration. However, as the captain said he could perceive no indication of danger, and as we were drifting in bodily to shore, he ordered the sails to be furled, and the anchor let go. No watch was set, and the crew, consisting principally of Malays, stretched themselves deliberately upon deck. I went below—not without a full presentiment of evil. Indeed, every appearance warranted me in apprehending a Simoon. I told the captain my fears; but he paid no attention to what I said, and left me without deigning to give a reply. My uneasiness, however, prevented me from sleeping, and about midnight I went upon deck. As I placed my foot upon the upper step of the companion-ladder, I was startled by a loud, humming noise, like that occasioned by the rapid revolution of a mill-wheel, and before I could ascertain its meaning, I found the ship

quivering to its center. In the next instant, a wilderness of foam hurled us upon our beam-ends, and, rushing over us fore and aft, swept the entire decks from stem to stern.

The extreme fury of the blast proved, in a great measure, the salvation of the ship. Although completely water-logged, yet, as her masts had gone by the board, she rose, after a minute, heavily from the sea, and, staggering awhile beneath the immense pressure of the tempest, finally righted.

By what miracle I escaped destruction, it is impossible to say. Stunned by the shock of the water, I found myself, upon recovery, jammed in between the stern-post and rudder. With great difficulty I gained my feet, and looking dizzily around, was at first struck with the idea of our being among breakers; so terrific, beyond the wildest imagination, was the whirlpool of mountainous and foaming ocean within which we were engulfed. After a while, I heard the voice of an old Swede, who had shipped with us at the moment of our leaving port. I hallooed to him with all my strength, and presently he came reeling aft. We soon discovered that we were the sole survivors of the accident. All on deck, with the exception of ourselves, had been swept overboard; the captain and mates must have perished as they slept, for the cabins were deluged with water. Without assistance, we could expect to do little for the security of the ship, and our exertions were at first paralyzed by the momentary expectation of going down. Our cable had, of course, parted like pack-thread, at the first breath of the hurricane, or we should have been instantaneously overwhelmed. We scudded with frightful velocity before the sea, and the water made clear breaches over us. The framework of our stern was shattered excessively, and, in almost every respect, we had received considerable injury; but to our extreme joy we found the pumps unchoked, and that we had made no great shifting of our ballast. The main fury of the blast had already blown over, and we apprehended little danger from the violence of the wind; but we looked forward to its total cessation with dismay; well believing, that in our shattered condition, we should inevitably perish in the tremendous swell which would ensue. But this very just apprehension seemed by no means likely to be soon verified. For five entire days and nights—during which our only subsistence was a small quantity of jaggeree, procured with great difficulty from the forecastle—the hulk flew at a rate defying computation, before rapidly succeeding flaws of wind, which, without equaling the first violence of the Simoon, were still more terrific than any tempest I had before encountered. Our course for the first four days was, with trifling variations, S.E. and by S.; and we must have run down the

coast of New Holland. On the fifth day the cold became extreme, although the wind had hauled round a point more to the northward. The sun arose with a sickly yellow luster, and clambered a very few degrees above the horizon—emitting no decisive light. There were no clouds apparent, yet the wind was upon the increase, and blew with a fitful and unsteady fury. About noon, as nearly as we could guess, our attention was again arrested by the appearance of the sun. It gave out no light, properly so called, but a dull and sullen glow without reflection, as if all its rays were polarized. Just before sinking within the turgid sea, its central fires suddenly went out, as if hurriedly extinguished by some unaccountable power. It was a dim, silver-like rim, alone, as it rushed down the unfathomable ocean.

We waited in vain for the arrival of the sixth day—that day to me has not arrived—to the Swede, never did arrive. Thenceforward we were enshrouded in patchy darkness, so that we could not have seen an object at twenty paces from the ship. Eternal night continued to envelop us, all unrelieved by the phosphoric sea-brilliancy to which we had been accustomed in the tropics. We observed too, that, although the tempest continued to rage with unabated violence, there was no longer to be discovered the usual appearance of surf, or foam, which had hitherto attended us. All around were horror, and thick gloom, and a black sweltering desert of ebony. Superstitious terror crept by degrees into the spirit of the old Swede, and my own soul was wrapped up in silent wonder. We neglected all care of the ship, as worse than useless, and securing ourselves, as well as possible, to the stump of the mizen-mast, looked out bitterly into the world of ocean. We had no means of calculating time, nor could we form any guess of our situation. We were, however, well aware of having made farther to the southward than any previous navigators, and felt great amazement at not meeting with the usual impediments of ice. In the meantime every moment threatened to be our last—every mountainous billow hurried to overwhelm us. The swell surpassed anything I had imagined possible, and that we were not instantly buried is a miracle. My companion spoke of the lightness of our cargo, and reminded me of the excellent qualities of our ship; but I could not help feeling the utter hopelessness of hope itself, and prepared myself gloomily for that death which I thought nothing could defer beyond an hour, as, with every knot of way the ship made, the swelling of the black stupendous seas became more dismally appalling. At times we gasped for breath at an elevation beyond the albatross—at times became dizzy with the velocity of our descent into some watery hell, where the air grew stagnant, and no sound disturbed the slumbers of the kraken.

We were at the bottom of one of these abysses, when a quick scream from my companion broke fearfully upon the night. "See! see!" cried he, shrieking in my ears, "Almighty God! see! see!" As he spoke, I became aware of a dull, sullen glare of red light which streamed down the sides of the vast chasm where we lay, and threw a fitful brilliancy upon our deck. Casting my eyes upwards, I beheld a spectacle which froze the current of my blood. At a terrific height directly above us, and upon the very verge of the precipitous descent, hovered a gigantic ship, of perhaps four thousand tons. Although upreared upon the summit of a wave more than a hundred times her own altitude, her apparent size still exceeded that of any ship of the line or East Indiaman in existence. Her huge hull was of a deep dingy black, unrelieved by any of the customary carvings of a ship. A single row of brass cannon protruded from her open ports, and dashed from their polished surfaces the fires of innumerable battle-lanterns, which swung to and fro about her rigging. But what mainly inspired us with horror and astonishment, was that she bore up under a press of sail in the very teeth of that supernatural sea, and of that ungovernable hurricane. When we first discovered her, her bows were alone to be seen, as she rose slowly from the dim and horrible gulf beyond her. For a moment of intense terror she paused upon the giddy pinnacle, as if in contemplation of her own sublimity, then trembled and tottered, and—came down.

At this instant, I know not what sudden self-possession came over my spirit. Staggering as far aft as I could, I awaited fearlessly the ruin that was to overwhelm. Our own vessel was at length ceasing from her struggles, and sinking with her head to the sea. The shock of the descending mass struck her, consequently, in that portion of her frame which was already under water, and the inevitable result was to hurl me, with irresistible violence, upon the rigging of the stranger.

As I fell, the ship hove in stays, and went about; and to the confusion ensuing I attributed my escape from the notice of the crew. With little difficulty I made my way, unperceived, to the main hatchway, which was partially open, and soon found an opportunity of secreting myself in the hold. Why I did so I can hardly tell. An indefinite sense of awe, which at first sight of the navigators of the ship had taken hold of my mind, was perhaps the principle of my concealment. I was unwilling to trust myself with a race of people who had offered, to the cursory glance I had taken, so many points of vague novelty, doubt, and apprehension. I therefore thought proper to contrive a hiding-place in the hold. This I did by

removing a small portion of the shifting-boards, in such a manner as to afford me a convenient retreat between the huge timbers of the ship.

I had scarcely completed my work, when a footstep in the hold forced me to make use of it. A man passed by my place of concealment with a feeble and unsteady gait. I could not see his face, but had an opportunity of observing his general appearance. There was about it an evidence of great age and infirmity. His knees tottered beneath a load of years, and his entire frame quivered under the burden. He muttered to himself, in a low broken tone, some words of a language which I could not understand, and groped in a corner among a pile of singular-looking instruments, and decayed charts of navigation. His manner was a wild mixture of the pee-vishness of second childhood and the solemn dignity of a God. He at length went on deck, and I saw him no more.

———

A feeling, for which I have no name, has taken possession of my soul—a sensation which will admit of no analysis, to which the lessons of by-gone time are inadequate, and for which I fear futurity itself will offer me no key. To a mind constituted like my own, the latter consideration is an evil. I shall never—I know that I shall never—be satisfied with regard to the nature of my conceptions. Yet it is not wonderful that these conceptions are indefinite, since they have their origin in sources so utterly novel. A new sense—a new entity is added to my soul.

———

It is long since I first trod the deck of this terrible ship, and the rays of my destiny are, I think, gathering to a focus. Incomprehensible men! Wrapped up in meditations of a kind which I cannot divine, they pass me by unno-ticed. Concealment is utter folly on my part, for the people *will not* see. It was but just now that I passed directly before the eyes of the mate; it was no long while ago that I ventured into the captain's own private cabin, and took thence the materials with which I write, and have written. I shall from time to time continue this journal. It is true that I may not find an opportunity of transmitting it to the world, but I will not fail to make the endeavor. At the last moment I will enclose the MS. in a bottle, and cast it within the sea.

———

An incident has occurred which has given me new room for meditation. Are such things the operation of ungoverned chance? I had ventured

upon deck and thrown myself down, without attracting any notice, among a pile of ratlin-stuff and old sails, in the bottom of the yawl. While musing upon the singularity of my fate, I unwittingly daubed with a tar-brush the edges of a neatly folded studding-sail which lay near me on a barrel. The studding-sail is now bent upon the ship, and the thoughtless touches of the brush are spread out into the word DISCOVERY.

I have made many observations lately upon the structure of the vessel. Although well armed, she is not, I think, a ship of war. Her rigging, build, and general equipment, all negative a supposition of this kind. What she *is not,* I can easily perceive; what she is I fear it is impossible to say. I know not how it is, but in scrutinizing her strange model and singular cast of spars, her huge size and overgrown suits of canvas, her severely simple bow and antiquated stern, there will occasionally flash across my mind a sensation of familiar things, and there is always mixed up with such indistinct shadows of recollection, an unaccountable memory of old foreign chronicles and ages long ago.

I have been looking at the timbers of the ship. She is built of a material to which I am a stranger. There is a peculiar character about the wood which strikes me as rendering it unfit for the purpose to which it has been applied. I mean its extreme *porousness,* considered independently of the worm-eaten condition which is a consequence of navigation in these seas, and apart from the rottenness attendant upon age. It will appear perhaps an observation somewhat over-curious, but this wood would have every characteristic of Spanish oak, if Spanish oak were distended by any unnatural means.

In reading the above sentence, a curious apothegm of an old weather-beaten Dutch navigator comes full upon my recollection. "It is as sure," he was wont to say, when any doubt was entertained of his veracity, "as sure as there is a sea where the ship itself will grow in bulk like the living body of the seaman."

About an hour ago, I made bold to thrust myself among a group of the crew. They paid me no manner of attention, and, although I stood in the very midst of them all, seemed utterly unconscious of my presence. Like the one I had at first seen in the hold, they all bore about them the marks of a hoary old age. Their knees trembled with infirmity; their shoulders

were bent double with decrepitude; their shriveled skins rattled in the wind; their voices were low, tremulous and broken; their eyes glistened with the rheum of years; and their gray hairs streamed terribly in the tempest. Around them, on every part of the deck, lay scattered mathematical instruments of the most quaint and obsolete construction.

I mentioned, some time ago, the bending of a studding-sail. From that period, the ship, being thrown dead off the wind, has continued her terrific course due south, with every rag of canvas packed upon her, from her trucks to her lower studding-sail booms, and rolling every moment her top-gallant yard-arms into the most appalling hell of water which it can enter into the mind of man to imagine. I have just left the deck, where I find it impossible to maintain a footing, although the crew seem to experience little inconvenience. It appears to me a miracle of miracles that our enormous bulk is not swallowed up at once and forever. We are surely doomed to hover continually upon the brink of eternity, without taking a final plunge into the abyss. From billows a thousand times more stupendous than any I have ever seen, we glide away with the facility of the arrowy sea-gull; and the colossal waters rear their heads above us like demons of the deep, but like demons confined to simple threats, and forbidden to destroy. I am led to attribute these frequent escapes to the only natural cause which can account for such effect. I must suppose the ship to be within the influence of some strong current, or impetuous under-tow.

I have seen the captain face to face, and in his own cabin—but, as I expected, he paid me no attention. Although in his appearance there is, to a casual observer, nothing which might bespeak him more or less than man, still, a feeling of irrepressible reverence and awe mingled with the sensation of wonder with which I regarded him. In stature, he is nearly my own height; that is, about five feet eight inches. He is of a well-knit and compact frame of body, neither robust nor remarkably otherwise. But it is the singularity of the expression which reigns upon the face—it is the intense, the wonderful, the thrilling evidence of old age, so utter, so extreme, which excites within my spirit a sense—a sentiment ineffable. His forehead, although little wrinkled, seems to bear upon it the stamp of a myriad of years. His gray hairs are records of the past, and his grayer eyes are sibyls of the future. The cabin floor was thickly strewn with strange, iron-clasped folios, and moldering

instruments of science, and obsolete long-forgotten charts. His head was bowed down upon his hands, and he pored, with a fiery, unquiet eye, over a paper which I took to be a commission, and which, at all events, bore the signature of a monarch. He muttered to himself—as did the first seaman whom I saw in the hold—some low peevish syllables of a foreign tongue; and although the speaker was close at my elbow, his voice seemed to reach my ears from the distance of a mile.

The ship and all in it are imbued with the spirit of Eld. The crew glide to and fro like the ghosts of buried centuries; their eyes have an eager and uneasy meaning; and when their fingers fall athwart my path in the wild glare of the battle-lanterns, I feel as I have never felt before, although I have been all my life a dealer in antiquities, and have imbibed the shadows of fallen columns at Balbec, and Tadmor, and Persepolis, until my very soul has become a ruin.

When I look around me, I feel ashamed of my former apprehensions. If I trembled at the blast which has hitherto attended us, shall I not stand aghast at a warring of wind and ocean, to convey any idea of which, the words tornado and simoon are trivial and ineffective? All in the immediate vicinity of the ship is the blackness of eternal night, and a chaos of foamless water; but, about a league on either side of us, may be seen, indistinctly and at intervals, stupendous ramparts of ice, towering away into the desolate sky, and looking like the walls of the universe.

As I imagined, the ship proves to be in a current—if that appellation can properly be given to a tide which, howling and shrieking by the white ice, thunders on to the southward with a velocity like the headlong dashing of a cataract.

To conceive the horror of my sensations is, I presume, utterly impossible; yet a curiosity to penetrate the mysteries of these awful regions, predominates even over my despair, and will reconcile me to the most hideous aspect of death. It is evident that we are hurrying onwards to some exciting knowledge—some never-to-be-imparted secret, whose attainment is

destruction. Perhaps this current leads us to the southern pole itself. It must be confessed that a supposition apparently so wild has every probability in its favor.

The crew pace the deck with unquiet and tremulous step; but there is upon their countenances an expression more of the eagerness of hope than of the apathy of despair.

In the meantime the wind is still in our poop, and, as we carry a crowd of canvas, the ship is at times lifted bodily from out the sea! Oh, horror upon horror!—the ice opens suddenly to the right, and to the left, and we are whirling dizzily, in immense concentric circles, round and round the borders of a gigantic amphitheater, the summit of whose walls is lost in the darkness and the distance. But little time will be left me to ponder upon my destiny! The circles rapidly grow small—we are plunging madly within the grasp of the whirlpool—and amid a roaring, and bellowing, and thundering of ocean and of tempest, the ship is quivering—oh God! and—going down.

NOTE. The "MS. Found in a Bottle," was originally published in 1831; and it was not until many years afterwards that I became acquainted with the maps of Mercator, in which the ocean is represented as rushing, by four mouths, into the (northern) Polar Gulf, to be absorbed into the bowels of the earth; the Pole itself being represented by a black rock, towering to a prodigious height.

SHADOW—A PARABLE

Yea! though I walk through the valley of the Shadow:

· —PSALM OF DAVID

YE WHO READ ARE STILL AMONG THE LIVING; BUT I WHO WRITE SHALL HAVE long since gone my way into the region of shadows. For indeed strange things shall happen, and secret things be known, and many centuries shall pass away, ere these memorials be seen of men. And, when seen, there will be some to disbelieve, and some to doubt, and yet a few who will find much to ponder upon in the characters here graven with a stylus of iron.

The year had been a year of terror, and of feelings more intense than terror for which there is no name upon the earth. For many prodigies and signs had taken place, and far and wide, over sea and land, the black wings of the Pestilence were spread abroad. To those, nevertheless, cunning in the stars, it was not unknown that the heavens wore an aspect of ill; and to me, the Greek Oinos, among others, it was evident that now had arrived the alternation of that seven hundred and ninety-fourth year when, at the entrance of Aries, the planet Jupiter is conjoined with the red ring of the terrible Saturnus. The peculiar spirit of the skies, if I mistake not greatly, made itself manifest, not only in the physical orb of the earth, but in the souls, imaginations, and meditations of mankind.

Over some flasks of the red Chian wine, within the walls of a noble hall, in a dim city called Ptolemais, we sat, at night, a company of seven. And to our chamber there was no entrance save by a lofty door of brass: and the door was fashioned by the artisan Corinos, and, being of rare workmanship, was fastened from within. Black draperies, likewise, in the

21

)m, shut out from our view the moon, the lurid stars, and the
streets—but the boding and the memory of Evil, they would
excluded. There were things around us and about of which I can
render no distinct account—things material and spiritual—heaviness in
the atmosphere—a sense of suffocation—anxiety—and, above all, that
terrible state of existence which the nervous experience when the senses
are keenly living and awake, and meanwhile the powers of thought lie
dormant. A dead weight hung upon us. It hung upon our limbs—upon
the household furniture—upon the goblets from which we drank; and all
things were depressed, and borne down thereby—all things save only the
flames of the seven lamps which illumined our revel. Uprearing them-
selves in tall slender lines of light, they thus remained burning all pallid
and motionless; and in the mirror which their luster formed upon the
round table of ebony at which we sat, each of us there assembled beheld
the pallor of his own countenance, and the unquiet glare in the downcast
eyes of his companions. Yet we laughed and were merry in our proper
way—which was hysterical; and sang the songs of Anacreon—which are
madness; and drank deeply—although the purple wine reminded us of
blood. For there was yet another tenant of our chamber in the person
of young Zoilus. Dead, and at full length he lay, enshrouded; the genius
and the demon of the scene. Alas! he bore no portion in our mirth, save
that his countenance, distorted with the plague, and his eyes, in which
Death had but half extinguished the fire of the pestilence, seemed to take
such interest in our merriment as the dead may haply take in the merri-
ment of those who are to die. But although I, Oinos, felt that the eyes of
the departed were upon me, still I forced myself not to perceive the bitter-
ness of their expression, and, gazing down steadily into the depths of the
ebony mirror, sang with a loud and sonorous voice the songs of the son of
Teios. But gradually my songs they ceased, and their echoes, rolling afar
off among the sable draperies of the chamber, became weak, and undis-
tinguishable, and so faded away. And lo! from among those sable
draperies where the sounds of the song departed, there came forth a dark
and undefined shadow—a shadow such as the moon, when low in heaven,
might fashion from the figure of a man: but it was the shadow neither of
man, nor of God, nor of any familiar thing. And, quivering awhile among
the draperies of the room, it at length rested in full view upon the surface
of the door of brass. But the shadow was vague, and formless, and indefi-
nite, and was the shadow neither of man nor of God—neither God of
Greece, nor God of Chaldæa, nor any Egyptian God. And the shadow

rested upon the brazen doorway, and under the arch of the entablature of the door, and moved not, nor spoke any word, but there became stationary and remained. And the door whereupon the shadow rested was, if I remember aright, over against the feet of the young Zoilus enshrouded. But we, the seven there assembled, having seen the shadow as it came out from among the draperies, dared not steadily behold it, but cast down our eyes, and gazed continually into the depths of the mirror of ebony. And at length I, Oinos, speaking some low words, demanded of the shadow its dwelling and its appellation. And the shadow answered, "I am SHADOW, and my dwelling is near to the Catacombs of Ptolemais, and hard by those dim plains of Helusion which border upon the foul Charonian canal." And then did we, the seven, start from our seats in horror, and stand trembling, and shuddering, and aghast: for the tones in the voice of the shadow were not the tones of any one being, but of a multitude of beings, and, varying in their cadences from syllable to syllable, fell duskily upon our ears in the well remembered and familiar accents of many thousand departed friends.

SILENCE—A FABLE

'Ενδουσιν δ' ορωνκορυΦαι τε καὶ Φάραγγες
Πρώονές τε καὶχάράδραι

The mountain pinnacles slumber; valleys,
crags and caves are silent.

—ALCMAN

"LISTEN TO *ME*," SAID THE DEMON, AS HE PLACED HIS HAND UPON MY HEAD. "The region of which I speak is a dreary region in Libya, by the borders of the river Zaire. And there is no quiet there, nor silence.

"The waters of the river have a saffron and sickly hue; and they flow not onwards to the sea, but palpitate forever and forever beneath the red eye of the sun with a tumultuous and convulsive motion. For many miles on either side of the river's oozy bed is a pale desert of gigantic water-lilies. They sigh one unto the other in that solitude, and stretch towards the heaven their long and ghastly necks, and nod to and fro their everlasting heads. And there is an indistinct murmur which cometh out from among them like the rushing of subterrene water. And they sigh one unto the other.

"But there is a boundary to their realm—the boundary of the dark, horrible, lofty forest. There, like the waves about the Hebrides, the low underwood is agitated continually. But there is no wind throughout the heaven. And the tall primeval trees rock eternally hither and thither with a crashing and mighty sound. And from their high summits, one by one, drop everlasting dews. And at the roots strange poisonous flowers lie writhing in perturbed slumber. And overhead, with a rustling and loud noise, the gray clouds rush westwardly forever, until they roll, a cataract, over the

24

fiery wall of the horizon. But there is no wind throughout the heaven. And by the shores of the river Zaire there is neither quiet nor silence.

"It was night, and the rain fell; and, falling, it was rain, but, having fallen, it was blood. And I stood in the morass among the tall lilies, and the rain fell upon my head—and the lilies sighed one unto the other in the solemnity of their desolation.

"And, all at once, the moon arose through the thin ghastly mist, and was crimson in color. And mine eyes fell upon a huge gray rock which stood by the shore of the river, and was lighted by the light of the moon. And the rock was gray, and ghastly, and tall—and the rock was gray. Upon its front were characters engraven in the stone; and I walked through the morass of water-lilies, until I came close unto the shore, that I might read the characters upon the stone. But I could not decipher them. And I was going back into the morass, when the moon shone with a fuller red, and I turned and looked again upon the rock, and upon the characters; and the characters were DESOLATION.

"And I looked upwards, and there stood a man upon the summit of the rock; and I hid myself among the water-lilies that I might discover the actions of the man. And the man was tall and stately in form, and was wrapped up from his shoulders to his feet in the toga of old Rome. And the outlines of his figure were indistinct—but his features were the features of a deity; for the mantle of the night, and of the mist, and of the moon, and of the dew, had left uncovered the features of his face. And his brow was lofty with thought, and his eye wild with care; and, in the few furrows upon his cheek I read the fables of sorrow, and weariness, and disgust with mankind, and a longing after solitude.

"And the man sat upon the rock, and leaned his head upon his hand, and looked out upon the desolation. He looked down into the low unquiet shrubbery, and up into the tall primeval trees, and up higher at the rustling heaven, and into the crimson moon. And I lay close within shelter of the lilies, and observed the actions of the man. And the man trembled in the solitude; but the night waned, and he sat upon the rock.

"And the man turned his attention from the heaven, and looked out upon the dreary river Zaire, and upon the yellow ghastly waters, and upon the pale legions of the water-lilies. And the man listened to the sighs of the water-lilies, and to the murmur that came up from among them. And I lay close within my covert and observed the actions of the man. And the man trembled in the solitude; but the night waned and he sat upon the rock.

"Then I went down into the recesses of the morass, and waded afar in among the wilderness of the lilies, and called unto the hippopotami which dwelt among the fens in the recesses of the morass. And the hippopotami heard my call, and came, with the behemoth, unto the foot of the rock, and roared loudly and fearfully beneath the moon. And I lay close within my covert and observed the actions of the man. And the man trembled in the solitude; but the night waned and he sat upon the rock.

"Then I cursed the elements with the curse of tumult; and a frightful tempest gathered in the heaven where, before, there had been no wind. And the heaven became livid with the violence of the tempest—and the rain beat upon the head of the man—and the floods of the river came down—and the river was tormented into foam—and the water-lilies shrieked within their beds—and the forest crumbled before the wind— and the thunder rolled—and the lightning fell—and the rock rocked to its foundation. And I lay close within my covert and observed the actions of the man. And the man trembled in the solitude; but the night waned and he sat upon the rock.

"Then I grew angry and cursed, with the curse of *silence*, the river, and the lilies, and the wind, and the forest, and the heaven, and the thunder, and the sighs of the water-lilies. And they became accursed, and *were still*. And the moon ceased to totter up its pathway to heaven—and the thunder died away—and the lightning did not flash—and the clouds hung motionless—and the waters sunk to their level and remained—and the trees ceased to rock—and the water-lilies sighed no more—and the murmur was heard no longer from among them, nor any shadow of sound throughout the vast illimitable desert. And I looked upon the characters of the rock, and they were changed; and the characters were SILENCE.

"And mine eyes fell upon the countenance of the man, and his countenance was wan with terror. And, hurriedly, he raised his head from his hand, and stood forth upon the rock and listened. But there was no voice throughout the vast illimitable desert, and the characters upon the rock were SILENCE. And the man shuddered, and turned his face away, and fled afar off, in haste, so that I beheld him no more."

Now there are fine tales in the volumes of the Magi—in the iron-bound, melancholy volumes of the Magi. Therein, I say, are glorious histories of the Heaven, and of the Earth, and of the mighty sea—and of the Genii that over-ruled the sea, and the earth, and the lofty heaven. There was much lore too in the sayings which were said by the Sybils; and holy, holy

things were heard of old by the dim leaves that trembled around Dodona—but, as Allah liveth, that fable which the Demon told me as he sat by my side in the shadow of the tomb, I hold to be the most wonderful of all! And as the Demon made an end of his story, he fell back within the cavity of the tomb and laughed. And I could not laugh with the Demon, and he cursed me because I could not laugh. And the lynx which dwelleth forever in the tomb, came out therefrom, and lay down at the feet of the Demon, and looked at him steadily in the face.

BERENICE

*Dicebant mihi sodales, si sepulchrum amicae visitarem,
curas meas aliquantulum fore levatas.*[1]

—EBN ZAIAT

MISERY IS MANIFOLD. THE WRETCHEDNESS OF EARTH IS MULTIFORM. Overreaching the wide horizon as the rainbow, its hues are as various as the hues of that arch—as distinct too, yet as intimately blended. Overreaching the wide horizon as the rainbow! How is it that from beauty I have derived a type of unloveliness?—from the covenant of peace a simile of sorrow? But as, in ethics, evil is a consequence of good, so, in fact, out of joy is sorrow born. Either the memory of past bliss is the anguish of today, or the agonies which *are* have their origin in the ecstasies which *might have been.*

My baptismal name is Egæus; that of my family I will not mention. Yet there are no towers in the land more time-honored than my gloomy, gray, hereditary halls. Our line has been called a race of visionaries; and in many striking particulars—in the character of the family mansion—in the frescos of the chief saloon—in the tapestries of the dormitories—in the chiseling of some buttresses in the armory—but more especially in the gallery of antique paintings—in the fashion of the library chamber—and, lastly, in the very peculiar nature of the library's contents, there is more than sufficient evidence to warrant the belief.

The recollections of my earliest years are connected with that chamber, and with its volumes—of which latter I will say no more. Here died my mother. Herein was I born. But it is mere idleness to say that I had not lived before—that the soul has no previous existence. You deny it?—let us

28

not argue the matter. Convinced myself, I seek not to convince. There is, however, a remembrance of aerial forms—of spiritual and meaning eyes—of sounds, musical yet sad—a remembrance which will not be excluded; a memory like a shadow, vague, variable, indefinite, unsteady; and like a shadow, too, in the impossibility of my getting rid of it while the sunlight of my reason shall exist.

In that chamber was I born. Thus awaking from the long night of what seemed, but was not, nonentity, at once into the very regions of fairy-land— into a palace of imagination—into the wild dominions of monastic thought and erudition—it is not singular that I gazed around me with a startled and ardent eye—that I loitered away my boyhood in books, and dissipated my youth in reverie; but it *is* singular that as years rolled away, and the noon of manhood found me still in the mansion of my fathers—it *is* wonderful what stagnation there fell upon the springs of my life— wonderful how total an inversion took place in the character of my commonest thought. The realities of the world affected me as visions, and as visions only, while the wild ideas of the land of dreams became, in turn—not the material of my everyday existence—but in very deed that existence utterly and solely in itself.

Berenice and I were cousins, and we grew up together in my paternal halls. Yet differently we grew—I ill of health and buried in gloom—she agile, graceful, and overflowing with energy—hers the ramble on the hill-side— mine the studies of the cloister—I living within my own heart, and addicted body and soul to the most intense and painful meditation—she roaming carelessly through life with no thought of the shadows in her path, or the silent flight of the raven-winged hours. Berenice! I call upon her name— Berenice!—and from the gray ruins of memory a thousand tumultuous recollections are startled at the sound! Ah! vividly is her image before me now, as in the early days of her light-heartedness and joy!—Oh! gorgeous yet fantastic beauty! Oh! sylph amid the shrubberies of Arnheim!—Oh! Naiad among its fountains!—and then—then all is mystery and terror, and a tale which should not be told. Disease—a fatal disease—fell like the simoon upon her frame; and, even while I gazed upon her, the spirit of change swept over her, pervading her mind, her habits, and her character, and, in a manner the most subtle and terrible, disturbing even the identity of her person! Alas! the destroyer came and went, and the victim—where was she? I knew her not—or knew her no longer as Berenice.

Among the numerous train of maladies superinduced by that fatal and primary one which effected a revolution of so horrible a kind in the moral and physical being of my cousin, may be mentioned as the most distressing and obstinate in its nature, a species of epilepsy not unfrequently terminating in *trance* itself—trance very nearly resembling positive dissolution, and from which her manner of recovery was, in most instances, startlingly abrupt. In the meantime my own disease—for I have been told that I should call it by no other appellation—my own disease, then, grew rapidly upon me, and assumed finally a monomaniac character of a novel and extraordinary form—hourly and momently gaining vigor—and at length obtaining over me the most incomprehensible ascendancy. This monomania, if I must so term it, consisted in a morbid irritability of those properties of the mind in metaphysical science termed the *attentive*. It is more than probable that I am not understood; but I fear, indeed, that it is in no manner possible to convey to the mind of the merely general reader, an adequate idea of that nervous *intensity of interest* with which, in my case, the powers of meditation (not to speak technically) busied and buried themselves, in the contemplation of even the most ordinary objects of the universe.

To muse for long unwearied hours with my attention riveted to some frivolous device on the margin, or in the typography of a book; to become absorbed, for the better part of a summer's day in a quaint shadow falling aslant upon the tapestry, or upon the floor; to lose myself for an entire night in watching the steady flame of a lamp, or the embers of a fire; to dream away whole days over the perfume of a flower; to repeat monotonously some common word, until the sound, by dint of frequent repetition, ceased to convey any idea whatever to the mind; to lose all sense of motion or physical existence, by means of absolute bodily quiescence long and obstinately persevered in: such were a few of the most common and least pernicious vagaries induced by a condition of the mental faculties, not, indeed, altogether unparalleled, but certainly bidding defiance to anything like analysis or explanation.

Yet let me not be misapprehended. The undue, earnest, and morbid attention thus excited by objects in their own nature frivolous, must not be confounded in character with that ruminating propensity common to all mankind, and more especially indulged in by persons of ardent imagination. It was not even, as might be at first supposed, an extreme condition, or exaggeration of such propensity, but primarily and essentially distinct and different. In the one instance, the dreamer, or

enthusiast, being interested by an object usually *not* frivolous, imperceptibly loses sight of this object in a wilderness of deductions and suggestions issuing therefrom, until, at the conclusion of a day dream *often replete with luxury*, he finds the *incitamentum* or first cause of his musings entirely vanished and forgotten. In my case the primary object was *invariably frivolous*, although assuming, through the medium of my distempered vision, a refracted and unreal importance. Few deductions, if any, were made; and those few pertinaciously returning in upon the original object as a center. The meditations were *never* pleasurable; and, at the termination of the reverie, the first cause, so far from being out of sight, had attained that supernaturally exaggerated interest which was the prevailing feature of the disease. In a word, the powers of mind more particularly exercised were, with me, as I have said before, the *attentive*, and are, with the daydreamer, the *speculative*.

My books, at this epoch, if they did not actually serve to irritate the disorder, partook, it will be perceived, largely, in their imaginative and inconsequential nature, of the characteristic qualities of the disorder itself. I well remember, among others, the treatise of the noble Italian Cœlius Secundus Curio *"de Amplitudine Beati Regni Dei;"* St. Austin's great work, the "City of God;" and Tertullian's *"De Carne Christi,"* in which the paradoxical sentence *"Mortuus est Dei filius; credible est quia ineptum est; et sepultus resurrexit; certum est quia impossibile est"*[2] occupied my undivided time, for many weeks of laborious and fruitless investigation.

Thus it will appear that, shaken from its balance only by trivial things, my reason bore resemblance to that ocean-crag spoken of by Ptolemy Hephestion, which steadily resisting the attacks of human violence, and the fiercer fury of the waters and the winds, trembled only to the touch of the flower called Asphodel.[3] And although, to a careless thinker, it might appear a matter beyond doubt, that the alteration produced by her unhappy malady, in the *moral* condition of Berenice, would afford me many objects for the exercise of that intense and abnormal meditation whose nature I have been at some trouble in explaining, yet such was not in any degree the case. In the lucid intervals of my infirmity, her calamity, indeed, gave me pain, and, taking deeply to heart that total wreck of her fair and gentle life, I did not fail to ponder frequently and bitterly upon the wonder-working means by which so strange a revolution had been so suddenly brought to pass. But these reflections partook not of the idiosyncrasy of my disease, and were such as would have occurred, under similar circumstances, to the ordinary mass of mankind. True to its own character,

my disorder reveled in the less important but more startling changes wrought in the *physical* frame of Berenice—in the singular and most appalling distortion of her personal identity.

During the brightest days of her unparalleled beauty, most surely I had never loved her. In the strange anomaly of my existence, feelings with me, *had never been* of the heart, and my passions *always were* of the mind. Through the gray of the early morning—among the trellised shadows of the forest at noon-day—and in the silence of my library at night, she had flitted by my eyes, and I had seen her—not as the living and breathing Berenice, but as the Berenice of a dream—not as a being of the earth, earthy, but as the abstraction of such a being—not as a thing to admire, but to analyze—not as an object of love, but as the theme of the most abstruse although desultory speculation. And *now*—now I shuddered in her presence, and grew pale at her approach; yet bitterly lamenting her fallen and desolate condition, I called to mind that she had loved me long, and, in an evil moment, I spoke to her of marriage.

And at length the period of our nuptials was approaching, when, upon an afternoon in the winter of the year—one of those unseasonably warm, calm, and misty days which are the nurse of the beautiful Halcyon,*[4] I sat (and sat, as I thought, alone), in the inner apartment of the library. But, uplifting my eyes, I saw that Berenice stood before me.

Was it my own excited imagination—or the misty influence of the atmosphere—or the uncertain twilight of the chamber—or the gray draperies which fell around her figure—that caused in it so vacillating and indistinct an outline? I could not tell. She spoke no word, and I—not for worlds could I have uttered a syllable. An icy chill ran through my frame; a sense of insufferable anxiety oppressed me; a consuming curiosity pervaded my soul; and sinking back upon the chair, I remained for some time breathless and motionless, with my eyes riveted upon her person. Alas! its emaciation was excessive, and not one vestige of the former being lurked in any single line of the contour. My burning glances at length fell upon the face.

The forehead was high, and very pale, and singularly placid; and the once jetty hair fell partially over it, and overshadowed the hollow temples

* For as Jove, during the winter season, gives twice seven days of warmth, men have called this element and temperate time the nurse of the beautiful Halcyon—*Simonides.*

with innumerable ringlets now of a vivid yellow, and jarring discordantly, in their fantastic character, with the reigning melancholy of the countenance. The eyes were lifeless, and lusterless, and seemingly pupil-less, and I shrank involuntarily from their glassy stare to the contemplation of the thin and shrunken lips. They parted; and in a smile of peculiar meaning, *the teeth* of the changed Berenice disclosed themselves slowly to my view. Would to God that I had never beheld them, or that, having done so, I had died!

The shutting of a door disturbed me, and, looking up, I found that my cousin had departed from the chamber. But from the disordered chamber of my brain, had not, alas! departed, and would not be driven away, the white and ghastly *spectrum* of the teeth. Not a speck on their surface— not a shade on their enamel—not an indenture in their edges—but what that period of her smile had sufficed to brand in upon my memory. I saw them *now* even more unequivocally than I beheld them *then*. The teeth!—the teeth!—they were here, and there, and everywhere, and visibly and palpably before me; long, narrow, and excessively white, with the pale lips writhing about them, as in the very moment of their first terrible development. Then came the full fury of my *monomania*, and I struggled in vain against its strange and irresistible influence. In the multiplied objects of the external world I had no thoughts but for the teeth. For these I longed with a frenzied desire. All other matters and all different interests became absorbed in their single contemplation. They—they alone were present to the mental eye, and they, in their sole individuality, became the essence of my mental life. I held them in every light. I turned them in every attitude. I surveyed their characteristics. I dwelt upon their peculiarities. I pondered upon their conformation. I mused upon the alteration in their nature. I shuddered as I assigned to them in imagination a sensitive and sentient power, and even when unassisted by the lips, a capability of moral expression. Of Mad'selle Sallé it has been well said, "*que tous ses pas etaient des sentiments*," and of Berenice I more seriously believed *que toutes ses dents etaient des idées. Des idées!*—ah here was the idiotic thought that destroyed me! *Des idées!*—ah *therefore* it was that I coveted them so madly! I felt that their possession could alone ever restore me to peace, in giving me back to reason.

And the evening closed in upon me thus—and then the darkness came, and tarried, and went—and the day again dawned—and the mists of a second night were now gathering around—and still I sat motionless

in that solitary room, and still I sat buried in meditation, and still the *phantasma* of the teeth maintained its terrible ascendancy as, with the most vivid and hideous distinctness, it floated about amid the changing lights and shadows of the chamber. At length there broke in upon my dreams a cry as of horror and dismay; and thereunto, after a pause, succeeded the sound of troubled voices, intermingled with many low moanings of sorrow, or of pain. I arose from my seat, and, throwing open one of the doors of the library, saw standing out in the antechamber a servant maiden, all in tears, who told me that Berenice was—no more. She had been seized with epilepsy in the early morning, and now, at the closing in of the night, the grave was ready for its tenant, and all the preparations for the burial were completed.

I found myself sitting in the library, and again sitting there alone. It seemed that I had newly awakened from a confused and exciting dream. I knew that it was now midnight, and I was well aware that since the setting of the sun Berenice had been interred. But of that dreary period which intervened I had no positive—at least no definite comprehension. Yet its memory was replete with horror—horror more horrible from being vague, and terror more terrible from ambiguity. It was a fearful page in the record of my existence, written all over with dim, and hideous, and unintelligible recollections. I strived to decipher them, but in vain; while ever and anon, like the spirit of a departed sound, the shrill and piercing shriek of a female voice seemed to be ringing in my ears. I had done a deed—what was it? I asked myself the question aloud, and the whispering echoes of the chamber answered me, *"what was it?"*

On the table beside me burned a lamp, and near it lay a little box. It was of no remarkable character, and I had seen it frequently before, for it was the property of the family physician; but how came it *there,* upon my table, and why did I shudder in regarding it? These things were in no manner to be accounted for, and my eyes at length dropped to the open pages of a book, and to a sentence underscored therein. The words were the singular but simple ones of the poet Ebn Zaiat: *"Dicebant mihi sodales si sepulchrum amicae visitarem, curas meas aliquantulum fore levatas."* Why then, as I perused them, did the hairs of my head erect themselves on end, and the blood of my body become congealed within my veins?

There came a light tap at the library door, and pale as the tenant of a tomb, a menial entered upon tiptoe. His looks were wild with terror,

and he spoke to me in a voice tremulous, husky, and very low. What said he?—some broken sentences I heard. He told of a wild cry disturbing the silence of the night—of the gathering together of the household—of a search in the direction of the sound; and then his tones grew thrillingly distinct as he whispered me of a violated grave—of a disfigured body enshrouded, yet still breathing, still palpitating, *still alive!*

He pointed to garments; they were muddy and clotted with gore. I spoke not, and he took me gently by the hand; it was indented with the impress of human nails. He directed my attention to some object against the wall; I looked at it for some minutes; it was a spade. With a shriek I bounded to the table, and grasped the box that lay upon it. But I could not force it open; and in my tremor, it slipped from my hands, and fell heavily, and burst into pieces; and from it, with a rattling sound, there rolled out some instruments of dental surgery, intermingled with thirty-two small, white and ivory-looking substances that were scattered to and fro about the floor.

MORELLA

Αυτο καθ' αυτο μεθ' αυτου, μονο ειδες αιει ον.
Itself, by itself solely, ONE everlastingly, and single.

<div align="right">—PLATO. SYMPOS.</div>

WITH A FEELING OF DEEP YET MOST SINGULAR AFFECTION I REGARDED MY friend Morella. Thrown by accident into her society many years ago, my soul, from our first meeting, burned with fires it had never before known; but the fires were not of Eros, and bitter and tormenting to my spirit was the gradual conviction that I could in no manner define their unusual meaning, or regulate their vague intensity. Yet we met; and fate bound us together at the altar, and I never spoke of passion, nor thought of love. She, however, shunned society, and, attaching herself to me alone, rendered me happy. It is a happiness to wonder; it is a happiness to dream.

Morella's erudition was profound. As I hope to live, her talents were of no common order—her powers of mind were gigantic. I felt this, and, in many matters, became her pupil. I soon, however, found that, perhaps on account of her Presburg education, she placed before me a number of those mystical writings which are usually considered the mere dross of the early German literature. These, for what reason I could not imagine, were her favorite and constant study—and that in process of time they became my own, should be attributed to the simple but effectual influence of habit and example.

In all this, if I err not, my reason had little to do. My convictions, or I forget myself, were in no manner acted upon by the ideal, nor was any tincture of the mysticism which I read, to be discovered, unless I am greatly mistaken, either in my deeds or in my thoughts. Persuaded of this,

I abandoned myself implicitly to the guidance of my wife, and entered with an unflinching heart into the intricacies of her studies. And then— then, when, poring over forbidden pages, I felt a forbidden spirit enkindling within me—would Morella place her cold hand upon my own, and rake up from the ashes of a dead philosophy some low, singular words, whose strange meaning burned themselves in upon my memory. And then, hour after hour, would I linger by her side, and dwell upon the music of her voice—until, at length, its melody was tainted with terror— and there fell a shadow upon my soul—and I grew pale, and shuddered inwardly at those too unearthly tones. And thus, joy suddenly faded into horror, and the most beautiful became the most hideous, as Hinnon became Ge-Henna.

It is unnecessary to state the exact character of those disquisitions which, growing out of the volumes I have mentioned, formed, for so long a time, almost the sole conversation of Morella and myself. By the learned in what might be termed theological morality they will be readily con- ceived, and by the unlearned they would, at all events, be little understood. The wild Pantheism of Fichte; the modified Παλιγγενεσια[1] of the Pythagoreans; and, above all, the doctrines of *Identity* as urged by Schelling, were generally the points of discussion presenting the most of beauty to the imaginative Morella. That identity which is termed per- sonal, Mr. Locke, I think, truly defines to consist in the saneness of a rational being. And since by person we understand an intelligent essence having reason, and since there is a consciousness which always accompa- nies thinking, it is this which makes us all to be that which we call *ourselves*—thereby distinguishing us from other beings that think, and giving us our personal identity. But the *principium indivduationis*—the notion of that identity *which at death is or is not lost forever,* was to me—at all times, a consideration of intense interest; not more from the per- plexing and exciting nature of its consequences, than from the marked and agitated manner in which Morella mentioned them.

But, indeed, the time had now arrived when the mystery of my wife's manner oppressed me as a spell. I could no longer bear the touch of her wan fingers, nor the low tone of her musical language, nor the luster of her melancholy eyes. And she knew all this, but did not upbraid; she seemed conscious of my weakness or my folly, and, smiling, called it Fate. She seemed, also, conscious of a cause, to me unknown, for the gradual alienation of my regard; but she gave me no hint or token of its nature. Yet was she woman, and pined away daily. In time, the crimson spot settled

steadily upon the cheek, and the blue veins upon the pale forehead became prominent; and, one instant, my nature melted into pity, but, in the next, I met the glance of her meaning eyes, and then my soul sickened and became giddy with the giddiness of one who gazes downward into some dreary and unfathomable abyss.

Shall I then say that I longed with an earnest and consuming desire for the moment of Morella's decease? I did; but the fragile spirit clung to its tenement of clay for many days—for many weeks and irksome months—until my tortured nerves obtained the mastery over my mind, and I grew furious through delay, and, with the heart of a fiend, cursed the days and the hours, and the bitter moments, which seemed to lengthen and lengthen as her gentle life declined—like shadows in the dying of the day.

But one autumnal evening, when the winds lay still in heaven, Morella called me to her bed-side. There was a dim mist over all the earth, and a warm glow upon the waters, and, amid the rich October leaves of the forest, a rainbow from the firmament had surely fallen.

"It is a day of days," she said, as I approached; "a day of all days either to live or die. It is a fair day for the sons of earth and life—ah, more fair for the daughters of heaven and death!"

I kissed her forehead, and she continued:

"I am dying, yet shall I live."

"Morella!"

"The days have never been when thou couldst love me—but her whom in life thou didst abhor, in death thou shalt adore."

"Morella!"

"I repeat that I am dying. But within me is a pledge of that affection—ah, how little!—which thou didst feel for me, Morella. And when my spirit departs shall the child live—thy child and mine, Morella's. But thy days shall be days of sorrow—that sorrow which is the most lasting of impressions, as the cypress is the most enduring of trees. For the hours of thy happiness are over; and joy is not gathered twice in a life, as the roses of Pæstum twice in a year. Thou shalt no longer, then, play the Teian with time, but, being ignorant of the myrtle and the vine, thou shalt bear about with thee thy shroud on the earth, as do the Moslemin at Mecca."

"Morella!" I cried, "Morella! how knowest thou this?" but she turned away her face upon the pillow, and, a slight tremor coming over her limbs, she thus died, and I heard her voice no more.

Yet, as she had foretold, her child—to which in dying she had given birth, and which breathed not until the mother breathed no more—her

child, a daughter, lived. And she grew strangely in stature and intellect, and was the perfect resemblance of her who had departed, and I loved her with a love more fervent than I had believed it possible to feel for any denizen of earth.

But, ere long, the heaven of this pure affection became darkened, and gloom, and horror, and grief, swept over it in clouds. I said the child grew strangely in stature and intelligence. Strange, indeed, was her rapid increase in bodily size—but terrible, oh! terrible were the tumultuous thoughts which crowded upon me while watching the development of her mental being. Could it be otherwise, when I daily discovered in the conceptions of the child the adult powers and faculties of the woman?— when the lessons of experience fell from the lips of infancy? and when the wisdom or the passions of maturity I found hourly gleaming from its full and speculative eye? When, I say, all this became evident to my appalled senses, when I could no longer hide it from my soul, nor throw it off from those perceptions which trembled to receive it—is it to be wondered at that suspicions, of a nature fearful and exciting, crept in upon my spirit, or that my thoughts fell back aghast upon the wild tales and thrilling theories of the entombed Morella? I snatched from the scrutiny of the world a being whom destiny compelled me to adore, and in the rigorous seclusion of my home, watched with an agonizing anxiety over all which concerned the beloved.

And, as years rolled away, and I gazed, day after day, upon her holy, and mild, and eloquent face, and poured over her maturing form, day after day did I discover new points of resemblance in the child to her mother, the melancholy and the dead. And, hourly, grew darker these shadows of similitude, and more full, and more definite, and more per-plexing, and more hideously terrible in their aspect. For that her smile was like her mother's I could bear; but then I shuddered at its too perfect *identity*—that her eyes were like Morella's I could endure; but then they too often looked down into the depths of my soul with Morella's own intense and bewildering meaning. And in the contour of the high fore-head, and in the ringlets of the silken hair, and in the wan fingers which buried themselves therein, and in the sad musical tones of her speech, and above all—oh, above all—in the phrases and expressions of the dead on the lips of the loved and the living, I found food for consuming thought and horror—for a worm that *would* not die.

Thus passed away two lustra of her life, and, as yet, my daughter remained nameless upon the earth. "My child" and "my love" were the

designations usually prompted by a father's affection, and the rigid seclu-sion of her days precluded all other intercourse. Morella's name died with her at her death. Of the mother I had never spoken to the daughter; it was impossible to speak. Indeed, during the brief period of her existence the latter had received no impressions from the outward world save such as might have been afforded by the narrow limits of her privacy. But at length the ceremony of baptism presented to my mind, in its unnerved and agi-tated condition, a present deliverance from the terrors of my destiny. And at the baptismal font I hesitated for a name. And many titles of the wise and beautiful, of old and modern times, of my own and foreign lands, came thronging to my lips, with many, many fair titles of the gentle, and the happy, and the good. What prompted me then to disturb the memory of the buried dead? What demon urged me to breathe that sound, which, in its very recollection was wont to make ebb the purple blood in torrents from the temples to the heart? What fiend spoke from the recesses of my soul, when, amid those dim aisles, and in the silence of the night, I whis-pered within the ears of the holy man the syllables—Morella? What more than fiend convulsed the features of my child, and overspread them with hues of death, as, starting at that scarcely audible sound, she turned her glassy eyes from the earth to heaven, and falling prostrate on the black slabs of our ancestral vault, responded—"I am here!"

Distinct, coldly, calmly distinct, fell those few simple sounds within my ear, and thence, like molten lead, rolled hissingly into my brain. Years—years may pass away, but the memory of that epoch—never! Nor was I indeed ignorant of the flowers and the vine—but the hemlock and the cypress overshadowed me night and day. And I kept no reckoning of time or place, and the stars of my fate faded from heaven, and therefore the earth grew dark, and its figures passed by me, like flitting shadows, and among them all I beheld only—Morella. The winds of the firmament breathed but one sound within my ears, and the ripples upon the sea mur-mured evermore—Morella. But she died; and with my own hands I bore her to the tomb; and I laughed with a long and bitter laugh as I found no traces of the first, in the channel where I laid the second—Morella.

LIGEIA

And the will therein lieth, which dieth not. Who knoweth the myster-
ies of the will, with its vigor? For God is but a great will pervading
all things by nature of its intentness. Man doth not yield himself to
the angels, nor unto death utterly, save only through the weakness
of his feeble will.

—JOSEPH GLANVILL

I CANNOT, FOR MY SOUL, REMEMBER HOW, WHEN, OR EVEN PRECISELY
where, I first became acquainted with the lady Ligeia. Long years have
since elapsed, and my memory is feeble through much suffering. Or, per
haps, I cannot *now* bring these points to mind, because, in truth, the
character of my beloved, her rare learning, her singular yet placid cast of
beauty, and the thrilling and enthralling eloquence of her low musical
language, made their way into my heart by paces so steadily and stealthily
progressive that they have been unnoticed and unknown. Yet I believe that
I met her first and most frequently in some large, old, decaying city near
the Rhine. Of her family—I have surely heard her speak. That it is of a
remotely ancient date cannot be doubted. Ligeia! Ligeia! Buried in stud-
ies of a nature more than all else adapted to deaden impressions of the
outward world, it is by that sweet word alone—by Ligeia—that I bring
before mine eyes in fancy the image of her who is no more. And now,
while I write, a recollection flashes upon me that I have *never known* the
paternal name of her who was my friend and my betrothed, and who
became the partner of my studies, and finally the wife of my bosom. Was
it a playful charge on the part of my Ligeia? Or was it a test of my strength
of affection, that I should institute no inquiries upon this point? or was it

rather a caprice of my own—a wildly romantic offering on the shrine of the most passionate devotion? I but indistinctly recall the fact itself— what wonder that I have utterly forgotten the circumstances which originated or attended it? And, indeed, if ever that spirit which is entitled *Romance*—if ever she, the wan and the misty-winged *Ashtophet* of idolatrous Egypt, presided, as they tell, over marriages ill-omened, then most surely she presided over mine.

There is one dear topic, however, on which my memory fails me not. It is the *person* of Ligeia. In stature she was tall, somewhat slender, and, in her latter days, even emaciated. I would in vain attempt to portray the majesty, the quiet ease of her demeanor, or the incomprehensible light- ness and elasticity of her footfall. She came and departed as a shadow. I was never made aware of her entrance into my closed study, save by the dear music of her low sweet voice, as she placed her marble hand upon my shoulder. In beauty of face no maiden ever equaled her. It was the radiance of an opium-dream—an airy and spirit-lifting vision more wildly divine than the fantasies which hovered vision about the slumbering souls of the daughters of Delos. Yet her features were not of that regular mold which we have been falsely taught to worship in the classical labors of the heathen. "There is no exquisite beauty," says Bacon, Lord Verulam, speaking truly of all the forms and *genera* of beauty, "without some *strange- ness* in the proportion." Yet, although I saw that the features of Ligeia were not of a classic regularity—although I perceived that her loveliness was indeed "exquisite," and felt that there was much of "strangeness" pervading it, yet I have tried in vain to detect the irregularity and to trace home my own perception of "the strange." I examined the contour of the lofty and pale forehead—it was faultless—how cold indeed that word when applied to a majesty so divine!—the skin rivaling the purest ivory, the commanding extent and repose, the gentle prominence of the regions above the temples; and then the raven-black, the glossy, the luxu- riant, and naturally curling tresses, setting forth the full force of the Homeric epithet, "hyacinthine!" I looked at the delicate outlines of the nose—and nowhere but in the graceful medallions of the Hebrews had I beheld a similar perfection. There were the same luxurious smooth- ness of surface, the same scarcely perceptible tendency to the aquiline, the same harmoniously curved nostrils speaking the free spirit. I regarded the sweet mouth. Here was indeed the triumph of all things heavenly—the magnificent turn of the short upper lip—the soft, volup- tuous slumber of the under—the dimples which sported, and the color

which spoke—the teeth glancing back, with a brilliancy almost startling, every ray of the holy light which fell upon them in her serene and placid, yet most exultingly radiant of all smiles. I scrutinized the formation of the chin—and here too, I found the gentleness of breadth, the softness and the majesty, the fullness and the spirituality, of the Greek—the contour which the god Apollo revealed but in a dream, to Cleomenes, the son of the Athenian. And then I peered into the large eyes of Ligeia.

For eyes we have no models in the remotely antique. It might have been, too, that in these eyes of my beloved lay the secret to which Lord Verulam alludes. They were, I must believe, far larger than the ordinary eyes of our own race. They were even fuller than the fullest of the gazelle eyes of the tribe of the valley of Nourjahad. Yet it was only at intervals—in moments of intense excitement—that this peculiarity became more than slightly noticeable in Ligeia. And at such moments was her beauty—in my heated fancy thus it appeared perhaps—the beauty of beings either above or apart from the earth—the beauty of the fabulous Houri of the Turk. The hue of the orbs was the most brilliant of black, and far over them, hung jetty lashes of great length. The brows, slightly irregular in outline, had the same tint. The "strangeness," however, which I found in the eyes was of a nature distinct from the formation, or the color, or the brilliancy of the features, and must, after all, be referred to the *expression*. Ah, word of no meaning! behind whose vast latitude of mere sound we entrench our ignorance of so much of the spiritual. The expression of the eyes of Ligeia! How for long hours have I pondered upon it! How have I, through the whole of a midsummer night, struggled to fathom it! What *was* it—that something more profound than the well of Democritus— which lay far within the pupils of my beloved? What was it? I was possessed with a passion to discover. Those eyes! those large, those shining, those divine orbs! they became to me twin stars of Leda, and I to them devoutest of astrologers.

There is no point, among the many incomprehensible anomalies of the science of mind, more thrillingly exciting than the fact—never, I believe, noticed in the schools—that, in our endeavors to recall to memory something long forgotten, we often find ourselves *upon the very verge* of remembrance, without being able, in the end, to remember. And thus how frequently, in my intense scrutiny of Ligeia's eyes, have I felt approaching the full knowledge of their expression—felt it approaching—yet not quite be mine—and so at length entirely depart! And (strange, oh, strangest mystery of all!) I found, in the commonest objects of the universe, a circle

of analogies to that expression. I mean to say that, subsequently to the period when Ligeia's beauty passed into my spirit, there dwelling as in a shrine, I derived, from many existences in the material world, a sentiment such as I felt always aroused within me by her large and luminous orbs. Yet not the more could I define that sentiment, or analyze, or even steadily view it. I recognized it, let me repeat, sometimes in the survey of a rapidly growing vine—in the contemplation of a moth, a butterfly, a chrysalis, a stream of running water. I have felt it in the ocean; in the falling of a meteor. I have felt it in the glances of unusually aged people. And there are one or two stars in heaven (one especially, a star of the sixth magnitude, double and changeable, to be found near the large star in Lyra) in a telescopic scrutiny of which I have been made aware of the feeling. I have been filled with it by certain sounds from stringed instruments, and not unfrequently by passages from books. Among innumerable other instances, I well remember something in a volume of Joseph Glanvill, which (perhaps merely from its quaintness—who shall say?) never failed to inspire me with the sentiment: "And the will therein lieth, which dieth not. Who knoweth the mysteries of the will, with its vigor? For God is but a great will pervading all things by nature of its intentness. Man doth not yield him to the angels, nor unto death utterly, save only through the weakness of his feeble will."

Length of years and subsequent reflection have enabled me to trace, indeed, some remote connection between this passage in the English moralist and a portion of the character of Ligeia. An *intensity* in thought, action, or speech was possibly, in her, a result, or at least an index, of that gigantic volition which, during our long intercourse, failed to give other and more immediate evidence of its existence. Of all the women whom I have ever known, she, the outwardly calm, the ever-placid Ligeia, was the most violently a prey to the tumultuous vultures of stern passion. And of such passion I could form no estimate, save by the miraculous expansion of those eyes which at once so delighted and appalled me—by the almost magical melody, modulation, distinctness, and placidity of her very low voice—and by the fierce energy (rendered doubly effective by contrast with her manner of utterance) of the wild words which she habitually uttered.

I have spoken of the learning of Ligeia: it was immense—such as I have never known in woman. In the classical tongues was she deeply proficient, and as far as my own acquaintance extended in regard to the modern dialects of Europe, I have never known her at fault. Indeed upon any theme of the most admired, because simply the most abstruse of the

boasted erudition of the Academy, have I *ever* found Ligeia at fault? How singularly—how thrillingly, this one point in the nature of my wife has forced itself, at this late period only, upon my attention! I said her knowledge was such as I have never known in woman—but where breathes the man who has traversed, and successfully, *all* the wide areas of moral, physical, and mathematical science? I saw not then what I now clearly perceive, that the acquisitions of Ligeia were gigantic, were astounding; yet I was sufficiently aware of her infinite supremacy to resign myself, with a child-like confidence, to her guidance through the chaotic world of metaphysical investigation at which I was most busily occupied during the earlier years of our marriage. With how vast a triumph—with how vivid a delight—with how much of all that is ethereal in hope did I *feel*, as she bent over me in studies but little sought—but less known—that delicious vista by slow degrees expanding before me, down whose long, gorgeous, and all untrodden path, I might at length pass onward to the goal of a wisdom too divinely precious not to be forbidden!

How poignant, then, must have been the grief with which, after some years, I beheld my well-grounded expectations take wings to themselves and fly away! Without Ligeia I was but as a child groping benighted. Her presence, her readings alone, rendered vividly luminous the many mysteries of the transcendentalism in which we were immersed. Wanting the radiant luster of her eyes, letters, lambent and golden, grew duller than Saturnian lead. And now those eyes shone less and less frequently upon the pages over which I pored. Ligeia grew ill. The wild eyes blazed with a too—too glorious effulgence; the pale fingers became of the transparent waxen hue of the grave and the blue veins upon the lofty forehead swelled and sank impetuously with the tides of the most gentle emotion. I saw that she must die—and I struggled desperately in spirit with the grim Azrael.[1] And the struggles of the passionate wife were, to my astonishment, even more energetic than my own. There had been much in her stern nature to impress me with the belief that, to her, death would have come without its terrors; but not so. Words are impotent to convey any just idea of the fierceness of resistance with which she wrestled with the Shadow. I groaned in anguish at the pitiable spectacle. I would have soothed— I would have reasoned; but, in the intensity of her wild desire for life—for life—*but* for life—solace and reason were alike the uttermost folly. Yet not until the last instance, amid the most convulsive writhings of her fierce spirit, was shaken the external placidity of her demeanor. Her voice grew more gentle—grew more low—yet I would not wish to dwell upon the wild

meaning of the quietly uttered words. My brain reeled as I harkened, entranced to a melody more than mortal—to assumptions and aspirations which mortality had never before known.

That she loved me I should not have doubted; and I might have been easily aware that, in a bosom such as hers, love would have reigned no ordinary passion. But in death only was I fully impressed with the strength of her affection. For long hours, detaining my hand, would she pour out before me the overflowing of a heart whose more than passionate devotion amounted to idolatry. How had I deserved to be so blessed by such confessions?—how had I deserved to be so cursed with the removal of my beloved in the hour of her making them? But upon this subject I cannot bear to dilate. Let me say only, that in Ligeia's more than womanly abandonment to a love, alas! all unmerited, all unworthily bestowed, I at length recognized the principle of her longing, with so wildly earnest a desire for the life which was now fleeing so rapidly away. It is this wild longing—it is this eager vehemence of desire for life—*but* for life—that I have no power to portray—no utterance capable of expressing.

At high noon of the night on which she departed, beckoning me, peremptorily, to her side, she bade me repeat certain verses composed by herself not many days before. I obeyed her. They were these:

> *Lo! 'tis a gala night*
> *Within the lonesome latter years!*
> *An angel throng, bewinged, bedight*
> *In veils, and drowned in tears,*
> *Sit in a theater, to see*
> *A play of hopes and fears,*
> *While the orchestra breathes fitfully*
> *The music of the spheres.*
>
> *Mimes, in the form of God on high,*
> *Mutter and mumble low,*
> *And hither and thither fly—*
> *Mere puppets they, who come and go*
> *At bidding of vast formless things*
> *That shift the scenery to and fro,*
> *Flapping from out their Condor wings*
> *Invisible Wo!*

That motley drama—oh, be sure
 It shall not be forgot!
With its Phantom chased for evermore,
 By a crowd that seize it not,
Through a circle that ever returneth in
 To the self-same spot,
And much of Madness, and more of Sin,
 And Horror the soul of the plot.

But see, amid the mimic rout,
 A crawling shape intrude!
A blood-red thing that writhes from out
 The scenic solitude!
It writhes!—it writhes!—with mortal pangs
 The mimes become its food,
And the seraphs sob at vermin fangs
 In human gore imbued.

Out—out are the lights—out all!
 And over each quivering form,
The curtain, a funeral pall,
 Comes down with the rush of a storm,
And the angels, all pallid and wan,
 Uprising, unveiling, affirm
That the play is the tragedy, "Man,"
 And its hero, the Conqueror Worm.

"O God!" half shrieked Ligeia, leaping to her feet and extending her arms aloft with a spasmodic movement, as I made an end of these lines— "O God! O Divine Father!—shall these things be undeviatingly so?—shall this Conqueror be not once conquered? Are we not part and parcel in Thee? Who—who knoweth the mysteries of the will with its vigor? Man doth not yield him to the angels, *nor unto death utterly,* save only through the weakness of his feeble will."

And now, as if exhausted with emotion, she suffered her white arms to fall, and returned solemnly to her bed of death. And as she breathed her last sighs, there came mingled with them a low murmur from her lips. I bent to them my ear and distinguished, again, the concluding words of

the passage in Glanvill— *"Man doth not yield him to the angels, nor unto death utterly, save only through the weakness of his feeble will."*

She died: and I, crushed into the very dust with sorrow, could no longer endure the lonely desolation of my dwelling in the dim and decaying city by the Rhine. I had no lack of what the world calls wealth, Ligeia had brought me far more, very far more than ordinarily falls to the lot of mortals. After a few months, therefore, of weary and aimless wandering, I purchased and put in some repair, an abbey, which I shall not name, in one of the wildest and least frequented portions of fair England. The gloomy and dreary grandeur of the building, the almost savage aspect of the domain, the many melancholy and time-honored memories connected with both, had much in unison with the feelings of utter abandonment which had driven me into that remote and unsocial region of the country. Yet although the external abbey, with its verdant decay hanging about it, suffered but little alteration, I gave way, with a child-like perversity, and perchance with a faint hope of alleviating my sorrows, to a display of more than regal magnificence within. For such follies, even in childhood, I had imbibed a taste, and now they came back to me as if in the dotage of grief. Alas, I feel how much even of incipient madness might have been discovered in the gorgeous and fantastic draperies, in the solemn carvings of Egypt, in the wild cornices and furniture, in the Bedlam patterns of the carpets of tufted gold! I had become a bounden slave in the trammels of opium, and my labors and my orders had taken a coloring from my dreams. But these absurdities I must not pause to detail. Let me speak only of that one chamber, ever accursed, whither, in a moment of mental alienation, I led from the altar as my bride—as the successor of the unforgotten Ligeia—the fair-haired and blue-eyed Lady Rowena Trevanion, of Tremaine.

There is no individual portion of the architecture and decoration of that bridal chamber which is not now visibly before me. Where were the souls of the haughty family of the bride, when, through thirst of gold, they permitted to pass the threshold of an apartment *so* bedecked, a maiden and a daughter so beloved? I have said that I minutely remember the details of the chamber—yet I am sadly forgetful on topics of deep moment—and here there was no system, no keeping, in the fantastic display, to take hold upon the memory. The room lay in a high turret of the castellated abbey, was pentagonal in shape, and of capacious size. Occupying the whole southern face of the pentagon was the sole window—an immense sheet of unbroken glass from Venice—a single pane, and tinted of a leaden hue, so that the rays of either the sun or moon, passing

through it, fell with a ghastly luster on the objects within. Over the upper portion of this huge window, extended the trellis-work of an aged vine, which clambered up the massy walls of the turret. The ceiling, of gloomy-looking oak, was excessively lofty, vaulted, and elaborately fretted with the wildest and most grotesque specimens of a semi-Gothic, semi-Druidical device. From out the most central recess of this melancholy vaulting, depended, by a single chain of gold with long links, a huge censer of the same metal, Saracenic in pattern, and with many perforations so contrived that there writhed in and out of them, as if endued with a serpent vitality, a continual succession of parti-colored fires.

Some few ottomans and golden candelabra, of Eastern figure, were in various stations about; and there was the couch, too—the bridal couch—of an Indian model, and low, and sculptured of solid ebony, with a pall-like canopy above. In each of the angles of the chamber stood on end a gigantic sarcophagus of black granite, from the tombs of the kings over against Luxor, with their aged lids full of immemorial sculpture. But in the draping of the apartment lay, alas! the chief fantasy of all. The lofty walls, gigantic in height—even unproportionably so—were hung from summit to foot, in vast folds, with a heavy and massive-looking tapestry—tapestry of a material which was found alike as a carpet on the floor, as a covering for the ottomans and the ebony bed, as a canopy for the bed and as the gorgeous volutes of the curtains which partially shaded the window. The material was the richest cloth of gold. It was spotted all over, at irregular intervals, with arabesque figures, about a foot in diameter, and wrought upon the cloth in patterns of the most jetty black. But these figures partook of the true character of the arabesque only when regarded from a single point of view. By a contrivance now common, and indeed traceable to a very remote period of antiquity, they were made changeable in aspect. To one entering the room, they bore the appearance of simple monstrosities; but upon a farther advance, this appearance gradually departed; and, step by step, as the visiter moved his station in the chamber, he saw himself surrounded by an endless succession of the ghastly forms which belong to the superstition of the Norman, or arise in the guilty slumbers of the monk. The phantasmagoric effect was vastly heightened by the artificial introduction of a strong continual current of wind behind the draperies—giving a hideous and uneasy animation to the whole.

In halls such as these—in a bridal chamber such as this—I passed, with the Lady of Tremaine, the unhallowed hours of the first month of our marriage—passed them with but little disquietude. That my wife

dreaded the fierce moodiness of my temper—that she shunned me and loved me but little—I could not help perceiving; but it gave me rather pleasure than otherwise. I loathed her with a hatred belonging more to demon than to man. My memory flew back (oh, with what intensity of regret!) to Ligeia, the beloved, the august, the beautiful, the entombed. I reveled in recollections of her purity, of her wisdom, of her lofty—her ethereal nature, of her passionate, her idolatrous love. Now, then, did my spirit fully and freely burn with more than all the fires of her own. In the excitement of my opium dreams (for I was habitually fettered in the shackles of the drug), I would call aloud upon her name, during the silence of the night, or among the sheltered recesses of the glens by day, as if, through the wild eagerness, the solemn passion, the consuming ardor of my longing for the departed, I could restore her to the pathway she had abandoned—ah, *could* it be forever?—upon the earth.

About the commencement of the second month of the marriage, the Lady Rowena was attacked with sudden illness, from which her recovery was slow. The fever which consumed her rendered her nights uneasy; and in her perturbed state of half-slumber, she spoke of sounds, and of motions, in and about the chamber of the turret, which I concluded had no origin save in the distemper of her fancy, or perhaps in the phantasmagoric influences of the chamber itself. She became at length convalescent—finally, well. Yet but a brief period elapsed, ere a second more violent disorder again threw her upon a bed of suffering; and from this attack her frame, at all times feeble, never altogether recovered. Her illnesses were, after this epoch, of alarming character, and of more alarming recurrence, defying alike the knowledge and the great exertions of her physicians. With the increase of the chronic disease, which had thus, apparently, taken too sure hold upon her constitution to be eradicated by human means, I could not fail to observe a similar increase in the nervous irritation of her temperament, and in her excitability by trivial causes of fear. She spoke again, and now more frequently and pertinaciously, of the sounds—of the slight sounds—and of the unusual motions among the tapestries, to which she had formerly alluded.

One night, near the closing in of September, she pressed this distressing subject with more than usual emphasis upon my attention. She had just awakened from an unquiet slumber, and I had been watching, with feelings half of anxiety, half of vague terror, the workings of her emaciated countenance. I sat by the side of her ebony bed, upon one of the ottomans of India. She partly arose, and spoke, in an earnest low whisper,

of sounds which she *then* heard, but which I could not hear—of motions which she *then* saw, but which I could not perceive. The wind was rushing hurriedly behind the tapestries, and I wished to show her (what, let me confess it, I could not *all* believe) that those almost inarticulate breathings, and those very gentle variations of the figures upon the wall, were but the natural effects of that customary rushing of the wind. But a deadly pallor, over-spreading her face, had proved to me that my exertions to reassure her would be fruitless. She appeared to be fainting, and no attendants were within call. I remembered where was deposited a decanter of light wine which had been ordered by her physicians, and hastened across the chamber to procure it. But, as I stepped beneath the light of the censer, two circumstances of a startling nature attracted my attention. I had felt that some palpable although invisible object had passed lightly by my person; and I saw that there lay upon the golden carpet, in the very middle of the rich luster thrown from the censer, a shadow—a faint, indefinite shadow of angelic aspect—such as might be fancied for the shadow of a shade. But I was wild with the excitement of an immoderate dose of opium, and heeded these things but little, nor spoke of them to Rowena. Having found the wine, I recrossed the chamber, and poured out a gobletful, which I held to the lips of the fainting lady. She had now partially recovered, however, and took the vessel herself, while I sank upon an ottoman near me, with my eyes fastened upon her person. It was then that I became distinctly aware of a gentle foot-fall upon the carpet, and near the couch; and in a second thereafter, as Rowena was in the act of raising the wine to her lips, I saw, or may have dreamed that I saw, fall within the goblet, as if from some invisible spring in the atmosphere of the room, three or four large drops of a brilliant and ruby colored fluid. If this I saw—not so Rowena. She swallowed the wine unhesitatingly, and I forbore to speak to her of a circumstance which must, after all, I considered, have been but the suggestion of a vivid imagination, rendered morbidly active by the terror of the lady, by the opium, and by the hour.

Yet I cannot conceal it from my own perception that, immediately subsequent to the fall of the ruby-drops, a rapid change for the worse took place in the disorder of my wife; so that, on the third subsequent night, the hands of her menials prepared her for the tomb, and on the fourth, I sat alone, with her shrouded body, in that fantastic chamber which had received her as my bride. Wild visions, opium-engendered, flitted, shadow-like, before me. I gazed with unquiet eye upon the sarcophagi in the angles of the room, upon the varying figures of the

drapery, and upon the writhing of the parti-colored fires in the censer overhead. My eyes then fell, as I called to mind the circumstances of a former night, to the spot beneath the glare of the censer where I had seen the faint traces of the shadow. It was there, however, no longer; and breathing with greater freedom, I turned my glances to the pallid and rigid figure upon the bed. Then rushed upon me a thousand memories of Ligeia—and then came back upon my heart, with the turbulent violence of a flood, the whole of that unutterable wo with which I had regarded *her* thus enshrouded. The night waned; and still, with a bosom full of bitter thoughts of the one only and supremely beloved, I remained gazing upon the body of Rowena.

It might have been midnight, or perhaps earlier, or later, for I had taken no note of time, when a sob, low, gentle, but very distinct, startled me from my reverie. I *felt* that it came from the bed of ebony—the bed of death. I listened in an agony of superstitious terror—but there was no repetition of the sound. I strained my vision to detect any motion in the corpse—but there was not the slightest perceptible. Yet I could not have been deceived. I *had* heard the noise, however faint, and my soul was awakened within me. I resolutely and perseveringly kept my attention riveted upon the body. Many minutes elapsed before any circumstance occurred tending to throw light upon the mystery. At length it became evident that a slight, a very feeble, and barely noticeable tinge of color had flushed up within the cheeks, and along the sunken small veins of the eyelids. Through a species of unutterable horror and awe, for which the language of mortality has no sufficiently energetic expression, I felt my heart cease to beat, my limbs grow rigid where I sat. Yet a sense of duty finally operated to restore my self-possession. I could no longer doubt that we had been precipitate in our preparations—that Rowena still lived. It was necessary that some immediate exertion be made; yet the turret was altogether apart from the portion of the abbey tenanted by the servants— there were none within call—I had no means of summoning them to my aid without leaving the room for many minutes—and this I could not venture to do. I therefore struggled alone in my endeavors to call back the spirit ill hovering. In a short period it was certain, however, that a relapse had taken place; the color disappeared from both eyelid and cheek, leaving a wanness even more than that of marble; the lips became doubly shriveled and pinched up in the ghastly expression of death; a repulsive clamminess and coldness over-spread rapidly the surface of the body; and all the usual rigorous stiffness immediately supervened. I fell back with a

shudder upon the couch from which I had been so startlingly aroused, and again gave myself up to passionate waking visions of Ligeia.

An hour thus elapsed, when (could it be possible?) I was a second time aware of some vague sound issuing from the region of the bed. I listened—in extremity of horror. The sound came again—it was a sigh. Rushing to the corpse, I saw—distinctly saw—a tremor upon the lips. In a minute afterward they relaxed, disclosing a bright line of the pearly teeth. Amazement now struggled in my bosom with the profound awe which had hitherto reigned there alone. I felt that my vision grew dim, that my reason wandered; and it was only by a violent effort that I at length succeeded in nerving myself to the task which duty thus once more had pointed out. There was now a partial glow upon the forehead and upon the cheek and throat; a perceptible warmth pervaded the whole frame; there was even a slight pulsation at the heart. The lady *lived;* and with redoubled ardor I betook myself to the task of restoration. I chafed and bathed the temples and the hands, and used every exertion which experience, and no little medical reading, could suggest. But in vain. Suddenly, the color fled, the pulsation ceased, the lips resumed the expression of the dead, and, in an instant afterward, the whole body took upon itself the icy chilliness, the livid hue, the intense rigidity, the sunken outline, and all the loathsome peculiarities of that which has been, for many days, a tenant of the tomb.

And again I sunk into visions of Ligeia—and again (what marvel that I shudder while I write?) *again* there reached my ears a low sob from the region of the ebony bed. But why shall I minutely detail the unspeakable horrors of that night? Why shall I pause to relate how, time after time, until near the period of the gray dawn, this hideous drama of revivification was repeated; how each terrific relapse was only into a sterner and apparently more irredeemable death; how each agony wore the aspect of a struggle with some invisible foe; and how each struggle was succeeded by I know not what of wild change in the personal appearance of the corpse? Let me hurry to a conclusion.

The greater part of the fearful night had worn away, and she who had been dead, once again stirred—and now more vigorously than hitherto, although arousing from a dissolution more appalling in its utter hopelessness than any. I had long ceased to struggle or to move, and remained sitting rigidly upon the ottoman, a helpless prey to a whirl of violent emotions, of which extreme awe was perhaps the least terrible, the least consuming. The corpse, I repeat, stirred, and now more vigorously than

before. The hues of life flushed up with unwonted energy into the countenance—the limbs relaxed—and, save that the eyelids were yet pressed heavily together, and that the bandages and draperies of the grave still imparted their charnel character to the figure, I might have dreamed that Rowena had indeed shaken off, utterly, the fetters of Death. But if this idea was not, even then, altogether adopted, I could at least doubt no longer, when, arising from the bed, tottering, with feeble steps, with closed eyes, and with the manner of one bewildered in a dream, the thing that was enshrouded advanced boldly and palpably into the middle of the apartment.

I trembled not—I stirred not—for a crowd of unutterable fancies connected with the air, the stature, the demeanor of the figure, rushing hurriedly through my brain, had paralyzed—had chilled me into stone. I stirred not—but gazed upon the apparition. There was a mad disorder in my thoughts—a tumult unappeasable. Could it, indeed, be the *living* Rowena who confronted me? Could it, indeed, be Rowena *at all*—the fair-haired, the blue-eyed Lady Rowena Trevanion of Tremaine? Why, *why* should I doubt it? The bandage lay heavily about the mouth—but then might it not be the mouth of the breathing Lady of Tremaine? And the cheeks—there were the roses as in her noon of life—yes, these might indeed be the fair cheeks of the living Lady of Tremaine. And the chin, with its dimples, as in health, might it not be hers?—but *had she then grown taller since her malady?* What inexpressible madness seized me with that thought? One bound, and I had reached her feet! Shrinking from my touch, she let fall from her head, unloosened, the ghastly cerements which had confined it, and there streamed forth into the rushing atmosphere of the chamber huge masses of long and disheveled hair; *it was blacker than the raven wings of the midnight!* And now slowly opened *the eyes* of the figure which stood before me. "Here then, at least," I shrieked aloud, "can I never—can I never be mistaken—these are the full, and the black, and the wild eyes—of my lost love—of the lady—of the LADY LIGEIA."

The Fall of the House of
House of Usher

Son cœur est un luth suspendu;
Sitôt qu'on le touche il résonne.

—DE BÉRANGER

DURING THE WHOLE OF A DULL, DARK, AND SOUNDLESS DAY IN THE
autumn of the year, when the clouds hung oppressively low in the heav-
ens, I had been passing alone, on horseback, through a singularly dreary
tract of country; and at length found myself, as the shades of the evening
drew on, within view of the melancholy House of Usher. I know not how
it was—but, with the first glimpse of the building, a sense of insufferable
gloom pervaded my spirit. I say insufferable; for the feeling was unre-
lieved by any of that half-pleasurable, because poetic, sentiment, with
which the mind usually receives even the sternest natural images of the
desolate or terrible. I looked upon the scene before me—upon the mere
house, and the simple landscape features of the domain—upon the bleak
walls—upon the vacant eye-like windows—upon a few rank sedges—and
upon a few white trunks of decayed trees—with an utter depression of
soul which I can compare to no earthly sensation more properly than to
the after-dream of the reveler upon opium—the bitter lapse into every-
day life—the hideous dropping off of the veil. There was an iciness, a
sinking, a sickening of the heart—an unredeemed dreariness of thought
which no goading of the imagination could torture into aught of the
sublime. What was it—I paused to think—what was it that so unnerved me
in the contemplation of the House of Usher? It was a mystery all insoluble;
nor could I grapple with the shadowy fancies that crowded upon me as I

pondered. I was forced to fall back upon the unsatisfactory conclusion, that while, beyond doubt, there *are* combinations of very simple natural objects which have the power of thus affecting us, still the analysis of this power lies among considerations beyond our depth. It was possible, I reflected, that a mere different arrangement of the particulars of the scene, of the details of the picture, would be sufficient to modify, or per-haps to annihilate its capacity for sorrowful impression; and, acting upon this idea, I reined my horse to the precipitous brink of a black and lurid tarn that lay in unruffled luster by the dwelling, and gazed down—but with a shudder even more thrilling than before—upon the remodeled and inverted images of the gray sedge, and the ghastly tree-stems, and the vacant and eye-like windows.

Nevertheless, in this mansion of gloom I now proposed to myself a sojourn of some weeks. Its proprietor, Roderick Usher, had been one of my boon companions in boyhood; but many years had elapsed since our last meeting. A letter, however, had lately reached me in a distant part of the country—a letter from him—which, in its wildly importunate nature, had admitted of no other than a personal reply. The MS. gave evidence of nervous agitation. The writer spoke of acute bodily illness—of a mental disorder which oppressed him—and of an earnest desire to see me, as his best, and indeed his only personal friend, with a view of attempting, by the cheerfulness of my society, some alleviation of his malady. It was the manner in which all this, and much more, was said—it was the apparent *heart* that went with his request—which allowed me no room for hesita-tion; and I accordingly obeyed forthwith what I still considered a very singular summons.

Although, as boys, we had been even intimate associates, yet I really knew little of my friend. His reserve had been always excessive and habit-ual. I was aware, however, that his very ancient family had been noted, time out of mind, for a peculiar sensibility of temperament, displaying itself, through long ages, in many works of exalted art, and manifested, of late, in repeated deeds of munificent yet unobtrusive charity, as well as in a passionate devotion to the intricacies, perhaps even more than to the orthodox and easily recognizable beauties, of musical science. I had learned, too, the very remarkable fact, that the stem of the Usher race, all time-honored as it was, had put forth, at no period, any enduring branch; in other words, that the entire family lay in the direct line of descent, and had always, with very trifling and very temporary variation, so lain. It was this deficiency, I considered, while running over in thought the perfect

keeping of the character of the premises with the accredited character of the people, and while speculating upon the possible influence which the one, in the long lapse of centuries, might have exercised upon the other— it was this deficiency, perhaps, of collateral issue, and the consequent undeviating transmission, from sire to son, of the patrimony with the name, which had, at length, so identified the two as to merge the original title of the estate in the quaint and equivocal appellation of the "House of Usher"—an appellation which seemed to include, in the minds of the peasantry who used it, both the family and the family mansion.

I have said that the sole effect of my somewhat childish experiment— that of looking down within the tarn—had been to deepen the first singular impression. There can be no doubt that the consciousness of the rapid increase of my superstition—for why should I not so term it?—served mainly to accelerate the increase itself. Such, I have long known, is the paradoxical law of all sentiments having terror as a basis. And it might have been for this reason only, that, when I again uplifted my eyes to the house itself, from its image in the pool, there grew in my mind a strange fancy—a fancy so ridiculous, indeed, that I but mention it to show the vivid force of the sensations which oppressed me. I had so worked upon my imagination as really to believe that about the whole mansion and domain there hung an atmosphere peculiar to themselves and their immediate vicinity—an atmosphere which had no affinity with the air of heaven, but which had reeked up from the decayed trees, and the gray wall, and the silent tarn—a pestilent and mystic vapor, dull, sluggish, faintly discernible, and leaden-hued.

Shaking off from my spirit what *must* have been a dream, I scanned more narrowly the real aspect of the building. Its principal feature seemed to be that of an excessive antiquity. The discoloration of ages had been great. Minute fungi overspread the whole exterior, hanging in a fine tangled web-work from the eaves. Yet all this was apart from any extraordinary dilapidation. No portion of the masonry had fallen; and there appeared to be a wild inconsistency between its still perfect adaptation of parts, and the crumbling condition of the individual stones. In this there was much that reminded me of the specious totality of old wood-work which has rotted for long years in some neglected vault, with no disturbance from the breath of the external air. Beyond this indication of extensive decay, however, the fabric gave little token of instability. Perhaps the eye of a scrutinizing observer might have discovered a barely perceptible fissure, which, extending from the roof of the building in front,

made its way down the wall in a zigzag direction, until it became lost in the sullen waters of the tarn.

Noticing these things, I rode over a short causeway to the house. A servant in waiting took my horse, and I entered the Gothic archway of the hall. A valet, of stealthy step, thence conducted me, in silence, through many dark and intricate passages in my progress to the *studio* of his master. Much that I encountered on the way contributed, I know not how, to heighten the vague sentiments of which I have already spoken. While the objects around me—while the carvings of the ceilings, the somber tapestries of the walls, the ebon blackness of the floors, and the phantasmagoric armorial trophies which rattled as I strode, were but matters to which, or to such as which, I had been accustomed from my infancy—while I hesitated not to acknowledge how familiar was all this—I still wondered to find how unfamiliar were the fancies which ordinary images were stirring up. On one of the staircases, I met the physician of the family. His countenance, I thought, wore a mingled expression of low cunning and perplexity. He accosted me with trepidation and passed on. The valet now threw open a door and ushered me into the presence of his master.

The room in which I found myself was very large and lofty. The windows were long, narrow, and pointed, and at so vast a distance from the black oaken floor as to be altogether inaccessible from within. Feeble gleams of encrimsoned light made their way through the trellissed panes, and served to render sufficiently distinct the more prominent objects around; the eye, however, struggled in vain to reach the remoter angles of the chamber, or the recesses of the vaulted and fretted ceiling. Dark draperies hung upon the walls. The general furniture was profuse, comfortless, antique, and tattered. Many books and musical instruments lay scattered about, but failed to give any vitality to the scene. I felt that I breathed an atmosphere of sorrow. An air of stern, deep, and irredeemable gloom hung over and pervaded all.

Upon my entrance, Usher arose from a sofa on which he had been lying at full length, and greeted me with a vivacious warmth which had much in it, I at first thought, of an overdone cordiality—of the constrained effort of the *ennuyé*[1] man of the world. A glance, however, at his countenance, convinced me of his perfect sincerity. We sat down; and for some moments, while he spoke not, I gazed upon him with a feeling half of pity, half of awe. Surely, man had never before so terribly altered, in so brief a period, as had Roderick Usher! It was with difficulty that I could bring myself to admit the identity of the wan being before me with the companion

of my early boyhood. Yet the character of his face had been at all times remarkable. A cadaverousness of complexion; an eye large, liquid, and luminous beyond comparison; lips somewhat thin and very pallid, but of a surpassingly beautiful curve; a nose of a delicate Hebrew model, but with a breadth of nostril unusual in similar formations; a finely molded chin, speaking, in its want of prominence, of a want of moral energy; hair of a more than web-like softness and tenuity; these features, with an inordinate expansion above the regions of the temple, made up altogether a countenance not easily to be forgotten. And now in the mere exaggeration of the prevailing character of these features, and of the expression they were wont to convey, lay so much of change that I doubted to whom I spoke. The now ghastly pallor of the skin, and the now miraculous luster of the eye, above all things startled and even awed me. The silken hair, too, had been suffered to grow all unheeded, and as, in its wild gossamer texture, it floated rather than fell about the face, I could not, even with effort, connect its Arabesque expression with any idea of simple humanity.

In the manner of my friend I was at once struck with an incoherence— an inconsistency; and I soon found this to arise from a series of feeble and futile struggles to overcome an habitual trepidancy—an excessive nervous agitation. For something of this nature I had indeed been prepared, no less by his letter, than by reminiscences of certain boyish traits, and by conclusions deduced from his peculiar physical conformation and temperament. His action was alternately vivacious and sullen. His voice varied rapidly from a tremulous indecision (when the animal spirits seemed utterly in abeyance) to that species of energetic concision—that abrupt, weighty, unhurried, and hollow-sounding enunciation—that leaden, self-balanced and perfectly modulated guttural utterance, which may be observed in the lost drunkard, or the irreclaimable eater of opium, during the periods of his most intense excitement.

It was thus that he spoke of the object of my visit, of his earnest desire to see me, and of the solace he expected me to afford him. He entered, at some length, into what he conceived to be the nature of his malady. It was, he said, a constitutional and a family evil, and one for which he despaired to find a remedy—a mere nervous affection, he immediately added, which would undoubtedly soon pass off. It displayed itself in a host of unnatural sensations. Some of these, as he detailed them, interested and bewildered me; although, perhaps, the terms, and the general manner of the narration had their weight. He suffered much from a morbid acuteness of the senses; the most insipid food was alone endurable; he could wear only

garments of certain texture; the odors of all flowers were oppressive; his eyes were tortured by even a faint light; and there were but peculiar sounds, and these from stringed instruments, which did not inspire him with horror.

To an anomalous species of terror I found him a bounden slave. "I shall perish," said he, "I *must* perish in this deplorable folly. Thus, thus, and not otherwise, shall I be lost. I dread the events of the future, not in themselves, but in their results. I shudder at the thought of any, even the most trivial, incident, which may operate upon this intolerable agitation of soul. I have, indeed, no abhorrence of danger, except in its absolute effect—in terror. In this unnerved—in this pitiable condition—I feel that the period will sooner or later arrive when I must abandon life and reason together, in some struggle with the grim phantasm, FEAR."

I learned, moreover, at intervals, and through broken and equivocal hints, another singular feature of his mental condition. He was enchained by certain superstitious impressions in regard to the dwelling which he tenanted, and whence, for many years, he had never ventured forth—in regard to an influence whose supposititious force was conveyed in terms too shadowy here to be restated—an influence which some peculiarities in the mere form and substance of his family mansion, had, by dint of long sufferance, he said, obtained over his spirit—an effect which the *physique* of the gray walls and turrets, and of the dim tarn[2] into which they all looked down, had, at length, brought about upon the *morale* of his existence.

He admitted, however, although with hesitation, that much of the peculiar gloom which thus afflicted him could be traced to a more natural and far more palpable origin—to the severe and long-continued illness—indeed to the evidently approaching dissolution—of a tenderly beloved sister—his sole companion for long years—his last and only relative on earth. "Her decease," he said, with a bitterness which I can never forget, "would leave him (him the hopeless and the frail) the last of the ancient race of the Ushers." While he spoke, the lady Madeline (for so was she called) passed slowly through a remote portion of the apartment, and, without having noticed my presence, disappeared. I regarded her with an utter astonishment not unmingled with dread—and yet I found it impossible to account for such feelings. A sensation of stupor oppressed me, as my eyes followed her retreating steps. When a door, at length, closed upon her, my glance sought instinctively and eagerly the countenance of the brother—but he had buried his face in his hands, and I could only perceive that a far more than ordinary wanness

had over-spread the emaciated fingers through which trickled many passionate tears.

The disease of the lady Madeline had long baffled the skill of her physicians. A settled apathy, a gradual wasting away of the person, and frequent although transient affections of a partially cataleptical character, were the unusual diagnosis. Hitherto she had steadily borne up against the pressure of her malady, and had not betaken herself finally to bed; but, on the closing in of the evening of my arrival at the house, she succumbed (as her brother told me at night with inexpressible agitation) to the prostrating power of the destroyer; and I learned that the glimpse I had obtained of her person would thus probably be the last I should obtain—that the lady, at least while living, would be seen by me no more.

For several days ensuing, her name was unmentioned by either Usher or myself: and during this period I was busied in earnest endeavors to alleviate the melancholy of my friend. We painted and read together; or I listened, as if in a dream, to the wild improvisations of his speaking guitar. And thus, as a closer and still closer intimacy admitted me more unreservedly into the recesses of his spirit, the more bitterly did I perceive the futility of all attempt at cheering a mind from which darkness, as if an inherent positive quality, poured forth upon all objects of the moral and physical universe, in one unceasing radiation of gloom.

I shall ever bear about me a memory of the many solemn hours I thus spent alone with the master of the House of Usher. Yet I should fail in any attempt to convey an idea of the exact character of the studies, or of the occupations, in which he involved me, or led me the way. An excited and highly distempered ideality threw a sulfurous luster over all. His long improvised dirges will ring forever in my ears. Among other things, I hold painfully in mind a certain singular perversion and amplification of the wild air of the last waltz of Von Weber. From the paintings over which his elaborate fancy brooded, and which grew, touch by touch, into vaguenesses at which I shuddered the more thrillingly, because I shuddered knowing not why; from these paintings (vivid as their images now are before me) I would in vain endeavor to educe more than a small portion which should lie within the compass of merely written words. By the utter simplicity, by the nakedness of his designs, he arrested and overawed attention. If ever mortal painted an idea, that mortal was Roderick Usher. For me at least—in the circumstances then surrounding me—there arose out of the pure abstractions which the hypochondriac contrived to throw upon his canvas, an intensity of intolerable awe, no shadow of which felt I

ever yet in the contemplation of the certainly glowing yet too concrete reveries of Fuseli.

One of the phantasmagoric conceptions of my friend, partaking not so rigidly of the spirit of abstraction, may be shadowed forth, although feebly, in words. A small picture presented the interior of an immensely long and rectangular vault or tunnel, with low walls, smooth, white, and without interruption or device. Certain accessory points of the design served well to convey the idea that this excavation lay at an exceeding depth below the surface of the earth. No outlet was observed in any portion of its vast extent, and no torch, or other artificial source of light was discernible; yet a flood of intense rays rolled throughout, and bathed the whole in a ghastly and inappropriate splendor.

I have just spoken of that morbid condition of the auditory nerve which rendered all music intolerable to the sufferer, with the exception of certain effects of stringed instruments. It was, perhaps, the narrow limits to which he thus confined himself upon the guitar, which gave birth, in great measure, to the fantastic character of his performances. But the fervid *facility* of his *impromptus* could not be so accounted for. They must have been, and were, in the notes, as well as in the words of his wild fantasias (for he not unfrequently accompanied himself with rhymed verbal improvisations), the result of that intense mental collectedness and concentration to which I have previously alluded as observable only in particular moments of the highest artificial excitement. The words of one of these rhapsodies I have easily remembered. I was, perhaps, the more forcibly impressed with it, as he gave it, because, in the under or mystic current of its meaning, I fancied that I perceived, and for the first time, a full consciousness on the part of Usher, of the tottering of his lofty reason upon her throne. The verses, which were entitled "The Haunted Palace," ran very nearly, if not accurately, thus:

I

In the greenest of our valleys
By good angels tenanted,
Once a fair and stately palace—
Radiant palace—reared its head.
In the monarch Thought's dominion—
It stood there!
Never seraph spread a pinion
Over fabric half so fair.

II

Banners yellow, glorious, golden,
 On its roof did float and flow;
(This—all this—was in the olden
 Time long ago)
And every gentle air that dallied,
 In that sweet day,
Along the ramparts plumed and pallid,
 A winged odor went away.

III

Wanderers in that happy valley
 Through two luminous windows saw
Spirits moving musically
 To a lute's well-tunéd law,
Round about a throne, where sitting
 (Porphyrogene!)
In state his glory well befitting,
 The ruler of the realm was seen.

IV

And all with pearl and ruby glowing
 Was the fair palace door,
Through which came flowing, flowing, flowing,
 And sparkling evermore,
A troop of Echoes, whose sweet duty
 Was but to sing,
In voices of surpassing beauty,
 The wit and wisdom of their king.

V

But evil things, in robes of sorrow,
 Assailed the monarch's high estate;
(Ah, let us mourn, for never morrow
 Shall dawn upon him, desolate!)

And, round about his home, the glory
That blushed and bloomed
Is but a dim-remembered story
Of the old time entombed.

VI

And travelers now within that valley,
Through the red-litten windows, see
Vast forms that move fantastically
To a discordant melody;
While, like a rapid ghastly river,
Through the pale door,
A hideous throng rush out forever,
And laugh—but smile no more.

I well remember that suggestions arising from this ballad led us into a train of thought wherein there became manifest an opinion of Usher's which I mention not so much on account of its novelty (for other men[*] have thought thus), as on account of the pertinacity with which he maintained it. This opinion, in its general form, was that of the sentience of all vegetable things. But, in his disordered fancy, the idea had assumed a more daring character, and trespassed, under certain conditions, upon the kingdom of inorganization. I lack words to express the full extent, or the earnest *abandon* of his persuasion. The belief, however, was connected (as I have previously hinted) with the gray stones of the home of his forefathers. The conditions of the sentience had been here, he imagined, fulfilled in the method of collocation of these stones—in the order of their arrangement, as well as in that of the many *fungi* which overspread them, and of the decayed trees which stood around—above all, in the long undisturbed endurance of this arrangement, and in its reduplication in the still waters of the tarn. Its evidence—the evidence of the sentience—was to be seen, he said (and I here started as he spoke), in the gradual yet certain condensation of an atmosphere of their own about the waters and the walls. The result was discoverable, he added, in

[*] Watson, Dr. Percival, Spallanzani, and especially the Bishop of Landaff. See *Chemical Essays*, vol. v.

that silent, yet importunate and terrible influence which for centuries had molded the destinies of his family, and which made *him* what I now saw him—what he was. Such opinions need no comment, and I will make none.

Our books—the books which, for years, had formed no small portion of the mental existence of the invalid—were, as might be supposed, in strict keeping with this character of phantasm. We pored together over such works as the Ververt et Chartreuse of Gresset; the Belphegor of Machiavelli; the Heaven and Hell of Swedenborg; the Subterranean Voyage of Nicholas Klimm by Holberg; the Chiromancy of Robert Flud, of Jean D'Indaginé, and of De la Chambre; the Journey into the Blue Distance of Tieck; and the City of the Sun of Campanella. One favorite volume was a small octavo edition of the *Directorium Inquisitorium,* by the Dominican Eymeric de Gironne; and there were passages in Pomponius Mela, about the old African Satyrs and Œgipans,[3] over which Usher would sit dreaming for hours. His chief delight, however, was found in the perusal of an exceedingly rare and curious book in quarto Gothic—the manual of a forgotten church—the *Vigiliae Mortuorum secundum Chorum Ecclesiae Maguntinae.*

I could not help thinking of the wild ritual of this work, and of its probable influence upon the hypochondriac, when, one evening, having informed me abruptly that the lady Madeline was no more, he stated his intention of preserving her corpse for a fortnight (previously to its final interment), in one of the numerous vaults within the main walls of the building. The worldly reason, however, assigned for this singular proceeding, was one which I did not feel at liberty to dispute. The brother had been led to his resolution (so he told me) by consideration of the unusual character of the malady of the deceased, of certain obtrusive and eager inquiries on the part of her medical men, and of the remote and exposed situation of the burial-ground of the family. I will not deny that when I called to mind the sinister countenance of the person whom I met upon the staircase, on the day of my arrival at the house, I had no desire to oppose what I regarded as at best but a harmless, and by no means an unnatural, precaution.

At the request of Usher, I personally aided him in the arrangements for the temporary entombment. The body having been encoffined, we two alone bore it to its rest. The vault in which we placed it (and which had been so long unopened that our torches, half smothered in its oppressive atmosphere, gave us little opportunity for investigation) was small, damp, and entirely without means of admission for light; lying, at

great depth, immediately beneath that portion of the building in which was my own sleeping apartment. It had been used, apparently, in remote feudal times, for the worst purposes of a donjon-keep, and, in later days, as a place of deposit for powder, or some other highly combustible substance, as a portion of its floor, and the whole interior of a long archway through which we reached it, were carefully sheathed with copper. The door, of massive iron, had been, also, similarly protected. Its immense weight caused an unusually sharp grating sound, as it moved upon its hinges.

Having deposited our mournful burden upon tressels within this region of horror, we partially turned aside the yet unscrewed lid of the coffin, and looked upon the face of the tenant. A striking similitude between the brother and sister now first arrested my attention; and Usher, divining, perhaps, my thoughts, murmured out some few words from which I learned that the deceased and himself had been twins, and that sympathies of a scarcely intelligible nature had always existed between them. Our glances, however, rested not long upon the dead— for we could not regard her unawed. The disease which had thus entombed the lady in the maturity of youth, had left, as usual in all maladies of a strictly cataleptical character, the mockery of a faint blush upon the bosom and the face, and that suspiciously lingering smile upon the lip which is so terrible in death. We replaced and screwed down the lid, and, having secured the door of iron, made our way, with toil, into the scarcely less gloomy apartments of the upper portion of the house.

And now, some days of bitter grief having elapsed, an observable change came over the features of the mental disorder of my friend. His ordinary manner had vanished. His ordinary occupations were neglected or forgotten. He roamed from chamber to chamber with hurried, unequal, and objectless step. The pallor of his countenance had assumed, if possible, a more ghastly hue—but the luminousness of his eye had utterly gone out. The once occasional huskiness of his tone was heard no more; and a tremulous quaver, as if of extreme terror, habitually characterized his utterance. There were times, indeed, when I thought his unceasingly agitated mind was laboring with some oppressive secret, to divulge which he struggled for the necessary courage. At times, again, I was obliged to resolve all into the mere inexplicable vagaries of madness, for I beheld him gazing upon vacancy for long hours, in an attitude of the profoundest attention, as if listening to some imaginary sound. It was no wonder that his condition terrified—that it infected me. I felt creeping

upon me, by slow yet certain degrees, the wild influences of his own fantastic yet impressive superstitions.

It was, especially, upon retiring to bed late in the night of the seventh or eighth day after the placing of the lady Madeline within the donjon, that I experienced the full power of such feelings. Sleep came not near my couch—while the hours waned and waned away. I struggled to reason off the nervousness which had dominion over me. I endeavored to believe that much, if not all of what I felt, was due to the bewildering influence of the gloomy furniture of the room—of the dark and tattered draperies, which, tortured into motion by the breath of a rising tempest, swayed fitfully to and fro upon the walls, and rustled uneasily about the decorations of the bed. But my efforts were fruitless. An irrepressible tremor gradually pervaded my frame; and, at length, there sat upon my very heart an incubus of utterly causeless alarm. Shaking this off with a gasp and a struggle, I uplifted myself upon the pillows, and, peering earnestly within the intense darkness of the chamber, harkened—I know not why, except that an instinctive spirit prompted me—to certain low and indefinite sounds which came, through the pauses of the storm, at long intervals, I knew not whence. Overpowered by an intense sentiment of horror, unaccountable yet unendurable, I threw on my clothes with haste (for I felt that I should sleep no more during the night), and endeavored to arouse myself from the pitiable condition into which I had fallen, by pacing rapidly to and fro through the apartment.

I had taken but few turns in this manner, when a light step on an adjoining staircase arrested my attention. I presently recognized it as that of Usher. In an instant afterward he rapped, with a gentle touch, at my door, and entered, bearing a lamp. His countenance was, as usual, cadaverously wan—but, moreover, there was a species of mad hilarity in his eyes—an evidently restrained *hysteria* in his whole demeanor. His air appalled me—but anything was preferable to the solitude which I had so long endured, and I even welcomed his presence as a relief.

"And you have not seen it?" he said abruptly, after having stared about him for some moments in silence—"you have not then seen it?—but, stay! you shall." Thus speaking, and having carefully shaded his lamp, he hurried to one of the casements, and threw it freely open to the storm.

The impetuous fury of the entering gust nearly lifted us from our feet. It was, indeed, a tempestuous yet sternly beautiful night, and one wildly singular in its terror and its beauty. A whirlwind had apparently collected its force in our vicinity; for there were frequent and violent alterations in

the direction of the wind; and the exceeding density of the clouds (which hung so low as to press upon the turrets of the house) did not prevent our perceiving the life-like velocity with which they flew careering from all points against each other, without passing away into the distance. I say that even their exceeding density did not prevent our perceiving this—yet we had no glimpse of the moon or stars—nor was there any flashing forth of the lightning. But the under surfaces of the huge masses of agitated vapor, as well as all terrestrial objects immediately around us, were glowing in the unnatural light of a faintly luminous and distinctly visible gaseous exhalation which hung about and enshrouded the mansion.

"You must not—you shall not behold this!" said I, shudderingly, to Usher, as I led him, with a gentle violence, from the window to a seat. "These appearances, which bewilder you, are merely electrical phenomena not uncommon—or it may be that they have their ghastly origin in the rank miasma of the tarn. Let us close this casement; the air is chilling and dangerous to your frame. Here is one of your favorite romances. I will read, and you shall listen; and so we will pass away this terrible night together."

The antique volume which I had taken up was the *Mad Trist* of Sir Launcelot Canning; but I had called it a favorite of Usher's more in sad jest than in earnest; for, in truth, there is little in its uncouth and unimaginative prolixity which could have had interest for the lofty and spiritual ideality of my friend. It was, however, the only book immediately at hand; and I indulged a vague hope that the excitement which now agitated the hypochondriac, might find relief (for the history of mental disorder is full of similar anomalies) even in the extremeness of the folly which I should read. Could I have judged, indeed, by the wild overstrained air of vivacity with which he harkened, or apparently harkened, to the words of the tale, I might well have congratulated myself upon the success of my design.

I had arrived at that well-known portion of the story where Ethelred, the hero of the Trist, having sought in vain for peaceable admission into the dwelling of the hermit, proceeds to make good an entrance by force. Here, it will be remembered, the words of the narrative run thus:

"And Ethelred, who was by nature of a doughty heart, and who was now mighty withal, on account of the powerfulness of the wine which he had drunken, waited no longer to hold parley with the hermit, who, in sooth, was of an obstinate and maliceful turn, but, feeling the rain upon his shoulders, and fearing the rising of the tempest, uplifted his mace outright, and, with blows, made quickly room in the plankings of the door for his gauntleted hand; and now pulling therewith sturdily, he so cracked,

and ripped, and tore all asunder, that the noise of the dry and hollow-sounding wood alarummed and reverberated throughout the forest."

At the termination of this sentence I started, and for a moment, paused; for it appeared to me (although I at once concluded that my excited fancy had deceived me)—it appeared to me that, from some very remote portion of the mansion, there came, indistinctly, to my ears, what might have been, in its exact similarity of character, the echo (but a stifled and dull one certainly) of the very cracking and ripping sound which Sir Launcelot had so particularly described. It was, beyond doubt, the coincidence alone which had arrested my attention; for, amid the rattling of the sashes of the casements, and the ordinary commingled noises of the still increasing storm, the sound, in itself, had nothing, surely, which should have interested or disturbed me. I continued the story:

"But the good champion Ethelred, now entering within the door, was sore enraged and amazed to perceive no signal of the maliceful hermit; but, in the stead thereof, a dragon of a scaly and prodigious demeanor, and of a fiery tongue, which sate in guard before a palace of gold, with a floor of silver; and upon the wall there hung a shield of shining brass with this legend enwritten—

> Who entereth herein, a conqueror hath bin;
> Who slayeth the dragon, the shield he shall win;

And Ethelred uplifted his mace, and struck upon the head of the dragon, which fell before him, and gave up his pesty breath, with a shriek so horrid and harsh, and withal so piercing, that Ethelred had fain to close his ears with his hands against the dreadful noise of it, the like whereof was never before heard."

Here again I paused abruptly, and now with a feeling of wild amazement—for there could be no doubt whatever that, in this instance, I did actually hear (although from what direction it proceeded I found it impossible to say) a low and apparently distant, but harsh, protracted, and most unusual screaming or grating sound—the exact counterpart of what my fancy had already conjured up for the dragon's unnatural shriek as described by the romancer.

Oppressed, as I certainly was, upon the occurrence of this second and most extraordinary coincidence, by a thousand conflicting sensations, in which wonder and extreme terror were predominant, I still retained sufficient presence of mind to avoid exciting, by any observation, the sensitive

nervousness of my companion. I was by no means certain that he had noticed the sounds in question; although, assuredly, a strange alteration had, during the last few minutes, taken place in his demeanor. From a position fronting my own, he had gradually brought round his chair, so as to sit with his face to the door of the chamber; and thus I could but partially perceive his features, although I saw that his lips trembled as if he were murmuring inaudibly. His head had dropped upon his breast—yet I knew that he was not asleep, from the wide and rigid opening of the eye as I caught a glance of it in profile. The motion of his body, too, was at variance with this idea—for he rocked from side to side with a gentle yet constant and uniform sway. Having rapidly taken notice of all this, I resumed the narrative of Sir Launcelot, which thus proceeded:

"And now, the champion, having escaped from the terrible fury of the dragon, bethinking himself of the brazen shield, and of the breaking up of the enchantment which was upon it, removed the carcass from out of the way before him, and approached valorously over the silver pavement of the castle to where the shield was upon the wall; which in sooth tarried not for his full coming, but fell down at his feet upon the silver floor, with a mighty great and terrible ringing sound."

No sooner had these syllables passed my lips, than—as if a shield of brass had indeed, at the moment, fallen heavily upon a floor of silver—I became aware of a distinct, hollow, metallic, and clangorous, yet apparently muffled reverberation. Completely unnerved, I leaped to my feet; but the measured rocking movement of Usher was undisturbed. I rushed to the chair in which he sat. His eyes were bent fixedly before him, and throughout his whole countenance there reigned a stony rigidity. But, as I placed my hand upon his shoulder, there came a strong shudder over his whole person; a sickly smile quivered about his lips; and I saw that he spoke in a low, hurried, and gibbering murmur, as if unconscious of my presence. Bending closely over him, I at length drank in the hideous import of his words.

"Not hear it?—yes, I hear it, and *have* heard it. Long—long—long— many minutes, many hours, many days, have I heard it—yet I dared not—oh, pity me, miserable wretch that I am! I dared not—I *dared* not speak! *We have put her living in the tomb!* Said I not that my senses were acute? I *now* tell you that I heard her first feeble movements in the hollow coffin. I heard them—many, many days ago—yet I dared not—*I dared not speak!* And now—tonight—Ethelred—ha! ha!—the breaking of the hermit's door, and the death-cry of the dragon, and the clangor of the

shield!—say, rather, the rending of her coffin, and the grating of the iron hinges of her prison, and her struggles within the coppered archway of the vault! Oh whither shall I fly? Will she not be here anon? Is she not hurrying to upbraid me for my haste? Have I not heard her footstep on the stair? Do I not distinguish that heavy and horrible beating of her heart? Madman!" here he sprang furiously to his feet, and shrieked out his syllables, as if in the effort he were giving up his soul— *"Madman! I tell you that she now stands without the door!"*

As if in the superhuman energy of his utterance there had been found the potency of a spell—the huge antique panels to which the speaker pointed, threw slowly back, upon the instant, their ponderous and ebony jaws. It was the work of the rushing gust—but then without those doors there *did* stand the lofty and enshrouded figure of the lady Madeline of Usher. There was blood upon her white robes, and the evidence of some bitter struggle upon every portion of her emaciated frame. For a moment she remained trembling and reeling to and fro upon the threshold—then, with a low moaning cry, fell heavily inward upon the person of her brother, and in her violent and now final death-agonies, bore him to the floor a corpse, and a victim to the terrors he had anticipated.

From that chamber, and from that mansion, I fled aghast. The storm was still abroad in all its wrath as I found myself crossing the old causeway. Suddenly there shot along the path a wild light, and I turned to see whence a gleam so unusual could have issued; for the vast house and its shadows were alone behind me. The radiance was that of the full, setting, and blood-red moon, which now shone vividly through that once barely discernible fissure, of which I have before spoken as extending from the roof of the building, in a zigzag direction, to the base. While I gazed, this fissure rapidly widened—there came a fierce breath of the whirl-wind— the entire orb of the satellite burst at once upon my sight—my brain reeled as I saw the mighty walls rushing asunder—there was a long tumultuous shouting sound like the voice of a thousand waters—and the deep and dank tarn at my feet closed sullenly and silently over the fragments of the *"House of Usher."*

WILLIAM WILSON

What say of it? what say CONSCIENCE *grim,*
That specter in my path?

—CHAMBERLAYNE'S *PHARRONIDA*

LET ME CALL MYSELF, FOR THE PRESENT, WILLIAM WILSON. THE FAIR PAGE now lying before me need not be sullied with my real appellation. This has been already too much an object for the scorn—for the horror—for the detestation of my race. To the uttermost regions of the globe have not the indignant winds bruited its unparalleled infamy? Oh, outcast of all outcasts most abandoned!—to the earth art thou not forever dead?—to its honors, to its flowers, to its golden aspirations?—and a cloud, dense, dismal, and limitless, does it not hang eternally between thy hopes and heaven?

I would not, if I could, here or today, embody a record of my later years of unspeakable misery, and unpardonable crime. This epoch—these later years—took unto themselves a sudden elevation in turpitude, whose origin alone it is my present purpose to assign. Men usually grow base by degrees. From me, in an instant, all virtue dropped bodily as a mantle. From comparatively trivial wickedness I passed, with the stride of a giant, into more than the enormities of an Elah-Gabalus. What chance—what one event brought this evil thing to pass, bear with me while I relate. Death approaches; and the shadow which foreruns him has thrown a softening influence over my spirit. I long, in passing through the dim valley, for the sympathy—I had nearly said for the pity—of my fellow-men. I would fain have them believe that I have been, in some measure, the slave of circumstances beyond human control. I would wish them to seek out for me, in the details I am about to give, some little oasis of *fatality* amid a

wilderness of error. I would have them allow—what they cannot refrain from allowing—that, although temptation may have erewhile existed as great, man was never *thus*, at least, tempted before—certainly, never *thus* fell. And is it therefore that he has never thus suffered? Have I not indeed been living in a dream? And am I not now dying a victim to the horror and the mystery of the wildest of all sublunary visions?

I am the descendant of a race whose imaginative and easily excitable temperament has at all times rendered them remarkable; and, in my earliest infancy, I gave evidence of having fully inherited the family character. As I advanced in years it was more strongly developed; becoming, for many reasons, a cause of serious disquietude to my friends, and of positive injury to myself. I grew self-willed, addicted to the wildest caprices, and a prey to the most ungovernable passions. Weak-minded, and beset with constitutional infirmities akin to my own, my parents could do but little to check the evil propensities which distinguished me. Some feeble and ill-directed efforts resulted in complete failure on their part, and, of course, in total triumph on mine. Thenceforward my voice was a household law; and at an age when few children have abandoned their leading-strings, I was left to the guidance of my own will, and became, in all but name, the master of my own actions.

My earliest recollections of a school-life, are connected with a large, rambling, Elizabethan house, in a misty-looking village of England, where were a vast number of gigantic and gnarled trees, and where all the houses were excessively ancient. In truth, it was a dream-like and spirit-soothing place, that venerable old town. At this moment, in fancy, I feel the refreshing chilliness of its deeply shadowed avenues, inhale the fragrance of its thousand shrubberies, and thrill anew with undefinable delight, at the deep hollow note of the church-bell, breaking, each hour, with sullen and sudden roar, upon the stillness of the dusky atmosphere in which the fretted Gothic steeple lay imbedded and asleep.

It gives me, perhaps, as much of pleasure as I can now in any manner experience, to dwell upon minute recollections of the school and its concerns. Steeped in misery as I am—misery, alas! only too real—I shall be pardoned for seeking relief, however slight and temporary, in the weakness of a few rambling details. These, moreover, utterly trivial, and even ridiculous in themselves, assume, to my fancy, adventitious importance, as connected with a period and a locality when and where I recognize the first ambiguous monitions of the destiny which afterward so fully overshadowed me. Let me then remember.

The house, I have said, was old and irregular. The grounds were extensive, and a high and solid brick wall, topped with a bed of mortar and broken glass, encompassed the whole. This prison-like rampart formed the limit of our domain; beyond it we saw but thrice a week—once every Saturday afternoon, when, attended by two ushers, we were permitted to take brief walks in a body through some of the neighboring fields—and twice during Sunday, when we were paraded in the same formal manner to the morning and evening service in the one church of the village. Of this church the principal of our school was pastor. With how deep a spirit of wonder and perplexity was I wont to regard him from our remote pew in the gallery, as, with step solemn and slow, he ascended the pulpit! This reverend man, with countenance so demurely benign, with robes so glossy and so clerically flowing, with wig so minutely powdered, so rigid and so vast—could this be he who, of late, with sour visage, and in snuffy habiliments, administered, ferule in hand, the Draconian laws of the academy? Oh, gigantic paradox, too utterly monstrous for solution!

At an angle of the ponderous wall frowned a more ponderous gate. It was riveted and studded with iron bolts, and surmounted with jagged iron spikes. What impressions of deep awe did it inspire! It was never opened save for the three periodical egressions and ingressions already mentioned; then, in every creak of its mighty hinges, we found a plenitude of mystery— a world of matter for solemn remark, or for more solemn meditation.

The extensive enclosure was irregular in form, having many capacious recesses. Of these, three or four of the largest constituted the play-ground. It was level, and covered with fine hard gravel. I well remember it had no trees, nor benches, nor anything similar within it. Of course it was in the rear of the house. In front lay a small parterre, planted with box and other shrubs; but through this sacred division we passed only upon rare occasions indeed—such as a first advent to school or final departure thence, or perhaps, when a parent or friend having called for us, we joyfully took our way home for the Christmas or Midsummer holidays.

But the house!—how quaint an old building was this!—to me how veritably a palace of enchantment! There was really no end to its windings—to its incomprehensible subdivisions. It was difficult, at any given time, to say with certainty upon which of its two stories one happened to be. From each room to every other there were sure to be found three or four steps either in ascent or descent. Then the lateral branches were innumerable— inconceivable—and so returning in upon themselves, that our most exact ideas in regard to the whole mansion were not very far different from

those with which we pondered upon infinity. During the five years of my residence here, I was never able to ascertain with precision, in what remote locality lay the little sleeping apartment assigned to myself and some eighteen or twenty other scholars.

The school-room was the largest in the house—I could not help thinking, in the world. It was very long, narrow, and dismally low, with pointed Gothic windows and a ceiling of oak. In a remote and terror-inspiring angle was a square enclosure of eight or ten feet, comprising the *sanctum,* "during hours," of our principal, the Reverend Dr. Bransby. It was a solid structure, with massy door, sooner than open which in the absence of the "Dominie," we would all have willingly perished by the *peine forte et dure.*[1] In other angles were two other similar boxes, far less reverenced, indeed, but still greatly matters of awe. One of these was the pulpit of the "classical" usher, one of the "English and mathematical." Interspersed about the room, crossing and recrossing in endless irregularity, were innumerable benches and desks, black, ancient, and time-worn, piled desperately with much-bethumbed books, and so beseamed with initial letters, names at full length, grotesque figures, and other multiplied efforts of the knife, as to have entirely lost what little of original form might have been their portion in days long departed. A huge bucket with water stood at one extremity of the room, and a clock of stupendous dimensions at the other.

Encompassed by the massy walls of this venerable academy, I passed, yet not in tedium or disgust, the years of the third lustrum[2] of my life. The teeming brain of childhood requires no external world of incident to occupy or amuse it; and the apparently dismal monotony of a school was replete with more intense excitement than my riper youth has derived from luxury, or my full manhood from crime. Yet I must believe that my first mental development had in it much of the uncommon—even much of the *outré.* Upon mankind at large the events of very early existence rarely leave in mature age any definite impression. All is gray shadow—a weak and irregular remembrance—an indistinct regathering of feeble pleasures and phantasmagoric pains. With me this is not so. In childhood I must have felt with the energy of a man what I now find stamped upon memory in lines as vivid, as deep, and as durable as the *exergues* of the Carthaginian medals.

Yet in fact—in the fact of the world's view—how little was there to remember! The morning's awakening, the nightly summons to bed; the connings, the recitations; the periodical half-holidays, and perambulations; the play-ground, with its broils, its pastimes, its intrigues; these, by

a mental sorcery long forgotten, were made to involve a wilderness of sensation, a world of rich incident, an universe of varied emotion, of excitement the most passionate and spirit-stirring. *"Oh, le bon temps, que ce siecle de fer!"*

In truth, the ardor, the enthusiasm, and the imperiousness of my disposition, soon rendered me a marked character among my school-mates, and by slow, but natural gradations, gave me an ascendancy over all not greatly older than myself; over all with a single exception. This exception was found in the person of a scholar, who, although no rela-tion, bore the same Christian and surname as myself; a circumstance, in fact, little remarkable; for, notwithstanding a noble descent, mine was one of those everyday appellations which seem, by prescriptive right, to have been, time out of mind, the common property of the mob. In this narrative I have therefore designated myself as William Wilson—a ficti-tious title not very dissimilar to the real. My namesake alone, of those who in school phraseology constituted "our set," presumed to compete with me in the studies of the class—in the sports and broils of the play-ground—to refuse implicit belief in my assertions, and submission to my will—indeed, to interfere with my arbitrary dictation in any respect what-soever. If there is on earth a supreme and unqualified despotism, it is the despotism of a master mind in boyhood over the less energetic spirits of its companions.

Wilson's rebellion was to me a source of the greatest embarrassment; the more so as, in spite of the bravado with which in public I made a point of treating him and his pretensions, I secretly felt that I feared him, and could not help thinking the equality which he maintained so easily with myself, a proof of his true superiority; since not to be overcome cost me a perpetual struggle. Yet this superiority—even this equality—was in truth acknowledged by no one but myself; our associates, by some unaccount-able blindness, seemed not even to suspect it. Indeed, his competition, his resistance, and especially his impertinent and dogged interference with my purposes, were not more pointed than private. He appeared to be destitute alike of the ambition which urged, and of the passionate energy of mind which enabled me to excel. In his rivalry he might have been supposed actuated solely by a whimsical desire to thwart, astonish, or mortify myself; although there were times when I could not help observing, with a feeling made up of wonder, abasement, and pique, that he mingled with his inju-ries, his insults, or his contradictions, a certain most inappropriate, and assuredly most unwelcome *affectionateness* of manner. I could only conceive

this singular behavior to arise from a consummate self-conceit assuming the vulgar airs of patronage and protection.

Perhaps it was this latter trait in Wilson's conduct, conjoined with our identity of name, and the mere accident of our having entered the school upon the same day, which set afloat the notion that we were brothers, among the senior classes in the academy. These do not usually inquire with much strictness into the affairs of their juniors. I have before said, or should have said, that Wilson was not, in the most remote degree, connected with my family. But assuredly if we *had* been brothers we must have been twins; for, after leaving Dr. Bransby's, I casually learned that my namesake was born on the nineteenth of January, 1813—and this is a somewhat remarkable coincidence; for the day is precisely that of my own nativity.

It may seem strange that in spite of the continual anxiety occasioned me by the rivalry of Wilson, and his intolerable spirit of contradiction, I could not bring myself to hate him altogether. We had, to be sure, nearly every day a quarrel in which, yielding me publicly the palm of victory, he, in some manner, contrived to make me feel that it was he who had deserved it; yet a sense of pride on my part, and a veritable dignity on his own, kept us always upon what are called "speaking terms," while there were many points of strong congeniality in our tempers, operating to awake in me a sentiment which our position alone, perhaps, prevented from ripening into friendship. It is difficult, indeed, to define, or even to describe, my real feelings towards him. They formed a motley and heterogeneous admixture; some petulant animosity, which was not yet hatred, some esteem, more respect, much fear, with a world of uneasy curiosity. To the moralist it will be unnecessary to say, in addition, that Wilson and myself were the most inseparable of companions.

It was no doubt the anomalous state of affairs existing between us, which turned all my attacks upon him, (and they were many, either open or covert) into the channel of banter or practical joke (giving pain while assuming the aspect of mere fun) rather than into a more serious and determined hostility. But my endeavors on this head were by no means uniformly successful, even when my plans were the most wittily concocted; for my namesake had much about him, in character, of that unassuming and quiet austerity which, while enjoying the poignancy of its own jokes, has no heel of Achilles in itself, and absolutely refuses to be laughed at. I could find, indeed, but one vulnerable point, and that, lying in a personal peculiarity, arising, perhaps, from constitutional disease, would have been spared by any antagonist less at his wit's end than myself; my rival had a

weakness in the faucial or guttural organs, which precluded him from rais-
ing his voice at any time *above a very low whisper.* Of this defect I did not fail
to take what poor advantage lay in my power.

Wilson's retaliations in kind were many; and there was one form of his
practical wit that disturbed me beyond measure. How his sagacity first
discovered at all that so petty a thing would vex me, is a question I never
could solve; but, having discovered, he habitually practiced the annoy-
ance. I had always felt aversion to my uncourtly patronymic, and its very
common, if not plebeian praenomen. The words were venom in my ears;
and when, upon the day of my arrival, a second William Wilson came also
to the academy, I felt angry with him for bearing the name, and doubly
disgusted with the name because a stranger bore it, who would be the
cause of its twofold repetition, who would be constantly in my presence,
and whose concerns, in the ordinary routine of the school business, must
inevitably, on account of the detestable coincidence, be often confounded
with my own.

The feeling of vexation thus engendered grew stronger with every
circumstance tending to show resemblance, moral or physical, between
my rival and myself. I had not then discovered the remarkable fact that we
were of the same age; but I saw that we were of the same height, and I
perceived that we were even singularly alike in general contour of person
and outline of feature. I was galled, too, by the rumor touching a relation-
ship, which had grown current in the upper forms. In a word, nothing
could more seriously disturb me (although I scrupulously concealed such
disturbance), than any allusion to a similarity of mind, person, or con-
dition existing between us. But, in truth, I had no reason to believe that
(with the exception of the matter of relationship, and in the case of Wilson
himself), this similarity had ever been made a subject of comment, or even
observed at all by our schoolfellows. That *he* observed it in all its bearings,
and as fixedly as I, was apparent; but that he could discover in such cir-
cumstances so fruitful a field of annoyance, can only be attributed, as I
said before, to his more than ordinary penetration.

His cue, which was to perfect an imitation of myself, lay both in words
and in actions; and most admirably did he play his part. My dress it was an
easy matter to copy; my gait and general manner were, without difficulty,
appropriated; in spite of his constitutional defect, even my voice did not
escape him. My louder tones were, of course, unattempted, but then the
key, it was identical; *and his singular whisper, it grew the very echo of my own.*

How greatly this most exquisite portraiture harassed me (for it could not justly be termed a caricature), I will not now venture to describe. I had but one consolation—in the fact that the imitation, apparently, was noticed by myself alone, and that I had to endure only the knowing and strangely sarcastic smiles of my namesake himself. Satisfied with having produced in my bosom the intended effect, he seemed to chuckle in secret over the sting he had inflicted, and was characteristically disregardful of the public applause which the success of his witty endeavors might have so easily elicited. That the school, indeed, did not feel his design, perceive its accomplishment, and participate in his sneer, was, for many anxious months, a riddle I could not resolve. Perhaps the *gradation* of his copy rendered it not so readily perceptible; or, more possibly, I owed my security to the master air of the copyist, who, disdaining the letter (which in a painting is all the obtuse can see), gave but the full spirit of his original for my individual contemplation and chagrin.

I have already more than once spoken of the disgusting air of patronage which he assumed towards me, and of his frequent officious interference with my will. This interference often took the ungracious character of advice; advice not openly given, but hinted or insinuated. I received it with a repugnance which gained strength as I grew in years. Yet, at this distant day, let me do him the simple justice to acknowledge that I can recall no occasion when the suggestions of my rival were on the side of those errors or follies so usual to his immature age and seeming inexperience; that his moral sense, at least, if not his general talents and worldly wisdom, was far keener than my own; and that I might, today, have been a better, and thus a happier man, had I less frequently rejected the counsels embodied in those meaning whispers which I then but too cordially hated and too bitterly despised.

As it was, I at length grew restive in the extreme under his distasteful supervision, and daily resented more and more openly what I considered his intolerable arrogance. I have said that, in the first years of our connection as schoolmates, my feelings in regard to him might have been easily ripened into friendship; but, in the latter months of my residence at the academy, although the intrusion of his ordinary manner had, beyond doubt, in some measure, abated, my sentiments, in nearly similar proportion, partook very much of positive hatred. Upon one occasion he saw this, I think, and afterward avoided, or made a show of avoiding me.

It was about the same period, if I remember aright, that, in an altercation of violence with him, in which he was more than usually thrown off his guard, and spoke and acted with an openness of demeanor rather foreign to his nature, I discovered, or fancied I discovered, in his accent, his air, and general appearance, a something which first startled, and then deeply interested me, by bringing to mind dim visions of my earliest infancy—wild, confused and thronging memories of a time when memory herself was yet unborn. I cannot better describe the sensation which oppressed me than by saying that I could with difficulty shake off the belief of my having been acquainted with the being who stood before me, at some epoch very long ago—some point of the past even infinitely remote. The delusion, however, faded rapidly as it came; and I mention it at all but to define the day of the last conversation I there held with my singular namesake.

The huge old house, with its countless subdivisions, had several large chambers communicating with each other, where slept the greater number of the students. There were, however (as must necessarily happen in a building so awkwardly planned), many little nooks or recesses, the odds and ends of the structure; and these the economic ingenuity of Dr. Bransby had also fitted up as dormitories; although, being the merest closets, they were capable of accommodating but a single individual. One of these small apartments was occupied by Wilson.

One night, about the close of my fifth year at the school, and immediately after the altercation just mentioned, finding everyone wrapped in sleep, I arose from bed, and, lamp in hand, stole through a wilderness of narrow passages from my own bed-room to that of my rival. I had long been plotting one of those ill-natured pieces of practical wit at his expense in which I had hitherto been so uniformly unsuccessful. It was my intention, now, to put my scheme in operation, and I resolved to make him feel the whole extent of the malice with which I was imbued. Having reached his closet, I noiselessly entered, leaving the lamp, with a shade over it, on the outside. I advanced a step, and listened to the sound of his tranquil breathing. Assured of his being asleep, I returned, took the light, and with it again approached the bed. Close curtains were around it, which, in the prosecution of my plan, I slowly and quietly withdrew, when the bright rays fell vividly upon the sleeper, and my eyes, at the same moment, upon his countenance. I looked; and a numbness, an iciness of feeling instantly pervaded my frame. My breast heaved, my knees tottered, my whole spirit became possessed with an objectless yet intolerable horror. Gasping for breath, I

lowered the lamp in still nearer proximity to the face. Were these—*these* the lineaments of William Wilson? I saw, indeed, that they were his, but I shook as if with a fit of the ague in fancying they were not. What *was* there about them to confound me in this manner? I gazed; while my brain reeled with a multitude of incoherent thoughts. Not thus he appeared—assuredly not *thus*—in the vivacity of his waking hours. The same name! The same contour of person! The same day of arrival at the academy! And then his dogged and meaningless imitation of my gait, my voice, my habits, and my manner! Was it, in truth, within the bounds of human possibility, that *what I now saw* was the result, merely, of the habitual practice of this sarcastic imitation? Awe-stricken, and with a creeping shudder, I extinguished the lamp, passed silently from the chamber, and left, at once, the halls of that old academy, never to enter them again.

After a lapse of some months, spent at home in mere idleness, I found myself a student at Eton. The brief interval had been sufficient to enfeeble my remembrance of the events at Dr. Bransby's, or at least to effect a material change in the nature of the feelings with which I remembered them. The truth—the tragedy—of the drama was no more. I could now find room to doubt the evidence of my senses; and seldom called up the subject at all but with wonder at the extent of human credulity, and a smile at the vivid force of the imagination which I hereditarily possessed. Neither was this species of skepticism likely to be diminished by the character of the life I led at Eton. The vortex of thoughtless folly into which I there so immediately and so recklessly plunged, washed away all but the froth of my past hours, engulfed at once every solid or serious impression, and left to memory only the veriest levities of a former existence.

I do not wish, however, to trace the course of my miserable profligacy here—a profligacy which set at defiance the laws, while it eluded the vigilance of the institution. Three years of folly, passed without profit, had but given me rooted habits of vice, and added, in a somewhat unusual degree, to my bodily stature, when, after a week of soulless dissipation, I invited a small party of the most dissolute students to a secret carousal in my chambers. We met at a late hour of the night; for our debaucheries were to be faithfully protracted until morning. The wine flowed freely, and there were not wanting other and perhaps more dangerous seductions; so that the gray dawn had already faintly appeared in the east, while our delirious extravagance was at its height. Madly flushed with cards and intoxication, I was in the act of insisting upon a toast of more than wonted profanity, when my attention was suddenly diverted by the violent, although partial

unclosing of the door of the apartment, and by the eager voice of a servant from without. He said that some person, apparently in great haste, demanded to speak with me in the hall.

Wildly excited with wine, the unexpected interruption rather delighted than surprised me. I staggered forward at once, and a few steps brought me to the vestibule of the building. In this low and small room there hung no lamp; and now no light at all was admitted, save that of the exceedingly feeble dawn which made its way through the semi-circular window. As I put my foot over the threshold, I became aware of the figure of a youth about my own height, and habited in a white kerseymere morning frock, cut in the novel fashion of the one I myself wore at the moment. This the faint light enabled me to perceive; but the features of his face I could not distinguish. Upon my entering he strode hurriedly up to me, and, seizing me by the arm with a gesture of petulant impatience, whispered the words "William Wilson!" in my ear.

I grew perfectly sober in an instant.

There was that in the manner of the stranger, and in the tremulous shake of his uplifted finger, as he held it between my eyes and the light, which filled me with unqualified amazement; but it was not this which had so violently moved me. It was the pregnancy of solemn admonition in the singular, low, hissing utterance; and, above all, it was the character, the tone, *the key,* of those few, simple, and familiar, yet *whispered* syllables, which came with a thousand thronging memories of by-gone days, and struck upon my soul with the shock of a galvanic battery. Ere I could recover the use of my senses he was gone.

Although this event failed not of a vivid effect upon my disordered imagination, yet was it evanescent as vivid. For some weeks, indeed, I busied myself in earnest inquiry, or was wrapped in a cloud of morbid speculation. I did not pretend to disguise from my perception the identity of the singular individual who thus perseveringly interfered with my affairs, and harassed me with his insinuated counsel. But who and what was this Wilson?—and whence came he?—and what were his purposes? Upon neither of these points could I be satisfied; merely ascertaining, in regard to him, that a sudden accident in his family had caused his removal from Dr. Bransby's academy on the afternoon of the day in which I myself had eloped. But in a brief period I ceased to think upon the subject; my attention being all absorbed in a contemplated departure for Oxford. Thither I soon went; the uncalculating vanity of my parents furnishing me with an outfit, and annual establishment, which would enable me to

indulge at will in the luxury already so dear to my heart—to vie in profuseness of expenditure with the haughtiest heirs of the wealthiest earldoms in Great Britain.

Excited by such appliances to vice, my constitutional temperament broke forth with redoubled ardor, and I spurned even the common restraints of decency in the mad infatuation of my revels. But it were absurd to pause in the detail of my extravagance. Let it suffice, that among spendthrifts I out-Heroded Herod, and that, giving name to a multitude of novel follies, I added no brief appendix to the long catalogue of vices then usual in the most dissolute university of Europe.

It could hardly be credited, however, that I had, even here, so utterly fallen from the gentlemanly estate, as to seek acquaintance with the vilest arts of the gambler by profession, and, having become an adept in his despicable science, to practice it habitually as a means of increasing my already enormous income at the expense of the weak-minded among my fellow-collegians. Such, nevertheless, was the fact. And the very enormity of this offence against all manly and honorable sentiment proved, beyond doubt, the main if not the sole reason of the impunity with which it was committed. Who, indeed, among my most abandoned associates, would not rather have disputed the clearest evidence of his senses, than have suspected of such courses, the gay, the frank, the generous William Wilson—the noblest and most liberal commoner at Oxford—him whose follies (said his parasites) were but the follies of youth and unbridled fancy—whose errors but inimitable whim—whose darkest vice but a careless and dashing extravagance?

I had been now two years successfully busied in this way, when there came to the university a young *parvenu* nobleman, Glendinning—rich, said report, as Herodes Atticus—his riches, too, as easily acquired. I soon found him of weak intellect, and, of course, marked him as a fitting subject for my skill. I frequently engaged him in play, and contrived, with the gambler's usual art, to let him win considerable sums, the more effectually to entangle him in my snares. At length, my schemes being ripe, I met him (with the full intention that this meeting should be final and decisive) at the chambers of a fellow-commoner (Mr. Preston), equally intimate with both, but who, to do him justice, entertained not even a remote suspicion of my design. To give to this a better coloring, I had contrived to have assembled a party of some eight or ten, and was solicitously careful that the introduction of cards should appear accidental, and originate in the proposal of my contemplated dupe himself. To be brief upon a vile topic,

none of the low finesse was omitted, so customary upon similar occasions that it is a just matter for wonder how any are still found so besotted as to fall its victim.

We had protracted our sitting far into the night, and I had at length effected the maneuver of getting Glendinning as my sole antagonist. The game, too, was my favorite *écarté*. The rest of the company, interested in the extent of our play, had abandoned their own cards, and were standing around us as spectators. The *parvenu*, who had been induced by my artifices in the early part of the evening, to drink deeply, now shuffled, dealt, or played, with a wild nervousness of manner for which his intoxication, I thought, might partially, but could not altogether account. In a very short period he had become my debtor to a large amount, when, having taken a long draught of port, he did precisely what I had been coolly anticipating—he proposed to double our already extravagant stakes. With a well-feigned show of reluctance, and not until after my repeated refusal had seduced him into some angry words which gave a color of *pique* to my compliance, did I finally comply. The result, of course, did but prove how entirely the prey was in my toils; in less than an hour he had quadrupled his debt. For some time his countenance had been losing the florid tinge lent it by the wine; but now, to my astonishment, I perceived that it had grown to a pallor truly fearful. I say to my astonishment. Glendinning had been represented to my eager inquiries as immeasurably wealthy; and the sums which he had as yet lost, although in themselves vast, could not, I supposed, very seriously annoy, much less so violently affect him. That he was overcome by the wine just swallowed, was the idea which most readily presented itself; and, rather with a view to the preservation of my own character in the eyes of my associates, than from any less interested motive, I was about to insist, peremptorily, upon a discontinuance of the play, when some expressions at my elbow from among the company, and an ejaculation evincing utter despair on the part of Glendinning, gave me to understand that I had effected his total ruin under circumstances which, rendering him an object for the pity of all, should have protected him from the ill offices even of a fiend.

What now might have been my conduct it is difficult to say. The pitiable condition of my dupe had thrown an air of embarrassed gloom over all; and, for some moments, a profound silence was maintained, during which I could not help feeling my cheeks tingle with the many burning glances of scorn or reproach cast upon me by the less abandoned of the party. I will even own that an intolerable weight of anxiety was for a brief instant lifted

from my bosom by the sudden and extraordinary interruption which ensued. The wide, heavy folding doors of the apartment were all at once thrown open, to their full extent, with a vigorous and rushing impetuosity that extinguished, as if by magic, every candle in the room. Their light, in dying, enabled us just to perceive that a stranger had entered, about my own height, and closely muffled in a cloak. The darkness, however, was now total; and we could only *feel* that he was standing in our midst. Before anyone of us could recover from the extreme astonishment into which this rudeness had thrown all, we heard the voice of the intruder.

"Gentlemen," he said, in a low, distinct, and never-to-be-forgotten *whisper* which thrilled to the very marrow of my bones, "Gentlemen, I make no apology for this behavior, because in thus behaving, I am but fulfilling a duty. You are, beyond doubt, uninformed of the true character of the person who has tonight won at *écarté* a large sum of money from Lord Glendinning. I will therefore put you upon an expeditious and decisive plan of obtaining this very necessary information. Please to examine, at your leisure, the inner linings of the cuff of his left sleeve, and the several little packages which may be found in the somewhat capacious pockets of his embroidered morning wrapper."

While he spoke, so profound was the stillness that one might have heard a pin drop upon the floor. In ceasing, he departed at once, and as abruptly as he had entered. Can I—shall I describe my sensations?—must I say that I felt all the horrors of the damned? Most assuredly I had little time given for reflection. Many hands roughly seized me upon the spot, and lights were immediately reprocured. A search ensued. In the lining of my sleeve were found all the court cards essential in *écarté*, and, in the pockets of my wrapper, a number of packs, fac-similes of those used at our sittings, with the single exception that mine were of the species called, technically, *arrondées*; the honors being slightly convex at the ends, the lower cards slightly convex at the sides. In this disposition, the dupe who cuts, as customary, at the length of the pack, will invariably find that he cuts his antagonist an honor; while the gambler, cutting at the breadth, will, as certainly, cut nothing for his victim which may count in the records of the game.

Any burst of indignation upon this discovery would have affected me less than the silent contempt, or the sarcastic composure, with which it was received.

"Mr. Wilson," said our host, stooping to remove from beneath his feet an exceedingly luxurious cloak of rare furs, "Mr. Wilson, this is your

property." (The weather was cold; and, upon quitting my own room, I had thrown a cloak over my dressing wrapper, putting it off upon reaching the scene of play.) "I presume it is supererogatory to seek here (eyeing the folds of the garment with a bitter smile) for any farther evidence of your skill. Indeed, we have had enough. You will see the necessity, I hope, of quitting Oxford—at all events, of quitting instantly my chambers."

Abased, humbled to the dust as I then was, it is probable that I should have resented this galling language by immediate personal violence, had not my whole attention been at the moment arrested by a fact of the most startling character. The cloak which I had worn was of a rare description of fur; how rare, how extravagantly costly, I shall not venture to say. Its fashion, too, was of my own fantastic invention; for I was fastidious to an absurd degree of coxcombry, in matters of this frivolous nature. When, therefore, Mr. Preston reached me that which he had picked up upon the floor, and near the folding doors of the apartment, it was with an astonishment nearly bordering upon terror, that I perceived my own already hanging on my arm (where I had no doubt unwittingly placed it), and that the one presented me was but its exact counterpart in every, in even the minutest possible particular. The singular being who had so disastrously exposed me, had been muffled, I remembered, in a cloak; and none had been worn at all by any of the members of our party with the exception of myself. Retaining some presence of mind, I took the one offered me by Preston; placed it, unnoticed, over my own; left the apartment with a resolute scowl of defiance; and, next morning ere dawn of day, commenced a hurried journey from Oxford to the continent, in a perfect agony of horror and of shame.

I fled in vain. My evil destiny pursued me as if in exultation, and proved, indeed, that the exercise of its mysterious dominion had as yet only begun. Scarcely had I set foot in Paris ere I had fresh evidence of the detestable interest taken by this Wilson in my concerns. Years flew, while I experienced no relief. Villain!—at Rome, with how untimely, yet with how spectral an officiousness, stepped he in between me and my ambition! At Vienna, too—at Berlin—and at Moscow! Where, in truth, had I *not* bitter cause to curse him within my heart? From his inscrutable tyranny did I at length flee, panic-stricken, as from a pestilence; and to the very ends of the earth *I fled in vain.*

And again, and again, in secret communion with my own spirit, would I demand the questions "Who is he? Whence came he? And what are his objects?" But no answer was there found. And then I scrutinized, with a minute scrutiny, the forms, and the methods, and the leading traits of his

impertinent supervision. But even here there was very little upon which to base a conjecture. It was noticeable, indeed, that, in no one of the multiplied instances in which he had of late crossed my path, had he so crossed it except to frustrate those schemes, or to disturb those actions, which, if fully carried out, might have resulted in bitter mischief. Poor justification this, in truth, for an authority so imperiously assumed! Poor indemnity for natural rights of self-agency so pertinaciously, so insultingly denied!

I had also been forced to notice that my tormentor, for a very long period of time (while scrupulously and with miraculous dexterity maintaining his whim of an identity of apparel with myself), had so contrived it, in the execution of his varied interference with my will, that I saw not, at any moment, the features of his face. Be Wilson what he might, *this*, at least, was but the veriest of affectation, or of folly. Could he, for an instant, have supposed that, in my admonisher at Eton—in the destroyer of my honor at Oxford—in him who thwarted my ambition at Rome, my revenge at Paris, my passionate love at Naples, or what he falsely termed my avarice in Egypt—that in this, my arch-enemy and evil genius, I could fail to recognize the William Wilson of my school-boy days—the namesake, the companion, the rival—the hated and dreaded rival at Dr. Bransby's? Impossible!—But let me hasten to the last eventful scene of the drama.

Thus far I had succumbed supinely to this imperious domination. The sentiment of deep awe with which I habitually regarded the elevated character, the majestic wisdom, the apparent omnipresence and omnipotence of Wilson, added to a feeling of even terror, with which certain other traits in his nature and assumptions inspired me, had operated, hitherto, to impress me with an idea of my own utter weakness and helplessness, and to suggest an implicit, although bitterly reluctant submission to his arbitrary will. But, of late days, I had given myself up entirely to wine; and its maddening influence upon my hereditary temper rendered me more and more impatient of control. I began to murmur—to hesitate—to resist. And was it only fancy which induced me to believe that, with the increase of my own firmness, that of my tormentor underwent a proportional diminution? Be this as it may, I now began to feel the inspiration of a burning hope, and at length nurtured in my secret thoughts a stern and desperate resolution that I would submit no longer to be enslaved.

It was at Rome, during the Carnival of 18—, that I attended a masquerade in the palazzo of the Neapolitan Duke Di Broglio. I had indulged more freely than usual in the excesses of the wine-table; and now the suffocating atmosphere of the crowded rooms irritated me beyond endurance.

The difficulty, too, of forcing my way through the mazes of the company contributed not a little to the ruffling of my temper; for I was anxiously seeking, (let me not say with what unworthy motive) the young, the gay, the beautiful wife of the aged and doting Di Broglio. With a too unscrupulous confidence she had previously communicated to me the secret of the costume in which she would be habited, and now, having caught a glimpse of her person, I was hurrying to make my way into her presence. At this moment I felt a light hand placed upon my shoulder, and that ever-remembered, low, damnable *whisper* within my ear.

In an absolute frenzy of wrath, I turned at once upon him who had thus interrupted me, and seized him violently by the collar. He was attired, as I had expected, in a costume altogether similar to my own; wearing a Spanish cloak of blue velvet, begirt about the waist with a crimson belt sustaining a rapier. A mask of black silk entirely covered his face.

"Scoundrel!" I said, in a voice husky with rage, while every syllable I uttered seemed as new fuel to my fury, "scoundrel! impostor! accursed villain! you shall not—you *shall not* dog me unto death! Follow me, or I stab you where you stand!"—and I broke my way from the ball-room into a small antechamber adjoining—dragging him unresistingly with me as I went.

Upon entering, I thrust him furiously from me. He staggered against the wall, while I closed the door with an oath, and commanded him to draw. He hesitated but for an instant; then, with a slight sigh, drew in silence, and put himself upon his defence.

The contest was brief indeed. I was frantic with every species of wild excitement, and felt within my single arm the energy and power of a multitude. In a few seconds I forced him by sheer strength against the wainscoting, and thus, getting him at mercy, plunged my sword, with brute ferocity, repeatedly through and through his bosom.

At that instant some person tried the latch of the door. I hastened to prevent an intrusion, and then immediately returned to my dying antagonist. But what human language can adequately portray *that* astonishment, *that* horror which possessed me at the spectacle then presented to view? The brief moment in which I averted my eyes had been sufficient to produce, apparently, a material change in the arrangements at the upper or farther end of the room. A large mirror—so at first it seemed to me in my confusion—now stood where none had been perceptible before; and, as I stepped up to it in extremity of terror, mine own image, but with features all pale and dabbled in blood, advanced to meet me with a feeble and tottering gait.

Thus it appeared I say, but was not. It was my antagonist—it was Wilson, who then stood before me in the agonies of his dissolution. His mask and cloak lay, where he had thrown them, upon the floor. Not a thread in all his raiment—not a line in all the marked and singular lineaments of his face which was not, even in the most absolute identity, *mine own!*

It was Wilson; but he spoke no longer in a whisper, and I could have fancied that I myself was speaking while he said:

"You have conquered, and I yield. Yet, henceforward art thou also dead—dead to the World, to Heaven and to Hope! In me didst thou exist—and, in my death, see by this image, which is thine own, how utterly thou hast murdered thyself."

A Descent into the Maelström

The ways of God in Nature, as in Providence, are not as our ways;
nor are the models that we frame in any way commensurate to the
vastness, profundity, and unsearchableness of His works, which
have a depth in them greater than the well of Democritus.

—JOSEPH GLANVILLE

We had now reached the summit of the loftiest crag. For some minutes the old man seemed too much exhausted to speak.

"Not long ago," said he at length, "and I could have guided you on this route as well as the youngest of my sons; but, about three years past, there happened to me an event such as never happened before to mortal man—or at least such as no man ever survived to tell of—and the six hours of deadly terror which I then endured have broken me up body and soul. You suppose me a *very* old man—but I am not. It took less than a single day to change these hairs from a jetty black to white, to weaken my limbs, and to unstring my nerves, so that I tremble at the least exertion, and am frightened at a shadow. Do you know I can scarcely look over this little cliff without getting giddy?"

The "little cliff," upon whose edge he had so carelessly thrown himself down to rest that the weightier portion of his body hung over it, while he was only kept from falling by the tenure of his elbow on its extreme and slippery edge—this "little cliff" arose, a sheer unobstructed precipice of black shining rock, some fifteen or sixteen hundred feet from the world of crags beneath us. Nothing would have tempted me to be within half a dozen yards of its brink. In truth so deeply was I excited by the perilous

90

position of my companion, that I fell at full length upon the ground, clung to the shrubs around me, and dared not even glance upward at the sky—while I struggled in vain to divest myself of the idea that the foundations of the mountain were in danger from the fury of the winds. It was long before I could reason myself into sufficient courage to sit up and look out into the distance.

"You must get over these fancies," said the guide, "for I have brought you here that you might have the best possible view of the scene of that event I mentioned—and to tell you the whole story with the spot just under your eye."

"We are now," he continued, in that particularizing manner which distinguished him—"we are now close upon the Norwegian coast—in the sixty-eighth degree of latitude—in the great province of Nordland—and in the dreary district of Lofoden. The mountain upon whose top we sit is Helseggen, the Cloudy. Now raise yourself up a little higher—hold on to the grass if you feel giddy—so—and look out, beyond the belt of vapor beneath us, into the sea."

I looked dizzily, and beheld a wide expanse of ocean, whose waters wore so inky a hue as to bring at once to my mind the Nubian geographer's account of the *Mare Tenebrarum*. A panorama more deplorably desolate no human imagination can conceive. To the right and left, as far as the eye could reach, there lay outstretched, like ramparts of the world, lines of horridly black and beetling cliff, whose character of gloom was but the more forcibly illustrated by the surf which reared high up against it its white and ghastly crest, howling and shrieking forever. Just opposite the promontory upon whose apex we were placed, and at a distance of some five or six miles out at sea, there was visible a small, bleak-looking island; or, more properly, its position was discernible through the wilderness of surge in which it was enveloped. About two miles nearer the land, arose another of smaller size; hideously craggy and barren, and encompassed at various intervals by a cluster of dark rocks.

The appearance of the ocean, in the space between the more distant island and the shore, had something very unusual about it. Although, at the time, so strong a gale was blowing landward that a brig in the remote offing lay to under a double-reefed trysail, and constantly plunged her whole hull out of sight, still there was here nothing like a regular swell, but only a short, quick, angry cross-dashing of water in every direction—as well in the teeth of the wind as otherwise. Of foam there was little except in the immediate vicinity of the rocks.

"The island in the distance," resumed the old man, "is called by the Norwegians Vurrgh. The one midway is Moskoe. That a mile to the northward is Ambaaren. Yonder are Islesen, Hotholm, Keildhelm, Suarven, and Buckholm. Further off—between Moskoe and Vurrgh—are Otterholm, Flimen, Sandflesen, and Stockholm. These are the true names of the places—but why it has been thought necessary to name them at all, is more than either you or I can understand. Do you hear anything? Do you see any change in the water?"

We had now been about ten minutes upon the top of Helseggen, to which we had ascended from the interior of Lofoden, so that we had caught no glimpse of the sea until it had burst upon us from the summit. As the old man spoke, I became aware of a loud and gradually increasing sound, like the moaning of a vast herd of buffaloes upon an American prairie; and at the same moment I perceived that what seamen term the *chopping* character of the ocean beneath us, was rapidly changing into a current which set to the eastward. Even while I gazed, this current acquired a monstrous velocity. Each moment added to its speed—to its headlong impetuosity. In five minutes the whole sea, as far as Vurrgh, was lashed into ungovernable fury; but it was between Moskoe and the coast that the main uproar held its sway. Here the vast bed of the waters, seamed and scarred into a thousand conflicting channels, burst suddenly into frenzied convulsion—heaving, boiling, hissing—gyrating in gigantic and innumerable vortices, and all whirling and plunging on to the eastward with a rapidity which water never elsewhere assumes, except in precipitous descents.

In a few minutes more, there came over the scene another radical alteration. The general surface grew somewhat more smooth, and the whirlpools, one by one, disappeared, while prodigious streaks of foam became apparent where none had been seen before. These streaks, at length, spreading out to a great distance, and entering into combination, took unto themselves the gyratory motion of the subsided vortices, and seemed to form the germ of another more vast. Suddenly—very suddenly—this assumed a distinct and definite existence, in a circle of more than a mile in diameter. The edge of the whirl was represented by a broad belt of gleaming spray; but no particle of this slipped into the mouth of the terrific funnel, whose interior, as far as the eye could fathom it, was a smooth, shining, and jet-black wall of water, inclined to the horizon at an angle of some forty-five degrees, speeding dizzily round and round with a swaying and sweltering motion, and sending forth to the winds an appalling voice, half

shriek, half roar, such as not even the mighty cataract of Niagara ever lifts up in its agony to Heaven.

The mountain trembled to its very base, and the rock rocked. I threw myself upon my face, and clung to the scant herbage in an excess of nervous agitation.

"This," said I at length, to the old man—"this *can* be nothing else than the great whirlpool of the Maelström."

"So it is sometimes termed," said he. "We Norwegians call it the Moskoe-ström, from the island of Moskoe in the midway."

The ordinary accounts of this vortex had by no means prepared me for what I saw. That of Jonas Ramus, which is perhaps the most circumstantial of any, cannot impart the faintest conception either of the magnificence, or of the horror of the scene—or of the wild bewildering sense of *the novel* which confounds the beholder. I am not sure from what point of view the writer in question surveyed it, nor at what time; but it could neither have been from the summit of Helseggen, nor during a storm. There are some passages of his description, nevertheless, which may be quoted for their details, although their effect is exceedingly feeble in conveying an impression of the spectacle.

"Between Lofoden and Moskoe," he says, "the depth of the water is between thirty-six and forty fathoms; but on the other side, towards Ver (Vurrgh) this depth decreases so as not to afford a convenient passage for a vessel, without the risk of splitting on the rocks, which happens even in the calmest weather. When it is flood, the stream runs up the country between Lofoden and Moskoe with a boisterous rapidity; but the roar of its impetuous ebb to the sea is scarce equaled by the loudest and most dreadful cataracts; the noise being heard several leagues off, and the vortices or pits are of such an extent and depth, that if a ship comes within its attraction, it is inevitably absorbed and carried down to the bottom, and there beat to pieces against the rocks; and when the water relaxes, the fragments thereof are thrown up again. But these intervals of tranquility are only at the turn of the ebb and flood, and in calm weather, and last but a quarter of an hour, its violence gradually returning. When the stream is most boisterous, and its fury heightened by a storm, it is dangerous to come within a Norway mile of it. Boats, yachts, and ships have been carried away by not guarding against it before they were within its reach. It likewise happens frequently, that whales come too near the stream, and are overpowered by its violence; and then it is impossible to describe their howlings and bellowings in their fruitless struggles to disengage

themselves. A bear once, attempting to swim from Lofoden to Moskoe, was caught by the stream and borne down, while he roared terribly, so as to be heard on shore. Large stocks of firs and pine trees, after being absorbed by the current, rise again broken and torn to such a degree as if bristles grew upon them. This plainly shows the bottom to consist of craggy rocks, among which they are whirled to and fro. This stream is regulated by the flux and reflux of the sea—it being constantly high and low water every six hours. In the year 1645, early in the morning of Sexagesima Sunday, it raged with such noise and impetuosity that the very stones of the houses on the coast fell to the ground."

In regard to the depth of the water, I could not see how this could have been ascertained at all in the immediate vicinity of the vortex. The "forty fathoms" must have reference only to portions of the channel close upon the shore either of Moskoe or Lofoden. The depth in the center of the Moskoe-ström must be immeasurably greater: and no better proof of this fact is necessary than can be obtained from even the sidelong glance into the abyss of the whirl which may be had from the highest crag of Helseggen. Looking down from this pinnacle upon the howling Phlegethon[1] below, I could not help smiling at the simplicity with which the honest Jonas Ramus records, as a matter difficult of belief, the anecdotes of the whales and the bears, for it appeared to me, in fact, a self-evident thing, that the largest ships of the line in existence, coming within the influence of that deadly attraction, could resist it as little as a feather the hurricane, and must disappear bodily and at once.

The attempts to account for the phenomenon—some of which I remember, seemed to me sufficiently plausible in perusal—now wore a very different and unsatisfactory aspect. The idea generally received is that this, as well as three smaller vortices among the Ferroe islands, "have no other cause than the collision of waves rising and falling, at flux and reflux, against a ridge of rocks and shelves, which confines the water so that it precipitates itself like a cataract; and thus the higher the flood rises, the deeper must the fall be, and the natural result of all is a whirlpool or vortex, the prodigious suction of which is sufficiently known by lesser experiments." These are the words of the Encyclopaedia Brittanica. Kircher and others imagine that in the center of the channel of the Maelström is an abyss penetrating the globe, and issuing in some very remote part—the Gulf of Bothnia being somewhat decidedly named in one instance. This opinion, idle in itself, was the one to which, as I gazed, my imagination most readily assented; and, mentioning it to the guide, I was

rather surprised to hear him say that, although it was the view almost universally entertained of the subject by the Norwegians, it nevertheless was not his own. As to the former notion he confessed his inability to comprehend it; and here I agreed with him—for, however conclusive on paper, it becomes altogether unintelligible, and even absurd, amid the thunder of the abyss.

"You have had a good look at the whirl now," said the old man, "and if you will creep round this crag, so as to get in its lee, and deaden the roar of the water, I will tell you a story that will convince you I ought to know something of the Moskoe-ström."

I placed myself as desired, and he proceeded.

"Myself and my two brothers once owned a schooner-rigged smack of about seventy tons burden, with which we were in the habit of fishing among the islands beyond Moskoe, nearly to Vurrgh. In all violent eddies at sea there is good fishing, at proper opportunities, if one has only the courage to attempt it; but among the whole of the Lofoden coastmen, we three were the only ones who made a regular business of going out to the islands, as I tell you. The usual grounds are a great way lower down to the southward. There fish can be got at all hours, without much risk, and therefore these places are preferred. The choice spots over here among the rocks, however, not only yield the finest variety, but in far greater abundance; so that we often got in a single day, what the more timid of the craft could not scrape together in a week. In fact, we made it a matter of desperate speculation—the risk of life standing instead of labor, and courage answering for capital.

"We kept the smack in a cove about five miles higher up the coast than this; and it was our practice, in fine weather, to take advantage of the fifteen minutes' slack to push across the main channel of the Moskoe-ström, far above the pool, and then drop down upon anchorage somewhere near Otterholm, or Sandflesen, where the eddies are not so violent as elsewhere. Here we used to remain until nearly time for slack water again, when we weighed and made for home. We never set out upon this expedition without a steady side wind for going and coming— one that we felt sure would not fail us before our return—and we seldom made a miscalculation upon this point. Twice, during six years, we were forced to stay all night at anchor on account of a dead calm, which is a rare thing indeed just about here; and once we had to remain on the grounds nearly a week, starving to death, owing to a gale which blew up shortly after our arrival, and made the channel too boisterous to be

thought of. Upon this occasion we should have been driven out to sea in spite of everything, (for the whirlpools threw us round and round so violently, that, at length, we fouled our anchor and dragged it) if it had not been that we drifted into one of the innumerable cross-currents—here today and gone tomorrow—which drove us under the lee of Flimen, where, by good luck, we brought up.

"I could not tell you the twentieth part of the difficulties we encountered 'on the grounds'—it is a bad spot to be in, even in good weather—but we made shift always to run the gauntlet of the Moskoe-ström itself without accident; although at times my heart has been in my mouth when we happened to be a minute or so behind or before the slack. The wind sometimes was not as strong as we thought it at starting, and then we made rather less way than we could wish, while the current rendered the smack unmanageable. My eldest brother had a son eighteen years old, and I had two stout boys of my own. These would have been of great assistance at such times, in using the sweeps as well as afterward in fishing—but somehow, although we ran the risk ourselves, we had not the heart to let the young ones get into the danger—for, after all is said and done, it *was* a horrible danger, and that is the truth.

"It is now within a few days of three years since what I am going to tell you occurred. It was on the tenth day of July, 18—, a day which the people of this part of the world will never forget—for it was one in which blew the most terrible hurricane that ever came out of the heavens. And yet all the morning and indeed until late in the afternoon, there was a gentle and steady breeze from the southwest, while the sun shone brightly, so that the oldest seaman among us could not have foreseen what was to follow.

"The three of us—my two brothers and myself—had crossed over to the islands about two o'clock PM, and had soon nearly loaded the smack with fine fish, which, we all remarked, were more plenty that day than we had ever known them. It was just seven, *by my watch,* when we weighed and started for home, so as to make the worst of the Ström at slack water, which we knew would be at eight.

"We set out with a fresh wind on our starboard quarter, and for some time spanked along at a great rate, never dreaming of danger, for indeed we saw not the slightest reason to apprehend it. All at once we were taken aback by a breeze from over Helseggen. This was most unusual—something that had never happened to us before—and I began to feel a little uneasy, without exactly knowing why. We put the boat on the wind, but could make no headway at all for the eddies, and

I was upon the point of proposing to return to the anchorage, when looking astern, we saw the whole horizon covered with a singular copper-colored cloud that rose with the most amazing velocity.

"In the meantime the breeze that had headed us off fell away and we were dead becalmed, drifting about in every direction. This state of things, however, did not last long enough to give us time to think about it. In less than a minute the storm was upon us—in less than two the sky was entirely overcast—and what with this and the driving spray, it became suddenly so dark that we could not see each other in the smack.

"Such a hurricane as then blew it is folly to attempt describing. The oldest seaman in Norway never experienced anything like it. We had let our sails go by the run before it cleverly took us; but, at the first puff, both our masts went by the board as if they had been sawed off—the mainmast taking with it my youngest brother, who had lashed himself to it for safety.

"Our boat was the lightest feather of a thing that ever sat upon water. It had a complete flush deck, with only a small hatch near the bow, and this hatch it had always been our custom to batten down when about to cross the Ström, by way of precaution against the chopping seas. But for this circumstance we should have foundered at once—for we lay entirely buried for some moments. How my elder brother escaped destruction I cannot say, for I never had an opportunity of ascertaining. For my part, as soon as I had let the foresail run, I threw myself flat on deck, with my feet against the narrow gunwale of the bow, and with my hands grasping a ring-bolt near the foot of the foremast. It was mere instinct that prompted me to do this—which was undoubtedly the very best thing I could have done—for I was too much flurried to think.

"For some moments we were completely deluged, as I say, and all this time I held my breath, and clung to the bolt. When I could stand it no longer I raised myself upon my knees, still keeping hold with my hands, and thus got my head clear. Presently our little boat gave herself a shake, just as a dog does in coming out of the water, and thus rid herself, in some measure, of the sea. I was now trying to get the better of the stupor that had come over me, and to collect my senses so as to see what was to be done, when I felt somebody grasp my arm. It was my elder brother, and my heart leaped for joy, for I had made sure that he was overboard—but the next moment all this joy was turned into horror—for he put his mouth close to my ear, and screamed out the word '*Moskoe-ström!*'

"No one ever will know what my feelings were at that moment. I shook from head to foot as if I had had the most violent fit of the ague. I knew

what he meant by that one word well enough—I knew what he wished to make me understand. With the wind that now drove us on, we were bound for the whirl of the Ström, and nothing could save us!

"You perceive that in crossing the Ström *channel,* we always went a long way up above the whirl, even in the calmest weather, and then had to wait and watch carefully for the slack—but now we were driving right upon the pool itself, and in such a hurricane as this! 'To be sure,' I thought, 'we shall get there just about the slack—there is some little hope in that'—but in the next moment I cursed myself for being so great a fool as to dream of hope at all. I knew very well that we were doomed, had we been ten times a ninety-gun ship.

"By this time the first fury of the tempest had spent itself, or perhaps we did not feel it so much, as we scudded before it, but at all events the seas, which at first had been kept down by the wind, and lay flat and frothing, now got up into absolute mountains. A singular change, too, had come over the heavens. Around in every direction it was still as black as pitch, but nearly overhead there burst out, all at once, a circular rift of clear sky—as clear as I ever saw—and of a deep bright blue—and through it there blazed forth the full moon with a luster that I never before knew her to wear. She lit up everything about us with the greatest distinctness—but, oh God, what a scene it was to light up!

"I now made one or two attempts to speak to my brother—but in some manner which I could not understand, the din had so increased that I could not make him hear a single word, although I screamed at the top of my voice in his ear. Presently he shook his head, looking as pale as death, and held up one of his fingers, as if to say *'listen!'*

"At first I could not make out what he meant—but soon a hideous thought flashed upon me. I dragged my watch from its fob. It was not going. I glanced at its face by the moonlight, and then burst into tears as I flung it far away into the ocean. *It had run down at seven o'clock! We were behind the time of the slack, and the whirl of the Ström was in full fury!*

"When a boat is well built, properly trimmed, and not deep laden, the waves in a strong gale, when she is going large, seem always to slip from beneath her—which appears very strange to a landsman—and this is what is called *riding,* in sea phrase. Well, so far we had ridden the swells very cleverly; but presently a gigantic sea happened to take us right under the counter, and bore us with it as it rose—up—up—as if into the sky. I would not have believed that any wave could rise so high. And then down we came with a sweep, a slide, and a plunge that made me feel sick and dizzy,

as if I was falling from some lofty mountaintop in a dream. But while we were up I had thrown a quick glance around—and that one glance was all-sufficient. I saw our exact position in an instant. The Moskoe-ström whirlpool was about a quarter of a mile dead ahead—but no more like the every day Moskoe-ström than the whirl, as you now see it, is like a mill-race. If I had not known where we were, and what we had to expect, I should not have recognized the place at all. As it was, I involuntarily closed my eyes in horror. The lids clenched themselves together as if in a spasm.

"It could not have been more than two minutes afterward until we suddenly felt the waves subside, and were enveloped in foam. The boat made a sharp half turn to larboard, and then shot off in its new direction like a thunderbolt. At the same moment the roaring noise of the water was completely drowned in a kind of shrill shriek—such a sound as you might imagine given out by the waste-pipes of many thousand steam-vessels letting off their steam all together. We were now in the belt of surf that always surrounds the whirl; and I thought, of course, that another moment would plunge us into the abyss, down which we could only see indistinctly on account of the amazing velocity with which we were borne along. The boat did not seem to sink into the water at all, but to skim like an air-bubble upon the surface of the surge. Her starboard side was next the whirl, and on the larboard arose the world of ocean we had left. It stood like a huge writhing wall between us and the horizon.

"It may appear strange, but now, when we were in the very jaws of the gulf, I felt more composed than when we were only approaching it. Having made up my mind to hope no more, I got rid of a great deal of that terror which unmanned me at first. I supposed it was despair that strung my nerves.

"It may look like boasting—but what I tell you is truth—I began to reflect how magnificent a thing it was to die in such a manner, and how foolish it was in me to think of so paltry a consideration as my own individual life, in view of so wonderful a manifestation of God's power. I do believe that I blushed with shame when this idea crossed my mind. After a little while I became possessed with the keenest curiosity about the whirl itself. I positively felt a *wish* to explore its depths, even at the sacrifice I was going to make; and my principal grief was that I should never be able to tell my old companions on shore about the mysteries I should see. These, no doubt, were singular fancies to occupy a man's mind in such extremity—and I have often thought since, that the revolutions of the boat around the pool might have rendered me a little light-headed.

"There was another circumstance which tended to restore my self-possession; and this was the cessation of the wind, which could not reach us in our present situation—for, as you saw yourself, the belt of surf is considerably lower than the general bed of the ocean, and this latter now towered above us, a high black, mountainous ridge. If you have never been at sea in a heavy gale, you can form no idea of the confusion of mind occasioned by the wind and spray together. They blind, deafen, and strangle you, and take away all power of action or reflection. But we were now, in a great measure, rid of these annoyances—just us death-condemned felons in prison are allowed petty indulgences, forbidden them while their doom is yet uncertain.

"How often we made the circuit of the belt it is impossible to say. We careered round and round for perhaps an hour, flying rather than floating, getting gradually more and more into the middle of the surge, and then nearer and nearer to its horrible inner edge. All this time I had never let go of the ring-bolt. My brother was at the stern, holding on to a small empty water-cask which had been securely lashed under the coop of the counters, and was the only thing on deck that had not been swept overboard when the gale first took us. As we approached the brink of the pit he let go his hold upon this, and made for the ring, from which, in the agony of his terror, he endeavored to force my hands, as it was not large enough to afford us both a secure grasp. I never felt deeper grief than when I saw him attempt this act—although I knew he was a madman when he did it—a raving maniac through sheer fright. I did not care, however, to contest the point with him. I knew it could make no difference whether either of us held on at all; so I let him have the bolt, and went astern to the cask. This there was no great difficulty in doing; for the smack flew round steadily enough, and upon an even keel—only swaying to and fro with the immense sweeps and swelters of the whirl. Scarcely had I secured myself in my new position, when we gave a wild lurch to starboard, and rushed headlong into the abyss. I muttered a hurried prayer to God, and thought all was over.

"As I felt the sickening sweep of the descent, I had instinctively tightened my hold upon the barrel, and closed my eyes. For some seconds I dared not open them—while I expected instant destruction, and wondered that I was not already in my death-struggles with the water. But moment after moment elapsed. I still lived. The sense of falling had ceased; and the motion of the vessel seemed much as it had been before, while in the belt of foam, with the exception that she now lay more along. I took courage and looked once again upon the scene.

"Never shall I forget the sensation of awe, horror, and admiration with which I gazed about me. The boat appeared to be hanging, as if by magic, midway down, upon the interior surface of a funnel vast in circumference, prodigious in depth, and whose perfectly smooth sides might have been mistaken for ebony, but for the bewildering rapidity with which they spun around, and for the gleaming and ghastly radiance they shot forth, as the rays of the full moon, from that circular rift amid the clouds which I have already described, streamed in a flood of golden glory along the black walls, and far away down into the inmost recesses of the abyss.

"At first I was too much confused to observe anything accurately. The general burst of terrific grandeur was all that I beheld. When I recovered myself a little, however, my gaze fell instinctively downward. In this direction I was able to obtain an unobstructed view, from the manner in which the smack hung on the inclined surface of the pool. She was quite upon an even keel—that is to say, her deck lay in a plane parallel with that of the water—but this latter sloped at an angle of more than forty-five degrees, so that we seemed to be lying upon our beam-ends. I could not help observing, nevertheless, that I had scarcely more difficulty in maintaining my hold and footing in this situation, than if we had been upon a dead level; and this, I suppose, was owing to the speed at which we revolved.

"The rays of the moon seemed to search the very bottom of the profound gulf; but still I could make out nothing distinctly on account of a thick mist in which there hung a magnificent rainbow, like that narrow and tottering bridge which Mussulmen say is the only pathway between Time and Eternity. This mist, or spray, was no doubt occasioned by the clashing of the great walls of the funnel, as they all met together at the bottom—but the yell that went up to the Heavens from out of that mist I dare not attempt to describe.

"Our first slide into the abyss itself, from the belt of foam above, had carried us a great distance down the slope; but our farther descent was by no means proportionate. Round and round we swept—not with any uniform movement—but in dizzying swings and jerks, that sent us sometimes only a few hundred yards—sometimes nearly the complete circuit of the whirl. Our progress downward, at each revolution, was slow, but very perceptible.

"Looking about me upon the wide waste of liquid ebony on which we were thus borne, I perceived that our boat was not the only object in the embrace of the whirl. Both above and below us were visible fragments of

vessels, large masses of building-timber and trunks of trees, with many smaller articles, such as pieces of house furniture, broken boxes, barrels and staves. I have already described the unnatural curiosity which had taken the place of my original terrors. It appeared to grow upon me as I drew nearer and nearer to my dreadful doom. I now began to watch, with a strange interest, the numerous things that floated in our company. I *must* have been delirious, for I even sought *amusement* in speculating upon the relative velocities of their several descents towards the foam below. 'This fir-tree,' I found myself at one time saying, 'will certainly be the next thing that takes the awful plunge and disappears'—and then I was disappointed to find that the wreck of a Dutch merchant ship overtook it and went down before. At length, after making several guesses of this nature, and being deceived in all—this fact—the fact of my invariable miscalculation, set me upon a train of reflection that made my limbs again tremble, and my heart beat heavily once more.

"It was not a new terror that thus affected me, but the dawn of a more exciting *hope*. This hope arose partly from memory, and partly from present observation. I called to mind the great variety of buoyant matter that strewed the coast of Lofoden, having been absorbed and then thrown forth by the Moskoe-ström. By far the greater number of the articles were shattered in the most extraordinary way—so chafed and roughened as to have the appearance of being stuck full of splinters—but then I distinctly recollected that there were *some* of them which were not disfigured at all. Now I could not account for this difference except by supposing that the roughened fragments were the only ones which had been *completely* absorbed—that the others had entered the whirl at so late a period of the tide, or, for some reason, had descended so slowly after entering, that they did not reach the bottom before the turn of the flood came, or of the ebb, as the case might be. I conceived it possible, in either instance, that they might thus be whirled up again to the level of the ocean, without undergoing the fate of those which had been drawn in more early or absorbed more rapidly. I made, also, three important observations. The first was, that as a general rule, the larger the bodies were, the more rapid their descent—the second, that, between two masses of equal extent, the one spherical, and the other *of any other shape,* the superiority in speed of descent was with the sphere—the third, that, between two masses of equal size, the one cylindrical, and the other of any other shape, the cylinder was absorbed the more slowly. Since my escape, I have had several conversations on this subject with an old school-master of the district; and it was

from him that I learned the use of the words 'cylinder' and 'sphere.' He explained to me—although I have forgotten the explanation—how what I observed was, in fact, the natural consequence of the forms of the floating fragments—and showed me how it happened that a cylinder, swimming in a vortex, offered more resistance to its suction, and was drawn in with greater difficulty than an equally bulky body, of any form whatever.[*]

"There was one startling circumstance which went a great way in enforcing these observations, and rendering me anxious to turn them to account, and this was that, at every revolution, we passed something like a barrel, or else the yard or the mast of a vessel, while many of these things, which had been on our level when I first opened my eyes upon the wonders of the whirlpool, were now high up above us, and seemed to have moved but little from their original station.

"I no longer hesitated what to do. I resolved to lash myself securely to the water-cask upon which I now held, to cut it loose from the counter, and to throw myself with it into the water. I attracted my brother's attention by signs, pointed to the floating barrels that came near us, and did everything in my power to make him understand what I was about to do. I thought at length that he comprehended my design—but, whether this was the case or not, he shook his head despairingly, and refused to move from his station by the ring-bolt. It was impossible to reach him; the emergency admitted of no delay; and so, with a bitter struggle, I resigned him to his fate, fastened myself to the cask by means of the lashings which secured it to the counter, and precipitated myself with it into the sea, without another moment's hesitation.

"The result was precisely what I had hoped it might be. As it is myself who now tell you this tale—as you see that I *did* escape—and as you are already in possession of the mode in which this escape was effected, and must therefore anticipate all that I have farther to say—I will bring my story quickly to conclusion. It might have been an hour, or thereabout, after my quitting the smack, when, having descended to a vast distance beneath me, it made three or four wild gyrations in rapid succession, and, bearing my loved brother with it, plunged headlong, at once and forever, into the chaos of foam below. The barrel to which I was attached sunk very little farther than half the distance between the bottom of the gulf and the spot at which I leaped overboard before a great change took

[*] See Archimedes, *De Incidentibus in Fluido*. Lib. 2.

place in the character of the whirlpool. The slope of the sides of the vast funnel became momently less and less steep. The gyrations of the whirl grew, gradually, less and less violent. By degrees, the froth and the rainbow disappeared, and the bottom of the gulf seemed slowly to uprise. The sky was clear, and the winds had gone down, and the full moon was setting radiantly in the west, when I found myself on the surface of the ocean, in full view of the shores of Lofoden, and above the spot where the pool of the Moskoe-ström *had been*. It was the hour of the slack—but the sea still heaved in mountainous waves from the effects of the hurricane. I was borne violently into the channel of the Ström, and in a few minutes, was hurried down the coast into the 'grounds' of the fishermen. A boat picked me up—exhausted from fatigue—and (now that the danger was removed) speechless from the memory of its horror. Those who drew me on board were my old mates and daily companions—but they knew me no more than they would have known a traveler from the spirit-land. My hair, which had been raven black the day before, was as white as you see it now. They say too that the whole expression of my countenance had changed. I told them my story—they did not believe it. I now tell it to *you*—and I can scarcely expect you to put more faith in it than did the merry fishermen of Lofoden."

THE MASQUE OF THE RED DEATH

THE "RED DEATH" HAD LONG DEVASTATED THE COUNTRY. NO PESTILENCE had ever been so fatal, or so hideous. Blood was its Avatar and its seal—the redness and the horror of blood. There were sharp pains, and sudden dizziness, and then profuse bleeding at the pores, with dissolution. The scarlet stains upon the body and especially upon the face of the victim, were the pest ban which shut him out from the aid and from the sympathy of his fellow-men. And the whole seizure, progress and termination of the disease, were the incidents of half an hour.

But the Prince Prospero was happy and dauntless and sagacious. When his dominions were half depopulated, he summoned to his presence a thousand hale and light-hearted friends from among the knights and dames of his court, and with these retired to the deep seclusion of one of his castellated abbeys. This was an extensive and magnificent structure, the creation of the prince's own eccentric yet august taste. A strong and lofty wall girdled it in. This wall had gates of iron. The courtiers, having entered, brought furnaces and massy hammers and welded the bolts. They resolved to leave means neither of ingress or egress to the sudden impulses of despair or of frenzy from within. The abbey was amply provisioned. With such precautions the courtiers might bid defiance to contagion. The external world could take care of itself. In the meantime it was folly to grieve, or to think. The prince had provided all the appliances of pleasure. There were buffoons, there were improvisatori, there were ballet-dancers, there were musicians, there was Beauty, there was wine. All these and security were within. Without was the "Red Death."

It was toward the close of the fifth or sixth month of his seclusion, and while the pestilence raged most furiously abroad, that the Prince Prospero entertained his thousand friends at a masked ball of the most unusual magnificence.

It was a voluptuous scene, that masquerade. But first let me tell of the rooms in which it was held. There were seven—an imperial suite. In many palaces, however, such suites form a long and straight vista, while the folding doors slide back nearly to the walls on either hand, so that the view of the whole extent is scarcely impeded. Here the case was very different; as might have been expected from the duke's love of the *bizarre*. The apartments were so irregularly disposed that the vision embraced but little more than one at a time. There was a sharp turn at every twenty or thirty yards, and at each turn a novel effect. To the right and left, in the middle of each wall, a tall and narrow Gothic window looked out upon a closed corridor which pursued the windings of the suite. These windows were of stained glass whose color varied in accordance with the prevailing hue of the decorations of the chamber into which it opened. That at the eastern extremity was hung, for example, in blue—and vividly blue were its windows. The second chamber was purple in its ornaments and tapestries, and here the panes were purple. The third was green throughout, and so were the casements. The fourth was furnished and lighted with orange— the fifth with white—the sixth with violet. The seventh apartment was closely shrouded in black velvet tapestries that hung all over the ceiling and down the walls, falling in heavy folds upon a carpet of the same material and hue. But in this chamber only, the color of the windows failed to correspond with the decorations. The panes here were scarlet—a deep blood color. Now in no one of the seven apartments was there any lamp or candelabrum, amid the profusion of golden ornaments that lay scattered to and fro or depended from the roof. There was no light of any kind emanating from lamp or candle within the suite of chambers. But in the corridors that followed the suite, there stood, opposite to each window, a heavy tripod, bearing a brazier of fire that protected its rays through the tinted glass and so glaringly illumined the room. And thus were produced a multitude of gaudy and fantastic appearances. But in the western or black chamber the effect of the fire-light that streamed upon the dark hangings through the blood-tinted panes, was ghastly in the extreme, and produced so wild a look upon the countenances of those who entered, that there were few of the company bold enough to set foot within its precincts at all.

It was in this apartment, also, that there stood against the western wall, a gigantic clock of ebony. Its pendulum swung to and fro with a dull, heavy, monotonous clang; and when the minute-hand made the circuit of the face, and the hour was to be stricken, there came from the brazen lungs of the clock a sound which was clear and loud and deep and exceedingly musical, but of so peculiar a note and emphasis that, at each lapse of an hour, the musicians of the orchestra were constrained to pause, momentarily, in their performance, to harken to the sound; and thus the waltzers perforce ceased their evolutions; and there was a brief disconcert of the whole gay company; and, while the chimes of the clock yet rang, it was observed that the giddiest grew pale, and the more aged and sedate passed their hands over their brows as if in confused reverie or meditation. But when the echoes had fully ceased, a light laughter at once pervaded the assembly; the musicians looked at each other and smiled as if at their own nervousness and folly, and made whispering vows, each to the other, that the next chiming of the clock should produce in them no similar emotion; and then, after the lapse of sixty minutes (which embrace three thousand and six hundred seconds of the Time that flies), there came yet another chiming of the clock, and then were the same disconcert and tremulousness and meditation as before.

But, in spite of these things, it was a gay and magnificent revel. The tastes of the duke were peculiar. He had a fine eye for colors and effects. He disregarded the *decora* of mere fashion. His plans were bold and fiery, and his conceptions glowed with barbaric luster. There are some who would have thought him mad. His followers felt that he was not. It was necessary to hear and see and touch him to be *sure* that he was not.

He had directed, in great part, the moveable embellishments of the seven chambers, upon occasion of this great *fête;* and it was his own guiding taste which had given character to the masqueraders. Be sure they were grotesque. There were much glare and glitter and piquancy and phantasm—much of what has been since seen in "Hernani." There were arabesque figures with unsuited limbs and appointments. There were delirious fancies such as the madman fashions. There was much of the beautiful, much of the wanton, much of the *bizarre,* something of the terrible, and not a little of that which might have excited disgust. To and fro in the seven chambers there stalked, in fact, a multitude of dreams. And these—the dreams—writhed in and about, taking hue from the rooms, and causing the wild music of the orchestra to seem as the echo of their steps. And, anon, there strikes the ebony clock which stands in the hall

of the velvet. And then, for a moment, all is still, and all is silent save the voice of the clock. The dreams are stiff-frozen as they stand. But the echoes of the chime die away—they have endured but an instant—and a light, half-subdued laughter floats after them as they depart. And now again the music swells, and the dreams live, and writhe to and fro more merrily than ever, taking hue from the many tinted windows through which stream the rays from the tripods. But to the chamber which lies most westwardly of the seven, there are now none of the maskers who venture; for the night is waning away; and there flows a ruddier light through the blood-colored panes; and the blackness of the sable drapery appalls; and to him whose foot falls upon the sable carpet, there comes from the near clock of ebony a muffled peal more solemnly emphatic than any which reaches *their* ears who indulge in the more remote gaieties of the other apartments.

But these other apartments were densely crowded, and in them beat feverishly the heart of life. And the revel went whirlingly on, until at length there commenced the sounding of midnight upon the clock. And then the music ceased, as I have told; and the evolutions of the waltzers were quieted; and there was an uneasy cessation of all things as before. But now there were twelve strokes to be sounded by the bell of the clock; and thus it happened, perhaps, that more of thought crept, with more of time, into the meditations of the thoughtful among those who reveled. And thus, too, it happened, perhaps, that before the last echoes of the last chime had utterly sunk into silence, there were many individuals in the crowd who had found leisure to become aware of the presence of a masked figure which had arrested the attention of no single individual before. And the rumor of this new presence having spread itself whisperingly around, there arose at length from the whole company a buzz, or murmur, expressive of disapprobation and surprise—then, finally, of terror, of horror, and of disgust.

In an assembly of phantasms such as I have painted, it may well be supposed that no ordinary appearance could have excited such sensation. In truth the masquerade license of the night was nearly unlimited; but the figure in question had out-Heroded Herod, and gone beyond the bounds of even the prince's indefinite decorum. There are chords in the hearts of the most reckless which cannot be touched without emotion. Even with the utterly lost, to whom life and death are equally jests, there are matters of which no jest can be made. The whole company, indeed, seemed now deeply to feel that in the costume and bearing of the stranger neither wit

nor propriety existed. The figure was tall and gaunt, and shrouded from head to foot in the habiliments of the grave. The mask which concealed the visage was made so nearly to resemble the countenance of a stiffened corpse that the closest scrutiny must have had difficulty in detecting the cheat. And yet all this might have been endured, if not approved, by the mad revelers around. But the mummer had gone so far as to assume the type of the Red Death. His vesture was dabbled in *blood*—and his broad brow, with all the features of the face, was besprinkled with the scarlet horror.

When the eyes of Prince Prospero fell upon this spectral image (which with a slow and solemn movement, as if more fully to sustain its *rôle*, stalked to and fro among the waltzers) he was seen to be convulsed, in the first moment with a strong shudder either of terror or distaste; but, in the next, his brow reddened with rage.

"Who dares?" he demanded hoarsely of the courtiers who stood near him—"who dares insult us with this blasphemous mockery? Seize him and unmask him—that we may know whom we have to hang at sunrise, from the battlements!"

It was in the eastern or blue chamber in which stood the Prince Prospero as he uttered these words. They rang throughout the seven rooms loudly and clearly—for the prince was a bold and robust man, and the music had become hushed at the waving of his hand.

It was in the blue room where stood the prince, with a group of pale courtiers by his side. At first, as he spoke, there was a slight rushing movement of this group in the direction of the intruder, who at the moment was also near at hand, and now, with deliberate and stately step, made closer approach to the speaker. But from a certain nameless awe with which the mad assumptions of the mummer had inspired the whole party, there were found none who put forth hand to seize him; so that, unimpeded, he passed within a yard of the prince's person; and, while the vast assembly, as if with one impulse, shrank from the centers of the rooms to the walls, he made his way uninterruptedly, but with the same solemn and measured step which had distinguished him from the first, through the blue chamber to the purple—through the purple to the green—through the green to the orange—through this again to the white—and even thence to the violet, ere a decided movement had been made to arrest him. It was then, however, that the Prince Prospero, maddening with rage and the shame of his own momentary cowardice, rushed hurriedly through the six chambers, while none followed him on account of a deadly terror that had seized upon all. He bore aloft a drawn dagger,

and had approached, in rapid impetuosity, to within three or four feet of the retreating figure, when the latter, having attained the extremity of the velvet apartment, turned suddenly and confronted his pursuer. There was a sharp cry—and the dagger dropped gleaming upon the sable carpet, upon which, instantly afterward, fell prostrate in death the Prince Prospero. Then, summoning the wild courage of despair, a throng of the revelers at once threw themselves into the black apartment, and, seizing the mummer, whose tall figure stood erect and motionless within the shadow of the ebony clock, gasped in unutterable horror at finding the grave-cerements and corpse-like mask which they handled with so violent a rudeness, untenanted by any tangible form.

And now was acknowledged the presence of the Red Death. He had come like a thief in the night. And one by one dropped the revelers in the blood-bedewed halls of their revel, and died each in the despairing posture of his fall. And the life of the ebony clock went out with that of the last of the gay. And the flames of the tripods expired. And Darkness and Decay and the Red Death held illimitable dominion over all.

The Pit and the Pendulum

Impia tortorum longos hic turba furores
Sanguinis innocui, non satiata, aluit.
Sospite nunc patria, fracto nunc funeris antro,
Mors ubi dira fuit vita salusque patent.[1]

[Quatrain composed for the gates of a market to be erected
upon the site of the Jacobin Club House at Paris.]

I WAS SICK—SICK UNTO DEATH WITH THAT LONG AGONY; AND WHEN THEY
at length unbound me, and I was permitted to sit, I felt that my senses
were leaving me. The sentence—the dread sentence of death—was the
last of distinct accentuation which reached my ears. After that, the sound
of the inquisitorial voices seemed merged in one dreamy indeterminate
hum. It conveyed to my soul the idea of *revolution*—perhaps from its asso-
ciation in fancy with the burr of a mill-wheel. This only for a brief period;
for presently I heard no more. Yet, for a while, I saw; but with how terrible
an exaggeration! I saw the lips of the black-robed judges. They appeared
to me white—whiter than the sheet upon which I trace these words—and
thin even to grotesqueness; thin with the intensity of their expression of
firmness—of immoveable resolution—of stern contempt of human tor-
ture. I saw that the decrees of what to me was Fate, were still issuing from
those lips. I saw them writhe with a deadly locution. I saw them fashion the
syllables of my name; and I shuddered because no sound succeeded. I saw,
too, for a few moments of delirious horror, the soft and nearly impercep-
tible waving of the sable draperies which enwrapped the walls of the

apartment. And then my vision fell upon the seven tall candles upon the table. At first they wore the aspect of charity, and seemed white and slender angels who would save me; but then, all at once, there came a most deadly nausea over my spirit, and I felt every fiber in my frame thrill as if I had touched the wire of a galvanic battery, while the angel forms became meaningless specters, with heads of flame, and I saw that from them there would be no help. And then there stole into my fancy, like a rich musical note, the thought of what sweet rest there must be in the grave. The thought came gently and stealthily, and it seemed long before it attained full appreciation; but just as my spirit came at length properly to feel and entertain it, the figures of the judges vanished, as if magically, from before me; the tall candles sank into nothingness; their flames went out utterly; the blackness of darkness supervened; all sensations appeared swallowed up in a mad rushing descent as of the soul into Hades. Then silence, and stillness, and night were the universe.

I had swooned; but still will not say that all of consciousness was lost. What of it there remained I will not attempt to define, or even to describe; yet all was not lost. In the deepest slumber—no! In delirium—no! In a swoon—no! In death—no! even in the grave all *is not* lost. Else there is no immortality for man. Arousing from the most profound of slumbers, we break the gossamer web of *some* dream. Yet in a second afterward, (so frail may that web have been) we remember not that we have dreamed. In the return to life from the swoon there are two stages; first, that of the sense of mental or spiritual; secondly, that of the sense of physical, existence. It seems probable that if, upon reaching the second stage, we could recall the impressions of the first, we should find these impressions eloquent in memories of the gulf beyond. And that gulf is—what? How at least shall we distinguish its shadows from those of the tomb? But if the impressions of what I have termed the first stage, are not, at will, recalled, yet, after long interval, do they not come unbidden, while we marvel whence they come? He who has never swooned, is not he who finds strange palaces and wildly familiar faces in coals that glow; is not he who beholds floating in mid-air the sad visions that the many may not view; is not he who ponders over the perfume of some novel flower—is not he whose brain grows bewildered with the meaning of some musical cadence which has never before arrested his attention.

Amid frequent and thoughtful endeavors to remember; amid earnest struggles to regather some token of the state of seeming nothingness into which my soul had lapsed, there have been moments when I have dreamed

of success; there have been brief, very brief periods when I have conjured up remembrances which the lucid reason of a later epoch assures me could have had reference only to that condition of seeming unconsciousness. These shadows of memory tell, indistinctly, of tall figures that lifted and bore me in silence down—down—still down—till a hideous dizziness oppressed me at the mere idea of the interminableness of the descent. They tell also of a vague horror at my heart, on account of that heart's unnatural stillness. Then comes a sense of sudden motionlessness throughout all things; as if those who bore me (a ghastly train!) had outrun, in their descent, the limits of the limitless, and paused from the wearisomeness of their toil. After this I call to mind flatness and dampness; and then all is *madness*—the madness of a memory which busies itself among forbidden things.

Very suddenly there came back to my soul motion and sound the tumultuous motion of the heart, and, in my ears, the sound of its beating. Then a pause in which all is blank. Then again sound, and motion, and touch—a tingling sensation pervading my frame. Then the mere consciousness of existence, without thought—a condition which lasted long. Then, very suddenly, *thought*, and shuddering terror, and earnest endeavor to comprehend my true state. Then a strong desire to lapse into insensibility. Then a rushing revival of soul and a successful effort to move. And now a full memory of the trial, of the judges, of the sable draperies, of the sentence, of the sickness, of the swoon. Then entire forgetfulness of all that followed; of all that a later day and much earnestness of endeavor have enabled me vaguely to recall.

So far, I had not opened my eyes. I felt that I lay upon my back, unbound. I reached out my hand, and it fell heavily upon something damp and hard. There I suffered it to remain for many minutes, while I strove to imagine where and *what* I could be. I longed, yet dared not to employ my vision. I dreaded the first glance at objects around me. It was not that I feared to look upon things horrible, but that I grew aghast lest there should be *nothing* to see. At length, with a wild desperation at heart, I quickly unclosed my eyes. My worst thoughts, then, were confirmed. The blackness of eternal night encompassed me. I struggled for breath. The intensity of the darkness seemed to oppress and stifle me. The atmosphere was intolerably close. I still lay quietly, and made effort to exercise my reason. I brought to mind the inquisitorial proceedings, and attempted from that point to deduce my real condition. The sentence had passed; and it appeared to me that a very long interval of time

had since elapsed. Yet not for a moment did I suppose myself actually dead. Such a supposition, notwithstanding what we read in fiction, is altogether inconsistent with real existence; but where and in what state was I? The condemned to death, I knew, perished usually at the *auto-da-fè*,[2] and one of these had been held on the very night of the day of my trial. Had I been remanded to my dungeon, to await the next sacrifice, which would not take place for many months? This I at once saw could not be. Victims had been in immediate demand. Moreover, my dungeon, as well as all the condemned cells at Toledo, had stone floors, and light was not altogether excluded.

A fearful idea now suddenly drove the blood in torrents upon my heart, and for a brief period, I once more relapsed into insensibility. Upon recovering, I at once started to my feet, trembling convulsively in every fiber. I thrust my arms wildly above and around me in all directions. I felt nothing; yet dreaded to move a step, lest I should be impeded by the walls of a *tomb*. Perspiration burst from every pore, and stood in cold big beads upon my forehead. The agony of suspense grew at length intolerable, and I cautiously moved forward, with my arms extended, and my eyes straining from their sockets, in the hope of catching some faint ray of light. I proceeded for many paces; but still all was blackness and vacancy. I breathed more freely. It seemed evident that mine was not, at least, the most hideous of fates.

And now, as I still continued to step cautiously onward, there came thronging upon my recollection a thousand vague rumors of the horrors of Toledo. Of the dungeons there had been strange things narrated— fables I had always deemed them—but yet strange, and too ghastly to repeat, save in a whisper. Was I left to perish of starvation in this subterranean world of darkness; or what fate, perhaps even more fearful, awaited me? That the result would be death, and a death of more than customary bitterness, I knew too well the character of my judges to doubt. The mode and the hour were all that occupied or distracted me.

My outstretched hands at length encountered some solid obstruction. It was a wall, seemingly of stone masonry—very smooth, slimy, and cold. I followed it up; stepping with all the careful distrust with which certain antique narratives had inspired me. This process, however, afforded me no means of ascertaining the dimensions of my dungeon; as I might make its circuit, and return to the point whence I set out, without being aware of the fact; so perfectly uniform seemed the wall. I therefore sought the knife which had been in my pocket, when led into the inquisitorial chamber;

but it was gone; my clothes had been exchanged for a wrapper of coarse serge. I had thought of forcing the blade in some minute crevice of the masonry, so as to identify my point of departure. The difficulty, nevertheless, was but trivial; although, in the disorder of my fancy, it seemed at first insuperable. I tore a part of the hem from the robe and placed the fragment at full length, and at right angles to the wall. In groping my way around the prison, I could not fail to encounter this rag upon completing the circuit. So, at least, I thought: but I had not counted upon the extent of the dungeon, or upon my own weakness. The ground was moist and slippery. I staggered onward for some time, when I stumbled and fell. My excessive fatigue induced me to remain prostrate; and sleep soon overtook me as I lay.

Upon awaking, and stretching forth an arm, I found beside me a loaf and a pitcher with water. I was too much exhausted to reflect upon this circumstance, but ate and drank with avidity. Shortly afterward, I resumed my tour around the prison, and with much toil, came at last upon the fragment of the serge. Up to the period when I fell, I had counted fifty-two paces, and, upon resuming my walk, I had counted forty-eight more—when I arrived at the rag. There were in all, then, a hundred paces; and, admitting two paces to the yard, I presumed the dungeon to be fifty yards in circuit. I had met, however, with many angles in the wall, and thus I could form no guess at the shape of the vault; for vault I could not help supposing it to be.

I had little object—certainly no hope—in these researches; but a vague curiosity prompted me to continue them. Quitting the wall, I resolved to cross the area of the enclosure. At first, I proceeded with extreme caution, for the floor, although seemingly of solid material, was treacherous with slime. At length, however, I took courage, and did not hesitate to step firmly—endeavoring to cross in as direct a line as possible. I had advanced some ten or twelve paces in this manner, when the remnant of the torn hem of my robe became entangled between my legs. I stepped on it, and fell violently on my face.

In the confusion attending my fall, I did not immediately apprehend a somewhat startling circumstance, which yet, in a few seconds afterward, and while I still lay prostrate, arrested my attention. It was this: my chin rested upon the floor of the prison, but my lips, and the upper portion of my head, although seemingly at a less elevation than the chin, touched nothing. At the same time my forehead seemed bathed in a clammy vapor, and the peculiar smell of decayed fungus arose to my nostrils. I put forward

my arm, and shuddered to find that I had fallen at the very brink of a circular pit, whose extent, of course, I had no means of ascertaining at the moment. Groping about the masonry just below the margin, I succeeded in dislodging a small fragment, and let it fall into the abyss. For many seconds I harkened to its reverberations as it dashed against the sides of the chasm in its descent: at length there was a sullen plunge into water, succeeded by loud echoes. At the same moment, there came a sound resembling the quick opening, and as rapid closing of a door overhead, while a faint gleam of light flashed suddenly through the gloom, and as suddenly faded away.

I saw clearly the doom which had been prepared for me, and congratulated myself upon the timely accident by which I had escaped. Another step before my fall, and the world had seen me no more. And the death just avoided, was of that very character which I had regarded as fabulous and frivolous in the tales respecting the Inquisition. To the victims of its tyranny, there was the choice of death with its direst physical agonies, or death with its most hideous moral horrors. I had been reserved for the latter. By long suffering my nerves had been unstrung, until I trembled at the sound of my own voice, and had become in every respect a fitting subject for the species of torture which awaited me.

Shaking in every limb, I groped my way back to the wall—resolving there to perish rather than risk the terrors of the wells, of which my imagination now pictured many in various positions about the dungeon. In other conditions of mind, I might have had courage to end my misery at once, by a plunge into one of these abysses; but now I was the veriest of cowards. Neither could I forget what I had read of these pits—that the *sudden* extinction of life formed no part of their most horrible plan.

Agitation of spirit kept me awake for many long hours; but at length I again slumbered. Upon arousing, I found by my side, as before, a loaf and a pitcher of water. A burning thirst consumed me, and I emptied the vessel at a draught. It must have been drugged—for scarcely had I drunk, before I became irresistibly drowsy. A deep sleep fell upon me—a sleep like that of death. How long it lasted, of course, I know not; but when, once again, I unclosed my eyes, the objects around me were visible. By a wild sulfurous luster, the origin of which I could not at first determine, I was enabled to see the extent and aspect of the prison.

In its size I had been greatly mistaken. The whole circuit of its walls did not exceed twenty-five yards. For some minutes this fact occasioned me a world of vain trouble; vain indeed—for what could be of less importance,

under the terrible circumstances which environed me, than the mere dimensions of my dungeon? But my soul took a wild interest in trifles, and I busied myself in endeavors to account for the error I had committed in my measurement. The truth at length flashed upon me. In my first attempt at exploration, I had counted fifty-two paces, up to the period when I fell; I must then have been within a pace or two of the fragment of serge; in fact, I had nearly performed the circuit of the vault. I then slept, and upon awaking, I must have returned upon my steps—thus supposing the circuit nearly double what it actually was. My confusion of mind prevented me from observing that I began my tour with the wall to the left, and ended it with the wall to the right.

I had been deceived, too, in respect to the shape of the enclosure. In feeling my way I had found many angles, and thus deduced an idea of great irregularity; so potent is the effect of total darkness upon one arousing from lethargy or sleep! The angles were simply those of a few slight depressions, or niches, at odd intervals. The general shape of the prison was square. What I had taken for masonry, seemed now to be iron, or some other metal, in huge plates, whose sutures or joints occasioned the depression. The entire surface of this metallic enclosure was rudely daubed in all the hideous and repulsive devices to which the charnel superstition of the monks has given rise. The figures of fiends in aspects of menace, with skeleton forms, and other more really fearful images, over-spread and disfigured the walls. I observed that the outlines of these monstrosities were sufficiently distinct, but that the colors seemed faded and blurred, as if from the effects of a damp atmosphere. I now noticed the floor, too, which was of stone. In the center yawned the circular pit from whose jaws I had escaped; but it was the only one in the dungeon.

All this I saw indistinctly and by much effort—for my personal condition had been greatly changed during slumber. I now lay upon my back, and at full length, on a species of low framework of wood. To this I was securely bound by a long strap resembling a surcingle. It passed in many convolutions about my limbs and body, leaving at liberty only my head, and my left arm to such extent, that I could, by dint of much exertion, supply myself with food from an earthen dish which lay by my side on the floor. I saw, to my horror, that the pitcher had been removed. I say to my horror—for I was consumed with intolerable thirst. This thirst it appeared to be the design of my persecutors to stimulate—for the food in the dish was meat pungently seasoned.

Looking upward, I surveyed the ceiling of my prison. It was some thirty or forty feet overhead, and constructed much as the side walls. In one of its panels a very singular figure riveted my whole attention. It was the painted figure of Time as he is commonly represented, save that, in lieu of a scythe, he held what, at a casual glance, I supposed to be the pictured image of a huge pendulum, such as we see on antique clocks. There was something, however, in the appearance of this machine which caused me to regard it more attentively. While I gazed directly upward at it (for its position was immediately over my own) I fancied that I saw it in motion. In an instant afterward the fancy was confirmed. Its sweep was brief, and of course slow. I watched it for some minutes, somewhat in fear, but more in wonder. Wearied at length with observing its dull movement, I turned my eyes upon the other objects in the cell.

A slight noise attracted my notice, and, looking to the floor, I saw several enormous rats traversing it. They had issued from the well, which lay just within view to my right. Even then, while I gazed, they came up in troops, hurriedly, with ravenous eyes, allured by the scent of the meat. From this it required much effort and attention to scare them away.

It might have been half an hour, perhaps even an hour (for I could take but imperfect note of time), before I again cast my eyes upward. What I then saw, confounded and amazed me. The sweep of the pendulum had increased in extent by nearly a yard. As a natural consequence, its velocity was also much greater. But what mainly disturbed me was the idea that had perceptibly *descended*. I now observed—with what horror it is needless to say—that its nether extremity was formed of a crescent of glittering steel, about a foot in length from horn to horn; the horns upward, and the under edge evidently as keen as that of a razor. Like a razor also, it seemed massy and heavy, tapering from the edge into a solid and broad structure above. It was appended to a weighty rod of brass, and the whole *hissed* as it swung through the air.

I could no longer doubt the doom prepared for me by monkish ingenuity in torture. My cognizance of the pit had become known to the inquisitorial agents—*the pit*, whose horrors had been destined for so bold a recusant as myself—*the pit*, typical of hell, and regarded by rumor as the Ultima Thule of all their punishments. The plunge into this pit I had avoided by the merest of accidents, I knew that surprise, or entrapment into torment, formed an important portion of all the grotesquerie of these dungeon deaths. Having failed to fall, it was no part of the demon plan to hurl me into the abyss; and thus (there being no alternative) a different

and a milder destruction awaited me. Milder! I half smiled in my agony as I thought of such application of such a term.

What boots it to tell of the long, long hours of horror more than mortal, during which I counted the rushing oscillations of the steel! Inch by inch—line by line—with a descent only appreciable at intervals that seemed ages—down and still down it came! Days passed—it might have been that many days passed—ere it swept so closely over me as to fan me with its acrid breath. The odor of the sharp steel forced itself into my nostrils. I prayed—I wearied heaven with my prayer for its more speedy descent. I grew frantically mad, and struggled to force myself upward against the sweep of the fearful scimitar. And then I fell suddenly calm, and lay smiling at the glittering death, as a child at some rare bauble.

There was another interval of utter insensibility; it was brief; for, upon again lapsing into life, there had been no perceptible descent in the pendulum. But it might have been long—for I knew there were demons who took note of my swoon, and who could have arrested the vibration at pleasure. Upon my recovery, too, I felt very—oh, inexpressibly—sick and weak, as if through long inanition. Even amid the agonies of that period, the human nature craved food. With painful effort I outstretched my left arm as far as my bonds permitted, and took possession of the small remnant which had been spared me by the rats. As I put a portion of it within my lips, there rushed to my mind a half-formed thought of joy—of hope. Yet what business had *I* with hope? It was, as I say, a half-formed thought—man has many such, which are never completed. I felt that it was of joy—of hope; but felt also that it had perished in its formation. In vain I struggled to perfect—to regain it. Long suffering had nearly annihilated all my ordinary powers of mind. I was an imbecile—an idiot.

The vibration of the pendulum was at right angles to my length. I saw that the crescent was designed to cross the region of the heart. It would fray the serge of my robe—it would return and repeat its operations—again—and again. Notwithstanding its terrifically wide sweep (some thirty feet or more), and the hissing vigor of its descent, sufficient to sunder these very walls of iron, still the fraying of my robe would be all that, for several minutes, it would accomplish. And at this thought I paused. I dared not go farther than this reflection. I dwelt upon it with a pertinacity of attention—as if, in so dwelling, I could arrest *here* the descent of the steel. I forced myself to ponder upon the sound of the crescent as it should pass across the garment—upon the peculiar thrilling sensation

which the friction of cloth produces on the nerves. I pondered upon all this frivolity until my teeth were on edge.

Down—steadily down it crept. I took a frenzied pleasure in contrasting its downward with its lateral velocity. To the right—to the left—far and wide—with the shriek of a damned spirit! to my heart, with the stealthy pace of the tiger! I alternately laughed and howled, as the one or the other idea grew predominant.

Down—certainly, relentlessly down! It vibrated within three inches of my bosom! I struggled violently—furiously—to free my left arm. This was free only from the elbow to the hand. I could reach the latter, from the platter beside me, to my mouth, with great effort, but no farther. Could I have broken the fastenings above the elbow, I would have seized and attempted to arrest the pendulum. I might as well have attempted to arrest an avalanche!

Down—still unceasingly—still inevitably down! I gasped and struggled at each vibration. I shrunk convulsively at its every sweep. My eyes followed its outward or upward whirls with the eagerness of the most unmeaning despair; they closed themselves spasmodically at the descent, although death would have been a relief, oh, how unspeakable! Still I quivered in every nerve to think how slight a sinking of the machinery would precipitate that keen, glistening axe upon my bosom. It was *hope* that prompted the nerve to quiver—the frame to shrink. It was *hope*—the hope that triumphs on the rack—that whispers to the death-condemned even in the dungeons of the Inquisition.

I saw that some ten or twelve vibrations would bring the steel in actual contact with my robe—and with this observation there suddenly came over my spirit all the keen, collected calmness of despair. For the first time during many hours—or perhaps days—I *thought*. It now occurred to me, that the bandage, or surcingle, which enveloped me, was *unique*. I was tied by no separate cord. The first stroke of the razor-like crescent athwart any portion of the band, would so detach it that it might be unwound from my person by means of my left hand. But how fearful, in that case, the proximity of the steel! The result of the slightest struggle, how deadly! Was it likely, moreover, that the minions of the torturer had not foreseen and provided for this possibility! Was it probable that the bandage crossed my bosom in the track of the pendulum? Dreading to find my faint, and, as it seemed, in last hope frustrated, I so far elevated my head as to obtain a distinct view of my breast. The surcingle enveloped my limbs and body close in all directions—*save in the path of the destroying crescent.*

Scarcely had I dropped my head back into its original position, when there flashed upon my mind what I cannot better describe than as the unformed half of that idea of deliverance to which I have previously alluded, and of which a moiety only floated indeterminately through my brain when I raised food to my burning lips. The whole thought was now present—feeble, scarcely sane, scarcely definite—but still entire. I proceeded at once, with the nervous energy of despair, to attempt its execution.

For many hours the immediate vicinity of the low framework upon which I lay, had been literally swarming with rats. They were wild, bold, ravenous—their red eyes glaring upon me as if they waited but for motionlessness on my part to make me their prey. "To what food," I thought, "have they been accustomed in the well?"

They had devoured, in spite of all my efforts to prevent them, all but a small remnant of the contents of the dish. I had fallen into an habitual see-saw, or wave of the hand about the platter; and, at length, the unconscious uniformity of the movement deprived it of effect. In their voracity, the vermin frequently fastened their sharp fangs in my fingers. With the particles of the oily and spicy viand which now remained, I thoroughly rubbed the bandage wherever I could reach it; then, raising my hand from the floor, I lay breathlessly still.

At first the ravenous animals were startled and terrified at the change—at the cessation of movement. They shrank alarmedly back; many sought the well. But this was only for a moment. I had not counted in vain upon their voracity. Observing that I remained without motion, one or two of the boldest leaped upon the frame-work, and smelt at the surcingle. This seemed the signal for a general rush. Forth from the well they hurried in fresh troops. They clung to the wood—they overran it, and leaped in hundreds upon my person. The measured movement of the pendulum disturbed them not at all. Avoiding its strokes, they busied themselves with the anointed bandage. They pressed—they swarmed upon me in ever accumulating heaps. They writhed upon my throat; their cold lips sought my own; I was half stifled by their thronging pressure; disgust, for which the world has no name, swelled my bosom, and chilled, with a heavy clamminess, my heart. Yet one minute, and I felt that the struggle would be over. Plainly I perceived the loosening of the bandage. I knew that in more than one place it must be already severed. With a more than human resolution I lay *still*.

Nor had I erred in my calculations—nor had I endured in vain. I at length felt that I was *free*. The surcingle hung in ribands from my body. But

the stroke of the pendulum already pressed upon my bosom. It had divided the serge of the robe. It had cut through the linen beneath. Twice again it swung, and a sharp sense of pain shot through every nerve. But the moment of escape had arrived. At a wave of my hand my deliverers hurried tumultuously away. With a steady movement—cautious, sidelong, shrinking, and slow—I slid from the embrace of the bandage and beyond the reach of the scimitar. For the moment, at least, *I was free.*

Free!—and in the grasp of the Inquisition! I had scarcely stepped from my wooden bed of horror upon the stone floor of the prison, when the motion of the hellish machine ceased and I beheld it drawn up, by some invisible force, through the ceiling. This was a lesson which I took desperately to heart. My every motion was undoubtedly watched. Free! I had but escaped death in one form of agony, to be delivered unto worse than death in some other. With that thought I rolled my eyes nervously around on the barriers of iron that hemmed me in. Something unusual—some change which, at first, I could not appreciate distinctly—it was obvious, had taken place in the apartment. For many minutes of a dreamy and trembling abstraction, I busied myself in vain, unconnected conjecture. During this period, I became aware, for the first time, of the origin of the sulfurous light which illumined the cell. It proceeded from a fissure, about half an inch in width, extending entirely around the prison at the base of the walls, which thus appeared, and were completely separated from the floor. I endeavored, but of course in vain, to look through the aperture.

As I arose from the attempt, the mystery of the alteration in the chamber broke at once upon my understanding. I have observed that, although the outlines of the figures upon the walls were sufficiently distinct, yet the colors seemed blurred and indefinite. These colors had now assumed, and were momentarily assuming, a startling and most intense brilliancy, that gave to the spectral and fiendish portraitures an aspect that might have thrilled even firmer nerves than my own. Demon eyes, of a wild and ghastly vivacity, glared upon me in a thousand directions, where none had been visible before, and gleamed with the lurid luster of a fire that I could not force my imagination to regard as unreal.

Unreal! Even while I breathed there came to my nostrils the breath of the vapor of heated iron! A suffocating odor pervaded the prison! A deeper glow settled each moment in the eyes that glared at my agonies! A richer tint of crimson diffused itself over the pictured horrors of blood. I panted! I gasped for breath! There could be no doubt of the design of my tormentors—oh! most unrelenting! oh! most demoniac of men! I shrank

from the glowing metal to the center of the cell. Amid the thought of the fiery destruction that impended, the idea of the coolness of the well came over my soul like balm. I rushed to its deadly brink. I threw my straining vision below. The glare from the enkindled roof illumined its inmost recesses. Yet, for a wild moment, did my spirit refuse to comprehend the meaning of what I saw. At length it forced—it wrestled its way into my soul—it burned itself in upon my shuddering reason. Oh! for a voice to speak!—oh! horror!—oh! any horror but this! With a shriek, I rushed from the margin, and buried my face in my hands—weeping bitterly.

The heat rapidly increased, and once again I looked up, shuddering as with a fit of the ague. There had been a second change in the cell—and now the change was obviously in the *form*. As before, it was in vain that I at first, endeavored to appreciate or understand what was taking place. But not long was I left in doubt. The Inquisitorial vengeance had been hurried by my two-fold escape, and there was to be no more dallying with the King of Terrors. The room had been square. I saw that two of its iron angles were now acute—two, consequently, obtuse. The fearful difference quickly increased with a low rumbling or moaning sound. In an instant the apartment had shifted its form into that of a lozenge. But the alteration stopped not here—I neither hoped nor desired it to stop. I could have clasped the red walls to my bosom as a garment of eternal peace. "Death," I said, "any death but that of the pit!" Fool! might I not have known that *into the pit* it was the object of the burning iron to urge me? Could I resist its glow? or if even that, could I withstand its pressure? And now, flatter and flatter grew the lozenge, with a rapidity that left me no time for contemplation. Its center, and of course, its greatest width, came just over the yawning gulf. I shrank back—but the closing walls pressed me resistlessly onward. At length for my seared and writhing body there was no longer an inch of foothold on the firm floor of the prison. I struggled no more, but the agony of my soul found vent in one loud, long, and final scream of despair. I felt that I tottered upon the brink—I averted my eyes—

There was a discordant hum of human voices! There was a loud blast as of many trumpets! There was a harsh grating as of a thousand thunders! The fiery walls rushed back! An outstretched arm caught my own as I fell, fainting, into the abyss. It was that of General Lasalle. The French army had entered Toledo. The Inquisition was in the hands of its enemies.

THE TELL-TALE HEART

TRUE!—NERVOUS—VERY, VERY DREADFULLY NERVOUS I HAD BEEN AND AM; but why *will* you say that I am mad? The disease had sharpened my senses— not destroyed—not dulled them. Above all was the sense of hearing acute. I heard all things in the heaven and in the earth. I heard many things in hell. How, then, am I mad? Harken! and observe how healthily—how calmly I can tell you the whole story.

It is impossible to say how first the idea entered my brain; but once conceived, it haunted me day and night. Object there was none. Passion there was none. I loved the old man. He had never wronged me. He had never given me insult. For his gold I had no desire. I think it was his eye! yes, it was this! One of his eyes resembled that of a vulture—a pale blue eye, with a film over it. Whenever it fell upon me, my blood ran cold; and so by degrees—very gradually—I made up my mind to take the life of the old man, and thus rid myself of the eye forever.

Now this is the point. You fancy me mad. Madmen know nothing. But you should have seen *me*. You should have seen how wisely I proceeded— with what caution—with what foresight—with what dissimulation I went to work! I was never kinder to the old man than during the whole week before I killed him. And every night, about midnight, I turned the latch of his door and opened it—oh, so gently! And then, when I had made an opening sufficient for my head, I put in a dark lantern, all closed, closed, so that no light shone out, and then I thrust in my head. Oh, you would have laughed to see how cunningly I thrust it in! I moved it slowly—very, very slowly, so that I might not disturb the old man's sleep. It took me an hour to place my whole head within the opening so far that I could see

him as he lay upon his bed. Ha!—would a madman have been so wise as this? And then, when my head was well in the room, I undid the lantern cautiously—oh, so cautiously—cautiously (for the hinges creaked)—I undid it just so much that a single thin ray fell upon the vulture eye. And this I did for seven long nights—every night just at midnight—but I found the eye always closed; and so it was impossible to do the work; for it was not the old man who vexed me, but his Evil Eye. And every morning, when the day broke, I went boldly into the chamber, and spoke courageously to him, calling him by name in a hearty tone, and inquiring how he has passed the night. So you see he would have been a very profound old man, indeed, to suspect that every night, just at twelve, I looked in upon him while he slept.

Upon the eighth night I was more than usually cautious in opening the door. A watch's minute hand moves more quickly than did mine. Never before that night had I *felt* the extent of my own powers—of my sagacity. I could scarcely contain my feelings of triumph. To think that there I was, opening the door, little by little, and he not even to dream of my secret deeds or thoughts. I fairly chuckled at the idea; and perhaps he heard me; for he moved on the bed suddenly, as if startled. Now you may think that I drew back—but no. His room was as black as pitch with the thick darkness (for the shutters were close fastened, through fear of robbers), and so I knew that he could not see the opening of the door, and I kept pushing it on steadily, steadily.

I had my head in, and was about to open the lantern, when my thumb slipped upon the tin fastening, and the old man sprang up in bed, crying out—"Who's there?"

I kept quite still and said nothing. For a whole hour I did not move a muscle, and in the meantime I did not hear him lie down. He was still sitting up in the bed listening; just as I have done, night after night, harkening to the death watches in the wall.

Presently I heard a slight groan, and I knew it was the groan of mortal terror. It was not a groan of pain or of grief—oh, no!—it was the low stifled sound that arises from the bottom of the soul when overcharged with awe. I knew the sound well. Many a night, just at midnight, when all the world slept, it has welled up from my own bosom, deepening, with its dreadful echo, the terrors that distracted me. I say I knew it well. I knew what the old man felt, and pitied him, although I chuckled at heart. I knew that he had been lying awake ever since the first slight noise, when he had turned in the bed. His fears had been ever since growing upon him. He had been

trying to fancy them causeless, but could not. He had been saying to himself—"It is nothing but the wind in the chimney—it is only a mouse crossing the floor," or "It is merely a cricket which has made a single chirp." Yes, he has been trying to comfort himself with these suppositions: but he had found all in vain. *All in vain;* because Death, in approaching him, had stalked with his black shadow before him, and enveloped the victim. And it was the mournful influence of the unperceived shadow that caused him to feel—although he neither saw nor heard—to *feel* the presence of my head within the room.

When I had waited a long time, very patiently, without hearing him lie down, I resolved to open a little—a very, very little crevice in the lantern. So I opened it—you cannot imagine how stealthily, stealthily—until, at length a single dim ray, like the thread of the spider, shot from out the crevice and fell upon the vulture eye.

It was open—wide, wide open—and I grew furious as I gazed upon it. I saw it with perfect distinctness—all a dull blue, with a hideous veil over it that chilled the very marrow in my bones; but I could see nothing else of the old man's face or person: for I had directed the ray as if by instinct, precisely upon the damned spot.

And now have I not told you that what you mistake for madness is but over-acuteness of the senses?—now, I say, there came to my ears a low, dull, quick sound, such as a watch makes when enveloped in cotton. I knew *that* sound well, too. It was the beating of the old man's heart. It increased my fury, as the beating of a drum stimulates the soldier into courage.

But even yet I refrained and kept still. I scarcely breathed. I held the lantern motionless. I tried how steadily I could maintain the ray upon the eye. Meantime the hellish tattoo of the heart increased. It grew quicker and quicker, and louder and louder every instant. The old man's terror *must* have been extreme! It grew louder, I say, louder every moment!—do you mark me well? I have told you that I am nervous: so I am. And now at the dead hour of the night, amid the dreadful silence of that old house, so strange a noise as this excited me to uncontrollable terror. Yet, for some minutes longer I refrained and stood still. But the beating grew louder, louder! I thought the heart must burst. And now a new anxiety seized me—the sound would be heard by a neighbor! The old man's hour had come! With a loud yell, I threw open the lantern and leaped into the room. He shrieked once—once only. In an instant I dragged him to the floor, and pulled the heavy bed over him. I then smiled gaily, to find the deed so far done. But, for many minutes, the

heart beat on with a muffled sound. This, however, did not vex me; it would not be heard through the wall. At length it ceased. The old man was dead. I removed the bed and examined the corpse. Yes, he was stone, stone dead. I placed my hand upon the heart and held it there many minutes. There was no pulsation. He was stone dead. His eye would trouble me no more.

If still you think me mad, you will think so no longer when I describe the wise precautions I took for the concealment of the body. The night waned, and I worked hastily, but in silence. First of all I dismembered the corpse. I cut off the head and the arms and the legs.

I then took up three planks from the flooring of the chamber, and deposited all between the scantlings. I then replaced the boards so cleverly, so cunningly, that no human eye—not even *his*—could have detected anything wrong. There was nothing to wash out no stain of any kind no blood-spot whatever. I had been too wary for that. A tub had caught all—ha! ha!

When I had made an end of these labors, it was four o'clock—still dark as midnight. As the bell sounded the hour, there came a knocking at the street door. I went down to open it with a light heart—for what had I *now* to fear? There entered three men, who introduced themselves, with perfect suavity, as officers of the police. A shriek had been heard by a neighbor during the night; suspicion of foul play had been aroused; information had been lodged at the police office, and they (the officers) had been deputed to search the premises.

I smiled—for *what* had I to fear? I bade the gentlemen welcome. The shriek, I said, was my own in a dream. The old man, I mentioned, was absent in the country. I took my visitors all over the house. I bade them search—search *well*. I led them, at length, to *his* chamber. I showed them his treasures, secure, undisturbed. In the enthusiasm of my confidence, I brought chairs into the room, and desired them *here* to rest from their fatigues, while I myself, in the wild audacity of my perfect triumph, placed my own seat upon the very spot beneath which reposed the corpse of the victim.

The officers were satisfied. My *manner* had convinced them. I was singularly at ease. They sat, and while I answered cheerily, they chatted of familiar things. But, ere long, I felt myself getting pale and wished them gone. My head ached, and I fancied a ringing in my ears: but still they sat and still chatted. The ringing became more distinct: it continued and became more distinct: I talked more freely to get rid of the feeling: but it

continued and gained definiteness—until, at length, I found that the noise was *not* within my ears.

No doubt I now grew *very* pale; but I talked more fluently, and with a heightened voice. Yet the sound increased—and what could I do? It was *a low, dull, quick sound—much such a sound as a watch makes when enveloped in cotton.* I gasped for breath—and yet the officers heard it not. I talked more quickly—more vehemently; but the noise steadily increased. I arose and argued about trifles, in a high key and with violent gesticulations; but the noise steadily increased. Why *would* they not be gone? I paced the floor to and fro with heavy strides, as if excited to fury by the observations of the men—but the noise steadily increased. Oh God! what *could* I do? I foamed—I raved—I swore! I swung the chair upon which I had been sitting, and grated it upon the boards, but the noise arose over all and continually increased. It grew louder—louder—*louder!* And still the men chatted pleasantly, and smiled. Was it possible they heard not? Almighty God!—no, no! They heard!—they suspected!—they *knew!*—they were making a mockery of my horror!—this I thought, and this I think. But anything was better than this agony! Anything was more tolerable than this derision! I could bear those hypocritical smiles no longer! I felt that I must scream or die!—and now—again!—hark! louder! louder! louder! *louder!*

"Villains!" I shrieked, "dissemble no more! I admit the deed!—tear up the planks! here, here!—it is the beating of his hideous heart!"

THE BLACK CAT

For the most wild, yet most homely narrative which I am about to pen, I neither expect nor solicit belief. Mad indeed would I be to expect it, in a case where my very senses reject their own evidence. Yet, mad am I not—and very surely do I not dream. But tomorrow I die, and today I would unburden my soul. My immediate purpose is to place before the world, plainly, succinctly, and without comment, a series of mere household events. In their consequences, these events have terrified—have tortured—have destroyed me. Yet I will not attempt to expound them. To me, they have presented little but Horror—to many they will seem less terrible than *barroques.* Hereafter, perhaps, some intellect may be found which will reduce my phantasm to the common place—some intellect more calm, more logical, and far less excitable than my own, which will perceive, in the circumstances I detail with awe, nothing more than an ordinary succession of very natural causes and effects.

From my infancy I was noted for the docility and humanity of my disposition. My tenderness of heart was even so conspicuous as to make me the jest of my companions. I was especially fond of animals, and was indulged by my parents with a great variety of pets. With these I spent most of my time, and never was so happy as when feeding and caressing them. This peculiarity of character grew with my growth, and in my manhood, I derived from it one of my principal sources of pleasure. To those who have cherished an affection for a faithful and sagacious dog, I need hardly be at the trouble of explaining the nature or the intensity of the gratification thus derivable. There is something in the unselfish and self-sacrificing love of a brute, which goes directly to the heart of him who has had frequent occasion to test the paltry friendship and gossamer fidelity of mere *Man.*

I married early, and was happy to find in my wife a disposition not uncongenial with my own. Observing my partiality for domestic pets, she lost no opportunity of procuring those of the most agreeable kind. We had birds, gold-fish, a fine dog, rabbits, a small monkey, and *a cat.*

This latter was a remarkably large and beautiful animal, entirely black, and sagacious to an astonishing degree. In speaking of his intelligence, my wife, who at heart was not a little tinctured with superstition, made frequent allusion to the ancient popular notion, which regarded all black cats as witches in disguise. Not that she was ever *serious* upon this point—and I mention the matter at all for no better reason than that it happens, just now, to be remembered.

Pluto—this was the cat's name—was my favorite pet and playmate. I alone fed him, and he attended me wherever I went about the house. It was even with difficulty that I could prevent him from following me through the streets.

Our friendship lasted, in this manner, for several years, during which my general temperament and character—through the instrumentality of the Fiend Intemperance—had (I blush to confess it) experienced a radical alteration for the worse. I grew, day by day, more moody, more irritable, more regardless of the feelings of others. I suffered myself to use intemperate language to my wife. At length, I even offered her personal violence. My pets, of course, were made to feel the change in my disposition. I not only neglected, but ill-used them. For Pluto, however, I still retained sufficient regard to restrain me from maltreating him, as I made no scruple of maltreating the rabbits, the monkey, or even the dog, when by accident, or through affection, they came in my way. But my disease grew upon me—for what disease is like Alcohol!—and at length even Pluto, who was now becoming old, and consequently somewhat peevish—even Pluto began to experience the effects of my ill temper.

One night, returning home, much intoxicated, from one of my haunts about town, I fancied that the cat avoided my presence. I seized him; when, in his fright at my violence, he inflicted a slight wound upon my hand with his teeth. The fury of a demon instantly possessed me. I knew myself no longer. My original soul seemed, at once, to take its flight from my body; and a more than fiendish malevolence, gin-nurtured, thrilled every fiber of my frame. I took from my waistcoat-pocket a pen-knife, opened it, grasped the poor beast by the throat, and deliberately cut one of its eyes from the socket! I blush, I burn, I shudder, while I pen the damnable atrocity.

When reason returned with the morning—when I had slept off the fumes of the night's debauch—I experienced a sentiment half of horror, half of remorse, for the crime of which I had been guilty; but it was, at best, a feeble and equivocal feeling, and the soul remained untouched. I again plunged into excess, and soon drowned in wine all memory of the deed.

In the meantime the cat slowly recovered. The socket of the lost eye presented, it is true, a frightful appearance, but he no longer appeared to suffer any pain. He went about the house as usual, but, as might be expected, fled in extreme terror at my approach. I had so much of my old heart left, as to be at first grieved by this evident dislike on the part of a creature which had once so loved me. But this feeling soon gave place to irritation. And then came, as if to my final and irrevocable overthrow, the spirit of PERVERSENESS. Of this spirit philosophy takes no account. Yet I am not more sure that my soul lives, than I am that perverseness is one of the primitive impulses of the human heart—one of the indivisible primary faculties, or sentiments, which give direction to the character of Man. Who has not, a hundred times, found himself committing a vile or a silly action, for no other reason than because he knows he should *not*? Have we not a perpetual inclination, in the teeth of our best judgment, to violate that which is *Law,* merely because we understand it to be such? This spirit of perverseness, I say, came to my final overthrow. It was this unfathomable longing of the soul *to vex itself*—to offer violence to its own nature—to do wrong for the wrong's sake only—that urged me to continue and finally to consummate the injury I had inflicted upon the unoffending brute. One morning, in cool blood, I slipped a noose about its neck and hung it to the limb of a tree; hung it with the tears streaming from my eyes, and with the bitterest remorse at my heart; hung it *because* I knew that it had loved me, and *because* I felt it had given me no reason of offence; hung it *because* I knew that in so doing I was committing a sin—a deadly sin that would so jeopardize my immortal soul as to place it—if such a thing were possible—even beyond the reach of the infinite mercy of the Most Merciful and Most Terrible God.

On the night of the day on which this cruel deed was done, I was aroused from sleep by the cry of fire. The curtains of my bed were in flames. The whole house was blazing. It was with great difficulty that my wife, a servant, and myself, made our escape from the conflagration. The destruction was complete. My entire worldly wealth was swallowed up, and I resigned myself thenceforward to despair.

I am above the weakness of seeking to establish a sequence of cause and effect, between the disaster and the atrocity. But I am detailing a chain of facts—and wish not to leave even a possible link imperfect. On the day succeeding the fire, I visited the ruins. The walls, with one exception, had fallen in. This exception was found in a compartment wall, not very thick, which stood about the middle of the house, and against which had rested the head of my bed. The plastering had here, in great measure, resisted the action of the fire—a fact which I attributed to its having been recently spread. About this wall a dense crowd were collected, and many persons seemed to be examining a particular portion of it with very minute and eager attention. The words "strange!" "singular!" and other similar expressions, excited my curiosity. I approached and saw, as if graven in *bas relief* upon the white surface, the figure of a gigantic *cat*. The impression was given with an accuracy truly marvelous. There was a rope about the animal's neck.

When I first beheld this apparition—for I could scarcely regard it as less—my wonder and my terror were extreme. But at length reflection came to my aid. The cat, I remembered, had been hung in a garden adjacent to the house. Upon the alarm of fire, this garden had been immediately filled by the crowd—by some one of whom the animal must have been cut from the tree and thrown, through an open window, into my chamber. This had probably been done with the view of arousing me from sleep. The falling of other walls had compressed the victim of my cruelty into the substance of the freshly-spread plaster; the lime of which, with the flames, and the *ammonia* from the carcass, had then accomplished the portraiture as I saw it.

Although I thus readily accounted to my reason, if not altogether to my conscience, for the startling fact just detailed, it did not the less fail to make a deep impression upon my fancy. For months I could not rid myself of the phantasm of the cat; and, during this period, there came back into my spirit a half-sentiment that seemed, but was not, remorse. I went so far as to regret the loss of the animal, and to look about me, among the vile haunts which I now habitually frequented, for another pet of the same species, and of somewhat similar appearance, with which to supply its place.

One night as I sat, half stupefied, in a den of more than infamy, my attention was suddenly drawn to some black object, reposing upon the head of one of the immense hogsheads of Gin, or of Rum, which constituted the chief furniture of the apartment. I had been looking steadily at the top of this hogshead for some minutes, and what now caused me surprise was the fact

that I had not sooner perceived the object thereupon. I approached it, and touched it with my hand. It was a black cat—a very large one—fully as large as Pluto, and closely resembling him in every respect but one. Pluto had not a white hair upon any portion of his body; but this cat had a large, although indefinite splotch of white, covering nearly the whole region of the breast.

Upon my touching him, he immediately arose, purred loudly, rubbed against my hand, and appeared delighted with my notice. This, then, was the very creature of which I was in search. I at once offered to purchase it of the landlord; but this person made no claim to it—knew nothing of it—had never seen it before.

I continued my caresses, and, when I prepared to go home, the animal evinced a disposition to accompany me. I permitted it to do so; occasionally stooping and patting it as I proceeded. When it reached the house it domesticated itself at once, and became immediately a great favorite with my wife.

For my own part, I soon found a dislike to it arising within me. This was just the reverse of what I had anticipated; but—I know not how or why it was—its evident fondness for myself rather disgusted and annoyed. By slow degrees, these feelings of disgust and annoyance rose into the bitterness of hatred. I avoided the creature; a certain sense of shame, and the remembrance of my former deed of cruelty, preventing me from physically abusing it. I did not, for some weeks, strike, or otherwise violently ill-use it; but gradually—very gradually—I came to look upon it with unutterable loathing, and to flee silently from its odious presence, as from the breath of a pestilence.

What added, no doubt, to my hatred of the beast, was the discovery, on the morning after I brought it home, that, like Pluto, it also had been deprived of one of its eyes. This circumstance, however, only endeared it to my wife, who, as I have already said, possessed, in a high degree, that humanity of feeling which had once been my distinguishing trait, and the source of many of my simplest and purest pleasures.

With my aversion to this cat, however, its partiality for myself seemed to increase. It followed my footsteps with a pertinacity which it would be difficult to make the reader comprehend. Whenever I sat, it would crouch beneath my chair, or spring upon my knees, covering me with its loathsome caresses. If I arose to walk it would get between my feet and thus nearly throw me down, or, fastening its long and sharp claws in my dress, clamber, in this manner, to my breast. At such times, although I longed to destroy it with a blow, I was yet withheld from so doing, partly

by a memory of my former crime, but chiefly—let me confess it at once—by absolute *dread* of the beast.

This dread was not exactly a dread of physical evil—and yet I should be at a loss how otherwise to define it. I am almost ashamed to own—yes, even in this felon's cell, I am almost ashamed to own—that the terror and horror with which the animal inspired me, had been heightened by one of the merest chimaeras it would be possible to conceive. My wife had called my attention, more than once, to the character of the mark of white hair, of which I have spoken, and which constituted the sole visible difference between the strange beast and the one I had destroyed. The reader will remember that this mark, although large, had been originally very indefinite; but, by slow degrees—degrees nearly imperceptible, and which for a long time my Reason struggled to reject as fanciful—it had, at length, assumed a rigorous distinctness of outline. It was now the representation of an object that I shudder to name—and for this, above all, I loathed, and dreaded, and would have rid myself of the monster *had I dared*—it was now, I say, the image of a hideous—of a ghastly thing—of the Gallows!—oh, mournful and terrible engine of Horror and of Crime—of Agony and of Death!

And now was I indeed wretched beyond the wretchedness of mere Humanity. And *a brute beast*—whose fellow I had contemptuously destroyed—*a brute beast* to work out for *me*—for me a man, fashioned in the image of the High God—so much of insufferable wo! Alas! neither by day nor by night knew I the blessing of Rest anymore! During the former the creature left me no moment alone; and, in the latter, I started, hourly, from dreams of unutterable fear, to find the hot breath of *the thing* upon my face, and its vast weight—an incarnate Night-Mare that I had no power to shake off—incumbent eternally upon my *heart!*

Beneath the pressure of torments such as these, the feeble remnant of the good within me succumbed. Evil thoughts became my sole intimates—the darkest and most evil of thoughts. The moodiness of my usual temper increased to hatred of all things and of all mankind; while, from the sudden, frequent, and ungovernable outbursts of a fury to which I now blindly abandoned myself, my uncomplaining wife, alas! was the most usual and the most patient of sufferers.

One day she accompanied me, upon some household errand, into the cellar of the old building which our poverty compelled us to inhabit. The cat followed me down the steep stairs, and, nearly throwing me headlong, exasperated me to madness. Uplifting an axe, and forgetting, in my wrath,

the childish dread which had hitherto stayed my hand, I aimed a blow at the animal which, of course, would have proved instantly fatal had it descended as I wished. But this blow was arrested by the hand of my wife. Goaded, by the interference, into a rage more than demoniacal, I withdrew my arm from her grasp and buried the axe in her brain. She fell dead upon the spot, without a groan.

This hideous murder accomplished, I set myself forthwith, and with entire deliberation, to the task of concealing the body. I knew that I could not remove it from the house, either by day or by night, without the risk of being observed by the neighbors. Many projects entered my mind. At one period I thought of cutting the corpse into minute fragments, and destroying them by fire. At another, I resolved to dig a grave for it in the floor of the cellar. Again, I deliberated about casting it in the well in the yard—about packing it in a box, as if merchandise, with the usual arrangements, and so getting a porter to take it from the house. Finally I hit upon what I considered a far better expedient than either of these. I determined to wall it up in the cellar—as the monks of the middle ages are recorded to have walled up their victims.

For a purpose such as this the cellar was well adapted. Its walls were loosely constructed, and had lately been plastered throughout with a rough plaster, which the dampness of the atmosphere had prevented from hardening. Moreover, in one of the walls was a projection, caused by a false chimney, or fireplace, that had been filled up, and made to resemble the red of the cellar. I made no doubt that I could readily displace the bricks at this point, insert the corpse, and wall the whole up as before, so that no eye could detect anything suspicious.

And in this calculation I was not deceived. By means of a crow-bar I easily dislodged the bricks, and, having carefully deposited the body against the inner wall, I propped it in that position, while, with little trouble, I relaid the whole structure as it originally stood. Having procured mortar, sand, and hair, with every possible precaution, I prepared a plaster which could not be distinguished from the old, and with this I very carefully went over the new brickwork. When I had finished, I felt satisfied that all was right. The wall did not present the slightest appearance of having been disturbed. The rubbish on the floor was picked up with the minutest care. I looked around triumphantly, and said to myself—"Here at least, then, my labor has not been in vain."

My next step was to look for the beast which had been the cause of so much wretchedness; for I had, at length, firmly resolved to put it to death.

Had I been able to meet with it, at the moment, there could have been no doubt of its fate; but it appeared that the crafty animal had been alarmed at the violence of my previous anger, and forbore to present itself in my present mood. It is impossible to describe, or to imagine, the deep, the blissful sense of relief which the absence of the detested creature occasioned in my bosom. It did not make its appearance during the night—and thus for one night at least, since its introduction into the house, I soundly and tranquilly slept; aye, *slept* even with the burden of murder upon my soul!

The second and the third day passed, and still my tormentor came not. Once again I breathed as a freeman. The monster, in terror, had fled the premises forever! I should behold it no more! My happiness was supreme! The guilt of my dark deed disturbed me but little. Some few inquiries had been made, but these had been readily answered. Even a search had been instituted—but of course nothing was to be discovered. I looked upon my future felicity as secured.

Upon the fourth day of the assassination, a party of the police came, very unexpectedly, into the house, and proceeded again to make rigorous investigation of the premises. Secure, however, in the inscrutability of my place of concealment, I felt no embarrassment whatever. The officers bade me accompany them in their search. They left no nook or corner unexplored. At length, for the third or fourth time, they descended into the cellar. I quivered not in a muscle. My heart beat calmly as that of one who slumbers in innocence. I walked the cellar from end to end. I folded my arms upon my bosom, and roamed easily to and fro. The police were thoroughly satisfied and prepared to depart. The glee at my heart was too strong to be restrained. I burned to say if but one word, by way of triumph, and to render doubly sure their assurance of my guiltlessness.

"Gentlemen," I said at last, as the party ascended the steps, "I delight to have allayed your suspicions. I wish you all health, and a little more courtesy. By the by, gentlemen, this—this is a very well constructed house." [In the rabid desire to say something easily, I scarcely knew what I uttered at all.]—"I may say an *excellently* well constructed house. These walls—are you going, gentlemen?—these walls are solidly put together"; and here, through the mere frenzy of bravado, I rapped heavily, with a cane which I held in my hand, upon that very portion of the brickwork behind which stood the corpse of the wife of my bosom.

But may God shield and deliver me from the fangs of the Arch-Fiend! No sooner had the reverberation of my blows sunk into silence, than I was answered by a voice from within the tomb!—by a cry, at first muffled

and broken, like the sobbing of a child, and then quickly swelling into one long, loud, and continuous scream, utterly anomalous and inhuman—a howl—a wailing shriek, half of horror and half of triumph, such as might have arisen only out of hell, conjointly from the throats of the dammed in their agony and of the demons that exult in the damnation.

Of my own thoughts it is folly to speak. Swooning, I staggered to the opposite wall. For one instant the party upon the stairs remained motionless, through extremity of terror and of awe. In the next, a dozen stout arms were toiling at the wall. It fell bodily. The corpse, already greatly decayed and clotted with gore, stood erect before the eyes of the spectators. Upon its head, with red extended mouth and solitary eye of fire, sat the hideous beast whose craft had seduced me into murder, and whose informing voice had consigned me to the hangman. I had walled the monster up within the tomb!

The Premature Burial

There are certain themes of which the interest is all-absorbing, but which are too entirely horrible for the purposes of legitimate fiction. These the mere romanticist must eschew, if he do not wish to offend, or to disgust. They are with propriety handled, only when the severity and majesty of Truth sanctify and sustain them. We thrill, for example, with the most intense of "pleasurable pain" over the accounts of the Passage of the Beresina, of the Earthquake at Lisbon, of the Plague at London, of the Massacre of St. Bartholomew, or of the stifling of the hundred and twenty-three prisoners in the Black Hole at Calcutta. But, in these accounts, it is the fact—it is the reality—it is the history which excites. As inventions, we should regard them with simple abhorrence.

I have mentioned some few of the more prominent and august calamities on record; but, in these, it is the extent, not less than the character of the calamity, which so vividly impresses the fancy. I need not remind the reader that, from the long and weird catalogue of human miseries, I might have selected many individual instances more replete with essential suffering than any of these vast generalities of disaster. The true wretchedness, indeed—the ultimate wo—is particular, not diffuse. That the ghastly extremes of agony are endured by man the unit, and never by man the mass—for this let us thank a merciful God!

To be buried while alive is, beyond question, the most terrific of these extremes which has ever fallen to the lot of mere mortality. That it has frequently, very frequently, so fallen will scarcely be denied by those who think. The boundaries which divide Life from Death, are at best shadowy and vague. Who shall say where the one ends, and where the other begins?

We know that there are diseases in which occur total cessations of all the apparent functions of vitality, and yet in which these cessations are merely suspensions, properly so called. They are only temporary pauses in the incomprehensible mechanism. A certain period elapses, and some unseen mysterious principle again sets in motion the magic pinions and the wizard wheels. The silver cord was not forever loosed, nor the golden bowl irreparably broken. But where, meantime, was the soul?

Apart, however, from the inevitable conclusion, *à priori,* that such causes must produce such effects—that the well-known occurrence of such cases of suspended animation must naturally give rise, now and then, to premature interments—apart from this consideration, we have the direct testimony of medical and ordinary experience to prove that a vast number of such interments have actually taken place. I might refer at once, if necessary, to a hundred well authenticated instances. One of very remarkable character, and of which the circumstances may be fresh in the memory of some of my readers, occurred, not very long ago, in the neighboring city of Baltimore, where it occasioned a painful, intense, and widely extended excitement. The wife of one of the most respectable citizens—a lawyer of eminence and a member of Congress—was seized with a sudden and unaccountable illness, which completely baffled the skill of her physicians. After much suffering she died, or was supposed to die. No one suspected, indeed, or had reason to suspect, that she was not actually dead. She presented all the ordinary appearances of death. The face assumed the usual pinched and sunken outline. The lips were of the usual marble pallor. The eyes were lusterless. There was no warmth. Pulsation had ceased. For three days the body was preserved unburied, during which it had acquired a stony rigidity. The funeral, in short, was hastened, on account of the rapid advance of what was supposed to be decomposition.

The lady was deposited in her family vault, which, for three subsequent years, was undisturbed. At the expiration of this term, it was opened for the reception of a sarcophagus; but, alas! how fearful a shock awaited the husband, who, personally, threw open the door. As its portals swung outwardly back, some white-appareled object fell rattling within his arms. It was the skeleton of his wife in her yet unmoldered shroud.

A careful investigation rendered it evident that she had revived within two days after her entombment—that her struggles within the coffin had caused it to fall from a ledge, or shelf to the floor, where it was so broken as to permit her escape. A lamp which had been accidentally left, full of

oil, within the tomb, was found empty; it might have been exhausted, however, by evaporation. On the uppermost of the steps which led down into the dread chamber was a large fragment of the coffin, with which, it seemed, that she had endeavored to arrest attention, by striking the iron door. While thus occupied, she probably swooned, or possibly died, through sheer terror; and, in failing, her shroud became entangled in some ironwork which projected interiorly. Thus she remained, and thus she rotted, erect.

In the year 1810, a case of living inhumation happened in France, attended with circumstances which go far to warrant the assertion that truth is, indeed, stranger than fiction. The heroine of the story was a Mademoiselle Victorine Lafourcade, a young girl of illustrious family, of wealth, and of great personal beauty. Among her numerous suitors was Julien Bossuet, a poor *littérateur,* or journalist, of Paris. His talents and general amiability had recommended him to the notice of the heiress, by whom he seems to have been truly beloved; but her pride of birth decided her, finally, to reject him, and to wed a Monsieur Rénelle, a banker and a diplomatist of some eminence. After marriage, however, this gentleman neglected, and, perhaps, even more positively ill-treated her. Having passed with him some wretched years, she died—at least her condition so closely resembled death as to deceive everyone who saw her. She was buried—not in a vault—but in an ordinary grave in the village of her nativity. Filled with despair, and still inflamed by the memory of a profound attachment, the lover journeys from the capital to the remote province in which the village lies, with the romantic purpose of disinterring the corpse, and possessing himself of its luxuriant tresses. He reaches the grave. At midnight he unearths the coffin, opens it, and is in the act of detaching the hair, when he is arrested by the unclosing of the beloved eyes. In fact, the lady had been buried alive. Vitality had not altogether departed, and she was aroused by the caresses of her lover, from the lethargy which had been mistaken for death. He bore her frantically to his lodgings in the village. He employed certain powerful restoratives suggested by no little medical learning. In fine, she revived. She recognized her preserver. She remained with him until, by slow degrees, she fully recovered her original health. Her woman's heart was not adamant, and this last lesson of love sufficed to soften it. She bestowed it upon Bossuet. She returned no more to her husband, but, concealing from him her resurrection, fled with her lover to America. Twenty years afterward, the two returned to France, in the persuasion that time had so greatly altered the lady's appearance that

her friends would be unable to recognize her. They were mistaken, how-
ever, for, at the first meeting, Monsieur Rénelle did actually recognize and
make claim to his wife. This claim she resisted, and a judicial tribunal
sustained her in her resistance; deciding that the peculiar circumstances,
with the long lapse of years, had extinguished, not only equitably, but
legally, the authority of the husband.

The *Chirurgical Journal*[1] of Leipsic—a periodical, of high authority
and merit, which some American bookseller would do well to translate and
republish—records, in a late number, a very distressing event of the char-
acter in question.

An officer of artillery, a man of gigantic stature and of robust health,
being thrown from an unmanageable horse, received a very severe contu-
sion upon the head, which rendered him insensible at once; the skull
was slightly fractured; but no immediate danger was apprehended. Tre-
panning was accomplished successfully. He was bled, and many other of
the ordinary means of relief were adopted. Gradually, however, he fell
into a more and more hopeless state of stupor; and, finally, it was thought
that he died.

The weather was warm; and he was buried, with indecent haste, in one
of the public cemeteries. His funeral took place on Thursday. On the
Sunday following, the grounds of the cemetery were, as usual, much
thronged with visiters; and, about noon, an intense excitement was cre-
ated by the declaration of a peasant that, while sitting upon the grave of
the officer, he had distinctly felt a commotion of the earth, as if occa-
sioned by someone struggling beneath. At first little attention was paid to
the man's asseveration; but his evident terror, and the dogged obstinacy
with which he persisted in his story, had, at length, their natural effect
upon the crowd. Spades were hurriedly procured, and the grave, which
was shamefully shallow, was, in a few minutes, so far thrown open that the
head of its occupant appeared. He was then, seemingly, dead; but he sat
nearly erect within his coffin, the lid of which, in his furious struggles, he
had partially uplifted.

He was forthwith conveyed to the nearest hospital, and there pro-
nounced to be still living, although in an asphytic condition. After some
hours he revived, recognized individuals of his acquaintance, and, in bro-
ken sentences, spoke of his agonies in the grave.

From what he related, it was clear that he must have been conscious of
life for more than an hour, while inhumed, before lapsing into insensibil-
ity. The grave was carelessly and loosely filled with an exceedingly porous

soil; and thus some air was necessarily admitted. He heard the footsteps of the crowd overhead, and endeavored to make himself heard in turn. It was the tumult within the grounds of the cemetery, he said, which appeared to awaken him from a deep sleep—but no sooner was he awake than he became fully aware of the awful horrors of his position.

This patient, it is recorded, was doing well, and seemed to be in a fair way of ultimate recovery, but fell a victim to the quackeries of medical experiment. The galvanic battery was applied, and he suddenly expired in one of those ecstatic paroxysms which, occasionally, it superinduces.

The mention of the galvanic battery, nevertheless, recalls to my memory a well known and very extraordinary case in point, where its action proved the means of restoring to animation a young attorney of London who had been interred for two days. This occurred in 1831, and created, at the time, a very profound sensation wherever it was made the subject of converse.

The patient, Mr. Edward Stapleton, had died, apparently, of typhus fever, accompanied with some anomalous symptoms which had excited the curiosity of his medical attendants. Upon his seeming decease, his friends were requested to sanction a *post mortem* examination, but declined to permit it. As often happens, when such refusals are made, the practitioners resolved to disinter the body and dissect it at leisure, in private. Arrangements were easily effected with some of the numerous corps of body-snatchers with which London abounds; and, upon the third night after the funeral, the supposed corpse was unearthed from a grave eight feet deep, and deposited in the opening chamber of one of the private hospitals.

An incision of some extent had been actually made in the abdomen, when the fresh and undecayed appearance of the subject suggested an application of the battery. One experiment succeeded another, and the customary effects supervened, with nothing to characterize them in any respect, except, upon one or two occasions, a more than ordinary degree of life-likeliness in the convulsive action.

It grew late. The day was about to dawn; and it was thought expedient, at length, to proceed at once to the dissection. A student, however, was especially desirous of testing a theory of his own, and insisted upon apply-ing the battery to one of the pectoral muscles. A rough gash was made, and a wire hastily brought in contact; when the patient, with a hurried but quite unconvulsive movement, arose from the table, stepped into the middle of the floor, gazed about him uneasily for a few seconds, and then—spoke.

What he said was unintelligible, but words were uttered; the syllabification was distinct. Having spoken, he fell heavily to the floor.

For some moments all were paralyzed with awe—but the urgency of the case soon restored them their presence of mind. It was seen that Mr. Stapleton was alive, although in a swoon. Upon exhibition of ether he revived and was rapidly restored to health, and to the society of his friends—from whom, however, all knowledge of his resuscitation was withheld, until a relapse was no longer to be apprehended. Their wonder—their rapturous astonishment—may be conceived.

The most thrilling peculiarity of this incident, nevertheless, is involved in what Mr. S. himself asserts. He declares that at no period was he altogether insensible—that, dully and confusedly, he was aware of everything which happened to him, from the moment in which he was pronounced *dead* by his physicians, to that in which he fell swooning to the floor of the hospital. "I am alive" were the uncomprehended words which, upon recognizing the locality of the dissecting-room, he had endeavored, in his extremity, to utter.

It were an easy matter to multiply such histories as these—but I forbear—for, indeed, we have no need of such to establish the fact that premature interments occur. When we reflect how very rarely, from the nature of the case, we have it in our power to detect them, we must admit that they may *frequently* occur without our cognizance. Scarcely, in truth, is a graveyard ever encroached upon, for any purpose, to any great extent, that skeletons are not found in postures which suggest the most fearful of suspicions.

Fearful indeed the suspicion—but more fearful the doom! It may be asserted, without hesitation, that *no* event is so terribly well adapted to inspire the supremeness of bodily and of mental distress, as is burial before death. The unendurable oppression of the lungs—the stifling fumes from the damp earth—the clinging to the death garments—the rigid embrace of the narrow house—the blackness of the absolute Night— the silence like a sea that overwhelms—the unseen but palpable presence of the Conqueror Worm—these things, with thoughts of the air and grass above, with memory of dear friends who would fly to save us if but informed of our fate, and with consciousness that of this fate they can *never* be informed—that our hopeless portion is that of the really dead— these considerations, I say, carry into the heart, which still palpitates, a degree of appalling and intolerable horror from which the most daring imagination must recoil. We know of nothing so agonizing upon Earth—

we can dream of nothing half so hideous in the realms of the nethermost Hell. And thus all narratives upon this topic have an interest profound; an interest, nevertheless, which, through the sacred awe of the topic itself, very properly and very peculiarly depends upon our conviction of the *truth* of the matter narrated. What I have now to tell, is of my own actual knowledge—of my own positive and personal experience.

For several years I had been subject to attacks of the singular disorder which physicians have agreed to term catalepsy, in default of a more definitive title. Although both the immediate and the predisposing causes, and even the actual diagnosis, of this disease, are still mysteries, its obvious and apparent character is sufficiently well understood. Its variations seem to be chiefly of degree. Sometimes the patient lies, for a day only, or even for a shorter period, in a species of exaggerated lethargy. He is senseless and externally motionless; but the pulsation of the heart is still faintly perceptible; some traces of warmth remain; a slight color lingers within the center of the cheek; and, upon application of a mirror to the lips, we can detect a torpid, unequal, and vacillating action of the lungs. Then again the duration of the trance is for weeks—even for months; while the closest scrutiny, and the most rigorous medical tests, fail to establish any material distinction between the state of the sufferer and what we conceive of absolute death. Very usually, he is saved from premature interment solely by the knowledge of his friends that he has been previously subject to catalepsy, by the consequent suspicion excited, and, above all, by the non-appearance of decay. The advances of the malady are, luckily, gradual. The first manifestations, although marked, are unequivocal. The fits grow successively more and more distinctive, and endure each for a longer term than the preceding. In this lies the principal security from inhumation. The unfortunate whose *first* attack should be of the extreme character which is occasionally seen, would almost inevitably be consigned alive to the tomb.

My own case differed in no important particular from those mentioned in medical books. Sometimes, without any apparent cause, I sank, little by little, into a condition of hemi-syncope, or half swoon; and, in this condition, without pain, without ability to stir, or, strictly speaking, to think, but with a dull lethargic consciousness of life and of the presence of those who surrounded my bed, I remained, until the crisis of the disease restored me, suddenly, to perfect sensation. At other times I was quickly and impetuously smitten. I grew sick, and numb, and chilly, and dizzy, and so fell prostrate at once. Then, for weeks all was void, and black, and silent, and Nothing became the universe. Total annihilation could be no more. From

these latter attacks I awoke, however, with a gradation slow in proportion to the suddenness of the seizure. Just as the day dawns to the friendless and houseless beggar who roams the streets throughout the long desolate winter night—just so tardily—just so wearily—just so cheerily came back the light of the Soul to me.

Apart from the tendency to trance, however, my general health appeared to be good; nor could I perceive that it was at all affected by the one prevalent malady—unless, indeed, an idiosyncrasy in my ordinary *sleep* may be looked upon as superinduced. Upon awaking from slumber, I could never gain, at once, thorough possession of my senses, and always remained, for many minutes, in much bewilderment and perplexity; the mental faculties in general, but the memory in especial, being in a condition of absolute abeyance.

In all that I endured there was no physical suffering, but of moral distress an infinitude. My fancy grew charnal, I talked "of worms, of tombs, and epitaphs." I was lost in reveries of death, and the idea of premature burial held continual possession of my brain. The ghastly Danger to which I was subjected, haunted me day and night. In the former, the torture of meditation was excessive—in the latter, supreme. When the grim Darkness overspread the Earth, then, with every horror of thought, I shook—shook as the quivering plumes upon the hearse. When Nature could endure wakefulness no longer, it was with a struggle that I consented to sleep—for I shuddered to reflect that, upon awaking, I might find myself the tenant of a grave. And when, finally, I sank into slumber, it was only to rush at once into a world of phantasms, above which, with vast, sable, overshadowing wing, hovered, predominant, the one sepulchral Idea.

From the innumerable images of gloom which thus oppressed me in dreams, I select for record but a solitary vision. Methought I was immersed in a cataleptic trance of more than usual duration and profundity. Suddenly there came an icy hand upon my forehead, and an impatient, gibbering voice whispered the word "Arise!" within my ear.

I sat erect. The darkness was total. I could not see the figure of him who had aroused me. I could call to mind neither the period at which I had fallen into the trance, nor the locality in which I then lay. While I remained motionless, and busied in endeavors to collect my thought, the cold hand grasped me fiercely by the wrist, shaking it petulantly, while the gibbering voice said again:

"Arise! did I not bid thee arise?"

"And who," I demanded, "art thou?"

"I have no name in the regions which I inhabit," replied the voice mournfully; "I was mortal, but am fiend. I was merciless, but am pitiful. Thou dost feel that I shudder. My teeth chatter as I speak, yet it is not with the chilliness of the night—of the night without end. But this hideousness is insufferable. How canst *thou* tranquilly sleep? I cannot rest for the cry of these great agonies. These sights are more than I can bear. Get thee up! Come with me into the outer Night, and let me unfold to thee the graves. Is not this a spectacle of wo?—Behold!"

I looked; and the unseen figure, which still grasped me by the wrist, had caused to be thrown open the graves of all mankind, and from each issued the faint phosphoric radiance of decay, so that I could see into the innermost recesses, and there view the shrouded bodies in their sad and solemn slumbers with the worm. But, alas! the real sleepers were fewer, by many millions, than those who slumbered not at all; and there was a feeble struggling; and there was a general sad unrest; and from out the depths of the countless pits there came a melancholy rustling from the garments of the buried. And, of those who seemed tranquilly to repose, I saw that a vast number had changed, in a greater or less degree, the rigid and uneasy position in which they had originally been entombed. And the voice again said to me, as I gazed:

"Is it not—oh, is it *not* a pitiful sight?" but, before I could find words to reply, the figure had ceased to grasp my wrist, the phosphoric lights expired, and the graves were closed with a sudden violence, while from out them arose a tumult of despairing cries, saying again: "Is it not—oh, God! Is it *not* a very pitiful sight?"

Phantasies such as these, presenting themselves at night, extended their terrific influence far into my waking hours. My nerves became thoroughly unstrung, and I fell a prey to perpetual horror. I hesitated to ride, or to walk, or to indulge in any exercise that would carry me from home. In fact I no longer dared trust myself out of the immediate presence of those who were aware of my proneness to catalepsy, lest, falling into one of my usual fits, I should be buried before my real condition could be ascertained. I doubted the care, the fidelity of my dearest friends. I dreaded that, in some trance of more than customary duration, they might be prevailed upon to regard me as irrecoverable. I even went so far as to fear that, as I occasioned much trouble, they might be glad to consider any very protracted attack as sufficient excuse for getting rid of me altogether. It was in vain they endeavored to reassure me by the most solemn promises. I exacted the most sacred oaths, that under no circumstances they would

bury me until decomposition had so materially advanced as to render far-
ther preservation impossible. And, even then, my mortal terrors would
listen to no reason—would accept no consolation. I entered into a series
of elaborate precautions. Among other things, I had the family vault so
remodeled as to admit of being readily opened from within. The slightest
pressure upon a long lever that extended far into the tomb would cause the
iron portal to fly back. There were arrangements also for the free admis-
sion of air and light, and convenient receptacles for food and water, within
immediate reach of the coffin intended for my reception. This coffin was
warmly and softly padded, and was provided with a lid, fashioned upon the
principle of the vault-door, with the addition of springs so contrived that
the feeblest movement of the body would be sufficient to set it at liberty.
Besides all this, there was suspended from the roof of the tomb, a large
bell, the rope of which, it was designed, should extend through a hole in
the coffin, and so be fastened to one of the hands of the corpse. But, alas!
what avails the vigilance against the Destiny of man? Not even these well-
contrived securities sufficed to save from the uttermost agonies of living
inhumation, a wretch to these agonies foredoomed!

There arrived an epoch—as often before there had arrived in which I
found myself emerging from total unconsciousness into the first feeble
and indefinite sense of existence. Slowly—with a tortoise gradation—
approached the faint gray dawn of the psychal day. A torpid uneasiness.
An apathetic endurance of dull pain. No care—no hope—no effort.
Then, after a long interval, a ringing in the ears; then, after a lapse still
longer, a prickling or tingling sensation in the extremities; then a seem-
ingly eternal period of pleasurable quiescence, during which the awakening
feelings are struggling into thought; then a brief resinking into non-entity;
then a sudden recovery. At length the slight quivering of an eyelid, and
immediately thereupon, an electric shock of a terror, deadly and indefi-
nite, which sends the blood in torrents from the temples to the heart. And
now the first positive effort to think. And now the first endeavor to remem-
ber. And now a partial and evanescent success. And now the memory has
so far regained its dominion that, in some measure, I am cognizant of my
state. I feel that I am not awaking from ordinary sleep. I recollect that I
have been subject to catalepsy. And now, at last, as if by the rush of an
ocean, my shuddering spirit is overwhelmed by the one grim Danger—by
the one spectral and ever-prevalent idea.

For some minutes after this fancy possessed me, I remained without
motion. And why? I could not summon courage to move. I dared not make

the effort which was to satisfy me of my fate—and yet there was something at my heart which whispered me *it was sure.* Despair—such as no other species of wretchedness ever calls into being—despair alone urged me, after long irresolution, to uplift the heavy lids of my eyes. I uplifted them. It was dark—all dark. I knew that the fit was over. I knew that the crisis of my disorder had long passed. I knew that I had now fully recovered the use of my visual faculties—and yet it was dark—all dark—the intense and utter raylessness of the Night that endureth for evermore.

I endeavored to shriek; and my lips and my parched tongue moved convulsively together in the attempt—but no voice issued from the cavernous lungs, which, oppressed as if by the weight of some incumbent mountain, gasped and palpitated, with the heart, at every elaborate and struggling inspiration.

The movement of the jaws, in this effort to cry aloud, showed me that they were bound up, as is usual with the dead. I felt, too, that I lay upon some hard substance, and by something similar my sides were, also, closely compressed. So far, I had not ventured to stir any of my limbs—but now I violently threw up my arms, which had been lying at length, with the wrists crossed. They struck a solid wooden substance, which extended above my person at an elevation of not more than six inches from my face. I could no longer doubt that I reposed within a coffin at last.

And now, amid all my infinite miseries, came sweetly the cherub Hope—for I thought of my precautions. I writhed, and made spasmodic exertions to force open the lid: it would not move. I felt my wrists for the bell-rope: it was not to be found. And now the Comforter fled forever, and a still sterner Despair reigned triumphant; for I could not help perceiving the absence of the paddings which I had so carefully prepared—and then, too, there came suddenly to my nostrils the strong peculiar odor of moist earth. The conclusion was irresistible. I was *not* within the vault. I had fallen into a trance while absent from home—while among strangers—when, or how, I could not remember—and it was they who had buried me as a dog—nailed up in some common coffin—and thrust deep, deep, and forever, into some ordinary and nameless *grave.*

As this awful conviction forced itself, thus, into the innermost chambers of my soul, I once again struggled to cry aloud. And in this second endeavor I succeeded. A long, wild, and continuous shriek, or yell of agony, resounded through the realms of the subterranean Night.

"Hillo! hillo, there!" said a gruff voice in reply.

"What the devil's the matter now!" said a second.

"Get out o' that!" said a third.

"What do you mean by yowling in that ere kind of style, like a cattymount?"[2] said a fourth; and hereupon I was seized and shaken without ceremony, for several minutes, by a junto of very rough-looking individuals. They did not arouse me from my slumber—for I was wide awake when I screamed—but they restored me to the full possession of my memory.

This adventure occurred near Richmond, in Virginia. Accompanied by a friend, I had proceeded, upon a gunning expedition, some miles down the banks of the James River. Night approached, and we were overtaken by a storm. The cabin of a small sloop lying at anchor in the stream, and laden with garden mold, afforded us the only available shelter. We made the best of it, and passed the night on board. I slept in one of the only two berths in the vessel—and the berths of a sloop of sixty or twenty tons need scarcely be described. That which I occupied had no bedding of any kind. Its extreme width was eighteen inches. The distance of its bottom from the deck overhead was precisely the same. I found it a matter of exceeding difficulty to squeeze myself in. Nevertheless, I slept soundly, and the whole of my vision—for it was no dream, and no nightmare—arose naturally from the circumstances of my position—from my ordinary bias of thought—and from the difficulty, to which I have alluded, of collecting my senses, and especially of regaining my memory, for a long time after awaking from slumber. The men who shook me were the crew of the sloop, and some laborers engaged to unload it. From the load itself came the earthly smell. The bandage about the jaws was a silk handkerchief in which I had bound up my head, in default of my customary nightcap.

The tortures endured, however, were indubitably quite equal, for the time, to those of actual sepulture. They were fearfully—they were inconceivably hideous; but out of Evil proceeded Good; for their very excess wrought in my spirit an inevitable revulsion. My soul acquired tone—acquired temper. I went abroad. I took vigorous exercise. I breathed the free air of Heaven. I thought upon other subjects than Death. I discarded my medical books. *Buchan* I burned. I read no *Night Thoughts*—no fustian about churchyards—no bugaboo tales—*such as this*. In short, I became a new man, and lived a man's life. From that memorable night, I dismissed forever my charnal apprehensions, and with them vanished the cataleptic disorder, of which, perhaps, they had been less the consequence than the cause.

There are moments when, even to the sober eye of Reason, the world of our sad Humanity may assume the semblance of a Hell—but the imagination of man is no Carathis, to explore with impunity its every cavern. Alas! the grim legion of sepulchral terrors cannot be regarded as altogether fanciful—but, like the Demons in whose company Afrasiab made his voyage down the Oxus, they must sleep, or they will devour us—they must be suffered to slumber, or we perish.

THE FACTS IN THE CASE OF
M. VALDEMAR

Of course I shall not pretend to consider it any matter for wonder, that the extraordinary case of M. Valdemar has excited discussion. It would have been a miracle had it not—especially under the circumstances. Through the desire of all parties concerned, to keep the affair from the public, at least for the present, or until we had farther opportunities for investigation—through our endeavors to effect this—a garbled or exaggerated account made its way into society, and became the source of many unpleasant misrepresentations; and, very naturally, of a great deal of disbelief.

It is now rendered necessary that I give the *facts*—as far as I comprehend them myself. They are, succinctly, these:

My attention, for the last three years, had been repeatedly drawn to the subject of Mesmerism; and, about nine months ago, it occurred to me, quite suddenly, that in the series of experiments made hitherto, there had been a very remarkable and most unaccountable omission: no person had as yet been mesmerized *in articulo mortis*.[1] It remained to be seen, first, whether, in such condition, there existed in the patient any susceptibility to the magnetic influence; secondly, whether, if any existed, it was impaired or increased by the condition; thirdly, to what extent, or for how long a period, the encroachments of Death might be arrested by the process. There were other points to be ascertained, but these most excited my curiosity—the last in especial, from the immensely important character of its consequences.

In looking around me for some subject by whose means I might test these particulars, I was brought to think of my friend, M. Ernest Valdemar, the well-known compiler of the "Bibliotheca Forensica," and author (under the *nom de plume* of Issachar Marx) of the Polish versions of *Wallenstein* and *Gargantua*. M. Valdemar, who has resided principally at Harlem, N.Y., since the year 1839, is (or was) particularly noticeable for the extreme spareness of his person—his lower limbs much resembling those of John Randolph; and, also, for the whiteness of his whiskers, in violent contrast to the blackness of his hair—the latter, in consequence, being very generally mistaken for a wig. His temperament was markedly nervous, and rendered him a good subject for mesmeric experiment. On two or three occasions I had put him to sleep with little difficulty, but was disappointed in other results which his peculiar constitution had naturally led me to anticipate. His will was at no period positively, or thoroughly, under my control, and in regard to *clairvoyance*, I could accomplish with him nothing to be relied upon. I always attributed my failure at these points to the disordered state of his health. For some months previous to my becoming acquainted with him, his physicians had declared him in a confirmed phthisis. It was his custom, indeed, to speak calmly of his approaching dissolution, as of a matter neither to be avoided nor regretted.

When the ideas to which I have alluded first occurred to me, it was of course very natural that I should think of M. Valdemar. I knew the steady philosophy of the man too well to apprehend any scruples from *him*; and he had no relatives in America who would be likely to interfere. I spoke to him frankly upon the subject; and, to my surprise, his interest seemed vividly excited. I say to my surprise, for, although he had always yielded his person freely to my experiments, he had never before given me any tokens of sympathy with what I did. His disease was of that character which would admit of exact calculation in respect to the epoch of its termination in death; and it was finally arranged between us that he would send for me about twenty-four hours before the period announced by his physicians as that of his decease.

It is now rather more than seven months since I received, from M. Valdemar himself, the subjoined note:

My Dear P—,
You may as well come now. D—— and F—— are agreed that I cannot hold out beyond tomorrow midnight; and I think they have hit the time very nearly.

Valdemar

I received this note within half an hour after it was written, and in fifteen minutes more I was in the dying man's chamber. I had not seen him for ten days, and was appalled by the fearful alteration which the brief interval had wrought in him. His face wore a leaden hue; the eyes were utterly lusterless; and the emaciation was so extreme that the skin had been broken through by the cheek-bones. His expectoration was excessive. The pulse was barely perceptible. He retained, nevertheless, in a very remarkable manner, both his mental power and a certain degree of physical strength. He spoke with distinctness—took some palliative medicines without aid—and, when I entered the room, was occupied in penciling memoranda in a pocket-book. He was propped up in the bed by pillows. Doctors D—— and F—— were in attendance.

After pressing Valdemar's hand, I took these gentlemen aside, and obtained from them a minute account of the patient's condition. The left lung had been for eighteen months in a semi-osseous or cartilaginous state, and was, of course, entirely useless for all purposes of vitality. The right, in its upper portion, was also partially, if not thoroughly, ossified, while the lower region was merely a mass of purulent tubercles, running one into another. Several extensive perforations existed; and, at one point, permanent adhesion to the ribs had taken place. These appearances in the right lobe were of comparatively recent date. The ossification had proceeded with very unusual rapidity; no sign of it had been discovered a month before, and the adhesion had only been observed during the three previous days. Independently of the phthisis, the patient was suspected of aneurism of the aorta; but on this point the osseous symptoms rendered an exact diagnosis impossible. It was the opinion of both physicians that M. Valdemar would die about midnight on the morrow (Sunday). It was then seven o'clock on Saturday evening.

On quitting the invalid's bed-side to hold conversation with myself, Doctors D—— and F—— had bidden him a final farewell. It had not been their intention to return; but, at my request, they agreed to look in upon the patient about ten the next night.

When they had gone, I spoke freely with M. Valdemar on the subject of his approaching dissolution, as well as, more particularly, of the experiment proposed. He still professed himself quite willing and even anxious to have it made, and urged me to commence it at once. A male and a female nurse were in attendance; but I did not feel myself altogether at liberty to engage in a task of this character with no more reliable witnesses than these people, in case of sudden accident, might prove. I therefore

postponed operations until about eight the next night, when the arrival of a medical student with whom I had some acquaintance (Mr. Theodore L——l), relieved me from farther embarrassment. It had been my design, originally, to wait for the physicians; but I was induced to proceed, first, by the urgent entreaties of M. Valdemar, and secondly, by my conviction that I had not a moment to lose, as he was evidently sinking fast.

Mr. L——l was so kind as to accede to my desire that he would take notes of all that occurred; and it is from his memoranda that what I now have to relate is, for the most part, either condensed or copied *verbatim*.

It wanted about five minutes of eight when, taking the patient's hand, I begged him to state, as distinctly as he could, to Mr. L——l, whether he (M. Valdemar) was entirely willing that I should make the experiment of mesmerizing him in his then condition.

He replied feebly, yet quite audibly: "Yes, I wish to be, mesmerized"— adding immediately afterward: "I fear you have deferred it too long."

While he spoke thus, I commenced the passes which I had already found most effectual in subduing him. He was evidently influenced with the first lateral stroke of my hand across his forehead; but, although I exerted all my powers, no farther perceptible effect was induced until some minutes after ten o'clock, when Doctors D—— and F—— called, according to appointment. I explained to them, in a few words, what I designed, and as they opposed no objection, saying that the patient was already in the death agony, I proceeded without hesitation—exchanging, however, the lateral passes for downward ones, and directing my gaze entirely into the right eye of the sufferer.

By this time his pulse was imperceptible and his breathing was stertorous, and at intervals of half a minute.

This condition was nearly unaltered for a quarter of an hour. At the expiration of this period, however, a natural although a very deep sigh escaped the bosom of the dying man, and the stertorous breathing ceased—that is to say, its stertorousness was no longer apparent; the intervals were undiminished. The patient's extremities were of an icy coldness.

At five minutes before eleven, I perceived unequivocal signs of the mesmeric influence. The glassy roll of the eye was changed for that expression of uneasy *inward* examination which is never seen except in cases of sleep-waking, and which it is quite impossible to mistake. With a few rapid lateral passes I made the lids quiver, as in incipient sleep, and with a few more I closed them altogether. I was not satisfied, however, with this, but continued the manipulations vigorously, and with the fullest exertion of

the will, until I had completely stiffened the limbs of the slumberer, after placing them in a seemingly easy position. The legs were at full length; the arms were nearly so, and reposed on the bed at a moderate distance from the loins. The head was very slightly elevated.

When I had accomplished this, it was fully midnight, and I requested the gentlemen present to examine M. Valdemar's condition. After a few experiments, they admitted him to be in an unusually perfect state of mesmeric trance. The curiosity of both the physicians was greatly excited. Dr. D—— resolved at once to remain with the patient all night, while Dr. F—— took leave with a promise to return at daybreak. Mr. L——l and the nurses remained.

We left M. Valdemar entirely undisturbed until about three o'clock in the morning, when I approached him and found him in precisely the same condition as when Dr. F—— went away—that is to say, he lay in the same position; the pulse was imperceptible; the breathing was gentle (scarcely noticeable, unless through the application of a mirror to the lips); the eyes were closed naturally; and the limbs were as rigid and as cold as marble. Still, the general appearance was certainly not that of death.

As I approached M. Valdemar I made a kind of half effort to influence his right arm into pursuit of my own, as I passed the latter gently to and fro above his person. In such experiments with this patient had never perfectly succeeded before, and assuredly I had little thought of succeeding now; but to my astonishment, his arm very readily, although feebly, followed every direction I assigned it with mine. I determined to hazard a few words of conversation.

"M. Valdemar," I said, "are you asleep?" He made no answer, but I perceived a tremor about the lips, and was thus induced to repeat the question, again and again. At its third repetition, his whole frame was agitated by a very slight shivering; the eyelids unclosed themselves so far as to display a white line of a ball; the lips moved sluggishly, and from between them, in a barely audible whisper, issued the words:

"Yes—asleep now. Do not wake me!—let me die so!"

I here felt the limbs, and found them as rigid as ever. The right arm, as before, obeyed the direction of my hand. I questioned the sleep-waker again:

"Do you still feel pain in the breast, M. Valdemar?"

The answer now was immediate, but even less audible than before:

"No pain—I am dying!"

I did not think it advisable to disturb him farther just then, and nothing more was said or done until the arrival of Dr. F——, who came a little before sunrise, and expressed unbounded astonishment at finding the patient still alive. After feeling the pulse and applying a mirror to the lips, he requested me to speak to the sleep-waker again. I did so, saying:

"M. Valdemar, do you still sleep?"

As before, some minutes elapsed ere a reply was made; and during the interval the dying man seemed to be collecting his energies to speak. At my fourth repetition of the question, he said very faintly, almost inaudibly:

"Yes; still asleep—dying."

It was now the opinion, or rather the wish, of the physicians, that M. Valdemar should be suffered to remain undisturbed in his present apparently tranquil condition, until death should supervene—and this, it was generally agreed, must now take place within a few minutes. I concluded, however, to speak to him once more, and merely repeated my previous question.

While I spoke, there came a marked change over the countenance of the sleep-waker. The eyes rolled themselves slowly open, the pupils disappearing upwardly; the skin generally assumed a cadaverous hue, resembling not so much parchment as white paper; and the circular hectic spots which, hitherto, had been strongly defined in the center of each cheek, *went out* at once. I use this expression, because the suddenness of their departure put me in mind of nothing so much as the extinguishment of a candle by a puff of the breath. The upper lip, at the same time, writhed itself away from the teeth, which it had previously covered completely; while the lower jaw fell with an audible jerk, leaving the mouth widely extended, and disclosing in full view the swollen and blackened tongue. I presume that no member of the party then present had been unaccustomed to death-bed horrors; but so hideous beyond conception was the appearance of M. Valdemar at this moment, that there was a general shrinking back from the region of the bed.

I now feel that I have reached a point of this narrative at which every reader will be startled into positive disbelief. It is my business, however, simply to proceed.

There was no longer the faintest sign of vitality in M. Valdemar; and concluding him to be dead, we were consigning him to the charge of the nurses, when a strong vibratory motion was observable in the tongue. This continued for perhaps a minute. At the expiration of this period, there issued from the distended and motionless jaws a voice—such as it would

be madness in me to attempt describing. There are, indeed, two or three epithets which might be considered as applicable to it in part; I might say, for example, that the sound was harsh, and broken and hollow; but the hideous whole is indescribable, for the simple reason that no similar sounds have ever jarred upon the ear of humanity. There were two particulars, nevertheless, which I thought then, and still think, might fairly be stated as characteristic of the intonation—as well adapted to convey some idea of its unearthly peculiarity. In the first place, the voice seemed to reach our ears—at least mine—from a vast distance, or from some deep cavern within the earth. In the second place, it impressed me (I fear, indeed, that it will be impossible to make myself comprehended) as gelatinous or glutinous matters impress the sense of touch.

I have spoken both of "sound" and of "voice." I mean to say that the sound was one of distinct—of even wonderfully, thrillingly distinct—syllabification. M. Valdemar *spoke*—obviously in reply to the question I had propounded to him a few minutes before. I had asked him, it will be remembered, if he still slept. He now said:

"Yes!—no;—I *have been* sleeping—and now—now—I *am dead*."

No person present even affected to deny, or attempted to repress, the unutterable, shuddering horror which these few words, thus uttered, were so well calculated to convey. Mr. L——l (the student) swooned. The nurses immediately left the chamber, and could not be induced to return. My own impressions I would not pretend to render intelligible to the reader. For nearly an hour, we busied ourselves, silently—without the utterance of a word—in endeavors to revive Mr. L——l. When he came to himself, we addressed ourselves again to an investigation of M. Valdemar's condition.

It remained in all respects as I have last described it, with the exception that the mirror no longer afforded evidence of respiration. An attempt to draw blood from the arm failed. I should mention, too, that this limb was no farther subject to my will. I endeavored in vain to make it follow the direction of my hand. The only real indication, indeed, of the mesmeric influence, was now found in the vibratory movement of the tongue, whenever I addressed M. Valdemar a question. He seemed to be making an effort to reply, but had no longer sufficient volition. To queries put to him by any other person than myself he seemed utterly insensible—although I endeavored to place each member of the company in mesmeric *rapport* with him. I believe that I have now related all that is necessary to an understanding of the sleep-waker's state at this epoch. Other nurses

were procured; and at ten o'clock I left the house in company with the two physicians and Mr. L——l.

In the afternoon we all called again to see the patient. His condition remained precisely the same. We had now some discussion as to the propriety and feasibility of awakening him; but we had little difficulty in agreeing that no good purpose would be served by so doing. It was evident that, so far, death (or what is usually termed death) had been arrested by the mesmeric process. It seemed clear to us all that to awaken M. Valdemar would be merely to insure his instant, or at least his speedy, dissolution.

From this period until the close of last week—*an interval of nearly seven months*—we continued to make daily calls at M. Valdemar's house, accompanied, now and then, by medical and other friends. All this time the sleeper-waker remained exactly as I have last described him. The nurses' attentions were continual.

It was on Friday last that we finally resolved to make the experiment of awakening, or attempting to awaken him; and it is the (perhaps) unfortunate result of this latter experiment which has given rise to so much discussion in private circles—to so much of what I cannot help thinking unwarranted popular feeling.

For the purpose of relieving M. Valdemar from the mesmeric trance, I made use of the customary passes. These, for a time, were unsuccessful. The first indication of revival was afforded by a partial descent of the iris. It was observed, as especially remarkable, that this lowering of the pupil was accompanied by the profuse outflowing of a yellowish ichor (from beneath the lids) of a pungent and highly offensive odor.

It was now suggested that I should attempt to influence the patient's arm as heretofore. I made the attempt and failed. Dr. F—— then intimated a desire to have me put a question. I did so, as follows:

"M. Valdemar, can you explain to us what are your feelings or wishes now?"

There was an instant return of the hectic circles on the cheeks: the tongue quivered, or rather rolled violently in the mouth (although the jaws and lips remained rigid as before), and at length the same hideous voice which I have already described, broke forth:

"For God's sake!—quick!—quick!—put me to sleep—or, quick!—waken me!—quick!—*I say to you that I am dead!*"

I was thoroughly unnerved, and for an instant remained undecided what to do. At first I made an endeavor to recompose the patient; but, failing in this through total abeyance of the will, I retracted my steps and

as earnestly struggled to awaken him. In this attempt I soon saw that I should be successful—or at least I soon fancied that my success would be complete—and I am sure that all in the room were prepared to see the patient awaken.

For what really occurred, however, it is quite impossible that any human being could have been prepared.

As I rapidly made the mesmeric passes, amid ejaculations of "dead! dead!" absolutely *bursting* from the tongue and not from the lips of the sufferer, his whole frame at once—within the space of a single minute, or even less, shrunk—crumbled, absolutely *rotted* away beneath my hands. Upon the bed, before that whole company, there lay a nearly liquid mass of loathsome—of detestable putridity.

THE CASK OF AMONTILLADO

THE THOUSAND INJURIES OF FORTUNATO I HAD BORNE AS I BEST COULD; but when he ventured upon insult, I vowed revenge. You, who so well know the nature of my soul, will not suppose, however, that I gave utterance to a threat. *At length* I would be avenged; this was a point definitively settled—but the very definitiveness with which it was resolved, precluded the idea of risk. I must not only punish, but punish with impunity. A wrong is unredressed when retribution overtakes its redresser. It is equally unredressed when the avenger fails to make himself felt as such to him who has done the wrong.

It must be understood, that neither by word nor deed had I given Fortunato cause to doubt my good will. I continued, as was my wont, to smile in his face, and he did not perceive that my smile *now* was at the thought of his immolation.

He had a weak point—this Fortunato—although in other regards he was a man to be respected and even feared. He prided himself on his connoisseurship in wine. Few Italians have the true virtuoso spirit. For the most part their enthusiasm is adopted to suit the time and opportunity—to practice imposture upon the British and Austrian *millionaires*. In painting and gemmary, Fortunato, like his countrymen, was a quack—but in the matter of old wines he was sincere. In this respect I did not differ from him materially: I was skilful in the Italian vintages myself, and bought largely whenever I could.

It was about dusk, one evening during the supreme madness of the carnival season, that I encountered my friend. He accosted me with excessive warmth, for he had been drinking much. The man wore motley. He

had on a tight-fitting parti-striped dress, and his head was surmounted by the conical cap and bells. I was so pleased to see him, that I thought I should never have done wringing his hand.

I said to him—"My dear Fortunato, you are luckily met. How remarkably well you are looking today! But I have received a pipe of what passes for Amontillado, and I have my doubts."

"How?" said he. "Amontillado? A pipe? Impossible! And in the middle of the carnival!"

"I have my doubts," I replied; "and I was silly enough to pay the full Amontillado price without consulting you in the matter. You were not to be found, and I was fearful of losing a bargain."

"Amontillado!"

"I have my doubts."

"Amontillado!"

"And I must satisfy them."

"Amontillado!"

"As you are engaged, I am on my way to Luchesi. If anyone has a critical turn, it is he. He will tell me—"

"Luchesi cannot tell Amontillado from Sherry."

"And yet some fools will have it that his taste is a match for your own."

"Come, let us go."

"Whither?"

"To your vaults."

"My friend, no; I will not impose upon your good nature. I perceive you have an engagement. Luchesi—"

"I have no engagement; come."

"My friend, no. It is not the engagement, but the severe cold with which I perceive you are afflicted. The vaults are insufferably damp. They are encrusted with niter."

"Let us go, nevertheless. The cold is merely nothing. Amontillado! You have been imposed upon. And as for Luchesi, he cannot distinguish Sherry from Amontillado."

Thus speaking, Fortunato possessed himself of my arm. Putting on a mask of black silk, and drawing a *roquelaire* closely about my person, I suffered him to hurry me to my palazzo.

There were no attendants at home; they had absconded to make merry in honor of the time. I had told them that I should not return until the morning, and had given them explicit orders not to stir from the house.

These orders were sufficient, I well knew, to insure their immediate disappearance, one and all, as soon as my back was turned.

I took from their sconces two flambeaux, and giving one to Fortunato, bowed him through several suites of rooms to the archway that led into the vaults. I passed down a long and winding staircase, requesting him to be cautious as he followed. We came at length to the foot of the descent, and stood together on the damp ground of the catacombs of the Montresors.

The gait of my friend was unsteady, and the bells upon his cap jingled as he strode.

"The pipe," said he.

"It is farther on," said I; "but observe the white web-work which gleams from these cavern walls."

He turned towards me, and looked into my eyes with two filmy orbs that distilled the rheum of intoxication.

"Niter?" he asked, at length.

"Niter," I replied. "How long have you had that cough?"

"Ugh! ugh! ugh!—ugh! ugh! ugh!—ugh! ugh! ugh!—ugh! ugh! ugh!—ugh! ugh! ugh!"

My poor friend found it impossible to reply for many minutes.

"It is nothing," he said, at last.

"Come," I said, with decision, "we will go back; your health is precious. You are rich, respected, admired, beloved; you are happy, as once I was. You are a man to be missed. For me it is no matter. We will go back; you will be ill, and I cannot be responsible. Besides, there is Luchesi—"

"Enough," he said; "the cough is a mere nothing; it will not kill me. I shall not die of a cough."

"True—true," I replied; "and, indeed, I had no intention of alarming you unnecessarily—but you should use all proper caution. A draught of this Medoc will defend us from the damps."

Here I knocked off the neck of a bottle which I drew from a long row of its fellows that lay upon the mold.

"Drink," I said, presenting him the wine.

He raised it to his lips with a leer. He paused and nodded to me familiarly, while his bells jingled.

"I drink," he said, "to the buried that repose around us."

"And I to your long life."

He again took my arm, and we proceeded.

"These vaults," he said, "are extensive."

"The Montresors," I replied, "were a great and numerous family."

"I forget your arms."

"A huge human foot d'or, in a field azure; the foot crushes a serpent rampant whose fangs are embedded in the heel."

"And the motto?"

"Nemo me impune lacessit."[1]

"Good!" he said.

The wine sparkled in his eyes and the bells jingled. My own fancy grew warm with the Medoc. We had passed through walls of piled bones, with casks and puncheons intermingling, into the inmost recesses of the catacombs. I paused again, and this time I made bold to seize Fortunato by an arm above the elbow.

"The niter!" I said: "see, it increases. It hangs like moss upon the vaults. We are below the river's bed. The drops of moisture trickle among the bones. Come, we will go back ere it is too late. Your cough—"

"It is nothing," he said; "let us go on. But first, another draught of the Medoc."

I broke and reached him a flaçon of De Grâve. He emptied it at a breath. His eyes flashed with a fierce light. He laughed and threw the bottle upwards with a gesticulation I did not understand.

I looked at him in surprise. He repeated the movement—a grotesque one.

"You do not comprehend?" he said.

"Not I," I replied.

"Then you are not of the brotherhood."

"How?"

"You are not of the masons."

"Yes, yes," I said, "yes, yes."

"You? Impossible! A mason?"

"A mason," I replied.

"A sign," he said.

"It is this," I answered, producing a trowel from beneath the folds of my *roquelaire.*

"You jest," he exclaimed, recoiling a few paces. "But let us proceed to the Amontillado."

"Be it so," I said, replacing the tool beneath the cloak, and again offering him my arm. He leaned upon it heavily. We continued our route in search of the Amontillado. We passed through a range of low arches, descended, passed on, and descending again, arrived at a deep

crypt, in which the foulness of the air caused our flambeaux rather to glow than flame.

At the most remote end of the crypt there appeared another less spacious. Its walls had been lined with human remains, piled to the vault overhead, in the fashion of the great catacombs of Paris. Three sides of this interior crypt were still ornamented in this manner. From the fourth the bones had been thrown down, and lay promiscuously upon the earth, forming at one point a mound of some size. Within the wall thus exposed by the displacing of the bones, we perceived a still interior recess, in depth about four feet, in width three, in height six or seven. It seemed to have been constructed for no especial use within itself, but formed merely the interval between two of the colossal supports of the roof of the catacombs, and was backed by one of their circumscribing walls of solid granite.

It was in vain that Fortunato, uplifting his dull torch, endeavored to pry into the depths of the recess. Its termination the feeble light did not enable us to see.

"Proceed," I said; "herein is the Amontillado. As for Luchesi—"

"He is an ignoramus," interrupted my friend, as he stepped unsteadily forward, while I followed immediately at his heels. In an instant he had reached the extremity of the niche, and finding his progress arrested by the rock, stood stupidly bewildered. A moment more and I had fettered him to the granite. In its surface were two iron staples, distant from each other about two feet, horizontally. From one of these depended a short chain, from the other a padlock. Throwing the links about his waist, it was but the work of a few seconds to secure it. He was too much astounded to resist. Withdrawing the key I stepped back from the recess.

"Pass your hand," I said, "over the wall; you cannot help feeling the niter. Indeed it is *very* damp. Once more let me *implore* you to return. No? Then I must positively leave you. But I must first render you all the little attentions in my power."

"The Amontillado!" ejaculated my friend, not yet recovered from his astonishment.

"True," I replied; "the Amontillado."

As I said these words I busied myself among the pile of bones of which I have before spoken. Throwing them aside, I soon uncovered a quantity of building stone and mortar. With these materials and with the aid of my trowel, I began vigorously to wall up the entrance of the niche.

I had scarcely laid the first tier of my masonry when I discovered that the intoxication of Fortunato had in a great measure worn off. The earliest

indication I had of this was a low moaning cry from the depth of the recess. It was *not* the cry of a drunken man. There was then a long and obstinate silence. I laid the second tier, and the third, and the fourth; and then I heard the furious vibrations of the chain. The noise lasted for several minutes, during which, that I might harken to it with the more satisfaction, I ceased my labors and sat down upon the bones. When at last the clanking subsided, I resumed the trowel, and finished without interruption the fifth, the sixth, and the seventh tier. The wall was now nearly upon a level with my breast. I again paused, and holding the flambeaux over the masonwork, threw a few feeble rays upon the figure within.

A succession of loud and shrill screams, bursting suddenly from the throat of the chained form, seemed to thrust me violently back. For a brief moment I hesitated—I trembled. Unsheathing my rapier, I began to grope with it about the recess; but the thought of an instant reassured me. I placed my hand upon the solid fabric of the catacombs, and felt satisfied. I reapproached the wall. I replied to the yells of him who clamored. I re-echoed—I aided—I surpassed them in volume and in strength. I did this, and the clamorer grew still.

It was now midnight, and my task was drawing to a close. I had completed the eighth, the ninth, and the tenth tier. I had finished a portion of the last and the eleventh; there remained but a single stone to be fitted and plastered in. I struggled with its weight; I placed it partially in its destined position. But now there came from out the niche a low laugh that erected the hairs upon my head. It was succeeded by a sad voice, which I had difficulty in recognizing as that of the noble Fortunato. The voice said—

"Ha! ha! ha!—he! he!—a very good joke indeed—an excellent jest. We will have many a rich laugh about it at the palazzo—he! he! he!—over our wine—he! he! he!"

"The Amontillado!" I said.

"He! he! he!—he! he! he!—yes, the Amontillado. But is it not getting late? Will not they be awaiting us at the palazzo, the Lady Fortunato and the rest? Let us be gone."

"Yes," I said, "let us be gone."

"For the love of God, Montresor!"

"Yes," I said, "for the love of God!"

But to these words I harkened in vain for a reply. I grew impatient. I called aloud—

"Fortunato!"

No answer. I called again—

"Fortunato!"

No answer still. I thrust a torch through the remaining aperture and let it fall within. There came forth in return only a jingling of the bells. My heart grew sick—on account of the dampness of the catacombs. I hastened to make an end of my labor. I forced the last stone into its position; I plastered it up. Against the new masonry I re-erected the old rampart of bones. For the half of a century no mortal has disturbed them. *In pace requiescat!*

HOP-FROG

I NEVER KNEW ANYONE SO KEENLY ALIVE TO A JOKE AS THE KING WAS. HE seemed to live only for joking. To tell a good story of the joke kind, and to tell it well, was the surest road to his favor. Thus it happened that his seven ministers were all noted for their accomplishments as jokers. They all took after the king, too, in being large, corpulent, oily men, as well as inimitable jokers. Whether people grow fat by joking, or whether there is something in fat itself which predisposes to a joke, I have never been quite able to determine; but certain it is that a lean joker is a *rara avis in terris*.

About the refinements, or, as he called them, the "ghosts" of wit, the king troubled himself very little. He had an especial admiration for *breadth* in a jest, and would often put up with *length*, for the sake of it. Over-niceties wearied him. He would have preferred Rabelais' *Gargantua* to the *Zadig* of Voltaire: and, upon the whole, practical jokes suited his taste far better than verbal ones.

At the date of my narrative, professing jesters had not altogether gone out of fashion at court. Several of the great continental "powers" still retained their "fools," who wore motley, with caps and bells, and who were expected to be always ready with sharp witticisms, at a moment's notice, in consideration of the crumbs that fell from the royal table.

Our king, as a matter of course, retained his "fool." The fact is, he *required* something in the way of folly—if only to counterbalance the heavy wisdom of the seven wise men who were his ministers—not to mention himself.

His fool, or professional jester, was not *only* a fool, however. His value was trebled in the eyes of the king, by the fact of his being also a dwarf and a cripple. Dwarfs were as common at court, in those days, as fools; and many

monarchs would have found it difficult to get through their days (days are rather longer at court than elsewhere) without both a jester to laugh *with,* and a dwarf to laugh *at.* But, as I have already observed, your jesters, in ninety-nine cases out of a hundred, are fat, round, and unwieldy—so that it was no small source of self-gratulation with our king that, in Hop-Frog (this was the fool's name), he possessed a triplicate treasure in one person.

I believe the name "Hop-Frog" was *not* that given to the dwarf by his sponsors at baptism, but it was conferred upon him, by general consent of the several ministers, on account of his inability to walk as other men do. In fact, Hop-Frog could only get along by a sort of interjectional gait—something between a leap and a wriggle—a movement that afforded illimitable amusement, and of course consolation, to the king, for (notwithstanding the protuberance of his stomach and a constitutional swelling of the head) the king, by his whole court, was accounted a capital figure.

But although Hop-Frog, through the distortion of his legs, could move only with great pain and difficulty along a road or floor, the prodigious muscular power which nature seemed to have bestowed upon his arms, by way of compensation for deficiency in the lower limbs, enabled him to perform many feats of wonderful dexterity, where trees or ropes were in question, or anything else to climb. At such exercises he certainly much more resembled a squirrel, or a small monkey, than a frog.

I am not able to say, with precision, from what country Hop-Frog originally came. It was from some barbarous region, however, that no person ever heard of—a vast distance from the court of our king. Hop-Frog, and a young girl very little less dwarfish than himself (although of exquisite proportions, and a marvelous dancer), had been forcibly carried off from their respective homes in adjoining provinces, and sent as presents to the king, by one of his ever-victorious generals.

Under these circumstances, it is not to be wondered at that a close intimacy arose between the two little captives. Indeed, they soon became sworn friends. Hop-Frog, who, although he made a great deal of sport, was by no means popular, had it not in his power to render Trippetta many services; but *she,* on account of her grace and exquisite beauty (although a dwarf), was universally admired and petted: so she possessed much influence; and never failed to use it, whenever she could, for the benefit of Hop-Frog.

On some grand state occasion—I forgot what—the king determined to have a masquerade; and whenever a masquerade, or anything of that

kind, occurred at our court, then the talents both of Hop-Frog and Trippetta were sure to be called into play. Hop-Frog, in especial, was so inventive in the way of getting up pageants, suggesting novel characters, and arranging costume, for masked balls, that nothing could be done, it seems, without his assistance.

The night appointed for the *fête* had arrived. A gorgeous hall had been fitted up, under Trippetta's eye, with every kind of device which could possibly give *éclât* to a masquerade. The whole court was in a fever of expectation. As for costumes and characters, it might well be supposed that everybody had come to a decision on such points. Many had made up their minds (as to what *rôles* they should assume) a week, or even a month, in advance; and, in fact, there was not a particle of indecision anywhere—except in the case of the king and his seven minsters. Why *they* hesitated I never could tell, unless they did it by way of a joke. More probably, they found it difficult, on account of being so fat, to make up their minds. At all events, time flew; and, as a last resource, they sent for Trippetta and Hop-Frog.

When the two little friends obeyed the summons of the king, they found him sitting at his wine with the seven members of his cabinet council; but the monarch appeared to be in a very ill humor. He knew that Hop-Frog was not fond of wine; for it excited the poor cripple almost to madness; and madness is no comfortable feeling. But the king loved his practical jokes, and took pleasure in forcing Hop-Frog to drink and (as the king called it) "to be merry."

"Come here, Hop Frog," said he, as the jester and his friend entered the room: "swallow this bumper to the health of your absent friends [here Hop-Frog sighed], and then let us have the benefit of your invention. We want characters—*characters*, man—something novel—out of the way. We are wearied with this everlasting sameness. Come, drink! the wine will brighten your wits."

Hop-Frog endeavored, as usual, to get up a jest in reply to these advances from the king; but the effort was too much. It happened to be the poor dwarf's birthday, and the command to drink to his "absent friends" forced the tears to his eyes. Many large, bitter drops fell into the goblet as he took it, humbly, from the hand of the tyrant.

"Ah! ha! ha! ha!" roared the latter, as the dwarf reluctantly drained the beaker. "See what a glass of good wine can do! Why, your eyes are shining already!"

Poor fellow! His large eyes *gleamed,* rather than shone; for the effect of wine on his excitable brain was not more powerful than instantaneous. He

placed the goblet nervously on the table, and looked round upon the company with a half-insane stare. They all seemed highly amused at the success of the king's *"joke."*

"And now to business," said the prime minister, a *very* fat man.

"Yes," said the king; "come, Hop-Frog, lend us your assistance. Characters, my fine fellow; we stand in need of characters—all of us—ha! ha! ha!" and as this was seriously meant for a joke, his laugh was chorused by the seven.

Hop-Frog also laughed, although feebly and somewhat vacantly.

"Come, come," said the king, impatiently, "have you nothing to suggest?"

"I am endeavoring to think of something *novel*," replied the dwarf, abstractedly, for he was quite bewildered by the wine.

"Endeavoring!" cried the tyrant, fiercely; "what do you mean by *that?* Ah, I perceive. You are sulky, and want more wine. Here, drink this!" and he poured out another goblet full and offered it to the cripple, who merely gazed at it, gasping for breath.

"Drink, I say!" shouted the monster, "or by the fiends—"

The dwarf hesitated. The king grew purple with rage. The courtiers smirked. Trippetta, pale as a corpse, advanced to the monarch's seat, and, falling on her knees before him, implored him to spare her friend.

The tyrant regarded her, for some moments, in evident wonder at her audacity. He seemed quite at a loss what to do or say—how most becomingly to express his indignation. At last, without uttering a syllable, he pushed her violently from him, and threw the contents of the brimming goblet in her face.

The poor girl got up as best she could, and, not daring even to sigh, resumed her position at the foot of the table.

There was a dead silence for about half a minute, during which the falling of a leaf, or of a feather, might have been heard. It was interrupted by a low, but harsh and protracted *grating* sound which seemed to come at once from every corner of the room.

"What—what—*what* are you making that noise for?" demanded the king, turning furiously to the dwarf.

The latter seemed to have recovered, in great measure, from his intoxication, and looking fixedly but quietly into the tyrant's face, merely ejaculated:

"I—I? How could it have been me?"

"The sound appeared to come from without," observed one of the courtiers. "I fancy it was the parrot at the window, whetting his bill upon his cage-wires."

"True," replied the monarch, as if much relieved by the suggestion; "but, on the honor of a knight, I could have sworn that it was the gritting of this vagabond's teeth."

Hereupon the dwarf laughed (the king was too confirmed a joker to object to anyone's laughing), and displayed a set of large, powerful, and very repulsive teeth. Moreover, he avowed his perfect willingness to swallow as much wine as desired. The monarch was pacified; and having drained another bumper with no very perceptible ill effect, Hop-Frog entered at once, and with spirit, into the plans for the masquerade.

"I cannot tell what was the association of idea," observed he, very tranquilly, and as if he had never tasted wine in his life, "but *just after* your majesty had struck the girl and thrown the wine in her face—*just after* your majesty had done this, and while the parrot was making that odd noise outside the window, there came into my mind a capital diversion—one of my own country frolics—often enacted among us, at our masquerades: but here it will be new altogether. Unfortunately, however, it requires a company of eight persons, and—"

"Here we *are!*" cried the king, laughing at his acute discovery of the coincidence; "eight to a fraction—I and my seven ministers. Come! what is the diversion?"

"We call it," replied the cripple, "the Eight Chained Ourang-Outangs, and it really is excellent sport if well enacted."

"*We* will enact it," remarked the king, drawing himself up, and lowering his eyelids.

"The beauty of the game," continued Hop-Frog, "lies in the fright it occasions among the women."

"Capital!" roared in chorus the monarch and his ministry.

"*I* will equip you as ourang-outangs," proceeded the dwarf; "leave all that to me. The resemblance shall be so striking, that the company of masqueraders will take you for real beasts—and of course, they will be as much terrified as astonished."

"O, this is exquisite!" exclaimed the king. "Hop-Frog! I will make a man of you."

"The chains are for the purpose of increasing the confusion by their jangling. You are supposed to have escaped, *en masse*, from your keepers. Your majesty cannot conceive the *effect* produced, at a masquerade, by eight chained ourang-outangs, imagined to be real ones by most of the company; and rushing in with savage cries, among the crowd of delicately and gorgeously habited men and women. The *contrast* is inimitable!"

"It *must* be," said the king: and the council arose hurriedly (as it was growing late), to put in execution the scheme of Hop-Frog.

His mode of equipping the party as ourang-outangs was very simple, but effective enough for his purposes. The animals in question had, at the epoch of my story, very rarely been seen in any part of the civilized world; and as the imitations made by the dwarf were sufficiently beast-like and more than sufficiently hideous, their truthfulness to nature was thus thought to be secured.

The king and his ministers were first encased in tight-fitting stockinet shirts and drawers. They were then saturated with tar. At this stage of the process, someone of the party suggested feathers; but the suggestion was at once overruled by the dwarf, who soon convinced the eight, by ocular demonstration, that the hair of such a brute as the ourang-outang was much more efficiently represented by *flax*. A thick coating of the latter was accordingly plastered upon the coating of tar. A long chain was now procured. First, it was passed about the waist of the king, *and tied*; then about another of the party, and also tied; then about all successively, in the same manner. When this chaining arrangement was complete, and the party stood as far apart from each other as possible, they formed a circle; and to make all things appear natural, Hop-Frog passed the residue of the chain, in two diameters, at right angles, across the circle, after the fashion adopted, at the present day, by those who capture Chimpanzees, or other large apes, in Borneo.

The grand saloon in which the masquerade was to take place, was a circular room, very lofty, and receiving the light of the sun only through a single window at top. At night (the season for which the apartment was especially designed), it was illuminated principally by a large chandelier, depending by a chain from the center of the sky-light, and lowered, or elevated, by means of a counterbalance as usual; but (in order not to look unsightly) this latter passed outside the cupola and over the roof.

The arrangements of the room had been left to Trippetta's superintendance; but, in some particulars, it seems, she had been guided by the calmer judgment of her friend the dwarf. At his suggestion it was that, on this occasion, the chandelier was removed. Its waxen drippings (which, in weather so warm, it was quite impossible to prevent), would have been seriously detrimental to the rich dresses of the guests, who, on account of the crowded state of the saloon, could not *all* be expected to keep from out its center—that is to say, from under the chandelier. Additional sconces were set in various parts of the hall, out of the way; and a flambeau,

emitting sweet odor, was placed in the right hand of each of the Caryatides that stood against the wall—some fifty or sixty altogether.

The eight ourang-outangs, taking Hop-Frog's advice, waited patiently until midnight (when the room was thoroughly filled with masqueraders) before making their appearance. No sooner had the clock ceased striking, however, than they rushed, or rather rolled in, all together—for the impediment of their chains caused most of the party to fall, and all to stumble as they entered.

The excitement among the masqueraders was prodigious, and filled the heart of the king with glee. As had been anticipated, there were not a few of the guests who supposed the ferocious-looking creatures to be beasts of *some* kind in reality, if not precisely ourang-outangs. Many of the women swooned with affright; and had not the king taken the precaution to exclude all weapons from the saloon, his party might soon have expiated their frolic in their blood. As it was, a general rush was made for the doors; but the king had ordered them to be locked immediately upon his entrance; and, at the dwarf's suggestion, the keys had been deposited with *him*.

While the tumult was at its height, and each masquerader attentive only to his own safety—(for, in fact, there was much *real* danger from the pressure of the excited crowd)—the chain by which the chandelier ordinarily hung, and which had been drawn up on its removal, might have been seen very gradually to descend, until its hooked extremity came within three feet of the floor.

Soon after this, the king and his seven friends, having reeled about the hall in all directions, found themselves, at length, in its center, and, of course, in immediate contact with the chain. While they were thus situated, the dwarf, who had followed closely at their heels, inciting them to keep up the commotion, took hold of their own chain at the intersection of the two portions which crossed the circle diametrically and at right angles. Here, with the rapidity of thought, he inserted the hook from which the chandelier had been wont to depend; and, in an instant, by some unseen agency, the chandelier-chain was drawn so far upwards as to take the hook out of reach, and, as an inevitable consequence, to drag the ourang-outangs together in close connection, and face to face.

The masqueraders, by this time, had recovered, in some measure, from their alarm; and, beginning to regard the whole matter as a well-contrived pleasantry, set up a loud shout of laughter at the predicament of the apes.

"Leave them to *me!*" now screamed Hop-Frog, his shrill voice making itself easily heard through all the din. "Leave them to *me*. I fancy *I* know them. If I can only get a good look at them, *I* can soon tell who they are."

Here, scrambling over the heads of the crowd, he managed to get to the wall; when, seizing a flambeau from one of the Caryatides, he returned, as he went, to the center of the room—leaping, with the agility of a monkey, upon the king's head—and thence clambered a few feet up the chain—holding down the torch to examine the group of ourang-outangs, and still screaming, "*I* shall soon find out who they are!"

And now, while the whole assembly (the apes included) were convulsed with laughter, the jester suddenly uttered a shrill whistle; when the chain flew violently up for about thirty feet—dragging with it the dismayed and struggling ourang-outangs, and leaving them suspended in midair between the sky-light and the floor. Hop-Frog, clinging to the chain as it rose, still maintained his relative position in respect to the eight maskers, and still (as if nothing were the matter) continued to thrust his torch down towards them, as though endeavoring to discover who they were.

So thoroughly astonished were the whole company at this ascent, that a dead silence, of about a minute's duration, ensued. It was broken by just such a low, harsh, *grating* sound, as had before attracted the attention of the king and his councilors, when the former threw the wine in the face of Trippetta. But, on the present occasion, there could be no question as to *whence* the sound issued. It came from the fang-like teeth of the dwarf, who ground them and gnashed them as he foamed at the mouth, and glared, with an expression of maniacal rage, into the upturned countenances of the king and his seven companions.

"Ah, ha!" said at length the infuriated jester. "Ah, ha! I begin to see who these people *are,* now!" Here, pretending to scrutinize the king more closely, he held the flambeau to the flaxen coat which enveloped him, and which instantly burst into a sheet of vivid flame. In less than half a minute the whole eight ourang-outangs were blazing fiercely, amid the shrieks of the multitude who gazed at them from below, horror-stricken, and without the power to render them the slightest assistance.

At length the flames, suddenly increasing in virulence, forced the jester to climb higher up the chain, to be out of their reach; and, as he made this movement, the crowd again sank, for a brief instant, into silence. The dwarf seized his opportunity, and once more spoke:

"I now see *distinctly,*" he said, "what manner of people these maskers are. They are a great king and his seven privy-councillors—a king who

does not scruple to strike a defenceless girl, and his seven councillors who abet him in the outrage. As for myself, I am simply Hop-Frog, the jester— and *this is my last jest.*"

Owing to the high combustibility of both the flax and the tar to which it adhered, the dwarf had scarcely made an end of his brief speech before the work of vengeance was complete. The eight corpses swung in their chains, a fetid, blackened, hideous, and indistinguishable mass. The cripple hurled his torch at them, clambered leisurely to the ceiling, and disappeared through the sky-light.

It is supposed that Trippetta, stationed on the roof of the saloon, had been the accomplice of her friend in his fiery revenge, and that, together, they effected their escape to their own country: for neither was seen again.

TALES OF DETECTION

The Murders in the
Rue Morgue

*What song the Syrens sang, or what name Achilles assumed when
he hid himself among women, although puzzling questions, are not
beyond all conjecture.*

—SIR THOMAS BROWNE

THE MENTAL FEATURES DISCOURSED OF AS THE ANALYTICAL, ARE, IN
themselves, but little susceptible of analysis. We appreciate them only
in their effects. We know of them, among other things, that they are always
to their possessor, when inordinately possessed, a source of the liveliest
enjoyment. As the strong man exults in his physical ability, delighting in
such exercises as call his muscles into action, so glories the analyst in that
moral activity which *disentangles.* He derives pleasure from even the most
trivial occupations bringing his talent into play. He is fond of enigmas, of
conundrums, of hieroglyphics; exhibiting in his solutions of each a degree
of *acumen* which appears to the ordinary apprehension preternatural. His
results, brought about by the very soul and essence of method, have, in
truth, the whole air of intuition.

The faculty of resolution is possibly much invigorated by mathemati-
cal study, and especially by that highest branch of it which, unjustly, and
merely on account of its retrograde operations, has been called, as if *par
excellence,* analysis. Yet to calculate is not in itself to analyze. A chess-
player, for example, does the one, without effort at the other. It follows
that the game of chess, in its effects upon mental character, is greatly
misunderstood. I am not now writing a treatise, but simply prefacing a

somewhat peculiar narrative by observations very much at random; I will, therefore, take occasion to assert that the higher powers of the reflective intellect are more decidedly and more usefully tasked by the unostentatious game of draughts[1] than by all the elaborate frivolity of chess. In this latter, where the pieces have different and *bizarre* motions, with various and variable values, what is only complex, is mistaken (a not unusual error) for what is profound. The *attention* is here called powerfully into play. If it flag for an instant, an oversight is committed, resulting in injury or defeat. The possible moves being not only manifold, but involute, the chances of such oversights are multiplied; and in nine cases out of ten, it is the more concentrative rather than the more acute player who conquers. In draughts, on the contrary, where the moves are *unique* and have but little variation, the probabilities of inadvertence are diminished, and the mere attention being left comparatively unemployed, what advantages are obtained by either party are obtained by superior *acumen*. To be less abstract, let us suppose a game of draughts where the pieces are reduced to four kings, and where, of course, no oversight is to be expected. It is obvious that here the victory can be decided (the players being at all equal) only by some *recherché*[2] movement, the result of some strong exertion of the intellect. Deprived of ordinary resources, the analyst throws himself into the spirit of his opponent, identifies himself therewith, and not unfrequently sees thus, at a glance, the sole methods (sometime indeed absurdly simple ones) by which he may seduce into error or hurry into miscalculation.

Whist has long been noted for its influence upon what is termed the calculating power; and men of the highest order of intellect have been known to take an apparently unaccountable delight in it, while eschewing chess as frivolous. Beyond doubt there is nothing of a similar nature so greatly tasking the faculty of analysis. The best chess-player in Christendom *may* be little more than the best player of chess; but proficiency in whist implies capacity for success in all those more important undertakings where mind struggles with mind. When I say proficiency, I mean that perfection in the game which includes a comprehension of *all* the sources whence legitimate advantage may be derived. These are not only manifold, but multiform, and lie frequently among recesses of thought altogether inaccessible to the ordinary understanding. To observe attentively is to remember distinctly; and, so far, the concentrative chess-player will do very well at whist; while the rules of Hoyle (themselves based upon the mere mechanism of the game) are sufficiently and generally

comprehensible. Thus to have a retentive memory, and proceed by "the book" are points commonly regarded as the sum total of good playing. But it is in matters beyond the limits of mere rule that the skill of the analyst is evinced. He makes, in silence, a host of observations and inferences. So, perhaps, do his companions; and the difference in the extent of the information obtained, lies not so much in the validity of the inference as in the quality of the observation. The necessary knowledge is that of *what* to observe. Our player confines himself not at all; nor, because the game is the object, does he reject deductions from things external to the game. He examines the countenance of his partner, comparing it carefully with that of each of his opponents. He considers the mode of assorting the cards in each hand; often counting trump by trump, and honor by honor, through the glances bestowed by their holders upon each. He notes every variation of face as the play progresses, gathering a fund of thought from the differences in the expression of certainty, of surprise, of triumph, or chagrin. From the manner of gathering up a trick he judges whether the person taking it can make another in the suit. He recognizes what is played through feint, by the air with which it is thrown upon the table. A casual or inadvertent word; the accidental dropping or turning of a card, with the accompanying anxiety or carelessness in regard to its concealment; the counting of the tricks, with the order of their arrangement; embarrassment, hesitation, eagerness, or trepidation—all afford, to his apparently intuitive perception, indications of the true state of affairs. The first two or three rounds having been played, he is in full possession of the contents of each hand, and thenceforward puts down his cards with as absolute a precision of purpose as if the rest of the party had turned outward the faces of their own.

The analytical power should not be confounded with simple ingenuity; for while the analyst is necessarily ingenious, the ingenious man is often remarkably incapable of analysis. The constructive or combining power, by which ingenuity is usually manifested, and to which the phrenologists (I believe erroneously) have assigned a separate organ, supposing it a primitive faculty, has been so frequently seen in those whose intellect bordered otherwise upon idiocy, as to have attracted general observation among writers on morals. Between ingenuity and the analytic ability there exists a difference far greater, indeed, than that between the fancy and the imagination, but of a character very strictly analogous. It will be found, in fact, that the ingenious are always fanciful, and the *truly* imaginative never otherwise than analytic.

The narrative which follows will appear to the reader somewhat in the light of a commentary upon the propositions just advanced.

Residing in Paris during the spring and part of the summer of 18—, I there became acquainted with a Monsieur C. Auguste Dupin. This young gentleman was of an excellent, indeed of an illustrious family, but, by a variety of untoward events, had been reduced to such poverty that the energy of his character succumbed beneath it, and he ceased to bestir himself in the world, or to care for the retrieval of his fortunes. By courtesy of his creditors, there still remained in his possession a small remnant of his patrimony; and, upon the income arising from this, he managed, by means of a rigorous economy, to procure the necessaries of life, without troubling himself about its superfluities. Books, indeed, were his sole luxuries, and in Paris these are easily obtained.

Our first meeting was at an obscure library in the Rue Montmartre, where the accident of our both being in search of the same very rare and very remarkable volume, brought us into closer communion. We saw each other again and again. I was deeply interested in the little family history which he detailed to me with all that candor which a Frenchman indulges whenever mere self is his theme. I was astonished, too, at the vast extent of his reading; and, above all, I felt my soul enkindled within me by the wild fervor, and the vivid freshness of his imagination. Seeking in Paris the objects I then sought, I felt that the society of such a man would be to me a treasure beyond price; and this feeling I frankly confided to him. It was at length arranged that we should live together during my stay in the city; and as my worldly circumstances were somewhat less embarrassed than his own, I was permitted to be at the expense of renting, and furnishing in a style which suited the rather fantastic gloom of our common temper, a time-eaten and grotesque mansion, long deserted through superstitions into which we did not inquire, and tottering to its fall in a retired and desolate portion of the Faubourg St. Germain.

Had the routine of our life at this place been known to the world, we should have been regarded as madmen—although, perhaps, as madmen of a harmless nature. Our seclusion was perfect. We admitted no visiters. Indeed the locality of our retirement had been carefully kept a secret from my own former associates; and it had been many years since Dupin had ceased to know or be known in Paris. We existed within ourselves alone.

It was a freak of fancy in my friend (for what else shall I call it?) to be enamored of the night for her own sake; and into this *bizarrerie*, as into all his others, I quietly fell; giving myself up to his wild whims with a perfect

abandon. The sable divinity would not herself dwell with us always; but we could counterfeit her presence. At the first dawn of the morning we closed all the messy shutters of our old building; lighting a couple of tapers which, strongly perfumed, threw out only the ghastliest and feeblest of rays. By the aid of these we then busied our souls in dreams—reading, writing, or conversing, until warned by the clock of the advent of the true Darkness. Then we sallied forth into the streets, arm in arm, continuing the topics of the day, or roaming far and wide until a late hour, seeking, amid the wild lights and shadows of the populous city, that infinity of mental excitement which quiet observation can afford.

At such times I could not help remarking and admiring (although from his rich ideality I had been prepared to expect it) a peculiar analytic ability in Dupin. He seemed, too, to take an eager delight in its exercise—if not exactly in its display—and did not hesitate to confess the pleasure thus derived. He boasted to me, with a low chuckling laugh, that most men, in respect to himself, wore windows in their bosoms, and was wont to follow up such assertions by direct and very startling proofs of his intimate knowledge of my own. His manner at these moments was frigid and abstract; his eyes were vacant in expression; while his voice, usually a rich tenor, rose into a treble which would have sounded petulantly but for the deliberateness and entire distinctness of the enunciation. Observing him in these moods, I often dwelt meditatively upon the old philosophy of the Bi-Part Soul, and amused myself with the fancy of a double Dupin—the creative and the resolvent.

Let it not be supposed, from what I have just said, that I am detailing any mystery, or penning any romance. What I have described in the Frenchman was merely the result of an excited, or perhaps of a diseased, intelligence, but of the character of his remarks at the periods in question an example will best convey the idea.

We were strolling one night down a long dirty street, in the vicinity of the Palais Royal. Being both, apparently, occupied with thought, neither of us had spoken a syllable for fifteen minutes at least. All at once Dupin broke forth with these words:

"He is a very little fellow, that's true, and would do better for the *Théâtre des Variétés.*"

"There can be no doubt of that," I replied unwittingly, and not at first observing (so much had I been absorbed in reflection) the extraordinary manner in which the speaker had chimed in with my meditations. In an instant afterward I recollected myself, and my astonishment was profound.

"Dupin," said I, gravely, "this is beyond my comprehension. I do not hesitate to say that I am amazed, and can scarcely credit my senses. How was it possible you should know I was thinking of ———?" Here I paused, to ascertain beyond a doubt whether he really knew of whom I thought.

"——— of Chantilly," said he, "why do you pause? You were remarking to yourself that his diminutive figure unfitted him for tragedy."

This was precisely what had formed the subject of my reflections. Chantilly was a *quondam* cobbler of the Rue St. Denis, who, becoming stage-mad, had attempted the *rôle* of Xerxes, in Crébillon's tragedy so called, and been notoriously Pasquinaded for his pains.

"Tell me, for Heaven's sake," I exclaimed, "the method—if method there is—by which you have been enabled to fathom my soul in this matter." In fact, I was even more startled than I would have been willing to express.

"It was the fruiterer," replied my friend, "who brought you to the conclusion that the mender of soles was not of sufficient height for Xerxes *et id genus omne.*"

"The fruiterer!—you astonish me—I know no fruiterer whomsoever."

"The man who ran up against you as we entered the street—it may have been fifteen minutes ago."

I now remembered that, in fact, a fruiterer, carrying upon his head a large basket of apples, had nearly thrown me down, by accident, as we passed from the Rue C—— into the thoroughfare where we stood; but what this had to do with Chantilly I could not possibly understand.

There was not a particle of *charlâtanerie* about Dupin. "I will explain," he said, "and that you may comprehend all clearly, we will first retrace the course of your meditations, from the moment in which I spoke to you until that of the *rencontre* with the fruiterer in question. The larger links of the chain run thus—Chantilly, Orion, Dr. Nichols, Epicurus, Stereotomy, the street stones, the fruiterer."

There are few persons who have not, at some period of their lives, amused themselves in retracing the steps by which particular conclusions of their own minds have been attained. The occupation is often full of interest; and he who attempts it for the first time is astonished by the apparently illimitable distance and incoherence between the starting-point and the goal. What, then, must have been my amazement, when I heard the Frenchman speak what he had just spoken, and I could not help acknowledging that he had spoken the truth. He continued:

"We had been talking of horses, if I remember aright, just before leaving the Rue C——. This was the last subject we discussed. As we

crossed into this street, a fruiterer, with a large basket upon his head, brushing quickly past us, thrust you upon a pile of paving-stones collected at a spot where the causeway is undergoing repair. You stepped upon one of the loose fragments, slipped, slightly strained your ankle, appeared vexed or sulky, muttered a few words, turned to look at the pile, and then proceeded in silence. I was not particularly attentive to what you did; but observation has become with me, of late, a species of necessity.

"You kept your eyes upon the ground—glancing, with a petulant expression, at the holes and ruts in the pavement (so that I saw you were still thinking of the stones), until we reached the little alley called Lamartine, which has been paved, by way of experiment, with the overlapping and riveted blocks. Here your countenance brightened up, and, perceiving your lips move, I could not doubt that you murmured the word 'stereotomy,' a term very affectedly applied to this species of pavement. I knew that you could not say to yourself 'stereotomy' without being brought to think of atomies, and thus of the theories of Epicurus; and since, when we discussed this subject not very long ago, I mentioned to you how singularly, yet with how little notice, the vague guesses of that noble Greek had met with confirmation in the late nebular cosmogony, I felt that you could not avoid casting your eyes upward to the great *nebula* in Orion, and I certainly expected that you would do so. You did look up; and I was now assured that I had correctly followed your steps. But in that bitter *tirade* upon Chantilly, which appeared in yesterday's '*Musée*,' the satirist, making some disgraceful allusions to the cobbler's change of name upon assuming the buskin, quoted a Latin line about which we have often conversed. I mean the line

Perdidit antiquum litera prima sonum.

I had told you that this was in reference to Orion, formerly written Urion; and, from certain pungencies connected with this explanation, I was aware that you could not have forgotten it. It was clear, therefore, that you would not fail to combine the two ideas of Orion and Chantilly. That you did combine them I saw by the character of the smile which passed over your lips. You thought of the poor cobbler's immolation. So far, you had been stooping in your gait; but now I saw you draw yourself up to your full height. I was then sure that you reflected upon the diminutive figure of Chantilly. At this point I interrupted your meditations to remark that

as, in fact, he was a very little fellow—that Chantilly—he would do better at the *Théâtre des Variétés.*"

Not long after this, we were looking over an evening edition of the *Gazette des Tribunaux,* when the following paragraphs arrested our attention.

EXTRAORDINARY MURDERS. This morning, about three o'clock, the inhabitants of the Quartier St. Roch were roused from sleep by a succession of terrific shrieks, issuing, apparently, from the fourth story of a house in the Rue Morgue, known to be in the sole occupancy of one Madame L'Espanaye, and her daughter, Mademoiselle Camille L'Espanaye. After some delay, occasioned by a fruitless attempt to procure admission in the usual manner, the gateway was broken in with a crowbar, and eight or ten of the neighbors entered, accompanied by two *gendarmes.* By this time the cries had ceased; but, as the party rushed up the first flight of stairs, two or more rough voices, in angry contention, were distinguished, and seemed to proceed from the upper part of the house. As the second landing was reached, these sounds, also, had ceased, and everything remained perfectly quiet. The party spread themselves, and hurried from room to room. Upon arriving at a large back chamber in the fourth story (the door of which, being found locked, with the key inside, was forced open), a spectacle presented itself which struck everyone present not less with horror than with astonishment.

The apartment was in the wildest disorder—the furniture broken and thrown about in all directions. There was only one bedstead; and from this the bed had been removed, and thrown into the middle of the floor. On a chair lay a razor, besmeared with blood. On the hearth were two or three long and thick tresses of gray human hair, also dabbled with blood, and seeming to have been pulled out by the roots. Upon the floor were found four Napoleons, an earring of topaz, three large silver spoons, three smaller of *métal d'Alger,* and two bags, containing nearly four thousand francs in gold. The drawers of a *bureau,* which stood in one corner, were open, and had been, apparently, rifled, although many articles still remained in them. A small iron safe was discovered under the *bed* (not under the bedstead). It was open, with the key still in the door. It had no contents beyond a few old letters, and other papers of little consequence.

Of Madame L'Espanaye no traces were here seen; but an unusual quantity of soot being observed in the fireplace, a search

was made in the chimney, and (horrible to relate!) the corpse of the daughter, head downward, was dragged therefrom; it having been thus forced up the narrow aperture for a considerable distance. The body was quite warm. Upon examining it, many excoriations were perceived, no doubt occasioned by the violence with which it had been thrust up and disengaged. Upon the face were many severe scratches, and, upon the throat, dark bruises, and deep indentations of finger nails, as if the deceased had been throttled to death.

After a thorough investigation of every portion of the house without farther discovery, the party made its way into a small paved yard in the rear of the building, where lay the corpse of the old lady, with her throat so entirely cut that, upon an attempt to raise her, the head fell off. The body, as well as the head, was fearfully mutilated—the former so much so as scarcely to retain any semblance of humanity.

To this horrible mystery there is not as yet, we believe, the slightest clue.

The next day's paper had these additional particulars:

The Tragedy in the Rue Morgue. Many individuals have been examined in relation to this most extraordinary and frightful affair, [the word affaire has not yet, in France, that levity of import which it conveys with us] but nothing whatever has transpired to throw light upon it. We give below all the material testimony elicited.

Pauline Dubourg, laundress, deposes that she has known both the deceased for three years, having washed for them during that period. The old lady and her daughter seemed on good terms—very affectionate towards each other. They were excellent pay. Could not speak in regard to their mode or means of living. Believed that Madame L. told fortunes for a living. Was reputed to have money put by. Never met any persons in the house when she called for the clothes or took them home. Was sure that they had no servant in employ. There appeared to be no furniture in any part of the building except in the fourth story.

Pierre Moreau, tobacconist, deposes that he has been in the habit of selling small quantities of tobacco and snuff to Madame L'Espanaye for nearly four years. Was born in the neighborhood, and has always resided there. The deceased and her daughter had occupied the house in which the corpses were found, for more

than six years. It was formerly occupied by a jeweler, who under-let the upper rooms to various persons. The house was the property of Madame L. She became dissatisfied with the abuse of the premises by her tenant, and moved into them herself, refusing to let any portion. The old lady was childish. Witness had seen the daughter some five or six times during the six years. The two lived an exceedingly retired life—were reputed to have money. Had heard it said among the neighbors that Madame L. told fortunes—did not believe it. Had never seen any person enter the door except the old lady and her daughter, a porter once or twice, and a physician some eight or ten times.

Many other persons, neighbors, gave evidence to the same effect. No one was spoken of as frequenting the house. It was not known whether there were any living connections of Madame L. and her daughter. The shutters of the front windows were seldom opened. Those in the rear were always closed, with the exception of the large back room, fourth story. The house was a good house—not very old.

Isidore Musèt, gendarme, deposes that he was called to the house about three o'clock in the morning, and found some twenty or thirty persons at the gateway, endeavoring to gain admittance. Forced it open, at length, with a bayonet—not with a crowbar. Had but little difficulty in getting it open, on account of its being a double or folding gate, and bolted neither at bottom nor top. The shrieks were continued until the gate was forced—and then suddenly ceased. They seemed to be screams of some person (or persons) in great agony—were loud and drawn out, not short and quick. Witness led the way upstairs. Upon reaching the first landing, heard two voices in loud and angry contention—the one a gruff voice, the other much shriller—a very strange voice. Could distinguish some words of the former, which was that of a Frenchman. Was positive that it was not a woman's voice. Could distinguish the words *"sacré"* and *"diable."* The shrill voice was that of a foreigner. Could not be sure whether it was the voice of a man or of a woman. Could not make out what was said, but believed the language to be Spanish. The state of the room and of the bodies was described by this witness as we described them yesterday.

Henri Duval, a neighbor, and by trade a silver-smith, deposes that he was one of the party who first entered the house. Corroborates the testimony of Musèt in general. As soon as they forced an

entrance, they reclosed the door, to keep out the crowd, which collected very fast, notwithstanding the lateness of the hour. The shrill voice, this witness thinks, was that of an Italian. Was certain it was not French. Could not be sure that it was a man's voice. It might have been a woman's. Was not acquainted with the Italian language. Could not distinguish the words, but was convinced by the intonation that the speaker was an Italian. Knew Madame L. and her daughter. Had conversed with both frequently. Was sure that the shrill voice was not that of either of the deceased.

———— *Odenheimer, restaurateur.* This witness volunteered his testimony. Not speaking French, was examined through an interpreter. Is a native of Amsterdam. Was passing the house at the time of the shrieks. They lasted for several minutes—probably ten. They were long and loud—very awful and distressing. Was one of those who entered the building. Corroborated the previous evidence in every respect but one. Was sure that the shrill voice was that of a man—of a Frenchman. Could not distinguish the words uttered. They were loud and quick—unequal—spoken apparently in fear as well as in anger. The voice was harsh—not so much shrill as harsh. Could not call it a shrill voice. The gruff voice said repeatedly "*sacré,*" "*diable,*" and once "*mon Dieu.*"

Jules Mignaud, banker, of the firm of Mignaud et Fils, Rue Deloraine. Is the elder Mignaud. Madame L'Espanaye had some property. Had opened an account with his banking house in the spring of the year ——— (eight years previously). Made frequent deposits in small sums. Had checked for nothing until the third day before her death, when she took out in person the sum of 4000 francs. This sum was paid in gold, and a clerk went home with the money.

Adolphe Le Bon, clerk to Mignaud et Fils, deposes that on the day in question, about noon, he accompanied Madame L'Espanaye to her residence with the 4000 francs, put up in two bags. Upon the door being opened, Mademoiselle L. appeared and took from his hands one of the bags, while the old lady relieved him of the other. He then bowed and departed. Did not see any person in the street at the time. It is a bye-street—very lonely.

William Bird, tailor, deposes that he was one of the party who entered the house. Is an Englishman. Has lived in Paris two years. Was one of the first to ascend the stairs. Heard the voices in contention. The gruff voice was that of a Frenchman. Could make out

several words, but cannot now remember all. Heard distinctly *"sacré"* and *"mon Dieu."* There was a sound at the moment as if of several persons struggling—a scraping and scuffling sound. The shrill voice was very loud—louder than the gruff one. Is sure that it was not the voice of an Englishman. Appeared to be that of a German. Might have been a woman's voice. Does not understand German.

Four of the above-named witnesses, being recalled, deposed that the door of the chamber in which was found the body of Mademoiselle L. was locked on the inside when the party reached it. Everything was perfectly silent—no groans or noises of any kind. Upon forcing the door no person was seen. The windows, both of the back and front room, were down and firmly fastened from within. A door between the two rooms was closed but not locked. The door leading from the front room into the passage was locked, with the key on the inside. A small room in the front of the house, on the fourth story, at the head of the passage was open, the door being ajar. This room was crowded with old beds, boxes, and so forth. These were carefully removed and searched. There was not an inch of any portion of the house which was not carefully searched. Sweeps were sent up and down the chimneys. The house was a four-story one, with garrets (*mansardes*). A trap-door on the roof was nailed down very securely— did not appear to have been opened for years. The time elapsing between the hearing of the voices in contention and the breaking open of the room door was variously stated by the witnesses. Some made it as short as three minutes—some as long as five. The door was opened with difficulty.

Alfonzo Garcio, undertaker, deposes that he resides in the Rue Morgue. Is a native of Spain. Was one of the party who entered the house. Did not proceed upstairs. Is nervous, and was apprehensive of the consequences of agitation. Heard the voices in contention. The gruff voice was that of a Frenchman. Could not distinguish what was said. The shrill voice was that of an Englishman—is sure of this. Does not understand the English language, but judges by the intonation.

Alberto Montani, confectioner, deposes that he was among the first to ascend the stairs. Heard the voices in question. The gruff voice was that of a Frenchman. Distinguished several words. The speaker appeared to be expostulating. Could not make out the words of the shrill voice. Spoke quick and unevenly. Thinks it the voice of a

Russian. Corroborates the general testimony. Is an Italian. Never conversed with a native of Russia.

Several witnesses, recalled, here testified that the chimneys of all the rooms on the fourth story were too narrow to admit the passage of a human being. By "sweeps" were meant cylindrical sweeping-brushes, such as are employed by those who clean chimneys. These brushes were passed up and down every flue in the house. There is no back passage by which anyone could have descended while the party proceeded upstairs. The body of Mademoiselle L'Espanaye was so firmly wedged in the chimney that it could not be got down until four or five of the party united their strength.

Paul Dumas, physician, deposes that he was called to view the bodies about daybreak. They were both then lying on the sacking of the bedstead in the chamber where Mademoiselle L. was found. The corpse of the young lady was much bruised and excoriated. The fact that it had been thrust up the chimney would sufficiently account for these appearances. The throat was greatly chafed. There were several deep scratches just below the chin, together with a series of livid spots which were evidently the impression of fingers. The face was fearfully discolored, and the eyeballs protruded. The tongue had been partially bitten through. A large bruise was discovered upon the pit of the stomach, produced, apparently, by the pressure of a knee. In the opinion of M. Dumas, Mademoiselle L'Espanaye had been throttled to death by some person or persons unknown. The corpse of the mother was horribly mutilated. All the bones of the right leg and arm were more or less shattered. The left *tibia* much splintered, as well as all the ribs of the left side. Whole body dreadfully bruised and discolored. It was not possible to say how the injuries had been inflicted. A heavy club of wood, or a broad bar of iron—a chair—any large, heavy, and obtuse weapon would have produced such results, if wielded by the hands of a very powerful man. No woman could have inflicted the blows with any weapon. The head of the deceased, when seen by witness, was entirely separated from the body, and was also greatly shattered. The throat had evidently been cut with some very sharp instrument—probably with a razor.

Alexandre Etienne, surgeon, was called with M. Dumas to view the bodies. Corroborated the testimony and the opinions of M. Dumas.

Nothing further of importance was elicited, although several other persons were examined. A murder so mysterious, and so

perplexing in all its particulars, was never before committed in Paris—if indeed a murder has been committed at all. The police are entirely at fault—an unusual occurrence in affairs of this nature. There is not, however, the shadow of a clue apparent.

The evening edition of the paper stated that the greatest excitement still continued in the Quartier St. Roch—that the premises in question had been carefully re-searched, and fresh examinations of witnesses instituted, but all to no purpose. A postscript, however, mentioned that Adolphe Le Bon had been arrested and imprisoned—although nothing appeared to criminate him beyond the facts already detailed.

Dupin seemed singularly interested in the progress of this affair—at least so I judged from his manner, for he made no comments. It was only after the announcement that Le Bon had been imprisoned, that he asked me my opinion respecting the murders.

I could merely agree with all Paris in considering them an insoluble mystery. I saw no means by which it would be possible to trace the murderer.

"We must not judge of the means," said Dupin, "by this shell of an examination. The Parisian police, so much extolled for *acumen,* are cunning, but no more. There is no method in their proceedings, beyond the method of the moment. They make a vast parade of measures; but, not unfrequently, these are so ill-adapted to the objects proposed, as to put us in mind of Monsieur Jourdain's calling for his *robe-de-chambre—pour mieux entendre la musique.* The results attained by them are not unfrequently surprising, but, for the most part, are brought about by simple diligence and activity. When these qualities are unavailing, their schemes fail. Vidocq, for example, was a good guesser, and a persevering man. But, without educated thought, he erred continually by the very intensity of his investigations. He impaired his vision by holding the object too close. He might see, perhaps, one or two points with unusual clearness, but in so doing he, necessarily, lost sight of the matter as a whole. Thus there is such a thing as being too profound. Truth is not always in a well. In fact, as regards the more important knowledge, I do believe that she is invariably superficial. The depth lies in the valleys where we seek her, and not upon the mountain-tops where she is found. The modes and sources of this kind of error are well typified in the contemplation of the heavenly bodies. To look at a star by glances—to view it in a side-long way, by turning towards it the exterior portions of the *retina* (more susceptible of feeble impressions of light than the interior), is to behold the star distinctly—is to have the best

appreciation of its luster—a luster which grows dim just in proportion as we turn our vision *fully* upon it. A greater number of rays actually fall upon the eye in the latter case, but in the former, there is the more refined capacity for comprehension. By undue profundity we perplex and enfeeble thought; and it is possible to make even Venus herself vanish from the firmament by a scrutiny too sustained, too concentrated, or too direct.

"As for these murders, let us enter into some examinations for ourselves, before we make up an opinion respecting them. An inquiry will afford us amusement," [I thought this an odd term, so applied, but said nothing] "and besides, Le Bon once rendered me a service for which I am not ungrateful. We will go and see the premises with our own eyes. I know G——, the Prefect of Police, and shall have no difficulty in obtaining the necessary permission."

The permission was obtained, and we proceeded at once to the Rue Morgue. This is one of those miserable thoroughfares which intervene between the Rue Richelieu and the Rue St. Roch. It was late in the afternoon when we reached it, as this quarter is at a great distance from that in which we resided. The house was readily found; for there were still many persons gazing up at the closed shutters, with an objectless curiosity, from the opposite side of the way. It was an ordinary Parisian house, with a gateway, on one side of which was a glazed watch-box, with a sliding panel in the window, indicating a *loge de concierge*. Before going in we walked up the street, turned down an alley, and then, again turning, passed in the rear of the building—Dupin, meanwhile, examining the whole neighborhood, as well as the house, with a minuteness of attention for which I could see no possible object.

Retracing our steps we came again to the front of the dwelling, rang, and having shown our credentials, were admitted by the agents in charge. We went upstairs—into the chamber where the body of Mademoiselle L'Espanaye had been found, and where both the deceased still lay. The disorders of the room had, as usual, been suffered to exist. I saw nothing beyond what had been stated in the *Gazette des Tribunaux*. Dupin scrutinized everything—not excepting the bodies of the victims. We then went into the other rooms, and into the yard; a *gendarme* accompanying us throughout. The examination occupied us until dark, when we took our departure. On our way home my companion stepped in for a moment at the office of one of the daily papers.

I have said that the whims of my friend were manifold, and that *Je les ménageais*: for this phrase there is no English equivalent. It was his humor,

now, to decline all conversation on the subject of the murder, until about noon the next day. He then asked me, suddenly, if I had observed anything *peculiar* at the scene of the atrocity.

There was something in his manner of emphasizing the word "peculiar," which caused me to shudder, without knowing why.

"No, nothing," I said; "nothing more, at least, than we both saw stated in the paper."

"The *Gazette*," he replied, "has not entered, I fear, into the unusual horror of the thing. But dismiss the idle opinions of this print. It appears to me that this mystery is considered insoluble, for the very reason which should cause it to be regarded as easy of solution—I mean for the *outré* character of its features. The police are confounded by the seeming absence of motive—not for the murder itself—but for the atrocity of the murder. They are puzzled, too, by the seeming impossibility of reconciling the voices heard in contention, with the facts that no one was discovered upstairs but the assassinated Mademoiselle L'Espanaye, and that there were no means of egress without the notice of the party ascending. The wild disorder of the room; the corpse thrust, with the head downward, up the chimney; the frightful mutilation of the body of the old lady; these considerations, with those just mentioned, and others which I need not mention, have sufficed to paralyze the powers, by putting completely at fault the boasted *acumen,* of the government agents. They have fallen into the gross but common error of confounding the unusual with the abstruse. But it is by these deviations from the plane of the ordinary, that reason feels its way, if at all, in its search for the true. In investigations such as we are now pursuing, it should not be so much asked 'what has occurred,' as 'what has occurred that has never occurred before.' In fact, the facility with which I shall arrive, or have arrived, at the solution of this mystery, is in the direct ratio of its apparent insolubility in the eyes of the police."

I stared at the speaker in mute astonishment.

"I am now awaiting," continued he, looking towards the door of our apartment—"I am now awaiting a person who, although perhaps not the perpetrator of these butcheries, must have been in some measure implicated in their perpetration. Of the worst portion of the crimes committed, it is probable that he is innocent. I hope that I am right in this supposition; for upon it I build my expectation of reading the entire riddle. I look for the man here—in this room—every moment. It is true that he may not arrive; but the probability is that he will. Should he come, it will be necessary to detain him. Here are pistols; and we both know how to use them when occasion demands their use."

I took the pistols, scarcely knowing what I did, or believing what I heard, while Dupin went on, very much as if in a soliloquy. I have already spoken of his abstract manner at such times. His discourse was addressed to myself; but his voice, although by no means loud, had that intonation which is commonly employed in speaking to someone at a great distance. His eyes, vacant in expression, regarded only the wall.

"That the voices heard in contention," he said, "by the party upon the stairs, were not the voices of the women themselves, was fully proved by the evidence. This relieves us of all doubt upon the question whether the old lady could have first destroyed the daughter, and afterward have committed suicide. I speak of this point chiefly for the sake of method; for the strength of Madame L'Espanaye would have been utterly unequal to the task of thrusting her daughter's corpse up the chimney as it was found; and the nature of the wounds upon her own person entirely preclude the idea of self-destruction. Murder, then, has been committed by some third party; and the voices of this third party were those heard in contention. Let me now advert—not to the whole testimony respecting these voices—but to what was *peculiar* in that testimony. Did you observe anything peculiar about it?"

I remarked that, while all the witnesses agreed in supposing the gruff voice to be that of a Frenchman, there was much disagreement in regard to the shrill, or, as one individual termed it, the harsh voice.

"That was the evidence itself," said Dupin, "but it was not the peculiarity of the evidence. You have observed nothing distinctive. Yet there *was* something to be observed. The witnesses, as you remark, agreed about the gruff voice; they were here unanimous. But in regard to the shrill voice, the peculiarity is—not that they disagreed—but that, while an Italian, an Englishman, a Spaniard, a Hollander, and a Frenchman attempted to describe it, each one spoke of it as that of *a foreigner.* Each is sure that it was not the voice of one of his own countrymen. Each likens it—not to the voice of an individual of any nation with whose language he is conversant—but the converse. The Frenchman supposes it the voice of a Spaniard, and 'might have distinguished some words *had he been acquainted with the Spanish.*' The Dutchman maintains it to have been that of a Frenchman; but we find it stated that '*not understanding French this witness was examined through an interpreter.*' The Englishman thinks it the voice of a German, and '*does not understand German.*' The Spaniard 'is sure' that it was that of an Englishman, but 'judges by the intonation' altogether, '*as he has no knowledge of the English.*' The Italian believes it the voice of a Russian, but '*has never conversed with a native of Russia.*' A second Frenchman differs, moreover, with the first, and is positive that the voice was that of an Italian; but, *not being cognizant*

of that tongue, is, like the Spaniard, 'convinced by the intonation.' Now, how strangely unusual must that voice have really been, about which such testimony as this *could* have been elicited!—in whose *tones,* even, denizens of the five great divisions of Europe could recognize nothing familiar! You will say that it might have been the voice of an Asiatic—of an African. Neither Asiatics nor Africans abound in Paris; but, without denying the inference, I will now merely call your attention to three points. The voice is termed by one witness 'harsh rather than shrill.' It is represented by two others to have been 'quick and *unequal.*' No words—no sounds resembling words—were by any witness mentioned as distinguishable.

"I know not," continued Dupin, "what impression I may have made, so far, upon your own understanding; but I do not hesitate to say that legitimate deductions even from this portion of the testimony—the portion respecting the gruff and shrill voices—are in themselves sufficient to engender a suspicion which should give direction to all farther progress in the investigation of the mystery. I said 'legitimate deductions'; but my meaning is not thus fully expressed. I designed to imply that the deductions are the *sole* proper ones, and that the suspicion arises *inevitably* from them as the single result. What the suspicion is, however, I will not say just yet. I merely wish you to bear in mind that, with myself, it was sufficiently forcible to give a definite form—a certain tendency—to my inquiries in the chamber.

"Let us now transport ourselves, in fancy, to this chamber. What shall we first seek here? The means of egress employed by the murderers. It is not too much to say that neither of us believe in preternatural events. Madame and Mademoiselle L'Espanaye were not destroyed by spirits. The doers of the deed were material, and escaped materially. Then how? Fortunately, there is but one mode of reasoning upon the point, and that mode *must* lead us to a definite decision. Let us examine, each by each, the possible means of egress. It is clear that the assassins were in the room where Mademoiselle L'Espanaye was found, or at least in the room adjoining, when the party ascended the stairs. It is, then, only from these two apartments that we have to seek issues. The police have laid bare the floors, the ceiling, and the masonry of the walls, in every direction. No *secret* issues could have escaped their vigilance. But, not trusting to *their* eyes, I examined with my own. There were, then, *no* secret issues. Both doors leading from the rooms into the passage were securely locked, with the keys inside. Let us turn to the chimneys. These, although of ordinary width for some eight or ten feet above the hearths, will not admit, throughout their extent, the body of a large cat. The impossibility of egress, by means already stated,

being thus absolute, we are reduced to the windows. Through those of the front room no one could have escaped without notice from the crowd in the street. The murderers *must* have passed, then, through those of the back room. Now, brought to this conclusion in so unequivocal a manner as we are, it is not our part, as reasoners, to reject it on account of apparent impossibilities. It is only left for us to prove that these apparent 'impossibilities' are, in reality, not such.

"There are two windows in the chamber. One of them is unobstructed by furniture, and is wholly visible. The lower portion of the other is hidden from view by the head of the unwieldy bedstead which is thrust close up against it. The former was found securely fastened from within. It resisted the utmost force of those who endeavored to raise it. A large gimlet-hole had been pierced in its frame to the left, and a very stout nail was found fitted therein, nearly to the head. Upon examining the other window, a similar nail was seen similarly fitted in it, and a vigorous attempt to raise this sash failed also. The police were now entirely satisfied that egress had not been in these directions. And, *therefore*, it was thought a matter of supererogation to withdraw the nails and open the windows.

"My own examination was somewhat more particular, and was so for the reason I have just given—because here it was, I knew, that all apparent impossibilities *must* be proved to be not such in reality.

"I proceeded to think thus—*a posteriori*. The murderers did escape from one of these windows. This being so, they could not have refastened the sashes from the inside, as they were found fastened—the consideration which put a stop, through its obviousness, to the scrutiny of the police in this quarter. Yet the sashes *were* fastened. They *must*, then, have the power of fastening themselves. There was no escape from this conclusion. I stepped to the unobstructed casement, withdrew the nail with some difficulty, and attempted to raise the sash. It resisted all my efforts, as I had anticipated. A concealed spring must, I now knew, exist; and this corroboration of my idea convinced me that my premises, at least, were correct, however mysterious still appeared the circumstances attending the nails. A careful search soon brought to light the hidden spring. I pressed it, and, satisfied with the discovery, forbore to upraise the sash.

"I now replaced the nail and regarded it attentively. A person passing out through this window might have reclosed it, and the spring would have caught—but the nail could not have been replaced. The conclusion was plain, and again narrowed in the field of my investigations. The assassins *must* have escaped through the other window. Supposing, then, the

springs upon each sash to be the same, as was probable, there *must* be found a difference between the nails, or at least between the modes of their fixture. Getting upon the sacking of the bedstead, I looked over the headboard minutely at the second casement. Passing my hand down behind the board, I readily discovered and pressed the spring, which was, as I had supposed, identical in character with its neighbor. I now looked at the nail. It was as stout as the other, and apparently fitted in the same manner—driven in nearly up to the head.

"You will say that I was puzzled; but, if you think so, you must have misunderstood the nature of the inductions. To use a sporting phrase, I had not been once 'at fault.' The scent had never for an instant been lost. There was no flaw in any link of the chain. I had traced the secret to its ultimate result—and that result was *the nail.* It had, I say, in every respect, the appearance of its fellow in the other window; but this fact was an absolute nullity (conclusive as it might seem to be) when compared with the consideration that here, at this point, terminated the clue. 'There *must* be something wrong,' I said, 'about the nail.' I touched it; and the head, with about a quarter of an inch of the shank came off in my fingers. The rest of the shank was in the gimlet-hole, where it had been broken off. The fracture was an old one (for its edges were incrusted with rust), and had apparently been accomplished by the blow of a hammer, which had partially imbedded, in the top of the bottom sash, the head portion of the nail. I now carefully replaced this head portion in the indentation whence I had taken it, and the resemblance to a perfect nail was complete—the fissure was invisible. Pressing the spring, I gently raised the sash for a few inches; the head went up with it, remaining firm in its bed. I closed the window, and the semblance of the whole nail was again perfect.

"The riddle, so far, was now unriddled. The assassin had escaped through the window which looked upon the bed. Dropping of its own accord upon his exit (or perhaps purposely closed), it had become fastened by the spring; and it was the retention of this spring which had been mistaken by the police for that of the nail—farther inquiry being thus considered unnecessary.

"The next question is that of the mode of descent. Upon this point I had been satisfied in my walk with you around the building. About five feet and a half from the casement in question there runs a lightning-rod. From this rod it would have been impossible for anyone to reach the window itself, to say nothing of entering it. I observed, however, that the shutters of the fourth story were of the peculiar kind called by Parisian carpenters *ferrades*—a kind rarely employed at the present day, but frequently seen

upon very old mansions at Lyons and Bourdeaux. They are in the form of an ordinary door (a single, not a folding door), except that the upper half is latticed or worked in open trellis—thus affording an excellent hold for the hands. In the present instance these shutters are fully three feet and a half broad. When we saw them from the rear of the house, they were both about half open—that is to say, they stood off at right angles from the wall. It is probable that the police, as well as myself, examined the back of the tenement; but, if so, in looking at these *ferrades* in the line of their breadth (as they must have done), they did not perceive this great breadth itself, or, at all events, failed to take it into due consideration. In fact, having once satisfied themselves that no egress could have been made in this quarter, they would naturally bestow here a very cursory examination. It was clear to me, however, that the shutter belonging to the window at the head of the bed, would, if swung fully back to the wall, reach to within two feet of the lightning-rod. It was also evident that, by exertion of a very unusual degree of activity and courage, an entrance into the window, from the rod, might have been thus effected. By reaching to the distance of two feet and a half (we now suppose the shutter open to its whole extent) a robber might have taken a firm grasp upon the trellis-work. Letting go, then, his hold upon the rod, placing his feet securely against the wall, and springing boldly from it, he might have swung the shutter so as to close it, and, if we imagine the window open at the time, might even have swung himself into the room.

"I wish you to bear especially in mind that I have spoken of a *very* unusual degree of activity as requisite to success in so hazardous and so difficult a feat. It is my design to show you first, that the thing might possibly have been accomplished: but, secondly and *chiefly*, I wish to impress upon your understanding the *very extraordinary*—the almost preternatural character of that agility which could have accomplished it.

"You will say, no doubt, using the language of the law, that 'to make out my case,' I should rather undervalue, than insist upon a full estimation of the activity required in this matter. This may be the practice in law, but it is not the usage of reason. My ultimate object is only the truth. My immediate purpose is to lead you to place in juxtaposition, that *very unusual* activity of which I have just spoken, with that *very peculiar* shrill (or harsh) and *unequal* voice, about whose nationality no two persons could be found to agree, and in whose utterance no syllabification could be detected."

At these words a vague and half-formed conception of the meaning of Dupin flitted over my mind. I seemed to be upon the verge of comprehension, without power to comprehend—as men, at times, find themselves

upon the brink of remembrance, without being able, in the end, to remember. My friend went on with his discourse.

"You will see," he said, "that I have shifted the question from the mode of egress to that of ingress. It was my design to convey the idea that both were effected in the same manner, at the same point. Let us now revert to the interior of the room. Let us survey the appearances here. The drawers of the bureau, it is said, had been rifled, although many articles of apparel still remained within them. The conclusion here is absurd. It is a mere guess—a very silly one—and no more. How are we to know that the articles found in the drawers were not all these drawers had originally contained? Madame L'Espanaye and her daughter lived an exceedingly retired life—saw no company—seldom went out—had little use for numerous changes of habiliment. Those found were at least of as good quality as any likely to be possessed by these ladies. If a thief had taken any, why did he not take the best—why did he not take all? In a word, why did he abandon four thousand francs in gold to encumber himself with a bundle of linen? The gold *was* abandoned. Nearly the whole sum mentioned by Monsieur Mignaud, the banker, was discovered, in bags, upon the floor. I wish you therefore, to discard from your thoughts the blundering idea of *motive,* engendered in the brains of the police by that portion of the evidence which speaks of money delivered at the door of the house. Coincidences ten times as remarkable as this (the delivery of the money, and murder committed within three days upon the party receiving it), happen to all of us every hour of our lives, without attracting even momentary notice. Coincidences, in general, are great stumbling-blocks in the way of that class of thinkers who have been educated to know nothing of the theory of probabilities—that theory to which the most glorious objects of human research are indebted for the most glorious of illustration. In the present instance, had the gold been gone, the fact of its delivery three days before would have formed something more than a coincidence. It would have been corroborative of this idea of motive. But, under the real circumstances of the case, if we are to suppose gold the motive of this outrage, we must also imagine the perpetrator so vacillating an idiot as to have abandoned his gold and his motive together.

"Keeping now steadily in mind the points to which I have drawn your attention—that peculiar voice, that unusual agility, and that startling absence of motive in a murder so singularly atrocious as this—let us glance at the butchery itself. Here is a woman strangled to death by manual strength, and thrust up a chimney head downward. Ordinary assassins

employ no such mode of murder as this. Least of all, do they thus dispose of the murdered. In the manner of thrusting the corpse up the chimney, you will admit that there was something *excessively outré*—something altogether irreconcilable with our common notions of human action, even when we suppose the actors the most depraved of men. Think, too, how great must have been that strength which could have thrust the body *up* such an aperture so forcibly that the united vigor of several persons was found barely sufficient to drag it *down!*

"Turn, now, to other indications of the employment of a vigor most marvelous. On the hearth were thick tresses—very thick tresses—of gray human hair. These had been torn out by the roots. You are aware of the great force necessary in tearing thus from the head even twenty or thirty hairs together. You saw the locks in question as well as myself. Their roots (a hideous sight!) were clotted with fragments of the flesh of the scalp—sure token of the prodigious power which had been exerted in uprooting perhaps half a million of hairs at a time. The throat of the old lady was not merely cut, but the head absolutely severed from the body: the instrument was a mere razor. I wish you also to look at the *brutal* ferocity of these deeds. Of the bruises upon the body of Madame L'Espanaye I do not speak. Monsieur Dumas, and his worthy coadjutor Monsieur Etienne, have pronounced that they were inflicted by some obtuse instrument; and so far these gentlemen are very correct. The obtuse instrument was clearly the stone pavement in the yard, upon which the victim had fallen from the window which looked in upon the bed. This idea, however simple it may now seem, escaped the police for the same reason that the breadth of the shutters escaped them—because, by the affair of the nails, their perceptions had been hermetically sealed against the possibility of the windows having ever been opened at all.

"If now, in addition to all these things, you have properly reflected upon the odd disorder of the chamber, we have gone so far as to combine the ideas of an agility astounding, a strength superhuman, a ferocity brutal, a butchery without motive, a *grotesquerie* in horror absolutely alien from humanity, and a voice foreign in tone to the ears of men of many nations, and devoid of all distinct or intelligible syllabification. What result, then, has ensued? What impression have I made upon your fancy?"

I felt a creeping of the flesh as Dupin asked me the question. "A madman," I said, "has done this deed—some raving maniac, escaping from a neighboring *Maison de Santé*."

"In some respects," he replied, "your idea is not irrelevant. But the voices of madmen, even in their wildest paroxysms, are never found to tally

with that peculiar voice heard upon the stairs. Madmen are of some nation, and their language, however incoherent in its words, has always the coherence of syllabification. Besides, the hair of a madman is not such as I now hold in my hand. I disentangled this little tuft from the rigidly clutched fingers of Madame L'Espanaye. Tell me what you can make of it."

"Dupin!" I said, completely unnerved; "this hair is most unusual—this is no *human* hair."

"I have not asserted that it is," said he; "but, before we decide this point, I wish you to glance at the little sketch I have here traced upon this paper. It is a fac-simile drawing of what has been described in one portion of the testimony as 'dark bruises, and deep indentations of finger nails' upon the throat of Mademoiselle L'Espanaye, and in another (by Messrs. Dumas and Etienne) as a 'series of livid spots, evidently the impression of fingers.'

"You will perceive," continued my friend, spreading out the paper upon the table before us, "that this drawing gives the idea of a firm and fixed hold. There is no *slipping* apparent. Each finger has retained— possibly until the death of the victim—the fearful grasp by which it originally embedded itself. Attempt, now, to place all your fingers, at the same time, in the respective impressions as you see them."

I made the attempt in vain.

"We are possibly not giving this matter a fair trial," he said. "The paper is spread out upon a plane surface; but the human throat is cylindrical. Here is a billet of wood, the circumference of which is about that of the throat. Wrap the drawing around it, and try the experiment again."

I did so; but the difficulty was even more obvious than before. "This," I said, "is the mark of no human hand."

"Read now," replied Dupin, "this passage from Cuvier."

It was a minute anatomical and generally descriptive account of the large fulvous Ourang-Outang of the East Indian islands. The gigantic stature, the prodigious strength and activity, the wild ferocity, and the imitative propensities of these mammalia are sufficiently well-known to all. I understood the full horrors of the murder at once.

"The description of the digits," said I, as I made an end of reading, "is in exact accordance with this drawing. I see that no animal but an Ourang-Outang, of the species here mentioned, could have impressed the indentations as you have traced them. This tuft of tawny hair, too, is identical in character with that of the beast of Cuvier. But I cannot possibly comprehend the particulars of this frightful mystery. Besides, there were

two voices heard in contention, and one of them was unquestionably the voice of a Frenchman."

"True; and you will remember an expression attributed almost unanimously, by the evidence, to this voice—the expression, '*mon Dieu!*' This, under the circumstances, has been justly characterized by one of the witnesses (Montani, the confectioner) as an expression of remonstrance or expostulation. Upon these two words, therefore, I have mainly built my hopes of a full solution of the riddle. A Frenchman was cognizant of the murder. It is possible—indeed it is far more than probable—that he was innocent of all participation in the bloody transaction which took place. The Ourang-Outang may have escaped from him. He may have traced it to the chamber; but, under the agitating circumstances which ensued, he could never have recaptured it. It is still at large. I will not pursue these guesses—for I have no right to call them more—since the shades of reflection upon which they are based are scarcely of sufficient depth to be appreciable by my own intellect, and since I could not pretend to make them intelligible to the understanding of another. We will call them guesses, then, and speak of them as such. If the Frenchman in question is indeed, as I suppose, innocent of this atrocity, this advertisement, which I left last night, upon our return home, at the office of *Le Monde* (a paper devoted to the shipping interest, and much sought by sailors), will bring him to our residence."

He handed me a paper, and I read thus:

CAUGHT—In the Bois de Boulogne, early in the morning of the —— inst. (the morning of the murder), a very large, tawny Ourang-Outang of the Bornese species. The owner (who is ascertained to be a sailor, belonging to a Maltese vessel) may have the animal again, upon identifying it satisfactorily, and paying a few charges arising from its capture and keeping. Call at No. ——, Rue ——, Faubourg St. Germain—au troisième.

"How was it possible," I asked, "that you should know the man to be a sailor, and belonging to a Maltese vessel?"

"I do *not know* it," said Dupin. "I am not *sure* of it. Here, however, is a small piece of ribbon, which from its form, and from its greasy appearance, has evidently been used in tying the hair in one of those long *queues* of which sailors are so fond. Moreover, this knot is one which few besides sailors can tie, and, is peculiar to the Maltese. I picked the ribbon up at

the foot of the lightning-rod. It could not have belonged to either of the deceased. Now if, after all, I am wrong in my induction from this ribbon, that the Frenchman was a sailor belonging to a Maltese vessel, still I can have done no harm in saying what I did in the advertisement. If I am right, a great point is gained. Cognizant although innocent of the murder, the Frenchman will naturally hesitate about replying to the advertisement— about demanding the Ourang-Outang. He will reason thus: 'I am innocent; I am poor; my Ourang-Outang is of great value—to one in my circumstances a fortune of itself—why should I lose it through idle apprehensions of danger? Here it is, within my grasp. It was found in the Bois de Boulogne—at a vast distance from the scene of that butchery. How can it ever be suspected that a brute beast should have done the deed? The police are at fault—they have failed to procure the slightest clue. Should they even trace the animal, it would be impossible to prove me cognizant of the murder, or to implicate me in guilt on account of that cognizance. Above all, *I am known*. The advertiser designates me as the possessor of the beast. I am not sure to what limit his knowledge may extend. Should I avoid claiming a property of so great value, which it is known that I possess, I will render the animal at least, liable to suspicion. It is not my policy to attract attention either to myself or to the beast. I will answer the advertisement, get the Ourang-Outang, and keep it close until this matter has blown over.'"

At this moment we heard a step upon the stairs.

"Be ready," said Dupin, "with your pistols, but neither use them nor show them until at a signal from myself."

The front door of the house had been left open, and the visiter had entered, without ringing, and advanced several steps upon the staircase. Now, however, he seemed to hesitate. Presently we heard him descending. Dupin was moving quickly to the door, when we again heard him coming up. He did not turn back a second time, but stepped up with decision, and rapped at the door of our chamber.

"Come in," said Dupin, in a cheerful and hearty tone.

A man entered. He was a sailor, evidently—a tall, stout, and muscular-looking person, with a certain dare-devil expression of countenance, not altogether unprepossessing. His face, greatly sunburnt, was more than half hidden by whisker and *mustachio*. He had with him a huge oaken cudgel, but appeared to be otherwise unarmed. He bowed awkwardly, and bade us "good evening," in French accents, which, although somewhat Neufchatelish, were still sufficiently indicative of a Parisian origin.

"Sit down, my friend," said Dupin. "I suppose you have called about the Ourang-Outang. Upon my word, I almost envy you the possession of him; a remarkably fine, and no doubt a very valuable animal. How old do you suppose him to be?"

The sailor drew a long breath, with the air of a man relieved of some intolerable burden, and then replied, in an assured tone:

"I have no way of telling—but he can't be more than four or five years old. Have you got him here?"

"Oh, no; we had no conveniences for keeping him here. He is at a livery stable in the Rue Dubourg, just by. You can get him in the morning. Of course you are prepared to identify the property?"

"To be sure I am, sir."

"I shall be sorry to part with him," said Dupin.

"I don't mean that you should be at all this trouble for nothing, sir," said the man. "Couldn't expect it. Am very willing to pay a reward for the finding of the animal—that is to say, anything in reason."

"Well," replied my friend, "that is all very fair, to be sure. Let me think!—what should I have? Oh! I will tell you. My reward shall be this. You shall give me all the information in your power about these murders in the Rue Morgue."

Dupin said the last words in a very low tone, and very quietly. Just as quietly, too, he walked towards the door, locked it, and put the key in his pocket. He then drew a pistol from his bosom and placed it, without the least flurry, upon the table.

The sailor's face flushed up as if he were struggling with suffocation. He started to his feet and grasped his cudgel; but the next moment he fell back into his seat, trembling violently, and with the countenance of death itself. He spoke not a word. I pitied him from the bottom of my heart.

"My friend," said Dupin, in a kind tone, "you are alarming yourself unnecessarily—you are indeed. We mean you no harm whatever. I pledge you the honor of a gentleman, and of a Frenchman, that we intend you no injury. I perfectly well know that you are innocent of the atrocities in the Rue Morgue. It will not do, however, to deny that you are in some measure implicated in them. From what I have already said, you must know that I have had means of information about this matter—means of which you could never have dreamed. Now the thing stands thus. You have done nothing which you could have avoided—nothing, certainly, which renders you culpable. You are not even guilty of robbery, when you might have robbed with impunity. You have nothing to conceal. You have no reason

for concealment. On the other hand, you are bound by every principle of honor to confess all you know. An innocent man is now imprisoned, charged with that crime of which you can point out the perpetrator."

The sailor had recovered his presence of mind, in a great measure, while Dupin uttered these words; but his original boldness of bearing was all gone.

"So help me God!" said he, after a brief pause, "I *will* tell you all I know about this affair; but I do not expect you to believe one half I say—I would be a fool indeed if I did. Still, I *am* innocent, and I will make a clean breast if I die for it."

What he stated was, in substance, this. He had lately made a voyage to the Indian Archipelago. A party, of which he formed one, landed at Borneo, and passed into the interior on an excursion of pleasure. Himself and a companion had captured the Ourang-Outang. This companion dying, the animal fell into his own exclusive possession. After a great trouble, occasioned by the intractable ferocity of his captive during the home voyage, he at length succeeded in lodging it safely at his own residence in Paris, where, not to attract towards himself the unpleasant curiosity of his neighbors, he kept it carefully secluded, until such time as it should recover from a wound in the foot, received from a splinter on board ship. His ultimate design was to sell it.

Returning home from some sailor's frolic on the night, or rather in the morning, of the murder, he found the beast occupying his own bedroom, into which it had broken from a closet adjoining, where it had been, as was thought, securely confined. Razor in hand, and fully lathered, it was sitting before a looking-glass, attempting the operation of shaving, in which it had no doubt previously watched its master through the keyhole of the closet. Terrified at the sight of so dangerous a weapon in the possession of an animal so ferocious, and so well able to use it, the man, for some moments, was at a loss what to do. He had been accustomed, however, to quiet the creature, even in its fiercest moods, by the use of a whip, and to this he now resorted. Upon sight of it, the Ourang-Outang sprang at once through the door of the chamber, down the stairs, and thence, through a window, unfortunately open, into the street.

The Frenchman followed in despair; the ape, razor still in hand, occasionally stopping to look back and gesticulate at its pursuer, until the latter had nearly come up with it. It then again made off. In this manner the chase continued for a long time. The streets were profoundly quiet, as it was nearly three o'clock in the morning. In passing down an alley in the rear of the Rue

Morgue, the fugitive's attention was arrested by a light gleaming from the open window of Madame L'Espanaye's chamber, in the fourth story of her house. Rushing to the building, it perceived the lightning-rod, clambered up with inconceivable agility, grasped the shutter, which was thrown fully back against the wall, and, by its means, swung itself directly upon the headboard of the bed. The whole feat did not occupy a minute. The shutter was kicked open again by the Ourang-Outang as it entered the room.

The sailor, in the meantime, was both rejoiced and perplexed. He had strong hopes of now recapturing the brute, as it could scarcely escape from the trap into which it had ventured, except by the rod, where it might be intercepted as it came down. On the other hand, there was much cause for anxiety as to what it might do in the house. This latter reflection urged the man still to follow the fugitive. A lightning-rod is ascended without difficulty, especially by a sailor; but, when he had arrived as high as the window, which lay far to his left, his career was stopped; the most that he could accomplish was to reach over so as to obtain a glimpse of the interior of the room. At this glimpse he nearly fell from his hold through excess of horror. Now it was that those hideous shrieks arose upon the night, which had startled from slumber, the inmates of the Rue Morgue. Madame L'Espanaye and her daughter, habited in their night clothes, had apparently been occupied in arranging some papers in the iron chest already mentioned, which had been wheeled into the middle of the room. It was open, and its contents lay beside it on the floor. The victims must have been sitting with their backs towards the window; and, from the time elapsing between the ingress of the beast and the screams, it seems probable that it was not immediately perceived. The flapping to of the shutter would naturally have been attributed to the wind.

As the sailor looked in, the gigantic animal had seized Madame L'Espanaye by the hair (which was loose, as she had been combing it), and was flourishing the razor about her face, in imitation of the motions of a barber. The daughter lay prostrate and motionless; she had swooned. The screams and struggles of the old lady (during which the hair was torn from her head) had the effect of changing the probably pacific purposes of the Ourang-Outang into those of wrath. With one determined sweep of its muscular arm it nearly severed her head from her body. The sight of blood inflamed its anger into frenzy. Gnashing its teeth, and flashing fire from its eyes, it flew upon the body of the girl and embedded its fearful talons in her throat, retaining its grasp until she expired. Its wandering and wild glances fell at this moment upon the head of the bed, over

which the face of its master, rigid with horror, was just discernible. The fury of the beast, who no doubt bore still in mind the dreaded whip, was instantly converted into fear. Conscious of having deserved punishment, it seemed desirous of concealing its bloody deeds, and skipped about the chamber in an agony of nervous agitation; throwing down and breaking the furniture as it moved, and dragging the bed from the bedstead. In conclusion, it seized first the corpse of the daughter, and thrust it up the chimney, as it was found; then that of the old lady, which, it immediately hurled through the window headlong.

As the ape approached the casement with its mutilated burden, the sailor shrank aghast to the rod, and, rather gliding than clambering down it, hurried at once home—dreading the consequences of the butchery, and gladly abandoning, in his terror, all solicitude about the fate of the Ourang-Outang. The words heard by the party upon the staircase were the Frenchman's exclamations of horror and affright, commingled with the fiendish jabberings of the brute.

I have scarcely anything to add. The Ourang-Outang must have escaped from the chamber, by the rod, just before the breaking of the door. It must have closed the window as it passed through it. It was subsequently caught by the owner himself, who obtained for it a very large sum at the *Jardin des Plantes*. Le Bon was instantly released, upon our narration of the circumstances (with some comments from Dupin) at the *bureau* of the Prefect of Police. This functionary, however, well disposed to my friend, could not altogether conceal his chagrin at the turn which affairs had taken, and was fain to indulge in a sarcasm or two about the propriety of every person minding his own business.

"Let him talk," said Dupin, who had not thought it necessary to reply. "Let him discourse; it will ease his conscience, I am satisfied with having defeated him in his own castle. Nevertheless, that he failed in the solution of this mystery, is by no means that matter for wonder which he supposes it; for, in truth, our friend the prefect is somewhat too cunning to be profound. In his wisdom is no *stamen*. It is all head and no body, like the pictures of the Goddess Laverna—or, at best, all head and shoulders, like a codfish. But he is a good creature after all. I like him especially for one master stroke of cant, by which he has attained his reputation for ingenuity. I mean the way he has *'de nier ce qui est, et d'expliquer ce qui n'est pas.'*"*[3]

* Rousseau—*Nouvelle Heloise*.

THE MYSTERY OF MARIE ROGÊT[*]

A SEQUEL TO "THE MURDERS IN THE RUE MORGUE"

Es giebt eine Reihe idealischer Begebenheiten, die der Wirklichkeit parallel läuft. Selten fallen sie zusammen. Menchen und zufalle modificiren gewohulich die idealische Begebenheit, so dass sie unvollkommen erscheint, und ihre Felgen gleichfalls unvollkommen sind. So bei der Reformation; statt des Protestantismus kam das Lutherum hervor.

There are ideal series of events which run parallel with the real ones. They rarely coincide. Men and circumstances generally modify the ideal train of events, so that it seems imperfect, and its consequences are equally imperfect. Thus with the Reformation; instead of Protestantism came Lutheranism.

NOVALIS.[†] MORAL ANSICHTEN

THERE ARE FEW PERSONS, EVEN AMONG THE CALMEST THINKERS, WHO have not occasionally been startled into a vague yet thrilling half-credence in the supernatural, by *coincidences* of so seemingly marvelous a character that, as *mere* coincidences, the intellect has been unable to receive them. Such sentiments—for the half-credences of which I speak

[*] Upon the original publication of "Marie Rogêt," the footnotes now appended were considered unnecessary; but the lapse of several years since the tragedy upon which the tale is based, renders it expedient to give them, and also to say a few words in explanation of the general design. A young girl, *Mary Cecilia Rogers*, was murdered in the vicinity of New York; and although her death occasioned an intense and long-enduring excitement, the mystery attending it

[†] The *nom de plume* of Von Hardenburg.

have never the full force of *thought*—such sentiments are seldom thoroughly stifled unless by reference to the doctrine of chance, or, as it is technically termed, the Calculus of Probabilities. Now this Calculus is, in its essence, purely mathematical; and thus we have the anomaly of the most rigidly exact in science applied to the shadow and spirituality of the most intangible in speculation.

The extraordinary details which I am now called upon to make public, will be found to form, as regards sequence of time, the primary branch of a series of scarcely intelligible *coincidences,* whose secondary or concluding branch will be recognized by all readers in the late murder of MARY CECILIA ROGERS, at New York.

When, in an article entitled "The Murders in the Rue Morgue," I endeavored, about a year ago, to depict some very remarkable features in the mental character of my friend, the Chevalier C. Auguste Dupin, it did not occur to me that I should ever resume the subject. This depicting of character constituted my design; and this design was thoroughly fulfilled in the wild train of circumstances brought to instance Dupin's idiosyncrasy. I might have adduced other examples, but I should have proven no more. Late events, however, in their surprising development, have startled me into some farther details, which will carry with them the air of extorted confession. Hearing what I have lately heard, it would be indeed strange should I remain silent in regard to what I both heard and saw so long ago.

Upon the winding up of the tragedy involved in the deaths of Madame L'Espanaye and her daughter, the Chevalier dismissed the affair at once

had remained unsolved at the period when the present paper was written and published (November, 1842). Herein, under pretence of relating the fate of a Parisian *grisette*, the author has followed, in minute detail, the essential, while merely paralleling the inessential, facts of the real murder of Mary Rogers. Thus all argument founded upon the fiction is applicable to the truth: and the investigation of the truth was the object.

The "Mystery of Marie Rogêt" was composed at a distance from the scene of the atrocity, and with no other means of investigation than the newspapers afforded. Thus much escaped the writer of which he could have availed himself had he been upon the spot and visited the localities. It may not be improper to record, nevertheless, that the confessions of *two* persons (one of them the Madame Deluc of the narrative), made, at different periods, long subsequent to the publication, confirmed, in full, not only the general conclusion, but absolutely *all* the chief hypothetical details by which that conclusion was attained.

from his attention, and relapsed into his old habits of moody revery. Prone, at all times, to abstraction, I readily fell in with his humor; and continuing to occupy our chambers in the Faubourg Saint Germain, we gave the Future to the winds, and slumbered tranquilly in the Present, weaving the dull world around us into dreams.

But these dreams were not altogether uninterrupted. It may readily be supposed that the part played by my friend, in the drama at the Rue Morgue had not failed of its impression upon the fancies of the Parisian police. With its emissaries, the name of Dupin had grown into a household word. The simple character of those inductions by which he had disentangled the mystery never having been explained even to the Prefect, or to any other individual than myself, of course it is not surprising that the affair was regarded as little less than miraculous, or that the Chevalier's analytical abilities acquired for him the credit of intuition. His frankness would have led him to disabuse every inquirer of such prejudice; but his indolent humor forbade all further agitation of a topic whose interest to himself had long ceased. It thus happened that he found himself the cynosure of the policial eyes; and the cases were not few in which attempt was made to engage his services at the Prefecture. One of the most remarkable instances was that of the murder of a young girl named Marie Rogêt.

This event occurred about two years after the atrocity in the Rue Morgue. Marie, whose Christian and family name will at once arrest attention from their resemblance to those of the unfortunate "cigar-girl," was the only daughter of the widow Estelle Rogêt. The father had died during the child's infancy, and from the period of his death, until within eighteen months before the assassination which forms the subject of our narrative, the mother and daughter had dwelt together in the Rue Pavée Saint Andrée;* Madame there keeping a *pension,* assisted by Marie. Affairs went on thus until the latter had attained her twenty-second year, when her great beauty attracted the notice of a perfumer, who occupied one of the shops in the basement of the Palais Royal, and whose custom lay chiefly among the desperate adventurers infesting that neighborhood. Monsieur Le Blanc† was not unaware of the advantages to be derived from the attendance of the fair Marie in his perfumery; and his liberal proposals were accepted eagerly by the girl, although with somewhat more of hesitation by Madame.

* Nassau Street.
† Anderson.

The anticipations of the shopkeeper were realized, and his rooms soon became notorious through the charms of the sprightly *grisette*. She had been in his employ about a year, when her admirers were thrown into confusion by her sudden disappearance from the shop. Monsieur Le Blanc was unable to account for her absence, and Madame Rogêt was distracted with anxiety and terror. The public papers immediately took up the theme, and the police were upon the point of making serious investigations, when, one fine morning, after the lapse of a week, Marie, in good health, but with a somewhat saddened air, made her reappearance at her usual counter in the perfumery. All inquiry, except that of a private character, was of course, immediately hushed. Monsieur Le Blanc professed total ignorance, as before. Marie, with Madame, replied to all questions, that the last week had been spent at the house of a relation in the country. Thus the affair died away, and was generally forgotten; for the girl, ostensibly to relieve herself from the impertinence of curiosity soon bade a final adieu to the perfumer, and sought the shelter of her mother's residence in the Rue Pavée Saint Andrée.

It was about five months after this return home, that her friends were alarmed by her sudden disappearance for the second time. Three days elapsed, and nothing was heard of her. On the fourth her corpse was found floating in the Seine,[*] near the shore which is opposite the Quartier of the Rue Saint Andre, and at a point not very far distant from the secluded neighborhood of the Barrière du Roule.[†]

The atrocity of this murder (for it was at once evident that murder had been committed), the youth and beauty of the victim, and, above all her previous notoriety, conspired to produce intense excitement in the minds of the sensitive Parisians. I can call to mind no similar occurrence producing so general and so intense an effect. For several weeks, in the discussion of this one absorbing theme, even the momentous political topics of the day were forgotten. The Prefect made unusual exertions; and the powers of the whole Parisian police were, of course, tasked to the utmost extent.

Upon the first discovery of the corpse, it was not supposed that the murderer would be able to elude, for more than a very brief period, the inquisition which was immediately set on foot. It was not until the expiration of a week that it was deemed necessary to offer a reward; and

[*] The Hudson.
[†] Weehawken.

even then this reward was limited to a thousand francs. In the meantime the investigation proceeded with vigor, if not always with judgment, and numerous individuals were examined to no purpose; while, owing to the continual absence of all clue to the mystery, the popular excitement greatly increased. At the end of the tenth day it was thought advisable to double the sum originally proposed; and, at length, the second week having elapsed without leading to any discoveries, and the prejudice which always exists in Paris against the Police having given vent to itself in several serious *émeutes,* the Prefect took it upon himself to offer the sum of twenty thousand francs "for the conviction of the assassin," or, if more than one should prove to have been implicated, "for the conviction of any one of the assassins." In the proclamation setting forth this reward, a full pardon was promised to any accomplice who should come forward in evidence against his fellow; and to the whole was appended, wherever it appeared, the private placard of a committee of citizens, offering ten thousand francs, in addition to the amount proposed by the Prefecture. The entire reward thus stood at no less than thirty thousand francs, which will be regarded as an extraordinary sum when we consider the humble condition of the girl, and the great frequency, in large cities, of such atrocities as the one described.

No one doubted now that the mystery of this murder would be immediately brought to light. But although, in one or two instances, arrests were made which promised elucidation, yet nothing was elicited which could implicate the parties suspected; and they were discharged forthwith. Strange as it may appear, the third week from the discovery of the body had passed, and passed without any light being thrown upon the subject, before even a rumor of the events which had so agitated the public mind reached the ears of Dupin and myself. Engaged in researches which absorbed our whole attention, it had been nearly a month since either of us had gone abroad, or received a visiter, or more than glanced at the leading political articles in one of the daily papers. The first intelligence of the murder was brought us by G——, in person. He called upon us early in the afternoon of the thirteenth of July, 18—, and remained with us until late in the night. He had been piqued by the failure of all his endeavors to ferret out the assassins. His reputation—so he said with a peculiarly Parisian air—was at stake. Even his honor was concerned. The eyes of the public were upon him; and there was really no sacrifice which he would not be willing to make for the development of the mystery. He concluded a somewhat droll speech with a compliment upon what he was pleased to term the *tact* of

Dupin, and made him a direct, and certainly a liberal proposition, the precise nature of which I do not feel myself at liberty to disclose, but which has no bearing upon the proper subject of my narrative.

The compliment my friend rebutted as best he could, but the proposition he accepted at once, although its advantages were altogether provisional. This point being settled, the Prefect broke forth at once into explanations of his own views, interspersing them with long comments upon the evidence; of which latter we were not yet in possession. He discoursed much and, beyond doubt, learnedly; while I hazarded an occasional suggestion as the night wore drowsily away. Dupin, sitting steadily in his accustomed arm-chair, was the embodiment of respectful attention. He wore spectacles, during the whole interview; and an occasional glance beneath their green glasses sufficed to convince me that he slept not the less soundly, because silently, throughout the seven or eight leaden-footed hours which immediately preceded the departure of the Prefect.

In the morning, I procured, at the Prefecture, a full report of all the evidence elicited, and, at the various newspaper offices, a copy of every paper in which, from first to last, had been published any decisive information in regard to this sad affair. Freed from all that was positively disproved, this mass of information stood thus:

Marie Rogêt left the residence of her mother, in the Rue Pavée St. Andrée, about nine o'clock in the morning of Sunday, June the twenty-second, 18—. In going out, she gave notice to a Monsieur Jacques St. Eustache,[*] and to him only, of her intention to spend the day with an aunt, who resided in the Rue des Drômes. The Rue des Drômes is a short and narrow but populous thoroughfare, not far from the banks of the river, and at a distance of some two miles, in the most direct course possible, from the *pension* of Madame Rogêt. St. Eustache was the accepted suitor of Marie, and lodged, as well as took his meals, at the *pension*. He was to have gone for his betrothed at dusk, and to have escorted her home. In the afternoon, however, it came on to rain heavily; and, supposing that she would remain all night at her aunt's (as she had done under similar circumstances before), he did not think it necessary to keep his promise. As night drew on, Madame Rogêt (who was an infirm old lady, seventy years of age) was heard to express a fear "that she should never see Marie again"; but this observation attracted little attention at the time.

[*] Payne.

On Monday it was ascertained that the girl had not been to the Rue des Drômes; and when the day elapsed without tidings of her, a tardy search was instituted at several points in the city and its environs. It was not, however, until the fourth day from the period of her disappearance that anything satisfactory was ascertained respecting her. On this day (Wednesday, the twenty-fifth of June) a Monsieur Beauvais,* who, with a friend, had been making inquiries for Marie near the Barrière du Roule, on the shore of the Seine which is opposite the Rue Pavée St. Andrée, was informed that a corpse had just been towed ashore by some fishermen, who had found it floating in the river. Upon seeing the body, Beauvais, after some hesitation, identified it as that of the perfumery-girl. His friend recognized it more promptly.

The face was suffused with dark blood, some of which issued from the mouth. No foam was seen, as in the case of the merely drowned. There was no discoloration in the cellular tissue. About the throat were bruises and impressions of fingers. The arms were bent over on the chest, and were rigid. The right hand was clenched; the left partially open. On the left wrist were two circular excoriations, apparently the effect of ropes, or of a rope in more than one volution. A part of the right wrist, also, was much chafed, as well as the back throughout its extent, but more especially at the shoulder-blades. In bringing the body to the shore the fishermen had attached to it a rope, but none of the excoriations had been effected by this. The flesh of the neck was much swollen. There were no cuts apparent, or bruises which appeared the effect of blows. A piece of lace was found tied so tightly around the neck as to be hidden from sight; it was completely buried in the flesh, and was fasted by a knot which lay just under the left ear. This alone would have sufficed to produce death. The medical testimony spoke confidently of the virtuous character of the deceased. She had been subjected, it said, to brutal violence. The corpse was in such condition when found, that there could have been no difficulty in its recognition by friends.

The dress was much torn and otherwise disordered. In the outer garment, a slip, about a foot wide, had been torn upward from the bottom hem to the waist, but not torn off. It was wound three times around the waist, and secured by a sort of hitch in the back. The dress immediately beneath the frock was of fine muslin; and from this a slip eighteen inches wide had been torn entirely out—torn very evenly and with great care. It was found around her neck, fitting loosely, and secured with a hard knot.

* Crommelin.

Over this muslin slip and the slip of lace the strings of a bonnet were attached, the bonnet being appended. The knot by which the strings of the bonnet were fastened was not a lady's, but a slip or sailor's knot.

After the recognition of the corpse, it was not, as usual, taken to the Morgue (this formality being superfluous), but hastily interred not far from the spot at which it was brought ashore. Through the exertions of Beauvais, the matter was industriously hushed up, as far as possible; and several days had elapsed before any public emotion resulted. A weekly paper,[*] however, at length took up the theme; the corpse was disinterred, and a re-examination instituted; but nothing was elicited beyond what has been already noted. The clothes, however, were now submitted to the mother and friends of the deceased, and fully identified as those worn by the girl upon leaving home.

Meantime, the excitement increased hourly. Several individuals were arrested and discharged. St. Eustache fell especially under suspicion; and he failed, at first, to give an intelligible account of his whereabouts during the Sunday on which Marie left home. Subsequently, however, he submitted to Monsieur G——, affidavits, accounting satisfactorily for every hour of the day in question. As time passed and no discovery ensued, a thousand contradictory rumors were circulated, and journalists busied themselves in *suggestions*. Among these, the one which attracted the most notice, was the idea that Marie Rogêt still lived—that the corpse found in the Seine was that of some other unfortunate. It will be proper that I submit to the reader some passages which embody the suggestion alluded to. These passages are *literal* translations from *L'Etoile*,[†] a paper conducted, in general, with much ability.

Mademoiselle Rogêt left her mother's house on Sunday morning, June the twenty-second, 18—, with the ostensible purpose of going to see her aunt, or some other connection, in the Rue des Drômes. From that hour, nobody is proved to have seen her. There is no trace or tidings of her at all. . . . There has no person, whatever, come forward, so far, who saw her at all, in that day, after she left her mother's door. . . . Now, though we have no evidence that Marie Rogêt was in the land of the living after nine o'clock on Sunday, June the twenty-second, we have proof that, up to that hour, she was alive. On Wednesday noon, at twelve, a female body was discovered

[*] The New York *Mercury.*
[†] The New York *Brother Jonathan,* edited by H. Hastings Weld, Esq.

afloat on the shore of the Barriere de Roule. This was, even if we presume that Marie Rogêt was thrown into the river within three hours after she left her mother's house, only three days from the time she left her home—three days to an hour. But it is folly to suppose that the murder, if murder was committed on her body, could have been consummated soon enough to have enabled her murderers to throw the body into the river before midnight. Those who are guilty of such horrid crimes choose darkness rather than light. . . . Thus we see that if the body found in the river *was* that of Marie Rogêt, it could only have been in the water two and a half days, or three at the outside. All experience has shown that drowned bodies, or bodies thrown into the water immediately after death by violence, require from six to ten days for sufficient decomposition to take place to bring them to the top of the water. Even where a cannon is fired over a corpse, and it rises before at least five or six days' immersion, it sinks again, if left alone. Now, we ask, what was there in this case to cause a departure from the ordinary course of nature? . . . If the body had been kept in its mangled state on shore until Tuesday night, some trace would be found in shore of the murderers. It is a doubtful point, also, whether the body would be so soon afloat, even were it thrown in after having been dead two days. And, furthermore, it is exceedingly improbable that any villains who had committed such a murder as is here supposed, would have thrown the body in without weight to sink it, when such a precaution could have so easily been taken.

The editor here proceeds to argue that the body must have been in the water "not three days merely, but, at least, five times three days," because it was so far decomposed that Beauvais had great difficulty in recognizing it. This latter point, however, was fully disproved. I continue the translation:

What, then, are the facts on which M. Beauvais says that he has no doubt the body was that of Marie Rogêt? He ripped up the gown sleeve, and says he found marks which satisfied him of the identity. The public generally supposed those marks to have consisted of some description of scars. He rubbed the arm and found *hair* upon it—something as indefinite, we think, as can readily be imagined— as little conclusive as finding an arm in the sleeve. M. Beauvais did not return that night, but sent word to Madame Rogêt, at seven

o'clock, on Wednesday evening, that an investigation was still in progress respecting her daughter. If we allow that Madame Rogêt, from her age and grief, could not go over (which is allowing a great deal), there certainly must have been someone who would have thought it worthwhile to go over and attend the investigation, if they thought the body was that of Marie. Nobody went over. There was nothing said or heard about the matter in the Rue Pavée St. Andrée, that reached even the occupants of the same building. M. St. Eustache, the lover and intended husband of Marie, who boarded in her mother's house, deposes that he did not hear of the discovery of the body of his intended until the next morning, when M. Beauvais came into his chamber and told him of it. For an item of news like this, it strikes us it was very coolly received.

In this way the journal endeavored to create the impression of an apathy on the part of the relatives of Marie, inconsistent with the supposition that these relatives believed the corpse to be hers. Its insinuations amount to this: that Marie, with the connivance of her friends, had absented herself from the city for reasons involving a charge against her chastity; and that these friends upon the discovery of a corpse in the Seine, somewhat resembling that of the girl, had availed themselves of the opportunity to impress the public with the belief of her death. But *L'Etoile* was again overhasty. It was distinctly proved that no apathy, such as was imagined, existed; that the old lady was exceedingly feeble, and so agitated as to be unable to attend to any duty; that St. Eustache, so far from receiving the news coolly, was distracted with grief, and bore himself so frantically, that M. Beauvais prevailed upon a friend and relative to take charge of him, and prevent his attending the examination at the disinterment. Moreover, although it was stated by *L'Etoile,* that the corpse was reinterred at the public expense—that an advantageous offer of private sepulture was absolutely declined by the family—and that no member of the family attended the ceremonial: although, I say, all this was asserted by *L'Etoile* in furtherance of the impression it designed to convey—yet *all* this was satisfactorily disproved. In a subsequent number of the paper, an attempt was made to throw suspicion upon Beauvais himself. The editor says:

> Now, then, a change comes over the matter. We are told that, on one occasion, while a Madame B—— was at Madame Rogêt's house, M. Beauvais, who was going out, told her that a *gendarme* was

expected there, and that she, Madame B., must not say anything to the *gendarme* until he returned, but let the matter be for him. . . . In the present posture of affairs, M. Beauvais appears to have the whole matter locked up in his head. A single step cannot be taken without M. Beauvais, for, go which way you will, you run against him. . . . For some reason he determined that nobody shall have anything to do with the proceedings but himself, and he has elbowed the male relatives out of the way, according to their representations, in a very singular manner. He seems to have been very much averse to permitting the relatives to see the body.

By the following fact, some color was given to the suspicion thus thrown upon Beauvais. A visiter at his office, a few days prior to the girl's disappearance, and during the absence of its occupant, had observed *a rose* in the key-hole of the door, and the name *"Marie"* inscribed upon a slate which hung near at hand.

The general impression, so far as we were enabled to glean it from the newspapers, seemed to be, that Marie had been the victim of *a gang* of desperadoes—that by these she had been borne across the river, mal-treated, and murdered. *Le Commerciel,*[*] however, a print of extensive influence, was earnest in combatting this popular idea. I quote a passage or two from its columns:

> We are persuaded that pursuit has hitherto been on a false scent, so far as it has been directed to the Barrière du Roule. It is impos-sible that a person so well-known to thousands as this young woman was, should have passed three blocks without someone having seen her; and anyone who saw her would have remem-bered it, for she interested all who knew her. It was when the streets were full of people, when she went out. . . . It is impossible that she could have gone to the Barrière du Roule, or to the Rue des Drômes, without being recognized by a dozen persons; yet no one has come forward who saw her outside of her mother's door, and there is no evidence, except the testimony concerning her *expressed intentions,* that she did go out at all. Her gown was torn, bound round her, and tied; and by that the body was carried as a bundle. If the murder had been committed at the Barrière du

[*] New York *Journal of Commerce.*

Roule, there would have been no necessity for any such arrangement. The fact that the body was found floating near the Barriere, is no proof as to where it was thrown into the water. . . . A piece of one of the unfortunate girl's petticoats, two feet long and one foot wide, was torn out and tied under her chin around the back of her head, probably to prevent screams. This was done by fellows who had no pocket-handkerchief.

A day or two before the Prefect called upon us, however, some important information reached the police, which seemed to overthrow, at least, the chief portion of *Le Commerciel*'s argument. Two small boys, sons of a Madame Deluc, while roaming among the woods near the Barrière du Roule, chanced to penetrate a close thicket, within which were three or four large stones, forming a kind of seat with a back and footstool. On the upper stone lay a white petticoat; on the second, a silk scarf. A parasol, gloves, and a pocket-handkerchief were also here found. The handkerchief bore the name "Marie Rogêt." Fragments of dress were discovered on the brambles around. The earth was trampled, the bushes were broken, and there was every evidence of a struggle. Between the thicket and the river, the fences were found taken down, and the ground bore evidence of some heavy burden having been dragged along it.

A weekly paper, *Le Soleil*,* had the following comments upon this discovery—comments which merely echoed the sentiment of the whole Parisian press:

> The things had all evidently been there at least three or four weeks; they were all mildewed down hard with the action of the rain, and stuck together from mildew. The grass had grown around and over some of them. The silk on the parasol was strong, but the threads of it were run together within. The upper part, where it had been doubled and folded, was all mildewed and rotten, and tore on its being opened. . . . The pieces of her frock torn out by the bushes were about three inches wide and six inches long. One part was the hem of the frock, and it had been mended; the other piece was part of the skirt, not the hem. They looked like strips torn off, and were on the thorn bush, about a foot from the ground. . . . There can be no doubt, therefore, that the spot of this appalling outrage has been discovered.

* Philadelphia *Saturday Evening Post,* edited by C. I. Peterson, Esq.

Consequent upon this discovery, new evidence appeared. Madame Deluc testified that she keeps a road-side inn not far from the bank of the river, opposite the Barrière du Roule. The neighborhood is secluded—particularly so. It is the usual Sunday resort of blackguards from the city, who cross the river in boats. About three o'clock, in the afternoon of the Sunday in question, a young girl arrived at the inn, accompanied by a young man of dark complexion. The two remained here for some time. On their departure, they took the road to some thick woods in the vicinity. Madame Deluc's attention was called to the dress worn by the girl, on account of its resemblance to one worn by a deceased relative. A scarf was particularly noticed. Soon after the departure of the couple, a gang of miscreants made their appearance, behaved boisterously, ate and drank without making payment, followed in the route of the young man and girl, returned to the inn about dusk, and recrossed the river as if in great haste.

It was soon after dark, upon this same evening, that Madame Deluc, as well as her eldest son, heard the screams of a female in the vicinity of the inn. The screams were violent but brief. Madame D. recognized not only the scarf which was found in the thicket, but the dress which was discovered upon the corpse. An omnibus-driver, Valence,* now also testified that he saw Marie Rogêt cross a ferry on the Seine, on the Sunday in question, in company with a young man of dark complexion. He, Valence, knew Marie, and could not be mistaken in her identity. The articles found in the thicket were fully identified by the relatives of Marie.

The items of evidence and information thus collected by myself, from the newspapers, at the suggestion of Dupin, embraced only one more point—but this was a point of seemingly vast consequence. It appears that, immediately after the discovery of the clothes as above described, the lifeless or nearly lifeless body of St. Eustache, Marie's betrothed, was found in the vicinity of what all now supposed the scene of the outrage. A phial labeled "laudanum,"[1] and emptied, was found near him. His breath gave evidence of the poison. He died without speaking. Upon his person was found a letter, briefly stating his love for Marie, with his design of self-destruction.

"I need scarcely tell you," said Dupin, as he finished the perusal of my notes, "that this is a far more intricate case than that of the Rue Morgue;

* Adam

from which it differs in one important respect. This is an *ordinary*, although an atrocious, instance of crime. There is nothing peculiarly *outré* about it. You will observe that, for this reason, the mystery has been considered easy, when, for this reason, it should have been considered difficult, of solution. Thus, at first, it was thought unnecessary to offer a reward. The myrmidons[2] of G—— were able at once to comprehend how and why such an atrocity *might have been* committed. They could picture to their imaginations a mode—many modes—and a motive—many motives; and because it was not impossible that either of these numerous modes or motives *could* have been the actual one, they have taken it for granted that one of them *must*. But the ease with which these variable fancies were entertained, and the very plausibility which each assumed, should have been understood as indicative rather of the difficulties than of the facilities which must attend elucidation. I have before observed that it is by prominences above the plane of the ordinary, that reason feels her way, if at all, in her search for the true, and that the proper question in cases such as this, is not so much 'what has occurred?' as 'what has occurred that has never occurred before?' In the investigations at the house of Madame L'Espanaye,* the agents of G—— were discouraged and confounded by that very *unusualness* which, to a properly regulated intellect, would have afforded the surest omen of success; while this same intellect might have been plunged in despair at the ordinary character of all that met the eye in the case of the perfumery-girl, and yet told of nothing but easy triumph to the functionaries of the Prefecture.

"In the case of Madame L'Espanaye and her daughter, there was, even at the beginning of our investigation, no doubt that murder had been committed. The idea of suicide was excluded at once. Here, too, we are freed, at the commencement, from all supposition of self-murder. The body found at the Barrière du Roule was found under such circumstances as to leave us no room for embarrassment upon this important point. But it has been suggested that the corpse discovered is not that of the Marie Rogêt for the conviction of whose assassin, or assassins, the reward is offered, and respecting whom, solely, our agreement has been arranged with the Prefect. We both know this gentleman well. It will not do to trust him too far. If, dating our inquiries from the body found, and thence tracing a murderer, we yet discover this body to be that of some other

* See "Murders in the Rue Morgue."

individual than Marie; or if, starting from the living Marie, we find her, yet find her unassassinated—in either case we lose our labor; since it is Monsieur G—— with whom we have to deal. For our own purpose, therefore, if not for the purpose of justice, it is indispensable that our first step should be the determination of the identity of the corpse with the Marie Rogêt who is missing.

"With the public the arguments of *L'Etoile* have had weight; and that the journal itself is convinced of their importance would appear from the manner in which it commences one of its essays upon the subject— 'Several of the morning papers of the day,' it says, 'speak of the *conclusive* article in Monday's *Etoile.'* To me, this article appears conclusive of little beyond the zeal of its inditer. We should bear in mind that, in general, it is the object of our newspapers rather to create a sensation—to make a point—than to further the cause of truth. The latter end is only pursued when it seems coincident with the former. The print which merely falls in with ordinary opinion (however well founded this opinion may be) earns for itself no credit with the mob. The mass of the people regard as profound only him who suggests *pungent contradictions* of the general idea. In ratiocination, not less than in literature, it is the *epigram* which is the most immediately and the most universally appreciated. In both, it is of the lowest order of merit.

"What I mean to say is, that it is the mingled epigram and melodrame of the idea, that Marie Rogêt still lives, rather than any true plausibility in this idea, which have suggested it to *L'Etoile*, and secured it a favorable reception with the public. Let us examine the heads of this journal's argument; endeavoring to avoid the incoherence with which it is originally set forth.

"The first aim of the writer is to show, from the brevity of the interval between Marie's disappearance and the finding of the floating corpse, that this corpse cannot be that of Marie. The reduction of this interval to its smallest possible dimension, becomes thus, at once, an object with the reasoner. In the rash pursuit of this object, he rushes into mere assumption at the outset. 'It is folly to suppose,' he says, 'that the murder, if murder was committed on her body, could have been consummated soon enough to have enabled her murderers to throw the body into the river before midnight.' We demand at once, and very naturally, *why?* Why is it folly to suppose that the murder was committed *within five minutes* after the girl's quitting her mother's house? Why is it folly to suppose that the murder was committed at any given period of the day? There have been

assassinations at all hours. But, had the murder taken place at any moment between nine o'clock in the morning of Sunday and a quarter before midnight, there would still have been time enough 'to throw the body into the river before midnight.' This assumption, then, amounts precisely to this—that the murder was not committed on Sunday at all—and, if we allow *L'Etoile* to assume this, we may permit it any liberties whatever. The paragraph beginning 'It is folly to suppose that the murder, etc.,' however it appears as printed in *L'Etoile,* may be imagined to have existed actually *thus* in the brain of its inditer: 'It is folly to suppose that the murder, if murder was committed on the body, could have been committed soon enough to have enabled her murderers to throw the body into the river before midnight; it is folly, we say, to suppose all this, and to suppose at the same time (as we are resolved to suppose), that the body was *not* thrown in until *after* midnight'—a sentence sufficiently inconsequential in itself, but not so utterly preposterous as the one printed.

"Were it my purpose," continued Dupin, "merely to *make out a case* against this passage of *L'Etoile*'s argument, I might safely leave it where it is. It is not, however, with *L'Etoile* that we have to do, but with the truth. The sentence in question has but one meaning, as it stands; and this meaning I have fairly stated; but it is material that we go behind the mere words, for an idea which these words have obviously intended, and failed to convey. It was the design of the journalist to say that at whatever period of the day or night Sunday this murder was committed, it was improbable that the assassins would have ventured to bear the corpse to the river before midnight. And herein lies, really, the assumption of which I complain. It is assumed that the murder was committed at such a position, and under such circumstances, that *the bearing it* to the river became necessary. Now, the assassination might have taken place upon the river's brink, or on the river itself; and, thus, the throwing the corpse in the water might have been resorted to at any period of the day or night, as the most obvious and most immediate mode of disposal. You will understand that I suggest nothing here as probable, or as coincident with my own opinion. My design, so far, has no reference to the *facts* of the case. I wish merely to caution you against the whole tone of *L'Etoile*'s *suggestion,* by calling your attention to its *ex parte* character at the outset.

"Having prescribed thus a limit to suit its own preconceived notions; having assumed that, if this were the body of Marie, it could have been in the water but a very brief time, the journal goes on to say:

All experience has shown that drowned bodies, or bodies thrown into the water immediately after death by violence, require from six to ten days for sufficient decomposition to take place to bring them to the top of the water. Even when a cannon is fired over a corpse, and it rises before at least five or six days' immersion, it sinks again if let alone.

"These assertions have been tacitly received by every paper in Paris, with the exception of *Le Moniteur*.* This latter print endeavors to combat that portion of the paragraph which has reference to 'drowned bodies' only, by citing some five or six instances in which the bodies of individuals known to be drowned were found floating after the lapse of less time than is insisted upon by *L'Etoile*. But there is something excessively unphilosophical in the attempt, on the part of *Le Moniteur*, to rebut the general assertion of *L'Etoile*, by a citation of particular instances militating against that assertion. Had it been possible to adduce fifty instead of five examples of bodies found floating at the end of two or three days, these fifty examples could still have been properly regarded only as exceptions to *L'Etoile*'s rule, until such time as the rule itself should be confuted. Admitting the rule (and this *Le Moniteur* does not deny, insisting merely upon its exceptions), the argument of *L'Etoile* is suffered to remain in full force; for this argument does not pretend to involve more than a question of the probability of the body having risen to the surface in less than three days; and this *probability* will be in favor of *L'Etoile*'s position until the instances so childishly adduced shall be sufficient in number to establish an antagonistical rule.

"You will see at once that all argument upon this head should be urged, if at all, against the rule itself; and for this end we must examine the *rationale* of the rule. Now the human body, in general, is neither much lighter nor much heavier than the water of the Seine; that is to say, the specific gravity of the human body, in its natural condition, is about equal to the bulk of fresh water which it displaces. The bodies of fat and fleshy persons, with small bones, and of women generally, are lighter than those of the lean and large-boned, and of men; and the specific gravity of the water of a river is somewhat influenced by the presence of the tide from sea. But, leaving this tide out of the question, it may be said that *very* few human bodies will sink at all, even in fresh water, *of their own accord*. Almost

* The New York *Commercial Advertiser*, edited by Col. Stone.

anyone, falling into a river, will be enabled to float, if he suffer the specific gravity of the water fairly to be adduced in comparison with his own—that is to say, if he suffer his whole person to be immersed, with as little exception as possible. The proper position for one who cannot swim, is the upright position of the walker on land, with the head thrown fully back, and immersed; the mouth and nostrils alone remaining above the surface. Thus circumstanced, we shall find that we float without difficulty and without exertion. It is evident, however, that the gravities of the body, and of the bulk of water displaced, are very nicely balanced, and that a trifle will cause either to preponderate. An arm, for instance, uplifted from the water, and thus deprived of its support, is an additional weight sufficient to immerse the whole head, while the accidental aid of the smallest piece of timber will enable us to elevate the head so as to look about. Now, in the struggles of one unused to swimming, the arms are invariably thrown upward, while an attempt is made to keep the head in its usual perpendicular position. The result is the immersion of the mouth and nostrils, and the inception, during efforts to breathe while beneath the surface, of water into the lungs. Much is also received into the stomach, and the whole body becomes heavier by the difference between the weight of the air originally distending these cavities, and that of the fluid which now fills them. This difference is sufficient to cause the body to sink, as a general rule; but is insufficient in the case of individuals with small bones and an abnormal quantity of flaccid or fatty matter. Such individuals float even after drowning.

"The corpse, being supposed at the bottom of the river, will there remain until, by some means, its specific gravity again becomes less than that of the bulk of water which it displaces. This effect is brought about by decomposition, or otherwise. The result of decomposition is the generation of gas, distending the cellular tissues and all the cavities, and giving the *puffed* appearance which is so horrible. When this distension has so far progressed that the bulk of the corpse is materially increased without a corresponding increase of *mass* or weight, its specific gravity becomes less than that of the water displaced, and it forthwith makes its appearance at the surface. But decomposition is modified by innumerable circumstances—is hastened or retarded by innumerable agencies; for example, by the heat or cold of the season, by the mineral impregnation or purity of the water, by its depth or shallowness, by its currency or stagnation, by the temperament of the body, by its infection or freedom from disease before death. Thus it is evident that we can assign no period, with

anything like accuracy, at which the corpse shall rise through decomposition. Under certain conditions this result would be brought about within an hour; under others it might not take place at all. There are chemical infusions by which the animal frame can be preserved *forever* from corruption; the Bichloride of Mercury is one. But, apart from decomposition, there may be, and very usually is, a generation of gas within the stomach, from the acetous fermentation of vegetable matter (or within other cavities from other causes), sufficient to induce a distension which will bring the body to the surface. The effect produced by the firing of a cannon is that of simple vibration. This may either loosen the corpse from the soft mud or ooze in which it is embedded, thus permitting it to rise when other agencies have already prepared it for so doing; or it may overcome the tenacity of some putrescent portions of the cellular tissue, allowing the cavities to distend under the influence of the gas.

"Having thus before us the whole philosophy of this subject, we can easily test by it the assertions of *L'Etoile*. 'All experience shows,' says this paper, 'that drowned bodies, or bodies thrown into the water immediately after death by violence, require from six to ten days for sufficient decomposition to take place to bring them to the top of the water. Even when a cannon is fired over a corpse, and it rises before at least five or six days' immersion, it sinks again if let alone.'

"The whole of this paragraph must now appear a tissue of inconsequence and incoherence. All experience does *not* show that 'drowned bodies' *require* from six to ten days for sufficient decomposition to take place to bring them to the surface. Both science and experience show that the period of their rising is, and necessarily must be, indeterminate. If, moreover, a body has risen to the surface through firing of cannon, it will *not* 'sink again if let alone,' until decomposition has so far progressed as to permit the escape of the generated gas. But I wish to call your attention to the distinction which is made between 'drowned bodies,' and 'bodies thrown into the water immediately after death by violence.' Although the writer admits the distinction, he yet includes them all in the same category. I have shown how it is that the body of a drowning man becomes specifically heavier than its bulk of water, and that he would not sink at all, except for the struggle by which he elevates his arms above the surface, and his gasps for breath while beneath the surface—gasps which supply by water the place of the original air in the lungs. But these struggles and these gasps would not occur in the body 'thrown into the water immediately after death by violence.' Thus, in the latter instance, *the body,*

as a general rule, would not sink at all—a fact of which *L'Etoile* is evidently ignorant. When decomposition had proceeded to a very great extent—when the flesh had in a great measure left the bones—then, indeed, but not *till* then, should we lose sight of the corpse.

"And now what are we to make of the argument, that the body found could not be that of Marie Rogêt, because, three days only having elapsed, this body was found floating? If drowned, being a woman, she might never have sunk; or, having sunk, might have reappeared in twenty-four hours or less. But no one supposes her to have been drowned; and, dying before being thrown into the river, she might have been found floating at any period afterward whatever.

"'But,' says *L'Etoile*, 'if the body had been kept in its mangled state on shore until Tuesday night, some trace would be found on shore of the murderers.' Here it is at first difficult to perceive the intention of the reasoner. He means to anticipate what he imagines would be an objection to his theory—viz.: that the body was kept on shore two days, suffering rapid decomposition—more rapid than if immersed in water. He supposes that, had this been the case, it *might* have appeared at the surface on the Wednesday, and thinks that *only* under such circumstances it could so have appeared. He is accordingly in haste to show that it *was not* kept on shore; for, if so, 'some trace would be found on shore of the murderers.' I presume you smile at the *sequitur*. You cannot be made to see how the mere *duration* of the corpse on the shore could operate to *multiply traces* of the assassins. Nor can I.

"'And furthermore it is exceedingly improbable,' continues our journal, 'that any villains who had committed such a murder as is here supposed, would have thrown the body in without weight to sink it, when such a precaution could have so easily been taken.' Observe, here, the laughable confusion of thought! No one—not even *L'Etoile*—disputes the murder committed *on the body found*. The marks of violence are too obvious. It is our reasoner's object merely to show that this body is not Marie's. He wishes to prove that *Marie* is not assassinated—not that the corpse was not. Yet his observation proves only the latter point. Here is a corpse without weight attached. Murderers, casting it in, would not have failed to attach a weight. Therefore it was not thrown in by murderers. This is all which is proved, if anything is. The question of identity is not even approached, and *L'Etoile* has been at great pains merely to gainsay now what it has admitted only a moment before. 'We are perfectly convinced,' it says, 'that the body found was that of a murdered female.'

"Nor is this the sole instance, even in this division of his subject, where our reasoner unwittingly reasons against himself. His evident object, I have already said, is to reduce, as much as possible, the interval between Marie's disappearance and the finding of the corpse. Yet we find him *urging* the point that no person saw the girl from the moment of her leaving her mother's house. 'We have no evidence,' he says, 'that Marie Rogêt was in the land of the living after nine o'clock on Sunday, June the twenty-second.' As his argument is obviously an *ex parte* one, he should, at least, have left this matter out of sight; for had anyone been known to see Marie, say on Monday, or on Tuesday, the interval in question would have been much reduced, and, by his own ratiocination, the probability much diminished of the corpse being that of the *grisette*. It is, nevertheless, amusing to observe that *L'Etoile* insists upon its point in the full belief of its furthering its general argument.

"Reperuse now that portion of this argument which has reference to the identification of the corpse by Beauvais. In regard to the *hair* upon the arm, *L'Etoile* has been obviously disingenuous. M. Beauvais, not being an idiot, could never have urged, in identification of the corpse, simply *hair upon its arm*. No arm is *without* hair. The *generality* of the expression of *L'Etoile* is a mere perversion of the witness' phraseology. He must have spoken of some *peculiarity* in this hair. It must have been a peculiarity of color, of quantity, of length, or of situation.

"'Her foot,' says the journal, 'was small—so are thousands of feet. Her garter is no proof whatever—nor is her shoe—for shoes and garters are sold in packages. The same may be said of the flowers in her hat. One thing upon which M. Beauvais strongly insists is, that the clasp on the garter found had been set back to take it in. This amounts to nothing; for most women find it proper to take a pair of garters home and fit them to the size of the limbs they are to encircle, rather than to try them in the store where they purchase.' Here it is difficult to suppose the reasoner in earnest. Had M. Beauvais, in his search for the body of Marie, discovered a corpse corresponding in general size and appearance to the missing girl, he would have been warranted (without reference to the question of habiliment at all) in forming an opinion that his search had been successful. If, in addition to the point of general size and contour, he had found upon the arm a peculiar hairy appearance which he had observed upon the living Marie, his opinion might have been justly strengthened; and the increase of positiveness might well have been in the ratio of the peculiarity, or unusualness, of the hairy mark. If, the feet

of Marie being small, those of the corpse were also small, the increase of probability that the body was that of Marie would not be an increase in a ratio merely arithmetical, but in one highly geometrical, or accumulative. Add to all this shoes such as she had been known to wear upon the day of her disappearance, and, although these shoes may be 'sold in packages,' you so far augment the probability as to verge upon the certain. What, of itself, would be no evidence of identity, becomes through its corroborative position, proof most sure. Give us, then, flowers in the hat corresponding to those worn by the missing girl, and we seek for nothing farther. If only *one* flower, we seek for nothing farther—what then if two or three, or more? Each successive one is multiple evidence—proof not *added* to proof, but *multiplied* by hundreds or thousands. Let us now discover, upon the deceased, garters such as the living used, and it is almost folly to proceed. But these garters are found to be tightened, by the setting back of a clasp, in just such a manner as her own had been tightened by Marie shortly previous to her leaving home. It is now madness or hypocrisy to doubt. What *L'Etoile* says in respect to this abbreviation of the garter's being an unusual occurrence, shows nothing beyond its own pertinacity in error. The elastic nature of the clasp-garter is self-demonstration of the *unusual-ness* of the abbreviation. What is made to adjust itself, must of necessity require foreign adjustment but rarely. It must have been by an accident, in its strictest sense, that these garters of Marie needed the tightening described. They alone would have amply established her identity. But it is not that the corpse was found to have the garters of the missing girl, or found to have her shoes, or her bonnet, or the flowers of her bonnet, or her feet, or a peculiar mark upon the arm, or her general size and appearance—it is that the corpse had each and *all collectively.* Could it be proved that the editor of *L'Etoile really* entertained a doubt, under the circumstances, there would be no need, in his case, of a commission *de lunatico inquirendo.* He has thought it sagacious to echo the small talk of the lawyers, who, for the most part, content themselves with echoing the rectangular precepts of the courts. I would here observe that very much of what is rejected as evidence by a court, is the best of evidence to the intellect. For the court, guiding itself by the general principles of evidence—the recognized and *booked* principles—is averse from swerving at particular instances. And this steadfast adherence to principle, with rigorous disregard of the conflicting exception, is a sure mode of attaining the *maximum* of attainable truth, in any long sequence of time. The practice, *in mass,*

is therefore philosophical; but it is not the less certain that it engenders vast individual error.*

"In respect to the insinuations leveled at Beauvais, you will be willing to dismiss them in a breath. You have already fathomed the true character of this good gentleman. He is a *busy-body,* with much of romance and little of wit. Anyone so constituted will readily so conduct himself, upon occasion of *real* excitement, as to render himself liable to suspicion on the part of the over-acute, or the ill-disposed. M. Beauvais (as it appears from your notes) had some personal interviews with the editor of *L'Etoile,* and offended him by venturing an opinion that the corpse, notwithstanding the theory of the editor, was, in sober fact, that of Marie. 'He persists,' says the paper, 'in asserting the corpse to be that of Marie, but cannot give a circumstance, in addition to those which we have commented upon, to make others believe.' Now, without readverting to the fact that stronger evidence 'to make others believe,' could *never* have been adduced, it may be remarked that a man may very well be understood to believe, in a case of this kind, without the ability to advance a single reason for the belief of a second party. Nothing is more vague than impressions of individual identity. Each man recognizes his neighbor, yet there are few instances in which anyone is prepared *to give a reason* for his recognition. The editor of *L'Etoile* had no right to be offended at M. Beauvais' unreasoning belief.

"The suspicious circumstances which invest him, will be found to tally much better with my hypothesis of *romantic busy-bodyism,* than with the reasoner's suggestion of guilt. Once adopting the more charitable interpretation, we shall find no difficulty in comprehending the rose in the key-hole; the 'Marie' upon the slate; the 'elbowing the male relatives out of the way'; the 'aversion to permitting them to see the body'; the caution given to Madame B——, that she must hold no conversation with the *gendarme* until his return (Beauvais'); and, lastly, his apparent determination 'that

* "A theory based on the qualities of an object, will prevent its being unfolded according to its objects; and he who arranges topics in reference to their causes, will cease to value them according to their results. Thus the jurisprudence of every nation will show that, when law becomes a science and a system, it ceases to be justice. The errors into which a blind devotion to *principles* of classification has led the common law, will be seen by observing how often the legislature has been obliged to come forward to restore the equity its scheme had lost."—*Landor.*

nobody should have anything to do with the proceedings except himself.' It seems to be unquestionable that Beauvais was a suitor of Marie's; that she coquetted with him; and that he was ambitious of being thought to enjoy her fullest intimacy and confidence. I shall say nothing more upon this point; and, as the evidence fully rebuts the assertion of *L'Etoile*, touching the matter of *apathy* on the part of the mother and other relatives—an apathy inconsistent with the supposition of their believing the corpse to be that of the perfumery-girl—we shall now proceed as if the question of *identity* were settled to our perfect satisfaction."

"And what," I here demanded, "do you think of the opinions of *Le Commerciel?*"

"That, in spirit, they are far more worthy of attention than any which have been promulgated upon the subject. The deductions from the premises are philosophical and acute; but the premises, in two instances, at least, are founded in imperfect observation. *Le Commerciel* wishes to intimate that Marie was seized by some gang of low ruffians not far from her mother's door. 'It is impossible,' it urges, 'that a person so well known to thousands as this young woman was, should have passed three blocks without someone having seen her.' This is the idea of a man long resident in Paris—a public man—and one whose walks to and fro in the city have been mostly limited to the vicinity of the public offices. He is aware that he seldom passes so far as a dozen blocks from his own *bureau*, without being recognized and accosted. And, knowing the extent of his personal acquaintance with others, and of others with him, he compares his notoriety with that of the perfumery-girl, finds no great difference between them, and reaches at once the conclusion that she, in her walks, would be equally liable to recognition with himself in his. This could only be the case were her walks of the same unvarying, methodical character, and within the same *species* of limited region as are his own. He passes to and fro, at regular intervals, within a confined periphery, abounding in individuals who are led to observation of his person through interest in the kindred nature of his occupation with their own. But the walks of Marie may, in general, be supposed discursive. In this particular instance, it will be understood as most probable, that she proceeded upon a route of more than average diversity from her accustomed ones. The parallel which we imagine to have existed in the mind of *Le Commerciel* would only be sustained in the event of the two individuals traversing the whole city. In this case, granting the personal acquaintances to be equal, the chances would be also equal that an equal number of personal rencounters would

be made. For my own part, I should hold it not only as possible, but as very far more than probable, that Marie might have proceeded, at any given period, by any one of the many routes between her own residence and that of her aunt, without meeting a single individual whom she knew, or by whom she was known. In viewing this question in its full and proper light, we must hold steadily in mind the great disproportion between the personal acquaintances of even the most noted individual in Paris, and the entire population of Paris itself.

"But whatever force there may still appear to be in the suggestion of *Le Commerciel*, will be much diminished when we take into consideration *the hour* at which the girl went abroad. 'It was when the streets were full of people,' says *Le Commerciel*, 'that she went out.' But not so. It was at nine o'clock in the morning. Now at nine o'clock of every morning in the week, *with the exception of Sunday*, the streets of the city are, it is true, thronged with people. At nine on Sunday, the populace are chiefly within doors *preparing for church*. No observing person can have failed to notice the peculiarly deserted air of the town, from about eight until ten on the morning of every Sabbath. Between ten and eleven the streets are thronged, but not at so early a period as that designated.

"There is another point at which there seems a deficiency of *observation* on the part of *Le Commerciel*. 'A piece,' it says, 'of one of the unfortunate girl's petticoats, two feet long, and one foot wide, was torn out and tied under her chin, and around the back of her head, probably to prevent screams. This was done by fellows who had no pocket-handkerchiefs.' Whether this idea is or is not well founded, we will endeavor to see hereafter; but by 'fellows who have no pocket-handkerchiefs,' the editor intends the lowest class of ruffians. These, however, are the very description of people who will always be found to have handkerchiefs even when destitute of shirts. You must have had occasion to observe how absolutely indispensable, of late years, to the thorough blackguard, has become the pocket-handkerchief."

"And what are we to think," I asked, "of the article in *Le Soleil?*"

"That it is a vast pity its inditer was not born a parrot—in which case he would have been the most illustrious parrot of his race. He has merely repeated the individual items of the already published opinion; collecting them, with a laudable industry, from this paper and from that. 'The things had all *evidently* been there,' he says, 'at least, three or four weeks, and there can be *no doubt* that the spot of this appalling outrage has been discovered.' The facts here restated by *Le Soleil*, are very far indeed from removing my

own doubts upon this subject, and we will examine them more particularly hereafter in connection with another division of the theme.

"At present we must occupy ourselves with other investigations. You cannot fail to have remarked the extreme laxity of the examination of the corpse. To be sure, the question of identity was readily determined, or should have been; but there were other points to be ascertained. Had the body been in any respect *despoiled?* Had the deceased any articles of jewelry about her person upon leaving home? If so, had she any when found? These are important questions utterly untouched by the evidence; and there are others of equal moment, which have met with no attention. We must endeavor to satisfy ourselves by personal inquiry. The case of St. Eustache must be re-examined. I have no suspicion of this person; but let us proceed methodically. We will ascertain beyond a doubt the validity of the *affidavits* in regard to his whereabouts on the Sunday. Affidavits of this character are readily made matter of mystification. Should there be nothing wrong here, however, we will dismiss St. Eustache from our investigations. His suicide, however, corroborative of suspicion, were there found to be deceit in the affidavits, is, without such deceit, in no respect an unaccountable circumstance, or one which need cause us to deflect from the line of ordinary analysis.

"In that which I now propose, we will discard the interior points of this tragedy, and concentrate our attention upon its outskirts. Not the least usual error in investigations such as this, is the limiting of inquiry to the immediate, with total disregard of the collateral or circumstantial events. It is the malpractice of the courts to confine evidence and discussion to the bounds of apparent relevancy. Yet experience has shown, and a true philosophy will always show, that a vast, perhaps the larger, portion of truth arises from the seemingly irrelevant. It is through the spirit of this principle, if not precisely through its letter, that modern science has resolved to *calculate upon the unforeseen.* But perhaps you do not comprehend me. The history of human knowledge has so uninterruptedly shown that to collateral, or incidental, or accidental events we are indebted for the most numerous and most valuable discoveries, that it has at length become necessary, in any prospective view of improvement, to make not only large, but the largest allowances for inventions that shall arise by chance, and quite out of the range of ordinary expectation. It is no longer philosophical to base upon what has been a vision of what is to be. *Accident* is admitted as a portion of the substructure. We make chance a matter of absolute calculation. We subject the unlooked for and unimagined to the mathematical *formulae* of the schools.

"I repeat that it is no more than fact that the *larger* portion of all truth has sprung from the collateral; and it is but in accordance with the spirit of the principle involved in this fact that I would divert inquiry, in the present case, from the trodden and hitherto unfruitful ground of the event itself to the contemporary circumstances which surround it. While you ascertain the validity of the affidavits, I will examine the newspapers more generally than you have as yet done. So far, we have only reconnoitered the field of investigation; but it will be strange, indeed, if a comprehensive survey, such as I propose, of the public prints will not afford us some minute points which shall establish a *direction* for inquiry."

In pursuance of Dupin's suggestion, I made scrupulous examination of the affair of the affidavits. The result was a firm conviction of their validity, and of the consequent innocence of St. Eustache. In the meantime my friend occupied himself, with what seemed to me a minuteness altogether objectless, in a scrutiny of the various newspaper files. At the end of a week he placed before me the following extracts:

About three years and a half ago, a disturbance very similar to the present was caused by the disappearance of this same Marie Rogêt from the *parfumerie* of Monsieur Le Blanc, in the Palais Royal. At the end of a week, however, she reappeared at her customary *comptoir,* as well as ever, with the exception of a slight paleness not altogether usual. It was given out by Monsieur Le Blanc and her mother that she had merely been on a visit to some friend in the country; and the affair was speedily hushed up. We presume that the present absence is a freak of the same nature, and that, at the expiration of a week or, perhaps, of a month, we shall have her among us again.—*Evening Paper,* Monday, June 23.*

An evening journal of yesterday refers to a former mysterious disappearance of Mademoiselle Rogêt. It is well known that, during the week of her absence from Le Blanc's *parfumerie,* she was in the company of a young naval officer much noted for his debaucheries. A quarrel, it is supposed, providentially, led to her return home. We have the name of the Lothario in question, who is at

* New York *Express.*

present stationed in Paris, but for obvious reasons forbear to make it public.—*Le Mercurie*, Tuesday Morning, June 24.*

An outrage of the most atrocious character was perpetrated near this city the day before yesterday. A gentleman, with his wife and daughter, engaged, about dusk, the services of six young men, who were idly rowing a boat to and fro near the banks of the Seine, to convey him across the river. Upon reaching the opposite shore the three passengers stepped out, and had proceeded so far as to be beyond the view of the boat, when the daughter discovered that she had left in it her parasol. She returned for it, was seized by the gang, carried out into the stream, gagged, brutally treated, and finally taken to the shore at a point not far from that at which she had originally entered the boat with her parents. The villains have escaped for the time, but the police are upon their trail, and some of them will soon be taken.—*Morning Paper*, June 25.†

We have received one or two communications, the object of which is to fasten the crime of the late atrocity upon Mennais;‡ but as this gentleman has been fully exonerated by a legal inquiry, and as the arguments of our several correspondents appear to be more zealous than profound, we do not think it advisable to make them public.—*Morning Paper*, June 28.§

We have received several forcibly written communications, apparently from various sources, and which go far to render it a matter of certainty that the unfortunate Marie Rogêt has become a victim of one of the numerous bands of blackguards which infest the vicinity of the city upon Sunday. Our own opinion is decidedly in favor of this supposition. We shall endeavor to make room for some of these arguments hereafter.—*Evening Paper*, Tuesday, June 31.**

* New York *Herald.*
† New York *Courier and Inquirer.*
‡ Mennais was one of the parties originally suspected and arrested, but discharged through total lack of evidence.
§ New York *Courier and Inquirer.*
** New York *Evening Post.*

On Monday, one of the bargemen connected with the revenue service saw an empty boat floating down the Seine. Sails were lying in the bottom of the boat. The bargeman towed it under the barge office. The next morning it was taken from thence without the knowledge of any of the officers. The rudder is now at the barge office.—*Le Diligence*, Thursday, June 26.[*]

Upon reading these various extracts, they not only seemed to me irrelevant, but I could perceive no mode in which any one of them could be brought to bear upon the matter in hand. I waited for some explanation from Dupin.

"It is not my present design," he said, "to *dwell* upon the first and second of those extracts. I have copied them chiefly to show you the extreme remissness of the police, who, as far as I can understand from the Prefect, have not troubled themselves, in any respect, with an examination of the naval officer alluded to. Yet it is mere folly to say that between the first and second disappearance of Marie there is no *supposable* connection. Let us admit the first elopement to have resulted in a quarrel between the lovers, and the return home of the betrayed. We are now prepared to view a second *elopement* (if we *know* that an elopement has again taken place) as indicating a renewal of the betrayer's advances, rather than as the result of new proposals by a second individual—we are prepared to regard it as a 'making up' of the old *amour,* rather than as the commencement of a new one. The chances are ten to one, that he who had once eloped with Marie would again propose an elopement, rather than that she to whom proposals of elopement had been made by one individual, should have them made to her by another. And here let me call your attention to the fact, that the time elapsing between the first ascertained and the second supposed elopement is a few months more than the general period of the cruises of our men-of-war. Had the lover been interrupted in his first villainy by the necessity of departure to sea, and had he seized the first moment of his return to renew the base designs not yet altogether accomplished—or not yet altogether accomplished *by him?* Of all these things we know nothing.

"You will say, however, that, in the second instance, there was *no* elopement as imagined. Certainly not—but are we prepared to say that there

[*] New York *Standard.*

was not the frustrated design? Beyond St. Eustache, and perhaps Beauvais, we find no recognized, no open, no honorable suitors of Marie. Of none other is there anything said. Who, then, is the secret lover, of whom the relatives (*at least most of them*) know nothing, but whom Marie meets upon the morning of Sunday, and who is so deeply in her confidence, that she hesitates not to remain with him until the shades of the evening descend, amid the solitary groves of the Barrière du Roule? Who is that secret lover, I ask, of whom, at least, *most* of the relatives know nothing? And what means the singular prophecy of Madame Rogêt on the morning of Marie's departure? 'I fear that I shall never see Marie again.'

"But if we cannot imagine Madame Rogêt privy to the design of elope-ment, may we not at least suppose this design entertained by the girl? Upon quitting home, she gave it to be understood that she was about to visit her aunt in the Rue des Drômes, and St. Eustache was requested to call for her at dark. Now, at first glance, this fact strongly militates against my suggestion; but let us reflect. That she *did* meet some companion, and proceed with him across the river, reaching the Barrière du Roule at so late an hour as three o'clock in the afternoon, is known. But in consent-ing so to accompany this individual (*for whatever purpose—to her mother known or unknown*), she must have thought of her expressed intention when leaving home, and of the surprise and suspicion aroused in the bosom of her affianced suitor, St. Eustache, when, calling for her, at the hour appointed, in the Rue des Drômes, he should find that she had not been there, and when, moreover, upon returning to the *pension* with this alarming intelligence, he should become aware of her continued absence from home. She must have thought of these things, I say. She must have foreseen the chagrin of St. Eustache, the suspicion of all. She could not have thought of returning to brave this suspicion; but the suspicion becomes a point of trivial importance to her, if we suppose her *not* intending to return.

"We may imagine her thinking thus—'I am to meet a certain person for the purpose of elopement, or for certain other purposes known only to myself. It is necessary that there be no chance of interruption—there must be sufficient time given us to elude pursuit—I will give it to be under-stood that I shall visit and spend the day with my aunt at the Rue des Drômes—I will tell St. Eustache not to call for me until dark—in this way, my absence from home for the longest possible period, without causing suspicion or anxiety, will be accounted for, and I shall gain more time than in any other manner. If I bid St. Eustache call for me at dark, he will

be sure not to call before; but if I wholly neglect to bid him call, my time for escape will be diminished, since it will be expected that I return the earlier, and my absence will the sooner excite anxiety. Now, if it were my design to return *at all*— if I had in contemplation merely a stroll with the individual in question—it would not be my policy to bid St. Eustache call; for, calling, he will be *sure* to ascertain that I have played him false—a fact of which I might keep him forever in ignorance, by leaving home without notifying him of my intention, by returning before dark, and by then stating that I had been to visit my aunt in the Rue des Drômes. But, as it is my design *never* to return—or not for some weeks—or not until certain concealments are effected—the gaining of time is the only point about which I need give myself any concern.'

"You have observed, in your notes, that the most general opinion in relation to this sad affair is, and was from the first, that the girl had been the victim of *a gang* of blackguards. Now, the popular opinion, under certain conditions, is not to be disregarded. When arising of itself—when manifesting itself in a strictly spontaneous manner—we should look upon it as analogous with that *intuition* which is the idiosyncrasy of the individual man of genius. In ninety-nine cases from the hundred I would abide by its decision. But it is important that we find no palpable traces of *suggestion*. The opinion must be rigorously *the public's own*; and the distinction is often exceedingly difficult to perceive and to maintain. In the present instance, it appears to me that this 'public opinion,' in respect to *a gang*, has been superinduced by the collateral event which is detailed in the third of my extracts. All Paris is excited by the discovered corpse of Marie, a girl young, beautiful, and notorious. This corpse is found, bearing marks of violence, and floating in the river. But it is now made known that, at the very period, or about the very period, in which it is supposed that the girl was assassinated, an outrage similar in nature to that endured by the deceased, although less in extent, was perpetuated by a gang of young ruffians, upon the person of a second young female. Is it wonderful that the one known atrocity should influence the popular judgment in regard to the other unknown? This judgment awaited direction, and the known outrage seemed so opportunely to afford it! Marie, too, was found in the river; and upon this very river was this known outrage committed. The connection of the two events had about it so much of the palpable, that the true wonder would have been a *failure* of the populace to appreciate and to seize it. But, in fact, the one atrocity, known to be so committed, is, if anything, evidence that the other, committed at a time nearly coincident, was *not* so

committed. It would have been a miracle indeed, if, while a gang of ruffians were perpetrating, at a given locality, a most unheard-of wrong, there should have been another similar gang, in a similar locality, in the same city, under the same circumstances, with the same means and appliances, engaged in a wrong of precisely the same aspect, at precisely the same period of time! Yet in what, if not in this marvelous train of coincidence, does the accidentally *suggested* opinion of the populace call upon us to believe?

"Before proceeding farther, let us consider the supposed scene of the assassination, in the thicket at the Barrière du Roule. This thicket, although dense, was in the close vicinity of a public road. Within were three or four large stones, forming a kind of seat with a back and footstool. On the upper stone was discovered a white petticoat; on the second, a silk scarf. A parasol, gloves, and a pocket-handkerchief, were also here found. The handkerchief bore the name 'Marie Rogêt.' Fragments of dress were seen on the branches around. The earth was trampled, the bushes were broken, and there was every evidence of a violent struggle.

"Notwithstanding the acclamation with which the discovery of this thicket was received by the press, and the unanimity with which it was supposed to indicate the precise scene of the outrage, it must be admitted that there was some very good reason for doubt. That it *was* the scene, I may or I may not believe—but there was excellent reason for doubt. Had the *true* scene been, as *Le Commerciel* suggested, in the neighborhood of the Rue Pavée St. Andrée, the perpetrators of the crime, supposing them still resident in Paris, would naturally have been stricken with terror at the public attention thus acutely directed into the proper channel; and, in certain classes of minds, there would have arisen, at once, a sense of the necessity of some exertion to redivert this attention. And thus, the thicket of the Barrière du Roule having been already suspected, the idea of placing the articles where they were found, might have been naturally entertained. There is no real evidence, although *Le Soleil* so supposes, that the articles discovered had been more than a very few days in the thicket; while there is much circumstantial proof that they could not have remained there, without attracting attention, during the twenty days elapsing between the fatal Sunday and the afternoon upon which they were found by the boys. 'They were all *mildewed* down hard,' says *Le Soleil*, adopting the opinions of its predecessors, 'with the action of the rain and stuck together from *mildew*. The grass had grown around and over some of them. The silk of the parasol was strong, but the threads of it were run together within. The upper part, where it had been doubled and

folded, was all *mildewed* and rotten, and tore on being opened.' In respect to the grass having 'grown around and over some of them,' it is obvious that the fact could only have been ascertained from the words, and thus from the recollections, of two small boys; for these boys removed the articles and took them home before they had been seen by a third party. But grass will grow, especially in warm and damp weather (such as was that of the period of the murder), as much as two or three inches in a single day. A parasol lying upon a newly turfed ground, might, in a single week, be entirely concealed from sight by the upspringing grass. And touching that *mildew* upon which the editor of *Le Soleil* so pertinaciously insists, that he employs the word no less than three times in the brief paragraph just quoted, is he really unaware of the nature of this *mildew?* Is he to be told that it is one of the many classes of *fungus,* of which the most ordinary feature is its up-springing and decadence within twenty-four hours?

"Thus we see, at a glance, that what has been most triumphantly adduced in support of the idea that the articles had been 'for at least three or four weeks' in the thicket, is most absurdly null as regards any evidence of that fact. On the other hand, it is exceedingly difficult to believe that these articles could have remained in the thicket specified for a longer period than a single week—for a longer period than from one Sunday to the next. Those who know anything of the vicinity of Paris, know the extreme difficulty of finding *seclusion,* unless at a great distance from its suburbs. Such a thing as an unexplored or even an unfrequently visited recess, amid its woods or groves, is not for a moment to be imagined. Let anyone who, being at heart a lover of nature, is yet chained by duty to the dust and heat of this great metropolis—let any such one attempt, even during the weekdays, to slake his thirst for solitude amid the scenes of natural loveliness which immediately surround us. At every second step, he will find the growing charm dispelled by the voice and personal intrusion of some ruffian or party of carousing blackguards. He will seek privacy amid the densest foliage, all in vain. Here are the very nooks where the unwashed most abound—here are the temples most desecrate. With sickness of the heart the wanderer will flee back to the polluted Paris as to a less odious because less incongruous sink of pollution. But if the vicinity of the city is so beset during the working days of the week, how much more so on the Sabbath! It is now especially that, released from the claims of labor, or deprived of the customary opportunities of crime, the town blackguard seeks the precincts of the town, not through love of the rural, which in his heart he despises, but by way of escape from the restraints and

conventionalities of society. He desires less the fresh air and the green trees, than the utter *licence* of the country. Here, at the road-side inn, or beneath the foliage of the woods, he indulges unchecked by any eye except those of his boon companions, in all the mad excess of a counterfeit hilarity—the joint offspring of liberty and of rum. I say nothing more than what must be obvious to every dispassionate observer, when I repeat that the circumstance of the articles in question having remained undiscovered, for a longer period than from one Sunday to another, in *any* thicket in the immediate neighborhood of Paris, is to be looked upon as little less than miraculous.

"But there are not wanting other grounds for the suspicion that the articles were placed in the thicket with the view of diverting attention from the real scene of the outrage. And first, let me direct your notice to the *date* of the discovery of the articles. Collate this with the date of the fifth extract made by myself from the newspapers. You will find that the discovery followed, almost immediately, the urgent communications sent to the evening paper. These communications, although various, and apparently from various sources, tended all to the same point—viz., the directing of attention to *a gang* as the perpetrators of the outrage, and to the neighborhood of the Barrière du Roule as its scene. Now, here, of course, the suspicion is not that, in consequence of these communications, or of the public attention by them directed, the articles were found by the boys; but the suspicion might and may well have been, that the articles were not *before* found by the boys, for the reason that the articles had not before been in the thicket; having been deposited there only at so late a period as at the date, or shortly prior to the date of the communications, by the guilty authors of these communications themselves.

"This thicket was a singular—an exceedingly singular one. It was unusually dense. Within its naturally walled enclosure were three extraordinary stones, *forming a seat with a back and a footstool.* And this thicket, so full of art, was in the immediate vicinity, *within a few rods,* of the dwelling of Madame Deluc, whose boys were in the habit of closely examining the shrubberies about them in search of the bark of the sassafras. Would it be a rash wager—a wager of one thousand to one—that *a day* never passed over the heads of these boys without finding at least one of them ensconced in the umbrageous hall, and enthroned upon its natural throne? Those who would hesitate at such a wager, have either never been boys themselves, or have forgotten the boyish nature. I repeat—it is exceedingly hard to comprehend how the articles could have remained

in this thicket undiscovered, for a longer period than one or two days; and that thus there is good ground for suspicion, in spite of the dogmatic ignorance of *Le Soleil*, that they were, at a comparatively late date, deposited where found.

"But there are still other and stronger reasons for believing them so deposited, than any which I have as yet urged. And, now, let me beg your notice to the highly artificial arrangement of the articles. On the *upper* stone lay a white petticoat; on the *second*, a silk scarf; scattered around, were a parasol, gloves, and a pocket-handkerchief bearing the name 'Marie Rogêt.' Here is just such an arrangement as would *naturally* be made by a not over-acute person wishing to dispose the articles *naturally*. But it is by no means a *really* natural arrangement. I should rather have looked to see the things *all* lying on the ground and trampled under foot. In the narrow limits of that bower, it would have been scarcely possible that the petticoat and scarf should have retained a position upon the stones, when subjected to the brushing to and fro of many struggling persons. 'There was evidence,' it is said, 'of a struggle; and the earth was trampled, the bushes were broken,'—but the petticoat and the scarf are found deposited as if upon shelves. 'The pieces of the frock torn out by the bushes were about three inches wide and six inches long. One part was the hem of the frock and it had been mended. They *looked like strips torn off.*' Here, inadvertently, *Le Soleil* has employed an exceedingly suspicious phrase. The pieces, as described, do indeed 'look like strips torn off'; but purposely and by hand. It is one of the rarest of accidents that a piece is 'torn off,' from any garment such as is now in question, by the agency *of a thorn*. From the very nature of such fabrics, a thorn or nail becoming entangled in them, tears them rectangularly—divides them into two longitudinal rents, at right angles with each other, and meeting at an apex where the thorn enters—but it is scarcely possible to conceive the piece 'torn off.' I never so knew it, nor did you. To tear a piece *off* from such fabric, two distinct forces, in different directions, will be, in almost every case, required. If there be two edges to the fabric—if, for example, it be a pocket-handkerchief, and it is desired to tear from it a slip, then, and then only, will the one force serve the purpose. But in the present case the question is of a dress, presenting but one edge. To tear a piece from the interior, where no edge is presented, could only be effected by a miracle through the agency of thorns, and no *one* thorn could accomplish it. But, even where an edge is presented, two thorns will be necessary, operating, the one in two distinct directions, and the

other in one. And this in the supposition that the edge is unhemmed. If hemmed, the matter is nearly out of the question. We thus see the numerous and great obstacles in the way of pieces being 'torn off' through the simple agency of 'thorns'; yet we are required to believe not only that one piece but that many have been so torn. 'And one part,' too, '*was the hem of the frock!*' Another piece was '*part of the skirt, not the hem,*'— that is to say, was torn completely out, through the agency of thorns, from the unedged interior of the dress! These, I say, are things which one may well be pardoned for disbelieving; yet, taken collectedly, they form, perhaps, less of reasonable ground for suspicion, than the one startling circumstance of the articles having been left in this thicket at all, by any *murderers* who had enough precaution to think of removing the corpse. You will not have apprehended me rightly, however, if you suppose it my design to *deny* this thicket as the scene of the outrage. There might have been a wrong *here,* or more possibly, an accident at Madame Deluc's. But, in fact, this is a point of minor importance. We are not engaged in an attempt to discover the scene, but to produce the perpetrators of the murder. What I have adduced, notwithstanding the minuteness with which I have adduced it, has been with the view, first, to show the folly of the positive and headlong assertions of *Le Soleil,* but secondly and chiefly, to bring you, by the most natural route, to a further contemplation of the doubt whether this assassination has, or has not, been the work of *a gang.*

"We will resume this question by mere allusion to the revolting details of the surgeon examined at the inquest. It is only necessary to say that his published *inferences,* in regard to the number of ruffians, have been properly ridiculed as unjust and totally baseless, by all the reputable anatomists of Paris. Not that the matter *might not* have been as inferred, but that there was no ground for the inference: was there not much for another?

"Let us reflect now upon 'the traces of a struggle'; and let me ask what these traces have been supposed to demonstrate. A gang. But do they not rather demonstrate the absence of a gang? What *struggle* could have taken place—what struggle so violent and so enduring as to have left its 'traces' in all directions—between a weak and defenceless girl and *a gang* of ruffians imagined? The silent grasp of a few rough arms and all would have been over. The victim must have been absolutely passive at their will. You will here bear in mind that the arguments urged against the thicket as the scene, are applicable, in chief part, only against it as the scene of an outrage committed by *more than a single individual.* If we imagine but *one*

violator, we can conceive, and thus only conceive, the struggle of so vio-
lent and so obstinate a nature as to have left the 'traces' apparent.

"And again. I have already mentioned the suspicion to be excited by
the fact that the articles in question were suffered to remain *at all* in the
thicket where discovered. It seems almost impossible that these evi-
dences of guilt should have been accidentally left where found. There
was sufficient presence of mind (it is supposed) to remove the corpse;
and yet a more positive evidence than the corpse itself (whose features
might have been quickly obliterated by decay), is allowed to lie con-
spicuously in the scene of the outrage—I allude to the handkerchief
with the *name* of the deceased. If this was accident, it was not the acci-
dent *of a gang*. We can imagine it only the accident of an individual. Let
us see. An individual has committed the murder. He is alone with the
ghost of the departed. He is appalled by what lies motionless before
him. The fury of his passion is over, and there is abundant room in his
heart for the natural awe of the deed. His is none of that confidence
which the presence of numbers inevitably inspires. He is *alone* with the
dead. He trembles and is bewildered. Yet there is a necessity for dispos-
ing of the corpse. He bears it to the river, but leaves behind him the
other evidences of guilt; for it is difficult, if not impossible to carry all
the burden at once, and it will be easy to return for what is left. But in
his toilsome journey to the water his fears redouble within him. The
sounds of life encompass his path. A dozen times he hears or fancies he
hears the step of an observer. Even the very lights from the city bewilder
him. Yet, in time, and by long and frequent pauses of deep agony, he
reaches the river's brink, and disposes of his ghastly charge—perhaps
through the medium of a boat. But *now* what treasure does the world
hold—what threat of vengeance could it hold out—which would have
power to urge the return of that lonely murderer over that toilsome and
perilous path, to the thicket and its blood-chilling recollections? He
returns *not,* let the consequences be what they may. He *could* not return
if he would. His sole thought is immediate escape. He turns his back *for-
ever* upon those dreadful shrubberies, and flees as from the wrath to come.

"But how with a gang? Their number would have inspired them with
confidence; if, indeed, confidence is ever wanting in the breast of the
arrant blackguard; and of arrant blackguards alone are the supposed
gangs ever constituted. Their number, I say, would have prevented the
bewildering and unreasoning terror which I have imagined to paralyze
the single man. Could we suppose an oversight in one, or two, or three,

this oversight would have been remedied by a fourth. They would have left nothing behind them; for their number would have enabled them to carry *all* at once. There would have been no need of *return*.

"Consider now the circumstance that, in the outer garment of the corpse when found, 'a slip, about a foot wide, had been torn upward from the bottom hem to the waist, wound three times around the waist, and secured by a sort of hitch in the back.' This was done with the obvious design of affording *a handle* by which to carry the body. But would any *number* of men have dreamed of resorting to such an expedient? To three or four, the limbs of the corpse would have afforded not only a sufficient, but the best possible, hold. The device is that of a single individual; and this brings us to the fact that 'between the thicket and the river, the rails of the fences were found taken down, and the ground bore evident traces of some heavy burden having been dragged along it!' But would a *number* of men have put themselves to the superfluous trouble of taking down a fence, for the purpose of dragging through it a corpse which they might have *lifted over* any fence in an instant? Would a *number* of men have so *dragged* a corpse at all as to have left evident *traces* of the dragging?

"And here we must refer to an observation of *Le Commerciel;* an observation upon which I have already, in some measure, commented. 'A piece,' says this journal, 'of one of the unfortunate girl's petticoats was torn out and tied under her chin, and around the back of her head, probably to prevent screams. This was done by fellows who had no pocket-handkerchiefs.'

"I have before suggested that a genuine blackguard is never *without* a pocket-handkerchief. But it is not to this fact that I now especially advert. That it was not through want of a handkerchief for the purpose imagined by *Le Commerciel,* that this bandage was employed, is rendered apparent by the handkerchief left in the thicket; and that the object was not 'to prevent screams' appears, also, from the bandage having been employed in preference to what would so much better have answered the purpose. But the language of the evidence speaks of the strip in question as 'found around the neck, fitting loosely, and secured with a hard knot.' These words are sufficiently vague, but differ materially from those of *Le Commerciel.* The slip was eighteen inches wide, and therefore, although of muslin, would form a strong band when folded or rumpled longitudinally. And thus rumpled it was discovered. My inference is this. The solitary murderer, having borne the corpse for some distance (whether from the thicket or elsewhere) by means of the bandage *hitched* around its middle, found the weight, in this mode of procedure, too much for his

strength. He resolved to drag the burden—the evidence goes to show that it *was* dragged. With this object in view, it became necessary to attach something like a rope to one of the extremities. It could be best attached about the neck, where the head would prevent it slipping off. And now the murderer bethought him, unquestionably, of the bandage about the loins. He would have used this, but for its volution about the corpse, the *hitch* which embarrassed it, and the reflection that it had not been 'torn off' from the garment. It was easier to tear a new slip from the petticoat. He tore it, made it fast about the neck, and so *dragged* his victim to the brink of the river. That this 'bandage,' only attainable with trouble and delay, and but imperfectly answering its purpose—that this bandage was employed *at all,* demonstrates that the necessity for its employment sprang from circumstances arising at a period when the handkerchief was no longer attainable—that is to say, arising, as we have imagined, after quitting the thicket (if the thicket it was), and on the road between the thicket and the river.

"But the evidence, you will say, of Madame Deluc (!) points especially to the presence of *a gang* in the vicinity of the thicket, at or about the epoch of the murder. This I grant. I doubt if there were not a *dozen* gangs, such as described by Madame Deluc, in and about the vicinity of the Barrière du Roule at or *about* the period of this tragedy. But the gang which has drawn upon itself the pointed animadversion, although the somewhat tardy and very suspicious evidence, of Madame Deluc, is the *only* gang which is represented by that honest and scrupulous old lady as having eaten her cakes and swallowed her brandy, without putting themselves to the trouble of making her payment. *Et hinc illae irae?*

"But what *is* the precise evidence of Madame Deluc? 'A gang of miscreants made their appearance, behaved boisterously, ate and drank without making payment, followed in the route of the young man and the girl, returned to the inn *about dusk,* and recrossed the river as if in great haste.'

"Now this 'great haste' very possibly seemed *greater* haste in the eyes of Madame Deluc, since she dwelt lingeringly and lamentingly upon her violated cakes and ale—cakes and ale for which she might still have entertained a faint hope of compensation. Why, otherwise, since it was *about dusk,* should she make a point of the *haste?* It is no cause for wonder, surely, that even a gang of blackguards should make *haste* to get home when a wide river is to be crossed in small boats, when storm impends, and when night *approaches.*

"I say *approaches*; for the night had *not yet arrived*. It was only *about dusk* that the indecent haste of these 'miscreants' offended the sober eyes of Madame Deluc. But we are told that it was upon this very evening that Madame Deluc, as well as her eldest son, 'heard the screams of a female in the vicinity of the inn.' And in what words does Madame Deluc designate the period of the evening at which these screams were heard? 'It was *soon after dark*,' she says. But 'soon after dark' is, at least, *dark*; and '*about dusk*' is as certainly daylight. Thus it is abundantly clear that the gang quitted the Barrière du Roule *prior* to the screams overheard (?) by Madame Deluc. And although, in all the many reports of the evidence, the relative expressions in question are distinctly and invariably employed just as I have employed them in this conversation with yourself, no notice whatever of the gross discrepancy has, as yet, been taken by any of the public journals, or by any of the myrmidons of police.

"I shall add but one to the arguments against *a gang*; but this *one* has, to my own understanding at least, a weight altogether irresistible. Under the circumstances of large reward offered, and full pardon to any king's evidence, it is not to be imagined, for a moment, that some member of *a gang* of low ruffians, or of any body of men would not long ago have betrayed his accomplices. Each one of a gang, so placed, is not so much greedy of reward, or anxious for escape, as *fearful of betrayal*. He betrays eagerly and early that *he may not himself be betrayed*. That the secret has not been divulged is the very best of proof that it is, in fact, a secret. The horrors of this dark deed are known only to *one*, or two, living human beings, and to God.

"Let us sum up now the meager yet certain fruits of our long analysis. We have attained the idea either of a fatal accident under the roof of Madame Deluc, or of a murder perpetrated, in the thicket at the Barrière du Roule, by a lover, or at least by an intimate and secret associate of the deceased. This associate is of swarthy complexion. This complexion, the 'hitch' in the bandage, and the 'sailor's knot' with which the bonnet-ribbon is tied, point to a seaman. His companionship with the deceased, a gay but not an abject young girl, designates him as above the grade of the common sailor. Here the well-written and urgent communications to the journals are much in the way of corroboration. The circumstance of the first elopement, as mentioned by *Le Mercurie*, tends to blend the idea of this seaman with that of the 'naval officer' who is first known to have led the unfortunate into crime.

"And here, most fitly, comes the consideration of the continued absence of him of the dark complexion. Let me pause to observe that the complexion of this man is dark and swarthy; it was no common swarthiness which constituted the *sole* point of remembrance, both as regards Valence and Madame Deluc. But why is this man absent? Was he murdered by the gang? If so, why are there only *traces* of the assassinated *girl*? The scene of the two outrages will naturally be supposed identical. And where is his corpse? The assassins would most probably have disposed of both in the same way. But it may be said that this man lives, and is deterred from making himself known, through dread of being charged with the murder. This consideration might be supposed to operate upon him now—at this late period—since it has been given in evidence that he was seen with Marie—but it would have had no force at the period of the deed. The first impulse of an innocent man would have been to announce the outrage, and to aid in identifying the ruffians. This, *policy* would have suggested. He had been seen with the girl. He had crossed the river with her in an open ferry-boat. The denouncing of the assassins would have appeared, even to an idiot, the surest and sole means of relieving himself from suspicion. We cannot suppose him, on the night of the fatal Sunday, both innocent himself and incognizant of an outrage committed. Yet only under such circumstances is it possible to imagine that he would have failed, if alive, in the denouncement of the assassins.

"And what means are ours of attaining the truth? We shall find these means multiplying and gathering distinctness as we proceed. Let us sift to the bottom this affair of the first elopement. Let us know the full history of 'the officer,' with his present circumstances, and his whereabouts at the precise period of the murder. Let us carefully compare with each other the various communications sent to the evening paper, in which the object was to inculpate *a gang*. This done, let us compare these communications, both as regards style and MS., with those sent to the morning paper, at a previous period, and insisting so vehemently upon the guilt of Mennais. And, all this done, let us again compare these various communications with the known MSS. of the officer. Let us endeavor to ascertain, by repeated questionings of Madame Deluc and her boys, as well as of the omnibus-driver, Valence, something more of the personal appearance and bearing of the 'man of dark complexion.' Queries, skillfully directed will not fail to elicit, from some of these parties, information on this particular point (or upon others)—information which the parties themselves may not even be aware of possessing. And let us

now trace *the boat* picked up by the bargeman on the morning of Monday the twenty-third of June, and which was removed from the barge-office, without the cognizance of the officer in attendance, and *without the rudder*, at some period prior to the discovery of the corpse. With a proper caution and perseverance we shall infallibly trace this boat; for not only can the bargeman who picked it up identify it, but the *rudder is at hand*. The rudder *of a sailboat* would not have been abandoned, without inquiry, by one altogether at ease in heart. And here let me pause to insinuate a question. There was no *advertisement* of the picking up of this boat. It was silently taken to the barge-office and as silently removed. But its owner or employer—how *happened* he, at so early a period as Tuesday morning, to be informed, without the agency of advertisement, of the locality of the boat taken up on Monday, unless we imagine some connection with the *navy*—some personal permanent connection leading to cognizance of its minute interests—its petty local news?

"In speaking of the lonely assassin dragging his burden to the shore, I have already suggested the probability of his availing himself *of a boat*. Now we are to understand that Marie Rogêt *was* precipitated from a boat. This would naturally have been the case. The corpse could not have been trusted to the shallow waters of the shore. The peculiar marks on the back and shoulders of the victim tell of the bottom ribs of a boat. That the body was found without weight is also corroborative of the idea. If thrown from the shore a weight would have been attached. We can only account for its absence by supposing the murderer to have neglected the precaution of supplying himself with it before pushing off. In the act of consigning the corpse to the water, he would unquestionably have noticed his oversight; but then no remedy would have been at hand. Any risk would have been preferred to a return to that accursed shore. Having rid himself of his ghastly charge, the murderer would have hastened to the city. There, at some obscure wharf, he would have leaped on land. But the boat—would he have secured it? He would have been in too great haste for such things as securing a boat. Moreover, in fastening it to the wharf, he would have felt as if securing evidence against himself. His natural thought would have been to cast from him, as far as possible, all that had held connection with his crime. He would not only have fled from the wharf, but he would not have permitted *the boat* to remain. Assuredly he would have cast it adrift. Let us pursue our fancies. In the morning, the wretch is stricken with unutterable horror at finding that the boat has been picked up and detained at a locality which he is in the

daily habit of frequenting—at a locality, perhaps, which his duty compels him to frequent. The next night, *without daring to ask for the rudder*, he removes it. Now *where* is that rudderless boat? Let it be one of our first purposes to discover. With the first glimpse we obtain of it, the dawn of our success shall begin. This boat shall guide us, with a rapidity which will surprise even ourselves, to him who employed it in the midnight of the fatal Sabbath. Corroboration will rise upon corroboration, and the murderer will be traced."

[For reasons which we shall not specify, but which to many readers will appear obvious, we have taken the liberty of here omitting, from the MSS. placed in our hands, such portion as details the *following up* of the apparently slight clue obtained by Dupin. We feel it advisable only to state, in brief, that the result desired was brought to pass; and that the Prefect fulfilled punctually, although with reluctance, the terms of his compact with the Chevalier. Mr. Poe's article concludes with the following words.—Eds.]*

It will be understood that I speak of coincidences and *no more*. What I have said above upon this topic must suffice. In my own heart there dwells no faith in preter-nature. That Nature and its God are two, no man who thinks will deny. That the latter, creating the former, can, at will, control or modify it, is also unquestionable. I say "at will"; for the question is of will, and not, as the insanity of logic has assumed, of power. It is not that the Deity *cannot* modify his laws, but that we insult him in imagining a possible necessity for modification. In their origin these laws were fashioned to embrace *all* contingencies which *could* lie in the Future. With God all is *Now*.

I repeat, then, that I speak of these things only as of coincidences. And farther: in what I relate it will be seen that between the fate of the unhappy Mary Cecilia Rogers, so far as that fate is known, and the fate of one Marie Rogêt up to a certain epoch in her history, there has existed a parallel in the contemplation of whose wonderful exactitude the reason becomes embarrassed. I say all this will be seen. But let it not for a moment be supposed that, in proceeding with the sad narrative of Marie from the epoch just mentioned, and in tracing to its *dénouement* the mystery which enshrouded her, it is my covert design to hint at an extension of the parallel, or even to suggest that the measures adopted in Paris for

* Of the Magazine in which the article was originally published.

the discovery of the assassin of a grisette, or measures founded in any similar ratiocination would produce any similar result.

For, in respect to the latter branch of the supposition, it should be considered that the most trifling variation in the facts of the two cases might give rise to the most important miscalculations, by diverting thoroughly the two courses of events; very much as, in arithmetic, an error which, in its own individuality, may be inappreciable, produces, at length, by dint of multiplication at all points of the process, a result enormously at variance with truth. And, in regard to the former branch, we must not fail to hold in view that the very Calculus of Probabilities to which I have referred, forbids all idea of the extension of the parallel— forbids it with a positiveness strong and decided just in proportion as this parallel has already been long-drawn and exact. This is one of those anomalous propositions which, seemingly appealing to thought altogether apart from the mathematical, is yet one which only the mathematician can fully entertain. Nothing, for example, is more difficult than to convince the merely general reader that the fact of sixes having been thrown twice in succession by a player at dice, is sufficient cause for betting the largest odds that sixes will not be thrown in the third attempt. A suggestion to this effect is usually rejected by the intellect at once. It does not appear that the two throws which have been completed, and which lie now absolutely in the Past, can have influence upon the throw which exists only in the Future. The chance for throwing sixes seems to be precisely as it was at any ordinary time—that is to say, subject only to the influence of the various other throws which may be made by the dice. And this is a reflection which appears so exceedingly obvious that attempts to controvert it are received more frequently with a derisive smile than with anything like respectful attention. The error here involved—a gross error redolent of mischief—I cannot pretend to expose within the limits assigned me at present; and with the philosophical it needs no exposure. It may be sufficient here to say that it forms one of an infinite series of mistakes which arise in the path of Reason through her propensity for seeking truth *in detail*.

THE PURLOINED LETTER

Nil sapientiae odiosius acumine nimio.

—SENECA

AT PARIS, JUST AFTER DARK ONE GUSTY EVENING IN THE AUTUMN OF 18—,
I was enjoying the twofold luxury of meditation and a meerschaum, in
company with my friend, C. Auguste Dupin, in his little back library, or
book-closet, au troisième, No. 33, Rue Dunôt, Faubourg St. Germain. For
one hour at least we had maintained a profound silence; while each, to
any casual observer, might have seemed intently and exclusively occupied
with the curling eddies of smoke that oppressed the atmosphere of the
chamber. For myself, however, I was mentally discussing certain topics
which had formed matter for conversation between us at an earlier period
of the evening; I mean the affair of the Rue Morgue, and the mystery
attending the murder of Marie Rogêt. I looked upon it, therefore, as
something of a coincidence, when the door of our apartment was thrown
open and admitted our old acquaintance, Monsieur G——, the Prefect of
the Parisian police.

We gave him a hearty welcome; for there was nearly half as much of
the entertaining as of the contemptible about the man, and we had not
seen him for several years. We had been sitting in the dark, and Dupin
now arose for the purpose of lighting a lamp, but sat down again, without
doing so, upon G.'s saying that he had called to consult us, or rather to
ask the opinion of my friend, about some official business which had occa-
sioned a great deal of trouble.

"If it is any point requiring reflection," observed Dupin, as he forbore
to enkindle the wick, "we shall examine it to better purpose in the dark."

"That is another of your odd notions," said the Prefect, who had the fashion of calling everything "odd" that was beyond his comprehension, and thus lived amid an absolute legion of "oddities."

"Very true," said Dupin, as he supplied his visiter with a pipe, and rolled towards him a comfortable chair.

"And what is the difficulty now?" I asked. "Nothing more in the assassination way I hope?"

"Oh, no; nothing of that nature. The fact is, the business is *very* simple indeed, and I make no doubt that we can manage it sufficiently well ourselves; but then I thought Dupin would like to hear the details of it, because it is so excessively *odd.*"

"Simple and odd," said Dupin.

"Why, yes; and not exactly that either. The fact is, we have all been a good deal puzzled because the affair *is* so simple, and yet baffles us altogether."

"Perhaps it is the very simplicity of the thing which puts you at fault," said my friend.

"What nonsense you *do* talk!" replied the Prefect, laughing heartily.

"Perhaps the mystery is a little *too* plain," said Dupin.

"Oh, good heavens! who ever heard of such an idea?"

"A little *too* self-evident."

"Ha! ha! ha!—ha! ha! ha!—ho! ho! ho!" roared our visiter, profoundly amused, "oh, Dupin, you will be the death of me yet!"

"And what, after all, *is* the matter on hand?" I asked.

"Why, I will tell you," replied the Prefect, as he gave a long, steady, and contemplative puff, and settled himself in his chair. "I will tell you in a few words; but, before I begin, let me caution you that this is an affair demanding the greatest secrecy, and that I should most probably lose the position I now hold, were it known that I confided it to anyone."

"Proceed," said I.

"Or not," said Dupin.

"Well, then; I have received personal information, from a very high quarter, that a certain document of the last importance has been purloined from the royal apartments. The individual who purloined it is known; this beyond a doubt; he was seen to take it. It is known, also, that it still remains in his possession."

"How is this known?" asked Dupin.

"It is clearly inferred," replied the Prefect, "from the nature of the document, and from the non-appearance of certain results which would at once arise from its passing *out* of the robber's possession; that is to say, from his employing it as he must design in the end to employ it."

"Be a little more explicit," I said.

"Well, I may venture so far as to say that the paper gives its holder a certain power in a certain quarter where such power is immensely valuable." The Prefect was fond of the cant of diplomacy.

"Still I do not quite understand," said Dupin.

"No? Well; the disclosure of the document to a third person, who shall be nameless, would bring in question the honor of a personage of most exalted station; and this fact gives the holder of the document an ascendancy over the illustrious personage whose honor and peace are so jeopardized."

"But this ascendancy," I interposed, "would depend upon the robber's knowledge of the loser's knowledge of the robber. Who would dare—"

"The thief," said G., "is the Minister D——, who dares all things, those unbecoming as well as those becoming a man. The method of the theft was not less ingenious than bold. The document in question—a letter, to be frank—had been received by the personage robbed while alone in the royal *boudoir*. During its perusal she was suddenly interrupted by the entrance of the other exalted personage from whom especially it was her wish to conceal it. After a hurried and vain endeavor to thrust it in a drawer, she was forced to place it, open as it was, upon a table. The address, however, was uppermost, and, the contents thus unexposed, the letter escaped notice. At this juncture enters the Minister D——. His lynx eye immediately perceives the paper, recognizes the handwriting of the address, observes the confusion of the personage addressed, and fathoms her secret. After some business transactions, hurried through in his ordinary manner, he produces a letter somewhat similar to the one in question, opens it, pretends to read it, and then places it in close juxtaposition to the other. Again he converses, for some fifteen minutes, upon the public affairs. At length, in taking leave, he takes also from the table the letter to which he had no claim. Its rightful owner saw, but, of course, dared not call attention to the act, in the presence of the third personage who stood at her elbow. The minister decamped; leaving his own letter— one of no importance—upon the table."

"Here, then," said Dupin to me, "you have precisely what you demand to make the ascendancy complete—the robber's knowledge of the loser's knowledge of the robber."

"Yes," replied the Prefect; "and the power thus attained has, for some months past, been wielded, for political purposes, to a very dangerous extent. The personage robbed is more thoroughly convinced, every day, of the necessity of reclaiming her letter. But this, of course, cannot be done openly. In fine, driven to despair, she has committed the matter to me."

"Than whom," said Dupin, amid a perfect whirlwind of smoke, "no more sagacious agent could, I suppose, be desired, or even imagined."

"You flatter me," replied the Prefect; "but it is possible that some such opinion may have been entertained."

"It is clear," said I, "as you observe, that the letter is still in possession of the minister; since it is this possession, and not any employment of the letter, which bestows the power. With the employment the power departs."

"True," said G.; "and upon this conviction I proceeded. My first care was to make thorough search of the minister's hotel; and here my chief embarrassment lay in the necessity of searching without his knowledge. Beyond all things, I have been warned of the danger which would result from giving him reason to suspect our design."

"But," said I, "you are quite *au fait* in these investigations. The Parisian police have done this thing often before."

"Oh, yes; and for this reason I did not despair. The habits of the minister gave me, too, a great advantage. He is frequently absent from home all night. His servants are by no means numerous. They sleep at a distance from their master's apartment, and, being chiefly Neapolitans, are readily made drunk. I have keys, as you know, with which I can open any chamber or cabinet in Paris. For three months a night has not passed, during the greater part of which I have not been engaged, personally, in ransacking the D—— Hotel. My honor is interested, and, to mention a great secret, the reward is enormous. So I did not abandon the search until I had become fully satisfied that the thief is a more astute man than myself. I fancy that I have investigated every nook and corner of the premises in which it is possible that the paper can be concealed."

"But is it not possible," I suggested, "that although the letter may be in possession of the minister, as it unquestionably is, he may have concealed it elsewhere than upon his own premises?"

"This is barely possible," said Dupin. "The present peculiar condition of affairs at court, and especially of those intrigues in which D—— is known to be involved, would render the instant availability of the document—its susceptibility of being produced at a moment's notice—a point of nearly equal importance with its possession."

"Its susceptibility of being produced?" said I.

"That is to say, of being *destroyed*," said Dupin.

"True," I observed; "the paper is clearly then upon the premises. As for its being upon the person of the minister, we may consider that as out of the question."

"Entirely," said the Prefect. "He has been twice waylaid, as if by foot-pads, and his person rigorously searched under my own inspection."

"You might have spared yourself this trouble," said Dupin. "D——, I presume, is not altogether a fool, and, if not, must have anticipated these waylayings, as a matter of course."

"Not *altogether* a fool," said G., "but then he's a poet, which I take to be only one remove from a fool."

"True," said Dupin, after a long and thoughtful whiff from his meer-schaum, "although I have been guilty of certain doggerel myself."

"Suppose you detail," said I, "the particulars of your search."

"Why, the fact is, we took our time, and we searched *everywhere*. I have had long experience in these affairs. I took the entire building, room by room; devoting the nights of a whole week to each. We examined, first, the furniture of each apartment. We opened every possible drawer; and I presume you know that, to a properly trained police agent, such a thing as a *'secret'* drawer is impossible. Any man is a dolt who permits a 'secret' drawer to escape him in a search of this kind. The thing is *so* plain. There is a certain amount of bulk—of space—to be accounted for in every cabi-net. Then we have accurate rules. The fiftieth part of a line could not escape us. After the cabinets we took the chairs. The cushions we probed with the fine long needles you have seen me employ. From the tables we removed the tops."

"Why so?"

"Sometimes the top of a table, or other similarly arranged piece of furniture, is removed by the person wishing to conceal an article; then the leg is excavated, the article deposited within the cavity, and the top replaced. The bottoms and tops of bedposts are employed in the same way."

"But could not the cavity be detected by sounding?" I asked.

"By no means, if, when the article is deposited, a sufficient wadding of cotton be placed around it. Besides, in our case, we were obliged to pro-ceed without noise."

"But you could not have removed—you could not have taken to pieces *all* articles of furniture in which it would have been possible to make a deposit in the manner you mention. A letter may be compressed into a thin spiral roll, not differing much in shape or bulk from a large knitting-needle, and in this form it might be inserted into the rung of a chair, for example. You did not take to pieces all the chairs?"

"Certainly not; but we did better—we examined the rungs of every chair in the hotel, and, indeed, the jointings of every description of furniture, by

the aid of a most powerful microscope. Had there been any traces of recent disturbance we should not have failed to detect it instantly. A single grain of gimlet-dust, for example, would have been as obvious as an apple. Any disorder in the gluing—any unusual gaping in the joints—would have sufficed to insure detection."

"I presume you looked to the mirrors, between the boards and the plates, and you probed the beds and the bedclothes, as well as the curtains and carpets."

"That of course; and when we had absolutely completed every particle of the furniture in this way, then we examined the house itself. We divided its entire surface into compartments, which we numbered, so that none might be missed; then we scrutinized each individual square inch throughout the premises, including the two houses immediately adjoining, with the microscope, as before."

"The two houses adjoining!" I exclaimed; "you must have had a great deal of trouble."

"We had; but the reward offered is prodigious."

"You include the *grounds* about the houses?"

"All the grounds are paved with brick. They gave us comparatively little trouble. We examined the moss between the bricks, and found it undisturbed."

"You looked among D——'s papers, of course, and into the books of the library?"

"Certainly; we opened every package and parcel; we not only opened every book, but we turned over every leaf in each volume, not contenting ourselves with a mere shake, according to the fashion of some of our police officers. We also measured the thickness of every book-*cover*, with the most accurate admeasurement, and applied to each the most jealous scrutiny of the microscope. Had any of the bindings been recently meddled with, it would have been utterly impossible that the fact should have escaped observation. Some five or six volumes, just from the hands of the binder, we carefully probed, longitudinally, with the needles."

"You explored the floors beneath the carpets?"

"Beyond doubt. We removed every carpet, and examined the boards with the microscope."

"And the paper on the walls?"

"Yes."

"You looked into the cellars?"

"We did."

"Then," I said, "you have been making a miscalculation, and the letter is *not* upon the premises, as you suppose."

"I fear you are right there," said the Prefect. "And now, Dupin, what would you advise me to do?"

"To make a thorough research of the premises."

"That is absolutely needless," replied G——. "I am not more sure that I breathe than I am that the letter is not at the hotel."

"I have no better advice to give you," said Dupin. "You have, of course, an accurate description of the letter?"

"Oh yes!"—And here the Prefect, producing a memorandum-book, proceeded to read aloud a minute account of the internal, and especially of the external appearance of the missing document. Soon after finishing the perusal of this description, he took his departure, more entirely depressed in spirits than I had ever known the good gentleman before.

In about a month afterward he paid us another visit, and found us occupied very nearly as before. He took a pipe and a chair and entered into some ordinary conversation. At length I said:

"Well, but G——, what of the purloined letter? I presume you have at last made up your mind that there is no such thing as overreaching the Minister?"

"Confound him, say I—yes; I made the re-examination, however, as Dupin suggested—but it was all labor lost, as I knew it would be."

"How much was the reward offered, did you say?" asked Dupin.

"Why, a very great deal—a *very* liberal reward—I don't like to say how much, precisely; but one thing I *will* say, that I wouldn't mind giving my individual check for fifty thousand francs to anyone who could obtain me that letter. The fact is, it is becoming of more and more importance every day; and the reward has been lately doubled. If it were trebled, however, I could do no more than I have done."

"Why, yes," said Dupin, drawlingly between the whiffs of his meerschaum. "I really—think, G——, you have not exerted yourself—to the utmost in this matter. You might—do a little more, I think, eh?"

"How?—in what way?'

"Why—puff, puff—you might—puff, puff—employ counsel in the matter, eh?—puff, puff, puff. Do you remember the story they tell of Abernethy?"

"No; hang Abernethy!"

"To be sure! hang him and welcome. But, once upon a time, a certain rich miser conceived the design of sponging upon this Abernethy for a medical opinion. Getting up, for this purpose, an ordinary conversation

in a private company, he insinuated his case to the physician, as that of an imaginary individual.

"'We will suppose,' said the miser, 'that his symptoms are such and such; now, doctor, what would *you* have directed him to take?'

"'Take!' said Abernethy, 'why, take *advice*, to be sure.'"

"But," said the Prefect, a little discomposed, "*I* am *perfectly* willing to take advice, and to pay for it. I would *really* give fifty thousand francs to anyone who would aid me in the matter."

"In that case," replied Dupin, opening a drawer, and producing a check-book, "you may as well fill me up a check for the amount mentioned. When you have signed it, I will hand you the letter."

I was astounded. The Prefect appeared absolutely thunder-stricken. For some minutes he remained speechless and motionless, looking incredulously at my friend with open mouth, and eyes that seemed starting from their sockets; then apparently recovering himself in some measure, he seized a pen, and after several pauses and vacant stares, finally filled up and signed a check for fifty thousand francs, and handed it across the table to Dupin. The latter examined it carefully and deposited it in his pocket-book; then, unlocking an *escritoire*, took thence a letter and gave it to the Prefect. This functionary grasped it in a perfect agony of joy, opened it with a trembling hand, cast a rapid glance at its contents, and then scrambling and struggling to the door, rushed at length unceremoniously from the room and from the house, without having uttered a syllable since Dupin had requested him to fill up the check.

When he had gone, my friend entered into some explanations.

"The Parisian police," he said, "are exceedingly able in their way. They are persevering, ingenious, cunning, and thoroughly versed in the knowledge which their duties seem chiefly to demand. Thus, when G—— detailed to us his mode of searching the premises at the Hotel D——, I felt entire confidence in his having made a satisfactory investigation—so far as his labors extended."

"So far as his labors extended?" said I.

"Yes," said Dupin. "The measures adopted were not only the best of their kind, but carried out to absolute perfection. Had the letter been deposited within the range of their search, these fellows would, beyond a question, have found it."

I merely laughed—but he seemed quite serious in all that he said.

"The measures then," he continued, "were good in their kind, and well executed; their defect lay in their being inapplicable to the case and to the man. A certain set of highly ingenious resources are, with the

Prefect, a sort of Procrustean bed, to which he forcibly adapts his designs. But he perpetually errs by being too deep or too shallow for the matter in hand; and many a school-boy is a better reasoner than he. I knew one about eight years of age, whose success at guessing in the game of 'even and odd' attracted universal admiration. This game is simple, and is played with marbles. One player holds in his hand a number of these toys, and demands of another whether that number is even or odd. If the guess is right, the guesser wins one; if wrong, he loses one. The boy to whom I allude won all the marbles of the school. Of course he had some principle of guessing; and this lay in mere observation and admeasurement of the astuteness of his opponents. For example, an arrant simpleton is his opponent, and, holding up his closed hand, asks, 'Are they even or odd?' Our school-boy replies, 'Odd,' and loses; but upon the second trial he wins, for he then says to himself: 'The simpleton had them even upon the first trial, and his amount of cunning is just sufficient to make him have them odd upon the second; I will therefore guess odd'; he guesses odd, and wins. Now, with a simpleton a degree above the first, he would have reasoned thus: 'This fellow finds that in the first instance I guessed odd, and, in the second, he will propose to himself, upon the first impulse, a simple variation from even to odd, as did the first simpleton; but then a second thought will suggest that this is too simple a variation, and finally he will decide upon putting it even as before. I will therefore guess even'; he guesses even, and wins. Now this mode of reasoning in the school-boy, whom his fellows termed 'lucky'—what, in its last analysis, is it?"

"It is merely," I said, "an identification of the reasoner's intellect with that of his opponent."

"It is," said Dupin; "and, upon inquiring of the boy by what means he effected the *thorough* identification in which his success consisted, I received answer as follows: 'When I wish to find out how wise, or how stupid, or how good, or how wicked is anyone, or what are his thoughts at the moment, I fashion the expression of my face, as accurately as possible, in accordance with the expression of his, and then wait to see what thoughts or sentiments arise in my mind or heart, as if to match or correspond with the expression.' This response of the school-boy lies at the bottom of all the spurious profundity which has been attributed to Rochefoucault, to La Bougive, to Machiavelli, and to Campanella."

"And the identification," I said, "of the reasoner's intellect with that of his opponent, depends, if I understand you aright, upon the accuracy with which the opponent's intellect is admeasured."

"For its practical value it depends upon this," replied Dupin; "and the Prefect and his cohort fail so frequently, first by default of this identification, and, secondly, by ill-admeasurement, or rather through non-admeasurement, of the intellect with which they are engaged. They consider only their *own* ideas of ingenuity; and, in searching for anything hidden advert only to the modes in which *they* would have hidden it. They are right in this much—that their own ingenuity is a faithful representative of that of the *mass*; but when the cunning of the individual felon is diverse in character from their own, the felon foils them, of course. This always happens when it is above their own, and very usually when it is below. They have no variation of principle in their investigations; at best, when urged by some unusual emergency—by some extraordinary reward—they extend or exaggerate their old modes of *practice*, without touching their principles. What, for example, in this case of D——, has been done to vary the principle of action? What is all this boring, and probing, and sounding, and scrutinizing with the microscope, and dividing the surface of the building into registered square inches—what is it all but an exaggeration *of the application* of the one principle or set of principles of search, which are based upon the one set of notions regarding human ingenuity, to which the Prefect, in the long routine of his duty, has been accustomed? Do you not see he has taken it for granted that *all* men proceed to conceal a letter—not exactly in a gimlet-hole bored in a chair-leg, but, at least, in *some* out-of-the-way hole or corner suggested by the same tenor of thought which would urge a man to secrete a letter in a gimlet-hole bored in a chair-leg? And do you not see also that such *recherchés* nooks for concealment are adapted only for ordinary occasions, and would be adopted only by ordinary intellects; for, in all cases of concealment, a disposal of the article concealed—a disposal of it in this *recherché* manner—is in the very first instance, presumable and presumed; and thus its discovery depends, not at all upon the acumen, but altogether upon the mere care, patience, and determination of the seekers; and where the case is of importance—or, what amounts to the same thing in the political eyes, when the reward is of magnitude—the qualities in question have *never* been known to fail. You will now understand what I meant in suggesting that, had the purloined letter been hidden anywhere within the limits of the Prefect's examination—in other words, had the principle of its concealment been comprehended within the principles of the Prefect—its discovery would have been a matter altogether beyond question. This functionary, however, has been thoroughly mystified; and the remote

source of his defeat lies in the supposition that the Minister is a fool, because he has acquired renown as a poet. All fools are poets; this the Prefect feels; and he is merely guilty of a *non distributio medii* in thence inferring that all poets are fools."

"But is this really the poet?" I asked. "There are two brothers, I know; and both have attained reputation in letters. The minister I believe has written learnedly on the Differential Calculus. He is a mathematician, and no poet."

"You are mistaken; I know him well; he is both. As poet *and* mathematician, he would reason well; as mere mathematician, he could not have reasoned at all, and thus would have been at the mercy of the Prefect."

"You surprise me," I said, "by these opinions, which have been contradicted by the voice of the world. You do not mean to set at naught the well-digested idea of centuries. The mathematical reason has long been regarded as *the reason par excellence*,"

"'*Il y à parièr,*'" replied Dupin, quoting from Chamfort, "'*que toute idée publique, toute convention reçue, est une sottise, car elle a convenue au plus grand nombre.*' The mathematicians, I grant you, have done their best to promulgate the popular error to which you allude, and which is none the less an error for its promulgation as truth. With an art worthy a better cause, for example, they have insinuated the term 'analysis' into application to algebra. The French are the originators of this particular deception; but if a term is of any importance—if words derive any value from applicability—then 'analysis' conveys 'algebra' about as much as, in Latin, '*ambitus*' implies 'ambition,' '*religio*' 'religion,' or '*homines honesti*' a set of *honorable* men."

"You have a quarrel on hand, I see," said I, "with some of the algebraists of Paris; but proceed."

"I dispute the availability, and thus the value, of that reason which is cultivated in any especial form other than the abstractly logical. I dispute, in particular, the reason educed by mathematical study. The mathematics are the science of form and quantity; mathematical reasoning is merely logic applied to observation upon form and quantity. The great error lies in supposing that even the truths of what is called *pure* algebra are abstract or general truths. And this error is so egregious that I am confounded at the universality with which it has been received. Mathematical axioms are *not* axiom; of general truth. What is true of *relation*—of form and quantity—is often grossly false in regard to morals, for example. In this latter science it is very usually *un*true that the aggregated parts are

equal to the whole. In chemistry also the axiom fails. In the consideration of motive it fails; for two motives, each of a given value, have not necessarily, a value when united, equal to the sum of their values apart. There are numerous other mathematical truths which are only truths within the limits of *relation*. But the mathematician argues from his *finite truths*, through habit, as if they were of an absolutely general applicability—as the world indeed imagines them to be. Bryant, in his very learned *Mythology*, mentions an analogous source of error, when he says that 'although the Pagan fables are not believed, yet we forget ourselves continually, and make inferences from them as existing realities.' With the algebraists, however, who are Pagans themselves, the 'Pagan fables' *are* believed, and the inferences are made, not so much through lapse of memory as through an unaccountable addling of the brains. In short, I never yet encountered the mere mathematician who could be trusted out of equal roots, or one who did not clandestinely hold it as a point of his faith that $x^2 + px$ was absolutely and unconditionally equal to q. Say to one of these gentlemen, by way of experiment, if you please, that you believe occasions may occur where $x^2 + px$ is not altogether equal to q, and, having made him understand what you mean, get out of his reach as speedily as convenient, for, beyond doubt, he will endeavor to knock you down.

"I mean to say," continued Dupin, while I merely laughed at his last observations, "that if the Minister had been no more than a mathematician, the Prefect would have been under no necessity of giving me this check. I know him, however, as both mathematician and poet, and my measures were adapted to his capacity, with reference to the circumstances by which he was surrounded. I knew him as a courtier, too, and as a bold *intriguant*. Such a man, I considered, could not fail to be aware of the ordinary political modes of action. He could not have failed to anticipate—and events have proved that he did not fail to anticipate—the waylayings to which he was subjected. He must have foreseen, I reflected, the secret investigations of his premises. His frequent absences from home at night, which were hailed by the Prefect as certain aids to his success, I regarded only as *ruses*, to afford opportunity for thorough search to the police, and thus the sooner to impress them with the conviction to which G——, in fact, did finally arrive—the conviction that the letter was not upon the premises. I felt, also, that the whole train of thought, which I was at some pains in detailing to you just now, concerning the invariable principle of political action in searches for articles concealed—I felt that this whole train of thought would necessarily pass through the mind of the Minister.

It would imperatively lead him to despise all the ordinary *nooks* of conceal-
ment. *He* could not, I reflected, be so weak as not to see that the most
intricate and remote recess of his hotel would be as open as his commonest
closets to the eyes, to the probes, to the gimlets, and to the microscopes of
the Prefect. I saw, in fine, that he would be driven, as a matter of course, to
simplicity, if not deliberately induced to it as a matter of choice. You will
remember, perhaps, how desperately the Prefect laughed when I sug-
gested, upon our first interview, that it was just possible this mystery
troubled him so much on account of its being so *very* self-evident."

"Yes," said I, "I remember his merriment well. I really thought he
would have fallen into convulsions."

"The material world," continued Dupin, "abounds with very strict
analogies to the immaterial; and thus some color of truth has been given
to the rhetorical dogma, that metaphor, or simile, may be made to
strengthen an argument as well as to embellish a description. The princi-
ple of the *vis inertiae,* for example, seems to be identical in physics and
metaphysics. It is not more true in the former, that a large body is with
more difficulty set in motion than a smaller one, and that its subsequent
momentum is commensurate with this difficulty, than it is, in the latter, that
intellects of the vaster capacity, while more forcible, more constant, and
more eventful in their movements than those of inferior grade, are yet the
less readily moved, and more embarrassed, and full of hesitation in the first
few steps of their progress. Again: have you ever noticed which of the
street signs, over the shop doors, are the most attractive of attention?"

"I have never given the matter a thought," I said.

"There is a game of puzzles," he resumed, "which is played upon a
map. One party playing requires another to find a given word—the name
of town, river, state, or empire—any word, in short, upon the motley and
perplexed surface of the chart. A novice in the game generally seeks to
embarrass his opponents by giving them the most minutely lettered
names; but the adept selects such words as stretch, in large characters,
from one end of the chart to the other. These, like the over-largely let-
tered signs and placards of the street, escape observation by dint of being
excessively obvious; and here the physical oversight is precisely analogous
with the moral inapprehension by which the intellect suffers to pass unno-
ticed those considerations which are too obtrusively and too palpably
self-evident. But this is a point, it appears, somewhat above or beneath the
understanding of the Prefect. He never once thought it probable, or pos-
sible, that the Minister had deposited the letter immediately beneath the

nose of the whole world by way of best preventing any portion of that world from perceiving it.

"But the more I reflected upon the daring, dashing, and discriminating ingenuity of D——; upon the fact that the document must always have been *at hand*, if he intended to use it to good purpose; and upon the decisive evidence, obtained by the Prefect, that it was not hidden within the limits of that dignitary's ordinary search—the more satisfied I became that, to conceal this letter, the Minister had resorted to the comprehensive and sagacious expedient of not attempting to conceal it at all.

"Full of these ideas, I prepared myself with a pair of green spectacles, and called one fine morning quite by accident, at the Ministerial hotel. I found D—— at home, yawning, lounging, and dawdling, as usual, and pretending to be in the last extremity of *ennui*. He is, perhaps, the most really energetic human being now alive—but that is only when nobody sees him.

"To be even with him, I complained of my weak eyes, and lamented the necessity of the spectacles, under cover of which I cautiously and thoroughly surveyed the whole apartment, while seemingly intent only upon the conversation of my host.

"I paid especial attention to a large writing-table near which he sat, and upon which lay confusedly, some miscellaneous letters and other papers, with one or two musical instruments and a few books. Here, however, after a long and very deliberate scrutiny, I saw nothing to excite particular suspicion.

"At length my eyes, in going the circuit of the room, fell upon a trumpery filigree card-rack of pasteboard, that hung dangling by a dirty blue ribbon, from a little brass knob just beneath the middle of the mantelpiece. In this rack, which had three or four compartments, were five or six visiting cards and a solitary letter. This last was much soiled and crumpled. It was torn nearly in two, across the middle—as if a design, in the first instance, to tear it entirely up as worthless, had been altered or stayed in the second. It had a large black seal, bearing the D—— cipher *very* conspicuously, and was addressed, in a diminutive female hand, to D——, the minister, himself. It was thrust carelessly, and even, as it seemed, contemptuously, into one of the uppermost divisions of the rack.

"No sooner had I glanced at this letter than I concluded it to be that of which I was in search. To be sure, it was, to all appearance, radically different from the one of which the Prefect had read us so minute a description. Here the seal was large and black, with the D—— cipher; there it was small and red, with the ducal arms of the S—— family. Here,

the address, to the Minister, was diminutive and feminine; there the super-scription, to a certain royal personage, was markedly bold and decided; the size alone formed a point of correspondence. But, then, the *radicalness* of these differences, which was excessive; the dirt; the soiled and torn con-dition of the paper, so inconsistent with the *true* methodical habits of D——, and so suggestive of a design to delude the beholder into an idea of the worthlessness of the document; these things, together with the hyperobtrusive situation of this document, full in the view of every visiter, and thus exactly in accordance with the conclusions to which I had previ-ously arrived; these things, I say, were strongly corroborative of suspicion, in one who came with the intention to suspect.

"I protracted my visit as long as possible, and, while I maintained a most animated discussion with the Minister, upon a topic which I knew well had never failed to interest and excite him, I kept my attention really riveted upon the letter. In this examination, I committed to memory its external appearance and arrangement in the rack; and also fell, at length, upon a discovery which set at rest whatever trivial doubt I might have entertained. In scrutinizing the edges of the paper, I observed them to be more *chafed* than seemed necessary. They presented the *broken* appearance which is manifested when a stiff paper, having been once folded and pressed with a folder, is refolded in a reversed direction, in the same creases or edges which had formed the original fold. This discovery was sufficient. It was clear to me that the letter had been turned as a glove, inside out, redirected and re-sealed. I bade the Minister good morning, and took my departure at once, leaving a gold snuff-box upon the table.

"The next morning I called for the snuff-box, when we resumed, quite eagerly, the conversation of the preceding day. While thus engaged, how-ever, a loud report, as if of a pistol, was heard immediately beneath the windows of the hotel, and was succeeded by a series of fearful screams, and the shoutings of a terrified mob. D—— rushed to a casement, threw it open, and looked out. In the meantime I stepped to the card-rack, took the letter, put it in my pocket, and replaced it by a *fac-simile* (so far as regards externals) which I had carefully prepared at my lodgings—imitating the D—— cipher, very readily, by means of a seal formed of bread.

"The disturbance in the street had been occasioned by the frantic behavior of a man with a musket. He had fired it among a crowd of women and children. It proved, however, to have been without ball, and the fellow was suffered to go his way as a lunatic or a drunkard. When he had gone, D—— came from the window, whither I had followed him immediately

upon securing the object in view. Soon afterward I bade him farewell. The pretended lunatic was a man in my own pay."

"But what purpose had you," I asked, "in replacing the letter by a *facsimile?* Would it not have been better at the first visit, to have seized it openly, and departed?"

"D——," replied Dupin, "is a desperate man, and a man of nerve. His hotel, too, is not without attendants devoted to his interests. Had I made the wild attempt you suggest, I might never have left the Ministerial presence alive. The good people of Paris might have heard of me no more. But I had an object apart from these considerations. You know my political prepossessions. In this matter, I act as a partisan of the lady concerned. For eighteen months the Minister has had her in his power. She has now him in hers—since, being unaware that the letter is not in his possession, he will proceed with his exactions as if it was. Thus will he inevitably commit himself, at once, to his political destruction. His downfall, too, will not be more precipitate than awkward. It is all very well to talk about the *facilis descensus Averni*; but in all kinds of climbing, as Catalani said of singing, it is far more easy to get up than to come down. In the present instance I have no sympathy—at least no pity—for him who descends. He is that *monstrum horrendum*, an unprincipled man of genius. I confess, however, that I should like very well to know the precise character of his thoughts, when, being defied by her whom the Prefect terms 'a certain personage,' he is reduced to opening the letter which I left for him in the card-rack."

"How? did you put anything particular in it?"

"Why—it did not seem altogether right to leave the interior blank— that would have been insulting. D——, at Vienna once, did me an evil turn, which I told him, quite good-humoredly, that I should remember. So, as I knew he would feel some curiosity in regard to the identity of the person who had outwitted him, I thought it a pity not to give him a clue. He is well acquainted with my MS., and I just copied into the middle of the blank sheet the words—

"'—— ——*Un dessein si funeste,*
S'il n'est digne d'Atrée, est digne de Thyeste.'

They are to be found in Crébillon's *Atrée.*"

THE GOLD BUG

What ho! what ho! this fellow is dancing mad!
He hath been bitten by the Tarantula.

—ALL IN THE WRONG

MANY YEARS AGO, I CONTRACTED AN INTIMACY WITH A MR. WILLIAM Legrand. He was of an ancient Huguenot family, and had once been wealthy; but a series of misfortunes had reduced him to want. To avoid the mortification consequent upon his disasters, he left New Orleans, the city of his forefathers, and took up his residence at Sullivan's Island, near Charleston, South Carolina.

This Island is a very singular one. It consists of little else than the sea sand, and is about three miles long. Its breadth at no point exceeds a quarter of a mile. It is separated from the main land by a scarcely perceptible creek, oozing its way through a wilderness of reeds and slime, a favorite resort of the marsh-hen. The vegetation, as might be supposed, is scant, or at least dwarfish. No trees of any magnitude are to be seen. Near the western extremity, where Fort Moultrie stands, and where are some miserable frame buildings, tenanted, during summer, by the fugitives from Charleston dust and fever, may be found, indeed, the bristly palmetto; but the whole island, with the exception of this western point, and a line of hard, white beach on the seacoast, is covered with a dense undergrowth of the sweet myrtle, so much prized by the horticulturists of England. The shrub here often attains the height of fifteen or twenty feet, and forms an almost impenetrable coppice, burdening the air with its fragrance.

In the inmost recesses of this coppice, not far from the eastern or more remote end of the island, Legrand had built himself a small hut,

which he occupied when I first, by mere accident, made his acquaintance. This soon ripened into friendship—for there was much in the recluse to excite interest and esteem. I found him well educated, with unusual powers of mind, but infected with misanthropy, and subject to perverse moods of alternate enthusiasm and melancholy. He had with him many books, but rarely employed them. His chief amusements were gunning and fishing, or sauntering along the beach and through the myrtles, in quest of shells or entomological specimens; his collection of the latter might have been envied by a Swammerdamm. In these excursions he was usually accompanied by an old negro, called Jupiter, who had been manumitted before the reverses of the family, but who could be induced, neither by threats nor by promises, to abandon what he considered his right of attendance upon the footsteps of his young "Massa Will." It is not improbable that the relatives of Legrand, conceiving him to be somewhat unsettled in intellect, had contrived to instill this obstinacy into Jupiter, with a view to the supervision and guardianship of the wanderer.

The winters in the latitude of Sullivan's Island are seldom very severe, and in the fall of the year it is a rare event indeed when a fire is considered necessary. About the middle of October, 18—, there occurred, however, a day of remarkable chilliness. Just before sunset I scrambled my way through the evergreens to the hut of my friend, whom I had not visited for several weeks—my residence being, at that time, in Charleston, a distance of nine miles from the island, while the facilities of passage and repassage were very far behind those of the present day. Upon reaching the hut I rapped, as was my custom, and getting no reply, sought for the key where I knew it was secreted, unlocked the door, and went in. A fine fire was blazing upon the hearth. It was a novelty, and by no means an ungrateful one. I threw off an overcoat, took an arm-chair by the crackling logs, and awaited patiently the arrival of my hosts.

Soon after dark they arrived, and gave me a most cordial welcome. Jupiter, grinning from ear to ear, bustled about to prepare some marsh-hens for supper. Legrand was in one of his fits—how else shall I term them?—of enthusiasm. He had found an unknown bivalve, forming a new genus, and, more than this, he had hunted down and secured, with Jupiter's assistance a *scarabaeus* which he believed to be totally new, but in respect to which he wished to have my opinion on the morrow.

"And why not tonight?" I asked, rubbing my hands over the blaze, and wishing the whole tribe of scarabaei at the devil.

"Ah, if I had only known you were here!" said Legrand, "but it's so long since I saw you; and how could I foresee that you would pay me a visit this very night of all others? As I was coming home I met Lieutenant G——, from the fort, and, very foolishly, I lent him the bug; so it will be impossible for you to see it until the morning. Stay here tonight, and I will send Jup down for it at sunrise. It is the loveliest thing in creation!"

"What?—sunrise?"

"Nonsense! no!—the bug. It is of a brilliant gold color—about the size of a large hickory-nut—with two jet black spots near one extremity of the back, and another, somewhat longer, at the other. The *antennae* are—"

"Dey aint *no* tin in him, Massa Will, I keep a tellin' on you," here interrupted Jupiter; "de bug is a goole-bug, solid, ebery bit of him, inside and all, sep him wing—neber feel half so hebby a bug in my life."

"Well, suppose it is, Jup," replied Legrand, somewhat more earnestly, it seemed to me, than the case demanded; "is that any reason for your letting the birds burn? The color"—here he turned to me—"is really almost enough to warrant Jupiter's idea. You never saw a more brilliant metallic luster that the scales emit—but of this you cannot judge till tomorrow. In the meantime I can give you some idea of the shape." Saying this, he seated himself at a small table, on which were a pen and ink, but no paper. He looked for some in a drawer, but found none.

"Never mind," he said at length, "this will answer"; and he drew from his waistcoat pocket a scrap of what I took to be very dirty foolscap, and made upon it a rough drawing with the pen. While he did this, I retained my seat by the fire, for I was still chilly. When the design was complete, he handed it to me without rising. As I received it, a loud growl was heard, succeeded by a scratching at the door. Jupiter opened it, and a large Newfoundland, belonging to Legrand, rushed in, leaped upon my shoulders, and loaded me with caresses; for I had shown him much attention during previous visits. When his gambols were over, I looked at the paper, and, to speak the truth, found myself not a little puzzled at what my friend had depicted.

"Well!" I said, after contemplating it for some minutes, "This *is* a strange *scarabaeus*, I must confess; new to me; never saw anything like it before—unless it was a skull, or a death's-head, which it more nearly resembles than anything else that has come under *my* observation."

"A death's-head!" echoed Legrand. "Oh—yes—well, it has something of that appearance upon paper, no doubt. The two upper black spots look like eyes, eh? and the longer one at the bottom like a mouth—and then the shape of the whole is oval."

"Perhaps so," said I; "but, Legrand, I fear you are no artist. I must wait until I see the beetle itself, if I am to form any idea of its personal appearance."

"Well, I don't know," said he, a little nettled, "I draw tolerably—*should* do it at least—have had good masters, and flatter myself that I am not quite a blockhead."

"But, my dear fellow, you are joking, then," said I, "this is a very passable *skull*—indeed, I may say that it is a very *excellent* skull, according to the vulgar notions about such specimens of physiology—and your *scarabaeus* must be the queerest *scarabaeus* in the world if it resembles it. Why, we may get up a very thrilling bit of superstition upon this hint. I presume you will call the bug *scarabaeus caput hominis*, or something of that kind—there are many similar titles in the Natural Histories. But where are the *antennae* you spoke of?"

"The *antennae!*" said Legrand, who seemed to be getting unaccountably warm upon the subject; "I am sure you must see the *antennae*. I made them as distinct as they are in the original insect, and I presume that is sufficient."

"Well, well," I said, "perhaps you have—still I don't see them"; and I handed him the paper without additional remark, not wishing to ruffle his temper; but I was much surprised at the turn affairs had taken; his ill humor puzzled me—and, as for the drawing of the beetle, there were positively *no antennae* visible, and the whole *did* bear a very close resemblance to the ordinary cuts of a death's-head.

He received the paper very peevishly, and was about to crumple it, apparently to throw it in the fire, when a casual glance at the design seemed suddenly to rivet his attention. In an instant his face grew violently red—in another excessively pale. For some minutes he continued to scrutinize the drawing minutely where he sat. At length he arose, took a candle from the table, and proceeded to seat himself upon a sea-chest in the farthest corner of the room. Here again he made an anxious examination of the paper; turning it in all directions. He said nothing however, and his conduct greatly astonished me; yet I thought it prudent not to exacerbate the growing moodiness of his temper by any comment. Presently he took from his coat-pocket a wallet, placed the paper carefully in it, and deposited both in a writing-desk, which he locked. He now grew more composed in his demeanor; but his original air of enthusiasm had quite disappeared. Yet he seemed not so much sulky as abstracted. As the evening wore away he became more and more absorbed in reverie, from which no sallies of mine could arouse him. It had been my intention to pass the night at the hut, as I had frequently done before, but, seeing my host in this mood, I

deemed it proper to take leave. He did not press me to remain, but, as I departed, he shook my hand with even more than his usual cordiality.

It was about a month after this (and during the interval I had seen nothing of Legrand) when I received a visit, at Charleston, from his man, Jupiter. I had never seen the good old negro look so dispirited, and I feared that some serious disaster had befallen my friend.

"Well, Jup," said I, "what is the matter now?—how is your master?"

"Why, to speak de troof, massa, him not so berry well as mought be."

"Not well! I am truly sorry to hear it. What does he complain of?"

"Dar! dat's it!—him neber plain of notin—but him berry sick for all dat."

"*Very* sick, Jupiter!—why didn't you say so at once? Is he confined to bed?"

"No, dat he aint!—he aint find nowhar—dat's just whar he shoe pinch—my mind is got to be berry hebby bout poor Massa Will."

"Jupiter, I should like to understand what it is you are talking about. You say your master is sick. Hasn't he told you what ails him?"

"Why, massa, taint worfwhile for to git mad about de matter—Massa Will say noffin at all aint de matter wid him—but den what make him go about looking dis here way, wid he head down and he soldiers up, and as white as a gose? And den he keep a syphon all de time—"

"Keeps a what, Jupiter?"

"Keeps a syphon wid de figgurs on de slate—de queerest figgurs I ebber did see. Ise gittin to be skeered, I tell you. Hab for to keep mighty tight eye pon him noovers. Todder day he gib me slip fore de sun up and was gone de whole ob de blessed day. I had a big stick ready cut for to gib him deuced good beating when he did come—but Ise sich a fool dat I hadn't de heart arter all—he looked so berry poorly."

"Eh?—what?—ah yes!—upon the whole I think you had better not be too severe with the poor fellow—don't flog him, Jupiter—he can't very well stand it—but can you form no idea of what has occasioned this illness, or rather this change of conduct? Has anything unpleasant happened since I saw you?"

"No, massa, dey aint bin noffin onpleasant *since* den—'twas *fore* den I'm feared—'twas be berry day you was dare."

"How? what do you mean?"

"Why, massa, I mean de bug—dare now."

"The what?"

"De bug—I'm berry sartain dat Massa Will bin bit somewhere 'bout de head by dat goole-bug."

"And what cause have you, Jupiter, for such a supposition?"

"Claws enuff, massa, and mouff too. I never did see sich a deuced bug—he kick and he bite eberyting what cum near him. Massa Will cotch him fuss, but had for to let him go gin mighty quick, I tell you—den was de time he must ha got de bite. I didn't like de look ob de bug mouff, myself, no how, so I wouldn't take hold ob him wid my finger, but I cotch him wid a piece ob paper dat I found. I rap him up in de paper and stuff a piece of it in he mouff—dat was de way."

"And you think, then, that your master was really bitten by the beetle, and that the bite made him sick?"

"I don't think noffin about it—I nose it. What make him dream bout de goole so much, if taint cause he bit by the goole-bug? Ise heerd bout dem goole-bugs fore dis."

"But how do you know he dreams about gold?"

"How I know? why, cause he talk about it in he sleep—dat's how I nose."

"Well, Jup, perhaps you are right; but to what fortunate circumstance am I to attribute the honor of a visit from you today?"

"What de matter, massa?"

"Did you bring any message from Mr. Legrand?"

"No, massa, I bring dis here pissel"; and here Jupiter handed me a note which ran thus:

My Dear—

Why have I not seen you for so long a time? I hope you have not been so foolish as to take offence at any little brusquerie *of mine; but no, that is improbable.*

Since I saw you I have had great cause for anxiety. I have something to tell you, yet scarcely know how to tell it, or whether I should tell it at all.

I have not been quite well for some days past, and poor old Jup annoys me, almost beyond endurance, by his well-meant attentions. Would you believe it?—he had prepared a huge stick, the other day, with which to chastise me for giving him the slip, and spending the day, solus, *among the hills on the main land. I verily believe that my ill looks alone saved me a flogging.*

I have made no addition to my cabinet since we met.

If you can, in any way, make it convenient, come over with Jupiter. Do come. I wish to see you tonight, *upon business of importance. I assure you that it is of the* highest *importance.*

Ever yours,
William Legrand

There was something in the tone of this note which gave me great uneasiness. Its whole style differed materially from that of Legrand. What could he be dreaming of? What new crotchet possessed his excitable brain? What "business of the highest importance" could *he* possibly have to transact? Jupiter's account of him boded no good. I dreaded lest the continued pressure of misfortune had, at length, fairly unsettled the reason of my friend. Without a moment's hesitation, therefore, I prepared to accompany the negro.

Upon reaching the wharf, I noticed a scythe and three spades, all apparently new, lying in the bottom of the boat in which we were to embark.

"What is the meaning of all this, Jup?" I inquired.

"Him syfe, massa, and spade."

"Very true; but what are they doing here?"

"Him de syfe and de spade what Massa Will sis pon my buying for him in de town, and de debbils own lot of money I had to gib for em."

"But what, in the name of all that is mysterious, is your 'Massa Will' going to do with scythes and spades?"

"Dat's more dan *I* know, and debbil take me if I don't blieve 'tis more dan he know too. But it's all cum ob de bug."

Finding that no satisfaction was to be obtained of Jupiter, whose whole intellect seemed to be absorbed by "de bug," I now stepped into the boat, and made sail. With a fair and strong breeze we soon ran into the little cove to the northward of Fort Moultrie, and a walk of some two miles brought us to the hut. It was about three in the afternoon when we arrived. Legrand had been awaiting us in eager expectation. He grasped my hand with a nervous *empressement* which alarmed me and strengthened the suspicions already entertained. His countenance was pale even to ghastliness, and his deep-set eyes glared with unnatural luster. After some inquiries respecting his health, I asked him, not knowing what better to say, if he had yet obtained the *scarabaeus* from Lieutenant G——.

"Oh, yes," he replied, coloring violently, "I got it from him the next morning. Nothing should tempt me to part with that *scarabaeus*. Do you know that Jupiter is quite right about it?"

"In what way?" I asked, with a sad foreboding at heart.

"In supposing it to be a bug of *real gold*." He said this with an air of profound seriousness, and I felt inexpressibly shocked.

"This bug is to make my fortune," he continued, with a triumphant smile; "to reinstate me in my family possessions. Is it any wonder, then, that I prize it? Since Fortune has thought fit to bestow it upon me, I have

only to use it properly, and I shall arrive at the gold of which it is the index. Jupiter, bring me that *scarabaeus!*"

"What! de bug, massa? I'd rudder not go fer trubble dat bug; you mus git him for your own self." Hereupon Legrand arose, with a grave and stately air, and brought me the beetle from a glass case in which it was enclosed. It was a beautiful *scarabaeus,* and, at that time, unknown to naturalists—of course a great prize in a scientific point of view. There were two round black spots near one extremity of the back, and a long one near the other. The scales were exceedingly hard and glossy, with all the appearance of burnished gold. The weight of the insect was very remarkable, and, taking all things into consideration, I could hardly blame Jupiter for his opinion respecting it; but what to make of Legrand's concordance with that opinion, I could not, for the life of me, tell.

"I sent for you," said he, in a grandiloquent tone, when I had completed my examination of the beetle, "I sent for you that I might have your counsel and assistance in furthering the views of Fate and of the bug—"

"My dear Legrand," I cried, interrupting him, "you are certainly unwell, and had better use some little precautions. You shall go to bed, and I will remain with you a few days, until you get over this. You are feverish and—"

"Feel my pulse," said he.

I felt it, and, to say the truth, found not the slightest indication of fever.

"But you may be ill and yet have no fever. Allow me this once to prescribe for you. In the first place go to bed. In the next—"

"You are mistaken," he interposed, "I am as well as I can expect to be under the excitement which I suffer. If you really wish me well, you will relieve this excitement."

"And how is this to be done?"

"Very easily. Jupiter and myself are going upon an expedition into the hills, upon the main land, and, in this expedition, we shall need the aid of some person in whom we can confide. You are the only one we can trust. Whether we succeed or fail, the excitement which you now perceive in me will be equally allayed."

"I am anxious to oblige you in any way," I replied; "but do you mean to say that this infernal beetle has any connection with your expedition into the hills?"

"It has."

"Then, Legrand, I can become a party to no such absurd proceeding."

"I am sorry—very sorry—for we shall have to try it by ourselves."

"Try it by yourselves! The man is surely mad!—but stay!—how long do you propose to be absent?"

"Probably all night. We shall start immediately, and be back, at all events, by sunrise."

"And will you promise me, upon your honor, that when this freak of yours is over, and the bug business (good God!) settled to your satisfaction, you will then return home and follow my advice implicitly, as that of your physician?"

"Yes; I promise; and now let us be off, for we have no time to lose."

With a heavy heart I accompanied my friend. We started about four o'clock—Legrand, Jupiter, the dog, and myself. Jupiter had with him the scythe and spades—the whole of which he insisted upon carrying—more through fear, it seemed to me, of trusting either of the implements within reach of his master, than from any excess of industry or complaisance. His demeanor was dogged in the extreme, and "dat deuced bug" were the sole words which escaped his lips during the journey. For my own part, I had charge of a couple of dark lanterns, while Legrand contented himself with the *scarabaeus,* which he carried attached to the end of a bit of whipcord: twirling it to and fro, with the air of a conjurer, as he went. When I observed this last, plain evidence of my friend's aberration of mind, I could scarcely refrain from tears. I thought it best, however, to humor his fancy, at least for the present, or until I could adopt some more energetic measures with a chance of success. In the meantime I endeavored, but all in vain, to sound him in regard to the object of the expedition. Having succeeded in inducing me to accompany him, he seemed unwilling to hold conversation upon any topic of minor importance, and to all my questions vouchsafed no other reply than "we shall see!"

We crossed the creek at the head of the island by means of a skiff, and, ascending the high grounds on the shore of the main land, proceeded in a northwesterly direction, through a tract of country excessively wild and desolate, where no trace of a human footstep was to be seen. Legrand led the way with decision; pausing only for an instant, here and there, to consult what appeared to be certain landmarks of his own contrivance upon a former occasion.

In this manner we journeyed for about two hours, and the sun was just setting when we entered a region infinitely more dreary than any yet seen. It was a species of table-land, near the summit of an almost inaccessible hill, densely wooded from base to pinnacle, and interspersed with huge

crags that appeared to lie loosely upon the soil, and in many cases were prevented from precipitating themselves into the valleys below, merely by the support of the trees against which they reclined. Deep ravines, in various directions, gave an air of still sterner solemnity to the scene.

The natural platform to which we had clambered was thickly overgrown with brambles, through which we soon discovered that it would have been impossible to force our way but for the scythe; and Jupiter, by direction of his master, proceeded to clear for us a path to the foot of an enormously tall tulip-tree, which stood, with some eight or ten oaks, upon the level, and far surpassed them all, and all other trees which I had then ever seen, in the beauty of its foliage and form, in the wide spread of its branches, and in the general majesty of its appearance. When we reached this tree, Legrand turned to Jupiter, and asked him if he thought he could climb it. The old man seemed a little staggered by the question, and for some moments made no reply. At length he approached the huge trunk, walked slowly around it, and examined it with minute attention. When he had completed his scrutiny, he merely said:

"Yes, massa, Jup climb any tree he ebber see in he life."

"Then up with you as soon as possible, for it will soon be too dark to see what we are about."

"How far mus go up, massa?" inquired Jupiter.

"Get up the main trunk first, and then I will tell you which way to go—and here—stop! take this beetle with you."

"De bug, Massa Will!—de goole-bug!" cried the negro, drawing back in dismay—"What for mus tote de bug way up de tree?—d——n if I do!"

"If you are afraid, Jup, a great big negro like you, to take hold of a harmless little dead beetle, why you can carry it up by this string—but, if you do not take it up with you in some way, I shall be under the necessity of breaking your head with this shovel."

"What de matter now, massa?" said Jup, evidently shamed into compliance; "always want for to raise fuss wid old nigger. Was only funnin anyhow. Me *feered* de bug! what I keer for de bug?" Here he took cautiously hold of the extreme end of the string, and, maintaining the insect as far from his person as circumstances would permit, prepared to ascend the tree.

In youth, the tulip-tree, or *Liriodendron Tulipiferum*, the most magnificent of American foresters, has a trunk peculiarly smooth, and often rises to a great height without lateral branches; but, in its riper age, the bark becomes gnarled and uneven, while many short limbs make their appearance on the stem. Thus the difficulty of ascension, in the present case, lay

more in semblance than in reality. Embracing the huge cylinder, as closely as possible, with his arms and knees, seizing with his hands some projections, and resting his naked toes upon others, Jupiter, after one or two narrow escapes from falling, at length wriggled himself into the first great fork, and seemed to consider the whole business as virtually accomplished. The *risk* of the achievement was, in fact, now over, although the climber was some sixty or seventy feet from the ground.

"Which way mus go now, Massa Will?" he asked.

"Keep up the largest branch—the one on this side," said Legrand. The negro obeyed him promptly, and apparently with but little trouble; ascending higher and higher, until no glimpse of his squat figure could be obtained through the dense foliage which enveloped it. Presently his voice was heard in a sort of halloo.

"How much fudder is got for go?"

"How high up are you?" asked Legrand.

"Ebber so fur," replied the negro; "can see de sky fru de top oh de tree."

"Never mind the sky, but attend to what I say. Look down the trunk and count the limbs below you on this side. How many limbs have you passed?"

"One, two, tree, four, fibe—I done pass fibe big limb, massa, pon dis side."

"Then go one limb higher."

In a few minutes the voice was heard again, announcing that the seventh limb was attained.

"Now, Jup," cried Legrand, evidently much excited, "I want you to work your way out upon that limb as far as you can. If you see anything strange let me know."

By this time what little doubt I might have entertained of my poor friend's insanity was put finally at rest. I had no alternative but to conclude him stricken with lunacy, and I became seriously anxious about getting him home. While I was pondering upon what was best to be done, Jupiter's voice was again heard.

"Mos feered for to ventur pon dis limb berry far—'tis dead limb putty much all de way."

"Did you say it was a *dead* limb, Jupiter?" cried Legrand in a quavering voice.

"Yes, massa, him dead as de doornail—done up for sartain—done departed dis here life."

"What in the name of heaven shall I do?" asked Legrand, seemingly in the greatest distress.

"Do!" said I, glad of an opportunity to interpose a word, "why come home and go to bed. Come now!—that's a fine fellow. It's getting late, and, besides, you remember your promise."

"Jupiter," cried he, without heeding me in the least, "do you hear me?"

"Yes, Massa Will, hear you ebber so plain."

"Try the wood well, then, with your knife, and see if you think it *very* rotten."

"Him rotten, massa, sure nuff," replied the negro in a few moments, "but not so berry rotten as mought be. Mought ventur out leetle way pon de limb by myself, dat's true."

"By yourself! What do you mean?"

"Why, I mean de bug. 'Tis *berry* hebby bug. Spose I drop him down fuss, and den de limb won't break wid just de weight of one nigger."

"You infernal scoundrel!" cried Legrand, apparently much relieved, "what do you mean by telling me such nonsense as that? As sure as you drop that beetle I'll break your neck. Look here, Jupiter, do you hear me?"

"Yes, massa, needn't hollo at poor nigger dat style."

"Well! now listen!—if you will venture out on the limb as far as you think safe, and not let go the beetle, I'll make you a present of a silver dollar as soon as you get down."

"I'm gwine, Massa Will—deed I is," replied the negro very promptly— "mos out to the eend now."

"*Out to the end!*" here fairly screamed Legrand; "do you say you are out to the end of that limb?"

"Soon be to de eend, massa—o-o-o-o-oh! Lor-gol-a-marcy! what *is* dis here pon de tree?"

"Well!" cried Legrand, highly delighted, "what is it?"

"Why 'taint noffin but a skull—somebody bin lef him head up de tree, and de crows done gobble ebery bit ob de meat off."

"A skull, you say!—very well—how is it fastened to the limb?—what holds it on?"

"Sure nuff, massa; mus look. Why dis berry curious sarcumstance, pon my word—dare's a great big nail in de skull, what fastens ob it on to de tree."

"Well now, Jupiter, do exactly as I tell you—do you hear?"

"Yes, massa."

"Pay attention, then—find the left eye of the skull."

"Hum! hoo! dat's good! why dare ain't no eye lef at all."

"Curst your stupidity! Do you know your right hand from your left?"

"Yes, I nose dat—nose all bout dat—tis my lef hand what I chops de wood wid."

"To be sure! you are left-handed; and your left eye is on the same side as your left hand. Now, I suppose, you can find the left eye of the skull, or the place where the left eye has been. Have you found it?"

Here was a long pause. At length the negro asked,

"Is de lef eye of de skull pon de same side as de lef hand of de skull too?—cause de skull aint got not a bit ob a hand at all—nebber mind! I got de lef eye now—here de lef eye! what mus do wid it?"

"Let the beetle drop through it, as far as the string will reach—but be careful and not let go your hold of the string."

"All dat done, Massa Will; mighty easy ting for to put de bug fru de hole—look out for him dare below!"

During this colloquy no portion of Jupiter's person could be seen; but the beetle, which he had suffered to descend, was now visible at the end of the string, and glistened, like a globe of burnished gold, in the last rays of the setting sun, some of which still faintly illumined the eminence upon which we stood. The *scarabaeus* hung quite clear of any branches, and, if allowed to fall, would have fallen at our feet. Legrand immediately took the scythe, and cleared with it a circular space, three or four yards in diameter, just beneath the insect, and, having accomplished this, ordered Jupiter to let go the string and come down from the tree.

Driving a peg, with great nicety, into the ground, at the precise spot where the beetle fell, my friend now produced from his pocket a tape-measure. Fastening one end of this at that point of the trunk of the tree which was nearest the peg, he unrolled it till it reached the peg, and thence farther unrolled it, in the direction already established by the two points of the tree and the peg, for the distance of fifty feet—Jupiter clearing away the brambles with the scythe. At the spot thus attained a second peg was driven, and about this, as a center, a rude circle, about four feet in diameter, described. Taking now a spade himself, and giving one to Jupiter and one to me, Legrand begged us to set about digging as quickly as possible.

To speak the truth, I had no especial relish for such amusement at any time, and, at that particular moment, would willingly have declined it; for the night was coming on, and I felt much fatigued with the exercise already taken; but I saw no mode of escape, and was fearful of disturbing my poor friend's equanimity by a refusal. Could I have depended, indeed upon Jupiter's aid, I would have had no hesitation in attempting to get

the lunatic home by force; but I was too well assured of the old negro's disposition, to hope that he would assist me, under any circumstances, in a personal contest with his master. I made no doubt that the latter had been infected with some of the innumerable Southern superstitions about money buried, and that his fantasy had received confirmation by the finding of the *scarabaeus*, or, perhaps, by Jupiter's obstinacy in maintaining it to be "a bug of real gold." A mind disposed to lunacy would readily be led away by such suggestions—especially if chiming in with favorite preconceived ideas—and then I called to mind the poor fellow's speech about the beetle's being "the index of his fortune." Upon the whole, I was sadly vexed and puzzled, but, at length, I concluded to make a virtue of necessity—to dig with a good will, and thus the sooner to convince the visionary, by ocular demonstration, of the fallacy of the opinions he entertained.

The lanterns having been lit, we all fell to work with a zeal worthy a more rational cause; and, as the glare fell upon our persons and implements, I could not help thinking how picturesque a group we composed, and how strange and suspicious our labors must have appeared to any interloper who, by chance, might have stumbled upon our whereabouts.

We dug very steadily for two hours. Little was said; and our chief embarrassment lay in the yelpings of the dog, who took exceeding interest in our proceedings. He, at length, became so obstreperous that we grew fearful of his giving the alarm to some stragglers in the vicinity—or, rather, this was the apprehension of Legrand; for myself, I should have rejoiced at any interruption which might have enabled me to get the wanderer home. The noise was, at length, very effectually silenced by Jupiter, who, getting out of the hole with a dogged air of deliberation, tied the brute's mouth up with one of his suspenders, and then returned, with a grave chuckle, to his task.

When the time mentioned had expired, we had reached a depth of five feet, and yet no sign of any treasure became manifest. A general pause ensued, and I began to hope that the farce was at an end. Legrand, however, although evidently much disconcerted, wiped his brow thoughtfully and recommenced. We had excavated the entire circle of four feet diameter, and now we slightly enlarged the limit, and went to the farther depth of two feet. Still nothing appeared. The gold-seeker, whom I sincerely pitied, at length clambered from the pit, with the bitterest disappointment imprinted upon every feature, and proceeded, slowly and reluctantly, to

put on his coat, which he had thrown off at the beginning of his labor. In the meantime I made no remark. Jupiter, at a signal from his master, began to gather up his tools. This done, and the dog having been unmuzzled, we turned in profound silence towards home.

We had taken, perhaps, a dozen steps in this direction, when, with a loud oath, Legrand strode up to Jupiter, and seized him by the collar. The astonished negro opened his eyes and mouth to the fullest extent, let fall the spades, and fell upon his knees.

"You scoundrel!" said Legrand, hissing out the syllables from between his clenched teeth—"you infernal black villain!—speak, I tell you!—answer me this instant, without prevarication!—which—which is your left eye?"

"Oh, my golly, Massa Will! aint dis here my lef eye for sartain?" roared the terrified Jupiter, placing his hand upon his *right* organ of vision, and holding it there with a desperate pertinacity, as if in immediate dread of his master's attempt at a gouge.

"I thought so!—I knew it! hurrah!" vociferated Legrand, letting the negro go and executing a series of curvets and caracols, much to the astonishment of his valet, who, arising from his knees, looked, mutely, from his master to myself, and then from myself to his master.

"Come! we must go back," said the latter, "the game's not up yet": and he again led the way to the tulip-tree.

"Jupiter," said he, when we reached its foot, "come here! Was the skull nailed to the limb with the face outward, or with the face to the limb?"

"De face was out, massa, so dat de crows could get at de eyes good, widout any trouble."

"Well, then, was it this eye or that through which you dropped the beetle?" here Legrand touched each of Jupiter's eyes.

"'Twas dis eye, massa—de lef eye—jis as you tell me," and here it was his right eye that the negro indicated.

"That will do—must try it again."

Here my friend, about whose madness I now saw, or fancied that I saw, certain indications of method, removed the peg which marked the spot where the beetle fell, to a spot about three inches to the westward of its former position. Taking, now, the tape-measure from the nearest point of the trunk to the peg, as before, and continuing the extension in a straight line to the distance of fifty feet, a spot was indicated, removed, by several yards, from the point at which we had been digging.

Around the new position a circle, somewhat larger than in the former instance, was now described, and we again set to work with the spades. I

was dreadfully weary, but, scarcely understanding what had occasioned the change in my thoughts, I felt no longer any great aversion from the labor imposed. I had become most unaccountably interested—nay, even excited. Perhaps there was something, amid all the extravagant demeanor of Legrand—some air of forethought, or of deliberation, which impressed me. I dug eagerly, and now and then caught myself actually looking, with something that very much resembled expectation, for the fancied treasure, the vision of which had demented my unfortunate companion. At a period when such vagaries of thought most fully possessed me, and when we had been at work perhaps an hour and a half, we were again interrupted by the violent howlings of the dog. His uneasiness, in the first instance, had been, evidently, but the result of playfulness or caprice, but he now assumed a bitter and serious tone. Upon Jupiter's again attempting to muzzle him, he made furious resistance, and, leaping into the hole, tore up the mold frantically with his claws. In a few seconds he had uncovered a mass of human bones, forming two complete skeletons, intermingled with several buttons of metal, and what appeared to be the dust of decayed woolen. One or two strokes of a spade upturned the blade of a large Spanish knife, and, as we dug farther, three or four loose pieces of gold and silver coin came to light.

At sight of these the joy of Jupiter could scarcely be restrained, but the countenance of his master wore an air of extreme disappointment. He urged us, however, to continue our exertions, and the words were hardly uttered when I stumbled and fell forward, having caught the toe of my boot in a large ring of iron that lay half buried in the loose earth.

We now worked in earnest, and never did I pass ten minutes of more intense excitement. During this interval we had fairly unearthed an oblong chest of wood, which, from its perfect preservation and wonderful hardness, had plainly been subjected to some mineralizing process—perhaps that of the Bichloride of Mercury. This box was three feet and a half long, three feet broad, and two and a half feet deep. It was firmly secured by bands of wrought iron, riveted, and forming a kind of open trellis-work over the whole. On each side of the chest, near the top, were three rings of iron—six in all—by means of which a firm hold could be obtained by six persons. Our utmost united endeavors served only to disturb the coffer very slightly in its bed. We at once saw the impossibility of removing so great a weight. Luckily, the sole fastenings of the lid consisted of two sliding bolts. These we drew back—trembling and panting with anxiety. In an instant, a treasure of incalculable value lay gleaming before us. As the rays of the lanterns fell within

the pit, there flashed upwards a glow and a glare, from a confused heap of gold and of jewels, that absolutely dazzled our eyes.

I shall not pretend to describe the feelings with which I gazed. Amazement was, of course, predominant. Legrand appeared exhausted with excitement, and spoke very few words. Jupiter's countenance wore, for some minutes, as deadly a pallor as it is possible, in the nature of things, for any negro's visage to assume. He seemed stupefied—thunderstricken. Presently he fell upon his knees in the pit, and burying his naked arms up to the elbows in gold, let them there remain, as if enjoying the luxury of a bath. At length, with a deep sigh, he exclaimed, as if in a soliloquy:

"And dis all cum ob de goole-bug! de putty goole-bug! de poor little goole-bug, what I boosed in dat sabage kind ob style! Aint you shamed ob yourself, nigger?—answer me dat!"

It became necessary, at last, that I should arouse both master and valet to the expediency of removing the treasure. It was growing late, and it behooved us to make exertion, that we might get everything housed before daylight. It was difficult to say what should be done, and much time was spent in deliberation—so confused were the ideas of all. We, finally, lightened the box by removing two-thirds of its contents, when we were enabled, with some trouble to raise it from the hole. The articles taken out were deposited among the brambles, and the dog left to guard them, with strict orders from Jupiter neither, upon any pretence, to stir from the spot, nor to open his mouth until our return. We then hurriedly made for home with the chest; reaching the hut in safety, but after excessive toil, at one o'clock in the morning. Worn out as we were, it was not in human nature to do more immediately. We rested until two, and had supper; starting for the hills immediately afterward, armed with three stout sacks, which, by good luck, were upon the premises. A little before four we arrived at the pit, divided the remainder of the booty, as equally as might be, among us, and, leaving the holes unfilled, again set out for the hut, at which, for the second time, we deposited our golden burdens, just as the first faint streaks of the dawn gleamed from over the tree-tops in the East.

We were now thoroughly broken down; but the intense excitement of the time denied us repose. After an unquiet slumber of some three or four hours' duration, we arose, as if by preconcert, to make examination of our treasure.

The chest had been full to the brim, and we spent the whole day, and the greater part of the next night, in a scrutiny of its contents. There had been nothing like order or arrangement. Everything had been heaped in

promiscuously. Having assorted all with care we found ourselves possessed
of even vaster wealth than we had at first supposed. In coin there was
rather more than four hundred and fifty thousand dollars—estimating the
value of the pieces, as accurately as we could, by the tables of the period.
There was not a particle of silver. All was gold of antique date and of great
variety—French, Spanish, and German money, with a few English guineas,
and some counters, of which we had never seen specimens before. There
were several very large and heavy coins, so worn that we could make noth-
ing of their inscriptions. There was no American money. The value of the
jewels we found more difficulty in estimating. There were diamonds—
some of them exceedingly large and fine—a hundred and ten in all, and
not one of them small; eighteen rubies of remarkable brilliancy; three
hundred and ten emeralds, all very beautiful; and twenty-one sapphires,
with an opal. These stones had all been broken from their settings and
thrown loose in the chest. The settings themselves, which we picked out
from among the other gold, appeared to have been beaten up with ham-
mers, as if to prevent identification. Besides all this, there was a vast
quantity of solid gold ornaments; nearly two hundred massive finger and
earrings; rich chains—thirty of these, if I remember; eighty-three very
large and heavy crucifixes; five gold censers of great value; a prodigious
golden punch-bowl, ornamented with richly chased vine-leaves and Bac-
chanalian figures; with two sword-handles exquisitely embossed, and many
other smaller articles which I cannot recollect. The weight of these valu-
ables exceeded three hundred and fifty pounds avoirdupois; and in this
estimate I have not included one hundred and ninety-seven superb gold
watches; three of the number being worth each five hundred dollars, if
one. Many of them were very old, and as time-keepers valueless; the works
having suffered, more or less, from corrosion—but all were richly jeweled
and in cases of great worth. We estimated the entire contents of the chest,
that night, at a million and a half of dollars; and upon the subsequent
disposal of the trinkets and jewels (a few being retained for our own use),
it was found that we had greatly undervalued the treasure.

When, at length, we had concluded our examination, and the intense
excitement of the time had, in some measure, subsided, Legrand, who
saw that I was dying with impatience for a solution of this most extraordi-
nary riddle, entered into a full detail of all the circumstances connected
with it.

"You remember," said he, "the night when I handed you the rough
sketch I had made of the *scarabaeus*. You recollect also, that I became quite

vexed at you for insisting that my drawing resembled a death's-head. When you first made this assertion I thought you were jesting; but afterward I called to mind the peculiar spots on the back of the insect, and admitted to myself that your remark had some little foundation in fact. Still, the sneer at my graphic powers irritated me—for I am considered a good artist—and, therefore, when you handed me the scrap of parchment, I was about to crumple it up and throw it angrily into the fire."

"The scrap of paper, you mean," said I.

"No; it had much of the appearance of paper, and at first I supposed it to be such, but when I came to draw upon it, I discovered it at once to be a piece of very thin parchment. It was quite dirty, you remember. Well, as I was in the very act of crumpling it up, my glance fell upon the sketch at which you had been looking, and you may imagine my astonishment when I perceived, in fact, the figure of a death's-head just where, it seemed to me, I had made the drawing of the beetle. For a moment I was too much amazed to think with accuracy. I knew that my design was very different in detail from this—although there was a certain similarity in general outline. Presently I took a candle, and seating myself at the other end of the room, proceeded to scrutinize the parchment more closely. Upon turning it over, I saw my own sketch upon the reverse, just as I had made it. My first idea, now, was mere surprise at the really remarkable similarity of outline—at the singular coincidence involved in the fact that, unknown to me, there should have been a skull upon the other side of the parchment, immediately beneath my figure of the *scarabaeus,* and that this skull, not only in outline, but in size, should so closely resemble my drawing. I say the singularity of this coincidence absolutely stupefied me for a time. This is the usual effect of such coincidences. The mind struggles to establish a connection—a sequence of cause and effect—and, being unable to do so, suffers a species of temporary paralysis. But, when I recovered from this stupor, there dawned upon me gradually a conviction which startled me even far more than the coincidence. I began distinctly, positively, to remember that there had been *no* drawing upon the parchment, when I made my sketch of the *scarabaeus.* I became perfectly certain of this; for I recollected turning up first one side and then the other, in search of the cleanest spot. Had the skull been then there, of course I could not have failed to notice it. Here was indeed a mystery which I felt it impossible to explain; but, even at that early moment, there seemed to glimmer, faintly, within the most remote and secret chambers of my intellect, a glow-worm-like conception of that truth

which last night's adventure brought to so magnificent a demonstration. I arose at once, and putting the parchment securely away, dismissed all further reflection until I should be alone.

"When you had gone, and when Jupiter was fast asleep, I betook myself to a more methodical investigation of the affair. In the first place I considered the manner in which the parchment had come into my possession. The spot where we discovered the *scarabaeus* was on the coast of the main land, about a mile eastward of the island, and but a short distance above high-water mark. Upon my taking hold of it, it gave me a sharp bite, which caused me to let it drop. Jupiter, with his accustomed caution, before seizing the insect, which had flown towards him, looked about him for a leaf, or something of that nature, by which to take hold of it. It was at this moment that his eyes, and mine also, fell upon the scrap of parchment, which I then supposed to be paper. It was lying half buried in the sand, a corner sticking up. Near the spot where we found it, I observed the remnants of the hull of what appeared to have been a ship's long boat. The wreck seemed to have been there for a very great while; for the resemblance to boat timbers could scarcely be traced.

"Well, Jupiter picked up the parchment, wrapped the beetle in it, and gave it to me. Soon afterward we turned to go home, and on the way met Lieutenant G——. I showed him the insect, and he begged me to let him take it to the fort. Upon my consenting, he thrust it forthwith into his waistcoat pocket, without the parchment in which it had been wrapped, and which I had continued to hold in my hand during his inspection. Perhaps he dreaded my changing my mind, and thought it best to make sure of the prize at once—you know how enthusiastic he is on all subjects connected with Natural History. At the same time, without being conscious of it, I must have deposited the parchment in my own pocket.

"You remember that when I went to the table, for the purpose of making a sketch of the beetle, I found no paper where it was usually kept. I looked in the drawer, and found none there. I searched my pockets, hoping to find an old letter, when my hand fell upon the parchment. I thus detail the precise mode in which it came into my possession; for the circumstances impressed me with a peculiar force.

"No doubt you will think me fanciful—but I had already established a kind of *connection*. I had put together two links of a great chain. There was a boat lying upon a seacoast, and not far from the boat was a parchment—*not a paper*—with a skull depicted upon it. You will, of course, ask 'where is the

connection?' I reply that the skull, or death's-head, is the well-known emblem
of the pirate. The flag of the death's-head is hoisted in all engagements.

"I have said that the scrap was parchment, and not paper. Parchment
is durable—almost imperishable. Matters of little moment are rarely
consigned to parchment; since, for the mere ordinary purposes of draw-
ing or writing, it is not nearly so well adapted as paper. This reflection
suggested some meaning—some relevancy—in the death's-head. I did not
fail to observe, also, the *form* of the parchment. Although one of its cor-
ners had been, by some accident, destroyed, it could be seen that the
original form was oblong. It was just such a slip, indeed, as might have
been chosen for a memorandum—for a record of something to be long
remembered and carefully preserved."

"But," I interposed, "you say that the skull was *not* upon the parchment
when you made the drawing of the beetle. How then do you trace any
connection between the boat and the skull—since this latter, according to
your own admission, must have been designed (God only knows how or by
whom) at some period subsequent to your sketching the *scarabaeus?*"

"Ah, hereupon turns the whole mystery; although the secret, at this
point, I had comparatively little difficulty in solving. My steps were sure,
and could afford but a single result. I reasoned, for example, thus: When
I drew the *scarabaeus,* there was no skull apparent upon the parchment.
When I had completed the drawing I gave it to you, and observed you nar-
rowly until you returned it. *You,* therefore, did not design the skull, and
no one else was present to do it. Then it was not done by human agency.
And nevertheless it was done.

"At this stage of my reflections I endeavored to remember, and *did*
remember, with entire distinctness, every incident which occurred about
the period in question. The weather was chilly (oh, rare and happy acci-
dent!), and a fire was blazing upon the hearth. I was heated with exercise
and sat near the table. You, however, had drawn a chair close to the chim-
ney. Just as I placed the parchment in your hand, and as you were in the
act of inspecting it, Wolf, the Newfoundland, entered, and leaped upon
your shoulders. With your left hand you caressed him and kept him off,
while your right, holding the parchment, was permitted to fall listlessly
between your knees, and in close proximity to the fire. At one moment I
thought the blaze had caught it, and was about to caution you, but, before
I could speak, you had withdrawn it, and were engaged in its examination.
When I considered all these particulars, I doubted not for a moment that
heat had been the agent in bringing to light, upon the parchment, the

skull which I saw designed upon it. You are well aware that chemical preparations exist, and have existed time out of mind, by means of which it is possible to write upon either paper or vellum, so that the characters shall become visible only when subjected to the action of fire. Zaffre, digested in *aqua regia*, and diluted with four times its weight of water, is sometimes employed; a green tint results. The regulus of cobalt, dissolved in spirit of niter, gives a red. These colors disappear at longer or shorter intervals after the material written upon cools, but again become apparent upon the reapplication of heat.

"I now scrutinized the death's-head with care. Its outer edges—the edges of the drawing nearest the edge of the vellum—were far more *distinct* than the others. It was clear that the action of the caloric had been imperfect or unequal. I immediately kindled a fire, and subjected every portion of the parchment to a glowing heat. At first, the only effect was the strengthening of the faint lines in the skull; but, upon persevering in the experiment, there became visible, at the corner of the slip, diagonally opposite to the spot in which the death's-head was delineated, the figure of what I at first supposed to be a goat. A closer scrutiny, however, satisfied me that it was intended for a kid."

"Ha! ha!" said I, "to be sure I have no right to laugh at you—a million and a half of money is too serious a matter for mirth—but you are not about to establish a third link in your chain—you will not find any especial connection between your pirates and a goat—pirates, you know, have nothing to do with goats; they appertain to the farming interest."

"But I have just said that the figure was *not* that of a goat."

"Well, a kid then—pretty much the same thing."

"Pretty much, but not altogether," said Legrand. "You may have heard of one *Captain* Kidd. I at once looked upon the figure of the animal as a kind of punning or hieroglyphical signature. I say signature; because its position upon the vellum suggested this idea. The death's-head at the corner diagonally opposite, had, in the same manner, the air of a stamp, or seal. But I was sorely put out by the absence of all else—of the body to my imagined instrument—of the text for my context."

"I presume you expected to find a letter between the stamp and the signature."

"Something of that kind. The fact is, I felt irresistibly impressed with a presentiment of some vast good fortune impending. I can scarcely say why. Perhaps, after all, it was rather a desire than an actual belief; but do you know that Jupiter's silly words, about the bug being of solid gold, had a

remarkable effect upon my fancy? And then the series of accidents and coincidences—these were so *very* extraordinary. Do you observe how mere an accident it was that these events should have occurred upon the *sole* day of all the year in which it has been, or may be sufficiently cool for fire, and that without the fire, or without the intervention of the dog at the precise moment in which he appeared, I should never have become aware of the death's-head, and so never the possessor of the treasure."

"But proceed—I am all impatience."

"Well; you have heard, of course, the many stories current—the thousand vague rumors afloat about money buried, somewhere upon the Atlantic coast, by Kidd and his associates. These rumors must have had some foundation in fact. And that the rumors have existed so long and so continuous, could have resulted, it appeared to me, only from the circumstance of the buried treasure still *remaining* entombed. Had Kidd concealed his plunder for a time, and afterward reclaimed it, the rumors would scarcely have reached us in their present unvarying form. You will observe that the stories told are all about money-seekers, not about money-finders. Had the pirate recovered his money, there the affair would have dropped. It seemed to me that some accident—say the loss of a memorandum indicating its locality— had deprived him of the means of recovering it, and that this accident had become known to his followers, who otherwise might never have heard that treasure had been concealed at all, and who, busying themselves in vain, because unguided, attempts to regain it, had given first birth, and then universal currency, to the reports which are now so common. Have you ever heard of any important treasure being unearthed along the coast?"

"Never."

"But that Kidd's accumulations were immense, is well known. I took it for granted, therefore, that the earth still held them; and you will scarcely be surprised when I tell you that I felt a hope, nearly amounting to certainty, that the parchment so strangely found involved a lost record of the place of deposit."

"But how did you proceed?"

"I held the vellum again to the fire, after increasing the heat, but nothing appeared. I now thought it possible that the coating of dirt might have something to do with the failure: so I carefully rinsed the parchment by pouring warm water over it, and, having done this, I placed it in a tin pan, with the skull downward, and put the pan upon a furnace of lighted charcoal. In a few minutes, the pan having become thoroughly heated, I

removed the slip, and, to my inexpressible joy, found it spotted, in several places, with what appeared to be figures arranged in lines. Again I placed it in the pan, and suffered it to remain another minute. Upon taking it off, the whole was just as you see it now."

Here Legrand, having reheated the parchment, submitted it to my inspection. The following characters were rudely traced, in a red tint, between the death's-head and the goat:

53‡‡†305))6*;4826)4‡.)4‡);806*;48†8¶60))
85;1‡(;:‡*8†83(88)5*†;46(;88*96*?;8)*‡(;4
85);5*†2:*‡(;4956*2(5*—4)8¶8*;4069285);)
6†8)4‡‡;1(‡9;48081;8:8‡1;48†85;4)485†5288
06*81(‡9;48;(88;4(‡?34;48)4‡;161;:188;‡?;

"But," said I, returning him the slip, "I am as much in the dark as ever. Were all the jewels of Golconda awaiting me upon my solution of this enigma, I am quite sure that I should be unable to earn them."

"And yet," said Legrand, "the solution is by no means so difficult as you might be led to imagine from the first hasty inspection of the characters. These characters, as anyone might readily guess, form a cipher—that is to say, they convey a meaning; but then from what is known of Kidd, I could not suppose him capable of constructing any of the more abstruse crypto-graphs. I made up my mind, at once, that this was of a simple species—such, however, as would appear, to the crude intellect of the sailor, absolutely insoluble without the key."

"And you really solved it?"

"Readily; I have solved others of an abstruseness ten thousand times greater. Circumstances, and a certain bias of mind, have led me to take interest in such riddles, and it may well be doubted whether human inge-nuity can construct an enigma of the kind which human ingenuity may not, by proper application, resolve. In fact, having once established con-nected and legible characters, I scarcely gave a thought to the mere difficulty of developing their import.

"In the present case—indeed in all cases of secret writing—the first question regards the *language* of the cipher; for the principles of solution, so far, especially, as the more simple ciphers are concerned, depend upon, and are varied by, the genius of the particular idiom. In general, there is no alternative but experiment (directed by probabilities) of every tongue known to him who attempts the solution, until the true one be

attained. But, with the cipher now before us, all difficulty was removed by the signature. The pun upon the word 'Kidd' is appreciable in no other language than the English. But for this consideration I should have begun my attempts with the Spanish and French, as the tongues in which a secret of this kind would most naturally have been written by a pirate of the Spanish main. As it was, I assumed the cryptograph to be English.

"You observe there are no divisions between the words. Had there been divisions, the task would have been comparatively easy. In such cases I should have commenced with a collation and analysis of the shorter words, and, had a word of a single letter occurred, as is most likely (*a* or *I*, for example), I should have considered the solution as assured. But, there being no division, my first step was to ascertain the predominant letters, as well as the least frequent. Counting all, I constructed a table thus:

Of the character 8 there are 33.
; " 26.
4 " 19.
‡) " 16.
* " 13.
5 " 12.
6 " 11.
† 1 " 8.
0 " 6.
9 2 " 5.
: 3 " 4.
? " 3.
¶ " 2.
— . " 1.

"Now, in English, the letter which most frequently occurs is *e*. Afterward, the succession runs thus: *a o i d h n r s t u y c f g l m w b k p q x z*. E predominates so remarkably, that an individual sentence of any length is rarely seen, in which it is not the prevailing character.

"Here, then, we have, in the very beginning, the groundwork for something more than a mere guess. The general use which may be made of the table is obvious—but, in this particular cipher, we shall only very partially require its aid. As our predominant character is 8, we will commence by assuming it as the *e* of the natural alphabet. To verify the supposition, let

us observe if the 8 be seen often in couples—for *e* is doubled with great frequency in English—in such words, for example, as 'meet,' 'fleet,' 'speed,' 'seen,' 'been,' 'agree,' etc. In the present instance we see it doubled no less than five times, although the cryptograph is brief.

"Let us assume 8, then, as *e*. Now, of all *words* in the language, 'the' is most usual; let us see, therefore, whether there are not repetitions of any three characters, in the same order of collocation, the last of them being 8. If we discover repetitions of such letters, so arranged, they will most probably represent the word 'the.' Upon inspection, we find no less than seven such arrangements, the characters being ;48. We may, therefore, assume that ; represents *t*, 4 represents *h*, and 8 represents *e*—the last being now well confirmed. Thus a great step has been taken.

"But, having established a single word, we are enabled to establish a vastly important point; that is to say, several commencements and terminations of other words. Let us refer, for example, to the last instance but one, in which the combination ;48 occurs—not far from the end of the cipher. We know that the ; immediately ensuing is the commencement of a word, and, of the six characters succeeding this 'the,' we are cognizant of no less than five. Let us set these characters down, thus, by the letters we know them to represent, leaving a space for the unknown—

t eeth

"Here we are enabled, at once, to discard the *'th,'* as forming no portion of the word commencing with the first *t*; since, by experiment of the entire alphabet for a letter adapted to the vacancy, we perceive that no word can be formed of which this *th* can be a part. We are thus narrowed into

t ee

and, going through the alphabet, if necessary, as before, we arrive at the word 'tree,' as the sole possible reading. We thus gain another letter, *r*, represented by (, with the words 'the tree' in juxtaposition.

"Looking beyond these words, for a short distance, we again see the combination ;48, and employ it by way of *termination* to what immediately precedes. We have thus this arrangement:

the tree ;4(‡?34 the,

or, substituting the natural letters, where known, it reads thus:

the tree thr‡?3h the.

"Now, if, in place of the unknown characters, we leave blank spaces, or substitute dots, we read thus:

the tree thr . . . h the,

when the word '*through*' makes itself evident at once. But this discovery gives us three new letters, *o, u,* and *g,* represented by ‡, ?, and 3.

"Looking now, narrowly, through the cipher for combinations of known characters, we find, not very far from the beginning, this arrangement,

83(88, or egree,

which plainly, is the conclusion of the word 'degree,' and gives us another letter, *d,* represented by †.

"Four letters beyond the word 'degree,' we perceive the combination

;46(;88.

"Translating the known characters, and representing the unknown by dots, as before, we read thus:

th.rtee

an arrangement immediately suggestive of the word 'thirteen,' and again furnishing us with two new characters, *i* and *n,* represented by 6 and *.

"Referring, now, to the beginning of the cryptograph, we find the combination,

53‡‡†.

"Translating, as before, we obtain

good,

which assures us that the first letter is *A,* and that the first two words are 'A good.'

"It is now time that we arrange our key, as far as discovered, in a tabular form, to avoid confusion. It will stand thus:

5	represents	a
†	"	d
8	"	e
3	"	g
4	"	h
6	"	i
*	"	n
‡	"	o
("	r
;	"	t

"We have therefore, no less than ten of the most important letters represented, and it will be unnecessary to proceed with the details of the solution. I have said enough to convince you that ciphers of this nature are readily soluble, and to give you some insight into the *rationale* of their development. But be assured that the specimen before us appertains to the very simplest species of cryptograph. It now only remains to give you the full translation of the characters upon the parchment, as unriddled. Here it is:

A good glass in the bishop's hostel in the devil's seat forty-one degrees and thirteen minutes northeast and by north main branch seventh limb east side shoot from the left eye of the death's-head a bee-line from the tree through the shot fifty feet out."

"But," said I, "the enigma seems still in as bad a condition as ever. How is it possible to extort a meaning from all this jargon about 'devil's seats,' 'death's-heads,' and 'bishop's hostels'?"

"I confess," replied Legrand, "that the matter still wears a serious aspect, when regarded with a casual glance. My first endeavor was to divide the sentence into the natural division intended by the cryptographist."

"You mean, to punctuate it?"

"Something of that kind."

"But how was it possible to effect this?"

"I reflected that it had been a *point* with the writer to run his words together without division, so as to increase the difficulty of solution. Now, a not over-acute man, in pursuing such an object, would be nearly certain

to overdo the matter. When, in the course of his composition, he arrived at a break in his subject which would naturally require a pause, or a point, he would be exceedingly apt to run his characters, at this place, more than usually close together. If you will observe the MS., in the present instance, you will easily detect five such cases of unusual crowding. Acting upon this hint, I made the division thus:

A good glass in the Bishop's hostel in the Devil's seat—forty-one degrees and thirteen minutes—northeast and by north—main branch seventh limb east side—shoot from the left eye of the death's-head—a bee-line from the tree through the shot fifty feet out."

"Even this division," said I, "leaves me still in the dark."

"It left me also in the dark," replied Legrand, "for a few days; during which I made diligent inquiry in the neighborhood of Sullivan's Island, for any building which went by the name of the 'Bishop's Hotel'; for, of course, I dropped the obsolete word 'hostel.' Gaining no information on the subject, I was on the point of extending my sphere of search, and proceeding in a more systematic manner, when, one morning, it entered into my head, quite suddenly, that this 'Bishop's Hostel' might have some reference to an old family, of the name of Bessop, which, time out of mind, had held possession of an ancient manor-house, about four miles to the northward of the Island. I accordingly went over to the plantation, and reinstituted my inquiries among the older negroes of the place. At length one of the most aged of the women said that she had heard of such a place as *Bessop's Castle*, and thought that she could guide me to it, but that it was not a castle, nor a tavern, but a high rock.

"I offered to pay her well for her trouble, and, after some demur, she consented to accompany me to the spot. We found it without much diffi-culty, when, dismissing her, I proceeded to examine the place. The 'castle' consisted of an irregular assemblage of cliffs and rocks—one of the latter being quite remarkable for its height as well as for its insulated and artifi-cial appearance. I clambered to its apex, and then felt much at a loss as to what should be next done.

"While I was busied in reflection, my eyes fell upon a narrow ledge in the eastern face of the rock, perhaps a yard below the summit upon which I stood. This ledge projected about eighteen inches, and was not more than a foot wide, while a niche in the cliff just above it gave it a rude resem-blance to one of the hollow-backed chairs used by our ancestors. I made

no doubt that here was the 'devil's seat' alluded to in the MS., and now I seemed to grasp the full secret of the riddle.

"The 'good glass,' I knew, could have reference to nothing but a telescope; for the word 'glass' is rarely employed in any other sense by seamen. Now here, I at once saw, was a telescope to be used, and a definite point of view, *admitting no variation,* from which to use it. Nor did I hesitate to believe that the phrases 'forty-one degrees and thirteen minutes,' and 'northeast and by north,' were intended as directions for the leveling of the glass. Greatly excited by these discoveries, I hurried home, procured a telescope, and returned to the rock.

"I let myself down to the ledge, and found that it was impossible to retain a seat upon it except in one particular position. This fact confirmed my preconceived idea. I proceeded to use the glass. Of course, the 'forty-one degrees and thirteen minutes' could allude to nothing but elevation above the visible horizon, since the horizontal direction was clearly indicated by the words, 'northeast and by north.' This latter direction I at once established by means of a pocket-compass; then, pointing the glass as nearly at an angle of forty-one degrees of elevation as I could do it by guess, I moved it cautiously up or down, until my attention was arrested by a circular rift or opening in the foliage of a large tree that overtopped its fellows in the distance. In the center of this rift I perceived a white spot, but could not, at first, distinguish what it was. Adjusting the focus of the telescope, I again looked, and now made it out to be a human skull.

"Upon this discovery I was so sanguine as to consider the enigma solved; for the phrase 'main branch, seventh limb, east side,' could refer only to the position of the skull upon the tree, while 'shoot from the left eye of the death's-head' admitted, also, of but one interpretation, in regard to a search for buried treasure. I perceived that the design was to drop a bullet from the left eye of the skull, and that a bee-line, or, in other words, a straight line, drawn from the nearest point of the trunk through 'the shot' (or the spot where the bullet fell), and thence extended to a distance of fifty feet, would indicate a definite point—and beneath this point I thought it at least *possible* that a deposit of value lay concealed."

"All this," I said, "is exceedingly clear, and, although ingenious, still simple and explicit. When you left the Bishop's Hotel, what then?"

"Why, having carefully taken the bearings of the tree, I turned homeward. The instant that I left 'the devil's seat,' however, the circular rift vanished; nor could I get a glimpse of it afterward, turn as I would. What seems to me the chief ingenuity in this whole business, is the fact (for

repeated experiment has convinced me it *is* a fact) that the circular opening in question is visible from no other attainable point of view than that afforded by the narrow ledge upon the face of the rock.

"In this expedition to the 'Bishop's Hotel' I had been attended by Jupiter, who had, no doubt, observed, for some weeks past, the abstraction of my demeanor, and took especial care not to leave me alone. But, on the next day, getting up very early, I contrived to give him the slip, and went into the hills in search of the tree. After much toil I found it. When I came home at night my valet proposed to give me a flogging. With the rest of the adventure I believe you are as well acquainted as myself."

"I suppose," said I, "you missed the spot, in the first attempt at digging, through Jupiter's stupidity in letting the bug fall through the right instead of through the left eye of the skull."

"Precisely. This mistake made a difference of about two inches and a half in the 'shot'—that is to say, in the position of the peg nearest the tree; and had the treasure been *beneath* the 'shot,' the error would have been of little moment; but 'the shot,' together with the nearest point of the tree, were merely two points for the establishment of a line of direction; of course the error, however trivial in the beginning, increased as we proceeded with the line, and by the time we had gone fifty feet threw us quite off the scent. But for my deep-seated impressions that treasure was here somewhere actually buried, we might have had all our labor in vain."

"But your grandiloquence, and your conduct in swinging the beetle—how excessively odd! I was sure you were mad. And why did you insist upon letting fall the bug, instead of a bullet, from the skull?"

"Why, to be frank, I felt somewhat annoyed by your evident suspicions touching my sanity, and so resolved to punish you quietly, in my own way, by a little bit of sober mystification. For this reason I swung the beetle, and for this reason I let it fall it from the tree. An observation of yours about its great weight suggested the latter idea."

"Yes, I perceive; and now there is only one point which puzzles me. What are we to make of the skeletons found in the hole?"

"That is a question I am no more able to answer than yourself. There seems, however, only one plausible way of accounting for them—and yet it is dreadful to believe in such atrocity as my suggestion would imply. It is clear that Kidd—if Kidd indeed secreted this treasure, which I doubt not—it is clear that he must have had assistance in the labor. But this labor concluded, he may have thought it expedient to remove all participants in his secret. Perhaps a couple of blows with a mattock were sufficient, while his coadjutors were busy in the pit; perhaps it required a dozen—who shall tell?"

SKETCHES AND ESSAYS

THE IMP OF THE PERVERSE

IN THE CONSIDERATION OF THE FACULTIES AND IMPULSES OF THE *PRIMA mobilia*[1] of the human soul, the phrenologists have failed to make room for a propensity, which, although obviously existing as a radical, primitive, irreducible sentiment, has been equally overlooked by all the moralists who have preceded them. In the pure arrogance of the reason, we have all overlooked it. We have suffered its existence to escape our senses, solely through want of belief—of faith; whether it be faith in Revelation, or faith in the Kabbala. The idea of it has never occurred to us, simply because of its supererogation. We saw no *need* of the impulse—for the propensity. We could not perceive its necessity. We could not understand, that is to say, we could not have understood, had the notion of this *primum mobile* ever obtruded itself; we could not have understood in what manner it might be made to further the objects of humanity, either temporal or eternal. It cannot be denied that phrenology, and in great measure, all metaphysicianism have been concocted *à priori*. The intellectual or logical man, rather than the understanding or observant man, set himself to imagine designs—to dictate purposes to God. Having thus fathomed to his satisfaction, the intentions of Jehovah, out of these intentions he built his innumerable systems of mind. In the matter of phrenology, for example, we first determined, naturally enough, that it was the design of the Deity that man should eat. We then assigned to man an organ of alimentiveness, and this organ is the scourge with which the Deity compels man, will-I nill-I, into eating. Secondly, having settled it to be God's will that man should continue his species, we discovered an organ of amativeness, forthwith. And so with combativeness, with ideality, with causality, with constructiveness—

so, in short, with every organ, whether representing a propensity, a moral sentiment, or a faculty of the pure intellect. And in these arrangements of the *principia* of human action, the Spurzheimites, whether right or wrong, in part, or upon the whole, have but followed, in principle, the footsteps of their predecessors: deducing and establishing everything from the preconceived destiny of man, and upon the ground of the objects of his Creator.

It would have been wiser, it would have been safer to classify (if classify we must), upon the basis of what man usually or occasionally did, and was always occasionally doing, rather than upon the basis of what we took it for granted the Deity intended him to do. If we cannot comprehend God in his visible works, how then in his inconceivable thoughts, that call the works into being? If we cannot understand him in his objective creatures, how then in his substantive moods and phases of creation?

Induction, *à posteriori*, would have brought phrenology to admit, as an innate and primitive principle of human action, a paradoxical something, which we may call *perverseness*, for want of a more characteristic term. In the sense I intend, it is, in fact, a *mobile* without motive, a motive not *motivirt*. Through its promptings we act without comprehensible object; or, if this shall be understood as a contradiction in terms, we may so far modify the proposition as to say, that through its promptings we act, for the reason that we should *not*. In theory, no reason can be more unreasonable; but, in fact, there is none more strong. With certain minds, under certain conditions, it becomes absolutely irresistible. I am not more certain that I breathe, than that the assurance of the wrong or error of any action is often the one unconquerable *force* which impels us, and alone impels us to its prosecution. Nor will this overwhelming tendency to do wrong for the wrong's sake, admit of analysis, or resolution into ulterior elements. It is a radical, a primitive impulse—elementary. It will be said, I am aware, that when we persist in acts because we feel we should *not* persist in them, our conduct is but a modification of that which ordinarily springs from the *combativeness* of phrenology. But a glance will show the fallacy of this idea. The phrenological combativeness has for its essence, the necessity of self-defence. It is our safeguard against injury. Its principle regards our well-being; and thus the desire to be well, is excited simultaneously with its development. It follows, that the desire to be well must be excited simultaneously with any principle which shall be merely a modification of combativeness, but in the case of that something which I term *perverseness*, the desire to be well is not only not aroused, but a strongly antagonistical sentiment exists.

An appeal to one's own heart is, after all, the best reply to the sophistry just noticed. No one who trustingly consults and thoroughly questions his own soul, will be disposed to deny the entire radicalness of the propensity in question. It is not more incomprehensible than distinctive. There lives no man who at some period, has not been tormented, for example, by an earnest desire to tantalize a listener by circumlocution. The speaker is aware that he displeases; he has every intention to please; he is usually curt, precise, and clear; the most laconic and luminous language is struggling for utterance upon his tongue; it is only with difficulty that he restrains himself from giving it flow; he dreads and deprecates the anger of him whom he addresses; yet, the thought strikes him, that by certain involutions and parentheses, this anger may be engendered. That single thought is enough. The impulse increases to a wish, the wish to a desire, the desire to an uncontrollable longing, and the longing (to the deep regret and morti-fication of the speaker, and in defiance of all consequences), is indulged.

We have a task before us which must be speedily performed. We know that it will be ruinous to make delay. The most important crisis of our life calls, trumpet-tongued, for immediate energy and action. We glow, we are consumed with eagerness to commence the work, with the anticipation of whose glorious result our whole souls are on fire. It must, it shall be under-taken today, and yet we put it off until tomorrow: and why? There is no answer, except that we feel *perverse*, using the word with no comprehen-sion of the principle. Tomorrow arrives, and with it a more impatient anxiety to do our duty, but with this very increase of anxiety arrives, also, a nameless, a positively fearful, because unfathomable, craving for delay. This craving gathers strength as the moments fly. The last hour for action is at hand. We tremble with the violence of the conflict within us—of the definite with the indefinite—of the substance with the shadow. But, if the contest have proceeded thus far, it is the shadow which prevails—we struggle in vain. The clock strikes, and is the knell of our welfare. At the same time, it is the chanticleer-note to the ghost that has so long over-awed us. It flies—it disappears—we are free. The old energy returns. We will labor *now*. Alas, it is *too late!*

We stand upon the brink of a precipice. We peer into the abyss—we grow sick and dizzy. Our first impulse is to shrink from the danger. Unac-countably we remain. By slow degrees our sickness, and dizziness, and horror, become merged in a cloud of unnameable feeling. By gradations, still more imperceptible, this cloud assumes shape, as did the vapor from the bottle out of which arose the genius in the Arabian Nights. But out of

this *our* cloud upon the precipice's edge, there grows into palpability, a shape, far more terrible than any genius, or any demon of a tale, and yet it is but a thought, although a fearful one, and one which chills the very marrow of our bones with the fierceness of the delight of its horror. It is merely the idea of what would be our sensations during the sweeping precipitancy of a fall from such a height. And this fall—this rushing annihilation—for the very reason that it involves that one most ghastly and loathsome of all the most ghastly and loathsome images of death and suffering which have ever presented themselves to our imagination—for this very cause do we now the most vividly desire it. And because our reason violently deters us from the brink, *therefore,* do we the more impetuously approach it. There is no passion in nature so demoniacally impatient, as that of him, who shuddering upon the edge of a precipice, thus meditates a plunge. To indulge for a moment, in any attempt at *thought,* is to be inevitably lost; for reflection but urges us to forbear, and *therefore* it is, I say, that we *cannot.* If there be no friendly arm to check us, or if we fail in a sudden effort to prostrate ourselves backward from the abyss, we plunge, and are destroyed.

Examine these similar actions as we will, we shall find them resulting solely from the spirit of the *Perverse.* We perpetrate them merely because we feel that we should *not.* Beyond or behind this, there is no intelligible principle. And we might, indeed, deem this perverseness a direct instigation of the Arch-Fiend, were it not occasionally known to operate in furtherance of good.

I have said thus much, that in some measure I may answer your question, that I may explain to you why I am here, that I may assign to you something that shall have at least the faint aspect of a cause for my wearing these fetters, and for my tenanting this cell of the condemned. Had I not been thus prolix, you might either have misunderstood me altogether; or with the rabble, you might have fancied me mad. As it is, you will easily perceive that I am one of the many uncounted victims of the Imp of the Perverse.

It is impossible that any deed could have been wrought with a more thorough deliberation. For weeks, for months, I pondered upon the means of the murder. I rejected a thousand schemes because their accomplishment involved a *chance* of detection. At length, in reading some French Memoirs, I found an account of a nearly fatal illness that occurred to Madame Pilau, through the agency of a candle accidentally poisoned. The idea struck my fancy at once. I knew my victim's habit of reading in

bed. I knew, too, that his apartment was narrow and ill ventilated. But I need not vex you with impertinent details. I need not describe the easy artifices by which I substituted, in his bed-room candlestand, a wax-light of my own making, for the one which I there found. The next morning he was discovered dead in his bed, and the Coroner's verdict was, "Death by the visitation of God."

Having inherited his estate, all went well with me for years. The idea of detection never once entered my brain. Of the remains of the fatal taper, I had myself carefully disposed. I had left no shadow of a clue by which it would be possible to convict, or even to suspect me of the crime. It is inconceivable how rich a sentiment of satisfaction arose in my bosom as I reflected upon my absolute security. For a very long period of time, I was accustomed to revel in this sentiment. It afforded me more real delight than all the mere worldly advantages accruing from my sin. But there arrived at length an epoch, from which the pleasurable feeling grew, by scarcely perceptible gradations, into a haunting and harassing thought. It harassed because it haunted. I could scarcely get rid of it for an instant. It is quite a common thing to be thus annoyed with the ringing in our ears, or rather in our memories, of the burden of some ordinary song, or some unimpressive snatches from an opera. Nor will we be the less tormented if the song in itself be good, or the opera air meritorious. In this manner, at last, I would perpetually catch myself pondering upon my security, and repeating, in a low undertone, the phrase, "I am safe."

One day, whilst sauntering along the streets, I arrested myself in the act of murmuring, half aloud, these customary syllables. In a fit of petulance, I remodeled them thus: "I am safe—I am safe—yes—if I be not fool enough to make open confession!"

No sooner had I spoken these words, than I felt an icy chill creep to my heart. I had had some experience in these fits of perversity, whose nature I have been at some trouble to explain, and I remembered well, that in no instance, I had successfully resisted their attacks. And now my own casual self-suggestion, that I might possibly be fool enough to confess the murder of which I had been guilty, confronted me, as if the very ghost of him whom I had murdered—and beckoned me on to death.

At first, I made an effort to shake off this nightmare of the soul. I walked vigorously—faster—still faster—at length I ran. I felt a maddening desire to shriek aloud. Every succeeding wave of thought overwhelmed me with new terror, for, alas! I well, too well understood that, to *think*, in my situation, was to be lost. I still quickened my pace. I bounded like a

madman through the crowded thoroughfares. At length, the populace took the alarm, and pursued me. I felt *then* the consummation of my fate. Could I have torn out my tongue, I would have done it, but a rough voice resounded in my ears—a rougher grasp seized me by the shoulder. I turned—I gasped for breath. For a moment, I experienced all the pangs of suffocation; I became blind, and deaf, and giddy; and then, some invisible fiend, I thought, struck me with his broad palm upon the back. The long imprisoned secret burst forth from my soul.

They say that I spoke with a distinct enunciation, but with marked emphasis, and passionate hurry, as if in dread of interruption before concluding the brief, but pregnant sentences that consigned me to the hangman, and to hell.

Having related all that was necessary for the fullest judicial conviction, I fell prostrate in a swoon.

But why shall I say more? Today I wear these chains, and am *here!* Tomorrow I shall be fetterless!—*but where?*

DIDDLING CONSIDERED AS ONE
OF THE EXACT SCIENCES

Hey, diddle diddle,
The cat and the fiddle.

SINCE THE WORLD BEGAN THERE HAVE BEEN TWO JEREMYS. THE ONE wrote a Jeremiad about usury, and was called Jeremy Bentham. He has been much admired by Mr. John Neal, and was a great man in a small way. The other gave name to the most important of the Exact Sciences, and was a great man in a *great* way—I may say, indeed, in the very greatest of ways.

Diddling—or the abstract idea conveyed by the verb to diddle—is sufficiently well understood. Yet the fact, the deed, the thing *diddling*, is somewhat difficult to define. We may get, however, at a tolerably distinct conception of the matter in hand, by defining—not the thing, diddling, in itself—but man, as an animal that diddles. Had Plato but hit upon this, he would have been spared the affront of the picked chicken.

Very pertinently it was demanded of Plato, why a picked chicken, which was clearly "a biped without feathers," was not, according to his own definition, a man? But I am not to be bothered by any similar query. Man is an animal that diddles, and there is *no* animal that diddles *but* man. It will take an entire hen-coop of picked chickens to get over that.

What constitutes the essence, the nare, the principle of diddling is, in fact, peculiar to the class of creatures that wear coats and pantaloons. A crow thieves; a fox cheats; a weasel outwits; a man diddles. To diddle is his destiny. "Man was made to mourn," says the poet. But not so: he was made to diddle. This is his aim—his object—his *end*. And for this reason when a man's diddled we say he's *"done."*

Diddling, rightly considered, is a compound, of which the ingredients are minuteness, interest, perseverance, ingenuity, audacity, *nonchalance,* originality, impertinence, and *grin.*

Minuteness: Your diddler is minute. His operations are upon a small scale. His business is retail, for cash, or approved paper at sight. Should he ever be tempted into magnificent speculation, he then, at once, loses his distinctive features, and becomes what we term "financier." This latter word conveys the diddling idea in every respect except that of magnitude. A diddler may thus be regarded as a banker *in petto*—a "financial operation," as a diddle at Brobdignag. The one is to the other, as Homer to "Flaccus"—as a Mastodon to a mouse—as the tail of a comet to that of a pig.

Interest: Your diddler is guided by self-interest. He scorns to diddle for the mere *sake* of the diddle. He has an object in view—his pocket—and yours. He regards always the main chance. He looks to Number One. You are Number Two, and must look to yourself.

Perseverance: Your diddler perseveres. He is not readily discouraged. Should even the banks break, he cares nothing about it. He steadily pursues his end, and

> *Ut canis a corio nunquam absterrebitur uncto,*

so he never lets go of his game.

Ingenuity: Your diddler is ingenious. He has constructiveness large. He understands plot. He invents and circumvents. Were he not Alexander he would be Diogenes. Were he not a diddler, he would be a maker of patent rat-traps or an angler for trout.

Audacity: Your diddler is audacious. He is a bold man. He carries the war into Africa. He conquers all by assault. He would not fear the daggers of Frey Herren. With a little more prudence Dick Turpin would have made a good diddler; with a trifle less blarney, Daniel O'Connell; with a pound or two more brains, Charles the Twelfth.

Nonchalance: Your diddler is *nonchalant.* He is not at all nervous. He never *had* any nerves. He is never seduced into a flurry. He is never put out—unless put out of doors. He is cool—cool as a cucumber. He is calm—"calm as a smile from Lady Bury." He is easy—easy as an old glove, or the damsels of ancient Baiæ.

Originality: Your diddler is original—conscientiously so. His thoughts are his own. He would scorn to employ those of another. A stale trick is his aversion. He would return a purse, I am sure, upon discovering that he had obtained it by an unoriginal diddle.

Impertinence: Your diddler is impertinent. He swaggers. He sets his arms akimbo. He thrusts his hands in his trousers' pockets. He sneers in your face. He treads on your corns. He eats your dinner, he drinks your wine, he borrows your money, he pulls your nose, he kicks your poodle, and he kisses your wife.

Grin: Your *true* diddler winds up all with a grin. But this nobody sees but himself. He grins when his daily work is done—when his allotted labors are accomplished—at night in his own closet, and altogether for his own private entertainment. He goes home. He locks his door. He divests himself of his clothes. He puts out his candle. He gets into bed. He places his head upon the pillow. All this done, and your diddler *grins*. This is no hypothesis. It is a matter of course. I reason *à priori*, and a diddle would be *no* diddle without a grin.

The origin of the diddle is referrable to the infancy of the Human Race. Perhaps the first diddler was Adam. At all events, we can trace the science back to a very remote period of antiquity. The moderns, however, have brought it to a perfection never dreamed of by our thick-headed progenitors. Without pausing to speak of the "old saws," therefore, I shall content myself with a compendious account of some of the more "modern instances."

A very good diddle is this. A housekeeper in want of a sofa, for instance, is seen to go in and out of several cabinet warehouses. At length she arrives at one offering an excellent variety. She is accosted, and invited to enter, by a polite and voluble individual at the door. She finds a sofa well adapted to her views, and upon inquiring the price, is surprised and delighted to hear a sum named at least twenty per cent lower than her expectations. She hastens to make the purchase, gets a bill and receipt, leaves her address, with a request that the article be sent home as speedily as possible, and retires amid a profusion of bows from the shop-keeper. The night arrives and no sofa. The next day passes, and still none. A servant is sent to make inquiry about the delay. The whole transaction is denied. No sofa has been sold—no money received—except by the diddler who played shop-keeper for the nonce.

Our cabinet warehouses are left entirely unattended, and thus afford every facility for a trick of this kind. Visiters enter, look at furniture, and depart unheeded and unseen. Should anyone wish to purchase, or to inquire the price of an article, a bell is at hand, and this is considered amply sufficient.

Again, quite a respectable diddle is this. A well-dressed individual enters a shop; makes a purchase to the value of a dollar; finds, much to his

vexation, that he has left his pocket-book in another coat pocket: and so says to the shop-keeper—

"My dear sir, never mind! Just oblige me, will you, by sending the bundle home? But stay! I really believe that I have nothing less than a five dollar bill even *there*. However, you can send four dollars in change *with* the bundle, you know."

"Very good, sir," replies the shop-keeper, who entertains, at once, a lofty opinion of the high-mindedness of his customer. "I know fellows," he says to himself, "who would just have put the goods under their arm, and walked off with a promise to call and pay the dollar as they came by in the afternoon."

A boy is sent with the parcel and change. On the route, quite accidentally, he is met by the purchaser, who exclaims:

"Ah! This is my bundle, I see—I thought you had been home with it, long ago. Well, go on! My wife, Mrs. Trotter, will give you the five dollars—I left instructions with her to that effect. The change you might as well give to *me*—I shall want some silver for the Post Office. Very good! One, two—is this a good quarter?—three, four—quite right! Say to Mrs. Trotter that you met me, and be sure now and *do* not loiter on the way."

The boy doesn't loiter at all—but he is a very long time in getting back from his errand—for no lady of the precise name of Mrs. Trotter is to be discovered. He consoles himself, however, that he has not been such a fool as to leave the goods without the money, and re-entering his shop with a self satisfied air, feels sensibly hurt and indignant when his master asks him what has become of the change.

A very simple diddle, indeed, is this. The captain of a ship which is about to sail, is presented by an official looking person, with an unusually moderate bill of city charges. Glad to get off so easily, and confused by a hundred duties pressing upon him all at once, he discharges the claim forthwith. In about fifteen minutes, another and less reasonable bill is handed him by one who soon makes it evident that the first collector was a diddler, and the original collection a diddle.

And here, too, is a somewhat similar thing. A steamboat is casting loose from the wharf. A traveler, portmanteau in hand, is discovered running towards the wharf at full speed. Suddenly, he makes a dead halt, stoops, and picks up something from the ground in a very agitated manner. It is a pocket-book, and—"Has any gentleman lost a pocket-book?" he cries. No one can say that he has exactly lost a pocket-book; but a great excitement ensues, when the treasure trove is found to be of value. The boat however, must not be detained.

"Time and tide wait for no man," says the captain.

"For God's sake, stay only a few minutes," says the finder of the book—"the true claimant will presently appear."

"Can't wait!" replies the man in authority; "cast off there, d'ye hear?"

"What *am* I to do?" asks the finder, in great tribulation. "I am about to leave the country for some years, and I cannot conscientiously retain this large amount in my possession. I beg your pardon, sir," [here he addresses a gentleman on shore,] "but you have the air of an honest man. *Will* you confer upon me the favor of taking charge of this pocket-book—I *know* I can trust you—and of advertising it? The notes, you see, amount to a very considerable sum. The owner will, no doubt, insist upon rewarding you for your trouble—"

"*Me!*—no, *you!*—it was *you* who found the book."

"Well, if you *must* have it so—*I* will take a small reward—just to satisfy your scruples. Let me see—why these notes are all hundreds—bless my soul! a hundred is too much to take—fifty would be quite enough, I am sure—"

"Cast off there!" says the captain.

"But then I have no change for a hundred, and upon the whole, *you* had better—"

"Cast off there!" says the captain.

"Never mind!" cries the gentleman on shore, who has been examining his own pocket-book for the last minute or so—"never mind! *I* can fix it—here is a fifty on the Bank of North America—throw the book."

And the over-conscientious finder takes the fifty with marked reluctance, and throws the gentleman the book, as desired, while the steamboat fumes and fizzes on her way. In about half an hour after her departure, the "large amount" is seen to be a "counterfeit presentment," and the whole thing a capital diddle.

A bold diddle is this. A camp-meeting, or something similar, is to be held at a certain spot which is accessible only by means of a free bridge. A diddler stations himself upon this bridge, respectfully informs all passers by of the new county law, which establishes a toll of one cent for foot passengers, two for horses and donkeys, and so forth, and so forth. Some grumble but all submit, and the diddler goes home a wealthier man by some fifty or sixty dollars well earned. This taking a toll from a great crowd of people is an excessively troublesome thing.

A neat diddle is this. A friend holds one of the diddler's promises to pay, filled up and signed in due form, upon the ordinary blanks printed in red ink. The diddler purchases one or two dozen of these blanks, and every day dips one of them in his soup, makes his dog jump for it, and

finally gives it to him as a *bonne bouche*. The note arriving at maturity, the diddler, with the diddler's dog, calls upon the friend, and the promise to pay is made the topic of discussion. The friend produces it from his *escritoire*, and is in the act of reaching it to the diddler, when up jumps the diddler's dog and devours it forthwith. The diddler is not only surprised but vexed and incensed at the absurd behavior of his dog, and expresses his entire readiness to cancel the obligation at any moment when the evidence of the obligation shall be forthcoming.

A very minute diddle is this. A lady is insulted in the street by a diddler's accomplice. The diddler himself flies to her assistance, and, giving his friend a comfortable thrashing, insists upon attending the lady to her own door. He bows, with his hand upon his heart, and most respectfully bids her adieu. She entreats him, as her deliverer, to walk in and be introduced to her big brother and her papa. With a sigh, he declines to do so. "Is there *no* way, then, sir," she murmurs, "in which I may be permitted to testify my gratitude?"

"Why, yes, madam, there is. Will you be kind enough to lend me a couple of shillings?"

In the first excitement of the moment the lady decides upon fainting outright. Upon second thought, however, she opens her purse-strings and delivers the specie. Now this, I say, is a diddle minute—for one entire moiety of the sum borrowed has to be paid to the gentleman who had the trouble of performing the insult, and who had then to stand still and be thrashed for performing it.

Rather a small, but still a scientific diddle is this. The diddler approaches the bar of a tavern, and demands a couple of twists of tobacco. These are handed to him, when, having slightly examined them, he says:

"I don't much like this tobacco. Here, take it back, and give me a glass of brandy and water in its place."

The brandy and water is furnished and imbibed, and the diddler makes his way to the door. But the voice of the tavern-keeper arrests him.

"I believe, sir, you have forgotten to pay for your brandy and water."

"Pay for my brandy and water!—didn't I give you the tobacco for the brandy and water? What more would you have?"

"But sir, if you please, I don't remember that you paid me for the tobacco."

"What do you mean by that, you scoundrel?—Didn't I give you back your tobacco? Isn't *that* your tobacco lying *there*? Do you expect me to pay for what I did not take?"

"But, sir," says the publican, now rather at a loss what to say, "but, sir—"

"But me no buts, sir," interrupts the diddler, apparently in very high dudgeon, and slamming the door after him, as he makes his escape. "But me no buts, sir, and none of your tricks upon travelers."

Here again is a very clever diddle, of which the simplicity is not its least recommendation. A purse, or pocket-book, being really lost, the loser inserts in *one* of the daily papers of a large city a fully descriptive advertisement.

Whereupon our diddler copies the *facts* of this advertisement, with a change of heading, of general phraseology, and *address*. The original, for instance, is long, and verbose, is headed "A Pocket-Book Lost!" and requires the treasure, when found, to be left at No. 1 Tom street. The copy is brief, and being headed with "Lost" only, indicates No. 2 Dick, or No. 3 Harry street, as the locality at which the owner may be seen. Moreover, it is inserted in at least five or six of the daily papers of the day, while in point of time, it makes its appearance only a few hours after the original. Should it be read by the loser of the purse, he would hardly suspect it to have any reference to his own misfortune. But, of course, the chances are five or six to one, that the finder will repair to the address given by the diddler, rather than to that pointed out by the rightful proprietor. The former pays the reward, pockets the treasure and decamps.

Quite an analogous diddle is this. A lady of ton has dropped, somewhere in the street, a diamond ring of very unusual value. For its recovery, she offers some forty or fifty dollars reward—giving, in her advertisement, a very minute description of the gem, and of its settings, and declaring that, on its restoration at No. so and so, in such and such Avenue, the reward will be paid *instanter*, without a single question being asked. During the lady's absence from home, a day or two afterward, a ring is heard at the door of No. so and so, in such and such Avenue; a servant appears; the lady of the house is asked for and is declared to be out, at which astounding information, the visiter expresses the most poignant regret. His business is of importance and concerns the lady herself. In fact, he had the good fortune to find her diamond ring. But perhaps it would be as well that he should call again. "By no means!" says the servant; and "By no means!" says the lady's sister and the lady's sister-in-law, who are summoned forthwith. The ring is clamorously identified, the reward is paid, and the finder nearly thrust out of doors. The lady returns, and expresses some little dissatisfaction with her sister and sister-in-law, because they happen to have paid forty or fifty dollars for a *fac-simile* of her diamond ring—a *fac-simile* made out of real pinchbeck and unquestionable paste.

But as there is really no end to diddling, so there would be none to this essay, were I even to hint at half the variations, or inflections, of which this science is susceptible. I must bring this paper, perforce, to a conclusion, and this I cannot do better than by a summary notice of a very decent, but rather elaborate diddle, of which our own city was made the theater, not very long ago, and which was subsequently repeated with success, in other still more verdant localities of the Union. A middle-aged gentleman arrives in town from parts unknown. He is remarkably precise, cautious, staid, and deliberate in his demeanor. His dress is scrupulously neat, but plain, unostentatious. He wears a white cravat, an ample waistcoat, made with an eye to comfort alone; thick-soled cozy-looking shoes, and pantaloons without straps. He has the whole air, in fact, of your well-to-do, sober-sided, exact, and respectable "man of business," *par excellence*—one of the stern and outwardly hard, internally soft, sort of people that we see in the crack high comedies—fellows whose words are so many bonds, and who are noted for giving away guineas, in charity, with the one hand, while, in the way of mere bargain, they exact the uttermost fraction of a farthing, with the other.

He makes much ado before he can get suited with a boarding house. He dislikes children. He has been accustomed to quiet. His habits are methodical—and then he would prefer getting into a private and respectable small family, piously inclined. Terms, however, are no object—only he *must* insist upon settling his bill on the first of every month, (it is now the second) and begs his landlady, when he finally obtains one to his mind, *not* on any account, to forget his instructions upon this point—but to send in a bill, *and* receipt, precisely at ten o'clock, on the *first* day of every month, and under *no* circumstances to put it off to the second.

These arrangements made, our man of business rents an office in a reputable rather than a fashionable quarter of the town. There is nothing he more despises than pretence. "Where there is much show," he says, "there is seldom anything very solid behind"—an observation which so profoundly impresses his landlady's fancy, that she makes a pencil memorandum of it forthwith, in her great family Bible, on the broad margin of the Proverbs of Solomon.

The next step is to advertise, after some such fashion as this, in the principal business sixpennies of the city—the pennies are eschewed as not "respectable"—and as demanding payment for all advertisements in advance. Our man of business holds it as a point of his faith that work should never be paid for until done.

Wanted. The advertisers, being about to commence extensive business operations in this city, will require the services of three or four intelligent and competent clerks, to whom a liberal salary will be paid. The very best recommendations, not so much for capacity, as for integrity, will be expected. Indeed, as the duties to be performed, involve high responsibilities, and large amounts of money must necessarily pass through the hands of those engaged, it is deemed advisable to demand a deposit of fifty dollars from each clerk employed. No person need apply, therefore, who is not prepared to leave this sum in the possession of the advertisers, and who cannot furnish the most satisfactory testimonials of morality. Young gentlemen piously inclined will be preferred. Application should be made between the hours of ten and eleven AM, and four and five PM, of Messrs.

Boggs, Hogs, Logs, Frogs, & Co.

No. 110 dog street

By the thirty-first day of the month, this advertisement has brought to the office of Messrs. Boggs, Hogs, Logs, Frogs, and Company, some fifteen or twenty young gentlemen piously inclined. But our man of business is in no hurry to conclude a contract with any—no man of business is *ever* precipitate—and it is not until the most rigid catechism in respect to the piety of each young gentleman's inclination, that his services are engaged and his fifty dollars receipted for, *just* by way of proper precaution, on the part of the respectable firm of Boggs, Hogs, Logs, Frogs, and Company. On the morning of the first day of the next month, the landlady does *not* present her bill according to promise—a piece of neglect for which the comfortable head of the house ending in *ogs*, would no doubt have chided her severely, could he have been prevailed upon to remain in town a day or two for that purpose.

As it is, the constables have had a sad time of it, running hither and thither, and all they can do is to declare the man of business most emphatically, a "hen knee high"—by which some persons imagine them to imply that, in fact, he is n. e. i.—by which again the very classical phrase *non est inventus*, is supposed to be understood. In the meantime the young gentlemen, one and all, are somewhat less piously inclined than before, while the landlady purchases a shilling's worth of the Indian rubber, and very carefully obliterates the pencil memorandum that some fool has made in her great family Bible, on the broad margin of the Proverbs of Solomon.

THE PHILOSOPHY OF COMPOSITION

CHARLES DICKENS, IN A NOTE NOW LYING BEFORE ME, ALLUDING TO AN examination I once made of the mechanism of *Barnaby Rudge*, says—"By the way, are you aware that Godwin wrote his *Caleb Williams* backwards? He first involved his hero in a web of difficulties, forming the second volume, and then, for the first, cast about him for some mode of accounting for what had been done."

I cannot think this the *precise* mode of procedure on the part of Godwin—and indeed what he himself acknowledges, is not altogether in accordance with Mr. Dickens' idea—but the author of *Caleb Williams* was too good an artist not to perceive the advantage derivable from at least a somewhat similar process. Nothing is more clear than that every plot, worth the name, must be elaborated to its *dénouement* before anything be attempted with the pen. It is only with the *dénouement* constantly in view that we can give a plot its indispensable air of consequence, or causation, by making the incidents, and especially the tone at all points, tend to the development of the intention.

There is a radical error, I think, in the usual mode of constructing a story. Either history affords a thesis—or one is suggested by an incident of the day—or, at best, the author sets himself to work in the combination of striking events to form merely the basis of his narrative—designing, generally, to fill in with description, dialogue, or autorial comment, whatever crevices of fact, or action, may, from page to page, render themselves apparent.

I prefer commencing with the consideration of an *effect*. Keeping originality *always* in view—for he is false to himself who ventures to dispense with so obvious and so easily attainable a source of interest—I say to myself, in the first place, "Of the innumerable effects, or impressions, of which the heart, the intellect, or (more generally) the soul is susceptible, what one shall I, on the present occasion, select?" Having chosen a novel, first, and secondly a vivid effect, I consider whether it can be best wrought by incident or tone—whether by ordinary incidents and peculiar tone, or the converse, or by peculiarity both of incident and tone—afterward looking about me (or rather within) for such combinations of event, or tone, as shall best aid me in the construction of the effect.

I have often thought how interesting a magazine paper might be written by any author who would—that is to say, who could—detail, step by step, the processes by which any one of his compositions attained its ultimate point of completion. Why such a paper has never been given to the world, I am much at a loss to say—but, perhaps, the autorial vanity has had more to do with the omission than any one other cause. Most writers—poets in especial—prefer having it understood that they compose by a species of fine frenzy—an ecstatic intuition—and would positively shudder at letting the public take a peep behind the scenes, at the elaborate and vacillating crudities of thought—at the true purposes seized only at the last moment—at the innumerable glimpses of idea that arrived not at the maturity of full view—at the fully matured fancies discarded in despair as unmanageable—at the cautious selections and rejections—at the painful erasures and interpolations—in a word, at the wheels and pinions—the tackle for scene-shifting—the step-ladders and demon-traps—the cock's feathers, the red paint and the black patches, which, in ninety-nine cases out of the hundred, constitute the properties of the literary *histrio*.

I am aware, on the other hand, that the case is by no means common, in which an author is at all in condition to retrace the steps by which his conclusions have been attained. In general, suggestions, having arisen pell-mell, are pursued and forgotten in a similar manner.

For my own part, I have neither sympathy with the repugnance alluded to, nor, at any time, the least difficulty in recalling to mind the progressive steps of any of my compositions; and, since the interest of an analysis, or reconstruction, such as I have considered a *desideratum*, is quite independent of any real or fancied interest in the thing analyzed, it will not be regarded as a breach of decorum on my part to show the *modus operandi*

by which some one of my own works was put together. I select "The Raven," as the most generally known. It is my design to render it manifest that no one point in its composition is referable either to accident or intuition—that the work proceeded, step by step, to its completion with the precision and rigid consequence of a mathematical problem.

Let us dismiss, as irrelevant to the poem, *per se*, the circumstance—or say the necessity—which, in the first place, gave rise to the intention of composing *a* poem that should suit at once the popular and the critical taste.

We commence, then, with this intention.

The initial consideration was that of extent. If any literary work is too long to be read at one sitting, we must be content to dispense with the immensely important effect derivable from unity of impression—for, if two sittings be required, the affairs of the world interfere, and everything like totality is at once destroyed. But since, *ceteris paribus,* no poet can afford to dispense with *anything* that may advance his design, it but remains to be seen whether there is, in extent, any advantage to counterbalance the loss of unity which attends it. Here I say no, at once. What we term a long poem is, in fact, merely a succession of brief ones—that is to say, of brief poetical effects. It is needless to demonstrate that a poem is such, only inasmuch as it intensely excites, by elevating, the soul; and all intense excitements are, through a psychal necessity, brief. For this reason, at least one-half of the *Paradise Lost* is essentially prose—a succession of poetical excitements interspersed, *inevitably,* with corresponding depressions—the whole being deprived, through the extremeness of its length, of the vastly important artistic element, totality, or unity, of effect.

It appears evident, then, that there is a distinct limit, as regards length, to all works of literary art—the limit of a single sitting—and that, although in certain classes of prose composition, such as *Robinson Crusoe,* (demanding no unity,) this limit may be advantageously overpassed, it can never properly be overpassed in a poem. Within this limit, the extent of a poem may be made to bear mathematical relation to its merit—in other words, to the excitement or elevation—again in other words, to the degree of the true poetical effect which it is capable of inducing; for it is clear that the brevity must be in direct ratio of the intensity of the intended effect: this, with one proviso—that a certain degree of duration is absolutely requisite for the production of any effect at all.

Holding in view these considerations, as well as that degree of excitement which I deemed not above the popular, while not below the critical, taste, I

reached at once what I conceived the proper *length* for my intended poem—a length of about one hundred lines. It is, in fact, a hundred and eight.

My next thought concerned the choice of an impression, or effect, to be conveyed: and here I may as well observe that, throughout the construction, I kept steadily in view the design of rendering the work *universally* appreciable. I should be carried too far out of my immediate topic were I to demonstrate a point upon which I have repeatedly insisted, and which, with the poetical, stands not in the slightest need of demonstration—the point, I mean, that Beauty is the sole legitimate province of the poem. A few words, however, in elucidation of my real meaning, which some of my friends have evinced a disposition to misrepresent. That pleasure which is at once the most intense, the most elevating, and the most pure, is, I believe, found in the contemplation of the beautiful. When, indeed, men speak of Beauty, they mean, precisely, not a quality, as is supposed, but an effect—they refer, in short, just to that intense and pure elevation of *soul—not* of intellect, or of heart—upon which I have commented, and which is experienced in consequence of contemplating "the beautiful." Now I designate Beauty as the province of the poem, merely because it is an obvious rule of Art that effects should be made to spring from direct causes—that objects should be attained through means best adapted for their attainment—no one as yet having been weak enough to deny that the peculiar elevation alluded to is *most readily* attained in the poem. Now the object, Truth, or the satisfaction of the intellect, and the object Passion, or the excitement of the heart, are, although attainable, to a certain extent, in poetry, far more readily attainable in prose. Truth, in fact, demands a precision, and Passion, a *homeliness* (the truly passionate will comprehend me) which are absolutely antagonistic to that Beauty which, I maintain, is the excitement, or pleasurable elevation, of the soul. It by no means follows from anything here said, that passion, or even truth, may not be introduced, and even profitably introduced, into a poem—for they may serve in elucidation, or aid the general effect, as do discords in music, by contrast—but the true artist will always contrive, first, to tone them into proper subservience to the predominant aim, and, secondly, to enveil them, as far as possible, in that Beauty which is the atmosphere and the essence of the poem.

Regarding, then, Beauty as my province, my next question referred to the *tone* of its highest manifestation—and all experience has shown that this tone is one of *sadness*. Beauty of whatever kind, in its supreme

development, invariably excites the sensitive soul to tears. Melancholy is thus the most legitimate of all the poetical tones.

The length, the province, and the tone, being thus determined, I betook myself to ordinary induction, with the view of obtaining some artistic piquancy which might serve me as a key-note in the construction of the poem—some pivot upon which the whole structure might turn. In carefully thinking over all the usual artistic effects—or more properly *points*, in the theatrical sense—I did not fail to perceive immediately that no one had been so universally employed as that of the *refrain*. The universality of its employment sufficed to assure me of its intrinsic value, and spared me the necessity of submitting it to analysis. I considered it, however, with regard to its susceptibility of improvement, and soon saw it to be in a primitive condition. As commonly used, the *refrain*, or burden, not only is limited to lyric verse, but depends for its impression upon the force of monotone—both in sound and thought. The pleasure is deduced solely from the sense of identity—of repetition. I resolved to diversify, and so vastly heighten, the effect, by adhering, in general, to the monotone of sound, while I continually varied that of thought: that is to say, I determined to produce continuously novel effects, by the variation of *the application* of the *refrain*—the *refrain* itself remaining, for the most part, unvaried.

These points being settled, I next bethought me of the *nature* of my *refrain*. Since its application was to be repeatedly varied, it was clear that the *refrain* itself must be brief, for there would have been an insurmountable difficulty in frequent variations of application in any sentence of length. In proportion to the brevity of the sentence, would, of course, be the facility of the variation. This led me at once to a single word as the best *refrain*.

The question now arose as to the *character* of the word. Having made up my mind to a *refrain*, the division of the poem into stanzas was, of course, a corollary: the *refrain* forming the close to each stanza. That such a close, to have force, must be sonorous and susceptible of protracted emphasis, admitted no doubt: and these considerations inevitably led me to the long *o* as the most sonorous vowel, in connection with *r* as the most producible consonant.

The sound of the *refrain* being thus determined, it became necessary to select a word embodying this sound, and at the same time in the fullest possible keeping with that melancholy which I had predetermined as the tone of the poem. In such a search it would have been absolutely

impossible to overlook the word "Nevermore." In fact, it was the very first which presented itself.

The next *desideratum* was a pretext for the continuous use of the one word "nevermore." In observing the difficulty which I at once found in inventing a sufficiently plausible reason for its continuous repetition, I did not fail to perceive that this difficulty arose solely from the pre-assumption that the word was to be so continuously or monotonously spoken by a *human* being—I did not fail to perceive, in short, that the difficulty lay in the reconciliation of this monotony with the exercise of reason on the part of the creature repeating the word. Here, then, immediately arose the idea of a *non*-reasoning creature capable of speech; and, very naturally, a parrot, in the first instance, suggested itself, but was superseded forthwith by a Raven, as equally capable of speech, and infinitely more in keeping with the intended *tone*.

I had now gone so far as the conception of a Raven—the bird of ill omen—monotonously repeating the one word, "Nevermore," at the conclusion of each stanza, in a poem of melancholy tone, and in length about one hundred lines. Now, never losing sight of the object *supremeness*, or perfection, at all points, I asked myself—"Of all melancholy topics, what, according to the *universal* understanding of mankind, is the *most* melancholy?" Death—was the obvious reply. "And when," I said, "is this most melancholy of topics most poetical?" From what I have already explained at some length, the answer, here also, is obvious—"When it most closely allies itself to *Beauty:* the death, then, of a beautiful woman is, unquestionably, the most poetical topic in the world—equally is beyond doubt that the lips best suited for such topic are those of a bereaved lover."

I had now to combine the two ideas, of a lover lamenting his deceased mistress and a Raven continuously repeating the word "Nevermore"—I had to combine these, bearing in mind my design of varying, at every turn, the *application* of the word repeated; but the only intelligible mode of such combination is that of imagining the Raven employing the word in answer to the queries of the lover. And here it was that I saw at once the opportunity afforded for the effect on which I had been depending—that is to say, the effect of the *variation of application.* I saw that I could make the first query propounded by the lover—the first query to which the Raven should reply "Nevermore"—that I could make this first query a commonplace one—the second less so—the third still less, and so on—until at length the lover, startled from his original *nonchalance* by the

melancholy character of the word itself—by its frequent repetition—and by a consideration of the ominous reputation of the fowl that uttered it—is at length excited to superstition, and wildly propounds queries of a far different character—propounds them half in superstition and half in that species of despair which delights in self-torture—propounds them not altogether because he believes in the prophetic or demoniac character of the bird (which, reason assures him, is merely repeating a lesson learned by rote) but because he experiences a frenzied pleasure in so modeling his questions as to receive from the *expected* "Nevermore" the most delicious because the most intolerable of sorrow. Perceiving the opportunity thus afforded me—or, more strictly, thus forced upon me in the progress of the construction—I first established in mind the climax, or concluding query—that to which "Nevermore" should be in the last place an answer—that in reply to which this word "Nevermore" should involve the utmost conceivable amount of sorrow and despair.

Here then the poem may be said to have its beginning—at the end, where all works of art should begin—for it was here, at this point of my preconsiderations, that I first put pen to paper in the composition of the stanza:

> "Prophet," said I, "thing of evil! prophet still if bird or devil!
> By that heaven that bends above us—by that God we both adore,
> Tell this soul sorrow laden, if within the distant Aidenn,
> It shall clasp a sainted maiden whom the angels name Lenore—
> Clasp a rare and radiant maiden whom the angels name Lenore."
> Quoth the raven "Nevermore."

I composed this stanza, at this point, first that, by establishing the climax, I might the better vary and graduate, as regards seriousness and importance, the preceding queries of the lover—and, secondly, that I might definitely settle the rhythm, the meter, and the length and general arrangement of the stanza—as well as graduate the stanzas which were to precede, so that none of them might surpass this in rhythmical effect. Had I been able, in the subsequent composition, to construct more vigorous stanzas, I should, without scruple, have purposely enfeebled them, so as not to interfere with the climacteric effect.

And here I may as well say a few words of the versification. My first object (as usual) was originality. The extent to which this has been neglected, in versification, is one of the most unaccountable things in the world. Admitting that there is little possibility of variety in mere *rhythm*, it

is still clear that the possible varieties of meter and stanza are absolutely infinite—and yet, *for centuries, no man, in verse, has ever done, or ever seemed to think of doing, an original thing.* The fact is, originality (unless in minds of very unusual force) is by no means a matter, as some suppose, of impulse or intuition. In general, to be found, it must be elaborately sought, and although a positive merit of the highest class, demands in its attainment less of invention than negation.

Of course, I pretend to no originality in either the rhythm or meter of the "Raven." The former is trochaic—the latter is octameter acatalectic, alternating with heptameter catalectic repeated in the *refrain* of the fifth verse, and terminating with tetrameter catalectic. Less pedantically—the feet employed throughout (trochees) consist of a long syllable followed by a short: the first line of the stanza consists of eight of these feet—the second of seven and a half (in effect two-thirds)—the third of eight—the fourth of seven and a half—the fifth the same—the sixth three and a half. Now, each of these lines, taken individually, has been employed before, and what originality the "Raven" has, is in their *combination into stanza;* nothing even remotely approaching this combination has ever been attempted. The effect of this originality of combination is aided by other unusual, and some altogether novel effects, arising from an extension of the application of the principles of rhyme and alliteration.

The next point to be considered was the mode of bringing together the lover and the Raven—and the first branch of this consideration was the *locale.* For this the most natural suggestion might seem to be a forest, or the fields—but it has always appeared to me that a close *circumscription of space* is absolutely necessary to the effect of insulated incident: it has the force of a frame to a picture. It has an indisputable moral power in keeping concentrated the attention, and, of course, must not be confounded with mere unity of place.

I determined, then, to place the lover in his chamber—in a chamber rendered sacred to him by memories of her who had frequented it. The room is represented as richly furnished—this in mere pursuance of the ideas I have already explained on the subject of Beauty, as the sole true poetical thesis.

The *locale* being thus determined, I had now to introduce the bird—and the thought of introducing him through the window, was inevitable. The idea of making the lover suppose, in the first instance, that the flapping of the wings of the bird against the shutter, is a "tapping" at the door, originated in a wish to increase, by prolonging, the reader's curiosity, and in a desire to admit the incidental effect arising from the lover's throwing

open the door, finding all dark, and thence adopting the half-fancy that it was the spirit of his mistress that knocked.

I made the night tempestuous, first, to account for the Raven's seeking admission, and secondly, for the effect of contrast with the (physical) serenity within the chamber.

I made the bird alight on the bust of Pallas, also for the effect of contrast between the marble and the plumage—it being understood that the bust was absolutely *suggested* by the bird—the bust of *Pallas* being chosen, first, as most in keeping with the scholarship of the lover, and, secondly, for the sonorousness of the word, Pallas, itself.

About the middle of the poem, also, I have availed myself of the force of contrast, with a view of deepening the ultimate impression. For example, an air of the fantastic—approaching as nearly to the ludicrous as was admissible—is given to the Raven's entrance. He comes in "with many a flirt and flutter."

> Not the *least obeisance made he*—not a moment stopped or stayed he,
> But with *mien of lord or lady,* perched above my chamber door.

In the two stanzas which follow, the design is more obviously carried out:

> Then this ebony bird beguiling my sad fancy into smiling
> By the *grave and stern decorum of the countenance it wore,*
> "Though thy *crest be shorn and shaven* thou," I said, "art sure no craven,
> Ghastly grim and ancient Raven wandering from the nightly shore—
> Tell me what thy lordly name is on the Night's Plutonian shore!"
> Quoth the Raven "Nevermore."

> Much I marveled *this ungainly fowl* to hear discourse so plainly,
> Though its answer little meaning—little relevancy bore;
> For we cannot help agreeing that no living human being
> Ever yet was blessed with seeing bird above his chamber door—
> Bird or beast upon the sculptured bust above his chamber door,
> With such name as "Nevermore."

The effect of the *dénouement* being thus provided for, I immediately drop the fantastic for a tone of the most profound seriousness: this tone commencing in the stanza directly following the one last quoted, with the line,

But the Raven, sitting lonely on that placid bust, spoke only, etc.

From this epoch the lover no longer jests—no longer sees anything even of the fantastic in the Raven's demeanor. He speaks of him as a "grim, ungainly, ghastly, gaunt, and ominous bird of yore," and feels the "fiery eyes" burning into his "bosom's core." This revolution of thought, or fancy, on the lover's part, is intended to induce a similar one on the part of the reader—to bring the mind into a proper frame for the *dénouement*—which is now brought about as rapidly and as *directly* as possible.

With the *dénouement* proper—with the Raven's reply, "Nevermore," to the lover's final demand if he shall meet his mistress in another world— the poem, in its obvious phase, that of a simple narrative, may be said to have its completion. So far, everything is within the limits of the accountable—of the real. A raven, having learned by rote the single word "Nevermore," and having escaped from the custody of its owner, is driven at midnight, through the violence of a storm, to seek admission at a window from which a light still gleams—the chamber-window of a student, occupied half in poring over a volume, half in dreaming of a beloved mistress deceased. The casement being thrown open at the fluttering of the bird's wings, the bird itself perches on the most convenient seat out of the immediate reach of the student, who, amused by the incident and the oddity of the visitor's demeanor, demands of it, in jest and without looking for a reply, its name. The raven addressed, answers with its customary word, "Nevermore"—a word which finds immediate echo in the melancholy heart of the student, who, giving utterance aloud to certain thoughts suggested by the occasion, is again startled by the fowl's repetition of "Nevermore." The student now guesses the state of the case, but is impelled, as I have before explained, by the human thirst for self-torture, and in part by superstition, to propound such queries to the bird as will bring him, the lover, the most of the luxury of sorrow, through the anticipated answer "Nevermore." With the indulgence, to the utmost extreme, of this self-torture, the narration, in what I have termed its first or obvious phase, has a natural termination, and so far there has been no overstepping of the limits of the real.

But in subjects so handled, however skillfully, or with however vivid an array of incident, there is always a certain hardness or nakedness, which repels the artistical eye. Two things are invariably required—first, some amount of complexity, or more properly, adaptation; and, secondly, some amount of suggestiveness—some undercurrent, however indefinite, of

meaning. It is this latter, in especial, which imparts to a work of art so much of that *richness* (to borrow from colloquy a forcible term) which we are too fond of confounding with *the ideal.* It is the *excess* of the suggested meaning—it is the rendering this the upper instead of the under current of the theme—which turns into prose (and that of the very flattest kind) the so-called poetry of the so-called transcendentalists.

Holding these opinions, I added the two concluding stanzas of the poem—their suggestiveness being thus made to pervade all the narrative which has preceded them. The undercurrent of meaning is rendered first apparent in the lines—

> "Take thy beak from out *my heart,* and take thy form from off
> my door!"
> Quoth the Raven "Nevermore!"

It will be observed that the words, "from out my heart," involve the first metaphorical expression in the poem. They, with the answer, "Nevermore," dispose the mind to seek a moral in all that has been previously narrated. The reader begins now to regard the Raven as emblematical—but it is not until the very last line of the very last stanza, that the intention of making him emblematical of *Mournful and Never-ending Remembrance* is permitted distinctly to be seen:

> And the Raven, never flitting, still is sitting, still is sitting,
> On the pallid bust of Pallas just above my chamber door;
> And his eyes have all the seeming of a demon's that is dreaming,
> And the lamplight o'er him streaming throws his shadow on
> the floor;
> And my soul *from out that shadow* that lies floating on the floor
> Shall be lifted—nevermore.

The Narrative of Arthur Gordon Pym of Nantucket

PREFACE

Upon my return to the United States a few months ago, after the extraordinary series of adventure in the South Seas and elsewhere, of which an account is given in the following pages, accident threw me into the society of several gentlemen in Richmond, Va., who felt deep interest in all matters relating to the regions I had visited, and who were constantly urging it upon me, as a duty, to give my narrative to the public. I had several reasons, however, for declining to do so, some of which were of a nature altogether private, and concern no person but myself; others not so much so. One consideration which deterred me was, that, having kept no journal during a greater portion of the time in which I was absent, I feared I should not be able to write, from mere memory, a statement so minute and connected as to have the *appearance* of that truth it would really possess, barring only the natural and unavoidable exaggeration to which all of us are prone when detailing events which have had powerful influence in exciting the imaginative faculties. Another reason was, that the incidents to be narrated were of a nature so positively marvelous, that, unsupported as my assertions must necessarily be (except by the evidence of a single individual, and he a half-breed Indian), I could only hope for belief among my family, and those of my friends who have had reason, through life, to put faith in my veracity—the probability being that the public at large would regard what I should put forth as merely an impudent and ingenious fiction. A distrust in my own abilities as a writer was, nevertheless, one of the principal causes which prevented me from complying with the suggestions of my advisers.

Among those gentlemen in Virginia who expressed the greatest interest in my statement, more particularly in regard to that portion of it which related to the Antarctic Ocean, was Mr. Poe, lately editor of the *Southern Literary Messenger*, a monthly magazine, published by Mr. Thomas W. White, in the city of Richmond. He strongly advised me, among others, to prepare at once a full account of what I had seen and undergone, and trust to the shrewdness and common sense of the public—insisting, with great plausibility, that however roughly, as regards mere authorship, my book should be got up, its very uncouthness, if there were any, would give it all the better chance of being received as truth.

Notwithstanding this representation, I did not make up my mind to do as he suggested. He afterward proposed (finding that I would not stir in the matter) that I should allow him to draw up, in his own words, a narrative of the earlier portion of my adventures, from facts afforded by myself, publishing it in the *Southern Messenger under the garb of fiction*. To this, perceiving no objection, I consented, stipulating only that my real name should be retained. Two numbers of the pretended fiction appeared, consequently, in the *Messenger* for January and February (1837), and, in order that it might certainly be regarded as fiction, the name of Mr. Poe was affixed to the articles in the table of contents of the magazine.

The manner in which this *ruse* was received has induced me at length to undertake a regular compilation and publication of the adventures in question; for I found that, in spite of the air of fable which had been so ingeniously thrown around that portion of my statement which appeared in the *Messenger* (without altering or distorting a single fact), the public were still not at all disposed to receive it as fable, and several letters were sent to Mr. P.'s address distinctly expressing a conviction to the contrary. I thence concluded that the facts of my narrative would prove of such a nature as to carry with them sufficient evidence of their own authenticity, and that I had consequently little to fear on the score of popular incredulity.

This *exposé* being made, it will be seen at once how much of what follows I claim to be my own writing; and it will also be understood that no fact is misrepresented in the first few pages which were written by Mr. Poe. Even to those readers who have not seen the *Messenger*, it will be unnecessary to point out where his portion ends and my own commences; the difference in point of style will be readily perceived.

<div align="right">

A. G. PYM

NEW YORK, JULY, 1838

</div>

Chapter i

My name is Arthur Gordon Pym. My father was a respectable trader in sea-stores at Nantucket, where I was born. My maternal grandfather was an attorney in good practice. He was fortunate in everything, and had speculated very successfully in stocks of the Edgarton New-Bank, as it was formerly called. By these and other means he had managed to lay by a tolerable sum of money. He was more attached to myself, I believe, than to any other person in the world, and I expected to inherit the most of his property at his death. He sent me, at six years of age, to the school of old Mr. Ricketts, a gentleman with only one arm, and of eccentric manners— he is well known to almost every person who has visited New Bedford. I stayed at his school until I was sixteen, when I left him for Mr. E. Ronald's academy on the hill. Here I became intimate with the son of Mr. Barnard, a sea-captain, who generally sailed in the employ of Lloyd and Vredenburgh— Mr. Barnard is also very well known in New Bedford, and has many relations, I am certain, in Edgarton. His son was named Augustus, and he was nearly two years older than myself. He had been on a whaling voyage with his father in the John Donaldson, and was always talking to me of his adventures in the South Pacific Ocean. I used frequently to go home with him, and remain all day, and sometimes all night. We occupied the same bed, and he would be sure to keep me awake until almost light, telling me stories of the natives of the Island of Tinian, and other places he had visited in his travels. At last I could not help being interested in what he said, and by degrees I felt the greatest desire to go to sea. I owned a sailboat called the *Ariel*,[1] and worth about seventy-five dollars. She had a half-deck or cuddy, and was rigged sloop-fashion—I forget her tonnage, but

she would hold ten persons without much crowding. In this boat we were in the habit of going on some of the maddest freaks in the world; and, when I now think of them, it appears to me a thousand wonders that I am alive today.

I will relate one of these adventures by way of introduction to a longer and more momentous narrative. One night there was a party at Mr. Barnard's, and both Augustus and myself were not a little intoxicated towards the close of it. As usual, in such cases, I took part of his bed in preference to going home. He went to sleep, as I thought, very quietly (it being near one when the party broke up), and without saying a word on his favorite topic. It might have been half an hour from the time of our getting in bed, and I was just about falling into a doze, when he suddenly started up, and swore with a terrible oath that he would not go to sleep for any Arthur Pym in Christendom, when there was so glorious a breeze from the southwest. I never was so astonished in my life, not knowing what he intended, and thinking that the wines and liquors he had drunk had set him entirely beside himself. He proceeded to talk very coolly, however, saying he knew that I supposed him intoxicated, but that he was never more sober in his life. He was only tired, he added, of lying in bed on such a fine night like a dog, and was determined to get up and dress, and go out on a frolic with the boat. I can hardly tell what possessed me, but the words were no sooner out of his mouth than I felt a thrill of the greatest excitement and pleasure, and thought his mad idea one of the most delightful and most reasonable things in the world. It was blowing almost a gale, and the weather was very cold—it being late in October. I sprang out of bed, nevertheless, in a kind of ecstasy, and told him I was quite as brave as himself, and quite as tired as he was of lying in bed like a dog, and quite as ready for any fun or frolic as any Augustus Barnard in Nantucket.

We lost no time in getting on our clothes and hurrying down to the boat. She was lying at the old decayed wharf by the lumber-yard of Pankey & Co., and almost thumping her side out against the rough logs. Augustus got into her and bailed her, for she was nearly half full of water. This being done, we hoisted jib and mainsail, kept full, and started boldly out to sea.

The wind, as I before said, blew freshly from the southwest. The night was very clear and cold. Augustus had taken the helm, and I stationed myself by the mast, on the deck of the cuddy. We flew along at a great rate—neither of us having said a word since casting loose from the wharf. I now asked my companion what course he intended to steer, and what time he thought it probable we should get back. He whistled for a few minutes,

and then said crustily: "*I* am going to sea—*you* may go home if you think proper." Turning my eyes upon him, I perceived at once that, in spite of his assumed *nonchalance*, he was greatly agitated. I could see him distinctly by the light of the moon—his face was paler than any marble, and his hand shook so excessively that he could scarcely retain hold of the tiller. I found that something had gone wrong, and became seriously alarmed. At this period I knew little about the management of a boat, and was now depending entirely upon the nautical skill of my friend. The wind, too, had suddenly increased, as we were fast getting out of the lee of the land—still I was ashamed to betray any trepidation, and for almost half an hour maintained a resolute silence. I could stand it no longer, however, and spoke to Augustus about the propriety of turning back. As before, it was nearly a minute before he made answer, or took any notice of my suggestion. "By and by," said he at length—"time enough—home by and by." I had expected a similar reply, but there was something in the tone of these words which filled me with an indescribable feeling of dread. I again looked at the speaker attentively. His lips were perfectly livid, and his knees shook so violently together that he seemed scarcely able to stand. "For God's sake, Augustus," I screamed, now heartily frightened, "what ails you?—what is the matter?—what *are* you going to do?" "Matter!" he stammered, in the greatest apparent surprise, letting go the tiller at the same moment, and falling forward into the bottom of the boat—"matter—why, nothing is the—matter—going home—d—d—don't you see?" The whole truth now flashed upon me. I flew to him and raised him up. He was drunk—beastly drunk—he could no longer either stand, speak, or see. His eyes were perfectly glazed; and as I let him go in the extremity of my despair, he rolled like a mere log into the bilge-water, from which I had lifted him. It was evident that, during the evening, he had drunk far more than I suspected, and that his conduct in bed had been the result of a highly concentrated state of intoxication—a state which, like madness, frequently enables the victim to imitate the outward demeanor of one in perfect possession of his senses. The coolness of the night air, however, had had its usual effect—the mental energy began to yield before its influence—and the confused perception which he no doubt then had of his perilous situation had assisted in hastening the catastrophe. He was now thoroughly insensible, and there was no probability that he would be otherwise for many hours.

It is hardly possible to conceive the extremity of my terror. The fumes of the wine lately taken had evaporated, leaving me doubly timid and irresolute. I knew that I was altogether incapable of managing the boat,

and that a fierce wind and strong ebb tide were hurrying us to destruction. A storm was evidently gathering behind us; we had neither compass nor provisions; and it was clear that, if we held our present course, we should be out of sight of land before daybreak. These thoughts, with a crowd of others equally fearful, flashed through my mind with a bewildering rapidity, and for some moments paralyzed me beyond the possibility of making any exertion. The boat was going through the water at a terrible rate—full before the wind—no reef in either jib or mainsail—running her bows completely under the foam. It was a thousand wonders she did not broach to—Augustus having let go the tiller, as I said before, and I being too much agitated to think of taking it myself. By good luck, however, she kept steady, and gradually I recovered some degree of presence of mind. Still the wind was increasing fearfully; and whenever we rose from a plunge forward, the sea behind fell combing over our counter, and deluged us with water. I was so utterly benumbed, too, in every limb, as to be nearly unconscious of sensation. At length I summoned up the resolution of despair, and rushing to the mainsail, let it go by the run. As might have been expected, it flew over the bows, and, getting drenched with water, carried away the mast short off by the board. This latter accident alone saved me from instant destruction. Under the jib only, I now boomed along before the wind, shipping heavy seas occasionally over the counter, but relieved from the terror of immediate death. I took the helm, and breathed with greater freedom as I found that there yet remained to us a chance of ultimate escape. Augustus still lay senseless in the bottom of the boat; and as there was imminent danger of his drowning (the water being nearly a foot deep just where he fell), I contrived to raise him partially up, and keep him in a sitting position, by passing a rope round his waist, and lashing it to a ringbolt in the deck of the cuddy. Having thus arranged everything as well as I could in my chilled and agitated condition, I recommended myself to God, and made up my mind to bear whatever might happen with all the fortitude in my power.

Hardly had I come to this resolution, when, suddenly, a loud and long scream or yell, as if from the throats of a thousand demons, seemed to pervade the whole atmosphere around and above the boat. Never while I live shall I forget the intense agony of terror I experienced at that moment. My hair stood erect on my head—I felt the blood congealing in my veins—my heart ceased utterly to beat, and without having once raised my eyes to learn the source of my alarm, I tumbled headlong and insensible upon the body of my fallen companion.

I found myself, upon reviving, in the cabin of a large whaling-ship (the *Penguin*) bound to Nantucket. Several persons were standing over me, and Augustus, paler than death, was busily occupied in chafing my hands. Upon seeing me open my eyes, his exclamations of gratitude and joy excited alternate laughter and tears from the rough-looking personages who were present. The mystery of our being in existence was now soon explained. We had been run down by the whaling-ship, which was close-hauled, beating up to Nantucket with every sail she could venture to set, and consequently running almost at right angles to our own course. Several men were on the look-out forward, but did not perceive our boat until it was an impossibility to avoid coming in contact—their shouts of warning upon seeing us were what so terribly alarmed me. The huge ship, I was told, rode immediately over us with as much ease as our own little vessel would have passed over a feather, and without the least perceptible impediment to her progress. Not a scream arose from the deck of the victim—there was a slight grating sound to be heard mingling with the roar of wind and water, as the frail bark which was swallowed up rubbed for a moment along the keel of her destroyer—but this was all. Thinking our boat (which it will be remembered was dismasted) some mere shell cut adrift as useless, the captain (Captain E. T. V. Block, of New London) was for proceeding on his course without troubling himself further about the matter. Luckily, there were two of the look-out who swore positively to having seen some person at our helm, and represented the possibility of yet saving him. A discussion ensued, when Block grew angry, and, after a while, said that "it was no business of his to be eternally watching for egg-shells; that the ship should not put about for any such nonsense; and if there was a man run down, it was nobody's fault but his own—he might drown and be d——d" or some language to that effect. Henderson, the first mate, now took the matter up, being justly indignant, as well as the whole ship's crew, at a speech evincing so base a degree of heartless atrocity. He spoke plainly, seeing himself upheld by the men, told the captain he considered him a fit subject for the gallows, and that he would disobey his orders if he were hanged for it the moment he set his foot on shore. He strode aft, jostling Block (who turned pale and made no answer) on one side, and seizing the helm, gave the word, in a firm voice, *Hard-a-lee!* The men flew to their posts, and the ship went cleverly about. All this had occupied nearly five minutes, and it was supposed to be hardly within the bounds of possibility that any individual could be saved—allowing any to have been on board the boat. Yet, as the

reader has seen, both Augustus and myself were rescued; and our deliverance seemed to have been brought about by two of those almost inconceivable pieces of good fortune which are attributed by the wise and pious to the special interference of Providence.

While the ship was yet in stays, the mate lowered the jolly-boat and jumped into her with the very two men, I believe, who spoke up as having seen me at the helm. They had just left the lee of the vessel (the moon still shining brightly) when she made a long and heavy roll to windward, and Henderson, at the same moment, starting up in his seat, bawled out to his crew to *back water*. He would say nothing else—repeating his cry impatiently, *back water! black water!* The men put back as speedily as possible; but by this time the ship had gone round, and gotten fully under headway, although all hands on board were making great exertions to take in sail. In despite of the danger of the attempt, the mate clung to the main-chains as soon as they came within his reach. Another huge lurch now brought the starboard side of the vessel out of water nearly as far as her keel, when the cause of his anxiety was rendered obvious enough. The body of a man was seen to be affixed in the most singular manner to the smooth and shining bottom (the *Penguin* was coppered and copper-fastened), and beating violently against it with every movement of the hull. After several ineffectual efforts, made during the lurches of the ship, and at the imminent risk of swamping the boat, I was finally disengaged from my perilous situation and taken on board—for the body proved to be my own. It appeared that one of the timber-bolts having started and broken a passage through the copper, it had arrested my progress as I passed under the ship, and fastened me in so extraordinary a manner to her bottom. The head of the bolt had made its way through the collar of the green baize jacket I had on, and through the back part of my neck, forcing itself out between two sinews and just below the right ear. I was immediately put to bed—although life seemed to be totally extinct. There was no surgeon on board. The captain, however, treated me with every attention—to make amends, I presume, in the eyes of his crew, for his atrocious behavior in the previous portion of the adventure.

In the meantime, Henderson had again put off from the ship, although the wind was now blowing almost a hurricane. He had not been gone many minutes when he fell in with some fragments of our boat, and shortly afterward one of the men with him asserted that he could distinguish a cry for help at intervals amid the roaring of the tempest. This induced the hardy seamen to persevere in their search for more than half

an hour, although repeated signals to return were made them by Captain Block, and although every moment on the water in so frail a boat was fraught to them with the most imminent and deadly peril. Indeed, it is nearly impossible to conceive how the small jolly they were in could have escaped destruction for a single instant. She was built, however, for the whaling service, and was fitted, as I have since had reason to believe, with air-boxes, in the manner of some life-boats used on the coast of Wales.

After searching in vain for about the period of time just mentioned, it was determined to get back to the ship. They had scarcely made this resolve when a feeble cry arose from a dark object that floated rapidly by. They pursued and soon overtook it. It proved to be the entire deck of the *Ariel's* cuddy. Augustus was struggling near it, apparently in the last agonies. Upon getting hold of him it was found that he was attached by a rope to the floating timber. This rope, it will be remembered, I had myself tied around his waist, and made fast to a ringbolt, for the purpose of keeping him in an upright position, and my so doing, it appeared, had been ultimately the means of preserving his life. The *Ariel* was slightly put together, and in going down her frame naturally went to pieces; the deck of the cuddy, as might have been expected, was lifted, by the force of the water rushing in, entirely from the main timbers, and floated (with other fragments, no doubt) to the surface—Augustus was buoyed up with it, and thus escaped a terrible death.

It was more than an hour after being taken on board the *Penguin* before he could give any account of himself, or be made to comprehend the nature of the accident which had befallen our boat. At length he became thoroughly aroused, and spoke much of his sensations while in the water. Upon his first attaining any degree of consciousness, he found himself beneath the surface, whirling round and round with inconceivable rapidity, and with a rope wrapped in three or four folds tightly about his neck. In an instant afterward he felt himself going rapidly upwards, when, his head striking violently against a hard substance, he again relapsed into insensibility. Upon once more reviving he was in fuller possession of his reason—this was still, however, in the greatest degree clouded and confused. He now knew that some accident had occurred, and that he was in the water, although his mouth was above the surface, and he could breathe with some freedom. Possibly, at this period the deck was drifting rapidly before the wind, and drawing him after it, as he floated upon his back. Of course, as long as he could have retained this position, it would have been nearly impossible that he should be drowned. Presently a surge threw him

directly athwart the deck; and this post he endeavored to maintain, scream-
ing at intervals for help. Just before he was discovered by Mr. Henderson,
he had been obliged to relax his hold through exhaustion, and, falling into
the sea, had given himself up for lost. During the whole period of his strug-
gles he had not the faintest recollection of the *Ariel*, nor of the matters in
connection with the source of his disaster. A vague feeling of terror and
despair had taken entire possession of his faculties. When he was finally
picked up, every power of his mind had failed him; and, as before said, it
was nearly an hour after getting on board the *Penguin* before he became
fully aware of his condition. In regard to myself—I was resuscitated from a
state bordering very nearly upon death (and after every other means had
been tried in vain for three hours and a half) by vigorous friction with flan-
nels bathed in hot oil—a proceeding suggested by Augustus. The wound in
my neck, although of an ugly appearance, proved of little real conse-
quence, and I soon recovered from its effects.

The *Penguin* got into port about nine o'clock in the morning, after
encountering one of the severest gales ever experienced off Nantucket.
Both Augustus and myself managed to appear at Mr. Barnard's in time for
breakfast—which, luckily, was somewhat late, owing to the party over
night. I suppose all at the table were too much fatigued themselves to
notice our jaded appearance—of course, it would not have borne a very
rigid scrutiny. Schoolboys, however, can accomplish wonders in the way of
deception, and I verily believe not one of our friends in Nantucket had
the slightest suspicion that the terrible story told by some sailors in town
of their having run down a vessel at sea and drowned some thirty or forty
poor devils, had reference either to the *Ariel*, my companion, or myself.
We two have since very frequently talked the matter over—but never with-
out a shudder. In one of our conversations Augustus frankly confessed to
me, that in his whole life he had at no time experienced so excruciating a
sense of dismay, as when on board our little boat he first discovered the
extent of his intoxication, and felt himself sinking beneath its influence.

CHAPTER II

IN NO AFFAIRS OF MERE PREJUDICE, PRO OR CON, DO WE DEDUCE INFERENCES with entire certainty, even from the most simple data. It might be supposed that a catastrophe such as I have just related would have effectually cooled my incipient passion for the sea. On the contrary, I never experienced a more ardent longing for the wild adventures incident to the life of a navigator than within a week after our miraculous deliverance. This short period proved amply long enough to erase from my memory the shadows, and bring out in vivid light all the pleasurably exciting points of color, all the picturesqueness, of the late perilous accident. My conversations with Augustus grew daily more frequent and more intensely full of interest. He had a manner of relating his stories of the ocean (more than one half of which I now suspect to have been sheer fabrications) well adapted to have weight with one of my enthusiastic temperament and somewhat gloomy although glowing imagination. It is strange, too, that he most strongly enlisted my feelings in behalf of the life of a seaman, when he depicted his more terrible moments of suffering and despair. For the bright side of the painting I had a limited sympathy. My visions were of shipwreck and famine; of death or captivity among barbarian hordes; of a lifetime dragged out in sorrow and tears, upon some gray and desolate rock, in an ocean unapproachable and unknown. Such visions or desires—for they amounted to desires—are common, I have since been assured, to the whole numerous race of the melancholy among men—at the time of which I speak I regarded them only as prophetic glimpses of a destiny which I felt myself in a measure bound to fulfill. Augustus thoroughly entered into my state of mind. It is probable, indeed, that our intimate communion had resulted in a partial interchange of character.

About eighteen months after the period of the *Ariel*'s disaster, the firm of Lloyd and Vredenburgh (a house connected in some manner with the Messieurs Enderby, I believe, of Liverpool) were engaged in repairing and fitting out the brig *Grampus* for a whaling voyage. She was an old hulk, and scarcely seaworthy when all was done to her that could be done. I hardly know why she was chosen in preference to other good vessels belonging to the same owners—but so it was. Mr. Barnard was appointed to command her, and Augustus was going with him. While the brig was getting ready, he frequently urged upon me the excellency of the opportunity now offered for indulging my desire of travel. He found me by no means an unwilling listener—yet the matter could not be so easily arranged. My father made no direct opposition; but my mother went into hysterics at the bare mention of the design; and, more than all, my grandfather, from whom I expected much, vowed to cut me off with a shilling if I should ever broach the subject to him again. These difficulties, however, so far from abating my desire, only added fuel to the flame. I determined to go at all hazards; and, having made known my intentions to Augustus, we set about arranging a plan by which it might be accomplished. In the meantime I forbore speaking to any of my relations in regard to the voyage, and, as I busied myself ostensibly with my usual studies, it was supposed that I had abandoned the design. I have since frequently examined my conduct on this occasion with sentiments of displeasure as well as of surprise. The intense hypocrisy I made use of for the furtherance of my project—an hypocrisy pervading every word and action of my life for so long a period of time—could only have been rendered tolerable to myself by the wild and burning expectation with which I looked forward to the fulfillment of my long-cherished visions of travel.

In pursuance of my scheme of deception, I was necessarily obliged to leave much to the management of Augustus, who was employed for the greater part of every day on board the *Grampus,* attending to some arrangements for his father in the cabin and cabin hold. At night, however, we were sure to have a conference and talk over our hopes. After nearly a month passed in this manner, without our hitting upon any plan we thought likely to succeed, he told me at last that he had determined upon everything necessary. I had a relation living in New Bedford, a Mr. Ross, at whose house I was in the habit of spending occasionally two or three weeks at a time. The brig was to sail about the middle of June (June, 1827), and it was agreed that, a day or two before her putting to sea, my father was to receive a note, as usual, from Mr. Ross, asking me

to come over and spend a fortnight with Robert and Emmet (his sons). Augustus charged himself with the inditing of this note and getting it delivered. Having set out as supposed, for New Bedford, I was then to report myself to my companion, who would contrive a hiding-place for me in the *Grampus*. This hiding-place, he assured me, would be rendered sufficiently comfortable for a residence of many days, during which I was not to make my appearance. When the brig had proceeded so far on her course as to make any turning back a matter out of question, I should then, he said, be formally installed in all the comforts of the cabin; and as to his father, he would only laugh heartily at the joke. Vessels enough would be met with by which a letter might be sent home explaining the adventure to my parents.

The middle of June at length arrived, and everything had been matured. The note was written and delivered, and on a Monday morning I left the house for the New Bedford packet, as supposed. I went, however, straight to Augustus, who was waiting for me at the corner of a street. It had been our original plan that I should keep out of the way until dark, and then slip on board the brig; but, as there was now a thick fog in our favor, it was agreed to lose no time in secreting me. Augustus led the way to the wharf, and I followed at a little distance, enveloped in a thick seaman's cloak, which he had brought with him, so that my person might not be easily recognized. Just as we turned the second corner, after passing Mr. Edmund's well, who should appear, standing right in front of me, and looking me full in the face, but old Mr. Peterson, my grandfather. "Why, bless my soul, Gordon," said he, after a long pause, "why, why—*whose* dirty cloak is that you have on?" "Sir!" I replied, assuming, as well as I could, in the exigency of the moment, an air of offended surprise, and talking in the gruffest of all imaginable tones— "sir! you are a sum'mat mistaken —my name, in the first place, bee'nt nothing at all like Goddin, and I'd want you for to know better, you blackguard, than to call my new ober-coat a darty one." For my life I could hardly refrain from screaming with laughter at the odd manner in which the old gentleman received this handsome rebuke. He started back two or three steps, turned first pale and then excessively red, threw up his spectacles, then, putting them down, ran full tilt at me, with his umbrella uplifted. He stopped short, however, in his career, as if struck with a sudden recollection; and presently, turning round, hobbled off down the street, shaking all the while with rage, and muttering between his teeth: "Won't do—new glasses—thought it was Gordon—d——d good-for-nothing salt water Long Tom."

After this narrow escape we proceeded with greater caution, and arrived at our point of destination in safety. There were only one or two of the hands on board, and these were busy forward, doing something to the forecastle combings. Captain Barnard, we knew very well, was engaged at Lloyd and Vredenburgh's, and would remain there until late in the evening, so we had little to apprehend on his account. Augustus went first up the vessel's side, and in a short while I followed him, without being noticed by the men at work. We proceeded at once into the cabin, and found no person there. It was fitted up in the most comfortable style—a thing somewhat unusual in a whaling-vessel. There were four very excellent staterooms, with wide and convenient berths. There was also a large stove, I took notice, and a remarkably thick and valuable carpet covering the floor of both the cabin and staterooms. The ceiling was full seven feet high, and, in short, everything appeared of a more roomy and agreeable nature than I had anticipated. Augustus, however, would allow me but little time for observation, insisting upon the necessity of my concealing myself as soon as possible. He led the way into his own stateroom, which was on the starboard side of the brig, and next to the bulkheads. Upon entering, he closed the door and bolted it. I thought I had never seen a nicer little room than the one in which I now found myself. It was about ten feet long, and had only one berth, which, as I said before, was wide and convenient. In that portion of the closet nearest the bulkheads there was a space of four feet square, containing a table, a chair, and a set of hanging shelves full of books, chiefly books of voyages and travels. There were many other little comforts in the room, among which I ought not to forget a kind of safe or refrigerator, in which Augustus pointed out to me a host of delicacies, both in the eating and drinking department.

He now pressed with his knuckles upon a certain spot of the carpet in one corner of the space just mentioned, letting me know that a portion of the flooring, about sixteen inches square, had been neatly cut out and again adjusted. As he pressed, this portion rose up at one end sufficiently to allow the passage of his finger beneath. In this manner he raised the mouth of the trap (to which the carpet was still fastened by tacks), and I found that it led into the after hold. He next lit a small taper by means of a phosphorous match, and, placing the light in a dark lantern, descended with it through the opening, bidding me follow. I did so, and he then pulled the cover upon the hole, by means of a nail driven into the under side—the carpet, of course, resuming its original position on the floor of the stateroom, and all traces of the aperture being concealed.

The taper gave out so feeble a ray that it was with the greatest difficulty I could grope my way through the confused mass of lumber among which I now found myself. By degrees, however, my eyes became accustomed to the gloom, and I proceeded with less trouble, holding on to the skirts of my friend's coat. He brought me, at length, after creeping and winding through innumerable narrow passages, to an iron-bound box, such as is used sometimes for packing fine earthenware. It was nearly four feet high, and full six long, but very narrow. Two large empty oil-casks lay on the top of it, and above these, again, a vast quantity of straw matting, piled up as high as the floor of the cabin. In every other direction around was wedged as closely as possible, even up to the ceiling, a complete chaos of almost every species of ship-furniture, together with a heterogeneous medley of crates, hampers, barrels, and bales, so that it seemed a matter no less than miraculous that we had discovered any passage at all to the box. I afterward found that Augustus had purposely arranged the stowage in this hold with a view to affording me a thorough concealment, having had only one assistant in the labor, a man not going out in the brig.

My companion now showed me that one of the ends of the box could be removed at pleasure. He slipped it aside and displayed the interior, at which I was excessively amused. A mattress from one of the cabin berths covered the whole of its bottom, and it contained almost every article of mere comfort which could be crowded into so small a space, allowing me, at the same time, sufficient room for my accommodation, either in a sitting position or lying at full length. Among other things, there were some books, pen, ink, and paper, three blankets, a large jug full of water, a keg of sea-biscuit, three or four immense Bologna sausages, an enormous ham, a cold leg of roast mutton, and half a dozen bottles of cordials and liqueurs. I proceeded immediately to take possession of my little apartment, and this with feelings of higher satisfaction, I am sure, than any monarch ever experienced upon entering a new palace. Augustus now pointed out to me the method of fastening the open end of the box, and then, holding the taper close to the deck, showed me a piece of dark whipcord lying along it. This, he said, extended from my hiding-place throughout all the necessary windings among the lumber, to a nail which was driven into the deck of the hold, immediately beneath the trap-door leading into his stateroom. By means of this cord I should be enabled readily to trace my way out without his guidance, provided any unlooked-for accident should render such a step necessary. He now took his departure, leaving with me the lantern, together with a copious supply of tapers and phosphorous, and promising

to pay me a visit as often as he could contrive to do so without observation. This was on the seventeenth of June.

I remained three days and nights (as nearly as I could guess) in my hiding-place without getting out of it at all, except twice for the purpose of stretching my limbs by standing erect between two crates just opposite the opening. During the whole period I saw nothing of Augustus; but this occasioned me little uneasiness, as I knew the brig was expected to put to sea every hour, and in the bustle he would not easily find opportunities of coming down to me. At length I heard the trap open and shut, and presently he called in a low voice, asking if all was well, and if there was anything I wanted. "Nothing," I replied; "I am as comfortable as can be; when will the brig sail?" "She will be under weigh in less than half an hour," he answered. "I came to let you know, and for fear you should be uneasy at my absence. I shall not have a chance of coming down again for some time—perhaps for three or four days more. All is going on right aboveboard. After I go up and close the trap, do you creep along by the whipcord to where the nail is driven in. You will find my watch there—it may be useful to you, as you have no daylight to keep time by. I suppose you can't tell how long you have been buried—only three days—this is the twentieth. I would bring the watch to your box, but am afraid of being missed." With this he went up.

In about an hour after he had gone I distinctly felt the brig in motion, and congratulated myself upon having at length fairly commenced a voyage. Satisfied with this idea, I determined to make my mind as easy as possible, and await the course of events until I should be permitted to exchange the box for the more roomy, although hardly more comfortable, accommodations of the cabin. My first care was to get the watch. Leaving the taper burning, I groped along in the dark, following the cord through windings innumerable, in some of which I discovered that, after toiling a long distance, I was brought back within a foot or two of a former position. At length I reached the nail, and securing the object of my journey, returned with it in safety. I now looked over the books which had been so thoughtfully provided, and selected the expedition of Lewis and Clarke to the mouth of the Columbia. With this I amused myself for some time, when, growing sleepy, I extinguished the light with great care, and soon fell into a sound slumber.

Upon awaking I felt strangely confused in mind, and some time elapsed before I could bring to recollection all the various circumstances of my situation. By degrees, however, I remembered all. Striking a light, I

looked at the watch; but it was run down, and there were, consequently, no means of determining how long I slept. My limbs were greatly cramped, and I was forced to relieve them by standing between the crates. Presently feeling an almost ravenous appetite, I bethought myself of the cold mutton, some of which I had eaten just before going to sleep, and found excellent. What was my astonishment in discovering it to be in a state of absolute putrefaction! This circumstance occasioned me great disquietude; for, connecting it with the disorder of mind I experienced upon awaking, I began to suppose that I must have slept for an inordinately long period of time. The close atmosphere of the hold might have had something to do with this, and might, in the end, be productive of the most serious results. My head ached excessively; I fancied that I drew every breath with difficulty; and, in short, I was oppressed with a multitude of gloomy feelings. Still I could not venture to make any disturbance by opening the trap or otherwise, and, having wound up the watch, contented myself as well as possible.

Throughout the whole of the next tedious twenty-four hours no person came to my relief, and I could not help accusing Augustus of the grossest inattention. What alarmed me chiefly was, that the water in my jug was reduced to about half a pint, and I was suffering much from thirst, having eaten freely of the Bologna sausages after the loss of my mutton. I became very uneasy, and could no longer take any interest in my books. I was overpowered, too, with a desire to sleep, yet trembled at the thought of indulging it, lest there might exist some pernicious influence, like that of burning charcoal, in the confined air of the hold. In the meantime the roll of the brig told me that we were far in the main ocean, and a dull humming sound, which reached my ears as if from an immense distance, convinced me no ordinary gale was blowing. I could not imagine a reason for the absence of Augustus. We were surely far enough advanced on our voyage to allow of my going up. Some accident might have happened to him—but I could think of none which would account for his suffering me to remain so long a prisoner, except, indeed, his having suddenly died or fallen overboard, and upon this idea I could not dwell with any degree of patience. It was possible that we had been baffled by head winds, and were still in the near vicinity of Nantucket. This notion, however, I was forced to abandon; for such being the case, the brig must have frequently gone about; and I was entirely satisfied, from her continual inclination to the larboard, that she had been sailing all along with a steady breeze on her starboard quarter. Besides, granting

that we were still in the neighborhood of the island, why should not Augustus have visited me and informed me of the circumstance? Pondering in this manner upon the difficulties of my solitary and cheerless condition, I resolved to wait yet another twenty-four hours, when, if no relief were obtained, I would make my way to the trap, and endeavor either to hold a parley with my friend, or get at least a little fresh air through the opening, and a further supply of water from the stateroom. While occupied with this thought, however, I fell, in spite of every exertion to the contrary, into a state of profound sleep, or rather stupor. My dreams were of the most terrific description. Every species of calamity and horror befell me. Among other miseries I was smothered to death between huge pillows, by demons of the most ghastly and ferocious aspect. Immense serpents held me in their embrace, and looked earnestly in my face with their fearfully shining eyes. Then deserts, limitless, and of the most forlorn and awe-inspiring character, spread themselves out before me. Immensely tall trunks of trees, gray and leafless, rose up in endless succession as far as the eye could reach. Their roots were concealed in wide-spreading morasses, whose dreary water lay intensely black, still, and altogether terrible, beneath. And the strange trees seemed endowed with a human vitality, and waving to and fro their skeleton arms, were crying to the silent waters for mercy, in the shrill and piercing accents of the most acute agony and despair. The scene changed; and I stood, naked and alone, amidst the burning sand-plains of Sahara. At my feet lay crouched a fierce lion of the tropics. Suddenly his wild eyes opened and fell upon me. With a conculsive bound he sprang to his feet, and laid bare his horrible teeth. In another instant there burst from his red throat a roar like the thunder of the firmament, and I fell impetuously to the earth. Stifling in a paroxysm of terror, I at last found myself partially awake. My dream, then, was not all a dream. Now, at least, I was in possession of my senses. The paws of some huge and real monster were pressing heavily upon my bosom—his hot breath was in my ear—and his white and ghastly fangs were gleaming upon me through the gloom.

Had a thousand lives hung upon the movement of a limb or the utterance of a syllable, I could have neither stirred nor spoken. The beast, whatever it was, retained his position without attempting any immediate violence, while I lay in an utterly helpless, and, I fancied, a dying condition beneath him. I felt that my powers of body and mind were fast leaving me—in a word, that I was perishing, and perishing of sheer fright. My brain swam—I grew deadly sick—my vision failed—even the glaring

eyeballs above me grew dim. Making a last strong effort, I at length breathed a faint ejaculation to God, and resigned myself to die. The sound of my voice seemed to arouse all the latent fury of the animal. He precipitated himself at full length upon my body; but what was my astonishment, when, with a long and low whine, he commenced licking my face and hands with the greatest eagerness, and with the most extravagant demonstration of affection and joy! I was bewildered, utterly lost in amazement—but I could not forget the peculiar whine of my Newfoundland dog Tiger, and the odd manner of his caresses I well knew. It was he. I experienced a sudden rush of blood to my temples—a giddy and overpowering sense of deliverance and reanimation. I rose hurriedly from the mattress upon which I had been lying, and, throwing myself upon the neck of my faithful follower and friend, relieved the long oppression of my bosom in a flood of the most passionate tears.

As upon a former occasion my conceptions were in a state of the greatest indistinctness and confusion after leaving the mattress. For a long time I found it nearly impossible to connect any ideas—but, by very slow degrees, my thinking faculties returned, and I again called to memory the several incidents of my condition. For the presence of Tiger I tried in vain to account; and after busying myself with a thousand different conjectures respecting him, was forced to content myself with rejoicing that he was with me to share my dreary solitude, and render me comfort by his caresses. Most people love their dogs—but for Tiger I had an affection far more ardent than common; and never, certainly, did any creature more truly deserve it. For seven years he had been my inseparable companion, and in a multitude of instances had given evidence of all the noble qualities for which we value the animal. I had rescued him, when a puppy, from the clutches of a malignant little villain in Nantucket who was leading him, with a rope around his neck, to the water; and the grown dog repaid the obligation, about three years afterward, by saving me from the bludgeon of a street-robber.

Getting now hold of the watch, I found, upon applying it to my ear, that it had again run down; but at this I was not at all surprised, being convinced, from the peculiar state of my feelings, that I had slept, as before, for a very long period of time, how long, it was of course impossible to say. I was burning up with fever, and my thirst was almost intolerable. I felt about the box for my little remaining supply of water, for I had no light, the taper having burnt to the socket of the lantern, and the phosphorus-box not coming readily to hand. Upon finding the jug, however, I

discovered it to be empty—Tiger, no doubt, having been tempted to drink it, as well as to devour the remnant of mutton, the bone of which lay, well picked, by the opening of the box. The spoiled meat I could well spare, but my heart sank as I thought of the water. I was feeble in the extreme—so much so that I shook all over, as with an ague, at the slightest movement or exertion. To add to my troubles, the brig was pitching and rolling with great violence, and the oil-casks which lay upon my box were in momentary danger of falling down, so as to block up the only way of ingress or egress. I felt, also, terrible sufferings from sea-sickness. These considerations determined me to make my way, at all hazards, to the trap, and obtain immediate relief, before I should be incapacitated from doing so altogether. Having come to this resolve, I again felt about for the phosphorus-box and tapers. The former I found after some little trouble; but, not discovering the tapers as soon as I had expected (for I remembered very nearly the spot in which I had placed them), I gave up the search for the present, and bidding Tiger lie quiet, began at once my journey towards the trap.

In this attempt my great feebleness became more than ever apparent. It was with the utmost difficulty I could crawl along at all, and very frequently my limbs sank suddenly from beneath me; when, falling prostrate on my face, I would remain for some minutes in a state bordering on insensibility. Still I struggled forward by slow degrees, dreading every moment that I should swoon amid the narrow and intricate windings of the lumber, in which event I had nothing but death to expect as the result. At length, upon making a push forward with all the energy I could command, I struck my forehead violently against the sharp corner of an iron-bound crate. The accident only stunned me for a few moments; but I found, to my inexpressible grief, that the quick and violent roll of the vessel had thrown the crate entirely across my path, so as effectually to block up the passage. With my utmost exertions I could not move it a single inch from its position, it being closely wedged in among the surrounding boxes and ship-furniture. It became necessary, therefore, enfeebled as I was, either to leave the guidance of the whipcord and seek out a new passage, or to climb over the obstacle, and resume the path on the other side. The former alternative presented too many difficulties and dangers to be thought of without a shudder. In my present weak state of both mind and body, I should infallibly lose my way if I attempted it, and perish miserably amid the dismal and disgusting labyrinths of the hold. I proceeded, therefore, without hesitation, to summon up all my remaining strength and fortitude, and endeavor, as I best might, to clamber over the crate.

Upon standing erect, with this end in view, I found the undertaking even a more serious task than my fears had led me to imagine. On each side of the narrow passage arose a complete wall of various heavy lumber, which the least blunder on my part might be the means of bringing down upon my head; or, if this accident did not occur, the path might be effectually blocked up against my return by the descending mass, as it was in front by the obstacle there. The crate itself was a long and unwieldy box, upon which no foothold could be obtained. In vain I attempted, by every means in my power, to reach the top, with the hope of being thus enabled to draw myself up. Had I succeeded in reaching it, it is certain that my strength would have proved utterly inadequate to the task of getting over, and it was better in every respect that I failed. At length, in a desperate effort to force the crate from its ground, I felt a strong vibration in the side next me. I thrust my hand eagerly to the edge of the planks, and found that a very large one was loose. With my pocket-knife, which, luckily, I had with me, I succeeded, after great labor, in prying it entirely off; and getting it through the aperture, discovered, to my exceeding joy, that there were no boards on the opposite side—in other words, that the top was wanting, it being the bottom through which I had forced my way. I now met with no important difficulty in proceeding along the line until I finally reached the nail. With a beating heart I stood erect, and with a gentle touch pressed against the cover of the trap. It did not rise as soon as I had expected, and I pressed it with somewhat more determination, still dreading lest some other person than Augustus might be in his stateroom. The door, however, to my astonishment, remained steady, and I became somewhat uneasy, for I knew that it had formerly required but little or no effort to remove it. I pushed it strongly—it was nevertheless firm: with all my strength—it still did not give way: with rage, with fury, with despair—it set at defiance my utmost efforts; and it was evident, from the unyielding nature of the resistance, that the hole had either been discovered and effectually nailed up, or that some immense weight had been placed upon it, which it was useless to think of removing.

My sensations were those of extreme horror and dismay. In vain I attempted to reason on the probable cause of my being thus entombed. I could summon up no connected chain of reflection, and, sinking on the floor, gave way, unresistingly, to the most gloomy imaginings, in which the dreadful deaths of thirst, famine, suffocation, and premature interment crowded upon me as the prominent disasters to be encountered. At length there returned to me some portion of presence of mind. I arose,

and felt with my fingers for the seams or cracks of the aperture. Having found them, I examined them closely to ascertain if they emitted any light from the stateroom; but none was visible. I then forced the blade of my pen-knife through them, until I met with some hard obstacle. Scraping against it, I discovered it to be a solid mass of iron, which, from its peculiar wavy feel as I passed the blade along it, I concluded to be a chain-cable. The only course now left me was to retrace my way to the box, and there either yield to my sad fate, or try so to tranquilize my mind as to admit of my arranging some plan of escape. I immediately set about the attempt, and succeeded, after innumerable difficulties, in getting back. As I sank, utterly exhausted, upon the mattress, Tiger threw himself at full length by my side, and seemed as if desirous, by his caresses, of consoling me in my troubles, and urging me to bear them with fortitude.

The singularity of his behavior at length forcibly arrested my attention. After licking my face and hands for some minutes, he would suddenly cease doing so, and utter a low whine. Upon reaching out my hand towards him, I then invariably found him lying on his back, with his paws uplifted. This conduct, so frequently repeated, appeared strange, and I could in no manner account for it. As the dog seemed distressed, I concluded that he had received some injury; and, taking his paws in my hands, I examined them one by one, but found no sign of any hurt. I then supposed him hungry, and gave him a large piece of ham, which he devoured with avidity—afterward, however, resuming his extraordinary maneuvers. I now imagined that he was suffering, like myself, the torments of thirst, and was about adopting this conclusion as the true one, when the idea occurred to me that I had as yet only examined his paws, and that there might possibly be a wound upon some portion of his body or head. The latter I felt carefully over, but found nothing. On passing my hand, however, along his back, I perceived a slight erection of the hair extending completely across it. Probing this with my finger, I discovered a string, and tracing it up, found that it encircled the whole body. Upon a closer scrutiny, I came across a small slip of what had the feeling of letter paper, through which the string had been fastened in such a manner as to bring it immediately beneath the left shoulder of the animal.

CHAPTER III

THE THOUGHT INSTANTLY OCCURRED TO ME THAT THE PAPER WAS A NOTE from Augustus, and that some unaccountable accident having happened to prevent his relieving me from my dungeon, he had devised this method of acquainting me with the true state of affairs. Trembling with eagerness, I now commenced another search for my phosphorous matches and tapers. I had a confused recollection of having put them carefully away just before falling asleep; and, indeed, previously to my last journey to the trap, I had been able to remember the exact spot where I had deposited them. But now I endeavored in vain to call it to mind, and busied myself for a full hour in a fruitless and vexatious search for the missing articles; never, surely, was there a more tantalizing state of anxiety and suspense. At length, while groping about, with my head close to the ballast, near the opening of the box, and outside of it, I perceived a faint glimmering of light in the direction of the steerage. Greatly surprised, I endeavored to make my way towards it, as it appeared to be but a few feet from my position. Scarcely had I moved with this intention, when I lost sight of the glimmer entirely, and, before I could bring it into view again, was obliged to feel along by the box until I had exactly resumed my original situation. Now, moving my head with caution to and fro, I found that, by proceeding slowly, with great care, in an opposite direction to that in which I had at first started, I was enabled to draw near the light, still keeping it in view. Presently I came directly upon it (having squeezed my way through innumerable narrow windings), and found that it proceeded from some fragments of my matches lying in an empty barrel turned upon its side. I was wondering how they came in such a place, when my hand fell upon

two or three pieces of taper wax, which had been evidently mumbled by the dog. I concluded at once that he had devoured the whole of my supply of candles, and I felt hopeless of being ever able to read the note of Augustus. The small remnants of the wax were so mashed up among other rubbish in the barrel, that I despaired of deriving any service from them, and left them as they were. The phosphorus, of which there was only a speck or two, I gathered up as well as I could, and returned with it, after much difficulty, to my box, where Tiger had all the while remained.

What to do next I could not tell. The hold was so intensely dark that I could not see my hand, however close I would hold it to my face. The white slip of paper could barely be discerned, and not even that when I looked at it directly; by turning the exterior portions of the retina towards it—that is to say, by surveying it slightly askance, I found that it became in some measure perceptible. Thus the gloom of my prison may be imagined, and the note of my friend, if indeed it were a note from him, seemed only likely to throw me into further trouble, by disquieting to no purpose my already enfeebled and agitated mind. In vain I revolved in my brain a multitude of absurd expedients for procuring light—such expedients precisely as a man in the perturbed sleep occasioned by opium would be apt to fall upon for a similar purpose—each and all of which appear by turns to the dreamer the most reasonable and the most preposterous of conceptions, just as the reasoning or imaginative faculties flicker, alternately, one above the other. At last an idea occurred to me which seemed rational, and which gave me cause to wonder, very justly, that I had not entertained it before. I placed the slip of paper on the back of a book, and, collecting the fragments of the phosphorous matches which I had brought from the barrel, laid them together upon the paper. I then, with the palm of my hand, rubbed the whole over quickly, yet steadily. A clear light diffused itself immediately throughout the whole surface; and had there been any writing upon it, I should not have experienced the least difficulty, I am sure, in reading it. Not a syllable was there, however—nothing but a dreary and unsatisfactory blank; the illumination died away in a few seconds, and my heart died away within me as it went.

I have before stated more than once that my intellect, for some period prior to this, had been in a condition nearly bordering on idiocy. There were, to be sure, momentary intervals of perfect sanity, and, now and then, even of energy; but these were few. It must be remembered that I had been, for days certainly, inhaling the almost pestilential atmosphere of a close hold in a whaling vessel, and for a long portion of that time but

scantily supplied with water. For the last fourteen or fifteen hours I had none—nor had I slept during that time. Salt provisions of the most exciting kind had been my chief, and, indeed, since the loss of the mutton, my only supply of food, with the exception of the sea-biscuit; and these latter were utterly useless to me, as they were too dry and hard to be swallowed in the swollen and parched condition of my throat. I was now in a high state of fever, and in every respect exceedingly ill. This will account for the fact that many miserable hours of despondency elapsed after my last adventure with the phosphorus, before the thought suggested itself that I had examined only one side of the paper. I shall not attempt to describe my feelings of rage (for I believe I was more angry than anything else) when the egregious oversight I had committed flashed suddenly upon my perception. The blunder itself would have been unimportant, had not my own folly and impetuosity rendered it otherwise—in my disappointment at not finding some words upon the slip, I had childishly torn it in pieces and thrown it away, it was impossible to say where.

From the worst part of this dilemma I was relieved by the sagacity of Tiger. Having got, after a long search, a small piece of the note, I put it to the dog's nose, and endeavored to make him understand that he must bring me the rest of it. To my astonishment (for I had taught him none of the usual tricks for which his breed are famous), he seemed to enter at once into my meaning, and, rummaging about for a few moments, soon found another considerable portion. Bringing me this, he paused awhile, and, rubbing his nose against my hand, appeared to be waiting for my approval of what he had done. I patted him on the head, when he immediately made off again. It was now some minutes before he came back—but when he did come, he brought with him a large slip, which proved to be all the paper missing—it having been torn, it seems, only into three pieces. Luckily, I had no trouble in finding what few fragments of the phosphorus were left—being guided by the indistinct glow one or two of the particles still emitted. My difficulties had taught me the necessity of caution, and I now took time to reflect upon what I was about to do. It was very probable, I considered, that some words were written upon that side of the paper which had not been examined—but which side was that? Fitting the pieces together gave me no clue in this respect, although it assured me that the words (if there were any) would be found all on one side, and connected in a proper manner, as written. There was the greater necessity of ascertaining the point in question beyond a doubt, as the phosphorus remaining would be altogether insufficient for a third

attempt, should I fail in the one I was now about to make. I placed the paper on a book as before, and sat for some minutes thoughtfully revolving the matter over in my mind. At last I thought it barely possible that the written side might have some unevenness on its surface, which a delicate sense of feeling might enable me to detect. I determined to make the experiment, and passed my finger very carefully over the side which first presented itself. Nothing, however, was perceptible, and I turned the paper, adjusting it on the book. I now again carried my forefinger cautiously along, when I was aware of an exceedingly slight, but still discernible glow, which followed as it proceeded. This, I knew, must arise from some very minute remaining particles of the phosphorus with which I had covered the paper in my previous attempt. The other, or under side, then, was that on which lay the writing, if writing there should finally prove to be. Again I turned the note, and went to work as I had previously done. Having rubbed in the phosphorus, a brilliancy ensued as before—but this time several lines of MS. in a large hand, and apparently in red ink, became distinctly visible. The glimmer, although sufficiently bright, was but momentary. Still, had I not been too greatly excited, there would have been ample time enough for me to peruse the whole three sentences before me—for I saw there were three. In my anxiety, however, to read all at once, I succeeded only in reading the seven concluding words, which thus appeared— *"blood—your life depends upon lying close."*

Had I been able to ascertain the entire contents of the note—the full meaning of the admonition which my friend had thus attempted to convey, that admonition, even although it should have revealed a story of disaster the most unspeakable, could not, I am firmly convinced, have imbued my mind with one tithe of the harrowing and yet indefinable horror with which I was inspired by the fragmentary warning thus received. And *"blood,"* too, that word of all words—so rife at all times with mystery, and suffering, and terror—how trebly full of import did it now appear—how chillily and heavily (disjointed, as it thus was, from any foregoing words to qualify or render it distinct) did its vague syllables fall, amid the deep gloom of my prison, into the innermost recesses of my soul!

Augustus had, undoubtedly, good reasons for wishing me to remain concealed, and I formed a thousand surmises as to what they could be— but I could think of nothing affording a satisfactory solution of the mystery. Just after returning from my last journey to the trap, and before my attention had been otherwise directed by the singular conduct of Tiger, I had come to the resolution of making myself heard at all events by those on

board, or, if I could not succeed in this directly, of trying to cut my way through the orlop deck. The half certainty which I felt of being able to accomplish one of these two purposes in the last emergency, had given me courage (which I should not otherwise have had) to endure the evils of my situation. The few words I had been able to read, however, had cut me off from these final resources, and I now, for the first time, felt all the misery of my fate. In a paroxysm of despair I threw myself again upon the mattress, where, for about the period of a day and night, I lay in a kind of stupor, relieved only by momentary intervals of reason and recollection.

At length I once more arose, and busied myself in reflection upon the horrors which encompassed me. For another twenty-four hours it was barely possible that I might exist without water—for a longer time I could not do so. During the first portion of my imprisonment I had made free use of the cordials with which Augustus had supplied me, but they only served to excite fever, without in the least degree assuaging thirst. I had now only about a gill left, and this was of a species of strong peach liqueur at which my stomach revolted. The sausages were entirely consumed; of the ham nothing remained but a small piece of the skin; and all the biscuit, except a few fragments of one, had been eaten by Tiger. To add to my troubles, I found that my headache was increasing momentarily, and with it the species of delirium which had distressed me more or less since my first falling asleep. For some hours past it had been with the greatest difficulty I could breathe at all, and now each attempt at so doing was attended with the most depressing spasmodic action of the chest. But there was still another and very different source of disquietude, and one, indeed, whose harassing terrors had been the chief means of arousing me to exertion from my stupor on the mattress. It arose from the demeanor of the dog.

I first observed an alteration in his conduct while rubbing in the phosphorus on the paper in my last attempt. As I rubbed, he ran his nose against my hand with a slight snarl; but I was too greatly excited at the time to pay much attention to the circumstance. Soon afterward, it will be remembered, I threw myself on the mattress, and fell into a species of lethargy. Presently I became aware of a singular hissing sound close at my ears, and discovered it to proceed from Tiger, who was panting and wheezing in a state of the greatest apparent excitement, his eyeballs flashing fiercely through the gloom. I spoke to him, when he replied with a low growl, and then remained quiet. Presently I relapsed into my stupor, from which I was again awakened in a similar manner. This was repeated three or four times, until finally his behavior inspired me with so great a degree of fear, that I

became fully aroused. He was now lying close by the door of the box, snarling fearfully, although in a kind of undertone, and grinding his teeth as if strongly convulsed. I had no doubt whatever that the want of water or the confined atmosphere of the hold had driven him mad, and I was at a loss what course to pursue. I could not endure the thought of killing him, yet it seemed absolutely necessary for my own safety. I could distinctly perceive his eyes fastened upon me with an expression of the most deadly animosity, and I expected every instant that he would attack me. At last I could endure my terrible situation no longer, and determined to make my way from the box at all hazards, and dispatch him, if his opposition should render it necessary for me to do so. To get out, I had to pass directly over his body, and he already seemed to anticipate my design—missing himself upon his fore-legs (as I perceived by the altered position of his eyes), and displayed the whole of his white fangs, which were easily discernible. I took the remains of the ham-skin, and the bottle containing the liqueur, and secured them about my person, together with a large carving-knife which Augustus had left me—then, folding my cloak around me as closely as possible, I made a movement towards the mouth of the box. No sooner did I do this, than the dog sprang with a loud growl towards my throat. The whole weight of his body struck me on the right shoulder, and I fell violently to the left, while the enraged animal passed entirely over me. I had fallen upon my knees, with my head buried among the blankets, and these protected me from a second furious assault, during which I felt the sharp teeth pressing vigorously upon the woolen which enveloped my neck—yet, luckily, without being able to penetrate all the folds. I was now beneath the dog, and a few moments would place me completely in his power. Despair gave me strength, and I rose boldly up, shaking him from me by main force, and dragging with me the blankets from the mattress. These I now threw over him, and before he could extricate himself, I had got through the door and closed it effectually against his pursuit. In this struggle, however, I had been forced to drop the morsel of ham-skin, and I now found my whole stock of provisions reduced to a single gill of liqueur. As this reflection crossed my mind, I felt myself actuated by one of those fits of perverseness which might be supposed to influence a spoiled child in similar circumstances, and, raising the bottle to my lips, I drained it to the last drop, and dashed it furiously upon the floor.

Scarcely had the echo of the crash died away, when I heard my name pronounced in an eager but subdued voice, issuing from the direction of the steerage. So unexpected was anything of the kind, and so intense was the emotion excited within me by the sound, that I endeavored in vain

to reply. My powers of speech totally failed, and in an agony of terror lest my friend should conclude me dead, and return without attempting to reach me, I stood up between the crates near the door of the box, trembling convulsively, and gasping and struggling for utterance. Had a thousand words depended upon a syllable, I could not have spoken it. There was a slight movement now audible among the lumber somewhere forward of my station. The sound presently grew less distinct, then again less so, and still less. Shall I ever forget my feelings at this moment? He was going—my friend, my companion, from whom I had a right to expect so much— he was going—he would abandon me—he was gone! He would leave me to perish miserably, to expire in the most horrible and loathesome of dungeons—and one word, one little syllable would save me—yet that single syllable I could not utter! I felt, I am sure, more than ten thousand times the agonies of death itself. My brain reeled, and I fell, deadly sick, against the end of the box.

As I fell the carving-knife was shaken out from the waist-band of my pantaloons, and dropped with a rattling sound to the floor. Never did any strain of the richest melody come so sweetly to my ears! With the intensest anxiety I listened to ascertain the effect of the noise upon Augustus—for I knew that the person who called my name could be no one but himself. All was silent for some moments. At length I again heard the word "*Arthur!*" repeated in a low tone, and one full of hesitation. Reviving hope loosened at once my powers of speech, and I now screamed at the top of my voice, "*Augustus! oh, Augustus!*" "Hush—for God's sake be silent!" he replied, in a voice trembling with agitation; "I will be with you immediately—as soon as I can make my way through the hold." For a long time I heard him moving among the lumber, and every moment seemed to me an age. At length I felt his hand upon my shoulder, and he placed, at the same moment, a bottle of water to my lips. Those only who have been suddenly redeemed from the jaws of the tomb, or who have known the insufferable torments of thirst under circumstances as aggravated as those which encompassed me in my dreary prison, can form any idea of the unutterable transports which that one long draught of the richest of all physical luxuries afforded.

When I had in some degree satisfied my thirst, Augustus produced from his pocket three or four boiled potatoes, which I devoured with the greatest avidity. He had brought with him a light in a dark lantern, and the grateful rays afforded me scarcely less comfort than the food and drink. But I was impatient to learn the cause of his protracted absence, and he proceeded to recount what had happened on board during my incarceration.

CHAPTER IV

THE BRIG PUT TO SEA, AS I HAD SUPPOSED, IN ABOUT AN HOUR AFTER HE had left the watch. This was on the twentieth of June. It will be remembered that I had then been in the hold for three days; and, during this period, there was so constant a bustle on board, and so much running to and fro, especially in the cabin and staterooms, that he had had no chance of visiting me without the risk of having the secret of the trap discovered. When at length he did come, I had assured him that I was doing as well as possible; and, therefore, for the two next days he felt but little uneasiness on my account—still, however, watching an opportunity of going down. It was not *until the fourth day* that he found one. Several times during this interval he had made up his mind to let his father know of the adventure, and have me come up at once; but we were still within reaching distance of Nantucket, and it was doubtful, from some expressions which had escaped Captain Barnard, whether he would not immediately put back if he discovered me to be on board. Besides, upon thinking the matter over, Augustus, so he told me, could not imagine that I was in immediate want, or that I would hesitate, in such case, to make myself heard at the trap. When, therefore, he considered everything he concluded to let me stay until he could meet with an opportunity of visiting me unobserved. This, as I said before, did not occur until the fourth day after his bringing me the watch, and the seventh since I had first entered the hold. He then went down without taking with him any water or provisions, intending in the first place merely to call my attention, and get me to come from the box to the trap—when he would go up to the stateroom and thence hand me down a supply. When he descended for this purpose he found that I was asleep, for it seems that

I was snoring very loudly. From all the calculations I can make on the sub-
ject, this must have been the slumber into which I fell just after my return
from the trap with the watch, and which, consequently, must have lasted *for
more than three entire days and nights* at the very least. Latterly, I have had
reason both from my own experience and the assurance of others, to be
acquainted with the strong soporific effects of the stench arising from old
fish-oil when closely confined; and when I think of the condition of the
hold in which I was imprisoned, and the long period during which the brig
had been used as a whaling vessel, I am more inclined to wonder that I
awoke at all, after once falling asleep, than that I should have slept uninter-
ruptedly for the period specified above.

Augustus called to me at first in a low voice and without closing the
trap—but I made him no reply. He then shut the trap, and spoke to me
in a louder, and finally in a very loud tone—still I continued to snore. He
was now at a loss what to do. It would take him some time to make his way
through the lumber to my box, and in the meanwhile his absence would
be noticed by Captain Barnard, who had occasion for his services every
minute, in arranging and copying papers connected with the business of
the voyage. He determined, therefore, upon reflection, to ascend, and
await another opportunity of visiting me. He was the more easily induced
to this resolve, as my slumber appeared to be of the most tranquil nature,
and he could not suppose that I had undergone any inconvenience from
my incarceration. He had just made up his mind on these points when
his attention was arrested by an unusual bustle, the sound of which pro-
ceeded apparently from the cabin. He sprang through the trap as quickly
as possible, closed it, and threw open the door of his stateroom. No sooner
had he put his foot over the threshold than a pistol flashed in his face, and
he was knocked down, at the same moment, by a blow from a handspike.

A strong hand held him on the cabin floor, with a tight grasp upon his
throat; still he was able to see what was going on around him. His father
was tied hand and foot, and lying along the steps of the companion-way,
with his head down, and a deep wound in the forehead, from which the
blood was flowing in a continued stream. He spoke not a word, and was
apparently dying. Over him stood the first mate, eyeing him with an
expression of fiendish derision, and deliberately searching his pockets,
from which he presently drew forth a large wallet and a chronometer.
Seven of the crew (among whom was the cook, a negro) were rummaging
the staterooms on the larboard for arms, where they soon equipped
themselves with muskets and ammunition. Besides Augustus and Captain

Barnard, there were nine men altogether in the cabin, and these among the most ruffianly of the brig's company. The villains now went upon deck, taking my friend with them after having secured his arms behind his back. They proceeded straight to the forecastle, which was fastened down—two of the mutineers standing by it with axes—two also at the main hatch. The mate called out in a loud voice: "Do you hear there below? tumble up with you, one by one—now, mark that—and no grumbling!" It was some minutes before anyone appeared: at last an Englishman, who had shipped as a raw hand, came up, weeping piteously, and entreating the mate, in the most humble manner, to spare his life. The only reply was a blow on the forehead from an axe. The poor fellow fell to the deck without a groan, and the black cook lifted him up in his arms as he would a child, and tossed him deliberately into the sea. Hearing the blow and the plunge of the body, the men below could now be induced to venture on deck neither by threats nor promises, until a proposition was made to smoke them out. A general rush then ensued, and for a moment it seemed possible that the brig might be retaken. The mutineers, however, succeeded at last in closing the forecastle effectually before more than six of their opponents could get up. These six, finding themselves so greatly outnumbered and without arms, submitted after a brief struggle. The mate gave them fair words—no doubt with a view of inducing those below to yield, for they had no difficulty in hearing all that was said on deck. The result proved his sagacity, no less than his diabolical villainy. All in the forecastle presently signified their intention of submitting, and, ascending one by one, were pinioned and then thrown on their backs, together with the first six—there being in all, of the crew who were not concerned in the mutiny, twenty-seven.

A scene of the most horrible butchery ensued. The bound seamen were dragged to the gangway. Here the cook stood with an axe, striking each victim on the head as he was forced over the side of the vessel by the other mutineers. In this manner twenty-two perished, and Augustus had given himself up for lost, expecting every moment his own turn to come next. But it seemed that the villains were now either weary, or in some measure disgusted with their bloody labor; for the four remaining prisoners, together with my friend, who had been thrown on the deck with the rest, were respited while the mate sent below for rum, and the whole murderous party held a drunken carouse, which lasted until sunset. They now fell to disputing in regard to the fate of the survivors, who lay not more than four paces off, and could distinguish every word said. Upon some of the mutineers

the liquor appeared to have a softening effect, for several voices were heard in favor of releasing the captives altogether, on condition of joining the mutiny and sharing the profits. The black cook, however (who in all respects was a perfect demon, and who seemed to exert as much influence, if not more, than the mate himself), would listen to no proposition of the kind, and rose repeatedly for the purpose of resuming his work at the gangway. Fortunately he was so far overcome by intoxication as to be easily restrained by the less blood-thirsty of the party, among whom was a line-manager,[2] who went by the name of Dirk Peters. This man was the son of an Indian squaw of the tribe of Upsarokas, who live among the fastnesses of the Black Hills, near the source of the Missouri. His father was a fur-trader, I believe, or at least connected in some manner with the Indian trading-posts on Lewis river. Peter himself was one of the most ferocious-looking men I ever beheld. He was short in stature, not more than four feet eight inches high, but his limbs were of Herculean mold. His hands, especially, were so enormously thick and broad as hardly to retain a human shape. His arms, as well as legs, were *bowed* in the most singular manner, and appeared to possess no flexibility whatever. His head was equally deformed, being of immense size, with an indentation on the crown (like that on the head of most negroes), and entirely bald. To conceal this latter deficiency, which did not proceed from old age, he usually wore a wig formed of any hair-like material which presented itself—occasionally the skin of a Spanish dog or American grizzly bear. At the time spoken of, he had on a portion of one of these bearskins; and it added no little to the natural ferocity of his countenance, which betook of the Upsaroka character. The mouth extended nearly from ear to ear; the lips were thin, and seemed, like some other portions of his frame, to be devoid of natural pliancy, so that the ruling expression never varied under the influence of any emotion whatever. This ruling expression may be conceived when it is considered that the teeth were exceedingly long and protruding, and never even partially covered, in any instance, by the lips. To pass this man with a casual glance, one might imagine him to be convulsed with laughter—but a second look would induce a shuddering acknowledgment, that if such an expression were indicative of merriment, the merriment must be that of a demon. Of this singular being many anecdotes were prevalent among the seafaring men of Nantucket. These anecdotes went to prove his prodigious strength when under excitement, and some of them had given rise to a doubt of his sanity. But on board the *Grampus*, it seems, he was regarded, at the time of the mutiny, with feelings more of derision than of anything

else. I have been thus particular in speaking of Dirk Peters, because, ferocious as he appeared, he proved the main instrument in preserving the life of Augustus, and because I shall have frequent occasion to mention him hereafter in the course of my narrative—a narrative, let me here say, which, in its latter portions, will be found to include incidents of a nature so entirely out of the range of human experience, and for this reason so far beyond the limits of human credulity, that I proceed in utter hopelessness of obtaining credence for all that I shall tell, yet confidently trusting in time and progressing science to verify some of the most important and most improbable of my statements.

After much indecision and two or three violent quarrels, it was determined at last that all the prisoners (with the exception of Augustus, whom Peters insisted in a jocular manner upon keeping as his clerk) should be set adrift in one of the smallest whaleboats. The mate went down into the cabin to see if Captain Barnard was still living—for, it will be remembered, he was left below when the mutineers came up. Presently the two made their appearance, the captain pale as death, but somewhat recovered from the effects of his wound. He spoke to the men in a voice hardly articulate, entreated them not to set him adrift, but to return to their duty, and promising to land them wherever they chose, and to take no steps for bringing them to justice. He might as well have spoken to the winds. Two of the ruffians seized him by the arms and hurled him over the brig's side into the boat, which had been lowered while the mate went below. The four men who were lying on the deck were then untied and ordered to follow, which they did without attempting any resistance—Augustus being still left in his painful position, although he struggled and prayed only for the poor satisfaction of being permitted to bid his father farewell. A handful of sea-biscuit and a jug of water were now handed down; but neither mast, sail, oar, nor compass. The boat was towed astern for a few minutes, during which the mutineers held another consultation—it was then finally cut adrift. By this time night had come on—there were neither moon nor stars visible—and a short and ugly sea was running, although there was no great deal of wind. The boat was instantly out of sight, and little hope could be entertained for the unfortunate sufferers who were in it. This event happened, however, in latitude 35° 30' north, longitude 61° 20' west, and consequently at no very great distance from the Bermuda Islands. Augustus therefore endeavored to console himself with the idea that the boat might either succeed in reaching the land, or come sufficiently near to be fallen in with by vessels off the coast.

All sail was now put upon the brig, and she continued her original course to the southwest—the mutineers being bent upon some piratical expedition, in which, from all that could be understood, a ship was to be intercepted on her way from the Cape Verd Islands to Porto Rico. No attention was paid to Augustus, who was untied and suffered to go about anywhere forward of the cabin companion-way. Dirk Peters treated him with some degree of kindness, and on one occasion saved him from the brutality of the cook. His situation was still one of the most precarious, as the men were continually intoxicated, and there was no relying upon their continued good-humor or carelessness in regard to himself. His anxiety on my account he represented, however, as the most distressing result of his condition; and, indeed, I had never reason to doubt the sincerity of his friendship. More than once he had resolved to acquaint the muti- neers with the secret of my being on board, but was restrained from so doing, partly through recollection of the atrocities he had already beheld, and partly through a hope of being able soon to bring me relief. For the latter purpose he was constantly on the watch; but, in spite of the most constant vigilance, three days elapsed after the boat was cut adrift before any chance occurred. At length, on the night of the third day, there came on a heavy blow from the eastward, and all hands were called up to take in sail. During the confusion which ensued, he made his way below unob- served, and into the stateroom. What was his grief and horror in discovering that the latter had been rendered a place of deposit for a variety of sea-stores and ship-furniture, and that several fathoms of old chain-cable, which had been stowed away beneath the companion-ladder, had been dragged thence to make room for a chest, and were now lying immediately upon the trap! To remove it without discovery was impos- sible, and he returned on deck as quickly as he could. As he came up, the mate seized him by the throat, and demanding what he had been doing in the cabin, was about flinging him over the larboard bulwark, when his life was again preserved through the interference of Dirk Peters. Augustus was now put in handcuffs (of which there were several pairs on board), and his feet lashed tightly together. He was then taken into the steerage, and thrown into a lower berth next to the forecastle bulkheads, with the assurance that he should never put his foot on deck again "until the brig was no longer a brig." This was the expression of the cook, who threw him into the berth—it is hardly possible to say what precise meaning was intended by the phrase. The whole affair, however, proved the ultimate means of my relief, as will presently appear.

CHAPTER V

FOR SOME MINUTES AFTER THE COOK HAD LEFT THE FORECASTLE, AUGUSTUS abandoned himself to despair, never hoping to leave the berth alive. He now came to the resolution of acquainting the first of the men who should come down with my situation, thinking it better to let me take my chance with the mutineers than perish of thirst in the hold—for it had been ten days since I was first imprisoned, and my jug of water was not a plentiful supply even for four. As he was thinking on this subject, the idea came all at once into his head that it might be possible to communicate with me by the way of the main hold. In any other circumstances, the difficulty and hazard of the undertaking would have prevented him from attempting it; but now he had, at all events, little prospect of life, and consequently little to lose—he bent his whole mind, therefore, upon the task.

His handcuffs were the first consideration. At first he saw no method of removing them, and feared that he should thus be baffled in the very outset; but upon a closer scrutiny he discovered that the irons could be slipped off and on at pleasure, with very little effort or inconvenience, merely by squeezing his hands through them—this species of manacle being altogether ineffectual in confining young persons, in whom the smaller bones readily yield to pressure. He now untied his feet, and, leaving the cord in such a manner that it could easily be readjusted in the event of any person's coming down, proceeded to examine the bulkhead where it joined the berth. The partition here was of soft pine board, an inch thick, and he saw that he should have little trouble in cutting his way through. A voice was now heard at the forecastle companion-way, and he had just time to put his right hand into its handcuff (the left had not been

removed) and to draw the rope in a slip-knot around his ankle, when Dirk Peters came below, followed by Tiger, who immediately leaped into the berth and lay down. The dog had been brought on board by Augustus, who knew my attachment to the animal, and thought it would give me pleasure to have him with me during the voyage. He went up to our house for him immediately after first taking me into the hold, but did not think of mentioning the circumstance upon his bringing the watch. Since the mutiny, Augustus had not seen him before his appearance with Dirk Peters, and had given him up for lost, supposing him to have been thrown overboard by some of the malignant villains belonging to the mate's gang. It appeared afterward that he had crawled into a hole beneath a whale-boat, from which, not having room to turn round, he could not extricate himself. Peters at last let him out, and, with a species of good feeling which my friend knew well how to appreciate, had now brought him to him in the forecastle as a companion, leaving at the same time some salt junk and potatoes, with a can of water; he then went on deck, promising to come down with something more to eat on the next day.

When he had gone, Augustus freed both hands from the manacles and unfastened his feet. He then turned down the head of the mattress on which he had been lying, and with his penknife (for the ruffians had not thought it worthwhile to search him) commenced cutting vigorously across one of the partition planks, as closely as possible to the floor of the berth. He chose to cut here, because, if suddenly interrupted, he would be able to conceal what had been done by letting the head of the mattress fall into its proper position. For the remainder of the day, however, no disturbance occurred, and by night he had completely divided the plank. It should here be observed that none of the crew occupied the forecastle as a sleeping-place, living altogether in the cabin since the mutiny, drink-ing the wines and feasting on the sea-stores of Captain Barnard, and giving no more heed than was absolutely necessary to the navigation of the brig. These circumstances proved fortunate both for myself and Augustus; for, had matters been otherwise, he would have found it impossible to reach me. As it was, he proceeded with confidence in his design. It was near daybreak, however, before he completed the second division of the board (which was about a foot above the first cut), thus making an aperture quite large enough to admit his passage through with facility to the main orlop deck. Having got here, he made his way with but little trouble to the lower main hatch, although in so doing he had to scramble over tiers of oil-casks piled nearly as high as the upper deck, there being barely room enough

left for his body. Upon reaching the hatch he found that Tiger had followed him below, squeezing between two rows of the casks. It was now too late, however, to attempt getting to me before dawn, as the chief difficulty lay in passing through the close stowage in the lower hold. He therefore resolved to return, and wait till the next night. With this design, he proceeded to loosen the hatch, so that he might have as little detention as possible when he should come again. No sooner had he loosened it than Tiger sprang eagerly to the small opening produced, snuffed for a moment, and then uttered a long whine, scratching at the same time, as if anxious to remove the covering with his paws. There could be no doubt, from his behavior, that he was aware of my being in the hold, and Augustus thought it possible that he would be able to get to me if he put him down. He now hit upon the expedient of sending the note, as it was especially desirable that I should make no attempt at forcing my way out, at least under existing circumstances, and there could be no certainty of his getting to me himself on the morrow as he intended. After-events proved how fortunate it was that the idea occurred to him as it did; for, had it not been for the receipt of the note, I should undoubtedly have fallen upon some plan, however desperate, of alarming the crew, and both our lives would most probably have been sacrificed in consequence.

Having concluded to write, the difficulty was now to procure the materials for so doing. An old toothpick was soon made into a pen; and this by means of feeling altogether, for the between-decks was as dark as pitch. Paper enough was obtained from the back of a letter—a duplicate of the forged letter from Mr. Ross. This had been the original draught; but the handwriting not being sufficiently well imitated, Augustus had written another, thrusting the first, by good fortune, into his coat-pocket, where it was now most opportunely discovered. Ink alone was thus wanting, and a substitute was immediately found for this by means of a slight incision with the penknife on the back of a finger just above the nail—a copious flow of blood ensuing, as usual, from wounds in that vicinity. The note was now written, as well as it could be in the dark and under the circumstances. It briefly explained that a mutiny had taken place; that Captain Barnard was set adrift; and that I might expect immediate relief as far as provisions were concerned, but must not venture upon making any disturbance. It concluded with these words: *"I have scrawled this with blood—your life depends upon lying close."*

This slip of paper being tied upon the dog, he was now put down the hatchway, and Augustus made the best of his way back to the forecastle,

where be found no reason to believe that any of the crew had been in his absence. To conceal the hole in the partition, he drove his knife in just above it, and hung up a pea-jacket which he found in the berth. His handcuffs were then replaced, and also the rope around his ankles.

These arrangements were scarcely completed when Dirk Peters came below, very drunk, but in excellent humor, and bringing with him my friend's allowance of provision for the day. This consisted of a dozen large Irish potatoes roasted, and a pitcher of water. He sat for some time on a chest by the berth, and talked freely about the mate and the general concerns of the brig. His demeanor was exceedingly capricious, and even grotesque. At one time Augustus was much alarmed by his odd conduct. At last, however, he went on deck, muttering a promise to bring his prisoner a good dinner on the morrow. During the day two of the crew (harpooners) came down, accompanied by the cook, all three in nearly the last stage of intoxication. Like Peters, they made no scruple of talking unreservedly about their plans. It appeared that they were much divided among themselves as to their ultimate course, agreeing in no point, except the attack on the ship from the Cape Verd Islands, with which they were in hourly expectation of meeting. As far as could be ascertained, the mutiny had not been brought about altogether for the sake of booty; a private pique of the chief mate's against Captain Barnard having been the main instigation. There now seemed to be two principal factions among the crew—one headed by the mate, the other by the cook. The former party were for seizing the first suitable vessel which should present itself, and equipping it at some of the West India Islands for a piratical cruise. The latter division, however, which was the stronger, and included Dirk Peters among its partisans, were bent upon pursuing the course originally laid out for the brig into the South Pacific; there either to take whale, or act otherwise, as circumstances should suggest. The representations of Peters, who had frequently visited these regions, had great weight, apparently, with the mutineers, wavering, as they were, between half-engendered notions of profit and pleasure. He dwelt on the world of novelty and amusement to be found among the innumerable islands of the Pacific, on the perfect security and freedom from all restraint to be enjoyed, but, more particularly, on the deliciousness of the climate, on the abundant means of good living, and on the voluptuous beauty of the women. As yet, nothing had been absolutely determined upon; but the pictures of the hybrid line-manager were taking strong hold upon the ardent imaginations of the seamen, and there was every possibility that his intentions would be finally carried into effect.

The three men went away in about an hour, and no one else entered the forecastle all day. Augustus lay quiet until nearly night. He then freed himself from the rope and irons, and prepared for his attempt. A bottle was found in one of the berths, and this he filled with water from the pitcher left by Peters, storing his pockets at the same time with cold potatoes. To his great joy he also came across a lantern, with a small piece of tallow candle in it. This he could light at any moment, as he had in his possession a box of phosphorous matches. When it was quite dark, he got through the hole in the bulkhead, having taken the precaution to arrange the bedclothes in the berth so as to convey the idea of a person covered up. When through, he hung up the pea-jacket on his knife, as before, to conceal the aperture—this maneuver being easily effected, as he did not readjust the piece of plank taken out until afterward. He was now on the main orlop deck, and proceeded to make his way, as before, between the upper deck and the oil-casks to the main hatchway. Having reached this, he lit the piece of candle, and descended, groping with extreme difficulty among the compact stowage of the hold. In a few moments he became alarmed at the insufferable stench and the closeness of the atmosphere. He could not think it possible that I had survived my confinement for so long a period breathing so oppressive an air. He called my name repeatedly, but I made him no reply, and his apprehensions seemed thus to be confirmed. The brig was rolling violently, and there was so much noise in consequence, that it was useless to listen for any weak sound, such as those of my breathing or snoring. He threw open the lantern, and held it as high as possible, whenever an opportunity occurred, in order that, by observing the light, I might, if alive, be aware that succor was approaching. Still nothing was heard from me, and the supposition of my death began to assume the character of certainty. He determined, nevertheless, to force a passage, if possible, to the box, and at least ascertain beyond a doubt the truth of his surmises. He pushed on for some time in a most pitiable state of anxiety, until, at length, he found the pathway utterly blocked up, and that there was no possibility of making any farther way by the course in which he had set out. Overcome now by his feelings, he threw himself among the lumber in despair, and wept like a child. It was at this period that he heard the crash occasioned by the bottle which I had thrown down. Fortunate, indeed, was it that the incident occurred—for, upon this incident, trivial as it appears, the thread of my destiny depended. Many years elapsed, however, before I was aware of this fact. A natural shame and regret for his weakness and indecision prevented Augustus from confiding to me at

once what a more intimate and unreserved communion afterward induced him to reveal. Upon finding his further progress in the hold impeded by obstacles which he could not overcome, he had resolved to abandon his attempt at reaching me, and return at once to the forecastle. Before condemning him entirely on this head, the harassing circumstances which embarrassed him should be taken into consideration. The night was fast wearing away, and his absence from the forecastle might be discovered; and indeed would necessarily be so, if he should fail to get back to the berth by daybreak. His candle was expiring in the socket, and there would be the greatest difficulty in retracing his way to the hatchway in the dark. It must be allowed, too, that he had every good reason to believe me dead; in which event no benefit could result to me from his reaching the box, and a world of danger would be encountered to no purpose by himself. He had repeatedly called, and I had made him no answer. I had been now eleven days and nights with no more water than that contained in the jug which he had left with me, a supply which it was not at all probable I had hoarded in the beginning of my confinement, as I had every cause to expect a speedy release. The atmosphere of the hold, too, must have appeared to him, coming from the comparatively open air of the steerage, of a nature absolutely poisonous, and by far more intolerable than it had seemed to me upon my first taking up my quarters in the box—the hatchways at that time having been constantly open for many months previous. Add to these considerations that of the scene of bloodshed and terror so lately witnessed by my friend; his confinement, privations, and narrow escapes from death; together with the frail and equivocal tenure by which he still existed—circumstances all so well calculated to prostrate every energy of mind—and the reader will be easily brought, as I have been, to regard his apparent falling off in friendship and in faith with sentiments rather of sorrow than of anger.

The crash of the bottle was distinctly heard, yet Augustus was not sure that it proceeded from the hold. The doubt, however, was sufficient inducement to persevere. He clambered up nearly to the orlop deck by means of the stowage, and then, watching for a lull in the pitchings of the vessel, he called out to me in as loud a tone as he could command— regardless, for the moment, of being overheard by the crew. It will be remembered that on this occasion the voice reached me, but I was so entirely overcome by violent agitation as to be incapable of reply. Confident, now, that his worst apprehensions were well founded, he descended, with a view of getting back to the forecastle without loss of time. In his

haste some small boxes were thrown down, the noise occasioned by which I heard, as will be recollected. He had made considerable progress on his return when the fall of the knife again caused him to hesitate. He retraced his steps immediately, and, clambering up the stowage a second time, called out my name, loudly as before, having watched for a lull. This time I found voice to answer. Overjoyed at discovering me to be still alive, he now resolved to brave every difficulty and danger in reaching me. Having extricated himself as quickly as possible from the labyrinth of lumber by which he was hemmed in, he at length struck into an opening which promised better, and finally, after a series of struggles, arrived at the box in a state of utter exhaustion.

CHAPTER VI

The leading particulars of this narration were all that Augustus communicated to me while we remained near the box. It was not until afterward that he entered fully into all the details. He was apprehensive of being missed, and I was wild with impatience to leave my detested place of confinement. We resolved to make our way at once to the hole in the bulkhead, near which I was to remain for the present, while he went through to reconnoiter. To leave Tiger in the box was what neither of us could endure to think of; yet, how to act otherwise was the question. He now seemed to be perfectly quiet, and we could not even distinguish the sound of his breathing upon applying our ears closely to the box. I was convinced that he was dead, and determined to open the door. We found him lying at full length, apparently in a deep stupor, yet still alive. No time was to be lost, yet I could not bring myself to abandon an animal who had now been twice instrumental in saving my life, without some attempt at preserving him. We therefore dragged him along with us as well as we could, although with the greatest difficulty and fatigue; Augustus, during part of the time, being forced to clamber over the impediments in our way with the huge dog in his arms—a feat to which the feebleness of my frame rendered me totally inadequate. At length we succeeded in reaching the hole, when Augustus got through, and Tiger was pushed in afterward. All was found to be safe, and we did not fail to return sincere thanks to God for our deliverance from the imminent danger we had escaped. For the present, it was agreed that I should remain near the opening, through which my companion could readily supply me with a part of his daily provision, and where I could have the advantages of breathing an atmosphere comparatively pure.

In explanation of some portions of this narrative, wherein I have spoken of the stowage of the brig, and which may appear ambiguous to some of my readers who may have seen a proper or regular stowage, I must here state that the manner in which this most important duty had been performed on board the *Grampus* was a most shameful piece of neglect on the part of Captain Barnard, who was by no means as careful or as experienced a seaman as the hazardous nature of the service on which he was employed would seem necessarily to demand. A proper stowage cannot be accomplished in a careless manner, and many most disastrous accidents, even within the limits of my own experience, have arisen from neglect or ignorance in this particular. Coasting vessels, in the frequent hurry and bustle attendant upon taking in or discharging cargo, are the most liable to mishap from the want of a proper attention to stowage. The great point is to allow no possibility of the cargo or ballast shifting position even in the most violent rollings of the vessel. With this end, great attention must be paid, not only to the bulk taken in, but to the nature of the bulk, and whether there be a full or only a partial cargo. In most kinds of freight the stowage is accomplished by means of a screw. Thus, in a load of tobacco or flour, the whole is screwed so tightly into the hold of the vessel that the barrels or hogsheads, upon discharging, are found to be completely flattened, and take some time to regain their original shape. This screwing, however, is resorted to principally with a view of obtaining more room in the hold; for in a *full* load of any such commodities as flour or tobacco, there can be no danger of any shifting whatever, at least none from which inconvenience can result. There have been instances, indeed, where this method of screwing has resulted in the most lamentable consequences, arising from a cause altogether distinct from the danger attendant upon a shifting of cargo. A load of cotton, for example, tightly screwed while in certain conditions, has been known, through the expansion of its bulk, to rend a vessel asunder at sea. There can be no doubt, either that the same result would ensue in the case of tobacco, while undergoing its usual course of fermentation, were it not for the interstices consequent upon the rotundity of the hogsheads.

It is when a partial cargo is received that danger is chiefly to be apprehended from shifting, and that precautions should be always taken to guard against such misfortune. Only those who have encountered a violent gale of wind, or rather who have experienced the rolling of a vessel in a sudden calm after the gale, can form an idea of the tremendous force of the plunges, and of the consequent terrible impetus given to all loose

articles in the vessel. It is then that the necessity of a cautious stowage, when there is a partial cargo, becomes obvious. When lying-to (especially with a small head sail), a vessel which is not properly modeled in the bows is frequently thrown upon her beam-ends; this occurring even every fifteen or twenty minutes upon an average, yet without any serious consequences resulting, *provided there be a proper stowage.* If this, however, has not been strictly attended to, in the first of these heavy lurches the whole of the cargo tumbles over to the side of the vessel which lies upon the water, and, being thus prevented from regaining her equilibrium, as she would otherwise necessarily do, she is certain to fill in a few seconds and go down. It is not too much to say that at least one half of the instances in which vessels have foundered in heavy gales at sea may be attributed to a shifting of cargo or of ballast.

When a partial cargo of any kind is taken on board, the whole, after being first stowed as compactly as may be, should be covered with a layer of stout shifting-boards, extending completely across the vessel. Upon these boards strong temporary stanchions should be erected, reaching to the timbers above, and thus securing everything in its place. In cargoes consisting of grain, or any similar matter, additional precautions are requisite. A hold filled entirely with grain upon leaving port will be found not more than three fourths full upon reaching its destination—this, too, although the freight, when measured bushel by bushel by the consignee, will overrun by a vast deal (on account of the swelling of the grain) the quantity consigned. This result is occasioned by *settling* during the voyage, and is the more perceptible in proportion to the roughness of the weather experienced. If grain loosely thrown in a vessel, then, is ever so well secured by shifting-boards and stanchions, it will be liable to shift in a long passage so greatly as to bring about the most distressing calamities. To prevent these, every method should be employed before leaving port to *settle* the cargo as much as possible; and for this there are many contrivances, among which may be mentioned the driving of wedges into the grain. Even after all this is done, and unusual pains taken to secure the shifting-boards, no seaman who knows what he is about will feel altogether secure in a gale of any violence with a cargo of grain on board, and, least of all, with a partial cargo. Yet there are hundreds of our coasting vessels, and, it is likely, many more from the ports of Europe, which sail daily with partial cargoes, even of the most dangerous species, and without any precaution whatever. The wonder is that no more accidents occur than do actually happen. A lamentable instance of this heedlessness

occurred to my knowledge in the case of Captain Joel Rice of the schooner *Firefly*, which sailed from Richmond, Virginia, to Madeira, with a cargo of corn, in the year 1825. The captain had gone many voyages without serious accident, although he was in the habit of paying no attention whatever to his stowage, more than to secure it in the ordinary manner. He had never before sailed with a cargo of grain, and on this occasion had the corn thrown on board loosely, when it did not much more than half fill the vessel. For the first portion of the voyage he met with nothing more than light breezes; but when within a day's sail of Madeira there came on a strong gale from the N. N. E. which forced him to lie-to. He brought the schooner to the wind under a double-reefed foresail alone, when she rode as well as any vessel could be expected to do, and shipped not a drop of water. Towards night the gale somewhat abated, and she rolled with more unsteadiness than before, but still did very well, until a heavy lurch threw her upon her beam-ends to starboard. The corn was then heard to shift bodily, the force of the movement bursting open the main hatchway. The vessel went down like a shot. This happened within hail of a small sloop from Madeira, which picked up one of the crew (the only person saved), and which rode out the gale in perfect security, as indeed a jollyboat might have done under proper management.

The stowage on board the *Grampus* was most clumsily done, if stowage that could be called which was little better than a promiscuous huddling together of oil-casks* and ship furniture. I have already spoken of the condition of articles in the hold. On the orlop deck there was space enough for my body (as I have stated) between the oil-casks and the upper deck; a space was left open around the main hatchway; and several other large spaces were left in the stowage. Near the hole cut through the bulkhead by Augustus there was room enough for an entire cask, and in this space I found myself comfortably situated for the present.

By the time my friend had got safely into the berth, and readjusted his handcuffs and the rope, it was broad daylight. We had made a narrow escape indeed; for scarcely had he arranged all matters, when the mate came below, with Dirk Peters and the cook. They talked for some time about the vessel from the Cape Verds, and seemed to be excessively anxious for her appearance. At length the cook came to the berth in which

* Whaling vessels are usually fitted with iron oil-tanks—why the *Grampus* was not I have never been able to ascertain.

Augustus was lying, and seated himself in it near the head. I could see and hear everything from my hiding-place, for the piece cut out had not been put back, and I was in momentary expectation that the negro would fall against the pea-jacket, which was hung up to conceal the aperture, in which case all would have been discovered, and our lives would, no doubt, have been instantly sacrificed. Our good fortune prevailed, however; and although he frequently touched it as the vessel rolled, he never pressed against it sufficiently to bring about a discovery. The bottom of the jacket had been carefully fastened to the bulkhead, so that the hole might not be seen by its swinging to one side. All this time Tiger was lying in the foot of the berth, and appeared to have recovered in some measure his faculties, for I could see him occasionally open his eyes and draw a long breath.

After a few minutes the mate and cook went above, leaving Dirk Peters behind, who, as soon as they were gone, came and sat himself down in the place just occupied by the mate. He began to talk very sociably with Augustus, and we could now see that the greater part of his apparent intoxication, while the two others were with him, was a feint. He answered all my companion's questions with perfect freedom; told him that he had no doubt of his father's having been picked up, as there were no less than five sail in sight just before sundown on the day he was cut adrift; and used other language of a consolatory nature, which occasioned me no less surprise than pleasure. Indeed, I began to entertain hopes, that through the instrumentality of Peters we might be finally enabled to regain possession of the brig, and this idea I mentioned to Augustus as soon as I found an opportunity. He thought the matter possible, but urged the necessity of the greatest caution in making the attempt, as the conduct of the hybrid appeared to be instigated by the most arbitrary caprice alone; and, indeed, it was difficult to say if he was at any moment of sound mind. Peters went upon deck in about an hour, and did not return again until noon, when he brought Augustus a plentiful supply of junk beef and pudding. Of this, when we were left alone, I partook heartily, without returning through the hole. No one else came down into the forecastle during the day, and at night, I got into Augustus' berth, where I slept soundly and sweetly until nearly daybreak, when he awakened me upon hearing a stir upon deck, and I regained my hiding-place as quickly as possible. When the day was fully broke, we found that Tiger had recovered his strength almost entirely, and gave no indications of hydrophobia, drinking a little water that was offered him

with great apparent eagerness. During the day he regained all his former vigor and appetite. His strange conduct had been brought on, no doubt, by the deleterious quality of the air of the hold, and had no connection with canine madness. I could not sufficiently rejoice that I had persisted in bringing him with me from the box. This day was the thirtieth of June, and the thirteenth since the *Grampus* made sail from Nantucket.

On the second of July the mate came below drunk as usual, and in an excessively good humor. He came to Augustus' berth, and, giving him a slap on the back, asked him if he thought he could behave himself if he let him loose, and whether he would promise not to be going into the cabin again. To this, of course, my friend answered in the affirmative, when the ruffian set him at liberty, after making him drink from a flask of rum which he drew from his coat-pocket. Both now went on deck, and I did not see Augustus for about three hours. He then came below with the good news that he had obtained permission to go about the brig as he pleased anywhere forward of the mainmast, and that he had been ordered to sleep, as usual, in the forecastle. He brought me, too, a good dinner, and a plentiful supply of water. The brig was still cruising for the vessel from the Cape Verds, and a sail was now in sight, which was thought to be the one in question. As the events of the ensuing eight days were of little importance, and had no direct bearing upon the main incidents of my narrative, I will here throw them into the form of a journal, as I do not wish to omit them altogether.

July 3. Augustus furnished me with three blankets, with which I contrived a comfortable bed in my hiding-place. No one came below, except my companion, during the day. Tiger took his station in the berth just by the aperture, and slept heavily, as if not yet entirely recovered from the effects of his sickness. Towards night a flaw of wind struck the brig before sail could be taken in, and very nearly capsized her. The puff died away immediately, however, and no damage was done beyond the splitting of the foretopsail. Dirk Peters treated Augustus all this day with great kindness and entered into a long conversation with him respecting the Pacific Ocean, and the islands he had visited in that region. He asked him whether he would not like to go with the mutineers on a kind of exploring and pleasure voyage in those quarters, and said that the men were gradually coming over to the mate's views. To this Augustus thought it best to reply that he would be glad to go on such an adventure, since nothing better could be done, and that anything was preferable to a piratical life.

July 4ᵗʰ. The vessel in sight proved to be a small brig from Liverpool, and was allowed to pass unmolested. Augustus spent most of his time on deck, with a view of obtaining all the information in his power respecting the intentions of the mutineers. They had frequent and violent quarrels among themselves, in one of which a harpooner, Jim Bonner, was thrown overboard. The party of the mate was gaining ground. Jim Bonner belonged to the cook's gang, of which Peters was a partisan.

July 5ᵗʰ. About daybreak there came on a stiff breeze from the west, which at noon freshened into a gale, so that the brig could carry nothing more than her trysail and foresail. In taking in the foretopsail, Simms, one of the common hands, and belonging also to the cook's gang, fell overboard, being very much in liquor, and was drowned—no attempt being made to save him. The whole number of persons on board was now thirteen, to wit: Dirk Peters; Seymour, the black cook; —— Jones, —— Greely, Hartman Rogers; and William Allen, of the cook's party; the mate, whose name I never learned; Absalom Hicks; —— Wilson; John Hunt; Richard Parker, of the mate's party—besides Augustus and myself.

July 6ᵗʰ. The gale lasted all this day, blowing in heavy squalls, accompanied with rain. The brig took in a good deal of water through her seams, and one of the pumps was kept continually going, Augustus being forced to take his turn. Just at twilight a large ship passed close by us, without having been discovered until within hail. The ship was supposed to be the one for which the mutineers were on the look-out. The mate hailed her, but the reply was drowned in the roaring of the gale. At eleven, a sea was shipped amidships, which tore away a great portion of the larboard bulwarks, and did some other slight damage. Towards morning the weather moderated, and at sunrise there was very little wind.

July 7ᵗʰ. There was a heavy swell running all this day, during which the brig, being light, rolled excessively, and many articles broke loose in the hold, as I could hear distinctly from my hiding-place. I suffered a great deal from sea-sickness. Peters had a long conversation this day with Augustus, and told him that two of his gang, Greely and Allen, had gone over to the mate, and were resolved to turn pirates. He put several questions to Augustus which he did not then exactly understand. During a part of this evening the leak gained upon the vessel; and little could be done to remedy it, as it was occasioned by the brig's straining, and taking in the water

through her seams. A sail was thrummed, and got under the bows, which aided us in some measure, so that we began to gain upon the leak.

July 8th. A light breeze sprang up at sunrise from the eastward, when the mate headed the brig to the southwest, with the intention of making some of the West India islands in pursuance of his piratical designs. No opposition was made by Peters or the cook—at least none in the hearing of Augustus. All idea of taking the vessel from the Cape Verds was abandoned. The leak was now easily kept under by one pump going every three quarters of an hour. The sail was drawn from beneath the bows. Spoke two small schooners during the day.

July 9th. Fine weather. All hands employed in repairing bulwarks. Peters had again a long conversation with Augustus, and spoke more plainly than he had done heretofore. He said nothing should induce him to come into the mate's views, and even hinted his intention of taking the brig out of his hands. He asked my friend if he could depend upon his aid in such case, to which Augustus said, "Yes," without hesitation. Peters then said he would sound the others of his party upon the subject, and went away. During the remainder of the day Augustus had no opportunity of speaking with him privately.

CHAPTER VII

JULY 10. SPOKE A BRIG FROM RIO, BOUND TO NORFOLK. WEATHER HAZY, with a light baffling wind from the eastward. Today Hartman Rogers died, having been attacked on the eighth with spasms after drinking a glass of grog. This man was of the cook's party, and one upon whom Peters placed his main reliance. He told Augustus that he believed the mate had poisoned him, and that he expected, if he did not be on the look-out, his own turn would come shortly. There were now only himself, Jones, and the cook belonging to his own gang—on the other side there were five. He had spoken to Jones about taking the command from the mate; but the project having been coolly received, he had been deterred from pressing the matter any further, or from saying anything to the cook. It was well, as it happened, that he was so prudent, for in the afternoon the cook expressed his determination of siding with the mate, and went over formally to that party; while Jones took an opportunity of quarreling with Peters, and hinted that he would let the mate know of the plan in agitation. There was now, evidently, no time to be lost, and Peters expressed his determination of attempting to take the vessel at all hazards, provided Augustus would lend him his aid. My friend at once assured him of his willingness to enter into any plan for that purpose, and, thinking the opportunity a favorable one, made known the fact of my being on board. At this the hybrid was not more astonished than delighted, as he had no reliance whatever upon Jones, whom he already considered as belonging to the party of the mate. They went below immediately, when Augustus called to me by name, and Peters and myself were soon made acquainted. It was agreed that we should attempt to retake the vessel upon the first

good opportunity, leaving Jones altogether out of our councils. In the event of success, we were to run the brig into the first port that offered, and deliver her up. The desertion of his party had frustrated Peters' design of going into the Pacific—an adventure which could not be accomplished without a crew, and he depended upon either getting acquitted upon trial, on the score of insanity (which he solemnly avowed had actuated him in lending his aid to the mutiny), or upon obtaining a pardon, if found guilty, through the representations of Augustus and myself. Our deliberations were interrupted for the present by the cry of, "All hands take in sail," and Peters and Augustus ran up on deck.

As usual, the crew were nearly all drunk; and, before sail could be properly taken in, a violent squall laid the brig on her beam-ends. By keeping her away, however, she righted, having shipped a good deal of water. Scarcely was everything secure, when another squall took the vessel, and immediately afterward another—no damage being done. There was every appearance of a gale of wind, which, indeed, shortly came on, with great fury, from the northward and westward. All was made as snug as possible, and we laid-to, as usual, under a close-reefed foresail. As night drew on, the wind increased in violence, with a remarkably heavy sea. Peters now came into the forecastle with Augustus, and we resumed our deliberations.

We agreed that no opportunity could be more favorable than the present for carrying our designs into effect, as an attempt at such a moment would never be anticipated. As the brig was snugly laid-to, there would be no necessity of maneuvering her until good weather, when, if we succeeded in our attempt, we might liberate one, or perhaps two of the men, to aid us in taking her into port. The main difficulty was the great disproportion in our forces. There were only three of us, and in the cabin there were nine. All the arms on board, too, were in their possession, with the exception of a pair of small pistols which Peters had concealed about his person, and the large seaman's knife which he always wore in the waistband of his pantaloons. From certain indications, too, such, for example, as there being no such thing as an axe or a handspike lying in their customary places, we began to fear that the mate had his suspicions, at least in regard to Peters, and that he would let slip no opportunity of getting rid of him. It was clear, indeed, that what we should determine to do could not be done too soon. Still the odds were too much against us to allow of our proceeding without the greatest caution.

Peters proposed that he should go up on deck, and enter into conversation with the watch (Allen), when he would be able to throw him into

the sea without trouble, and without making any disturbance, by seizing a good opportunity; that Augustus and myself should then come up, and endeavor to provide ourselves with some kind of weapons from the deck; and that we should then make a rush together, and secure the companion-way before any opposition could be offered. I objected to this, because I could not believe that the mate (who was a cunning fellow in all matters which did not affect his superstitious prejudices) would suffer himself to be so easily entrapped. The very fact of there being a watch on deck at all was sufficient proof that he was upon the alert—it not being usual, except in vessels where discipline is most rigidly enforced, to station a watch on deck when a vessel is lying-to in a gale of wind. As I address myself principally, if not altogether, to persons who have never been to sea, it may be as well to state the exact condition of a vessel under such circumstances. Lying-to, or, in sea-parlance, "laying-to," is a measure resorted to for various purposes, and effected in various manners. In moderate weather it is frequently done with a view of merely bringing the vessel to a stand-still, to wait for another vessel, or any similar object. If the vessel which lies-to is under full sail, the maneuver is usually accomplished by throwing round some portion of her sails, so as to let the wind take them aback, when she becomes stationary. But we are now speaking of lying-to in a gale of wind. This is done when the wind is ahead, and too violent to admit of carrying sail without danger of capsizing; and sometimes even when the wind is fair, but the sea too heavy for the vessel to be put before it. If a vessel be suffered to scud before the wind in a very heavy sea, much damage is usually done her by the shipping of water over her stern, and sometimes by the violent plunges she makes forward. This maneuver, then, is seldom resorted to in such case, unless through necessity. When the vessel is in a leaky condition she is often put before the wind even in the heaviest seas; for, when lying-to, her seams are sure to be greatly opened by her violent straining, and it is not so much the case when scudding. Often, too, it becomes necessary to scud a vessel, either when the blast is so exceedingly furious as to tear in pieces the sail which is employed with a view of bringing her head to the wind, or when, through the false modeling of the frame or other causes, this main object cannot be effected.

Vessels in a gale of wind are laid-to in different manners, according to their peculiar construction. Some lie-to best under a foresail, and this, I believe, is the sail most usually employed. Large square-rigged vessels have sails for the express purpose, called storm-staysails. But the jib is occasionally employed by itself—sometimes the jib and foresail, or a double-reefed

foresail, and not unfrequently the after-sails, are made use of. Foretopsails are very often found to answer the purpose better than any other species of sail. The *Grampus* was generally laid-to under a close-reefed foresail.

When a vessel is to be laid-to, her head is brought up to the wind just so nearly as to fill the sail under which she lies when hauled flat aft, that is, when brought diagonally across the vessel. This being done, the bows point within a few degrees of the direction from which the wind issues, and the windward bow of course receives the shock of the waves. In this situation a good vessel will ride out a very heavy gale of wind without shipping a drop of water, and without any further attention being requisite on the part of the crew. The helm is usually lashed down, but this is altogether unnecessary (except on account of the noise it makes when loose), for the rudder has no effect upon the vessel when lying-to. Indeed, the helm had far better be left loose than lashed very fast, for the rudder is apt to be torn off by heavy seas if there be no room for the helm to play. As long as the sail holds, a well-modeled vessel will maintain her situation, and ride every sea, as if instinct with life and reason. If the violence of the wind, however, should tear the sail into pieces (a feat which it requires a perfect hurricane to accomplish under ordinary circumstances), there is then imminent danger. The vessel falls off from the wind, and, coming broadside to the sea, is completely at its mercy: the only resource in this case is to put her quietly before the wind, letting her scud until some other sail can be set. Some vessels will lie-to under no sail whatever, but such are not to be trusted at sea.

But to return from this digression. It had never been customary with the mate to have any watch on deck when lying-to in a gale of wind, and the fact that he had now one, coupled with the circumstance of the missing axes and handspikes, fully convinced us that the crew were too well on the watch to be taken by surprise in the manner Peters had suggested. Something, however, was to be done, and that with as little delay as practicable, for there could be no doubt that a suspicion having been once entertained against Peters, he would be sacrificed upon the earliest occasion, and one would certainly be either found or made upon the breaking of the gale.

Augustus now suggested that if Peters could contrive to remove, under any pretext, the piece of chain-cable which lay over the trap in the stateroom, we might possibly be able to come upon them unawares by means of the hold; but a little reflection convinced us that the vessel rolled and pitched too violently for any attempt of that nature.

By good fortune I at length hit upon the idea of working upon the superstitious terrors and guilty conscience of the mate. It will be remembered that one of the crew, Hartman Rogers, had died during the morning, having been attacked two days before with spasms after drinking some spirits and water. Peters had expressed to us his opinion that this man had been poisoned by the mate, and for this belief he had reasons, so he said, which were incontrovertible, but which he could not be prevailed upon to explain to us—this wayward refusal being only in keeping with other points of his singular character. But whether or not he had any better grounds for suspecting the mate than we had ourselves, we were easily led to fall in with his suspicion, and determined to act accordingly.

Rogers had died about eleven in the forenoon, in violent convulsions; and the corpse presented in a few minutes after death one of the most horrid and loathsome spectacles I ever remember to have seen. The stomach was swollen immensely, like that of a man who has been drowned and lain under water for many weeks. The hands were in the same condition, while the face was shrunken, shriveled, and of a chalky whiteness, except where relieved by two or three glaring red blotches like those occasioned by the erysipelas: one of these blotches extended diagonally across the face, completely covering up an eye as if with a band of red velvet. In this disgusting condition the body had been brought up from the cabin at noon to be thrown overboard, when the mate getting a glimpse of it (for he now saw it for the first time), and being either touched with remorse for his crime or struck with terror at so horrible a sight, ordered the men to sew the body up in its hammock, and allow it the usual rites of sea-burial. Having given these directions, he went below, as if to avoid any further sight of his victim. While preparations were making to obey his orders, the gale came on with great fury, and the design was abandoned for the present. The corpse, left to itself, was washed into the larboard scuppers, where it still lay at the time of which I speak, floundering about with the furious lurches of the brig.

Having arranged our plan, we set about putting it in execution as speedily as possible. Peters went upon deck, and, as he had anticipated, was immediately accosted by Allen, who appeared to be stationed more as a watch upon the forecastle than for any other purpose. The fate of this villain, however, was speedily and silently decided; for Peters, approaching him in a careless manner, as if about to address him, seized him by the throat, and, before he could utter a single cry, tossed him over the bulwarks. He then called to us, and we came up. Our first precaution was to

look about for something with which to arm ourselves, and in doing this we had to proceed with great care, for it was impossible to stand on deck an instant without holding fast, and violent seas broke over the vessel at every plunge forward. It was indispensable, too, that we should be quick in our operations, for every minute we expected the mate to be up to set the pumps going, as it was evident the brig must be taking in water very fast. After searching about for some time, we could find nothing more fit for our purpose than the two pump-handles, one of which Augustus took, and I the other. Having secured these, we stripped off the shirt of the corpse and dropped the body overboard. Peters and myself then went below, leaving Augustus to watch upon deck, where he took his station just where Allen had been placed, and with his back to the cabin companion-way, so that, if any of the mate's gang should come up, he might suppose it was the watch.

As soon as I got below I commenced disguising myself so as to represent the corpse of Rogers. The shirt which we had taken from the body aided us very much, for it was of singular form and character, and easily recognizable—a kind of smock, which the deceased wore over his other clothing. It was a blue stockinet, with large white stripes running across. Having put this on, I proceeded to equip myself with a false stomach, in imitation of the horrible deformity of the swollen corpse. This was soon effected by means of stuffing with some bedclothes. I then gave the same appearance to my hands by drawing on a pair of white woolen mittens, and filling them in with any kind of rags that offered themselves. Peters then arranged my face, first rubbing it well over with white chalk, and afterward blotching it with blood, which he took from a cut in his finger. The streak across the eye was not forgotten and presented a most shocking appearance.

CHAPTER VIII

As I viewed myself in a fragment of looking-glass which hung up in the cabin, and by the dim light of a kind of battle-lantern, I was so impressed with a sense of vague awe at my appearance, and at the recollection of the terrific reality which I was thus representing, that I was seized with a violent tremor, and could scarcely summon resolution to go on with my part. It was necessary, however, to act with decision, and Peters and myself went upon deck.

We there found everything safe, and, keeping close to the bulwarks, the three of us crept to the cabin companion-way. It was only partially closed, precautions having been taken to prevent its being suddenly pushed to from without, by means of placing billets of wood on the upper step so as to interfere with the shutting. We found no difficulty in getting a full view of the interior of the cabin through the cracks where the hinges were placed. It now proved to have been very fortunate for us that we had not attempted to take them by surprise, for they were evidently on the alert. Only one was asleep, and he lying just at the foot of the companion-ladder, with a musket by his side. The rest were seated on several mattresses, which had been taken from the berths and thrown on the floor. They were engaged in earnest conversation; and although they had been carousing, as appeared from two empty jugs, with some tin tumblers which lay about, they were not as much intoxicated as usual. All had knives, one or two of them pistols, and a great many muskets were lying in a berth close at hand.

We listened to their conversation for some time before we could make up our minds how to act, having as yet resolved on nothing determinate, except that we would attempt to paralyze their exertions, when we should

attack them, by means of the apparition of Rogers. They were discussing their piratical plans, in which all we could hear distinctly was, that they would unite with the crew of a schooner *Hornet,* and, if possible, get the schooner herself into their possession preparatory to some attempt on a large scale, the particulars of which could not be made out by either of us.

One of the men spoke of Peters, when the mate replied to him in a low voice which could not be distinguished, and afterward added more loudly, that "he could not understand his being so much forward with the captain's brat in the forecastle, and he thought the sooner both of them were overboard the better." To this no answer was made, but we could easily perceive that the hint was well received by the whole party, and more particularly by Jones. At this period I was excessively agitated, the more so as I could see that neither Augustus nor Peters could determine how to act. I made up my mind, however, to sell my life as dearly as possible, and not to suffer myself to be overcome by any feelings of trepidation.

The tremendous noise made by the roaring of the wind in the rigging, and the washing of the sea over the deck, prevented us from hearing what was said, except during momentary lulls. In one of these, we all distinctly heard the mate tell one of the men to "go forward, and order the d——d lubbers to come into the cabin, where he could have an eye upon them, for he wanted no such secret doings on board the brig." It was well for us that the pitching of the vessel at this moment was so violent as to prevent this order from being carried into instant execution. The cook got up from his mattress to go for us, when a tremendous lurch, which I thought would carry away the masts, threw him headlong against one of the larboard stateroom doors, bursting it open, and creating a good deal of other confusion. Luckily, neither of our party was thrown from his position, and we had time to make a precipitate retreat to the forecastle, and arrange a hurried plan of action before the messenger made his appearance, or rather before he put his head out of the companion-hatch, for he did not come on deck. From this station he could not notice the absence of Allen, and he accordingly bawled out, as if to him, repeating the orders of the mate. Peters cried out, "Ay, ay," in a disguised voice, and the cook immediately went below, without entertaining a suspicion that all was not right.

My two companions now proceeded boldly aft and down into the cabin, Peters closing the door after him in the same manner he had found it. The mate received them with feigned cordiality, and told Augustus that, since he had behaved himself so well of late, he might take up his quarters in the cabin and be one of them for the future. He then poured him out

a tumbler half full of rum, and made him drink it. All this I saw and heard, for I followed my friends to the cabin as soon as the door was shut, and took up my old point of observation. I had brought with me the two pump-handles, one of which I secured near the companion-way, to be ready for use when required.

I now steadied myself as well as possible so as to have a good view of all that was passing within, and endeavored to nerve myself to the task of descending among the mutineers when Peters should make a signal to me, as agreed upon. Presently he contrived to turn the conversation upon the bloody deeds of the mutiny, and by degrees led the men to talk of the thousand superstitions which are so universally current among seamen. I could not make out all that was said, but I could plainly see the effects of the conversation in the countenances of those present. The mate was evidently much agitated, and presently, when someone mentioned the terrific appearance of Rogers' corpse, I thought he was upon the point of swooning. Peters now asked him if he did not think it would be better to have the body thrown overboard at once as it was too horrible a sight to see it floundering about in the scuppers. At this the villain absolutely gasped for breath, and turned his head slowly round upon his companions, as if imploring someone to go up and perform the task. No one, however, stirred, and it was quite evident that the whole party were wound up to the highest pitch of nervous excitement. Peters now made me the signal. I immediately threw open the door of the companion-way, and, descending, without uttering a syllable, stood erect in the midst of the party.

The intense effect produced by this sudden apparition is not at all to be wondered at when the various circumstances are taken into consideration. Usually, in cases of a similar nature, there is left in the mind of the spectator some glimmering of doubt as to the reality of the vision before his eyes; a degree of hope, however feeble, that he is the victim of chicanery, and that the apparition is not actually a visitant from the old world of shadows. It is not too much to say that such remnants of doubt have been at the bottom of almost every such visitation, and that the appalling horror which has sometimes been brought about, is to be attributed, even in the cases most in point, and where most suffering has been experienced, more to a kind of anticipative horror, lest the apparition *might possibly be* real, than to an unwavering belief in its reality. But, in the present instance, it will be seen immediately, that in the minds of the mutineers there was not even the shadow of a basis upon which to rest a doubt that the apparition of Rogers was indeed a revivification of his

disgusting corpse, or at least its spiritual image. The isolated situation of the brig, with its entire inaccessibility on account of the gale, confined the apparently possible means of deception within such narrow and definite limits, that they must have thought themselves enabled to survey them all at a glance. They had now been at sea twenty-four days, without holding more than a speaking communication with any vessel whatever. The whole of the crew, too, at least all whom they had the most remote reason for suspecting to be on board, were assembled in the cabin, with the exception of Allen, the watch; and his gigantic stature (he was six feet six inches high) was too familiar in their eyes to permit the notion that he was the apparition before them to enter their minds even for an instant. Add to these considerations the awe-inspiring nature of the tempest, and that of the conversation brought about by Peters; the deep impression which the loathsomeness of the actual corpse had made in the morning upon the imaginations of the men; the excellence of the imitation in my person; and the uncertain and wavering light in which they beheld me, as the glare of the cabin lantern, swinging violently to and fro, fell dubiously and fitfully upon my figure, and there will be no reason to wonder that the deception had even more than the entire effect which we had anticipated. The mate sprang up from the mattress on which he was lying, and, without uttering a syllable, fell back, stone dead, upon the cabin floor, and was hurled to the leeward like a log by a heavy roll of the brig. Of the remaining seven, there were but three who had at first any degree of presence of mind. The four others sat for some time rooted apparently to the floor, the most pitiable objects of horror and utter despair my eyes ever encountered. The only opposition we experienced at all was from the cook, John Hunt, and Richard Parker; but they made but a feeble and irresolute defence. The two former were shot instantly by Peters, and I felled Parker with a blow on the head from the pump-handle which I had brought with me. In the meantime, Augustus seized one of the muskets lying on the floor and shot another mutineer (——Wilson) through the breast. There were now but three remaining; but by this time they had become aroused from their lethargy, and perhaps began to see that a deception had been practiced upon them, for they fought with great resolution and fury, and, but for the immense muscular strength of Peters, might have ultimately got the better of us. These three men were —— Jones, —— Greely, and Absalom Hicks. Jones had thrown Augustus to the floor, stabbed him in several places along the right arm, and would no doubt have soon dispatched

him (as neither Peters nor myself could immediately get rid of our own antagonists), had it not been for the timely aid of a friend, upon whose assistance we, surely, had never depended. This friend was no other than Tiger. With a low growl, he bounded into the cabin, at a most critical moment for Augustus, and throwing himself upon Jones, pinned him to the floor in an instant. My friend, however, was now too much injured to render us any aid whatever, and I was so encumbered with my disguise that I could do but little. The dog would not leave his hold upon the throat of Jones—Peters, nevertheless, was far more than a match for the two men who remained, and would, no doubt, have dispatched them sooner, had it not been for the narrow space in which he had to act, and the tremendous lurches of the vessel. Presently he was enabled to get hold of a heavy stool, several of which lay about the floor. With this he beat out the brains of Greely as he was in the act of discharging a musket at me, and immediately afterward a roll of the brig throwing him in contact with Hicks, he seized him by the throat, and, by dint of sheer strength, strangled him instantaneously. Thus, in far less time than I have taken to tell it, we found ourselves masters of the brig.

The only person of our opponents who was left alive was Richard Parker. This man, it will be remembered, I had knocked down with a blow from the pump-handle at the commencement of the attack. He now lay motionless by the door of the shattered stateroom; but, upon Peters touching him with his foot, he spoke, and entreated for mercy. His head was only slightly cut, and otherwise he had received no injury, having been merely stunned by the blow. He now got up, and, for the present, we secured his hands behind his back. The dog was still growling over Jones; but, upon examination, we found him completely dead, the blood issuing in a stream from a deep wound in the throat, inflicted, no doubt, by the sharp teeth of the animal.

It was now about one o'clock in the morning, and the wind was still blowing tremendously. The brig evidently labored much more than usual, and it became absolutely necessary that something should be done with a view of easing her in some measure. At almost every roll to leeward she shipped a sea, several of which came partially down into the cabin during our scuffle, the hatchway having been left open by myself when I descended. The entire range of bulwarks to larboard had been swept away, as well as the caboose, together with the jollyboat from the counter. The creaking and working of the mainmast, too, gave indication that it was nearly sprung. To make room for more stowage in the afterhold, the

heel of this mast had been stepped between decks (a very reprehensible practice, occasionally resorted to by ignorant ship-builders), so that it was in imminent danger of working from its step. But, to crown all our difficulties, we plumbed the well, and found no less than seven feet of water.

Leaving the bodies of the crew lying in the cabin, we got to work immediately at the pumps—Parker, of course, being set at liberty to assist us in the labor. Augustus' arm was bound up as well as we could effect it, and he did what he could, but that was not much. However, we found that we could just manage to keep the leak from gaining upon us by having one pump constantly going. As there were only four of us, this was severe labor; but we endeavored to keep up our spirits, and looked anxiously for daybreak, when we hoped to lighten the brig by cutting away the mainmast.

In this manner we passed a night of terrible anxiety and fatigue, and, when the day at length broke, the gale had neither abated in the least, nor were there any signs of its abating. We now dragged the bodies on deck and threw them overboard. Our next care was to get rid of the mainmast. The necessary preparations having been made, Peters cut away at the mast (having found axes in the cabin), while the rest of us stood by the stays and lanyards. As the brig gave a tremendous lee-lurch, the word was given to cut away the weather-lanyards, which being done, the whole mass of wood and rigging plunged into the sea, clear of the brig, and without doing any material injury. We now found that the vessel did not labor quite as much as before, but our situation was still exceedingly precarious, and in spite of the utmost exertions, we could not gain upon the leak without the aid of both pumps. The little assistance which Augustus could render us was not really of any importance. To add to our distress, a heavy sea, striking the brig to the windward, threw her off several points from the wind, and, before she could regain her position, another broke completely over her, and hurled her full upon her beam-ends. The ballast now shifted in a mass to leeward (the stowage had been knocking about perfectly at random for some time), and for a few moments we thought nothing could save us from capsizing. Presently, however, we partially righted; but the ballast still retaining its place to larboard, we lay so much along that it was useless to think of working the pumps, which indeed we could not have done much longer in any case, as our hands were entirely raw with the excessive labor we had undergone, and were bleeding in the most horrible manner.

Contrary to Parker's advice, we now proceeded to cut away the foremast, and at length accomplished it after much difficulty, owing to the

position in which we lay. In going overboard the wreck took with it the bowsprit, and left us a complete hulk.

So far we had had reason to rejoice in the escape of our longboat, which had received no damage from any of the huge seas which had come on board. But we had not long to congratulate ourselves; for the foremast having gone, and, of course, the foresail with it, by which the brig had been steadied, every sea now made a complete breach over us, and in five minutes our deck was swept from stem to stern, the longboat and starboard bulwarks torn off, and even the windlass shattered into fragments. It was, indeed, hardly possible for us to be in a more pitiable condition.

At noon there seemed to be some slight appearance of the gale's abating, but in this we were sadly disappointed, for it only lulled for a few minutes to blow with redoubled fury. About four in the afternoon it was utterly impossible to stand up against the violence of the blast; and, as the night closed in upon us, I had not a shadow of hope that the vessel would hold together until morning.

By midnight we had settled very deep in the water, which was now up to the orlop deck. The rudder went soon afterward, the sea which tore it away lifting the after portion of the brig entirely from the water, against which she thumped in her descent with such a concussion as would be occasioned by going ashore. We had all calculated that the rudder would hold its own to the last, as it was unusually strong, being rigged as I have never seen one rigged either before or since. Down its main timber there ran a succession of stout iron hooks, and others in the same manner down the stern-post. Through these hooks there extended a very thick wrought-iron rod, the rudder being thus held to the stern-post and swinging freely on the rod. The tremendous force of the sea which tore it off may be estimated by the fact, that the hooks in the stern-post, which ran entirely through it, being clinched on the inside, were drawn every one of them completely out of the solid wood.

We had scarcely time to draw breath after the violence of this shock, when one of the most tremendous waves I had then ever known broke right on board of us, sweeping the companion-way clear off, bursting in the hatchways, and filling every inch of the vessel with water.

CHAPTER IX

LUCKILY, JUST BEFORE NIGHT, ALL FOUR OF US HAD LASHED OURSELVES firmly to the fragments of the windlass, lying in this manner as flat upon the deck as possible. This precaution alone saved us from destruction. As it was, we were all more or less stunned by the immense weight of water which tumbled upon us, and which did not roll from above us until we were nearly exhausted. As soon as I could recover breath, I called aloud to my companions. Augustus alone replied, saying: "It is all over with us, and may God have mercy upon our souls!" By and by both the others were enabled to speak, when they exhorted us to take courage, as there was still hope; it being impossible, from the nature of the cargo, that the brig could go down, and there being every chance that the gale would blow over by the morning. These words inspired me with new life; for, strange as it may seem, although it was obvious that a vessel with a cargo of empty oil-casks would not sink, I had been hitherto so confused in mind as to have overlooked this consideration altogether; and the danger which I had for some time regarded as the most imminent was that of foundering. As hope revived within me, I made use of every opportunity to strengthen the lashings which held me to the remains of the windlass, and in this occupation I soon discovered that my companions were also busy. The night was as dark as it could possibly be, and the horrible shrieking din and confusion which surrounded us it is useless to attempt describing. Our deck lay level with the sea, or rather we were encircled with a towering ridge of foam, a portion of which swept over us every instant. It is not too much to say that our heads were not fairly out of the water more than one second in three. Although we lay close together, no one of us

could see the other, or, indeed, any portion of the brig itself, upon which we were so tempestuously hurled about. At intervals we called one to the other, thus endeavoring to keep alive hope, and render consolation and encouragement to such of us as stood most in need of it. The feeble condition of Augustus made him an object of solicitude with us all; and as, from the lacerated condition of his right arm, it must have been impossible for him to secure his lashings with any degree of firmness, we were in momentary expectation of finding that he had gone overboard—yet to render him aid was a thing altogether out of the question. Fortunately, his station was more secure than that of any of the rest of us; for the upper part of his body lying just beneath a portion of the shattered windlass, the seas, as they tumbled in upon him, were greatly broken in their violence. In any other situation than this (into which he had been accidentally thrown after having lashed himself in a very exposed spot) he must inevitably have perished before morning. Owing to the brig's lying so much along, we were all less liable to be washed off than otherwise would have been the case. The heel, as I have before stated, was to larboard,⁵ about one half of the deck being constantly under water. The seas, therefore, which struck us to starboard were much broken, by the vessel's side, only reaching us in fragments as we lay flat on our faces; while those which came from larboard being what are called back-water seas, and obtaining little hold upon us on account of our posture, had not sufficient force to drag us from our fastenings.

In this frightful situation we lay until the day broke so as to show us more fully the horrors which surrounded us. The brig was a mere log, rolling about at the mercy of every wave; the gale was upon the increase, if anything, blowing indeed a complete hurricane, and there appeared to us no earthly prospect of deliverance. For several hours we held on in silence, expecting every moment that our lashings would either give way, that the remains of the windlass would go by the board, or that some of the huge seas, which roared in every direction around us and above us, would drive the hulk so far beneath the water that we should be drowned before it could regain the surface. By the mercy of God, however, we were preserved from these imminent dangers, and about midday were cheered by the light of the blessed sun. Shortly afterward we could perceive a sensible diminution in the force of the wind, when, now for the first time since the latter part of the evening before, Augustus spoke, asking Peters, who lay closest to him, if he thought there was any possibility of our being saved. As no reply was at first made to this question, we all concluded that

the hybrid had been drowned where he lay; but presently, to our great joy, he spoke, although very feebly, saying that he was in great pain, being so cut by the tightness of his lashings across the stomach, that he must either find means of loosening them or perish, as it was impossible that he could endure his misery much longer. This occasioned us great distress, as it was altogether useless to think of aiding him in any manner while the sea continued washing over us as it did. We exhorted him to bear his sufferings with fortitude, and promised to seize the first opportunity which should offer itself to relieve him. He replied that it would soon be too late; that it would be all over with him before we could help him; and then, after moaning for some minutes, lay silent, when we concluded that he had perished.

As the evening drew on, the sea had fallen so much that scarcely more than one wave broke over the hulk from windward in the course of five minutes, and the wind had abated a great deal, although still blowing a severe gale. I had not heard any of my companions speak for hours, and now called to Augustus. He replied, although very feebly, so that I could not distinguish what he said. I then spoke to Peters and to Parker, neither of whom returned any answer.

Shortly after this period I fell into a state of partial insensibility, during which the most pleasing images floated in my imagination; such as green trees, waving meadows of ripe grain, processions of dancing girls, troops of cavalry, and other fantasies. I now remember that, in all which passed before my mind's eye, *motion* was a predominant idea. Thus, I never fancied any stationary object, such as a house, a mountain, or anything of that kind; but windmills, ships, large birds, balloons, people on horseback, carriages driving furiously, and similar moving objects, presented themselves in endless succession. When I recovered from this state, the sun was, as near as I could guess, an hour high. I had the greatest difficulty in bringing to recollection the various circumstances connected with my situation, and for some time remained firmly convinced that I was still in the hold of the brig, near the box, and that the body of Parker was that of Tiger.

When I at length completely came to my senses, I found that the wind blew no more than a moderate breeze, and that the sea was comparatively calm; so much so that it only washed over the brig amidships. My left arm had broken loose from its lashings, and was much cut about the elbow; my right was entirely benumbed, and the hand and wrist swollen prodigiously by the pressure of the rope, which had worked from the shoulder downward. I was also in great pain from another rope which went about my

waist, and had been drawn to an insufferable degree of tightness. Looking round upon my companions, I saw that Peters still lived, although a thick line was pulled so forcibly around his loins as to give him the appearance of being cut nearly in two; as I stirred, he made a feeble motion to me with his hand, pointing to the rope. Augustus gave no indication of life whatever, and was bent nearly double across a splinter of the windlass. Parker spoke to me when he saw me moving, and asked me if I had not sufficient strength to release him from his situation; saying that if I would summon up what spirits I could, and contrive to untie him, we might yet save our lives; but that otherwise we must all perish. I told him to take courage, and I would endeavor to free him. Feeling in my pantaloons' pocket, I got hold of my penknife, and, after several ineffectual attempts, at length succeeded in opening it. I then, with my left hand, managed to free my right from its fastenings, and afterward cut the other ropes which held me. Upon attempting, however, to move from my position, I found that my legs failed me altogether, and that I could not get up; neither could I move my right arm in any direction. Upon mentioning this to Parker, he advised me to lie quiet for a few minutes, holding on to the windlass with my left hand, so as to allow time for the blood to circulate. Doing this, the numbness presently began to die away so that I could move first one of my legs, and then the other; and, shortly afterward I regained the partial use of my right arm. I now crawled with great caution towards Parker, without getting on my legs, and soon cut loose all the lashings about him, when, after a short delay, he also recovered the partial use of his limbs. We now lost no time in getting loose the rope from Peters. It had cut a deep gash through the waistband of his woolen pantaloons, and through two shirts, and made its way into his groin, from which the blood flowed out copiously as we removed the cordage. No sooner had we removed it, however, than he spoke, and seemed to experience instant relief—being able to move with much greater ease than either Parker or myself—this was no doubt owing to the discharge of blood.

We had little hopes that Augustus would recover, as he evinced no signs of life; but, upon getting to him, we discovered that he had merely swooned from the loss of blood, the bandages we had placed around his wounded arm having been torn off by the water; none of the ropes which held him to the windlass were drawn sufficiently tight to occasion his death. Having relieved him from the fastenings, and got him clear of the broken wood about the windlass, we secured him in a dry place to windward, with his head somewhat lower than his body, and all three of us

busied ourselves in chafing his limbs. In about half an hour he came to himself, although it was not until the next morning that he gave signs of recognizing any of us, or had sufficient strength to speak. By the time we had thus got clear of our lashings it was quite dark, and it began to cloud up, so that we were again in the greatest agony lest it should come on to blow hard, in which event nothing could have saved us from perishing, exhausted as we were. By good fortune it continued very moderate during the night, the sea subsiding every minute, which gave us great hopes of ultimate preservation. A gentle breeze still blew from the N. W., but the weather was not at all cold. Augustus was lashed carefully to windward in such a manner as to prevent him from slipping overboard with the rolls of the vessel, as he was still too weak to hold on at all. For ourselves there was no such necessity. We sat close together, supporting each other with the aid of the broken ropes about the windlass, and devising methods of escape from our frightful situation. We derived much comfort from taking off our clothes and wringing the water from them. When we put them on after this, they felt remarkably warm and pleasant, and served to invigorate us in no little degree. We helped Augustus off with his, and wrung them for him, when he experienced the same comfort.

Our chief sufferings were now those of hunger and thirst, and when we looked forward to the means of relief in this respect, our hearts sunk within us, and we were induced to regret that we had escaped the less dreadful perils of the sea. We endeavored, however, to console ourselves with the hope of being speedily picked up by some vessel and encouraged each other to bear with fortitude the evils that might happen.

The morning of the fourteenth at length dawned, and the weather still continued clear and pleasant, with a steady but very light breeze from the N. W. The sea was now quite smooth, and as, from some cause which we could not determine, the brig did not lie so much along as she had done before, the deck was comparatively dry, and we could move about with freedom. We had now been better than three entire days and nights without either food or drink, and it became absolutely necessary that we should make an attempt to get up something from below. As the brig was completely full of water, we went to this work despondently, and with but little expectation of being able to obtain anything. We made a kind of drag by driving some nails which we broke out from the remains of the companion-hatch into two pieces of wood. Tying these across each other, and fastening them to the end of a rope, we threw them into the cabin, and dragged them to and fro, in the faint hope of being thus able to entangle

some article which might be of use to us for food, or which might at least render us assistance in getting it. We spent the greater part of the morning in this labor without effect, fishing up nothing more than a few bed-clothes, which were readily caught by the nails. Indeed, our contrivance was so very clumsy that any greater success was hardly to be anticipated.

We now tried the forecastle, but equally in vain, and were upon the brink of despair, when Peters proposed that we should fasten a rope to his body, and let him make an attempt to get up something by diving into the cabin. This proposition we hailed with all the delight which reviving hope could inspire. He proceeded immediately to strip off his clothes with the exception of his pantaloons; and a strong rope was then carefully fastened around his middle, being brought up over his shoulders in such a manner that there was no possibility of its slipping. The undertaking was one of great difficulty and danger; for, as we could hardly expect to find much, if any, provision in the cabin itself, it was necessary that the diver, after let-ting himself down, should make a turn to the right, and proceed under water a distance of ten or twelve feet, in a narrow passage, to the store-room, and return, without drawing breath.

Everything being ready, Peters now descended in the cabin, going down the companion-ladder until the water reached his chin. He then plunged in, head first, turning to the right as he plunged, and endeavor-ing to make his way to the storeroom. In this first attempt, however, he was altogether unsuccessful. In less than half a minute after his going down we felt the rope jerked violently (the signal we had agreed upon when he desired to be drawn up). We accordingly drew him up instantly, but so incautiously as to bruise him badly against the ladder. He had brought nothing with him, and had been unable to penetrate more than a very little way into the passage, owing to the constant exertions he found it necessary to make in order to keep himself from floating up against the deck. Upon getting out he was very much exhausted, and had to rest full fifteen minutes before he could again venture to descend.

The second attempt met with even worse success; for he remained so long under water without giving the signal, that, becoming alarmed for his safety, we drew him out without it, and found that he was almost at the last gasp, having, as he said, repeatedly jerked at the rope without our feeling it. This was probably owing to a portion of it having become entangled in the balustrade at the foot of the ladder. This balustrade was, indeed, so much in the way, that we determined to remove it, if possible, before pro-ceeding with our design. As we had no means of getting it away except by

main force, we all descended into the water as far as we could on the lad-
der, and giving a pull against it with our united strength, succeeded in
breaking it down.

The third attempt was equally unsuccessful with the two first, and it
now became evident that nothing could be done in this manner without
the aid of some weight with which the diver might steady himself, and
keep to the floor of the cabin while making his search. For a long time we
looked about in vain for something which might answer this purpose; but
at length, to our great joy, we discovered one of the weather-forechains so
loose that we had not the least difficulty in wrenching it off. Having fas-
tened this securely to one of his ankles, Peters now made his fourth
descent into the cabin, and this time succeeded in making his way to the
door of the steward's room. To his inexpressible grief, however, he found
it locked, and was obliged to return without effecting an entrance, as, with
the greatest exertion, he could remain under water not more, at the
utmost extent, than a single minute. Our affairs now looked gloomy
indeed, and neither Augustus nor myself could refrain from bursting into
tears, as we thought of the host of difficulties which encompassed us, and
the slight probability which existed of our finally making an escape. But
this weakness was not of long duration. Throwing ourselves on our knees
to God, we implored His aid in the many dangers which beset us; and
arose with renewed hope and vigor to think what could yet be done by
mortal means towards accomplishing our deliverance.

CHAPTER X

Shortly afterward an incident occurred which I am induced to look upon as more intensely productive of emotion, as far more replete with the extremes first of delight and then of horror, than even any of the thousand chances which afterward befell me in nine long years, crowded with events of the most startling and, in many cases, of the most unconceived and unconceivable character. We were lying on the deck near the companion-way, and debating the possibility of yet making our way into the storeroom, when, looking towards Augustus, who lay fronting myself, I perceived that he had become all at once deadly pale, and that his lips were quivering in the most singular and unaccountable manner. Greatly alarmed, I spoke to him, but he made me no reply, and I was beginning to think that he was suddenly taken ill, when I took notice of his eyes, which were glaring apparently at some object behind me. I turned my head, and shall never forget the ecstatic joy which thrilled through every particle of my frame, when I perceived a large brig bearing down upon us, and not more than a couple of miles off. I sprung to my feet as if a musket bullet had suddenly struck me to the heart; and, stretching out my arms in the direction of the vessel, stood in this manner, motionless, and unable to articulate a syllable. Peters and Parker were equally affected, although in different ways. The former danced about the deck like a madman, uttering the most extravagant rhodomontades, intermingled with howls and imprecations, while the latter burst into tears, and continued for many minutes weeping like a child.

The vessel in sight was a large hermaphrodite brig, of a Dutch build, and painted black, with a tawdry gilt figure-head. She had evidently seen a good deal of rough weather, and, we supposed, had suffered much in

the gale which had proved so disastrous to ourselves; for her foretopmast was gone, and some of her starboard bulwarks. When we first saw her, she was, as I have already said, about two miles off and to windward, bearing down upon us. The breeze was very gentle, and what astonished us chiefly was, that she had no other sails set than her foremast and mainsail, with a flying jib—of course she came down but slowly, and our impatience amounted nearly to frenzy. The awkward manner in which she steered, too, was remarked by all of us, even excited as we were. She yawed about so considerably, that once or twice we thought it impossible she could see us, or imagined that, having seen us, and discovered no person on board, she was about to tack and make off in another direction. Upon each of these occasions we screamed and shouted at the top of our voices, when the stranger would appear to change for a moment her intention, and again hold on towards us—this singular conduct being repeated two or three times, so that at last we could think of no other manner of accounting for it than by supposing the helmsman to be in liquor.

No person was seen upon her decks until she arrived within about a quarter of a mile of us. We then saw three seamen, whom by their dress we took to be Hollanders. Two of these were lying on some old sails near the forecastle, and the third, who appeared to be looking at us with great curiosity, was leaning over the starboard bow near the bowsprit. This last was a stout and tall man, with a very dark skin. He seemed by his manner to be encouraging us to have patience, nodding to us in a cheerful although rather odd way, and smiling constantly, so as to display a set of the most brilliantly white teeth. As his vessel drew nearer, we saw a red flannel cap which he had on fall from his head into the water; but of this he took little or no notice, continuing his odd smiles and gesticulations. I relate these things and circumstances minutely, and I relate them, it must be understood, precisely as they *appeared* to us.

The brig came on slowly, and now more steadily than before, and—I cannot speak calmly of this event—our hearts leaped up wildly within us, and we poured out our whole souls in shouts and thanksgiving to God for the complete, unexpected, and glorious deliverance that was so palpably at hand. Of a sudden, and all at once, there came wafted over the ocean from the strange vessel (which was now close upon us) a smell, a stench, such as the whole world has no name for—no conception of—hellish—utterly suffocating—insufferable, inconceivable. I gasped for breath, and turning to my companions, perceived that they were paler than marble. But we had now no time left for question or surmise—the brig was within fifty feet of

us, and it seemed to be her intention to run under our counter, that we might board her without putting out a boat. We rushed aft, when, suddenly, a wide yaw threw her off full five or six points from the course she had been running, and, as she passed under our stern at the distance of about twenty feet, we had a full view of her decks. Shall I ever forget the triple horror of that spectacle? Twenty-five or thirty human bodies, among whom were several females, lay scattered about between the counter and the galley in the last and most loathsome state of putrefaction! We plainly saw that not a soul lived in that fated vessel! Yet we could not help shouting to the dead for help! Yes, long and loudly did we beg, in the agony of the moment, that those silent and disgusting images would stay for us, would not abandon us to become like them, would receive us among their goodly company! We were raving with horror and despair—thoroughly mad through the anguish of our grievous disappointment.

As our first loud yell of terror broke forth, it was replied to by something, from near the bowsprit of the stranger, so closely resembling the scream of a human voice that the nicest ear might have been startled and deceived. At this instant another sudden yaw brought the region of the forecastle for a moment into view, and we beheld at once the origin of the sound. We saw the tall stout figure still leaning on the bulwark, and still nodding his head to and fro, but his face was now turned from us so that we could not behold it. His arms were extended over the rail, and the palms of his hands fell outward. His knees were lodged upon a stout rope, tightly stretched, and reaching from the heel of the bowsprit to a cat-head. On his back, from which a portion of the shirt had been torn, leaving it bare, there sat a huge sea-gull, busily gorging itself with the horrible flesh, its bill and talons deep buried, and its white plumage spattered all over with blood. As the brig moved farther round so as to bring us close in view, the bird, with much apparent difficulty, drew out its crimsoned head, and, after eyeing us for a moment as if stupefied, arose lazily from the body upon which it had been feasting, and, flying directly above our deck, hovered there awhile with a portion of clotted and liver-like substance in its beak. The horrid morsel dropped at length with a sullen splash immediately at the feet of Parker. May God forgive me, but now, for the first time, there flashed through my mind a thought, a thought which I will not mention, and I felt myself making a step towards the ensanguined spot. I looked upward, and the eyes of Augustus met my own with a degree of intense and eager meaning which immediately brought me to my senses. I sprang forward quickly, and, with a deep shudder, threw the frightful thing into the sea.

The body from which it had been taken, resting as it did upon the rope, had been easily swayed to and fro by the exertions of the carnivorous bird, and it was this motion which had at first impressed us with the belief of its being alive. As the gull relieved it of its weight, it swung round and fell partially over, so that the face was fully discovered. Never, surely, was any object so terribly full of awe! The eyes were gone, and the whole flesh around the mouth, leaving the teeth utterly naked. This, then, was the smile which had cheered us on to hope! this the—but I forbear. The brig, as I have already told, passed under our stern, and made its way slowly but steadily to leeward. With her and with her terrible crew went all our gay visions of deliverance and joy. Deliberately as she went by, we might possibly have found means of boarding her, had not our sudden disappointment and the appalling nature of the discovery which accompanied it, laid entirely prostrate every active faculty of mind and body. We had seen and felt, but we could neither think nor act, until, alas! too late. How much our intellects had been weakened by this incident may be estimated by the fact, that when the vessel had proceeded so far that we could perceive no more than the half of her hull, the proposition was seriously entertained of attempting to overtake her by swimming!

I have, since this period, vainly endeavored to obtain some clue to the hideous uncertainty which enveloped the fate of the stranger. Her build and general appearance, as I have before stated, led us to the belief that she was a Dutch trader, and the dresses of the crew also sustained this opinion. We might have easily seen the name upon her stern, and, indeed, taken other observations, which would have guided us in making out her character; but the intense excitement of the moment blinded us to everything of that nature. From the saffron-like hue of such of the corpses as were not entirely decayed, we concluded that the whole of her company had perished by the yellow fever, or some other virulent disease of the same fearful kind. If such were the case (and I know not what else to imagine), death, to judge from the positions of the bodies, must have come upon them in a manner awfully sudden and overwhelming, in a way totally distinct from that which generally characterizes even the most deadly pestilences with which mankind are acquainted. It is possible, indeed, that poison, accidentally introduced into some of their sea-stores, may have brought about the disaster, or that the eating of some unknown venomous species of fish, or other marine animal, or oceanic bird, might have induced it—but it is utterly useless to form conjectures where all is involved, and will, no doubt, remain forever involved, in the most appalling and unfathomable mystery.

Chapter XI

We spent the remainder of the day in a condition of stupid lethargy, gazing after the retreating vessel until the darkness, hiding her from our sight, recalled us in some measure to our senses. The pangs of hunger and thirst then returned, absorbing all other cares and considerations. Nothing, however, could be done until the morning, and, securing ourselves as well as possible, we endeavored to snatch a little repose. In this I succeeded beyond my expectations, sleeping until my companions, who had not been so fortunate, aroused me at daybreak to renew our attempts at getting up provisions from the hull.

It was now a dead calm, with the sea as smooth as I have ever known it—the weather warm and pleasant. The brig was out of sight. We commenced our operations by wrenching off, with some trouble, another of the forechains; and having fastened both to Peters' feet, he again made an endeavor to reach the door of the storeroom, thinking it possible that he might be able to force it open, provided he could get at it in sufficient time; and this he hoped to do, as the hulk lay much more steadily than before.

He succeeded very quickly in reaching the door, when, loosening one of the chains from his ankle, he made every exertion to force the passage with it, but in vain, the framework of the room being far stronger than was anticipated. He was quite exhausted with his long stay under water, and it became absolutely necessary that some other one of us should take his place. For this service Parker immediately volunteered; but, after making three ineffectual efforts, found that he could never even succeed in getting near the door. The condition of Augustus' wounded arm rendered it useless for him to attempt going down, as he would be unable to force the

room open should he reach it, and it accordingly now devolved upon me to exert myself for our common deliverance.

Peters had left one of the chains in the passage, and I found, upon plunging in, that I had not sufficient balance to keep me firmly down. I determined, therefore, to attempt no more, in my first effort, than merely to recover the other chain. In groping along the floor of the passage for this, I felt a hard substance, which I immediately grasped, not having time to ascertain what it was, but returning and ascending instantly to the surface. The prize proved to be a bottle, and our joy may be conceived when I say that it was found to be full of port wine. Giving thanks to God for this timely and cheering assistance, we immediately drew the cork with my pen-knife, and, each taking a moderate sup, felt the most indescribable comfort from the warmth, strength, and spirits with which it inspired us. We then carefully recorked the bottle, and, by means of a handkerchief, swung it in such a manner that there was no possibility of its getting broken.

Having rested awhile after this fortunate discovery, I again descended, and now recovered the chain, with which I instantly came up. I then fastened it on and went down for the third time, when I became fully satisfied that no exertions whatever, in that situation, would enable me to force open the door of the storeroom. I therefore returned in despair.

There seemed now to be no longer any room for hope, and I could perceive in the countenances of my companions that they had made up their minds to perish. The wine had evidently produced in them a species of delirium, which, perhaps, I had been prevented from feeling by the immersion I had undergone since drinking it. They talked incoherently, and about matters unconnected with our condition, Peters repeatedly asking me questions about Nantucket. Augustus, too, I remember, approached me with a serious air, and requested me to lend him a pocket-comb, as his hair was full of fish-scales, and he wished to get them out before going on shore. Parker appeared somewhat less affected, and urged me to dive at random into the cabin, and bring up any article which might come to hand. To this I consented, and, in the first attempt, after staying under a full minute, brought up a small leather trunk belonging to Captain Barnard. This was immediately opened in the faint hope that it might contain something to eat or drink. We found nothing, however, except a box of razors and two linen shirts. I now went down again, and returned without any success. As my head came above water I heard a crash on deck, and, upon getting up, saw that my companions had ungratefully taken advantage of my absence to drink the remainder of the wine, having let

the bottle fall in the endeavor to replace it before I saw them. I remonstrated with them on the heartlessness of their conduct, when Augustus burst into tears. The other two endeavored to laugh the matter off as a joke, but I hope never again to behold laughter of such a species: the distortion of countenance was absolutely frightful. Indeed, it was apparent that the stimulus, in the empty state of their stomachs, had taken instant and violent effect, and that they were all exceedingly intoxicated. With great difficulty I prevailed upon them to lie down, when they fell very soon into a heavy slumber, accompanied with loud stertorous breathing.

I now found myself, as it were, alone in the brig, and my reflections, to be sure, were of the most fearful and gloomy nature. No prospect offered itself to my view but a lingering death by famine, or, at the best, by being overwhelmed in the first gale which should spring up, for in our present exhausted condition we could have no hope of living through another.

The gnawing hunger which I now experienced was nearly insupportable, and I felt myself capable of going to any lengths in order to appease it. With my knife I cut off a small portion of the leather trunk, and endeavored to eat it, but found it utterly impossible to swallow a single morsel, although I fancied that some little alleviation of my suffering was obtained by chewing small pieces of it and spitting them out. Towards night my companions awoke, one by one, each in an indescribable state of weakness and horror, brought on by the wine, whose fumes had now evaporated. They shook as if with a violent ague, and uttered the most lamentable cries for water. Their condition affected me in the most lively degree, at the same time causing me to rejoice in the fortunate train of circumstances which had prevented me from indulging in the wine, and consequently from sharing their melancholy and most distressing sensations. Their conduct, however, gave me great uneasiness and alarm; for it was evident that, unless some favorable change took place, they could afford me no assistance in providing for our common safety. I had not yet abandoned all idea of being able to get up something from below; but the attempt could not possibly be resumed until some one of them was sufficiently master of himself to aid me by holding the end of the rope while I went down. Parker appeared to be somewhat more in possession of his senses than the others, and I endeavored, by every means in my power, to rouse him. Thinking that a plunge in the seawater might have a beneficial effect, I contrived to fasten the end of a rope around his body, and then, leading him to the companion-way (he remaining quite passive all the while), pushed him in, and immediately drew him out. I had good reason to congratulate myself

upon having made this experiment; for he appeared much revived and invigorated, and, upon getting out, asked me, in a rational manner, why I had so served him. Having explained my object, he expressed himself indebted to me, and said that he felt greatly better from the immersion, afterward conversing sensibly upon our situation. We then resolved to treat Augustus and Peters in the same way, which we immediately did, when they both experienced much benefit from the shock. This idea of sudden immersion had been suggested to me by reading in some medical work the good effect of the shower-bath in a case where the patient was suffering from *mania a potu.*[4]

Finding that I could now trust my companions to hold the end of the rope, I again made three or four plunges into the cabin, although it was now quite dark, and a gentle but long swell from the northward rendered the hulk somewhat unsteady. In the course of these attempts I succeeded in bringing up two case-knives, a three-gallon jug, empty, and a blanket, but nothing which could serve us for food. I continued my efforts, after getting these articles, until I was completely exhausted, but brought up nothing else. During the night Parker and Peters occupied themselves by turns in the same manner; but nothing coming to hand, we now gave up this attempt in despair, concluding that we were exhausting ourselves in vain.

We passed the remainder of this night in a state of the most intense mental and bodily anguish that can possibly be imagined. The morning of the sixteenth at length dawned, and we looked eagerly around the horizon for relief, but to no purpose. The sea was still smooth, with only a long swell from the northward, as on yesterday. This was the sixth day since we had tasted either food or drink, with the exception of the bottle of port wine, and it was clear that we could hold out but a very little while longer unless something could be obtained. I never saw before, nor wish to see again, human beings so utterly emaciated as Peters and Augustus. Had I met them on shore in their present condition I should not have had the slightest suspicion that I had ever beheld them. Their countenances were totally changed in character, so that I could not bring myself to believe them really the same individuals with whom I had been in company but a few days before. Parker, although sadly reduced, and so feeble that he could not raise his head from his bosom, was not so far gone as the other two. He suffered with great patience, making no complaint, and endeavoring to inspire us with hope in every manner he could devise. For myself, although at the commencement of the voyage I had been in bad health, and was at all times of a delicate constitution, I suffered less than any of

us, being much less reduced in frame, and retaining my powers of mind in a surprising degree, while the rest were completely prostrated in intellect, and seemed to be brought to a species of second childhood, generally simpering in their expressions, with idiotic smiles, and uttering the most absurd platitudes. At intervals, however, they would appear to revive suddenly, as if inspired all at once with a consciousness of their condition, when they would spring upon their feet in a momentary flash of vigor, and speak, for a short period, of their prospects, in a manner altogether rational, although full of the most intense despair. It is possible, however, that my companions may have entertained the same opinion of their own condition as I did of mine, and that I may have unwittingly been guilty of the same extravagances and imbecilities as themselves—this is a matter which cannot be determined.

About noon Parker declared that he saw land off the larboard quarter, and it was with the utmost difficulty I could restrain him from plunging into the sea with the view of swimming towards it. Peters and Augustus took little notice of what he said, being apparently wrapped up in moody contemplation. Upon looking in the direction pointed out, I could not perceive the faintest appearance of the shore—indeed, I was too well aware that we were far from any land to indulge in a hope of that nature. It was a long time, nevertheless, before I could convince Parker of his mistake. He then burst into a flood of tears, weeping like a child, with loud cries and sobs, for two or three hours, when becoming exhausted, he fell asleep.

Peters and Augustus now made several ineffectual efforts to swallow portions of the leather. I advised them to chew it and spit it out; but they were too excessively debilitated to be able to follow my advice. I continued to chew pieces of it at intervals, and found some relief from so doing; my chief distress was for water, and I was only prevented from taking a draught from the sea by remembering the horrible consequences which thus have resulted to others who were similarly situated with ourselves.

The day wore on in this manner, when I suddenly discovered a sail to the eastward, and on our larboard bow. She appeared to be a large ship, and was coming nearly athwart us, being probably twelve or fifteen miles distant. None of my companions had as yet discovered her, and I forbore to tell them of her for the present, lest we might again be disappointed of relief. At length upon her getting nearer, I saw distinctly that she was heading immediately for us, with her light sails filled. I could now contain myself no longer, and pointed her out to my fellow-sufferers. They immediately sprang to their feet, again indulging in the most extravagant

demonstrations of joy, weeping, laughing in an idiotic manner, jumping, stamping upon the deck, tearing their hair, and praying and cursing by turns. I was so affected by their conduct, as well as by what I considered a sure prospect of deliverance, that I could not refrain from joining in with their madness, and gave way to the impulses of my gratitude and ecstasy by lying and rolling on the deck, clapping my hands, shouting, and other similar acts, until I was suddenly called to my recollection, and once more to the extreme human misery and despair, by perceiving the ship all at once with her stern fully presented towards us, and steering in a direction nearly opposite to that in which I had at first perceived her.

It was some time before I could induce my poor companions to believe that this sad reverse in our prospects had actually taken place. They replied to all my assertions with a stare and a gesture implying that they were not to be deceived by such misrepresentations. The conduct of Augustus most sensibly affected me. In spite of all I could say or do to the contrary, he persisted in saying that the ship was rapidly nearing us, and in making preparations to go on board of her. Some seaweed floating by the brig, he maintained that it was the ship's boat, and endeavored to throw himself upon it, howling and shrieking in the most heartrending manner, when I forcibly restrained him from thus casting himself into the sea.

Having become in some degree pacified, we continued to watch the ship until we finally lost sight of her, the weather becoming hazy, with a light breeze springing up. As soon as she was entirely gone, Parker turned suddenly towards me with an expression of countenance which made me shudder. There was about him an air of self-possession which I had not noticed in him until now, and before he opened his lips my heart told me what he would say. He proposed, in a few words, that one of us should die to preserve the existence of the others.

CHAPTER XII

I HAD FOR SOME TIME PAST, DWELT UPON THE PROSPECT OF OUR BEING reduced to this last horrible extremity, and had secretly made up my mind to suffer death in any shape or under any circumstances rather than resort to such a course. Nor was this resolution in any degree weakened by the present intensity of hunger under which I labored. The proposition had not been heard by either Peters or Augustus. I therefore took Parker aside; and mentally praying to God for power to dissuade him from the horrible purpose he entertained, I expostulated with him for a long time, and in the most supplicating manner, begging him in the name of everything which he held sacred, and urging him by every species of argument which the extremity of the case suggested, to abandon the idea, and not to mention it to either of the other two.

He heard all I said without attempting to controvert any of my arguments, and I had begun to hope that he would be prevailed upon to do as I desired. But when I had ceased speaking, he said that he knew very well all I had said was true, and that to resort to such a course was the most horrible alternative which could enter into the mind of man; but that he had now held out as long as human nature could be sustained; that it was unnecessary for all to perish, when, by the death of one, it was possible, and even probable, that the rest might be finally preserved; adding that I might save myself the trouble of trying to turn him from his purpose, his mind having been thoroughly made up on the subject even before the appearance of the ship, and that only her heaving in sight had prevented him from mentioning his intention at an earlier period.

I now begged him, if he would not be prevailed upon to abandon his design, at least to defer it for another day, when some vessel might come

to our relief; again reiterating every argument I could devise, and which I thought likely to have influence with one of his rough nature. He said, in reply, that he had not spoken until the very last possible moment, that he could exist no longer without sustenance of some kind, and that therefore in another day his suggestion would be too late, as regarded himself at least.

Finding that he was not to be moved by anything I could say in a mild tone, I now assumed a different demeanor, and told him that he must be aware I had suffered less than any of us from our calamities; that my health and strength, consequently, were at that moment far better than his own, or than that either of Peters or Augustus; in short, that I was in a condition to have my own way by force if I found it necessary; and that if he attempted in any manner to acquaint the others with his bloody and cannibal designs, I would not hesitate to throw him into the sea. Upon this he immediately seized me by the throat, and drawing a knife, made several ineffectual efforts to stab me in the stomach; an atrocity which his excessive debility alone prevented him from accomplishing. In the meantime, being roused to a high pitch of anger, I forced him to the vessel's side, with the full intention of throwing him overboard. He was saved from his fate, however, by the interference of Peters, who now approached and separated us, asking the cause of the disturbance. This Parker told before I could find means in any manner to prevent him.

The effect of his words was even more terrible than what I had anticipated. Both Augustus and Peters, who, it seems, had long secretly entertained the same fearful idea which Parker had been merely the first to broach, joined with him in his design and insisted upon its immediately being carried into effect. I had calculated that one at least of the two former would be found still possessed of sufficient strength of mind to side with myself in resisting any attempt to execute so dreadful a purpose, and, with the aid of either one of them, I had no fear of being able to prevent its accomplishment. Being disappointed in this expectation, it became absolutely necessary that I should attend to my own safety, as a further resistance on my part might possibly be considered by men in their frightful condition a sufficient excuse for refusing me fair play in the tragedy that I knew would speedily be enacted.

I now told them I was willing to submit to the proposal, merely requesting a delay of about one hour, in order that the fog which had gathered around us might have an opportunity of lifting, when it was possible that the ship we had seen might be again in sight. After great difficulty I

obtained from them a promise to wait thus long; and, as I had anticipated (a breeze rapidly coming in), the fog lifted before the hour had expired, when, no vessel appearing in sight, we prepared to draw lots.

It is with extreme reluctance that I dwell upon the appalling scene which ensued; a scene which, with its minutest details, no after events have been able to efface in the slightest degree from my memory, and whose stern recollection will embitter every future moment of my existence. Let me run over this portion of my narrative with as much haste as the nature of the events to be spoken of will permit. The only method we could devise for the terrific lottery, in which we were to take each a chance, was that of drawing straws. Small splinters of wood were made to answer our purpose, and it was agreed that I should be the holder. I retired to one end of the hulk, while my poor companions silently took up their station in the other with their backs turned towards me. The bitterest anxiety which I endured at any period of this fearful drama was while I occupied myself in the arrangement of the lots. There are few conditions into which man can possibly fall where he will not feel a deep interest in the preservation of his existence; an interest momentarily increasing with the frailness of the tenure by which that existence may be held. But now that the silent, definite, and stern nature of the business in which I was engaged (so different from the tumultuous dangers of the storm or the gradually approaching horrors of famine) allowed me to reflect on the few chances I had of escaping the most appalling of deaths—a death for the most appalling of purposes—every particle of that energy which had so long buoyed me up departed like feathers before the wind, leaving me a helpless prey to the most abject and pitiable terror. I could not, at first, even summon up sufficient strength to tear and fit together the small splinters of wood, my fingers absolutely refusing their office, and my knees knocking violently against each other. My mind ran over rapidly a thousand absurd projects by which to avoid becoming a partner in the awful speculation. I thought of falling on my knees to my companions, and entreating them to let me escape this necessity; of suddenly rushing upon them, and, by putting one of them to death, of rendering the decision by lot useless—in short, of everything but of going through with the matter I had in hand. At last, after wasting a long time in this imbecile conduct, I was recalled to my senses by the voice of Parker, who urged me to relieve them at once from the terrible anxiety they were enduring. Even then I could not bring myself to arrange the splinters upon the spot, but thought over every species of

finesse by which I could trick some one of my fellow-sufferers to draw the short straw, as it had been agreed that whoever drew the shortest of four splinters from my hand was to die for the preservation of the rest. Before anyone condemn me for this apparent heartlessness, let him be placed in a situation precisely similar to my own.

At length delay was no longer possible, and, with a heart almost bursting from my bosom, I advanced to the region of the forecastle, where my companions were awaiting me. I held out my hand with the splinters, and Peters immediately drew. He was free—*his*, at least, was not the shortest; and there was now another chance against my escape. I summoned up all my strength, and passed the lots to Augustus. He also drew immediately, and he also was free; and now, whether I should live or die, the chances were no more than precisely even. At this moment all the fierceness of the tiger possessed my bosom, and I felt towards my poor fellow-creature, Parker, the most intense, the most diabolical hatred. But the feeling did not last; and, at length, with a convulsive shudder and closed eyes, I held out the two remaining splinters towards him. It was fully five minutes before he could summon resolution to draw, during which period of heartrending suspense I never once opened my eyes. Presently one of the two lots was quickly drawn from my hand. The decision was then over, yet I knew not whether it was for me or against me. No one spoke, and still I dared not satisfy myself by looking at the splinter I held. Peters at length took me by the hand, and I forced myself to look up, when I immediately saw by the countenance of Parker that I was safe, and that he it was who had been doomed to suffer. Gasping for breath, I fell senseless to the deck.

I recovered from my swoon in time to behold the consummation of the tragedy in the death of him who had been chiefly instrumental in bringing it about. He made no resistance whatever, and was stabbed in the back by Peters, when he fell instantly dead. I must not dwell upon the fearful repast which immediately ensued. Such things may be imagined, but words have no power to impress the mind with the exquisite horror of their reality. Let it suffice to say that, having in some measure appeased the raging thirst which consumed us by the blood of the victim, and having by common consent taken off the hands, feet, and head, throwing them together with the entrails, into the sea, we devoured the rest of the body, piecemeal, during the four ever memorable days of the seventeenth, eighteenth, nineteenth, and twentieth of the month.

On the nineteenth, there coming on a smart shower which lasted fifteen or twenty minutes, we contrived to catch some water by means of

a sheet which had been fished up from the cabin by our drag just after the gale. The quantity we took in all did not amount to more than half a gallon; but even this scanty allowance supplied us with comparative strength and hope.

On the twenty-first we were again reduced to the last necessity. The weather still remained warm and pleasant, with occasional fogs and light breezes, most usually from N. to W.

On the twenty-second, as we were sitting close huddled together, gloomily revolving over our lamentable condition, there flashed through my mind all at once an idea which inspired me with a bright gleam of hope. I remembered that, when the foremast had been cut away, Peters, being in the windward chains, passed one of the axes into my hand, requesting me to put it, if possible, in a place of security, and that a few minutes before the last heavy sea struck the brig and filled her I had taken this axe into the forecastle and laid it in one of the larboard berths. I now thought it possible that, by getting at this axe, we might cut through the deck over the storeroom, and thus readily supply ourselves with provisions

When I communicated this object to my companions, they uttered a feeble shout of joy, and we all proceeded forthwith to the forecastle. The difficulty of descending here was greater than that of going down in the cabin, the opening being much smaller, for it will be remembered that the whole framework about the cabin companion-hatch had been carried away, whereas the forecastle-way, being a simple hatch of only about three feet square, had remained uninjured. I did not hesitate, however, to attempt the descent; and a rope being fastened round my body as before, I plunged boldly in, feet foremost, made my way quickly to the berth, and at the first attempt brought up the axe. It was hailed with the most ecstatic joy and triumph, and the ease with which it had been obtained was regarded as an omen of our ultimate preservation.

We now commenced cutting at the deck with all the energy of rekindled hope, Peters and myself taking the axe by turns, Augustus' wounded arm not permitting him to aid us in any degree. As we were still so feeble as to be scarcely able to stand unsupported, and could consequently work but a minute or two without resting, it soon became evident that many long hours would be necessary to accomplish our task —that is, to cut an opening sufficiently large to admit of a free access to the storeroom. This consideration, however, did not discourage us; and, working all night by the light of the moon, we succeeded in effecting our purpose by daybreak on the morning of the twenty-third.

Peters now volunteered to go down; and, having made all arrange-
ments as before, he descended, and soon returned bringing up with him
a small jar, which, to our great joy, proved to be full of olives. Having
shared these among us, and devoured them with the greatest avidity, we
proceeded to let him down again. This time he succeeded beyond our
utmost expectations, returning instantly with a large ham and a bottle of
Madeira wine. Of the latter we each took a moderate sup, having learned
by experience the pernicious consequences of indulging too freely. The
ham, except about two pounds near the bone, was not in a condition to
be eaten, having been entirely spoiled by the salt water. The sound part
was divided among us. Peters and Augustus, not being able to restrain
their appetite, swallowed theirs upon the instant; but I was more cau-
tious, and ate but a small portion of mine, dreading the thirst which I
knew would ensue. We now rested awhile from our labors, which had
been intolerably severe.

By noon, feeling somewhat strengthened and refreshed, we again
renewed our attempt at getting up provisions, Peters and myself going
down alternately, and always with more or less success, until sundown. Dur-
ing this interval we had the good fortune to bring up, altogether, four
more small jars of olives, another ham, a carboy containing nearly three
gallons of excellent Cape Madeira wine, and, what gave us still more
delight, a small tortoise of the Gallipago breed, several of which had been
taken on board by Captain Barnard, as the *Grampus* was leaving port, from
the schooner *Mary Pitts*, just returned from a sealing voyage in the Pacific.

In a subsequent portion of this narrative I shall have frequent occa-
sion to mention this species of tortoise. It is found principally, as most of
my readers may know, in the group of islands called the Gallipagos,
which, indeed, derive their name from the animal—the Spanish word
Gallipago meaning a fresh-water terrapin. From the peculiarity of their
shape and action they have been sometimes called the elephant tortoise.
They are frequently found of an enormous size. I have myself seen sev-
eral which would weigh from twelve to fifteen hundred pounds, although
I do not remember that any navigator speaks of having seen them weigh-
ing more than eight hundred. Their appearance is singular, and even
disgusting. Their steps are very slow, measured, and heavy, their bodies
being carried about a foot from the ground. Their neck is long, and
exceedingly slender; from eighteen inches to two feet is a very common
length, and I killed one, where the distance from the shoulder to the
extremity of the head was no less than three feet ten inches. The head

has a striking resemblance to that of a serpent. They can exist without food for an almost incredible length of time, instances having been known where they have been thrown into the hold of a vessel and lain two years without nourishment of any kind—being as fat, and, in every respect, in as good order at the expiration of the time as when they were first put in. In one particular these extraordinary animals bear a resemblance to the dromedary, or camel of the desert. In a bag at the root of the neck they carry with them a constant supply of water. In some instances, upon killing them after a full year's deprivation of all nourishment, as much as three gallons of perfectly sweet and fresh water have been found in their bags. Their food is chiefly wild parsley and celery, with purslane, sea-kelp, and prickly pears, upon which latter vegetable they thrive wonderfully, a great quantity of it being usually found on the hill-sides near the shore wherever the animal itself is discovered. They are excellent and highly nutritious food, and have, no doubt, been the means of preserving the lives of thousands of seamen employed in the whale-fishery and other pursuits in the Pacific.

The one which we had the good fortune to bring up from the store-room was not of a large size, weighing probably sixty-five or seventy pounds. It was a female, and in excellent condition, being exceedingly fat, and having more than a quart of limpid and sweet water in its bag. This was indeed a treasure; and, falling on our knees with one accord, we returned fervent thanks to God for so seasonable a relief.

We had great difficulty in getting the animal up through the opening, as its struggles were fierce and its strength prodigious. It was upon the point of making its escape from Peter's grasp, and slipping back into the water, when Augustus, throwing a rope with a slip-knot around its throat, held it up in this manner until I jumped into the hole by the side of Peters, and assisted him in lifting it out.

The water we drew carefully from the bag into the jug; which, it will be remembered, had been brought up before from the cabin. Having done this, we broke off the neck of a bottle so as to form, with the cork, a kind of glass, holding not quite half a gill. We then each drank one of these measures full, and resolved to limit ourselves to this quantity per day as long as it should hold out.

During the last two or three days, the weather having been dry and pleasant, the bedding we had obtained from the cabin, as well as our clothing, had become thoroughly dry, so that we passed this night (that of the twenty-third) in comparative comfort, enjoying a tranquil repose, after

having supped plentifully on olives and ham, with a small allowance of the wine. Being afraid of losing some of our stores overboard during the night, in the event of a breeze springing up, we secured them as well as possible with cordage to the fragments of the windlass. Our tortoise, which we were anxious to preserve alive as long as we could, we threw on its back, and otherwise carefully fastened.

CHAPTER XIII

JULY 24. THIS MORNING SAW US WONDERFULLY RECRUITED IN SPIRITS AND strength. Notwithstanding the perilous situation in which we were still placed, ignorant of our position, although certainly at a great distance from land, without more food than would last us for a fortnight even with great care, almost entirely without water, and floating about at the mercy of every wind and wave on the merest wreck in the world, still the infinitely more terrible distresses and dangers from which we had so lately and so providentially been delivered caused us to regard what we now endured as but little more than an ordinary evil—so strictly comparative is either good or ill.

At sunrise we were preparing to renew our attempts at getting up something from the storeroom, when, a smart shower coming on, with some lightning, we turn our attention to the catching of water by means of the sheet we had used before for this purpose. We had no other means of collecting the rain than by holding the sheet spread out with one of the forechain-plates in the middle of it. The water, thus conducted to the center, was drained through into our jug. We had nearly filled it in this manner, when, a heavy squall coming on from the northward, obliged us to desist, as the hulk began once more to roll so violently that we could no longer keep our feet. We now went forward, and, lashing ourselves securely to the remnant of the windlass as before, awaited the event with far more calmness than could have been anticipated or would have been imagined possible under the circumstances. At noon the wind had freshened into a two-reef breeze, and by night into a stiff gale,

accompanied with a tremendously heavy swell. Experience having taught us, however, the best method of arranging our lashings, we weathered this dreary night in tolerable security, although thoroughly drenched at almost every instant by the sea, and in momentary dread of being washed off. Fortunately, the weather was so warm as to render the water rather grateful than otherwise.

July 25. This morning the gale had diminished to a mere ten-knot breeze, and the sea had gone down with it so considerably that we were able to keep ourselves dry upon the deck. To our great grief, however, we found that two jars of our olives, as well as the whole of our ham, had been washed overboard, in spite of the careful manner in which they had been fastened. We determined not to kill the tortoise as yet, and contented ourselves for the present with a breakfast on a few of the olives, and a measure of water each, which latter we mixed half and half, with wine, finding great relief and strength from the mixture, without the distressing intoxication which had ensued upon drinking the port. The sea was still far too rough for the renewal of our efforts at getting up provision from the storeroom. Several articles, of no importance to us in our present situation, floated up through the opening during the day, and were immediately washed overboard. We also now observed that the hulk lay more along than ever, so that we could not stand an instant without lashing ourselves. On this account we passed a gloomy and uncomfortable day. At noon the sun appeared to be nearly vertical, and we had no doubt that we had been driven down by the long succession of northward and northwesterly winds into the near vicinity of the equator. Towards evening we saw several sharks, and were somewhat alarmed by the audacious manner in which an enormously large one approached us. At one time, a lurch throwing the deck very far beneath the water, the monster actually swam in upon us, floundering for some moments just over the companion-hatch, and striking Peters violently with his tail. A heavy sea at length hurled him overboard, much to our relief. In moderate weather we might have easily captured him.

July 26. This morning, the wind having greatly abated, and the sea not being very rough, we determined to renew our exertions in the storeroom. After a great deal of hard labor during the whole day, we found that nothing further was to be expected from this quarter, the partitions of the room having been stove during the night, and its contents swept into the hold. This discovery, as may be supposed, filled us with despair.

July 27. The sea nearly smooth, with a light wind, and still from the north-ward and westward. The sun coming out hotly in the afternoon, we occupied ourselves in drying our clothes. Found great relief from thirst, and much comfort otherwise, by bathing in the sea; in this, however, we were forced to use great caution, being afraid of sharks, several of which were seen swimming around the brig during the day.

July 28. Good weather still. The brig now began to lie along so alarmingly that we feared she would eventually roll bottom up. Prepared ourselves as well as we could for this emergency, lashing our tortoise, water-jug, and two remaining jars of olives as far as possible over to the windward, placing them outside the hull, below the main-chains. The sea very smooth all day, with little or no wind.

July 29. A continuance of the same weather. Augustus' wounded arm began to evince symptoms of mortification. He complained of drowsiness and excessive thirst, but no acute pain. Nothing could be done for his relief beyond rubbing his wounds with a little of the vinegar from the olives, and from this no benefit seemed to be experienced. We did everything in our power for his comfort, and trebled his allowance of water.

July 30. An excessively hot day, with no wind. An enormous shark kept close by the hulk during the whole of the forenoon. We made several unsuccessful attempts to capture him by means of a noose. Augustus much worse, and evidently sinking as much from want of proper nourishment as from the effect of his wounds. He constantly prayed to be relieved from his sufferings, wishing for nothing but death. This evening we ate the last of our olives, and found the water in our jug so putrid that we could not swallow it at all without the addition of wine. Determined to kill our tortoise in the morning.

July 31. After a night of excessive anxiety and fatigue, owing to the position of the hulk, we set about killing and cutting up our tortoise. He proved to be much smaller than we had supposed, although in good condition—the whole meat about him not amounting to more than ten pounds. With a view of preserving a portion of this as long as possible, we cut it into fine pieces, and filled with them our three remaining olive-jars and the wine-bottle (all of which had been kept), pouring in afterward the vinegar from the olives. In this manner we put away about three pounds of the tortoise,

intending not to touch it until we had consumed the rest. We concluded to restrict ourselves to about four ounces of the meat per day; the whole would thus last us thirteen days. A brisk shower, with severe thunder and lightning, came on about dusk, but lasted so short a time that we only succeeded in catching about half a pint of water. The whole of this, by common consent, was given to Augustus, who now appeared to be in the last extremity. He drank the water from the sheet as we caught it (we holding it above him as he lay so as to let it run into his mouth), for we had now nothing left capable of holding water, unless we had chosen to empty out our wine from the carboy, or the stale water from the jug. Either of these expedients would have been resorted to had the shower lasted.

The sufferer seemed to derive but little benefit from the draught. His arm was completely black from the wrist to the shoulder, and his feet were like ice. We expected every moment to see him breathe his last. He was frightfully emaciated; so much so that, although he weighed a hundred and twenty-seven pounds upon his leaving Nantucket, he now did not weigh more than *forty or fifty at the farthest*. His eyes were sunk far in his head, being scarcely perceptible, and the skin of his cheeks hung so loosely as to prevent his masticating any food, or even swallowing any liquid, without great difficulty.

August 1. A continuance of the same calm weather, with an oppressively hot sun. Suffered exceedingly from thirst, the water in the jug being absolutely putrid and swarming with vermin. We contrived, nevertheless, to swallow a portion of it by mixing it with wine—our thirst, however, was but little abated. We found more relief by bathing in the sea, but could not avail ourselves of this expedient except at long intervals, on account of the continual presence of sharks. We now saw clearly that Augustus could not be saved; that he was evidently dying. We could do nothing to relieve his sufferings, which appeared to be great. About twelve o'clock he expired in strong convulsions, and without having spoken for several hours. His death filled us with the most gloomy forebodings, and had so great an effect upon our spirits that we sat motionless by the corpse during the whole day, and never addressed each other except in a whisper. It was not until some time after dark that we took courage to get up and throw the body overboard. It was then loathsome beyond expression, and so far decayed that, as Peters attempted to lift it, an entire leg came off in his grasp. As the mass of putrefaction slipped over the vessel's side into the water, the glare of phosphoric light with which it was surrounded plainly

discovered to us seven or eight large sharks, the clashing of whose horrible teeth, as their prey was torn to pieces among them, might have been heard at the distance of a mile. We shrunk within ourselves in the extremity of horror at the sound.

August 2. The same fearfully calm and hot weather. The dawn found us in a state of pitiable dejection as well as bodily exhaustion. The water in the jug was now absolutely useless, being a thick gelatinous mass; nothing but frightful-looking worms mingled with slime. We threw it out, and washed the jug well in the sea, afterward pouring a little vinegar in it from our bottles of pickled tortoise. Our thirst could now scarcely be endured, and we tried in vain to relieve it by wine, which seemed only to add fuel to the flame, and excited us to a high degree of intoxication. We afterward endeavored to relieve our sufferings by mixing the wine with seawater; but this instantly brought about the most violent retchings, so that we never again attempted it. During the whole day we anxiously sought an opportunity of bathing, but to no purpose; for the hulk was now entirely besieged on all sides with sharks—no doubt the identical monsters who had devoured our poor companion on the evening before, and who were in momentary expectation of another similar feast. This circumstance occasioned us the most bitter regret and filled us with the most depressing and melancholy forebodings. We had experienced indescribable relief in bathing, and to have this resource cut off in so frightful a manner was more than we could bear. Nor, indeed, were we altogether free from the apprehension of immediate danger, for the least slip or false movement would have thrown us at once within reach of those voracious fish, who frequently thrust themselves directly upon us, swimming up to leeward. No shouts or exertions on our part seemed to alarm them. Even when one of the largest was struck with an axe by Peters and much wounded, he persisted in his attempts to push in where we were. A cloud came up at dusk, but, to our extreme anguish, passed over without discharging itself. It is quite impossible to conceive our sufferings from thirst at this period. We passed a sleepless night, both on this account and through dread of the sharks.

August 3. No prospect of relief, and the brig lying still more and more along, so that now we could not maintain a footing upon deck at all. Busied ourselves in securing our wine and tortoise-meat, so that we might not lose them in the event of our rolling over. Got out two stout spikes from

the forechains, and, by means of the axe, drove them into the hull to windward within a couple of feet of the water, this not being very far from the keel, as we were nearly upon our beam-ends. To these spikes we now lashed our provisions, as being more secure than their former position beneath the chains. Suffered great agony from thirst during the whole day—no chance of bathing on account of the sharks, which never left us for a moment. Found it impossible to sleep.

August 4. A little before daybreak we perceived that the hulk was heeling over, and aroused ourselves to prevent being thrown off by the movement. At first the roll was slow and gradual, and we contrived to clamber over to windward very well, having taken the precaution to leave ropes hanging from the spikes we had driven in for the provision. But we had not calculated sufficiently upon the acceleration of the impetus; for, presently the heel became too violent to allow of our keeping pace with it; and, before either of us knew what was to happen, we found ourselves hurled furiously into the sea, and struggling several fathoms beneath the surface, with the huge hull immediately above us.

In going under the water I had been obliged to let go my hold upon the rope; and finding that I was completely beneath the vessel, and my strength nearly exhausted, I scarcely made a struggle for life, and resigned myself, in a few seconds, to die. But here again I was deceived, not having taken into consideration the natural rebound of the hull to windward. The whirl of the water upward, which the vessel occasioned in rolling partially back, brought me to the surface still more violently than I had been plunged beneath. Upon coming up I found myself about twenty yards from the hulk, as near as I could judge. She was lying keel up, rocking furiously from side to side, and the sea in all directions around was much agitated, and full of strong whirlpools. I could see nothing of Peters. An oil-cask was floating within a few feet of me, and various other articles from the brig were scattered about.

My principal terror was now on account of the sharks, which I knew to be in my vicinity. In order to deter these, if possible, from approaching me, I splashed the water vigorously with both hands and feet as I swam towards the hulk, creating a body of foam. I have no doubt that to this expedient, simple as it was, I was indebted for my preservation; for the sea all round the brig, just before her rolling over, was so crowded with these monsters, that I must have been, and really was, in actual contact with some of them during my progress. By great good fortune, however, I

reached the side of the vessel in safety, although so utterly weakened by the violent exertion I had used that I should never have been able to get upon it but for the timely assistance of Peters, who, now, to my great joy, made his appearance (having scrambled up to the keel from the opposite side of the hull), and threw me the end of a rope—one of those which had been attached to the spikes.

Having barely escaped this danger, our attention was now directed to the dreadful imminency of another—that of absolute starvation. Our whole stock of provision had been swept overboard in spite of all our care in securing it; and seeing no longer the remotest possibility of obtaining more, we gave way both of us to despair, weeping aloud like children, and neither of us attempting to offer consolation to the other. Such weakness can scarcely be conceived, and to those who have never been similarly situated will, no doubt, appear unnatural; but it must be remembered that our intellects were so entirely disordered by the long course of privation and terror to which we had been subjected, that we could not justly be considered, at that period, in the light of rational beings. In subsequent perils, nearly as great, if not greater, I bore up with fortitude against all the evils of my situation, and Peters, it will be seen, evinced a stoical philosophy nearly as incredible as his present childlike supineness and imbecility—the mental condition made the difference.

The overturning of the brig, even with the consequent loss of the wine and turtle, would not, in fact, have rendered our situation more deplorable than before, except for the disappearance of the bedclothes by which we had been hitherto enabled to catch rainwater, and of the jug in which we had kept it when caught; for we found the whole bottom, from within two or three feet of the bends as far as the keel, together with the keel itself, *thickly covered with large barnacles, which proved to be excellent and highly nutritious food.* Thus, in two important respects, the accident we had so greatly dreaded proved to be a benefit rather than an injury; it had opened to us a supply of provisions which we could not have exhausted, using it moderately, in a month; and it had greatly contributed to our comfort as regards position, we being much more at ease, and in infinitely less danger, than before.

The difficulty, however, of now obtaining water blinded us to all the benefits of the change in our condition. That we might be ready to avail ourselves, as far as possible, of any shower which might fall we took off our shirts, to make use of them as we had of the sheets—not hoping, of course, to get more in this way, even under the most favorable circumstances,

than half a gill at a time. No signs of a cloud appeared during the day, and the agonies of our thirst were nearly intolerable. At night, Peters obtained about an hour's disturbed sleep, but my intense sufferings would not permit me to close my eyes for a single moment.

August 5. Today, a gentle breeze springing up carried us through a vast quantity of seaweed, among which we were so fortunate as to find eleven small crabs, which afforded us several delicious meals. Their shells being quite soft, we ate them entire, and found that they irritated our thirst far less than the barnacles. Seeing no trace of sharks among the seaweed, we also ventured to bathe, and remained in the water for four or five hours, during which we experienced a very sensible diminution of our thirst. Were greatly refreshed, and spent the night somewhat more comfortably than before, both of us snatching a little sleep.

August 6. This day we were blessed by a brisk and continual rain, lasting from about noon until after dark. Bitterly did we now regret the loss of our jug and carboy; for, in spite of the little means we had of catching the water, we might have filled one, if not both of them. As it was, we contrived to satisfy the cravings of thirst by suffering the shirts to become saturated, and then wringing them so as to let the grateful fluid trickle into our mouths. In this occupation we passed the entire day.

August 7. Just at daybreak we both at the same instant descried a sail to the eastward, and *evidently coming towards us!* We hailed the glorious sight with a long, although feeble shout of rapture; and began instantly to make every signal in our power, by flaring the shirts in the air, leaping as high as our weak condition would permit, and even by hallooing with all the strength of our lungs, although the vessel could not have been less than fifteen miles distant. However, she still continued to near our hulk, and we felt that, if she but held her present course, she must eventually come so close as to perceive us. In about an hour after we first discovered her, we could clearly see the people on her decks. She was a long, low, and rakish-looking topsail schooner, with a black ball in her foretopsail, and had, apparently, a full crew. We now became alarmed, for we could hardly imagine it possible that she did not observe us, and were apprehensive that she meant to leave us to perish as we were—an act of fiendish barbarity, which, however incredible it may appear, has been repeatedly perpetuated at sea, under circumstances very nearly similar, and by

beings who were regarded as belonging to the human species.* In this instance, however, by the mercy of God, we were destined to be most happily deceived; for, presently we were aware of a sudden commotion on the deck of the stranger, who immediately afterward ran up a British flag, and, hauling her wind, bore up directly upon us. In half an hour more we found ourselves in her cabin. She proved to be the *Jane Guy*, of Liverpool, Captain Guy, bound on a sealing and trading voyage to the South Seas and Pacific.

* The case of the brig *Polly*, of Boston, is one so much in point, and her fate, in many respects, so remarkably similar to our own, that I cannot forbear alluding to it here. This vessel, of one hundred and thirty tons burden, sailed from Boston, with a cargo of lumber and provisions, for Santa Croix, on the twelfth of December, 1811, under the command of Captain Casneau. There were eight souls on board besides the captain—the mate, four seamen, and the cook, together with a Mr. Hunt, and a negro girl belonging to him. On the fifteenth, having cleared the shoal of Georges, she sprung a leak in a gale of wind from the southeast, and was finally capsized; but, the masts going by the board, she afterward righted. They remained in this situation, without fire, and with very little provision, for the period of *one hundred and ninety-one days* (from December the fifteenth to June the twentieth), when Captain Casneau and Samuel Badger, the only survivors, were taken off the wreck by the *Fame*, of Hull, Captain Featherstone, bound home from Rio Janeiro. When picked up, they were in *latitude 28° N., longitude 13° W., having drifted above two thousand miles!* On the ninth of July the *Fame* fell in with the brig *Dromero*, Captain Perkins, who landed the two sufferers in Kennebeck. The narrative from which we gather these details ends in the following words:

"It is natural to inquire how they could float such a vast distance, upon the most frequented part of the Atlantic, and not be discovered all this time. *They were passed by more than a dozen sail, one of which came so nigh them that they could distinctly see the people on deck and on the rigging looking at them; but, to the inexpressible disappointment of the starving and freezing men, they stifled the dictates of compassion, hoisted sail, and cruelly abandoned them to their fate.*"

CHAPTER XIV

THE *JANE GUY* WAS A FINE-LOOKING TOPSAIL SCHOONER OF A HUNDRED and eighty tons burden. She was unusually sharp in the bows, and on a wind, in moderate weather, the fastest sailer I have ever seen. Her qualities, however, as a rough sea-boat, were not so good, and her draught of water was by far too great for the trade to which she was destined. For this peculiar service, a larger vessel, and one of a light proportionate draught, is desirable—say a vessel of from three hundred to three hundred and fifty tons. She should be bark-rigged, and in other respects of a different construction from the usual South Sea ships. It is absolutely necessary that she should be well armed. She should have, say ten or twelve twelve-pound carronades, and two or three long twelves, with brass blunderbusses, and water-tight arm-chests for each top. Her anchors and cables should be of far greater strength than is required for any other species of trade, and, above all, her crew should be numerous and efficient—not less, for such a vessel as I have described, than fifty or sixty able-bodied men. The *Jane Guy* had a crew of thirty-five, all able seamen, besides the captain and mate, but she was not altogether as well armed or otherwise equipped, as a navigator acquainted with the difficulties and dangers of the trade could have desired.

Captain Guy was a gentleman of great urbanity of manner, and of considerable experience in the southern traffic, to which he had devoted a great portion of his life. He was deficient, however, in energy, and, consequently, in that spirit of enterprise which is here so absolutely requisite. He was part owner of the vessel in which he sailed, and was invested with discretionary powers to cruise in the South Seas for any cargo which

might come most readily to hand. He had on board, as usual in such voyages, beads, looking-glasses, tinder-works, axes, hatchets, saws, adzes, planes, chisels, gouges, gimlets, files, spokeshaves, rasps, hammers, nails, knives, scissors, razors, needles, thread, crockery-ware, calico, trinkets, and other similar articles.

The schooner sailed from Liverpool on the tenth of July, crossed the Tropic of Cancer on the twenty-fifth, in longitude twenty degrees west, and reached Sal, one of the Cape Verd islands, on the twenty-ninth, where she took in salt and other necessaries for the voyage. On the third of August, she left the Cape Verds and steered southwest, stretching over towards the coast of Brazil, so as to cross the equator between the meridians of twenty-eight and thirty degrees west longitude. This is the course usually taken by vessels bound from Europe to the Cape of Good Hope, or by that route to the East Indies. By proceeding thus they avoid the calms and strong contrary currents which continually prevail on the coast of Guinea, while, in the end, it is found to be the shortest track, as westerly winds are never wanting afterward by which to reach the Cape. It was Captain Guy's intention to make his first stoppage at Kerguelen's Land—I hardly know for what reason. On the day we were picked up the schooner was off Cape St. Roque, in longitude thirty-one degrees west; so that, when found, we had drifted probably, from north to south, *not less than five-and-twenty degrees!*

On board the Jane Guy we were treated with all the kindness our distressed situation demanded. In about a fortnight, during which time we continued steering to the southeast, with gentle breezes and fine weather, both Peters and myself recovered entirely from the effects of our late privation and dreadful sufferings, and we began to remember what had passed rather as a frightful dream from which we had been happily awakened, than as events which had taken place in sober and naked reality. I have since found that this species of partial oblivion is usually brought about by sudden transition, whether from joy to sorrow or from sorrow to joy—the degree of forgetfulness being proportioned to the degree of difference in the exchange. Thus, in my own case, I now feel it impossible to realize the full extent of the misery which I endured during the days spent upon the hulk. The incidents are remembered, but not the feelings which the incidents elicited at the time of their occurrence. I only know, that when they did occur, I *then* thought human nature could sustain nothing more of agony.

We continued our voyage for some weeks without any incidents of greater moment than the occasional meeting with whaling-ships, and more frequently with the black or right whale, so called in contradistinction to

the spermaceti. These, however, were chiefly found south of the twenty-fifth parallel. On the sixteenth of September, being in the vicinity of the Cape of Good Hope, the schooner encountered her first gale of any violence since leaving Liverpool. In this neighborhood, but more frequently to the south and east of the promontory (we were to the westward), navigators have often to contend with storms from the northward, which rage with great fury. They always bring with them a heavy sea, and one of their most dangerous features is the instantaneous chopping round of the wind, an occurrence almost certain to take place during the greatest force of the gale. A perfect hurricane will be blowing at one moment from the northward or northeast, and in the next not a breath of wind will be felt in that direction, while from the southwest it will come out all at once with a violence almost inconceivable. A bright spot to the southward is the sure forerunner of the change, and vessels are thus enabled to take the proper precautions.

It was about six in the morning when the blow came on with a white squall, and, as usual, from the northward. By eight it had increased very much, and brought down upon us one of the most tremendous seas I had then ever beheld. Everything had been made as snug as possible, but the schooner labored excessively, and gave evidence of her bad qualities as a seaboat, pitching her forecastle under at every plunge and with the greatest difficulty struggling up from one wave before she was buried in another. Just before sunset the bright spot for which we had been on the look-out made its appearance in the southwest, and in an hour afterward we perceived the little headsail we carried flapping listlessly against the mast. In two minutes more, in spite of every preparation, we were hurled on our beam-ends, as if by magic, and a perfect wilderness of foam made a clear breach over us as we lay. The blow from the southwest, however, luckily proved to be nothing more than a squall, and we had the good fortune to right the vessel without the loss of a spar. A heavy cross sea gave us great trouble for a few hours after this, but towards morning we found ourselves in nearly as good condition as before the gale. Captain Guy considered that he had made an escape little less than miraculous.

On the thirteenth of October we came in sight of Prince Edward's Island, in latitude 46° 53' S., longitude 37° 46' E. Two days afterward we found ourselves near Possession Island, and presently passed the islands of Crozet, in latitude 42° 59' S., longitude 48° E. On the eighteenth we made Kerguelen's or Desolation Island, in the Southern Indian

Ocean, and came to anchor in Christmas Harbor, having four fathoms of water.

This island, or rather group of islands, bears southeast from the Cape of Good Hope, and is distant therefrom nearly eight hundred leagues. It was first discovered in 1772, by the Baron de Kergulen, or Kerguelen, a Frenchman, who, thinking the land to form a portion of an extensive southern continent carried home information to that effect, which produced much excitement at the time. The government, taking the matter up, sent the baron back in the following year for the purpose of giving his new discovery a critical examination, when the mistake was discovered. In 1777, Captain Cook fell in with the same group, and gave to the principal one the name of Desolation Island, a title which it certainly well deserves. Upon approaching the land, however, the navigator might be induced to suppose otherwise, as the sides of most of the hills, from September to March, are clothed with very brilliant verdure. This deceitful appearance is caused by a small plant resembling saxifrage, which is abundant, growing in large patches on a species of crumbling moss. Besides this plant there is scarcely a sign of vegetation on the island, if we except some coarse rank grass near the harbor, some lichen, and a shrub which bears resemblance to a cabbage shooting into seed, and which has a bitter and acrid taste.

The face of the country is hilly, although none of the hills can be called lofty. Their tops are perpetually covered with snow. There are several harbors, of which Christmas Harbor is the most convenient. It is the first to be met with on the northeast side of the island after passing Cape Francois, which forms the northern shore, and, by its peculiar shape, serves to distinguish the harbor. Its projecting point terminates in a high rock, through which is a large hole, forming a natural arch. The entrance is in latitude 48° 40' S., longitude 69° 6' E. Passing in here, good anchorage may be found under the shelter of several small islands, which form a sufficient protection from all easterly winds. Proceeding on eastwardly from this anchorage you come to Wasp Bay, at the head of the harbor. This is a small basin, completely landlocked, into which you can go with four fathoms, and find anchorage in from ten to three, hard clay bottom. A ship might lie here with her best bower ahead all the year round without risk. To the westward, at the head of Wasp Bay, is a small stream of excellent water, easily procured.

Some seal of the fur and hair species are still to be found on Kerguelen's Island, and sea elephants abound. The feathered tribes are discovered

in great numbers. Penguins are very plenty, and of these there are four different kinds. The royal penguin, so called from its size and beautiful plumage, is the largest. The upper part of the body is usually gray, sometimes of a lilac tint; the under portion of the purest white imaginable. The head is of a glossy and most brilliant black, the feet also. The chief beauty of plumage, however, consists in two broad stripes of a gold color, which pass along from the head to the breast. The bill is long, and either pink or bright scarlet. These birds walk erect; with a stately carriage. They carry their heads high with their wings drooping like two arms, and, as their tails project from their body in a line with the legs, the resemblance to a human figure is very striking, and would be apt to deceive the spectator at a casual glance or in the gloom of the evening. The royal penguins which we met with on Kerguelen's Land were rather larger than a goose. The other kinds are the macaroni, the jackass, and the rookery penguin. These are much smaller, less beautiful in plumage, and different in other respects.

Besides the penguin many other birds are here to be found, among which may be mentioned seahens, blue petrels, teal, ducks, Port Egmont hens, shags, Cape pigeons, the nelly, seaswallows, terns, seagulls, Mother Carey's chickens, Mother Carey's geese, or the great petrel, and, lastly, the albatross.

The great petrel is as large as the common albatross, and is carnivorous. It is frequently called the break-bones, or osprey petrel. They are not at all shy, and, when properly cooked, are palatable food. In flying they sometimes sail very close to the surface of the water, with the wings expanded, without appearing to move them in the least degree, or make any exertion with them whatever.

The albatross is one of the largest and fiercest of the South Sea birds. It is of the gull species, and takes its prey on the wing, never coming on land except for the purpose of breeding. Between this bird and the penguin the most singular friendship exists. Their nests are constructed with great uniformity upon a plan concerted between the two species—that of the albatross being placed in the center of a little square formed by the nests of four penguins. Navigators have agreed in calling an assemblage of such encampments *a rookery*. These rookeries have been often described, but as my readers may not all have seen these descriptions, and as I shall have occasion hereafter to speak of the penguin and albatross, it will not be amiss to say something here of their mode of building and living.

When the season for incubation arrives, the birds assemble in vast numbers, and for some days appear to be deliberating upon the proper course to be pursued. At length they proceed to action. A level piece of ground is selected, of suitable extent, usually comprising three or four acres, and situated as near the sea as possible, being still beyond its reach. The spot is chosen with reference to its evenness of surface, and that is preferred which is the least encumbered with stones. This matter being arranged, the birds proceed, with one accord, and actuated apparently by one mind, to trace out, with mathematical accuracy, either a square or other parallelogram, as may best suit the nature of the ground, and of just sufficient size to accommodate easily all the birds assembled, and no more—in this particular seeming determined upon preventing the access of future stragglers who have not participated in the labor of the encampment. One side of the place thus marked out runs parallel with the water's edge, and is left open for ingress or egress.

Having defined the limits of the rookery, the colony now begin to clear it of every species of rubbish, picking up stone by stone, and carrying them outside of the lines, and close by them, so as to form a wall on the three inland sides. Just within this wall a perfectly level and smooth walk is formed, from six to eight feet wide, and extending around the encampment—thus serving the purpose of a general promenade.

The next process is to partition out the whole area into small squares exactly equal in size. This is done by forming narrow paths, very smooth, and crossing each other at right angles throughout the entire extent of the rookery. At each intersection of these paths the nest of an albatross is constructed, and a penguin's nest in the center of each square—thus every penguin is surrounded by four albatrosses, and each albatross by a like number of penguins. The penguin's nest consists of a hole in the earth, very shallow, being only just of sufficient depth to keep her single egg from rolling. The albatross is somewhat less simple in her arrangements, erecting a hillock about a foot high and two in diameter. This is made of earth, seaweed, and shells. On its summit she builds her nest.

The birds take especial care never to leave their nests unoccupied for an instant during the period of incubation, or, indeed, until the young progeny are sufficiently strong to take care of themselves. While the male is absent at sea in search of food, the female remains on duty, and it is only upon the return of her partner that she ventures abroad. The eggs are never left uncovered at all—while one bird leaves the nest the other

nestling in by its side. This precaution is rendered necessary by the thiev-
ing propensities prevalent in the rookery, the inhabitants making no
scruple to purloin each other's eggs at every good opportunity.

Although there are some rookeries in which the penguin and albatross
are the sole population, yet in most of them a variety of oceanic birds are
to be met with, enjoying all the privileges of citizenship, and scattering
their nests here and there, wherever they can find room, never interfer-
ing, however, with the stations of the larger species. The appearance of
such encampments, when seen from a distance, is exceedingly singular.
The whole atmosphere just above the settlement is darkened with the
immense number of the albatross (mingled with the smaller tribes) which
are continually hovering over it, either going to the ocean or returning
home. At the same time a crowd of penguins are to be observed, some
passing to and fro in the narrow alleys, and some marching with the mili-
tary strut so peculiar to them, around the general promenade ground
which encircles the rookery. In short, survey it as we will, nothing can be
more astonishing than the spirit of reflection evinced by these feathered
beings, and nothing surely can be better calculated to elicit reflection in
every well-regulated human intellect.

On the morning after our arrival in Christmas Harbor the chief mate,
Mr. Patterson, took the boats, and (although it was somewhat early in the
season) went in search of seal, leaving the captain and a young relation
of his on a point of barren land to the westward, they having some busi-
ness, whose nature I could not ascertain, to transact in the interior of the
island. Captain Guy took with him a bottle, in which was a sealed letter,
and made his way from the point on which he was set on shore towards
one of the highest peaks in the place. It is probable that his design was to
leave the letter on that height for some vessel which he expected to come
after him. As soon as we lost sight of him we proceeded (Peters and
myself being in the mate's boat) on our cruise around the coast, looking
for seal. In this business we were occupied about three weeks, examining
with great care every nook and corner, not only of Kerguelen's Land, but
of the several small islands in the vicinity. Our labors, however, were not
crowned with any important success. We saw a great many fur seal, but
they were exceedingly shy, and with the greatest exertions, we could only
procure three hundred and fifty skins in all. Sea elephants were abun-
dant, especially on the western coast of the mainland, but of these we
killed only twenty, and this with great difficulty. On the smaller islands

we discovered a good many of the hair seal, but did not molest them. We returned to the schooner: on the eleventh, where we found Captain Guy and his nephew, who gave a very bad account of the interior, representing it as one of the most dreary and utterly barren countries in the world. They had remained two nights on the island, owing to some misunderstanding, on the part of the second mate, in regard to the sending a jollyboat from the schooner to take them off.

CHAPTER XV

On the twelfth we made sail from Christmas Harbor retracing our way to the westward, and leaving Marion's Island, one of Crozet's group, on the larboard. We afterward passed Prince Edward's Island, leaving it also on our left; then, steering more to the northward, made, in fifteen days, the islands of Tristan d'Acunha, in latitude 37° 8' S., longitude 12° 8' W.

This group, now so well known, and which consists of three circular islands, was first discovered by the Portuguese, and was visited afterward by the Dutch in 1643, and by the French in 1767. The three islands together form a triangle, and are distant from each other about ten miles, there being fine open passages between. The land in all of them is very high, especially in Tristan d'Acunha, properly so called. This is the largest of the group, being fifteen miles in circumference, and so elevated that it can be seen in clear weather at the distance of eighty or ninety miles. A part of the land towards the north rises more than a thousand feet perpendicularly from the sea. A table-land at this height extends back nearly to the center of the island, and from this table-land arises a lofty cone like that of Teneriffe. The lower half of this cone is clothed with trees of good size, but the upper region is barren rock, usually hidden among the clouds, and covered with snow during the greater part of the year. There are no shoals or other dangers about the island, the shores being remarkably bold and the water deep. On the northwestern coast is a bay, with a beach of black sand where a landing with boats can be easily effected, provided there be a southerly wind. Plenty of excellent water may here be readily procured; also cod and other fish may be taken with hook and line.

The next island in point of size, and the most westwardly of the group, is that called the Inaccessible. Its precise situation is 37° 17' S. latitude, longitude 12° 24' W. It is seven or eight miles in circumference, and on all sides presents a forbidding and precipitous aspect. Its top is perfectly flat, and the whole region is sterile, nothing growing upon it except a few stunted shrubs.

Nightingale Island, the smallest and most southerly, is in latitude 37° 26' S., longitude 12° 12' W. Off its southern extremity is a high ledge of rocky islets; a few also of a similar appearance are seen to the northeast. The ground is irregular and sterile, and a deep valley partially separates it.

The shores of these islands abound, in the proper season, with sea lions, sea elephants, the hair and fur seal, together with a great variety of oceanic birds. Whales are also plenty in their vicinity. Owing to the ease with which these various animals were here formerly taken, the group has been much visited since its discovery. The Dutch and French frequented it at a very early period. In 1790, Captain Patten, of the ship *Industry*, of Philadelphia, made Tristan d'Acunha, where he remained seven months (from August, 1790, to April, 1791) for the purpose of collecting sealskins. In this time he gathered no less than five thousand six hundred, and says that he would have had no difficulty in loading a large ship with oil in three weeks. Upon his arrival he found no quadrupeds, with the exception of a few wild goats; the island now abounds with all our most valuable domestic animals, which have been introduced by subsequent navigators.

I believe it was not long after Captain Patten's visit that Captain Colquhoun, of the American brig *Betsey*, touched at the largest of the islands for the purpose of refreshment. He planted onions, potatoes, cabbages, and a great many other vegetables, an abundance of all which is now to be met with.

In 1811, a Captain Haywood, in the *Nereus*, visited Tristan. He found there three Americans, who were residing upon the island to prepare sealskins and oil. One of these men was named Jonathan Lambert, and he called himself the sovereign of the country. He had cleared and cultivated about sixty acres of land, and turned his attention to raising the coffee-plant and sugar-cane, with which he had been furnished by the American Minister at Rio Janeiro. This settlement, however, was finally abandoned, and in 1817 the islands were taken possession of by the British Government, who sent a detachment for that purpose from the Cape of Good Hope. They did not, however, retain them long; but, upon the evacuation of the country as a British possession, two or three English families took up their residence there independently of the Government. On the twenty-fifth of March,

1824, the *Berwick*, Captain Jeffrey, from London to Van Diemen's Land, arrived at the place, where they found an Englishman of the name of Glass, formerly a corporal in the British artillery. He claimed to be supreme governor of the islands, and had under his control twenty-one men and three women. He gave a very favorable account of the salubrity of the climate and of the productiveness of the soil. The population occupied themselves chiefly in collecting sealskins and sea elephant oil, with which they traded to the Cape of Good Hope, Glass owning a small schooner. At the period of our arrival the governor was still a resident, but his little community had multiplied, there being fifty-six persons upon Tristan, besides a smaller settlement of seven on Nightingale Island. We had no difficulty in procuring almost every kind of refreshment which we required—sheep, hogs, bullocks, rabbits, poultry, goats, fish in great variety, and vegetables were abundant. Having come to anchor close in with the large island, in eighteen fathoms, we took all we wanted on board very conveniently. Captain Guy also purchased of Glass five hundred sealskins and some ivory. We remained here a week, during which the prevailing winds were from the northward and westward, and the weather somewhat hazy. On the fifth of November we made sail to the southward and westward, with the intention of having a thorough search for a group of islands called the Auroras, respecting whose existence a great diversity of opinion has existed.

These islands are said to have been discovered as early as 1762, by the commander of the ship *Aurora*. In 1790, Captain Manuel de Oyarvido, in the ship *Princess*, belonging to the Royal Philippine Company, sailed, as he asserts, directly among them. In 1794, the Spanish corvette *Atrevida* went with the determination of ascertaining their precise situation, and, in a paper published by the Royal Hydrographical Society of Madrid in the year 1809, the following language is used respecting this expedition: "The corvette *Atrevida* practiced, in their immediate vicinity, from the twenty-first to the twenty-seventh of January, all the necessary observations, and measured by chronometers the difference of longitude between these islands and the port of Soledad in the Malninas. The islands are three, they are very nearly in the same meridian; the center one is rather low, and the other two may be seen at nine leagues' distance." The observations made on board the *Atrevida* give the following results as the precise situation of each island. The most northern is in latitude 52° 37' 24" S., longitude 47°, 43' 15" W.; the middle one in latitude 53° 2' 40" S., longitude 47° 55' 15" W.; and the most southern in latitude 53° 15' 22" S., longitude 47° 57' 15" W.

On the twenty-seventh of January, 1820, Captain James Weddel, of the British navy, sailed from Staten Land also in search of the Auroras. He reports that, having made the most diligent search and passed not only immediately over the spots indicated by the commander of the *Atrevida*, but in every direction throughout the vicinity of these spots, he could discover no indication of land. These conflicting statements have induced other navigators to look out for the islands; and, strange to say, while some have sailed through every inch of sea where they are supposed to lie without finding them, there have been not a few who declare positively that they have seen them; and even been close in with their shores. It was Captain Guy's intention to make every exertion within his power to settle the question so oddly in dispute.*

We kept on our course, between the south and west, with variable weather, until the twentieth of the month, when we found ourselves on the debated ground, being in latitude 53° 15' S., longitude 47° 58' W.—that is to say, very nearly upon the spot indicated as the situation of the most southern of the group. Not perceiving any sign of land, we continued to the westward of the parallel of fifty-three degrees south, as far as the meridian of fifty degrees west. We then stood to the north as far as the parallel of fifty-two degrees south, when we turned to the eastward, and kept our parallel by double altitudes, morning and evening, and meridian altitudes of the planets and moon. Having thus gone eastwardly to the meridian of the western coast of Georgia, we kept that meridian until we were in the latitude from which we set out. We then took diagonal courses throughout the entire extent of sea circumscribed, keeping a lookout constantly at the masthead, and repeating our examination with the greatest care for a period of three weeks, during which the weather was remarkably pleasant and fair, with no haze whatsoever. Of course we were thoroughly satisfied that, whatever islands might have existed in this vicinity at any former period, no vestige of them remained at the present day. Since my return home I find that the same ground was traced over, with equal care, in 1822, by Captain Johnson, of the American schooner *Henry*, and by Captain Morrell in the American schooner *Wasp*—in both cases with the same result as in our own.

* Among the vessels which at various times have professed to meet with the Auroras may be mentioned the ship *San Miguel*, in 1769; the ship *Aurora*, in 1774; the brig *Pearl*, in 1779; and the ship *Dolores*, in 1790. They all agree in giving the mean latitude fifty-three degrees south.

CHAPTER XVI

IT HAD BEEN CAPTAIN GUY'S ORIGINAL INTENTION, AFTER SATISFYING himself about the Auroras, to proceed through the Strait of Magellan, and up along the western coast of Patagonia; but information received at Tristan d'Acunha induced him to steer to the southward, in the hope of falling in with some small islands said to lie about the parallel of 60° S., longitude 41° 20' W. In the event of his not discovering these lands, he designed, should the season prove favorable, to push on towards the pole. Accordingly, on the twelfth of December, we made sail in that direction. On the eighteenth we found ourselves about the station indicated by Glass, and cruised for three days in that neighborhood without finding any traces of the islands he had mentioned. On the twenty-first, the weather being unusually pleasant, we again made sail to the southward, with the resolution of penetrating in that course as far as possible. Before entering upon this portion of my narrative, it may be as well, for the information of those readers who have paid little attention to the progress of discovery in these regions, to give some brief account of the very few attempts at reaching the southern pole which have hitherto been made.

That of Captain Cook was the first of which we have any distinct account. In 1772 he sailed to the south in the *Resolution*, accompanied by Lieutenant Furneaux in the *Adventure*. In December he found himself as far as the fifty-eighth parallel of south latitude, and in longitude 26° 57' E. Here he met with narrow fields of ice, about eight or ten inches thick, and running northwest and southeast. This ice was in large cakes, and usually it was packed so closely that the vessel had great difficulty in forcing a passage. At this period Captain Cook supposed, from the vast

number of birds to be seen, and from other indications, that he was in the near vicinity of land. He kept on to the southward, the weather being exceedingly cold, until he reached the sixty-fourth parallel, in longitude 38° 14' E. Here he had mild weather, with gentle breezes, for five days, the thermometer being at thirty-six. In January, 1773, the vessels crossed the Antarctic circle, but did not succeed in penetrating much farther; for upon reaching latitude 67° 15' they found all farther progress impeded by an immense body of ice, extending all along the southern horizon as far as the eye could reach. This ice was of every variety—and some large floes of it, miles in extent, formed a compact mass, rising eighteen or twenty feet above the water. It being late in the season, and no hope entertained of rounding these obstructions, Captain Cook now reluctantly turned to the northward.

In the November following he renewed his search in the Antarctic. In latitude 59° 40' he met with a strong current setting to the southward. In December, when the vessels were in latitude 67° 31', longitude 142° 54' W., the cold was excessive, with heavy gales and fog. Here also birds were abundant; the albatross, the penguin, and the petrel especially. In latitude 70° 23' some large islands of ice were encountered, and shortly afterward the clouds to the southward were observed to be of a snowy whiteness, indicating the vicinity of field ice. In latitude 71° 10', longitude 106° 54' W., the navigators were stopped, as before, by an immense frozen expanse, which filled the whole area of the southern horizon. The northern edge of this expanse was ragged and broken, so firmly wedged together as to be utterly impassible, and extending about a mile to the southward. Behind it the frozen surface was comparatively smooth for some distance, until terminated in the extreme background by gigantic ranges of ice mountains, the one towering above the other. Captain Cook concluded that this vast field reached the southern pole or was joined to a continent. Mr. J. N. Reynolds, whose great exertions and perseverance have at length succeeded in getting set on foot a national expedition, partly for the purpose of exploring these regions, thus speaks of the attempt of the *Resolution*. "We are not surprised that Captain Cook was unable to go beyond 71° 10', but we are astonished that he did attain that point on the meridian of 106° 54' west longitude. Palmer's Land lies south of the Shetland, latitude sixty-four degrees, and tends to the southward and westward farther than any navigator has yet penetrated. Cook was standing for this land when his progress was arrested by the ice; which, we apprehend, must always be the case in that point, and so early

in the season as the sixth of January—and we should not be surprised if a portion of the icy mountains described was attached to the main body of Palmer's Land, or to some other portions of land lying farther to the southward and westward."

In 1803, Captains Kreutzenstern and Lisiausky were dispatched by Alexander of Russia for the purpose of circumnavigating the globe. In endeavoring to get south, they made no farther than 59° 58', in longitude 70° 15' W. They here met with strong currents setting eastwardly. Whales were abundant, but they saw no ice. In regard to this voyage, Mr. Reynolds observes that, if Kreutzenstern had arrived where he did earlier in the season, he must have encountered ice—it was March when he reached the latitude specified. The winds, prevailing, as they do, from the southward and westward, had carried the floes, aided by currents, into that icy region bounded on the north by Georgia, east by Sandwich Land and the South Orkneys, and west by the South Shetland islands.

In 1822, Captain James Weddell, of the British navy, with two very small vessels, penetrated farther to the south than any previous navigator, and this, too, without encountering extraordinary difficulties. He states that although he was frequently hemmed in by ice *before* reaching the seventy-second parallel, yet, upon attaining it, not a particle was to be discovered, and that, upon arriving at the latitude of 74° 15', no fields, and only three islands of ice were visible. It is somewhat remarkable that, although vast flocks of birds were seen, and other usual indications of land, and although, south of the Shetlands, unknown coasts were observed from the masthead tending southwardly, Weddell discourages the idea of land existing in the polar regions of the south.

On the 11th of January, 1823, Captain Benjamin Morrell, of the American schooner *Wasp,* sailed from Kerguelen's Land with a view of penetrating as far south as possible. On the first of February he found himself in latitude 64° 52' S., longitude 118° 27' E. The following passage is extracted from his journal of that date. "The wind soon freshened to an eleven-knot breeze, and we embraced this opportunity of making to the west; being however convinced that the farther we went south beyond latitude sixty-four degrees, the less ice was to be apprehended, we steered a little to the southward, until we crossed the Antarctic circle, and were in latitude 69° 15' E. In this latitude there was *no field ice,* and very few ice islands in sight."

Under the date of March fourteenth I find also this entry. "The sea was now entirely free of field ice, and there were not more than a dozen ice

islands in sight. At the same time the temperature of the air and water was at least thirteen degrees higher (more mild) than we had ever found it between the parallels of sixty and sixty-two south. We were now in latitude 70° 14' S., and the temperature of the air was forty-seven, and that of the water forty-four. In this situation I found the variation to be 14° 27' easterly, per azimuth. . . . I have several times passed within the Antarctic circle, on different meridians, and have uniformly found the temperature, both of the air and the water, to become more and more mild the farther I advanced beyond the sixty-fifth degree of south latitude, and that the variation decreases in the same proportion. While north of this latitude, say between sixty and sixty-five south, we frequently had great difficulty in finding a passage for the vessel between the immense and almost innumerable ice islands, some of which were from one to two miles in circumference, and more than five hundred feet above the surface of the water."

Being nearly destitute of fuel and water, and without proper instruments, it being also late in the season, Captain Morrell was now obliged to put back, without attempting any further progress to the westward, although an entirely open sea lay before him. He expresses the opinion that, had not these overruling considerations obliged him to retreat, he could have penetrated, if not to the pole itself, at least to the eighty-fifth parallel. I have given his ideas respecting these matters somewhat at length, that the reader may have an opportunity of seeing how far they were borne out by my own subsequent experience.

In 1831, Captain Briscoe, in the employ of the Messieurs Enderby, whale-ship owners of London, sailed in the brig *Lively* for the South Seas, accompanied by the cutter *Tula*. On the twenty-eighth of February, being in latitude 66° 30' S., longitude 47° 31' E., he descried land, and "clearly discovered through the snow the black peaks of a range of mountains running E. S. E." He remained in this neighborhood during the whole of the following month, but was unable to approach the coast nearer than within ten leagues, owing to the boisterous state of the weather. Finding it impossible to make further discovery during this season, he returned northward to winter in Van Diemen's Land.

In the beginning of 1832 he again proceeded southwardly, and on the fourth of February was seen to the southeast in latitude 67° 15', longitude 69° 29' W. This was soon found to be an island near the headland of the country he had first discovered. On the twenty-first of the month he succeeded in landing on the latter, and took possession of it in the name of William IV, calling it Adelaide's Island, in honour of the English queen.

These particulars being made known to the Royal Geographical Society of London, the conclusion was drawn by that body "that there is a continuous tract of land extending from 47° 30' E. to 69° 29' W. longitude, running the parallel of from sixty-six to sixty-seven degrees south latitude." In respect to this conclusion Mr. Reynolds observes: "In the correctness of it we by no means concur; nor do the discoveries of Briscoe warrant any such indifference. It was within these limits that Weddel proceeded south on a meridian to the east of Georgia, Sandwich Land, and the South Orkney and Shetland Islands." My own experience will be found to testify most directly to the falsity of the conclusion arrived at by the society.

These are the principal attempts which have been made at penetrating to a high southern latitude, and it will now be seen that there remained, previous to the voyage of the *Jane*, nearly three hundred degrees of longitude in which the Antarctic circle had not been crossed at all. Of course a wide field lay before us for discovery, and it was with feelings of most intense interest that I heard Captain Guy express his resolution of pushing boldly to the southward.

CHAPTER XVII

WE KEPT OUR COURSE SOUTHWARDLY FOR FOUR DAYS AFTER GIVING UP the search for Glass' islands, without meeting with any ice at all. On the twenty-sixth, at noon, we were in latitude 63° 23' S., longitude 41° 25' W. We now saw several large ice islands, and a floe of field ice, not, however, of any great extent. The winds generally blew from the southeast, or the northeast, but were very light. Whenever we had a westerly wind, which was seldom, it was invariably attended with a rain squall. Every day we had more or less snow. The thermometer, on the twenty-seventh stood at thirty-five.

January 1, 1828. This day we found ourselves completely hemmed in by the ice, and our prospects looked cheerless indeed. A strong gale blew, during the whole forenoon, from the northeast, and drove large cakes of the drift against the rudder and counter with such violence that we all trembled for the consequences. Towards evening, the gale still blowing with fury, a large field in front separated, and we were enabled, by carrying a press of sail to force a passage through the smaller flakes into some open water beyond. As we approached this space we took in sail by degrees, and having at length got clear, lay-to under a single reefed foresail.

January 2. We had now tolerably pleasant weather. At noon we found ourselves in latitude 69° 10' S, longitude 42° 20' W, having crossed the Antarctic circle. Very little ice was to be seen to the southward, although large fields of it lay behind us. This day we rigged some sounding gear, using a large iron pot capable of holding twenty gallons, and a line of two hundred

fathoms. We found the current setting to the north, about a quarter of a mile per hour. The temperature of the air was now about thirty-three. Here we found the variation to be 14° 28' easterly, per azimuth.

January 5. We had still held on to the southward without any very great impediments. On this morning, however, being in latitude 73° 15' E., longitude 42° 10' W, we were again brought to a stand by an immense expanse of firm ice. We saw, nevertheless, much open water to the southward, and felt no doubt of being able to reach it eventually. Standing to the eastward along the edge of the floe, we at length came to a passage of about a mile in width, through which we warped our way by sundown. The sea in which we now were was thickly covered with ice islands, but had no field ice, and we pushed on boldly as before. The cold did not seem to increase, although we had snow very frequently, and now and then hail squalls of great violence. Immense flocks of the albatross flew over the schooner this day, going from southeast to northwest.

January 7. The sea still remained pretty well open, so that we had no difficulty in holding on our course. To the westward we saw some icebergs of incredible size, and in the afternoon passed very near one whose summit could not have been less than four hundred fathoms from the surface of the ocean. Its girth was probably, at the base, three quarters of a league, and several streams of water were running from crevices in its sides. We remained in sight of this island two days, and then only lost it in a fog.

January 10. Early this morning we had the misfortune to lose a man overboard. He was an American named Peter Vredenburgh, a native of New York, and was one of the most valuable hands on board the schooner. In going over the bows his foot slipped, and he fell between two cakes of ice, never rising again. At noon of this day we were in latitude 78° 30', longitude 40° 15' W. The cold was now excessive, and we had hail squalls continually from the northward and eastward. In this direction also we saw several more immense icebergs, and the whole horizon to the eastward appeared to be blocked up with field ice, rising in tiers, one mass above the other. Some driftwood floated by during the evening, and a great quantity of birds flew over, among which were Nellies, petrels, albatrosses, and a large bird of a brilliant blue plumage. The variation here, per azimuth, was less than it had been previously to our passing the Antarctic circle.

January 12. Our passage to the south again looked doubtful, as nothing was to be seen in the direction of the pole but one apparently limitless floe, backed by absolute mountains of ragged ice, one precipice of which arose frowningly above the other. We stood to the westward until the fourteenth, in the hope of finding an entrance.

January 14. This morning we reached the western extremity of the field which had impeded us, and, weathering it, came to an open sea, without a particle of ice. Upon sounding with two hundred fathoms, we here found a current setting southwardly at the rate of half a mile per hour. The temperature of the air was forty-seven, that of the water thirty-four. We now sailed to the southward without meeting any interruption of moment until the sixteenth, when, at noon, we were in latitude 81° 21', longitude 42° W. We here again sounded, and found a current setting still southwardly, and at the rate of three quarters of a mile per hour. The variation per azimuth had diminished, and the temperature of the air was mild and pleasant, the thermometer being as high as fifty-one. At this period not a particle of ice was to be discovered. All hands on board now felt certain of attaining the pole.

January 17. This day was full of incident. Innumerable flights of birds flew over us from the southward, and several were shot from the deck; one of them, a species of pelican, proved to be excellent eating. About midday a small floe of ice was seen from the masthead off the larboard bow, and upon it there appeared to be some large animal. As the weather was good and nearly calm, Captain Guy ordered out two of the boats to see what it was. Dirk Peters and myself accompanied the mate in the larger boat. Upon coming up with the floe, we perceived that it was in the possession of a gigantic creature of the race of the Arctic bear, but far exceeding in size the largest of these animals. Being well armed, we made no scruple of attacking it at once. Several shots were fired in quick succession, the most of which took effect, apparently, in the head and body. Nothing discouraged, however, the monster threw himself from the ice, and swam with open jaws, to the boat in which were Peters and myself. Owing to the confusion which ensued among us at this unexpected turn of the adventure, no person was ready immediately with a second shot, and the bear had actually succeeded in getting half his vast bulk across our gunwale, and seizing one of the men by the small of his back, before any efficient means were taken to repel him. In this extremity nothing but the promptness and agility of

Peters saved us from destruction. Leaping upon the back of the huge beast, he plunged the blade of a knife behind the neck, reaching the spinal marrow at a blow. The brute tumbled into the sea lifeless, and without a struggle, rolling over Peters as he fell. The latter soon recovered himself, and a rope being thrown him, he secured the carcass before entering the boat. We then returned in triumph to the schooner, towing our trophy behind us. This bear, upon admeasurement, proved to be full fifteen feet in his greatest length. His wool was perfectly white, and very coarse, curling tightly. The eyes were of a blood red, and larger than those of the Arctic bear; the snout also more rounded, rather resembling the snout of the bulldog. The meat was tender, but excessively rank and fishy, although the men devoured it with avidity, and declared it excellent eating.

Scarcely had we got our prize alongside, when the man at the mast-head gave the joyful shout of *"land on the starboard bow!"* All hands were now upon the alert, and, a breeze springing up very opportunely from the northward and eastward, we were soon close in with the coast. It proved to be a low rocky islet, of about a league in circumference, and altogether destitute of vegetation, if we except a species of prickly pear. In approaching it from the northward, a singular ledge of rock is seen projecting into the sea, and bearing a strong resemblance to corded bales of cotton. Around this ledge to the westward is a small bay, at the bottom of which our boats effected a convenient landing.

It did not take us long to explore every portion of the island, but, with one exception, we found nothing worthy of our observation. In the southern extremity, we picked up near the shore, half buried in a pile of loose stones, a piece of wood, which seemed to have formed the prow of a canoe. There had been evidently some attempt at carving upon it, and Captain Guy fancied that he made out the figure of a tortoise, but the resemblance did not strike me very forcibly. Besides this prow, if such it were, we found no other token that any living creature had ever been here before. Around the coast we discovered occasional small floes of ice—but these were very few. The exact situation of the islet (to which Captain Guy gave the name of Bennet's Islet, in honor of his partner in the ownership of the schooner) is 82° 50' S. latitude, 42° 20' W. longitude.

We had now advanced to the southward more than eight degrees farther than any previous navigators, and the sea still lay perfectly open before us. We found, too, that the variation uniformly decreased as we proceeded, and, what was still more surprising, that the temperature of the air, and latterly of the water, became milder. The weather might even

be called pleasant, and we had a steady but very gentle breeze always from some northern point of the compass. The sky was usually clear, with now and then a slight appearance of thin vapor in the southern horizon—this, however, was invariably of brief duration. Two difficulties alone presented themselves to our view; we were getting short of fuel, and symptoms of scurvy had occurred among several of the crew. These considerations began to impress upon Captain Guy the necessity of returning, and he spoke of it frequently. For my own part, confident as I was of soon arriving at land of some description upon the course we were pursuing, and having every reason to believe, from present appearances, that we should not find it the sterile soil met with in the higher Arctic latitudes, I warmly pressed upon him the expediency of persevering, at least for a few days longer, in the direction we were now holding. So tempting an opportunity of solving the great problem in regard to an Antarctic continent had never yet been afforded to man, and I confess that I felt myself bursting with indignation at the timid and ill-timed suggestions of our commander. I believe, indeed, that what I could not refrain from saying to him on this head had the effect of inducing him to push on. While, therefore, I cannot but lament the most unfortunate and bloody events which immediately arose from my advice, I must still be allowed to feel some degree of gratification at having been instrumental, however remotely, in opening to the eye of science one of the most intensely exciting secrets which has ever engrossed its attention.

CHAPTER XVIII

JANUARY 18. THIS MORNING* WE CONTINUED TO THE SOUTHWARD, WITH THE same pleasant weather as before. The sea was entirely smooth, the air tolerably warm and from the northeast, the temperature of the water fifty-three. We now again got our sounding-gear in order, and, with a hundred and fifty fathoms of line, found the current setting towards the pole at the rate of a mile an hour. This constant tendency to the southward, both in the wind and current, caused some degree of speculation, and even of alarm, in different quarters of the schooner, and I saw distinctly that no little impression had been made upon the mind of Captain Guy. He was exceedingly sensitive to ridicule, however, and I finally succeeded in laughing him out of his apprehensions. The variation was now very trivial. In the course of the day we saw several large whales of the right species, and innumerable flights of the albatross passed over the vessel. We also picked up a bush, full of red berries, like those of the hawthorn, and the carcass of a singular-looking land-animal. It was three feet in length, and but six inches in

* The terms *morning* and *evening*, which I have made use of to avoid confusion in my narrative, as far as possible, must not, of course, be taken in their ordinary sense. For a long time past we had had no night at all, the daylight being continual. The dates throughout are according to nautical time, and the bearing must be understood as per compass. I would also remark, in this place, that I cannot, in the first portion of what is here written, pretend to strict accuracy in respect to dates, or latitudes and longitudes, having kept no regular journal until after the period of which this first portion treats. In many instances I have relied altogether upon memory.

height, with four very short legs, the feet armed with long claws of a brilliant scarlet, and resembling coral in substance. The body was covered with a straight silky hair, perfectly white. The tail was peaked like that of a rat, and about a foot and a half long. The head resembled a cat's, with the exception of the ears—these were flopped like the ears of a dog. The *teeth* were of the same brilliant scarlet as the claws.

January 19. Today, being in latitude 83° 20', longitude 43° 5' W. (the sea being of an extraordinarily dark color), we again saw land from the mast-head, and, upon a closer scrutiny, found it to be one of a group of very large islands. The shore was precipitous, and the interior seemed to be well wooded, a circumstance which occasioned us great joy. In about four hours from our first discovering the land we came to anchor in ten fathoms, sandy bottom, a league from the coast, as a high surf, with strong ripples here and there, rendered a nearer approach of doubtful expediency. The two largest boats were now ordered out, and a party, well armed (among whom were Peters and myself), proceeded to look for an opening in the reef which appeared to encircle the island. After searching about for some time, we discovered an inlet, which we were entering, when we saw four large canoes put off from the shore, filled with men who seemed to be well armed. We waited for them to come up, and, as they moved with great rapidity, they were soon within hail. Captain Guy now held up a white handkerchief on the blade of an oar, when the strangers made a full stop, and commenced a loud jabbering all at once, intermingled with occasional shouts, in which we could distinguish the words *Anamoo-moo!* and *Lama-Lama!* They continued this for at least half an hour, during which we had a good opportunity of observing their appearance.

In the four canoes, which might have been fifty feet long and five broad, there were a hundred and ten savages in all. They were about the ordinary stature of Europeans, but of a more muscular and brawny frame. Their complexion a jet black, with thick and long woolly hair. They were clothed in skins of an unknown black animal, shaggy and silky, and made to fit the body with some degree of skill, the hair being inside, except where turned out about the neck, wrists, and ankles. Their arms consisted principally of clubs, of a dark, and apparently very heavy wood. Some spears, however, were observed among them, headed with flint, and a few slings. The bottoms of the canoes were full of black stones about the size of a large egg.

When they had concluded their harangue (for it was clear they intended their jabbering for such), one of them who seemed to be the

chief stood up in the prow of his canoe, and made signs for us to bring our boats alongside of him. This hint we pretended not to understand, thinking it the wiser plan to maintain, if possible, the interval between us, as their number more than quadrupled our own. Finding this to be the case, the chief ordered the three other canoes to hold back, while he advanced towards us with his own. As soon as he came up with us he leaped on board the largest of our boats, and seated himself by the side of Captain Guy, pointing at the same time to the schooner, and repeating the word *Anamoo-moo!* and *Lama-Lama!* We now put back to the vessel, the four canoes following at a little distance.

Upon getting alongside, the chief evinced symptoms of extreme surprise and delight, clapping his hands, slapping his thighs and breast, and laughing obstreperously. His followers behind joined in his merriment, and for some minutes the din was so excessive as to be absolutely deafening. Quiet being at length restored, Captain Guy ordered the boats to be hoisted up, as a necessary precaution, and gave the chief (whose name we soon found to be *Too-wit*) to understand that we could admit no more than twenty of his men on deck at one time. With this arrangement he appeared perfectly satisfied, and gave some directions to the canoes, when one of them approached, the rest remaining about fifty yards off. Twenty of the savages now got on board, and proceeded to ramble over every part of the deck, and scramble about among the rigging, making themselves much at home, and examining every article with great inquisitiveness.

It was quite evident that they had never before seen any of the white race—from whose complexion, indeed, they appeared to recoil. They believed the *Jane* to be a living creature, and seemed to be afraid of hurting it with the points of their spears, carefully turning them up. Our crew were much amused with the conduct of Too-wit in one instance. The cook was splitting some wood near the galley, and, by accident, struck his axe into the deck, making a gash of considerable depth. The chief immediately ran up, and pushing the cook on one side rather roughly, commenced a half whine, half howl, strongly indicative of sympathy in what he considered the sufferings of the schooner, patting and smoothing the gash with his hand, and washing it from a bucket of seawater which stood by. This was a degree of ignorance for which we were not prepared, and for my part I could not help thinking some of it affected.

When the visiters had satisfied, as well as they could, their curiosity in regard to our upper works, they were admitted below, when their amazement exceeded all bounds. Their astonishment now appeared to be far

too deep for words, for they roamed about in silence, broken only by low ejaculations. The arms afforded them much food for speculation, and they were suffered to handle and examine them at leisure. I do not believe that they had the least suspicion of their actual use, but rather took them for idols, seeing the care we had of them, and the attention with which we watched their movements while handling them. At the great guns their wonder was redoubled. They approached them with every mark of the profoundest reverence and awe, but forbore to examine them minutely. There were two large mirrors in the cabin, and here was the acme of their amazement. Too-wit was the first to approach them, and he had got in the middle of the cabin, with his face to one and his back to the other, before he fairly perceived them. Upon raising his eyes and seeing his reflected self in the glass, I thought the savage would go mad; but, upon turning short round to make a retreat, and beholding himself a second time in the opposite direction, I was afraid he would expire upon the spot. No persuasion could prevail upon him to take another look; but, throwing himself upon the floor, with his face buried in his hands, he remained thus until we were obliged to drag him upon deck.

The whole of the savages were admitted on board in this manner, twenty at a time, Too-wit being suffered to remain during the entire period. We saw no disposition to thievery among them, nor did we miss a single article after their departure. Throughout the whole of their visit they evinced the most friendly manner. There were, however, some points in their demeanor which we found it impossible to understand; for example, we could not get them to approach several very harmless objects—such as the schooner's sails, an egg, an open book, or a pan of flour. We endeavored to ascertain if they had among them any articles which might be turned to account in the way of traffic, but found great difficulty in being comprehended. We made out, nevertheless, what greatly astonished us, that the islands abounded in the large tortoise of the Gallipagos, one of which we saw in the canoe of Too-wit. We saw also some *biche de mer*[b] in the hands of one of the savages, who was greedily devouring it in its natural state. These anomalies—for they were such when considered in regard to the latitude—induced Captain Guy to wish for a thorough investigation of the country, in the hope of making a profitable speculation in his discovery. For my own part, anxious as I was to know something more of these islands, I was still more earnestly bent on prosecuting the voyage to the southward without delay. We had now fine weather, but there was no telling how long it would last; and being already in the eighty-fourth parallel,

with an open sea before us, a current setting strongly to the southward, and the wind fair, I could not listen with any patience to a proposition of stopping longer than was absolutely necessary for the health of the crew and the taking on board a proper supply of fuel and fresh provisions. I represented to the captain that we might easily make this group on our return, and winter here in the event of being blocked up by the ice. He at length came into my views (for in some way, hardly known to myself, I had acquired much influence over him), and it was finally resolved that, even in the event of our finding *biche de mer*, we should only stay here a week to recruit, and then push on to the southward while we might. Accordingly we made every necessary preparation, and, under the guidance of Too-wit, got the *Jane* through the reef in safety, coming to anchor about a mile from the shore, in an excellent bay, completely landlocked, on the southeastern coast of the main island, and in ten fathoms of water, black sandy bottom. At the head of this bay there were three fine springs (we were told) of good water, and we saw abundance of wood in the vicinity. The four canoes followed us in, keeping, however, at a respectful distance. Too-wit himself remained on board, and, upon our dropping anchor, invited us to accompany him on shore, and visit his village in the interior. To this Captain Guy consented; and ten savages being left on board as hostages, a party of us, twelve in all, got in readiness to attend the chief. We took care to be well armed, yet without evincing any distrust. The schooner had her guns run out, her boarding-nettings up, and every other proper precaution was taken to guard against surprise. Directions were left with the chief mate to admit no person on board during our absence, and, in the event of our not appearing in twelve hours, to send the cutter, with a swivel, around the island in search of us.

At every step we took inland the conviction forced itself upon us that we were in a country differing essentially from any hitherto visited by civilized men. We saw nothing with which we had been formerly conversant. The trees resembled no growth of either the torrid, the temperate, of the northern frigid zones, and were altogether unlike those of the lower southern latitudes we had already traversed. The very rocks were novel in their mass, their color, and their stratification; and the streams themselves, utterly incredible as it may appear, had so little in common with those of other climates, that we were scrupulous of tasting them, and, indeed, had difficulty in bringing ourselves to believe that their qualities were purely those of nature. At a small brook which crossed our path (the first we had reached) Too-wit and his attendants halted to drink. On

account of the singular character of the water, we refused to taste it, supposing it to be polluted; and it was not until some time afterward we came to understand that such was the appearance of the streams throughout the whole group. I am at a loss to give a distinct idea of the nature of this liquid, and cannot do so without many words. Although it flowed with rapidity in all declivities where common water would do so, yet never, except when falling in a cascade, had it the customary appearance of *limpidity*. It was, nevertheless, in point of fact, as perfectly limpid as any limestone water in existence, the difference being only in appearance. At first sight, and especially in cases where little declivity was found, it bore resemblance, as regards consistency, to a thick infusion of gum Arabic in common water. But this was only the least remarkable of its extraordinary qualities. It was *not* colorless, nor was it of any one uniform color—presenting to the eye, as it flowed, every possible shade of purple; like the hues of a changeable silk. This variation in shade was produced in a manner which excited as profound astonishment in the minds of our party as the mirror had done in the case of Too-wit. Upon collecting a basinful, and allowing it to settle thoroughly, we perceived that the whole mass of liquid was made up of a number of distinct veins, each of a distinct hue; that these veins did not commingle; and that their cohesion was perfect in regard to their own particles among themselves, and imperfect in regard to neighboring veins. Upon passing the blade of a knife athwart the veins, the water closed over it immediately, as with us, and also, in withdrawing it, all traces of the passage of the knife were instantly obliterated. If, however, the blade was passed down accurately between the two veins, a perfect separation was effected, which the power of cohesion did not immediately rectify. The phenomena of this water formed the first definite link in that vast chain of apparent miracles with which I was destined to be at length encircled.

Chapter XIX

We were nearly three hours in reaching the village, it being more than nine miles in the interior, and the path lying through a rugged country. As we passed along, the party of Too-wit (the whole hundred and ten savages of the canoes) was momentarily strengthened by smaller detachments, of from two to six or seven, which joined us, as if by accident, at different turns of the road. There appeared so much of system in this that I could not help feeling distrust, and I spoke to Captain Guy of my apprehensions. It was now too late, however, to recede, and we concluded that our best security lay in evincing a perfect confidence in the good faith of Too-wit. We accordingly went on, keeping a wary eye upon the maneuvers of the savages, and not permitting them to divide our numbers by pushing in between. In this way, passing through a precipitous ravine, we at length reached what we were told was the only collection of habitations upon the island. As we came in sight of them, the chief set up a shout, and frequently repeated the word *Klock-Klock;* which we supposed to be the name of the village, or perhaps the generic name for villages.

The dwellings were of the most miserable description imaginable, and, unlike those of even the lowest of the savage races with which mankind are acquainted, were of no uniform plan. Some of them (and these we found belonged to the *Wampoos* or *Yampoos*, the great men of the land) consisted of a tree cut down at about four feet from the root, with a large black skin thrown over it, and hanging in loose folds upon the ground. Under this the savage nestled. Others were formed by means of rough limbs of trees, with the withered foliage upon them, made to recline, at an angle of forty-five degrees, against a bank of clay, heaped up, without regular form, to

the height of five or six feet. Others, again, were mere holes dug in the earth perpendicularly, and covered over with similar branches, these being removed when the tenant was about to enter, and pulled on again when he had entered. A few were built among the forked limbs of trees as they stood, the upper limbs being partially cut through, so as to bend over upon the lower, thus forming thicker shelter from the weather. The greater number, however, consisted of small shallow caverns, apparently scratched in the face of a precipitous ledge of dark stone, resembling fuller's earth, with which three sides of the village were bounded. At the door of each of these primitive caverns was a small rock, which the tenant carefully placed before the entrance upon leaving his residence, for what purpose I could not ascertain, as the stone itself was never of sufficient size to close up more than a third of the opening.

This village, if it were worthy of the name, lay in a valley of some depth, and could only be approached from the southward, the precipitous ledge of which I have already spoken cutting off all access in other directions. Through the middle of the valley ran a brawling stream of the same magical-looking water which has been described. We saw several strange animals about the dwellings, all appearing to be thoroughly domesticated. The largest of these creatures resembled our common hog in the structure of the body and snout; the tail, however, was bushy, and the legs slender as those of the antelope. Its motion was exceedingly awkward and indecisive, and we never saw it attempt to run. We noticed also several animals very similar in appearance, but of a greater length of body, and covered with a black wool. There were a great variety of tame fowls running about, and these seemed to constitute the chief food of the natives. To our astonishment we saw black albatross among these birds in a state of entire domestication, going to sea periodically for food, but always returning to the village as a home, and using the southern shore in the vicinity as a place of incubation. There they were joined by their friends the pelicans as usual, but these latter never followed them to the dwellings of the savages. Among the other kinds of tame fowls were ducks, differing very little from the canvass-back of our own country, black gannets, and a large bird not unlike the buzzard in appearance, but not carnivorous. Of fish there seemed to be a great abundance. We saw, during our visit, a quantity of dried salmon, rock cod, blue dolphins, mackerel, blackfish, skate, conger eels, elephant-fish, mullets, soles, parrotfish, leather-jackets, gurnards, hake, flounders, paracutas, and innumerable other varieties. We noticed, too, that most of them were similar to the fish about the group of Lord Auckland Islands, in

a latitude as low as fifty-one degrees south. The Gallipago tortoise was also very plentiful. We saw but few wild animals, and none of a large size, or of a species with which we were familiar. One or two serpents of a formidable aspect crossed our path, but the natives paid them little attention, and we concluded that they were not venomous.

As we approached the village with Too-wit and his party, a vast crowd of the people rushed out to meet us, with loud shouts, among which we could only distinguish the everlasting *Anamoo-moo!* and *Lama-Lama!* We were much surprised at perceiving that, with one or two exceptions, these new comers were entirely naked, and skins being used only by the men of the canoes. All the weapons of the country seemed also to be in the possession of the latter, for there was no appearance of any among the villagers. There were a great many women and children, the former not altogether wanting in what might be termed personal beauty. They were straight, tall, and well formed, with a grace and freedom of carriage not to be found in civilized society. Their lips, however, like those of the men, were thick and clumsy, so that, even when laughing, the teeth were never disclosed. Their hair was of a finer texture than that of the males. Among these naked villagers there might have been ten or twelve who were clothed, like the party of Too-wit, in dresses of black skin, and armed with lances and heavy clubs. These appeared to have great influence among the rest, and were always addressed by the title *Wampoo.* These, too, were the tenants of the black skin palaces. That of Too-wit was situated in the center of the village, and was much larger and somewhat better constructed than others of its kind. The tree which formed its support was cut off at a distance of twelve feet or thereabouts from the root, and there were several branches left just below the cut, these serving to extend the covering, and in this way prevent its flapping about the trunk. The covering, too, which consisted of four very large skins fastened together with wooden skewers, was secured at the bottom with pegs driven through it and into the ground. The floor was strewed with a quantity of dry leaves by way of carpet.

To this hut we were conducted with great solemnity, and as many of the natives crowded in after us as possible. Too-wit seated himself on the leaves, and made signs that we should follow his example. This we did, and presently found ourselves in a situation peculiarly uncomfortable, if not indeed critical. We were on the ground, twelve in number, with the savages, as many as forty, sitting on their hams so closely around us that, if any disturbance had arisen, we should have found it impossible to make

use of our arms, or indeed to have risen to our feet. The pressure was not only inside the tent, but outside, where probably was every individual on the whole island, the crowd being prevented from trampling us to death only by the incessant exertions and vociferations of Too-wit. Our chief security lay, however, in the presence of Too-wit himself among us, and we resolved to stick by him closely, as the best chance of extricating ourselves from the dilemma, sacrificing him immediately upon the first appearance of hostile design.

After some trouble a certain degree of quiet was restored, when the chief addressed us in a speech of great length, and very nearly resembling the one delivered in the canoes, with the exception that the *Anamoo-moos!* were now somewhat more strenuously insisted upon than the *Lama-Lamas!* We listened in profound silence until the conclusion of this harangue, when Captain Guy replied by assuring the chief of his eternal friendship and goodwill, concluding what he had to say be a present of several strings of blue beads and a knife. At the former the monarch, much to our surprise, turned up his nose with some expression of contempt, but the knife gave him the most unlimited satisfaction, and he immediately ordered dinner. This was handed into the tent over the heads of the attendants, and consisted of the palpitating entrails of a specials of unknown animal, probably one of the slim-legged hogs which we had observed in our approach to the village. Seeing us at a loss how to proceed, he began, by way of setting us an example, to devour yard after yard of the enticing food, until we could positively stand it no longer, and evinced such manifest symptoms of rebellion of stomach as inspired his majesty with a degree of astonishment only inferior to that brought about by the looking-glasses. We declined, however, partaking of the delicacies before us, and endeavored to make him understand that we had no appetite whatever, having just finished a hearty *déjeuner.*

When the monarch had made an end of his meal, we commenced a series of cross-questioning in every ingenious manner we could devise, with a view of discovering what were the chief productions of the country, and whether any of them might be turned to profit. At length he seemed to have some idea of our meaning, and offered to accompany us to a part of coast where he assured us the *biche de mer* (pointing to a specimen of that animal) was to be found in great abundance. We were glad of this early opportunity of escaping from the oppression of the crowd, and signified our eagerness to proceed. We now left the tent, and, accompanied by the whole population of the village, followed the chief to the southeastern

extremity of the island, nor far from the bay where our vessel lay at anchor. We waited here for about an hour, until the four canoes were brought around by some of the savages to our station. The whole of our party then getting into one of them, we were paddled along the edge of the reef before mentioned, and of another still farther out, where we saw a far greater quantity of *biche de mer* than the oldest seamen among us had ever seen in those groups of the lower latitudes most celebrated for this article of commerce. We stayed near these reefs only long enough to satisfy ourselves that we could easily load a dozen vessels with the animal if necessary, when we were taken alongside the schooner, and parted with Too-wit, after obtaining from him a promise that he would bring us, in the course of twenty-four hours, as many of the canvass-back ducks and Gallipago tortoises as his canoes would hold. In the whole of this adventure we saw nothing in the demeanor of the natives calculated to create suspicion, with the single exception of the systematic manner in which their party was strengthened during our route from the schooner to the village.

CHAPTER XX

THE CHIEF WAS AS GOOD AS HIS WORD, AND WE WERE SOON PLENTIFULLY supplied with fresh provisions. We found the tortoises as fine as we had ever seen, and the ducks surpassed our best species of wild fowl, being exceedingly tender, juicy, and well-flavored. Besides these, the savages brought us, upon our making them comprehend our wishes, a vast quantity of brown celery and scurvy grass, with a canoe-load of fresh fish and some dried. The celery was a treat indeed, and the scurvy grass proved of incalculable benefit in restoring those of our men who had shown symptoms of disease. In a very short time we had not a single person on the sick-list. We had also plenty of other kinds of fresh provisions, among which may be mentioned a species of shellfish resembling the mussel in shape, but with the taste of an oyster. Shrimps, too, and prawns were abundant, and albatross and other birds' eggs with dark shells. We took in, too, a plentiful stock of the flesh of the hog which I have mentioned before. Most of the men found it a palatable food, but I thought it fishy and otherwise disagreeable. In return for these good things we presented the natives with blue beads, brass trinkets, nails, knives, and pieces of red cloth, they being fully delighted in the exchange. We established a regular market on shore, just under the guns of the schooner, where our barterings were carried on with every appearance of good faith, and a degree of order which their conduct at the village of *Klock-klock* had not led us to expect from the savages.

Matters went on thus very amicably for several days, during which parties of the natives were frequently on board the schooner, and parties of our men frequently on shore, making long excursions into the interior, and receiving no molestation whatever. Finding the ease with which the

vessel might be loaded with *biche de mer*, owing to the friendly disposition
of the islanders, and the readiness with which they would render us assis-
tance in collecting it, Captain Guy resolved to enter into negotiations with
Too-wit for the erection of suitable houses in which to cure the article, and
for the services of himself and tribe in gathering as much as possible, while
he himself took advantage of the fine weather to prosecute his voyage to
the southward. Upon mentioning this project to the chief he seemed very
willing to enter into an agreement. A bargain was accordingly struck, per-
fectly satisfactory to both parties, by which it was arranged that, after
making the necessary preparations, such as laying off the proper grounds,
erecting a portion of the buildings, and doing some other work in which
the whole of our crew would be required, the schooner should proceed
on her route, leaving three of her men on the island to superintend the
fulfillment of the project, and instruct the natives in drying the *biche de
mer*. In regard to terms, these were made to depend upon the exertions of
the savages in our absence. They were to receive a stipulated quantity
of blue beads, knives, red cloth, and so forth, for every certain number of
piculs of the *biche de mer* which should be ready on our return.

A description of the nature of this important article of commerce,
and the method of preparing it, may prove of some interest to my read-
ers, and I can find no more suitable place than this for introducing an
account of it. The following comprehensive notice of the substance is
taken from a modern history of a voyage to the South Seas.

"It is that *mollusca* from the Indian Seas which is known to commerce
by the French name *bouche de mer* (a nice morsel from the sea). If I am not
much mistaken, the celebrated Cuvier calls it *gasteropeda pulmonifera*. It is
abundantly gathered in the coasts of the Pacific islands, and gathered
especially for the Chinese market, where it commands a great price, per-
haps as much as their much-talked-of edible birds' nests, which are
properly made up of the gelatinous matter picked up by a species of swal-
low from the body of these molluscae. They have no shell, no legs, nor any
prominent part, except an *absorbing* and an *excretory*, opposite organs; but,
by their elastic wings, like caterpillars or worms, they creep in shallow
waters, in which, when low, they can be seen by a kind of swallow, the
sharp bill of which, inserted in the soft animal, draws a gummy and fila-
mentous substance, which, by drying, can be wrought into the solid walls
of their nest. Hence the name of *gasteropeda pulmonifera*.

"This mollusca is oblong, and of different sizes, from three to eighteen
inches in length; and I have seen a few that were not less than two feet long.

They were nearly round, a little flattish on one side, which lies next to the bottom of the sea; and they are from one to eight inches thick. They crawl up into shallow water at particular seasons of the year, probably for the purpose of gendering, as we often find them in pairs. It is when the sun has the most power on the water, rendering it tepid, that they approach the shore; and they often go up into places so shallow that, on the tide's receding, they are left dry, exposed to the heat of the sun. But they do not bring forth their young in shallow water, as we never see any of their progeny, and full-grown ones are always observed coming in from deep water. They feed principally on that class of zoophytes which produce the coral.

"The *biche de mer* is generally taken in three or four feet of water; after which they are brought on shore, and split at one end with a knife, the incision being one inch or more, according to the size of the mollusca. Through this opening the entrails are forced out by pressure, and they are much like those of any other small tenant of the deep. The article is then washed, and afterward boiled to a certain degree, which must not be too much or too little. They are then buried in the ground for four hours, then boiled again for a short time, after which they are dried, either by the fire or the sun. Those cured by the sun are worth the most; but where one picul (133⅓lbs.) can be cured that way, I can cure thirty piculs by the fire. When once properly cured, they can be kept in a dry place for two or three years without any risk; but they should be examined once in every few months, say four times a year, to see if any dampness is likely to affect them.

"The Chinese, as before stated, consider *biche de mer* a very great luxury, believing that it wonderfully strengthens and nourishes the system, and renews the exhausted system of the immoderate voluptuary. The first quality commands a high price in Canton, being worth ninety dollars a picul; the second quality, seventy-five dollars; the third, fifty dollars; the fourth, thirty dollars; the fifth, twenty dollars; the sixth, twelve dollars; the seventh, eight dollars; and the eighth, four dollars; small cargoes, however, will often bring more in Manila, Singapore, and Batavia."

An agreement having been thus entered into, we proceeded immediately to land everything necessary for preparing the buildings and clearing the ground. A large flat space near the eastern shore of the bay was selected, where there was plenty of both wood and water, and within a convenient distance of the principal reefs on which the *biche de mer* was to be procured. We now all set to work in good earnest, and soon, to the great astonishment of the savages, had felled a sufficient number of trees for our purpose, getting them quickly in order for the framework of the houses,

which in two or three days were so far under way that we could safely trust the rest of the work to the three men whom we intended to leave behind. These were John Carson, Alfred Harris, and —— Peterson (all natives of London, I believe), who volunteered their services in this respect.

By the last of the month we had everything in readiness for departure. We had agreed, however, to pay a formal visit of leave-taking to the village, and Too-wit insisted so pertinaciously upon our keeping the promise that we did not think it advisable to run the risk of offending him by a final refusal. I believe that not one of us had at this time the slightest suspicion of the good faith of the savages. They had uniformly behaved with the greatest decorum, aiding us with alacrity in our work, offering us their commodities, frequently without price, and never, in any instance, pilfering a single article, although the high value they set upon the goods we had with us was evident by the extravagant demonstrations of joy always manifested upon our making them a present. The women especially were most obliging in every respect, and, upon the whole, we should have been the most suspicious of human beings had we entertained a single thought of perfidy on the part of a people who treated us so well. A very short while sufficed to prove that this apparent kindness of disposition was only the result of a deeply-laid plan for our destruction, and that the islanders for whom we entertained such inordinate feelings of esteem, were among the most barbarous, subtle, and bloodthirsty wretches that ever contaminated the face of the globe.

It was on the first of February that we went on shore for the purpose of visiting the village. Although, as said before, we entertained not the slightest suspicion, still no proper precaution was neglected. Six men were left in the schooner, with instructions to permit none of the savages to approach the vessel during our absence, under any pretence whatever, and to remain constantly on deck. The boarding-nettings were up, the guns double-shotted with grape and canister, and the swivels loaded with canisters of musket-balls. She lay, with her anchor apeak, about a mile from the shore, and no canoe could approach her in any direction without being distinctly seen and exposed to the full fire of our swivels immediately.

The six men being left on board, our shore-party consisted of thirty-two persons in all. We were armed to the teeth, having with us muskets, pistols, and cutlasses; besides, each had a long kind of seaman's knife, somewhat resembling the bowie knife now so much used throughout our western and southern country. A hundred of the black-skin warriors met us at the landing for the purpose of accompanying us on our way. We noticed, however,

with some surprise, that they were now entirely without arms; and, upon questioning Too-wit in relation to this circumstance, he merely answered that *Mattee non we pa pa si*—meaning that there was no need of arms where all were brothers. We took this in good part, and proceeded.

We had passed the spring and rivulet of which I before spoke, and were now entering upon a narrow gorge leading through the chain of soapstone hills among which the village was situated. This gorge was very rocky and uneven, so much so that it was with no little difficulty we scrambled through it on our first visit to Klock-klock. The whole length of the ravine might have been a mile and a half, or probably two miles. It wound in every possible direction through the hills (having apparently formed, at some remote period, the bed of a torrent), in no instance proceeding more than twenty yards without an abrupt turn. The sides of this dell would have averaged, I am sure, seventy or eighty feet in perpendicular altitude throughout the whole of their extent, and in some portions they arose to an astonishing height, overshadowing the pass so completely that but little of the light of day could penetrate. The general width was about forty feet, and occasionally it diminished so as not to allow the passage of more than five or six persons abreast. In short, there could be no place in the world better adapted for the consummation of an ambuscade, and it was no more than natural that we should look carefully to our arms as we entered upon it. When I now think of our egregious folly, the chief subject of astonishment seems to be, that we should have ever ventured, under any circumstances, so completely into the power of unknown savages as to permit them to march both before and behind us in our progress through this ravine. Yet such was the order we blindly took up, trusting foolishly to the force of our party, the unarmed condition of Too-wit and his men, the certain efficacy of our firearms (whose effect was yet a secret to the natives), and, more than all, to the long-sustained pretension of friendship kept up by these infamous wretches. Five or six of them went on before, as if to lead the way, ostentatiously busying themselves in removing the larger stones and rubbish from the path. Next came our own party. We walked closely together, taking care only to prevent separation. Behind followed the main body of the savages, observing unusual order and decorum.

Dirk Peters, a man named Wilson Allen, and myself were on the right of our companions, examining, as we went along, the singular stratification of the precipice which overhung us. A fissure in the soft rock attracted our attention. It was about wide enough for one person to enter without squeezing, and extended back into the hill some eighteen or twenty feet

in a straight course, sloping afterward to the left. The height of the opening, as far as we could see into it from the main gorge, was perhaps sixty or seventy feet. There were one or two stunted shrubs growing from the crevices, bearing a species of filbert which I felt some curiosity to examine, and pushed in briskly for that purpose, gathering five or six of the nuts at a grasp, and then hastily retreating. As I turned, I found that Peters and Allen had followed me. I desired them to go back, as there was not room for two persons to pass, saying they should have some of my nuts. They accordingly turned, and were scrambling back, Allen being close to the mouth of the fissure, when I was suddenly aware of a concussion resembling nothing I had ever before experienced, and which impressed me with a vague conception, if indeed I then thought of anything, that the whole foundations of the solid globe were suddenly rent asunder, and that the day of universal dissolution was at hand.

CHAPTER XXI

As soon as I could collect my scattered senses, I found myself nearly suffocated, and groveling in utter darkness among a quantity of loose earth, which was also falling upon me heavily in every direction, threatening to bury me entirely. Horribly alarmed at this idea, I struggled to gain my feet, and at last succeeded. I then remained motionless for some moments, endeavoring to conceive what had happened to me, and where I was. Presently I heard a deep groan just at my ear, and afterward the smothered voice of Peters calling to me for aid in the name of God. I scrambled one or two paces forward, when I fell directly over the head and shoulders of my companion, who, I soon discovered, was buried in a loose mass of earth as far as his middle, and struggling desperately to free himself from the pressure. I tore the dirt from around him with all the energy I could command, and at length succeeded in getting him out.

As soon as we sufficiently recovered from our fright and surprise to be capable of conversing rationally, we both came to the conclusion that the walls of the fissure in which we had ventured had, by some convulsion of nature, or probably from their own weight, caved in overhead, and that we were consequently lost forever, being thus entombed alive. For a long time we gave up supinely to the most intense agony and despair, such as cannot be adequately imagined by those who have never been in a similar position. I firmly believed that no incident ever occurring in the course of human events is more adapted to inspire the supremeness of mental and bodily distress than a case like our own, of living inhumation. The blackness of darkness which envelops the victim, the terrific oppression of lungs, the stifling fumes from the damp earth, unite with the ghastly considerations

that we are beyond the remotest confines of hope, and that such is the allotted portion of *the dead,* to carry into the human heart a degree of appalling awe and horror not to be tolerated—never to be conceived.

At length Peters proposed that we should endeavor to ascertain precisely the extent of our calamity, and grope about our prison; it being barely possible, he observed, that some opening might yet be left us for escape. I caught eagerly at this hope, and, arousing myself to exertion, attempted to force my way through the loose earth. Hardly had I advanced a single step before a glimmer of light became perceptible, enough to convince me that, at all events, we should not immediately perish for want of air. We now took some degree of heart, and encouraged each other to hope for the best. Having scrambled over a bank of rubbish which impeded our farther progress in the direction of the light, we found less difficulty in advancing and also experienced some relief from the excessive oppression of lungs which had tormented us. Presently we were enabled to obtain a glimpse of the objects around, and discovered that we were near the extremity of the straight portion of the fissure, where it made a turn to the left. A few struggles more, and we reached the bend, when to our inexpressible joy, there appeared a long seam or crack extending upward a vast distance, generally at an angle of about forty-five degrees, although sometimes much more precipitous. We could not see through the whole extent of this opening; but, as a good deal of light came down it, we had little doubt of finding at the top of it (if we could by any means reach the top) a clear passage into the open air.

I now called to mind that three of us had entered the fissure from the main gorge, and that our companion, Allen, was still missing; we determined at once to retrace our steps and look for him. After a long search, and much danger from the farther caving in of the earth above us, Peters at length cried out to me that he had hold of our companion's foot, and that his whole body was deeply buried beneath the rubbish beyond the possibility of extricating him. I soon found that what he said was too true, and that, of course, life had been long extinct. With sorrowful hearts, therefore, we left the corpse to its fate, and again made our way to the bend.

The breadth of the seam was barely sufficient to admit us, and, after one or two ineffectual efforts at getting up, we began once more to despair. I have before said that the chain of hills through which ran the main gorge was composed of a species of soft rock resembling soapstone. The sides of the cleft we were now attempting to ascend were of the same material, and so excessively slippery, being wet, that we could get but little

foothold upon them even in their least precipitous parts; in some places, where the ascent was nearly perpendicular, the difficulty was, of course, much aggravated; and, indeed, for some time we thought insurmountable. We took courage, however, from despair; and what, by dint of cutting steps in the soft stone with our bowie knives, and swinging at the risk of our lives, to small projecting points of a harder species of slaty rock which now and then protruded from the general mass, we at length reached a natural platform, from which was perceptible a patch of blue sky, at the extremity of a thickly-wooded ravine. Looking back now, with somewhat more leisure, at the passage through which we had thus far proceeded, we clearly saw from the appearance of its sides, that it was of late formation, and we concluded that the concussion, whatever it was, which had so unexpectedly overwhelmed us, had also, at the same moment, laid open this path for escape. Being quite exhausted with exertion, and indeed, so weak that we were scarcely able to stand or articulate, Peters now proposed that we should endeavor to bring our companions to the rescue by firing the pistols which still remained in our girdles—the muskets as well as cutlasses had been lost among the loose earth at the bottom of the chasm. Subsequent events proved that, had we fired, we should have sorely repented it, but luckily a half suspicion of foul play had by this time arisen in my mind, and we forbore to let the savages know of our whereabouts.

After having reposed for about an hour, we pushed on slowly up the ravine, and had gone no great way before we heard a succession of tremendous yells. At length we reached what might be called the surface of the ground; for our path hitherto, since leaving the platform, had lain beneath an archway of high rock and foliage, at a vast distance overhead. With great caution we stole to a narrow opening, through which we had a clear sight of the surrounding country, when the whole dreadful secret of the concussion broke upon us in one moment and at one view.

The spot from which we looked was not far from the summit of the highest peak in the range of the soapstone hills. The gorge in which our party of thirty-two had entered ran within fifty feet to the left of us. But, for at least one hundred yards, the channel or bed of this gorge was entirely filled up with the chaotic ruins of more than a million tons of earth and stone that had been artificially tumbled within it. The means by which the vast mass had been precipitated were not more simple than evident, for sure traces of the murderous work were yet remaining. In several spots along the top of the eastern side of the gorge (we were now on the western) might be seen stakes of wood driven into the earth. In

these spots the earth had not given way; but throughout the whole extent of the face of the precipice from which the mass *had* fallen, it was clear, from marks left in the soil resembling those made by the drill of the rockblaster, that stakes similar to those we saw standing had been inserted, at not more than a yard apart, for the length of perhaps three hundred feet, and ranging at about ten feet back from the edge of the gulf. Strong cords of grape-vine were attached to the stakes still remaining on the hill, and it was evident that such cords had also been attached to each of the other stakes. I have already spoken of the singular stratification of these soapstone hills; and the description just given of the narrow and deep fissure through which we effected our escape from inhumation will afford a further conception of its nature. This was such that almost every natural convulsion would be sure to split the soil into perpendicular layers or ridges running parallel with one another; and a very moderate exertion of art would be sufficient for effecting the same purpose. Of this stratification the savages had availed themselves to accomplish their treacherous ends. There can be no doubt that, by the continuous line of stakes, a partial rupture of the soil had been brought about, probably to the depth of one or two feet, when by means of a savage pulling at the end of each of the cords (these cords being attached to the tops of the stakes, and extending back from the edge of the cliff), a vast leverage power was obtained, capable of hurling the whole face of the hill, upon a given signal, into the bosom of the abyss below. The fate of our poor companions was no longer a matter of uncertainty. We alone had escaped from the tempest of that overwhelming destruction. We were the only living white men upon the island.

CHAPTER XXII

OUR SITUATION, AS IT NOW APPEARED, WAS SCARCELY LESS DREADFUL than when we had conceived ourselves entombed forever. We saw before us no prospect but that of being put to death by the savages, or of dragging out a miserable existence in captivity among them. We might, to be sure, conceal ourselves for a time from their observation among the fastnesses of the hills, and, as a final resort, in the chasm from which we had just issued; but we must either perish in the long polar winter through cold and famine, or be ultimately discovered in our efforts to obtain relief.

The whole country around us seemed to be swarming with savages, crowds of whom, we now perceived, had come over from the islands to the southward on flat rafts, doubtless with a view of lending their aid in the capture and plunder of the *Jane*. The vessel still lay calmly at anchor in the bay, those on board being apparently quite unconscious of any danger awaiting them. How we longed at that moment to be with them! either to aid in effecting their escape, or to perish with them in attempting a defence. We saw no chance even of warning them of their danger without bringing immediate destruction upon our own heads, with but a remote hope of benefit to them. A pistol fired might suffice to apprise them that something wrong had occurred; but the report could not possibly inform them that their only prospect of safety lay in getting out of the harbor forthwith—it could not tell them that no principles of honor now bound them to remain, that their companions were no longer among the living. Upon hearing the discharge they could not be more thoroughly prepared to meet the foe, who were now getting ready to attack, than they already were, and always had been. No good,

therefore, and infinite harm, would result from our firing, and after mature deliberation, we forbore.

Our next thought was to attempt to rush towards the vessel, to seize one of the four canoes which lay at the head of the bay, and endeavor to force a passage on board. But the utter impossibility of succeeding in this desperate task soon became evident. The country, as I said before, was literally swarming with the natives, skulking among the bushes and recesses of the hills, so as not to be observed from the schooner. In our immediate vicinity especially, and blockading the sole path by which we could hope to attain the shore at the proper point were stationed the whole party of the black-skin warriors, with Too-wit at their head, and apparently only waiting for some re-enforcement to commence his onset upon the *Jane*. The canoes, too, which lay at the head of the bay, were manned with savages, unarmed, it is true, but who undoubtedly had arms within reach. We were forced, therefore, however unwillingly, to remain in our place of concealment, mere spectators of the conflict which presently ensued.

In about half an hour we saw some sixty or seventy rafts, or flatboats, without riggers, filled with savages, and coming round the southern bight of the harbor. They appeared to have no arms except short clubs, and stones which lay in the bottom of the rafts. Immediately afterward another detachment, still larger, appeared in an opposite direction, and with similar weapons. The four canoes, too, were now quickly filled with natives, starting up from the bushes at the head of the bay, and put off swiftly to join the other parties. Thus, in less time than I have taken to tell it, and as if by magic, the *Jane* saw herself surrounded by an immense multitude of desperadoes evidently bent upon capturing her at all hazards.

That they would succeed in so doing could not be doubted for an instant. The six men left in the vessel, however resolutely they might engage in her defence, were altogether unequal to the proper management of the guns, or in any manner to sustain a contest at such odds. I could hardly imagine that they would make resistance at all, but in this was deceived; for presently I saw them get springs upon the cable, and bring the vessel's starboard broadside to bear upon the canoes, which by this time were within pistol range, the rafts being nearly a quarter of a mile to windward. Owing to some cause unknown, but most probably to the agitation of our poor friends at seeing themselves in so hopeless a situation, the discharge was an entire failure. Not a canoe was hit or a single savage injured, the shots striking short and *ricochêting* over their heads. The only effect produced upon them was astonishment at the unexpected report

and smoke, which was so excessive that for some moments I almost thought they would abandon their design entirely, and return to the shore. And this they would most likely have done had our men followed up their broadside by a discharge of small arms, in which, as the canoes were now so near at hand, they could not have failed in doing some execution, sufficient, at least, to deter this party from a farther advance, until they could have given the rafts also a broadside. But, in place of this, they left the canoe party to recover from their panic, and, by looking about them, to see that no injury had been sustained, while they flew to the larboard to get ready for the rafts.

The discharge to larboard produced the most terrible effect. The star and double-headed shot of the large guns cut seven or eight of the rafts completely asunder, and killed, perhaps, thirty or forty of the savages outright, while a hundred of them, at least, were thrown into the water, the most of them dreadfully wounded. The remainder, frightened out of their senses, commenced at once a precipitate retreat, not even waiting to pick up their maimed companions, who were swimming about in every direction, screaming and yelling for aid. This great success, however, came too late for the salvation of our devoted people. The canoe party were already on board the schooner to the number of more than a hundred and fifty, the most of them having succeeded in scrambling up the chains and over the boarding-netting even before the matches had been applied to the larboard guns. Nothing now could withstand their brute rage. Our men were borne down at once, overwhelmed, trodden under foot, and absolutely torn to pieces in an instant.

Seeing this, the savages on the rafts got the better of their fears, and came up in shoals to the plunder. In five minutes the *Jane* was a pitiable scene indeed of havoc and tumultuous outrage. The decks were split open and ripped up; the cordage, sails, and everything moveable on deck demolished as if by magic; while, by dint of pushing at the stern, towing with the canoes, and hauling at the sides, as they swam in thousands around the vessel, the wretches finally forced her on shore (the cable having been slipped), and delivered her over to the good offices of Too-wit, who, during the whole of the engagement, had maintained, like a skillful general, his post of security and reconnaissance among the hills, but, now that the victory was completed to his satisfaction, condescended to scamper down with his warriors of the black skin, and become a partaker in the spoils.

Too-wit's descent left us at liberty to quit our hiding-place and reconnoiter the hill in the vicinity of the chasm. At about fifty yards from the

mouth of it we saw a small spring of water, at which we slaked the burning thirst that now consumed us. Not far from the spring we discovered several of the filbert-bushes which I mentioned before. Upon tasting the nuts we found them palatable, and very nearly resembling in flavour the common English filbert. We collected our hats full immediately, deposited them within the ravine, and returned for more. While we were busily employed in gathering these, a rustling in the bushes alarmed us, and we were upon the point of stealing back to our covert, when a large black bird of the bittern species strugglingly and slowly arose above the shrubs. I was so much startled that I could do nothing, but Peters had sufficient presence of mind to run up to it before it could make its escape, and seize it by the neck. Its struggles and screams were tremendous, and we had thoughts of letting it go, lest the noise should alarm some of the savages who might be still lurking in the neighborhood. A stab with a bowie knife, however, at length brought it to the ground, and we dragged it into the ravine, congratulating ourselves that, at all events, we had thus obtained a supply of food enough to last us for a week.

We now went out again to look about us, and ventured a considerable distance down the southern declivity of the hill, but met with nothing else which could serve us for food. We therefore collected a quantity of dry wood and returned, seeing one or two large parties of the natives on their way to the village, laden with the plunder of the vessel, and who, we were apprehensive, might discover us in passing beneath the hill.

Our next care was to render our place of concealment as secure as possible, and with this object, we arranged some brushwood over the aperture which I have before spoken of as the one through which we saw the patch of blue sky, on reaching the platform from the interior of the chasm. We left only a very small opening just wide enough to admit of our seeing the bay, without the risk of being discovered from below. Having done this, we congratulated ourselves upon the security of the position; for we were now completely excluded from observation, as long as we chose to remain within the ravine itself, and not venture out upon the hill. We could perceive no traces of the savages having ever been within this hollow; but, indeed, when we came to reflect upon the probability that the fissure through which we attained it had been only just now created by the fall of the cliff opposite, and that no other way of attaining it could be perceived, we were not so much rejoiced at the thought of being secure from molestation as fearful lest there should be absolutely no means left us for descent. We resolved to explore the summit of the hill thoroughly,

when a good opportunity should offer. In the meantime we watched the motions of the savages through our loophole.

They had already made a complete wreck of the vessel, and were now preparing to set her on fire. In a little while we saw the smoke ascending in huge volumes from her main hatchway, and, shortly afterward, a dense mass of flame burst up from the forecastle. The rigging, masts and what remained of the sails caught immediately, and the fire spread rapidly along the decks. Still a great many of the savages retained their stations about her, hammering with large stones, axes, and cannon-balls at the bolts and other iron and copper work. On the beach, and in canoes and rafts, there were not less, altogether, in the immediate vicinity of the schooner, than ten thousand natives, besides the shoals of them who, laden with booty, were making their way inland and over to the neighboring islands. We now anticipated a catastrophe, and were not disappointed. First of all there came a smart shock (which we felt as distinctly where we were as if we had been slightly galvanized), but unattended with any visible signs of an explosion. The savages were evidently startled, and paused for an instant from their labors and yellings. They were upon the point of recommencing, when suddenly a mass of smoke puffed up from the decks, resembling a black and heavy thunder-cloud—then, as if from its bowels, arose a tall stream of vivid fire to the height, apparently, of a quarter of a mile—then there came a sudden circular expansion of the flame—then the whole atmosphere was magically crowded, in a single instant, with a wild chaos of wood, and metal, and human limbs—and, lastly, came the concussion in its fullest fury, which hurled us impetuously from our feet, while the hills echoed and re-echoed the tumult, and a dense shower of the minutest fragments of the ruins tumbled headlong in every direction around us.

The havoc among the savages far exceeded our utmost expectation, and they had now, indeed, reaped the full and perfect fruits of their treachery. Perhaps a thousand perished by the explosion, while at least an equal number were desperately mangled. The whole surface of the bay was literally strewn with the struggling and drowning wretches, and on shore matters were even worse. They seemed utterly appalled by the suddenness and completeness of their discomfiture, and made no efforts at assisting one another. At length we observed a total change in their demeanor. From absolute stupor, they appeared to be, all at once, aroused to the highest pitch of excitement, and rushed wildly about, going to and from a certain point on the beach, with the strangest expressions of mingled

horror, rage, and intense curiosity depicted on their countenances, and shouting, at the top of their voices, *Tekeli-li! Tekeli-li!*

Presently we saw a large body go off into the hills, whence they returned in a short time, carrying stakes of wood. These they brought to the station where the crowd was the thickest, which now separated so as to afford us a view of the object of all this excitement. We perceived something white lying upon the ground, but could not immediately make out what it was. At length we saw that it was the carcass of the strange animal with the scarlet teeth and claws which the schooner had picked up at sea on the eighteenth of January. Captain Guy had had the body preserved for the purpose of stuffing the skin and taking it to England. I remember he had given some directions about it just before our making the island, and it had been brought into the cabin and stowed away in one of the lockers. It had now been thrown on shore by the explosion; but why it had occasioned so much concern among the savages was more than we could comprehend. Although they crowded around the carcass at a little distance, none of them seemed willing to approach it closely. By and by the men with the stakes drove them in a circle around it, and no sooner was this arrangement completed, than the whole of the vast assemblage rushed into the interior of the island, with loud screams of *Tekeli-li! Tekeli-li!*

CHAPTER XXIII

DURING THE SIX OR SEVEN DAYS IMMEDIATELY FOLLOWING WE REMAINED IN our hiding-place upon the hill, going out only occasionally, and then with the greatest precaution, for water and filberts. We had made a kind of penthouse on the platform, furnishing it with a bed of dry leaves, and placing in it three large flat stones, which served us for both fireplace and table. We kindled a fire without difficulty by rubbing two pieces of dry wood together, the one soft, the other hard. The bird we had taken in such good season proved excellent eating, although somewhat tough. It was not an oceanic fowl, but a species of bittern, with jet black and grizzly plumage, and diminutive wings in proportion to its bulk. We afterward saw three of the same kind in the vicinity of the ravine, apparently seeking for the one we had captured; but, as they never alighted, we had no opportunity of catching them.

As long as this fowl lasted we suffered nothing from our situation, but it was now entirely consumed, and it became absolutely necessary that we should look out for provision. The filberts would not satisfy the cravings of hunger, afflicting us, too, with severe gripings of the bowels, and, if freely indulged in, with violent headache. We had seen several large tortoises near the seashore to the eastward of the hill, and perceived they might be easily taken, if we could get at them without the observation of the natives. It was resolved, therefore, to make an attempt at descending.

We commenced by going down the southern declivity, which seemed to offer the fewest difficulties, but had not proceeded a hundred yards before (as we had anticipated from appearances on the hill-top) our progress was entirely arrested by a branch of the gorge in which our companions had perished. We now passed along the edge of this for about a quarter of

a mile, when we were again stopped by a precipice of immense depth, and, not being able to make our way along the brink of it, we were forced to retrace our steps by the main ravine.

We now pushed over to the eastward, but with precisely similar fortune. After an hour's scramble, at the risk of breaking our necks, we discovered that we had merely descended into a vast pit of black granite, with fine dust at the bottom, and whence the only egress was by the rugged path in which we had come down. Toiling again up this path, we now tried the northern edge of the hill. Here we were obliged to use the greatest possible caution in our maneuvers, as the least indiscretion would expose us to the full view of the savages in the village. We crawled along, therefore, on our hands and knees, and, occasionally, were even forced to throw ourselves at full length, dragging our bodies along by means of the shrubbery. In this careful manner we had proceeded but a little way, when we arrived at a chasm far deeper than any we had yet seen, and leading directly into the main gorge. Thus our fears were fully confirmed, and we found ourselves cut off entirely from access to the world below. Thoroughly exhausted by our exertions, we made the best of our way back to the platform, and throwing ourselves upon the bed of leaves, slept sweetly and soundly for some hours.

For several days after this fruitless search we were occupied in exploring every part of the summit of the hill, in order to inform ourselves of its actual resources. We found that it would afford us no food, with the exception of the unwholesome filberts, and a rank species of scurvy grass, which grew in a little patch of not more than four rods square, and would be soon exhausted. On the fifteenth of February, as near as I can remember, there was not a blade of this left, and the nuts were growing scarce; our situation, therefore, could hardly be more lamentable.* On the sixteenth we again went round the walls of our prison, in hope of finding some avenue of escape; but to no purpose. We also descended the chasm in which we had been overwhelmed, with the faint expectation of discovering, through this channel, some opening to the main ravine. Here, too, we were disappointed, although we found and brought up with us a musket.

On the seventeenth we set out with the determination of examining more thoroughly the chasm of black granite into which we had made our way in the first search. We remembered that one of the fissures in the sides

* This day was rendered remarkable by our observing in the south several huge wreaths of the grayish vapor I have spoken of.

of this pit had been but partially looked into, and we were anxious to explore it, although with no expectation of discovering here any opening.

We found no great difficulty in reaching the bottom of the hollow as before, and were now sufficiently calm to survey it with some attention. It was, indeed, one of the most singular-looking places imaginable, and we could scarcely bring ourselves to believe it altogether the work of nature. The pit, from its eastern to its western extremity, was about five hundred yards in length, when all its windings were threaded; the distance from east to west in a straight line not being more (I should suppose, having no means of accurate examination) than forty or fifty yards. Upon first descending into the chasm, that is to say, for a hundred feet downward from the summit of the hill, the sides of the abyss bore little resemblance to each other, and, apparently, had at no time been connected, the one surface being of the soapstone, and the other of marl, granulated with some metallic matter. The average breadth or interval between the two cliffs was probably here sixty feet, but there seemed to be no regularity of formation. Passing down, however, beyond the limit spoken of, the interval rapidly contracted, and the sides began to run parallel, although, for some distance farther, they were still dissimilar in their material and form of surface. Upon arriving within fifty feet of the bottom, a perfect regularity commenced. The sides were now entirely uniform in substance, in color, and in lateral direction, the material being a very black and shining granite, and the distance between the two sides, at all points facing each other,

Figure 1.

exactly twenty yards. The precise formation of the chasm will be best understood by means of a delineation taken upon the spot; for I had luckily with me a pocket-book and pencil, which I preserved with great care through a long series of subsequent adventure, and to which I am indebted for memoranda of many subjects which would otherwise have been crowded from my remembrance.

This figure (see figure 1) gives the general outlines of the chasm, without the minor cavities in the sides, of which there were several, each cavity having a corresponding protuberance opposite. The bottom of the gulf was covered to the depth of three or four inches with a powder almost impalpable, beneath which we found a continuation of the black granite. To the right, at the lower extremity, will be noticed the appearance of a small opening; this is the fissure alluded to above, and to examine which more minutely than before was the object of our second visit. We now pushed into it with vigor, cutting away a quantity of brambles which impeded us, and removing a vast heap of sharp flints somewhat resembling arrowheads in shape. We were encouraged to persevere, however, by perceiving some little light proceeding from the farther end. We at length squeezed our way for about thirty feet, and found that the aperture was a low and regularly formed arch, having a bottom of the same impalpable powder as that in the main chasm. A strong light now broke upon us, and, turning a short bend, we found ourselves in another lofty chamber, similar to the one we had left in every respect but longitudinal form. Its general figure is here given. (See figure 2.)

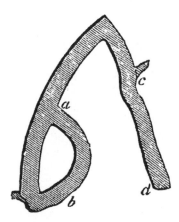

Figure 2.

The total length of this chasm, commencing at the opening *a* and proceeding round the curve *b* to the extremity *d,* is five hundred and fifty yards. At *c* we discovered a small aperture similar to the one through which we had issued from the other chasm, and this was choked up in the same manner with brambles and a quantity of the white arrowhead flints. We forced our way through it, finding it about forty feet long, and emerged into a third chasm. This, too, was precisely like the first, except in its longitudinal shape, which was thus. (See figure 3.)

Figure 3. Figure 5.

We found the entire length of the third chasm three hundred and twenty yards. At the point *a* was an opening about six feet wide, and extending fifteen feet into the rock, where it terminated in a bed of marl, there being no other chasm beyond, as we had expected. We were about leaving this fissure, into which very little light was admitted, when Peters called my attention to a range of singular-looking indentures in the surface of the marl forming the termination of the *cul-de-sac.* With a very slight exertion of the imagination, the left, or most northern of these indentures might have been taken for the intentional, although rude, representation of a human figure standing erect, with outstretched arm. The rest of them bore also some little resemblance to alphabetical characters, and Peters was willing, at all events, to adopt the idle opinion that they were really such. I convinced him of his error, finally, by directing his attention to the floor of the fissure, where, among the powder, we picked up, piece by piece, several large flakes of the marl, which had evidently been broken off by some convulsion from the surface where the indentures were found, and which had projecting points exactly fitting the indentures; thus proving them to have been the work of nature. Figure 4 presents an accurate copy of the whole.

After satisfying ourselves that these singular caverns afforded us no means of escape from our prison, we made our way back, dejected and

Figure 4.

dispirited, to the summit of the hill. Nothing worth mentioning occurred during the next twenty-four hours, except that, in examining the ground to the eastward of the third chasm, we found two triangular holes of great depth, and also with black granite sides. Into these holes we did not think it worthwhile to attempt descending, as they had the appearance of mere natural wells, without outlet. They were each about twenty yards in circumference, and their shape, as well as relative position in regard to the third chasm, is shown in figure 5.

CHAPTER XXIV

ON THE TWENTIETH OF THE MONTH, FINDING IT ALTOGETHER IMPOSSIBLE to subsist any longer upon the filberts, the use of which occasioned us the most excruciating torment, we resolved to make a desperate attempt at descending the southern declivity of the hill. The face of the precipice was here of the softest species of soapstone, although nearly perpendicular throughout its whole extent (a depth of a hundred and fifty feet at the least), and in many places even overarching. After a long search we discovered a narrow ledge about twenty feet below the brink of the gulf; upon this Peters contrived to leap, with what assistance I could render him by means of our pocket-handkerchiefs tied together. With somewhat more difficulty I also got down; and we then saw the possibility of descending the whole way by the process in which we had clambered up from the chasm when we had been buried by the fall of the hill—that is, by cutting steps in the face of the soapstone with our knives. The extreme hazard of the attempt can scarcely be conceived; but, as there was no other resource, we determined to undertake it.

Upon the ledge where we stood there grew some filbert-bushes; and to one of these we made fast an end of our rope of handkerchiefs. The other end being tied round Peters' waist, I lowered him down over the edge of the precipice until the handkerchiefs were stretched tight. He now proceeded to dig a deep hole in the soapstone (as far in as eight or ten inches), sloping away the rock above to the height of a foot, or thereabout, so as to allow of his driving, with the butt of a pistol, a tolerably strong peg into the leveled surface. I then drew him up for about four feet, when he made a hole similar to the one below, driving in a peg as before, and

having thus a resting-place for both feet and hands. I now unfastened the handkerchiefs from the bush, throwing him the end, which he tied to the peg in the uppermost hole, letting himself down gently to a station about three feet lower than he had yet been—that is, to the full extent of the handkerchiefs. Here he dug another hole, and drove another peg. He then drew himself up, so as to rest his feet in the hole just cut, taking hold with his hands upon the peg in the one above. It was now necessary to untie the handkerchiefs from the topmost peg, with the view of fastening them to the second; and here he found that an error had been committed in cutting the holes at so great a distance apart. However, after one or two unsuccessful and dangerous attempts at reaching the knot (having to hold on with his left hand while he labored to undo the fastening with his right), he at length cut the string, leaving six inches of it affixed to the peg. Tying the handkerchiefs now to the second peg, he descended to a station below the third, taking care not to go too far down. By these means (means which I should never have conceived of myself, and for which we were indebted altogether to Peters' ingenuity and resolution) my companion finally succeeded, with the occasional aid of projections in the cliff, in reaching the bottom without accident.

It was some time before I could summon sufficient resolution to follow him; but I did at length attempt it. Peters had taken off his shirt before descending, and this, with my own, formed the rope necessary for the adventure. After throwing down the musket found in the chasm, I fastened this rope to the bushes, and let myself down rapidly, striving, by the vigor of my movements, to banish the trepidation which I could overcome in no other manner. This answered sufficiently well for the first four or five steps; but presently I found my imagination growing terribly excited by thoughts of the vast depths yet to be descended, and the precarious nature of the pegs and soapstone holes which were my only support. It was in vain I endeavored to banish these reflections, and to keep my eyes steadily bent upon the flat surface of the cliff before me. The more earnestly I struggled *not to think*, the more intensely vivid became my conceptions, and the more horribly distinct. At length arrived that crisis of fancy, so fearful in all similar cases, the crisis in which we begin to anticipate the feelings with which we *shall* fall—to picture to ourselves the sickness, and dizziness, and the last struggle, and the half swoon, and the final bitterness of the rushing and headlong descent. And now I found these fancies creating their own realities, and all imagined horrors crowding upon me in fact. I felt my knees strike violently

together, while my fingers were gradually but certainly relaxing their grasp. There was a ringing in my ears, and I said, "This is my knell of death!" And now I was consumed with the irrepressible desire of looking below. I could not, I would not, confine my glances to the cliff; and, with a wild, indefinable emotion, half of horror, half of a relieved oppression, I threw my vision far down into the abyss. For one moment my fingers clutched convulsively upon their hold, while, with the movement, the faintest possible idea of ultimate escape wandered, like a shadow, through my mind—in the next my whole soul was pervaded with *a longing to fall;* a desire, a yearning, a passion utterly uncontrollable. I let go at once my grasp upon the peg, and, turning half round from the precipice, remained tottering for an instant against its naked face. But now there came a spinning of the brain; a shrill-sounding and phantom voice screamed within my ears; a dusky, fiendish, and filmy figure stood immediately beneath me; and, sighing, I sunk down with a bursting heart, and plunged within its arms.

I had swooned, and Peters had caught me as I fell. He had observed my proceedings from his station at the bottom of the cliff; and perceiving my imminent danger, had endeavored to inspire me with courage by every suggestion he could devise; although my confusion of mind had been so great as to prevent my hearing what he said, or being conscious that he had even spoken to me at all. At length, seeing me totter, he hastened to ascend to my rescue, and arrived just in time for my preservation. Had I fallen with my full weight, the rope of linen would inevitably have snapped, and I should have been precipitated into the abyss; as it was, he contrived to let me down gently, so as to remain suspended without danger until animation returned. This was in about fifteen minutes. On recovery, my trepidation had entirely vanished; I felt a new being, and, with some little further aid from my companion, reached the bottom also in safety.

We now found ourselves not far from the ravine which had proved the tomb of our friends, and to the southward of the spot where the hill had fallen. The place was one of singular wildness, and its aspect brought to my mind the descriptions given by travelers of those dreary regions marking the site of degraded Babylon. Not to speak of the ruins of the disrupted cliff, which formed a chaotic barrier in the vista to the northward, the surface of the ground in every other direction was strewn with huge tumuli, apparently the wreck of some gigantic structures of art; although, in detail, no semblance of art could be detected. Scoria were abundant,

and large shapeless blocks of the black granite, intermingled with others of marl,* and both granulated with metal. Of vegetation there were no traces whatsoever throughout the whole of the desolate area within sight. Several immense scorpions were seen, and various reptiles not elsewhere to be found in the high latitudes. As food was our most immediate object, we resolved to make our way to the seacoast, distant not more than half a mile, with a view of catching turtle, several of which we had observed from our place of concealment on the hill. We had proceeded some hundred yards, threading our route cautiously between the huge rocks and tumuli, when, upon turning a corner, five savages sprung upon us from a small cavern, felling Peters to the ground with a blow from a club. As he fell the whole party rushed upon him to secure their victim, leaving me time to recover from my astonishment. I still had the musket, but the barrel had received so much injury in being thrown from the precipice that I cast it aside as useless, preferring to trust my pistols, which had been carefully preserved in order. With these I advanced upon the assailants, firing one after the other in quick succession. Two savages fell, and one, who was in the act of thrusting a spear into Peters, sprung to his feet without accomplishing his purpose. My companion being thus released, we had no further difficulty. He had his pistols also, but prudently declined using them, confiding in his great personal strength, which far exceeded that of any person I have ever known. Seizing a club from one of the savages who had fallen, he dashed out the brains of the three who remained, killing each instantaneously with a single blow of the weapon, and leaving us completely masters of the field.

So rapidly had these events passed, that we could scarcely believe in their reality, and were standing over the bodies of the dead in a species of stupid contemplation, when we were brought to recollection by the sound of shouts in the distance. It was clear that the savages had been alarmed by the firing, and that we had little chance of avoiding discovery. To regain the cliff, it would be necessary to proceed in the direction of the shouts; and even should we succeed in arriving at its base, we should never be able to ascend it without being seen. Our situation was one of the greatest peril, and we were hesitating in which path to commence a flight, when one of the savages whom I had shot, and supposed dead, sprang briskly to

* The marl was also black; indeed, we noticed no light-colored substances of any kind upon the island.

his feet, and attempted to make his escape. We overtook him, however, before he had advanced many paces, and were about to put him to death, when Peters suggested that we might derive some benefit from forcing him to accompany us in our attempt to escape. We therefore dragged him with us, making him understand that we would shoot him if he offered resistance. In a few minutes he was perfectly submissive, and ran by our sides as we pushed in among the rocks, making for the seashore.

So far, the irregularities of the ground we had been traversing hid the sea, except at intervals, from our sight, and, when we first had it fairly in view, it was perhaps two hundred yards distant. As we emerged into the open beach we saw, to our great dismay, an immense crowd of the natives pouring from the village, and from all visible quarters of the island, making towards us with gesticulations of extreme fury, and howling like wild beasts. We were upon the point of turning upon our steps, and trying to secure a retreat among the fastnesses of the rougher ground, when I discovered the bows of two canoes projecting from behind a large rock which ran out into the water. Towards these we now ran with all speed, and, reaching them, found them unguarded, and without any other freight than three of the large Gallipago turtles and the usual supply of paddles for sixty rowers. We instantly took possession of one of them, and, forcing our captive on board, pushed out to sea with all the strength we could command.

We had not made, however, more than fifty yards from the shore before we became sufficiently calm to perceive the great oversight of which we had been guilty in leaving the other canoe in the power of the savages, who, by this time, were not more than twice as far from the beach as ourselves, and were rapidly advancing to the pursuit. No time was now to be lost. Our hope was, at best, a forlorn one, but we had none other. It was very doubtful whether, with the utmost exertion, we could get back in time to anticipate them in taking possession of the canoe; but yet there was a chance that we could. We might save ourselves if we succeeded, while not to make the attempt was to resign ourselves to inevitable butchery.

The canoe was modeled with the bow and stern alike, and, in place of turning it around, we merely changed our position in paddling. As soon as the savages perceived this they redoubled their yells, as well as their speed, and approached with inconceivable rapidity. We pulled, however, with all the energy of desperation, and arrived at the contested point before more than one of the natives had attained it. This man paid dearly for his superior agility, Peters shooting him through the head with a pistol as he approached the shore. The foremost among the rest of his party were probably some

twenty or thirty paces distant as we seized upon the canoe. We at first endeavored to pull her into the deep water, beyond the reach of the savages, but, finding her too firmly aground, and there being no time to spare, Peters, with one or two heavy strokes from the butt of the musket, succeeded in dashing out a large portion of the bow and of one side. We then pushed off. Two of the natives by this time had got hold of our boat, obstinately refusing to let go, until we were forced to dispatch them with our knives. We were now clear off, and making great way out to sea. The main body of the savages, upon reaching the broken canoe, set up the most tremendous yell of rage and disappointment conceivable. In truth, from everything I could see of these wretches, they appeared to be the most wicked, hypocritical, vindictive, bloodthirsty, and altogether fiendish race of men upon the face of the globe. It is clear we should have had no mercy had we fallen into their hands. They made a mad attempt at following us in the fractured canoe, but, finding it useless, again vented their rage in a series of hideous vociferations, and rushed up into the hills.

We were thus relieved from immediate danger, but our situation was still sufficiently gloomy. We knew that four canoes of the kind we had were at one time in the possession of the savages, and were not aware of the fact (afterward ascertained from our captive) that two of these had been blown to pieces in the explosion of the *Jane Guy*. We calculated, therefore, upon being yet pursued, as soon as our enemies could get round to the bay (distant about three miles) where the boats were usually laid up. Fearing this, we made every exertion to leave the island behind us, and went rapidly through the water, forcing the prisoner to take a paddle. In about half an hour, when we had gained, probably, five or six miles to the southward, a large fleet of the flat-bottomed canoes or rafts were seen to emerge from the bay evidently with the design of pursuit. Presently they put back, despairing to overtake us.

CHAPTER XXV

WE NOW FOUND OURSELVES IN THE WIDE AND DESOLATE ANTARCTIC Ocean, in a latitude exceeding eighty-four degrees, in a frail canoe, and with no provision but the three turtles. The long polar winter, too, could not be considered as far distant, and it became necessary that we should deliberate well upon the course to be pursued. There were six or seven islands in sight belonging to the same group, and distant from each other about five or six leagues; but upon neither of these had we any intention to venture. In coming from the northward in the *Jane Guy* we had been gradually leaving behind us the severest regions of ice—this, however little it may be in accordance with the generally received notions respecting the Antarctic, was a fact experience would not permit us to deny. To attempt, therefore, getting back would be folly—especially at so late a period of the season. Only one course seemed to be left open for hope. We resolved to steer boldly to the southward, where there was at least a probability of discovering other lands, and more than a probability of finding a still milder climate.

So far we had found the Antarctic, like the Arctic Ocean, peculiarly free from violent storms or immoderately rough water; but our canoe was, at best, of frail structure, although large, and we set busily to work with a view of rendering her as safe as the limited means in our possession would admit. The body of the boat was of no better material than bark—the bark of a tree unknown. The ribs were of a tough osier, well adapted to the purpose for which it was used. We had fifty feet room from stem to stern, from four to six in breadth, and in depth throughout four feet and a half—the boats thus differing vastly in shape from those of any other inhabitants of the Southern Ocean with whom civilized nations are acquainted. We never did believe

them the workmanship of the ignorant islanders who owned them; and some days after this period discovered, by questioning our captive, that they were in fact made by the natives of a group to the southwest of the country where we found them, having fallen accidentally into the hands of our barbarians. What we could do for the security of our boat was very little indeed. Several wide rents were discovered near both ends, and these we contrived to patch up with pieces of woolen jacket. With the help of the superfluous paddles, of which there were a great many, we erected a kind of framework about the bow, so as to break the force of any seas which might threaten to fill us in that quarter. We also set up two paddle-blades for masts, placing them opposite each other, one by each gunwale, thus saving the necessity of a yard. To these masts we attached a sail made of our shirts—doing this with some difficulty, as here we could get no assistance from our prisoner whatever, although he had been willing enough to labor in all the other operations. The sight of the linen seemed to affect him in a very singular manner. He could not be prevailed upon to touch it or go near it, shuddering when we attempted to force him, and shrieking out, *Tekeli-li!*

Having completed our arrangements in regard to the security of the canoe, we now set sail to the south-southeast for the present, with the view of weathering the most southerly of the group in sight. This being done, we turned the bow full to the southward. The weather could by no means be considered disagreeable. We had a prevailing and very gentle wind from the northward, a smooth sea, and continual daylight. No ice whatever was to be seen; *nor did I ever see one particle of this after leaving the parallel of Bennet's Islet.* Indeed, the temperature of the water was here far too warm for its existence in any quantity. Having killed the largest of our tortoises, and obtained from him not only food, but a copious supply of water, we continued on our course, without any incident of moment, for perhaps seven or eight days, during which period we must have proceeded a vast distance to the southward, as the wind blew constantly with us, and a very strong current set continually in the direction we were pursuing.

March 1.[*] Many unusual phenomena now indicated that we were entering upon a region of novelty and wonder. A high range of light gray vapor

[*] For obvious reasons I cannot pretend to strict accuracy in these dates. They are given principally with a view to perspicuity of narrative, and as set down in my pencil memoranda.

appeared constantly in the southern horizon, flaring up occasionally in lofty streaks, now darting from east to west, now from west to east, and again presenting a level and uniform summit—in short, having all the wild variations of the Aurora Borealis. The average height of this vapor, as apparent from our station, was about twenty-five degrees. The temperature of the sea seemed to be increasing momentarily, and there was a very perceptible alteration in its color.

March 2. Today, by repeated questioning of our captive, we came to the knowledge of many particulars in regard to the island of the massacre, its inhabitants, and customs—but with these how can I *now* detain the reader? I may say, however, that we learned there were eight islands in the group—that they were governed by a common king, named *Tsalemon* or *Psalemoun,* who resided in one of the smallest of the islands; that the black skins forming the dress of the warriors came from an animal of huge size to be found only in a valley near the court of the king—that the inhabitants of the group fabricated no other boats than the flat-bottomed rafts; the four canoes being all of the kind in their possession, and these having been obtained, by mere accident, from some large island in the southwest—that his own name was Nu-Nu—that he had no knowledge of Bennett's Islet—and that the appellation of the island he had left was *Tsalal.* The commencement of the words *Tsalemon* and *Tsalal* was given with a prolonged hissing sound, which we found it impossible to imitate, even after repeated endeavors, and which was precisely the same with the note of the black bittern we had eaten upon the summit of the hill.

March 3. The heat of the water was now truly remarkable, and its color was undergoing a rapid change, being no longer transparent, but of a milky consistency and hue. In our immediate vicinity it was usually smooth, never so rough as to endanger the canoe—but we were frequently surprised at perceiving, to our right and left, at different distances, sudden and extensive agitations of the surface—these, we at length noticed, were always preceded by wild flickerings in the region of vapor to the southward.

March 4. Today, with the view of widening our sail, the breeze from the northward dying away perceptibly, I took from my coat-pocket a white handkerchief. Nu-Nu was seated at my elbow, and the linen accidentally flaring in his face, he became violently affected with convulsions. These were succeeded by drowsiness and stupor, and low murmurings of *"Tekeli-li! Tekeli-li!"*

March 5. The wind had entirely ceased, but it was evident that we were still hurrying on to the southward, under the influence of a powerful current. And now, indeed, it would seem reasonable that we should experience some alarm at the turn events were taking—but we felt none. The countenance of Peters indicated nothing of this nature, although it wore at times an expression I could not fathom. The polar winter appeared to be coming on—but coming without its terrors. I felt a *numbness* of body and mind—a dreaminess of sensation—but this was all.

March 6. The gray vapor had now arisen many more degrees above the horizon, and was gradually losing its grayness of tint. The heat of the water was extreme, even unpleasant to the touch, and its milky hue was more evident than ever. Today a violent agitation of the water occurred very close to the canoe. It was attended, as usual, with a wild flaring up of the vapor at its summit, and a momentary division at its base. A fine white powder, resembling ashes—but certainly not such—fell over the canoe and over a large surface of the water, as the flickering died away among the vapor and the commotion subsided in the sea. Nu-Nu now threw himself on his face in the bottom of the boat, and no persuasions could induce him to arise.

March 7. This day we questioned Nu-Nu concerning the motives of his countrymen in destroying our companions; but he appeared to be too utterly overcome by terror to afford us any rational reply. He still obstinately lay in the bottom of the boat; and, upon reiterating the questions as to the motive, made use only of idiotic gesticulations, such as raising with his forefinger the upper lip, and displaying the teeth which lay beneath it. These were black. We had never before seen the teeth of an inhabitant of Tsalal.

March 8. Today there floated by us one of the white animals whose appearance upon the beach at Tsalal had occasioned so wild a commotion among the savages. I would have picked it up, but there came over me a sudden listlessness, and I forbore. The heat of the water still increased, and the hand could no longer be endured within it. Peters spoke little, and I knew not what to think of his apathy. Nu-Nu breathed, and no more.

March 9. The whole ashy material fell now continually around us, and in vast quantities. The range of vapor to the southward had arisen prodigiously in the horizon, and began to assume more distinctness of form.

I can liken it to nothing but a limitless cataract, rolling silently into the sea from some immense and far-distant rampart in the heaven. The gigantic curtain ranged along the whole extent of the southern horizon. It emitted no sound.

March 21. A sullen darkness now hovered above us—but from out the milky depths of the ocean a luminous glare arose, and stole up along the bulwarks of the boat. We were nearly overwhelmed by the white ashy shower which settled upon us and upon the canoe, but melted into the water as it fell. The summit of the cataract was utterly lost in the dimness and the distance. Yet we were evidently approaching it with a hideous velocity. At intervals there were visible in it wide, yawning, but momentary rents, and from out these rents, within which was a chaos of flitting and indistinct images, there came rushing and mighty, but soundless winds, tearing up the enkindled ocean in their course.

March 22. The darkness had materially increased, relieved only by the glare of the water thrown back from the white curtain before us. Many gigantic and pallidly white birds flew continuously now from beyond the veil, and their scream was the eternal *Tekeli-li!* as they retreated from our vision. Hereupon Nu-Nu stirred in the bottom of the boat; but upon touching him we found his spirit departed. And now we rushed into the embraces of the cataract, where a chasm threw itself open to receive us. But there arose in our pathway a shrouded human figure, very far larger in its proportions than any dweller among men. And the hue of the skin of the figure was of the perfect whiteness of the snow.

NOTE

THE CIRCUMSTANCES CONNECTED WITH THE LATE SUDDEN AND DISTRESSING death of Mr. Pym are already well known to the public through the medium of the daily press. It is feared that the few remaining chapters which were to have completed his narrative, and which were retained by him, while the above were in type, for the purpose of revision, have been irrecoverably lost through the accident by which he perished himself. This, however, may prove not to be the case, and the papers, if ultimately found, will be given to the public.

No means have been left untried to remedy the deficiency. The gentleman whose name is mentioned in the preface, and who, from the statement there made, might be supposed able to fill the vacuum, has declined the task—this, for satisfactory reasons connected with the general inaccuracy of the details afforded him, and his disbelief in the entire truth of the latter portions of the narration. Peters, from whom some information might be expected, is still alive, and a resident of Illinois, but cannot be met with at present. He may hereafter be found, and will, no doubt, afford material for a conclusion of Mr. Pym's account.

The loss of two or three final chapters (for there were but two or three) is the more deeply to be regretted, as it cannot be doubted they contained matter relative to the Pole itself, or at least to regions in its very near proximity; and as, too, the statements of the author in relation to these regions may shortly be verified or contradicted by means of the governmental expedition now preparing for the Southern Ocean.

On one point in the narrative some remarks may well be offered; and it would afford the writer of this appendix much pleasure if what he may here

observe should have a tendency to throw credit, in any degree, upon the very singular pages now published. We allude to the chasms found in the island of Tsalal, and to the whole of the figures upon pages 479–482.

Mr. Pym has given the figures of the chasms without comment, and speaks decidedly of the *indentures* found at the extremity of the most easterly of these chasms as having but a fanciful resemblance to alphabetical characters, and, in short, as being positively *not such*. This assertion is made in a manner so simple, and sustained by a species of demonstration so conclusive (viz., the fitting of the projections of the fragments found among the dust into the indentures upon the wall), that we are forced to believe the writer in earnest; and no reasonable reader should suppose otherwise. But as the facts in relation to *all* the figures are most singular (especially when taken in connection with statements made in the body of the narrative), it may be as well to say a word or two concerning them all—this, too, the more especially as the facts in question have, beyond doubt, escaped the attention of Mr. Poe.

Figure 1, then, figure 2, figure 3, and figure 5, when conjoined with one another in the precise order which the chasms themselves presented, and when deprived of the small lateral branches or arches (which, it will be remembered, served only as a means of communication between the main chambers, and were of totally distinct character), constitute an Ethiopian verbal root—the root ᚤᚦᚡ꞉ "To be shady"—whence all the inflections of shadow or darkness.

In regard to the "left or most northwardly" of the indentures in figure 4, it is more than probable that the opinion of Peters was correct, and that the hieroglyphical appearance was really the work of art, and intended as the representation of a human form. The delineation is before the reader, and he may, or may not, perceive the resemblance suggested; but the rest of the indentures afford strong confirmation of Peters' idea. The upper range is evidently the Arabic verbal root ꭗꞏꞈ "To be white," whence all the inflections of brilliancy and whiteness. The lower range is not so immediately perspicuous. The characters are somewhat broken and disjointed; nevertheless, it cannot be doubted that, in their perfect state, they formed the full Egyptian word ΠᚨᚼᏒPHC "The region of the south." It should be observed that these interpretations confirm the opinion of Peters in regard to the "most northwardly" of the figures. The arm is outstretched towards the south.

Conclusions such as these open a wide field for speculation and exciting conjecture. They should be regarded, perhaps, in connection with

some of the most faintly detailed incidents of the narrative; although in no visible manner is this chain of connection complete. Tekeli-li! was the cry of the affrighted natives of Tsalal upon discovering the carcase of the *white* animal picked up at sea. This also was the shuddering exclamation of the captive Tsalalian upon encountering the *white* materials in possession of Mr. Pym. This also was the shriek of the swift-flying, *white*, and gigantic birds which issued from the vapory *white* curtain of the South. Nothing *white* was to be found at Tsalal, and nothing otherwise in the subsequent voyage to the region beyond. It is not impossible that "Tsalal," the appellation of the island of the chasms, may be found, upon minute philological scrutiny, to betray either some alliance with the chasms themselves, or some reference to the Ethiopian characters so mysteriously written in their windings.

"*I have graven it within the hills, and my vengeance upon the dust within the rock.*"

POEMS

THE LAKE: TO _____

In spring of youth it was my lot
To haunt of the wide world a spot
The which I could not love the less—
So lovely was the loneliness
Of a wild lake, with black rock bound,
And the tall pines that towered around.

But when the Night had thrown her pall
Upon that spot, as upon all,
And the mystic wind went by
Murmuring in melody—
Then—ah then I would awake
To the terror of the lone lake.

Yet that terror was not fright,
But a tremulous delight—
A feeling not the jewelled mine
Could teach or bribe me to define—
Nor Love—although the Love were thine.

Death was in that poisonous wave,
And in its gulf a fitting grave
For him who thence could solace bring
To his lone imagining—
Whose solitary soul could make
An Eden of that dim lake.

FAIRY-LAND

DIM VALES—AND SHADOWY FLOODS—
And cloudy-looking woods,
Whose forms we can't discover
For the tears that drip all over
Huge moons there wax and wane—
Again—again—again—
Every moment of the night—
Forever changing places—
And they put out the star-light
With the breath from their pale faces.
About twelve by the moon-dial
One more filmy than the rest
(A kind which, upon trial,
They have found to be the best)
Comes down—still down—and down
With its center on the crown
Of a mountain's eminence,
While its wide circumference
In easy drapery falls
Over hamlets, over halls,
Wherever they may be—
O'er the strange woods—o'er the sea—

Over spirits on the wing—
Over every drowsy thing—
And buries them up quite

In a labyrinth of light—
And then, how deep!—O, deep!
Is the passion of their sleep.
In the morning they arise,
And their moony covering
Is soaring in the skies,
With the tempests as they toss,
Like——almost anything—
Or a yellow Albatross.
They use that moon no more
For the same end as before—
Videlicet a tent—[1]
Which I think extravagant:
Its atomies, however,
Into a shower dissever,
Of which those butterflies,
Of Earth, who seek the skies,
And so come down again
(Never-contented things!)
Have brought a specimen
Upon their quivering wings.

ALONE

From childhood's hour I have not been
As others were—I have not seen
As others saw—I could not bring
My passions from a common spring.
From the same source I have not taken
My sorrow; I could not awaken
My heart to joy at the same tone;
And all I lov'd—*I* lov'd alone.

Then—in my childhood—in the dawn
Of a most stormy life—was drawn
From ev'ry depth of good and ill
The mystery which binds me still:
From the torrent, or the fountain,
From the red cliff of the mountain,
From the sun that 'round me roll'd
In its autumn tint of gold—
From the lightning in the sky
As it pass'd me flying by—
From the thunder and the storm,
And the cloud that took the form
(When the rest of Heaven was blue)
Of a demon in my view.

ISRAFEL[*]

In Heaven a spirit doth dwell
 "Whose heart-strings are a lute";
None sing so wildly well
As the angel Israfel,
And the giddy stars (so legends tell),
Ceasing their hymns, attend the spell
 Of his voice, all mute.

Tottering above
 In her highest noon,
 The enamored moon
Blushes with love,
 While, to listen, the red levin
 (With the rapid Pleiads, even,
 Which were seven,)
 Pauses in Heaven

And they say (the starry choir
 And all the listening things)
That Israfeli's fire
Is owing to that lyre
 By which he sits and sings—
The trembling living wire
 Of those unusual strings.

[*] And the angel Israfel, whose heart-strings are a lute, and who has the sweetest voice of all God's creatures. Koran

But the skies that angel trod,
 Where deep thoughts are a duty,
Where Love's a grown-up God,
 Where the Houri glances are
Imbued with all the beauty
 Which we worship in a star.

Therefore, thou art not wrong,
 Israfeli, who despisest
An unimpassioned song;
To thee the laurels belong,
 Best bard, because the wisest!
Merrily live, and long!

The ecstasies above
 With thy burning measures suit—
Thy grief, thy joy, thy hate, thy love,
 With the fervor of thy lute—
 Well may the stars be mute!

Yes, Heaven is thine; but this
 Is a world of sweets and sours;
 Our flowers are merely—flowers,
And the shadow of thy perfect bliss
 Is the sunshine of ours.

If I could dwell
Where Israfel
 Hath dwelt, and he where I,
He might not sing so wildly well
 A mortal melody,
While a bolder note than this might swell
 From my lyre within the sky.

THE VALLEY OF UNREST

ONCE IT SMILED A SILENT DELL
Where the people did not dwell;
They had gone unto the wars,
Trusting to the mild eyed stars,
Nightly, from their azure towers,
To keep watch above the flowers,
In the midst of which all day
The red sun-light lazily lay.
Now each visitor shall confess
The sad valley's restlessness.
Nothing there is motionless—
Nothing save the airs that brood
Over the magic solitude.
Ah, by no wind are stirred those trees
That palpitate like the chill seas
Around the misty Hebrides!
Ah, by no wind those clouds are driven
That rustle through the unquiet Heaven
Uneasily, from morn till even,
Over the violets there that lie
In myriad types of the human eye—
Over the lilies there that wave
And weep above a nameless grave!
They wave: from out their fragrant tops
Eternal dews come down in drops.
They weep: from off their delicate stems
Perennial tears descend in gems.

THE CITY IN THE SEA

LO! DEATH HAS REARED HIMSELF A THRONE
In a strange city lying alone
Far down within the dim West,
Where the good and the bad and the worst and the best
Have gone to their eternal rest.
There shrines and palaces and towers
(Time-eaten towers that tremble not!)
Resemble nothing that is ours.
Around, by lifting winds forgot,
Resignedly beneath the sky
The melancholy waters lie.

No rays from the holy heaven come down
On the long night-time of that town;
But light from out the lurid sea
Streams up the turrets silently—
Gleams up the pinnacles far and free—
Up domes—up spires—up kingly halls—
Up fanes—up Babylon-like walls—
Up shadowy long-forgotten bowers
Of sculptured ivy and stone flowers—
Up many and many a marvelous shrine
Whose wreathéd friezes intertwine
The viol, the violet, and the vine.

Resignedly beneath the sky
The melancholy waters lie.

So blend the turrets and shadows there
That all seem pendulous in air,
While from a proud tower in the town
Death looks gigantically down.

There open fanes and gaping graves
Yawn level with the luminous waves;
But not the riches there that lie
In each idol's diamond eye—
Not the gaily-jeweled dead
Tempt the waters from their bed;
For no ripples curl, alas!
Along that wilderness of glass—
No swellings tell that winds may be
Upon some far-off happier sea—
No heavings hint that winds have been
On seas less hideously screne.

But lo, a stir is in the air!
The wave—there is a movement there!
As if the towers had thrown aside,
In slightly sinking, the dull tide—
As if their tops had feebly given
A void within the filmy Heaven.
The waves have now a redder glow—
The hours are breathing faint and low—
And when, amid no earthly moans,
Down, down that town shall settle hence.
Hell, rising from a thousand thrones,
Shall do it reverence.

LENORE

AH, BROKEN IS THE GOLDEN BOWL!—THE SPIRIT FLOWN FOREVER!
Let the bell toll!—a saintly soul floats on the Stygian river:
And, Guy De Vere, hast *thou* no tear?—weep now or never more!
See! on yon drear and rigid bier low lies thy love, Lenore!
Come! Let the burial rite be read—the funeral song be sung!—
An anthem for the queenliest dead that ever died so young—
A dirge for her the doubly dead in that she died so young.
"Wretches! ye loved her for her wealth and ye hated her for her pride;
And, when she fell in feeble health, ye blessed her—that she died:
How *shall* the ritual then be read?—the requiem how be sung
By you—by yours, the evil eye—by yours, the slanderous tongue
That did to death the innocence that died and died so young?"

Peccavimus:[1] yet rave not thus! but let a Sabbath song
Go up to God so solemnly the dead may feel no wrong!
The sweet Lenore hath gone before, with Hope that flew beside,
Leaving thee wild for the dear child that should have been thy bride—
For her, the fair and debonair, that now so lowly lies,
The life upon her yellow hair, but not within her eyes—
The life still there upon her hair, the death upon her eyes.

"Avaunt!—avaunt! to friends from fiends the indignant ghost is riven—
From Hell unto a high estate within the utmost Heaven—
From moan and groan to a golden throne beside the King of Heaven:
Let *no* bell toll, then, lest her soul, amid its hallowed mirth
Should catch the note as it doth float up from the damnéd Earth!
And I—tonight my heart is light: no dirge will I upraise,
But waft the angel on her flight with a Paean of old days!"

SONNET—SILENCE

THERE ARE SOME QUALITIES—SOME INCORPORATE THINGS,
 That have a double life, which thus is made
A type of that twin entity which springs
 From matter and light, evinced in solid and shade.
There is a two-fold *Silence*—sea and shore—
 Body and soul. One dwells in lonely places,
 Newly with grass o'ergrown; some solemn graces,
Some human memories and tearful lore,
Render him terrorless: his name's "No More."
He is the corporate Silence: dread him not!
 No power hath he of evil in himself;
But should some urgent fate (untimely lot!)
 Bring thee to meet his shadow (nameless elf,
That haunteth the lone regions where hath trod
No foot of man,) commend thyself to God!

THE HAUNTED PALACE

In the greenest of our valleys
 By good angels tenanted,
Once a fair and stately palace—
 Radiant palace—reared its head.
In the monarch Thought's dominion—
 It stood there!
Never seraph spread a pinion
 Over fabric half so fair!

Banners yellow, glorious, golden,
 On its roof did float and flow,
(This—all this—was in the olden
 Time long ago),
And every gentle air that dallied,
 In that sweet day,
Along the ramparts plumed and pallid,
 A wingéd odor went away.

Wanderers in that happy valley,
 Through two luminous windows, saw
Spirits moving musically,
 To a lute's well-tunéd law,
Round about a throne where, sitting
 Porphyrogene
In state his glory well befitting,
 The ruler of the realm was seen.

And all with pearl and ruby glowing
 Was the fair palace door,
Through which came flowing, flowing, flowing,
 And sparkling evermore,
A troop of Echoes, whose sweet duty
 Was but to sing,
In voices of surpassing beauty,
 The wit and wisdom of their king.

But evil things, in robes of sorrow,
 Assailed the monarch's high estate.
(Ah, let us mourn!—for never sorrow
 Shall dawn upon him, desolate!)
And round about his home the glory
 That blushed and bloomed,
Is but a dim-remembered story
 Of the old time entombed.

And travelers, now, within that valley,
 Through the red-litten windows see
Vast forms that move fantastically
 To a discordant melody,
While, like a ghastly rapid river,
 Through the pale door
A hideous throng rush out forever
 And laugh—but smile no more.

THE CONQUEROR WORM

Lo! 'TIS A GALA NIGHT
 Within the lonesome latter years!
An angel throng, bewinged, bedight
 In veils, and drowned in tears,
Sit in a theatre, to see
 A play of hopes and fears,
While the orchestra breathes fitfully
 The music of the spheres.

Mimes, in the form of God on high,
 Mutter and mumble low,
And hither and thither fly—
 Mere puppets they, who come and go
At bidding of vast formless things
 That shift the scenery to and fro,
Flapping from out their Condor wings
 Invisible Wo!

That motley drama—oh, be sure
 It shall not be forgot!
With its Phantom chased for evermore,
 By a crowd that seize it not,
Through a circle that ever returneth in
 To the self-same spot,
And much of Madness, and more of Sin,
 And Horror the soul of the plot.

But see, amid the mimic rout,
 A crawling shape intrude!
A blood-red thing that writhes from out
 The scenic solitude!
It writhes! It writhes! With mortal pangs
 The mimes become its food,
And seraphs sob at vermin fangs
 In human gore imbued.

Out—out are the lights—out all!
 And, over each quivering form,
The curtain, a funeral pall,
 Comes down with the rush of a storm,
While the angels, all pallid and wan,
 Uprising, unveiling, affirm
That the play is the tragedy, "Man,"
 And its hero, the Conqueror Worm.

DREAM-LAND

By a route obscure and lonely,
Haunted by ill angels only,
Where an Eidolon,[1] named NIGHT,
On a black throne reigns upright,
I have reached these lands but newly
From an ultimate dim Thule—
From a wild weird clime that lieth, sublime,
Out of SPACE—out of TIME.

Bottomless vales and boundless floods,
And chasms, and caves, and Titan woods,
With forms that no man can discover
For the tears that drip all over;
Mountains toppling evermore
Into seas without a shore;
Seas that restlessly aspire,
Surging, unto skies of fire;
Lakes that endlessly outspread
Their lone waters—lone and dead,
Their still waters—still and chilly
With the snows of the lolling lily.

By the lakes that thus outspread
Their lone waters, lone and dead,
Their sad waters, sad and chilly
With the snows of the lolling lily,

By the mountains—near the river
Murmuring lowly, murmuring ever,
By the grey woods, by the swamp
Where the toad and the newt encamp,
By the dismal tarns and pools
 Where dwell the Ghouls,
By each spot the most unholy—
In each nook most melancholy,
There the traveler meets, aghast,
Sheeted Memories of the Past—
Shrouded forms that start and sigh
As they pass the wanderer by—
White-robed forms of friends long given,
In agony, to the Earth—and Heaven.

For the heart whose woes are legion
'Tis a peaceful, soothing region—
For the spirit that walks in shadow
'Tis—oh, 't is an Eldorado!
But the traveler, traveling through it,
May not—dare not openly view it;
Never its mysteries are exposed
To the weak human eye unclosed;
So wills its King, who hath forbid
The uplifting of the fringéd lid;
And thus the sad Soul that here passes
Beholds it but through darkened glasses.

By a route obscure and lonely,
Haunted by ill angels only,
Where an Eidolon, named NIGHT,
On a black throne reigns upright,
I have wandered home but newly
From this ultimate dim Thule.

THE RAVEN

Once upon a midnight dreary, while I pondered, weak and weary,
Over many a quaint and curious volume of forgotten lore—
While I nodded, nearly napping, suddenly there came a tapping,
As of some one gently rapping, rapping at my chamber door.
"'Tis some visiter," I muttered, "tapping at my chamber door—
 Only this and nothing more."

Ah, distinctly I remember it was in the bleak December;
And each separate dying ember wrought its ghost upon the floor.
Eagerly I wished the morrow; vainly I had sought to borrow
From my books surcease of sorrow—sorrow for the lost Lenore—
For the rare and radiant maiden whom the angels name Lenore—
 Nameless *here* for evermore.

And the silken, sad, uncertain rustling of each purple curtain
Thrilled me—filled me with fantastic terrors never felt before;
So that now, to still the beating of my heart, I stood repeating
"'Tis some visiter entreating entrance at my chamber door—
Some late visiter entreating entrance at my chamber door;
 This it is and nothing more."

Presently my soul grew stronger; hesitating then no longer,
"Sir," said I, "or Madam, truly your forgiveness I implore;
But the fact is I was napping, and so gently you came rapping,
And so faintly you came tapping, tapping at my chamber door,
That I scarce was sure I heard you"—here I opened wide the door;
 Darkness there and nothing more.

Deep into that darkness peering, long I stood there wondering, fearing,
Doubting, dreaming dreams no mortal ever dared to dream before;
But the silence was unbroken, and the darkness gave no token,
And the only word there spoken was the whispered word, "Lenore?"
This I whispered, and an echo murmured back the word, "Lenore!"
 Merely this and nothing more.

Back into the chamber turning, all my soul within me burning,
Soon again I heard a tapping somewhat louder than before.
"Surely," said I, "surely that is something at my window lattice;
Let me see, then, what thereat is, and this mystery explore—
Let my heart be still a moment and this mystery explore;
 'Tis the wind and nothing more!"

Open here I flung the shutter, when, with many a flirt and flutter,
In there stepped a stately Raven of the saintly days of yore;
Not the least obeisance made he; not a minute stopped or stayed he;
But, with mien of lord or lady, perched above my chamber door—
Perched upon a bust of Pallas just above my chamber door—
 Perched, and sat, and nothing more.

Then this ebony bird beguiling my sad fancy into smiling,
By the grave and stern decorum of the countenance it wore,
"Though thy crest be shorn and shaven, thou," I said, "art sure no craven,
Ghastly grim and ancient Raven wandering from the Nightly shore—
Tell me what thy lordly name is on the Night's Plutonian shore!"
 Quoth the Raven "Nevermore."

Much I marvelled this ungainly fowl to hear discourse so plainly,
Though its answer little meaning—little relevancy bore;
For we cannot help agreeing that no living human being
Ever yet was blessed with seeing bird above his chamber door—
Bird or beast upon the sculptured bust above his chamber door,
 With such name as "Nevermore."

But the Raven, sitting lonely on the placid bust, spoke only
That one word, as if his soul in that one word he did outpour.

Nothing farther then he uttered—not a feather then he fluttered—
Till I scarcely more than muttered "Other friends have flown before—
On the morrow *he* will leave me, as my Hopes have flown before."
 Then the bird said "Nevermore."

Startled at the stillness broken by reply so aptly spoken,
"Doubtless," said I, "what it utters is its only stock and store
Caught from some unhappy master whom unmerciful Disaster
Followed fast and followed faster till his songs one burden bore—
Till the dirges of his Hope that melancholy burden bore
 Of 'Never—nevermore.'"

But the Raven still beguiling my sad fancy into smiling,
Straight I wheeled a cushioned seat in front of bird, and bust
 and door;
Then, upon the velvet sinking, I betook myself to linking
Fancy unto fancy, thinking what this ominous bird of yore—
What this grim, ungainly, ghastly, gaunt, and ominous bird of yore
 Meant in croaking "Nevermore."

This I sat engaged in guessing, but no syllable expressing
To the fowl whose fiery eyes now burned into my bosom's core;
This and more I sat divining, with my head at ease reclining
On the cushion's velvet lining that the lamp-light gloated o'er,
But whose velvet-violet lining with the lamp-light gloating o'er,
 She shall press, ah, nevermore!

Then, methought, the air grew denser, perfumed from an
 unseen censer
Swung by seraphim whose foot-falls tinkled on the tufted floor.
"Wretch," I cried, "thy God hath lent thee—by these angels he
 hath sent thee
Respite—respite and nepenthe from thy memories of Lenore;
Quaff, oh quaff this kind nepenthe and forget this lost Lenore!"
 Quoth the Raven "Nevermore."

"Prophet!" said I, "thing of evil!—prophet still, if bird or devil!
Whether Tempter sent, or whether tempest tossed thee here ashore,
Desolate yet all undaunted, on this desert land enchanted—

On this home by Horror haunted—tell me truly, I implore—
Is there—*is* there balm in Gilead?—tell me—tell me, I implore!"
 Quoth the Raven "Nevermore."

"Prophet!" said I, "thing of evil!—prophet still, if bird or devil!
By that Heaven that bends above us—by that God we both adore—
Tell this soul with sorrow laden if, within the distant Aidenn,
It shall clasp a sainted maiden whom the angels name Lenore—
Clasp a rare and radiant maiden whom the angels name Lenore."
 Quoth the Raven "Nevermore."

"Be that word our sign of parting, bird or fiend!" I shrieked,
 upstarting—
"Get thee back into the tempest and the Night's Plutonian shore!
Leave no black plume as a token of that lie thy soul hath spoken!
Leave my loneliness unbroken!—quit the bust above my door!
Take thy beak from out my heart, and take thy form from off
 my door!"
 Quoth the Raven "Nevermore."

And the Raven, never flitting, still is sitting, *still* is sitting
On the pallid bust of Pallas just above my chamber door;
And his eyes have all the seeming of a demon's that is dreaming,
And the lamp-light o'er him streaming throws his shadow on
 the floor;
And my soul from out that shadow that lies floating on the floor
 Shall be lifted—nevermore!

ULALUME—A BALLAD

THE SKIES THEY WERE ASHEN AND SOBER;
　　The leaves they were crispéd and sere—
　　The leaves they were withering and sere;
It was night, in the lonesome October
　　Of my most immemorial year:
It was hard by the dim lake of Auber,
　　In the misty mid region of Weir—
It was down by the dank tarn of Auber,
　　In the ghoul-haunted woodland of Weir.

Here once, through an alley Titanic,
　　Of cypress, I roamed with my Soul—
　　Of cypress, with Psyche, my Soul.
There were days when my heart was volcanic
　　As the scoriac rivers[1] that roll—
　　As the lavas that restlessly roll
Their sulphurous currents down Yaanek,
　　In the ultimate climes of the Pole—
That groan as they roll down Mount Yaanek
　　In the realms of the Boreal Pole.

Our talk had been serious and sober,
　　But our thoughts they were palsied and sere—
　　Our memories were treacherous and sere;
For we knew not the month was October,
　　And we marked not the night of the year

(Ah, night of all nights in the year!)
We noted not the dim lake of Auber,
 (Though once we had journeyed down here)—
We remembered not the dank tarn of Auber,
 Nor the ghoul-haunted woodland of Weir.

And now, as the night was senescent,
 And star-dials pointed to morn—
 As the star-dials hinted of morn—
At the end of our path a liquescent
 And nebulous luster was born,
Out of which a miraculous crescent
 Arose with a duplicate horn—
Astarte's bediamonded crescent,
 Distinct with its duplicate horn.

And I said: "She is warmer than Dian;
 She rolls through an ether of sighs—
 She revels in a region of sighs.
She has seen that the tears are not dry on
 These cheeks, where the worm never dies,
And has come past the stars of the Lion,
 To point us the path to the skies—
 To the Lethean peace of the skies—
Come up, in despite of the Lion,
 To shine on us with her bright eyes—
Come up, through the lair of the Lion,
 With love in her luminous eyes."

But Psyche, uplifting her finger,
 Said: "Sadly this star I mistrust—
 Her pallor I strangely mistrust:
Ah, hasten!—ah, let us not linger!
 Ah, fly!—let us fly!—for we must."
In terror she spoke, letting sink her
 Wings till they trailed in the dust—
In agony sobbed, letting sink her
 Plumes till they trailed in the dust—
 Till they sorrowfully trailed in the dust.

I replied—"This is nothing but dreaming.
 Let us on, by this tremulous light!
 Let us bathe in this crystalline light!
Its Sybillic splendor is beaming
 With Hope and in Beauty tonight—
 See!—it flickers up the sky through the night!
Ah, we safely may trust to its gleaming,
 And be sure it will lead us aright—
We safely may trust to a gleaming
 That cannot but guide us aright,
 Since it flickers up to Heaven through the night."

Thus I pacified Psyche and kissed her,
 And tempted her out of her gloom—
 And conquered her scruples and gloom;
And we passed to the end of the vista,
 But were stopped by the door of a tomb—
 By the door of a legended tomb;
And I said—"What is written, sweet sister,
 On the door of this legended tomb?"
 She replied—"Ulalume—Ulalume!
 'T is the vault of thy lost Ulalume!"

Then my heart it grew ashen and sober
 As the leaves that were crispéd and sere—
 As the leaves that were withering and sere;
And I cried: "It was surely October
 On *this* very night of last year,
 That I journeyed—I journeyed down here!
 That I brought a dread burden down here—
 On this night, of all nights in the year,
 Ah, what demon has tempted me here?
Well I know, now, this dim lake of Auber—
 This misty mid region of Weir—
Well I know, now, this dank tarn of Auber,
 This ghoul-haunted woodland of Weir."

Said we, then—the two, then: "Ah, can it
 Have been that the woodlandish ghouls—

 The pitiful, the merciful ghouls—
To bar up our way and to ban it
 From the secret that lies in these wolds
 From the thing that lies hidden in these wolds—
Have drawn up the specter of a planet
 From the limbo of lunary souls—
This sinfully scintillant planet
 From the Hell of the planetary souls?"

THE BELLS

HEAR THE SLEDGES WITH THE BELLS—
Silver bells!
What a world of merriment their melody foretells!
How they tinkle, tinkle, tinkle,
In the icy air of night!
While the stars that oversprinkle
All the heavens, seem to twinkle
With a crystalline delight;
Keeping time, time, time,
In a sort of Runic rhyme,
To the tintinnabulation that so musically wells
From the bells, bells, bells, bells,
Bells, bells, bells—
From the jingling and the tinkling of the bells.

Hear the mellow wedding bells—
Golden bells!
What a world of happiness their harmony foretells!
Through the balmy air of night
How they ring out their delight!
From the molten-golden notes,
And all in tune,

What a liquid ditty floats
To the turtle-dove that listens, while she gloats
On the moon!
Oh, from out the sounding cells,
What a gush of euphony voluminously wells!
How it swells!
How it dwells
On the Future!—how it tells
Of the rapture that impels
To the swinging and the ringing
Of the bells, bells, bells!
Of the bells, bells, bells, bells,
Bells, bells, bells—
To the rhyming and the chiming of the bells!

III

Hear the loud alarum bells—
Brazen bells!
What tale of terror, now, their turbulency tells!
In the startled ear of Night
How they scream out their affright!
Too much horrified to speak,
They can only shriek, shriek,
Out of tune,
In a clamorous appealing to the mercy of the fire—
In a mad expostulation with the deaf and frantic fire,
Leaping higher, higher, higher,
With a desperate desire,
And a resolute endeavor
Now—now to sit, or never,
By the side of the pale-faced moon.
Oh, the bells, bells, bells!
What a tale their terror tells
Of despair!
How they clang and clash and roar!
What a horror they outpour
On the bosom of the palpitating air!
Yet the ear, it fully knows,

By the twanging
And the clanging,
How the danger ebbs and flows;
Yet, the ear distinctly tells,
In the jangling
And the wrangling,
How the danger sinks and swells,
By the sinking or the swelling in the anger of the bells—
Of the bells,
Of the bells, bells, bells, bells,
Bells, bells, bells—
In the clamor and the clangor of the bells!

IV

Hear the tolling of the bells—
Iron bells!
What a world of solemn thought their monody compels!
In the silence of the night,
How we shiver with affright
At the melancholy meaning of the tone!
For every sound that floats
From the rust within their throats
Is a groan.
And the people—ah, the people
They that dwell up in the steeple,
All alone,
And who, tolling, tolling, tolling,
In that muffled monotone,
Feel a glory in so rolling
On the human heart a stone—
They are neither man nor woman—
They are neither brute nor human—
They are Ghouls:
And their king it is who tolls:
And he rolls, rolls, rolls, rolls
A Pæan from the bells!
And his merry bosom swells
With the Pæan of the bells!

And he dances and he yells;
Keeping time, time, time,
In a sort of Runic rhyme,
 To the Pæan of the bells—
 Of the bells:
Keeping time, time, time,
In a sort of Runic rhyme,
 To the throbbing of the bells—
Of the bells, bells, bells—
 To the sobbing of the bells:
Keeping time, time, time,
 As he knells, knells, knells,
In a happy Runic rhyme,
 To the rolling of the bells—
Of the bells, bells, bells:
 To the tolling of the bells—
Of the bells, bells, bells, bells,
 Bells, bells, bells—
To the moaning and the groaning of the bells.

TO HELEN

I SAW THEE ONCE—ONCE ONLY—YEARS AGO:
I must not say *how* many—but *not* many.
It was a July midnight; and from out
A full-orbed moon, that, like thine own soul, soaring,
Sought a precipitate pathway up through heaven,
There fell a silvery-silken veil of light,
With quietude, and sultriness, and slumber,
Upon the upturn'd faces of a thousand
Roses that grew in an enchanted garden,
Where no wind dared to stir, unless on tiptoe—
Fell on the upturn'd faces of these roses
That gave out, in return for the love-light,
Their odorous souls in an ecstatic death—
Fell on the upturn'd faces of these roses
That smiled and died in this parterre, enchanted
By thee, and by the poetry of thy presence.

Clad all in white, upon a violet bank
I saw thee half reclining; while the moon
Fell on the upturn'd faces of the roses,
And on thine own, upturn'd—alas, in sorrow!

Was it not Fate, that, on this July midnight—
Was it not Fate, (whose name is also Sorrow,)
That bade me pause before that garden-gate,
To breathe the incense of those slumbering roses?
No footstep stirred: the hated world all slept,
Save only thee and me. (Oh, Heaven!—oh, God!

How my heart beats in coupling those two words!)
Save only thee and me. I paused—I looked—
And in an instant all things disappeared.
(Ah, bear in mind this garden was enchanted!)
The pearly luster of the moon went out:
The mossy banks and the meandering paths,
The happy flowers and the repining trees,
Were seen no more: the very roses' odors
Died in the arms of the adoring airs.
All—all expired save thee—save less than thou:
Save only the divine light in thine eyes—
Save but the soul in thine uplifted eyes.
I saw but them—they were the world to me.
I saw but them—saw only them for hours—
Saw only them until the moon went down.
What wild heart-histories seemed to lie enwritten
Upon those crystalline, celestial spheres!
How dark a wo! yet how sublime a hope!
How silently serene a sea of pride!
How daring an ambition! yet how deep—
How fathomless a capacity for love!

But now, at length, dear Dian sank from sight,
Into a western couch of thunder-cloud;
And thou, a ghost, amid the entombing trees
Didst glide away. *Only thine eyes remained.*
They *would not* go—they never yet have gone.
Lighting my lonely pathway home that night,
They have not left me (as my hopes have) since.
They follow me—they lead me through the years.
They are my ministers—yet I their slave.
Their office is to illumine and enkindle—
My duty, *to be saved* by their bright light,
And purified in their electric fire,
And sanctified in their elysian fire.
They fill my soul with Beauty (which is Hope,)
And are far up in Heaven—the stars I kneel to
In the sad, silent watches of my night;
While even in the meridian glare of day
I see them still—two sweetly scintillant
Venuses, unextinguished by the sun!

A Dream within a Dream

Take this kiss upon the brow!
And, in parting from you now,
Thus much let me avow—
You are not wrong, who deem
That my days have been a dream;
Yet if Hope has flown away
In a night, or in a day,
In a vision, or in none,
Is it therefore the less *gone?*
All that we see or seem
Is but a dream within a dream.

I stand amid the roar
Of a surf-tormented shore,
And I hold within my hand
Grains of the golden sand—
How few! yet how they creep
Through my fingers to the deep,
While I weep—while I weep!
O God! can I not grasp
Them with a tighter clasp?
O God! can I not save
One from the pitiless wave?
Is *all* that we see or seem
But a dream within a dream?

ELDORADO

GAILY BEDIGHT,
 A gallant knight,
In sunshine and in shadow,
 Had journeyed long,
 Singing a song,
In search of Eldorado.

 But he grew old—
 This knight so bold—
And o'er his heart a shadow
 Fell, as he found
 No spot of ground
That looked like Eldorado.

 And, as his strength
 Failed him at length,
He met a pilgrim shadow—
 'Shadow,' said he,
 'Where can it be—
This land of Eldorado?'

 'Over the Mountains
 Of the Moon,
Down the Valley of the Shadow,
 Ride, boldly ride,'
 The shade replied,
'If you seek for Eldorado!'

Annabel Lee

It was many and many a year ago,
 In a kingdom by the sea,
That a maiden there lived whom you may know
 By the name of Annabel Lee;
And this maiden she lived with no other thought
 Than to love and be loved by me.

She was a child and *I* was a child,
 In this kingdom by the sea,
But we loved with a love that was more than love—
 I and my Annabel Lee—
With a love that the wingéd seraphs of Heaven
 Coveted her and me.

And this was the reason that, long ago,
 In this kingdom by the sea,
A wind blew out of a cloud by night
 Chilling my Annabel Lee;
So that her high-born kinsmen came
 And bore her away from me,
To shut her up in a sepulcher
 In this kingdom by the sea.

The angels, not half so happy in Heaven,
 Went envying her and me;
Yes! that was the reason (as all men know,
 In this kingdom by the sea)

That the wind came out of the cloud, chilling
 And killing my Annabel Lee.

But our love it was stronger by far than the love
 Of those who were older than we—
 Of many far wiser than we—
And neither the angels in Heaven above
 Nor the demons down under the sea
Can ever dissever my soul from the soul
 Of the beautiful Annabel Lee:

For the moon never beams without bringing me dreams
 Of the beautiful Annabel Lee;
And the stars never rise but I see the bright eyes
 Of the beautiful Annabel Lee;
And so, all the night-tide, I lie down by the side
Of my darling, my darling, my life and my bride
 In her sepulcher there by the sea—
 In her tomb by the side of the sea.

ENDNOTES

1. Thomas White, *Letters of Edgar Allan Poe*, vol. 7 of *The Complete Works of Edgar Allan Poe*, ed. James A. Harrison (1902; repr. New York: AMS Press, 1965), 20–21.
2. H. P. Lovecraft, *Supernatural Horror in Literature* (1927), full text (unpaginated) from The H. P. Lovecraft Archive, www.hplovecraft.com/writings.
3. Edgar Allan Poe, *Letters of Edgar Allan Poe*, vol. 7, 205.

TALES OF THE MACABRE
METZENGERSTEIN

1. (p. 3) *Pestis eram vivus . . . ero.:* This Latin quotation means, "I plagued you while living, and dying, I will be the death of you." Martin Luther is said to have addressed this statement to the popes of the Vatican.
2. (p. 3) *Metempsychosis:* Metempsychosis is the theory that when a person dies his or her soul is transferred to another person—or an animal.

MS. FOUND IN A BOTTLE

1. (p. 11) *Qui n'a plus . . . dissimuler.:* "He who has only a moment to live has no time for falsehoods."
2. (p. 11) *Pyrrhonism:* Skepticism.

BERENICE

1. (p. 28) *Dicebant mihi . . . fore levatas.:* "My companions told me my cares would be noticeably relieved if I visited the grave of my lover."
2. (p. 31) *"Mortuus est Dei filius . . . impossibile est":* This Latin phrase means: "The son of God died; this can be believed because it's foolish; he rose from the grave; this can be believed because it's impossible."
3. (p. 31) *Asphodel:* A flower, symbolic of death.

4. (p. 32) *Halcyon:* According to legend, the halcyon was a bird that could cast a spell on the sea to make the waves so calm it could make its nest on the water. The "halcyon days" were fourteen mild days around the winter solstice.

MORELLA

1. (p. 37) Παλιγγενεσια: The Greek word refers to the Pythagorean idea that people are reborn as humans or animals.

LIGEIA

1. (p. 45) *Azrael:* The Angel of Death.

THE FALL OF THE HOUSE OF USHER

1. (p. 58) *ennuyé:* Bored.
2. (p. 60) *tarn:* A lake in the mountains, often formed by glacial action.
3. (p. 65) *Œgipans:* Goat-like mythical beings.

WILLIAM WILSON

1. (p. 75) *peine forte et dure:* A type of medieval torture.
2. (p. 75) *lustrum:* A period of five years.

A DESCENT INTO THE MAELSTRÖM

1. (p. 94) *Phlegethon:* A river of fire in Greek mythology.

THE PIT AND THE PENDULUM

1. (p. 111) *Impia tortorum . . . salusque patent.:* "Here a group of insatiable torturers wickedly nourished their appetites for innocent blood."
2. (p. 114) *auto-da-fè:* Execution by burning at the stake, as during the Inquisition.

THE PREMATURE BURIAL

1. (p. 141) *Chirurgical:* Surgical.
2. (p. 149) *cattymount:* Mountain lion.

THE FACTS IN THE CASE OF M. VALDEMAR

1. (p. 151) *in articulo mortis:* "In the grip of death."

THE CASK OF AMONTILLADO

1. (p. 163) *"Nemo me impune lacessit."*: "No one insults me and gets away with it."

TALES OF DETECTION
THE MURDERS IN THE RUE MORGUE

1. (p. 180) *draughts:* Checkers.
2. (p. 180) *recherché:* Special, unusual.
3. (p. 208) *'de nier ce qui est, et d'expliquer ce qui n'est pas.'*: This French line translates to "of denying what is, and of explaining what is not."

THE MYSTERY OF MARIE ROGÊT

1. (p. 221) *"laudanum":* A liquid drug containing opium.
2. (p. 222) *myrmidons:* Followers or troops, here referring to the police.

SKETCHES AND ESSAYS
THE IMP OF THE PERVERSE

1. (p. 303) *prima mobilia:* Poe is showing off his Latin here. *Prima mobilia* is an unusual Latin plural form of *primum mobile,* meaning "prime mover," or "basic cause." Here it refers to the elements of the basic structure or essence of the soul. *Primum mobile* is also a term for the outermost sphere of the geocentric (Ptolemaic) model of the universe.

THE NARRATIVE OF ARTHUR GORDON PYM OF NANTUCKET

1. (p. 333) *Ariel:* Poe cannot resist allusions. *Ariel* was also the name of poet Percy Bysshe Shelley's boat, in which he drowned.
2. (p. 363) *line-manager:* Man in charge of the whale lines
3. (p. 395) *larboard:* The port, or left, side of a ship.
4. (p. 408) *mania a potu:* Delirium tremens from drinking too much alcohol.
5. (p. 453) *biche de mer:* A marine slug called a sea cucumber.

POEMS
FAIRY-LAND

1. (p. 501) *Videlicet a tent–:* "That is, a tent."

LENORE

1. (p. 508) *Peccavimus:* "We have sinned."

DREAM-LAND

1. (p. 514) *Eidolon:* A phantom image.

ULALUME—A BALLAD

1. (p. 520) *scoriac rivers:* Rivers of lava carrying volcanic ash.

BASED ON THE BOOK

POE-INSPIRED FICTION AND POETRY

MANY WRITERS HAVE BEEN INFLUENCED BY EDGAR ALLAN POE. JULES Verne admired Poe very much, and wrote a sequel to Poe's *The Narrative of Arthur Gordon Pym of Nantucket* called *An Antarctic Mystery; or, The Sphinx of the Ice Fields* (1897). Other works said to have been influenced by Poe include Herman Melville's *Moby-Dick* (1851), H. P. Lovecraft's *At the Mountains of Madness* (1936), and Stephen King's *Gerald's Game* (1992).

Sir Arthur Conan Doyle and Agatha Christie acknowledged their debt to Poe's detective character, Dupin, and Michael Harrison used Dupin in a series of detective stories collected as *The Exploits of Chevalier Dupin* (1968). Ray Bradbury used themes from "The Cask of Amontillado" and "The Fall of the House of Usher" in his story "Usher II" (1950), and contemporary author Matthew Pearl took things a bit further, making an investigation of the mysterious circumstances of Poe's death the main theme of *The Poe Shadow* (2006).

French poets Charles Baudelaire, Stéphane Mallarmé, Paul Verlaine, and Arthur Rimbaud were influenced by Poe, as was the Russian Symbolist poet Konstantin Balmont, who wrote several poems on Poe themes.

Among other writers influenced by Poe are authors as diverse as Rudyard Kipling, Walter de la Mare, Thomas Mann, the Argentine writer Jorge Luis Borges, Robert Louis Stevenson, and the modern Japanese writers Jun'ichirō Tanizaki and Kobo Abe.

POE IN ART

The list of artists who derived inspiration from Poe's writing, either as illustrators of Poe's tales and poems or in their own work, is an impressive

one. In 1875, the French painter Édouard Manet produced a masterful series of lithographs for "The Raven." Other famous illustrators of Poe include the Irishman Harry Clarke, the French artist Edmund Dulac, British artist W. Heath Robinson, and Frenchman Gustave Doré. Among the best-known depictions of Poe's tales is a series of color and black-and-white illustrations that Arthur Rackham did in 1935 for a special edition of Poe's *Tales of Mystery and Imagination.*

Artists who took inspiration in their own work from Poe include the Flemish-Belgian painter James Ensor, the Swiss artist Félix Vallotton, and the Japanese conceptual artist Shusaku Arakawa. Frenchman Paul Gauguin's famous painting of a reclining nude titled "Nevermore" (1897), complete with a raven in the background, has a very Poesque mood of beauty and sadness. Other art inspired by Poe includes the French painter Odilon Redon's charcoal and chalk presentation of the eye as a hot air balloon (1878), and the American artist Nathan Oliveira's series of black-and-white lithographs in a monumental suite of works paying tribute to Poe's writing (1971).

POE IN MUSIC

Numerous musical works have been inspired by Edgar Allen Poe's writing. One of the earliest was Roger Nichols' *Le palais hanté,* Opus 49 (1904). Rachmaninoff's choral symphony *The Bells* (1913) was inspired by the Poe poem of the same name. André Caplet's moody *Conte fantastique* for harp and string quartet (1924) was inspired by Poe's "The Masque of the Red Death" and his novel *The Narrative of Arthur Gordon Pym.*

Claude Debussy devoted a number of years to two operas on Poe themes, *La chute de la maison Usher* ("The Fall of the House of Usher") and *Le diable dans le beffroi* ("The Devil in the Belfry"), though he never finished either of them. More recently, Philip Glass composed *A Descent into the Maelström* (1986). In 2009, the Swedish composer Fredrik Klingwall released his *Works of Woe,* nine piano pieces based on Poe's poetry.

In recent years there has been something of a musical revival in Poe-themed works. Many rock and alternative musicians have brought a Poe theme to their music, including Blues Traveler's "Run-Around" (1994), Odes of Ecstasy's "Abstract Thoughts" (2000), Cinema Strange's "Legs and Tarpaulin" and even music by Lou Reed and Britney Spears. In 2011 Tangerine Dream issued an album called *Edgar Allan Poe's The Island of the Fay.*

POE IN THE CINEMA

Edgar Allan Poe's stories and poems have had a rich life in the cinema. From the period of silent films to the early 1990s, approximately one hundred films appeared that were inspired by Poe's works.

A number of silent films blended elements of Poe's life with quotations or plots from his poems and tales. *The Raven* (1912) combines aspects of Poe's personal history with images from the poem; this film is also of interest in that it features some actual footage of Poe's Fordham, New York, cottage. *The Avenging Conscience* (1914) takes the plot of "The Tell-Tale Heart," gives it some additional twists, and adds lines from "Annabel Lee" and other poems.

American International Pictures (which produced *I Was a Teenage Werewolf* [1957] and *Blood of Dracula* [1957]) perhaps created the greatest awareness of Poe's writing for Americans in the 1960s. The first and most famous of the Poe-inspired films from AIP was *The Fall of the House of Usher* (1960), directed and produced by Roger Corman, with screenwriting by Richard Matheson and Vincent Price playing Roderick Usher. Corman took a highly creative approach to the movie, filming the first scene of a galloping horse and rider in an area of the Hollywood Hills that had recently been rendered desolate by a forest fire. In his role as Roderick Usher, Vincent Price won the New York Herald Tribune award for Best Actor.

American International followed the commercial and critical success of *The Fall of the House of Usher* with *The Pit and the Pendulum* (1961), which with Vincent Price again in the lead role, is a tale of mystery, torture, and obsession in a haunted castle, based loosely on Poe's story. Lancer published a paperback of *The Pit and the Pendulum* to accompany the movie, and this was the first story to have a paperback book tie-in written from the screenplay, not the original story.

Other Poe-inspired films in the Corman/AIP partnership are *The Premature Burial* (1962), *Tales of Terror* (1962), *The Raven* (1963), *The Masque of the Red Death* (1964), and *The Tomb of Ligeia* (1965).

Another notable entry into the Poe-inspired film canon is *Histoires extraordinaires* or *Spirits of the Dead* (1967). This film is a triptych of three Poe tales, each segment directed by a famous filmmaker (Roger Vadim, Federico Fellini, and Louis Malle). The stories depicted are "Metzengerstein," "William Wilson," and "Never Bet the Devil Your Head."

FURTHER READING

Particularly recommended are the works by Quinn, and Thomas and Jackson

ACKROYD, PETER. *Poe: A Life Cut Short.* London: Chatto & Windus, 2008.

ALLEN, HERVEY. *Israfel, the Life and Times of Edgar Allan Poe.* New York: Farrar & Rinehart, 1926.

BITTNER, WILLIAM. *Poe, A Biography.* Boston: Little Brown, 1962.

BLOOM, HAROLD, ED. *Edgar Allan Poe.* New York: Chelsea House Publishers, 1985.

BURANELLI, VINCENT. *Edgar Allan Poe.* New York: Twayne Publishers, 1961.

DAVIDSON, EDWARD. *Poe, A Critical Study.* Cambridge, MA: Harvard University Press, 1957.

ELIOT, THOMAS STEARNS. *From Poe to Valery.* New York: Harcourt Brace, 1948.

FIEDLER, LESLIE. *Love and Death in the American Novel.* Champaign, IL: Dalkey Archive, 1998.

FOYE, GORTON, ED. *The Unknown Poe.* San Francisco: City Lights, 1980.

FRANK, FREDERICK S., AND ANTHONY MAGISTRALE. *The Poe Encyclopedia.* Westport, CT: Greenwood Press, 1997.

HUTCHINSON, JAMES M. *Poe.* Jackson: University Press of Mississippi, 2005.

KRUTCH, JOSEPH WOOD. *Edgar Allan Poe: A Study in Genius.* New York: Russell & Russell, 1965.

LAWRENCE, D. H. *Studies in Classic American Literature.* New York: Penguin Classics, 1990.

MEYERS, JEFFREY. *Edgar Allan Poe: His Life and Legacy.* New York: Cooper Square Press, 1992.

POE, EDGAR ALLAN. *The Letters of Edgar Allan Poe.* Edited by John Ostrom. New York: Gordian Press, 1966.

———. *Letters of Edgar Allan Poe.* Vol. 7 of *The Complete Works of Edgar Allan Poe,* edited by James A. Harrison. 1902. Reprint, New York: AMS Press Inc., 1965.

————. *Selected Poetry and Prose of Poe*. Edited by Thomas O. Mabbott. New York: McGraw-Hill, 1951.

POE, HARRY LEE. *Edgar Allan Poe: An Illustrated Companion to His Tell-Tale Stories*. New York: Metro Books, 2008.

POPE-HENNESSY, UNA. *Edgar Allan Poe, A Critical Biography*. New York: Haskell House, 1971.

QUINN, ARTHUR HOBSON. *Edgar Allan Poe, A Critical Biography*. Baltimore: Johns Hopkins University Press, 1997.

SILVERMAN, KENNETH. *Edgar A. Poe: Mournful and Never-Ending Remembrance*. New York: Harper Perennial, 1991.

SMITH, DON G. *The Poe Cinema: A Critical Filmography*. Jefferson, NC: McFarland & Company Inc., Publishers, 1999.

SOVA, DAWN B. *Edgar Allan Poe: A to Z*. New York: Checkmark Books, 2001.

THOMAS, DWIGHT, AND DAVID K. JACKSON. *The Poe Log: A Documentary Life of Edgar Allan Poe 1809–1849*. Boston: G. K. Hall & Co., 1987.

WAGENKNECHT, EDWARD. *Edgar Allan Poe: The Man Behind the Legend*. New York: Oxford University Press, 1963.

INDEX OF TITLES